FAMILY

April 2010

80p

Dennis Russell

AVETON BOOKS

FAMILY

First published in the UK by Aveton Books, 2005

A CIP catalogue record for this book is available from the British Library.

ISBN 0-9549742-0-4

Typeset by TW Typesetting, Plymouth, Devon
Printed by Biddles, Kings Lynn

Aveton Books, The Eyrie, Sandhills Road, Salcombe, Devon, TQ8 8JP, England

Contents

For Averil

DEATH IN THE FAMILY

Chapter One

"I didn't scream when I saw the body. I mean, up in Crabbes Wood at that time on a Sunday morning, there's probably no one to hear you if you do. Scream, that is." Elizabeth Dyer looked up from the tape-recorder into which she was dictating her statement. D.S. Alison Clarke was reassuring.

"It's all right, Elizabeth, just tell it any way you like. I'll turn it into a neater statement if necessary."

Elizabeth was a thin, nervous girl in her late teens, with dark curly hair, cut quite short, and a face that was pert and lively rather than pretty. She nodded, and continued.

"It was Rip, my Golden Retriever that found her. I was walking quickly along the path, trying to keep up with him when he jumped off to the left into a sort of clearing, and started barking in a bush. The first thing I saw was this white little dress, fluttering like a rag on one side of the bush. Then I saw a shoe, sort of silver strappy thing . . ."

She had been speaking more slowly, as though straining with the effort to recall every detail, and now she stopped again, breathing deeply, and stroking the dog that sat beside her. She was clearly very close to tears.

"I know it's painful and frightening, but just a little more now and we'll be done."

"Then I looked into the bush, and there was this body. A girl, fair hair, naked except for the other shoe. She seemed so small and helpless, like a little doll. I didn't exactly recognise her, she was on her side, with her face turned away. Though I know now it was Susan Stevens. We were at school together. She was a couple of years older than me."

"Did you touch her?"

There was another long pause. "I . . . I put my hand on her shoulder, it was so cold . . . I put Rip's lead on and more or less ran back to the Tennis Club. I called 999 from there."

"Thank you, thank you very much. You've been very sensible and helpful. I'm sure you're due home for lunch now, but if you'd like to pop back into the Police Station here early tomorrow evening, say, we'll have this typed up for you to sign. Can I see you out?"

At about six o'clock on the evening of the next day, Monday July 16th, a press conference was beginning in the Georgian white and gold Meeting Room of Lynchester's Town Hall. Detective Chief Inspector James Renton had at first protested to the Assistant Chief Constable that it was too soon to go public, "Makes us appear helpless", he objected, but the A.C.C. had insisted,

"This is your first time in charge of a murder investigation, Jim, and I want it to go well for you. Local girl, no obvious clues, take my word for it, there are two likely scenarios, either an angry local lover, or a random nutter. Either way you'll need all the help you can get to turn up some leads quickly, and going public is the best way to get it. And by the way don't use the Lynchester nick for the conference, it's a mess, needs complete refurbishing, as soon as we've got the funds. On the other hand, the Town Hall's Assembly Room is quite grand so you should get a good turnout from the vultures."

His forecast of a good turnout proved accurate. In addition to Midlands T.V. News, there were reporters from Birmingham, Nottingham, Derby, Rugby and Coventry. No national press, but Jim guessed that the local reporters would have their London contacts if the story was a good one. The official press release had been carefully worded, and Jim Renton followed it closely in his presentation,

"I am Detective Chief Inspector Jim Renton, and I'm in charge of a murder investigation, in which we are seeking your help. Yesterday morning, that's Sunday, a young woman with her dog were walking through Crabbe's Wood."

He pointed to a large blow-up map of the town on the wall behind him,

"The wood is here, across the bridge from the town and on high ground immediately behind Crabbe's Marsh. It's an old coppice wood, almost a mile across, popular as a place to walk, with nice views in several places looking east across the town. She came across the body of a young woman. She had been strangled, probably late on Saturday evening. We have since identified her as Susan Stevens, aged 20. Susan grew up in Lynchester, but relocated to Birmingham almost two years ago, after her parents had split up. Susan came back to the town on Saturday to stay with a friend. The two girls played tennis at the Lynchester Tennis Club on Saturday afternoon, and returned to the club in the evening for a meal, drinks and the disco. Her friend lost sight of her after about 9.30. We believe Susan left the club at around that time. As you can see, the club is here, behind the Hawkins Timber Yard, if you are coming across the bridge from the town. Just alongside the club is Crabbe's Lane, which leads up into the wood. Susan's body was found here, alongside a path and about two hundred yards into the wood. We're fairly sure she walked there, possibly alone, possibly with someone else.

We want to talk to anyone who saw Susan on Saturday, afternoon or evening. Who did she talk to? Who did she dance with? And we also want to hear, more generally, from anyone who knew her, either in Lynchester, or Birmingham, or anywhere else. I'll take questions now."

"Was she raped?"

"We're keeping an open mind on that one. Sexual activity had taken place, possibly under duress, but there were no obvious signs of violence or assault, apart from the manual strangulation of course."

"Did you say manual strangulation?"

"Yes."

"Big hands? Powerful squeezing?"

"No. More like a sudden jerk."

"Like a judo or karate trick?"

"Possibly."

"So she did not put up a desperate fight for her life?"

"As far as we can tell, no."

"Lynchester's a small place, and a murder will make a lot of people very nervous. Why have you kept quiet about it for almost thirty-six hours?"

"We had to be sure of the identification, which meant finding and informing her parents. Really, I think we've moved very quickly."

"Did she have a boy-friend?"

"She was actually engaged. He's a salesman, away on a weekend sales conference in Spain with his company. We reached him too, late this afternoon."

"So he's not a suspect?"

"Pass. Any more? Right, if there are no more urgent questions, you'll find copies of the press release on the table here, together with the map and two fairly recent pictures of Susan. As I said, I'm leading the inquiry, but if I'm not available you can talk to Detective Sergeant Andrew Wilson, or Detective Sergeant Alison Clarke. We are setting up an Operations Centre in the T.A. Drill Hall, telephone number on the release. Thank you for your help."

"Thanks Andrew. You make a great cup of coffee."

D.S. Alison Clarke sat down gratefully with the steaming mug. The Drill Hall might have come straight out of the last century, and equipping and organising it to be an efficient Incident Room, able to process and collate perhaps hundreds of statements and reports, had been an exhausting job. Alison was in her late twenties, stocky with fair, curly hair, a graduate of Exeter University, and marked for rapid promotion. Of course D.C.I. Renton would get the major credit – or blame – for handling this murder, but Alison could do herself a lot of good also, particularly if the administration was seen to have gone well. She put down her coffee thoughtfully.

"How about the girl friend as a murder suspect?"

Andrew Wilson looked at Alison in some astonishment,

"You mean the girl she stayed with?" He thumbed through the already growing pile of papers in front of him, "Ah, yes, here we are, Joyce Clumber. I see you took her statement this afternoon. Seems straightforward – any thing about it strike you as fishy? She and Susan were classmates at school, and stayed friends afterwards. Susan used to come back from Birmingham fairly regularly to stay with her. Susan had recently got engaged to this salesman, but came this weekend because her boy-friend was off to Spain. They play singles first, then some mixed doubles, go home to smarten up, come back for a meal some drinks and the disco. When the disco finishes around midnight, Joyce looks around for Susan and, finding no sign of her, assumes she has gone off with one of the boys, so after waiting around for twenty minutes she drives her car home by herself and goes to bed. There's a note from you that she seemed very shocked and upset when told about the murder, and refused point-blank to make the identification. So why the suspicions?"

"Here's the hypothesis then, Andrew. See if you can poke holes in it, will you? Let's just suppose that Susan and Joyce were more than just pals. Suppose there was a long-running, full-bloodied lesbian affair in place".

"Possible, I suppose. What's Joyce like?"

"You mean does she have short hair and wear jackboots?" Alison picked up the photographs of Susan. A pale pretty face, eyes wide-set, a slightly snub nose. A weak face? Easily led?

"Joyce is not the obvious stereotype, I'm afraid. She is not what you'd call pretty, but very attractive I'd say. Tall, dark, rather bold features, and a super figure."

"Athletic, would you say?"

"You mean strong enough to kill with her bare hands? I'd guess so. Susan strikes me as a rather fragile girl, from the look of her. Maybe Joyce had some training in karate or judo? The pathologist says that 'Susan's neck was broken with a single, sudden jerk, rather than a powerful squeeze'. Taken by surprise, no sign of a struggle, nothing beneath the finger nails."

"Hangs together so far. Go on with the hypothesis."

"When Susan is seventeen or eighteen there's a big trauma over her parent's divorce, and she gets away herself, lands a reasonable job as a secretary with a merchant bank in Brum'. This starts to cause real stress in her relationship with Joyce. Perhaps Susan is finding her feet, growing away from Joyce, growing up in fact, getting interested in men."

Andrew wondered momentarily if any of this was Alison's own story, but said nothing,

"Then she meets her salesman, and agrees to marry him. She returns one last time to Lynchester, and breaks the news to Joyce, perhaps over supper that evening. Joyce begs for one last night of love, and then kills her in a fit of jealous rage and rejection".

"The D.C.I. suggested that the absence of semen could be explained if the murderer used a condom. And we don't have any DNA information back yet. Your story is at least as plausible at this stage, I'd say. Just a minute though. Susan was staying at Joyce's flat. Why go off into a dark wood full of heaven-knows-what for a night of love, when they've a comfortable bed to go back to?"

"Fair point. Let's see then . . . Could be that Joyce objects to the way Susan is flirting with one of the boys, and persuades Susan to go for a walk to talk it over. There's a passionate reconciliation, then another fatal quarrel. Does that fit all the evidence?"

"Closely enough to be worth a run. We certainly don't have anything better to go at. You try it on the D.C.I. in the morning. I'm for my bed".

Alison watched him go with some affection. Andrew was two or three years older than herself, a gangling six-footer with irregular, craggy features and a warm personality that radiated honesty. She was already his superior by seniority, but, in the three years they had known one another, he had never shown the slightest sign of envy or resentment. In fact he seemed to enjoy her success, and to look forward to her next promotion.

"You're a good friend, Andrew Wilson", she thought, and tidied her desk for the morning.

Chapter Two

St. Saviour's Hospice occupies a couple of well-wooded acres on the south side of Lynchester. On the evening of Saturday June 30th. Jennifer Hawkins visited her husband, Joe, as she had done every day now for five long months.

"How much longer can he live, do you think?"

The question could have been brutal, but the pain and concern in Jennifer's voice was only too obvious. The visiting consultant at the hospice looked up from his desk, as she came into the small office next door to the private room where Joe Hawkins lay, and stood before him. He knew that Jennifer was Joe's second wife, and wondered idly how old she was. Thirty-something, he guessed. Jennifer had looked after herself well, and no doubt Joe's money had helped. Her glossy-black hair was elegantly coiled and pinned, her face was delicately made-up to emphasise her finely-moulded high cheekbones and her generous mouth. She was tall enough for her full figure not to seem out of proportion, and her high-necked dark green silk dress was matched by the plain leather high heels. "An interesting woman," he thought, as she sat down and he tried to frame an appropriate answer to her question.

"To be honest, we don't know. He is in no pain of course."

He paused, trying to weigh his words carefully. He had been careful, over the preceding months, to ensure that Jennifer had a good understanding of the decline in her husband that was to be expected after the catastrophic stroke he had suffered. He had perceived – and shared – her relief when Joe, after agonising weeks of increasingly total paralysis and loss of mental faculties, had finally slipped into permanent unconsciousness. He decided she was ready for him to be clinically frank,

"In a way it has to be your decision, Mrs. Hawkins. We have known cases where the patient can be kept alive, in a technical sense of course, for many months, even years."

He saw the alarm evidenced in a slight frown that crinkled her high forehead, and continued reassuringly,

"Of course that's not recommended in Mr. Hawkins' case. In a truly meaningful sense he is no longer alive, if you understand me?"

She nodded,

"You could say that we are just using technology to simulate the symptoms of life. There is no obligation really to keep on doing that, you know. To be honest, we feel that we have to wait until his nearest and dearest are ready, if you take my meaning?"

He stopped at that point, and waited for a response. Jennifer gazed steadily at him, comprehension dawning in her wide dark eyes, hoping he would tell her the right answer. He remained silent. Suddenly she heaved a great sigh,

"Oh let him go, let him go, the poor, poor man."

George and Alan Hawkins were Joe's twin sons, with George the older by two hours. They were not identical, but one could see the strong family likeness. Both were fair, with pale blue eyes and a prominent beaky nose. George, as befitted the elder brother, looked permanently worried. He was putting on some weight, and had long ago given up trying to conceal his increasing baldness. He resented Alan's capacity to sail blithely through life without apparent concern or fuss, and particularly he envied Alan for his still full head of hair, with the boyish wave that he habitually pushed back so appealingly from his forehead.

That Saturday evening George and his wife Helen had gone out for a stroll along the towpath, beside the river Lyn. They had been careful to be back by nine, because they wanted to catch the Michael Caine thriller on television.

Afterwards George was quickly into bed first. He greatly enjoyed the covert pleasure of watching Helen undress. She was a tall, blonde, bony woman who still worked occasional days most weeks in the Cottage Hospital. Having no children, a good deal of her energy went into trying to get George to cut down on his drinking, and to stiffen his ambition, so that he concentrated on the family business rather than on his beloved fishing.

"I saw your father this afternoon."

This reminder of a duty that he had shirked served to warn George that the evening was probably not going to be rounded off with cosy lovemaking.

"Oh. Yes. How was he then?"

"Much the same. I mean he's just about a complete vegetable now, poor chap. Sometimes I think it's cruel of the hospice to keep him alive, don't you? I mean, what hope is there? None, I'd say. Why not just pull the plug and have done with it? I think we should say as much to Jennifer in the morning, don't you?"

George could see that she was deeply affected by the recollection of her visit, and put his arm protectively around her shoulder as he made room for her in the bed.

"I don't know love. Should we talk to one of the doctors? It upsets me just as much as it does you."

In truth, George was more disturbed than he cared to admit by the rapid degeneration he had seen in his father over the few short months since the stroke. Of course Joe had been well into his sixties, but until this last year he had been so vigorous and hearty, involved full time in every aspect of the family builders merchant business, and physically dominating Alan and himself, so that disagreements were quickly flattened out by the sheer weight of his personality. Now George felt exposed and uncertain. His life was losing its ballast, and he was at the mercy of others. More and more he was becoming aware that his brother expected to be allowed to make all the important decisions, without offering anything like his fair share of the work.

He felt the need for a drink, but for the moment it was Helen who needed reassurance,

"I think we've done everything we can. At least everything I can think of. We've just got to leave it to the doctors. I suppose they have to take the view that any minute now some miracle cure may be found. Pulling the plug would be like killing you know, even with the kindest of intentions, and you shouldn't ask anyone to do that. It's not as though he's in pain, is he?"

"They say he feels nothing at all. But how can they know? Perhaps his mind is still racing away inside, screaming to be let out. It's so horrible."

George said nothing more. Indeed he shared Helen's feelings of horror only too personally. What if it was hereditary in some way? What if that same unspeakable fate was lying in wait for himself?

He moved his hand gently across Helen's lean body, but she arrested his exploration with a friendly pressure.

At 11.30p.m. the night was warm and still. Grace Hawkins lay face-down on the bed in the half-darkness of her front bedroom. From outside, the perfume of the honeysuckle that climbed the wall drifted in through the open window, and the street lantern illuminated the pale curves of her naked body through a chink in the curtains.

The man who knelt beside her was also naked, and, from the smile on his face, obviously enjoying himself. He was massaging her back, pressing strongly at first as he kneaded her shoulder muscles, then moving more gently down her spine, to finish with delicate, feathery strokes across the back of her thighs and buttocks. After a few minutes of silent pleasure her body began to rock a little from side to side as she responded to the excitement that was transmitted through the pressure of his fingers.

"Alan, oh Alan that's lovely," she murmured, and as he covered her back with his body she raised herself up to receive him comfortably inside her.

Alan Hawkins rather fancied himself as a lover. He read the usual books of advice with interest as well as amusement, and in the time before he had met and married Grace he had experimented, with considerable success, with a fair proportion of the girls at the Lynchester Tennis Club. And there had been the more or less casual pick-ups too from the Saturday night discos at the Alhambra. But that life was fifteen years ago. Someone else had brought Grace, the daughter of a prominent local builder, to the Club's Christmas dance, but Alan had taken her home. Grace was petite, with dark straight hair cut in the very short boyish style that was fashionable that year, and large dark eyes that promised much.

Fifteen years and three children had added twenty pounds of flesh, but Grace kept herself in firm condition with tennis in the summer and year-round swimming, and Alan enjoyed every moment of their love-making. Mostly it was, as now, Saturday night when he really fancied her, after four or five pints of lager at the Club, with his imagination heightened by mentally undressing other women around the bar or the dining room.

Grace turned over onto her back and spread herself for him, aware that, as often, he was more excited than she was, but not greatly perturbed or disappointed. As that "Woman's Own " article had said last week, "Your orgasm is your own responsibility." She felt him moving with a more insistent, pounding motion and, recognising the signs, began to gasp a little and gripped him encouragingly until his hands tightened fiercely under her shoulders as his body jerked and pushed into her with a great shuddering spasm. Unsatisfied, but with a vague feeling that her husband had paid a kind of tribute to her continuing appeal for him, she whispered,

"That was gorgeous, Alan. I do love you so much."

Chapter Three

Lynchester is a small town in the English Midlands, important long ago as the place, fortified by the Romans, where their Watling Street crossed the river Lyn. It flourished greatly during the Coaching era, two hundred years ago. Then it sank into a long, genteel decline when the railways were built, its consolation being the survival of a piazza-style Market Square, with a mediaeval church and handsome Georgian buildings on three sides and a river walk on the fourth.

The death of Joe Hawkins on July 2nd caused great interest and speculation in the small town's business community. Joe had lived there all his life, and was known either socially or commercially to many. 'Hawkins Timber Yard' had been handed down through the family for six generations. Joe inherited it, as a very young man, when his father was killed during the assault across the Rhine in 1945. In the post-war boom in the building industry he had transformed it, retaining its reputation for good, seasoned timber, but also extending the business into every kind of component – bricks, cement, plumbing, windows, roof-trusses – "30,000 products always in stock" was his new motto. Joe used his big jovial personality to make friends, especially with the small local builders. He would meet them on site in winter, when his full flask of whisky made a welcome addition to the brew of tea. He knew them all by name when they came to the yard for supplies. Often he allowed extended credit, sometimes in exchange for a modest share of the profit when the development was sold.

Joe's first wife, Mary, was killed by a hit-and-run driver, and Joe was left to grieve, and to drink, with two sons, aged eighteen then, to bring up. A few months before, Mary had persuaded him to let her open a Cash-and-Carry counter, principally to supply a growing number of self-employed 'moonlighters', carrying out small works in their spare time, and not caring to be bothered with invoices and credit and their inevitable paper trail that might make life easier for the Inland Revenue.

After Mary's death, her cash-and-carry business was neglected. Indeed Joe could barely bring himself to touch her cash-register, so painful were the memories. Eventually he advertised for a manageress – cheaper than a manager, he thought – and Jennifer was the outcome. He could scarcely have made a better choice. Trained as a bright school-leaver in Lynchester's small branch of Woolworth's, Jennifer had transferred to the big branch in Birmingham, and over the next five years had earned successive promotions to become Assistant Manager, supervising the store's Hardware, D.I.Y. and Household Goods sections. She was twenty-three years old when they first met, tall, dark, top-heavy by the 'Twiggy' standards of the early eighties, and unattached. She liked men, but somehow the ones she liked were put off – frightened away perhaps – by a certain fierce competitiveness in her personality which she refused to dissemble. And she had no time for the softer, more dependent types that probably wanted her as a mother-substitute.

Joe Hawkins was something totally different. From the beginning, when she came to the yard for interview, he set their relationship on a straightforward business footing.

"Look here Jenny – I may call you Jenny mayn't I? – my poor Mary thought there was a real business to be built around that cash-register, and maybe she was right. Anyway, I'd like to give it a go, for her sake, d'you see? You'd need to keep proper books of account, separate from the credit side. I'd pay you a salary, same as you've been getting at Woolworth's and you'd save the travelling into Birmingham. In addition, you could have a bonus on your side of the business – say ten per cent of the profit on trading after deducting overheads."

"With respect, Mr. Hawkins . . ."

"It's Joe, everyone calls me Joe."

"With respect then Joe, from a look around the place, I doubt very much if there is a real profit at this time. Not much in the way of sales even. So there'd be a long wait for my bonus, wouldn't there? And meantime I'd be giving up my prospects of promotion in Woolworth's, where I've done pretty well so far. Fifty percent of the profit would be a more interesting incentive."

Privately, Joe had some sympathy for her appraisal, which recalled the way Mary had poured cold water on some of his dafter notions in the old days. But male pride would not allow any instant concession,

"I like your brass neck, Jenny. Let me think on it till tomorrow. Can you meet me in the Three Feathers about seven o'clock?"

Heads turned when Jennifer entered the Feathers that next evening, and there were some knowing looks exchanged as she moved towards Joe Hawkins at his usual corner table. Dark hair pinned up smoothly, huge dark eyes that widened as she picked him out, a well-filled white blouse with a neat collar and shapely black slacks. Old Joe must be coming to life again! Joe looked up from his pint to catch her smile as she made her way across the crowded bar. As he confided a year later to a crony at their wedding,

"That smile was the best thing that had happened to me since poor Mary was taken from us."

They haggled ritually over Jennifer's profit-share – if there was a profit to share – and settled on one third. On his side, Joe was intuitive enough to suspect that he might have done more than recruit another employee, and was content to have won back a little ground. Jennifer at that time had thoughts only for the business opportunity. The prospects for developing cash sales to jobbing tradesmen and moonlighters were obvious. But beyond that, she was keenly aware of how rapidly her Woolworth branch had been expanding its sales to "do-it-yourself" homeowners, and she thought that Hawkins must have good prospects in that business too, with its long history and good reputation in the district. They shook hands formally on the deal, and perhaps Joe held her hand in his a moment longer than was strictly necessary,

"Have you had your tea already, Jenny, or do you fancy having a bite with me? We could go over to the Crown Hotel if you like, I've heard they do a good steak there."

Jennifer looked at him steadily for a few seconds, as though appraising him as a man for the first time,

"We're comfortable here now. Besides, I think the tongues would never stop wagging if we left together now. Do you think they would make us a couple of sandwiches if you asked them nicely?"

Chapter Four

Charles Harrison F.C.A. had built up for himself a prosperous practice in Lynchester as a Chartered Accountant. Joe Hawkins started to employ him almost thirty years previously, "To keep the tax man out of my hair." It was natural therefore that, once the decencies of the funeral were over, the family should turn to Charles for advice. Jennifer telephoned him soon after the formal reading of Joe's will,

"Joe has left me the house of course, but I am also to have a one-third share in the business, with Alan and George having a third each also. The thing is, Joe seems to have assumed that we would want to carry on as before. But, well, with Joe gone . . ."

She paused, drew a deep slow breath to help to control the tremor that she felt in her voice, then continued firmly,

"Now that Joe's no longer here to be in charge, I'm not sure that I do want to go on. So we're looking to you for advice. Could you give it some thought, please, Charles and then give us your views as to what the possibilities might be? Say a week from now? We'll come to your office then, next Monday July 9th, at two."

Monday afternoon was hot and humid, and Charles opened the casement windows of his big office overlooking the Market Square, used on that day only as a car park. He let down the Venetian blinds to filter out the sunlight. The result was to produce a cool, shuttered formality, which he reinforced with his dark suit, black tie and quiet deferential manner as he greeted them. Alan and George had equally responded to their sense of the occasion by wearing dark suits, as if continuing to mourn for their father. Only Jennifer struck a discordant note, arriving ten minutes late wearing high-heeled white sandals, a swirling flower-print cotton skirt and a lacy white blouse that emphasised the generous lines of her body.

"Charles, I really don't think we need treat this meeting as a kind of wake you know. I said goodbye to the Joe Hawkins I knew a long time ago. Alan, George, it's so hot today, you look boiled in those suits. Wouldn't you like to take off those jackets, so that we can relax and concentrate on getting some work done?"

All three responded with relief to the lightness of her mood, and they sat down, Charles behind his impressive Georgian desk, his three clients at the polished table that was fitted up to the front of it. A pretty secretary discreetly offered lemon squash tinkling with ice-cubes. Charles began,

"I thought it might be helpful if I brought you up to date with the latest unaudited figures for the Hawkins business, as we haven't had a Board meeting since, since, ah . . ."

"Since February" Jennifer broke in, "When Joe's illness was confirmed."

"Thank you, just so. If you remember, the company showed a profit of £86,000 before tax for the year ending December 31st. For the first time the Retail side made a larger contribution than the Merchanting side, which I suggested was a healthy trend, when one takes into account the amount of money tied up in credit given, and so at risk, on the Merchanting side, whilst the Retail business is nearly all immediate cash and payment from guaranteed credit-cards. No dividend was declared, the funds being mainly required to continue the expansion and fitting out of the Retail premises.

For the first six months of this year, you've shown further nice sales growth on the Retail side, and sales remaining steady on the credit side. In total therefore I would expect an audit to show you as likely to hit the £100,000 mark for the full year. The build-up of Retail cash business has helped to reduce the overdraft to a nominal couple of thousand. As a quick summary then, the company is in fine shape."

"So how much might it be worth, as a going concern I mean, if we decide to sell?"

"That's exactly what Jennifer asked me to look at last week, Alan, so I've concentrated my efforts over the last few days on coming up with an answer. I won't bore you with enumerating all the points of the calculation, because anyway putting a value on any business is not a very exact science. It's got to be a bit broad-brush I'm afraid."

"So how much then?"

"Not less than half a million pounds, not more than one and a half million. Best guess around a million."

"A million would do very nicely, don't you think", said Alan, leaning back in his chair with a broad smile "Just like winning the Lottery."

"Well, I wouldn't say no to a million", Jennifer agreed.

"Well, I would. Say no, I mean. Definitely no sale."

The others looked at George in surprise. He had said almost nothing since he had arrived, mostly just looking glumly down at the empty writing-pad on the table in front of him, or fiddling a pencil through the fingers of his big hands. Jennifer knew that he had always been closer to his father than Alan, and wondered if he was finding Joe's death that much harder to take. She fixed her eyes on his face as he continued, trying to read the intent behind the words.

"There's no need to look at me like that, just because I don't sit up and wag my tail when Charles mentions a million quid. What's a million these days? Take out the lawyers' fees and the accountants' fees and the Bank's fees and God knows what other pickings, and we'd be lucky to see three hundred thou' each. And that's before tax. Bet you'd forgotten tax hadn't you? But the bloody tax man doesn't forget. I'd say we'd be doing well if we cleared two hundred thousand each. And, what's more important, at least to me, we'd almost certainly be out of a job. Could I get another job round here that would pay me twenty-five even, plus car and expenses? I don't think so. Could you, Alan? I doubt it. It's all right for you, Jenny, you've got the big house to do what you like with. And I'm not saying you didn't love Dad, but you're young enough to find another man, if you've a mind to. But Hawkins Timber is my place in the world. This business is where I stand, so I'm sticking to it. There's no way you can make me sell out and I'm not selling, that's all there is to it."

He sat back, having delivered what was obviously a prepared speech, and looked straight down at the writing-pad again.

"Is he right, I mean about the tax and all that?" The elation had entirely left Alan's voice,

"I'm afraid so. A sale for cash would be heavily penalised, as I was about to remind you, before George did it for me. Your father fortunately transferred his shares in the company into a trust for the three of you about ten years ago, so there are no death duties to pay. But by the same token if you sell up now you would have a very hefty Capital Gains Tax to pay, which is what I imagine George was referring to. Would you like me to try to estimate how much?"

"Don't bother, Charles". Jennifer's tone was despondent too "It's obvious that a sale on those terms would be stupid, even if George could be persuaded. Business is still growing, we'd do better to at least wait a few years."

"Alan?"

Alan opened his mouth as if to speak, then shook his head slowly, disappointment obvious from the slump of his body into the chair. The meeting had come to a natural conclusion, and they stood up as Charles arranged for tea and biscuits to be brought in.

"What will you do now, Jenny? Will you stay on? Your retail side seems to be going from strength to strength."

"I suppose so. These last few months have been such a strain, I just felt that I needed to make a change. Silly really. I mean, where would I go? I've lived here most of my life, all my friends are here."

Even as she was speaking, she knew that the words were just empty platitudes. "All my friends . . ." Really, she had no friends of her own now, only friends of Joe's generation, twenty years or more older than herself. She had a sudden vision of the rest of her life, working in the business, coffee mornings, bridge evenings, ever more frequent funerals . . .

There was a large framed photograph of the Square on the wall behind Charles, and glancing casually at it as she made small talk, she caught sight of a clear reflection of Alan. The bony profile, with the wavy fair hair reminded her sharply of Joe, when they had first met. Then she realised, with a sudden shock, that Alan was himself watching her closely whilst she talked. There was that hungry, predatory look she had seen before at parties, when Alan was sizing up the next woman to add to his collection.

"Good Lord", she thought in momentary confusion, "He fancies me. Perhaps I'm the next one on his list. I wonder how much Grace knows? What would Freud have said, I wonder?"

And, despite herself, a small shiver of excitement ran through her body.

Later that evening Jennifer awoke with a start, and stood up in sudden alarm. She had been dozing over a Ruth Rendell in the evening sunshine that had filled the rose-garden at the back of her handsome Edwardian house. A feeling of panic took hold of her. Something, or someone had broken into her sleep. What was it?

"Good evening,"

Jennifer realised that the speaker was standing in the deep shadows of the tall yew hedge that ran down the north side of her garden. Was it possible that Alan was already on the prowl? *No, it's not Alan . . .*

She stood up. "Who's there? Who are you? What are you doing in my garden?"

"Mrs. Hawkins? I'm sorry if I disturbed you, But I did knock at the front door for quite a while, and I've come a long way . . ."

The intruder stepped forward into the last of the sunlight. He wore a well-cut dark suit, was very tall and lean to the point of emaciation, "He looks like Mephistopheles on a bad day," Jennifer thought.

"My name is Layton, Christopher Layton. If I might have a few minutes of your time, Mrs Hawkins, I know that you will find it very beneficial."

"Are you selling something?"

Jennifer was no longer frightened, and the hostility in her voice was only too obvious.

"No, not really. I represent a London firm of property development consultants, Benson and Partners. This is my card . . . you won't know of us probably, but we are regularly retained by the most prestigious retailers – Marks and Spencer, Sainsburys, that sort of thing. I really do have something of value to say, if you could spare me half an hour?"

She read the card carefully, felt its thickness and the embossed lettering. "Of course. I'm sorry if I sounded cross, but you did startle me. Please, sit down won't you?"

She indicated a patio table, surrounded by big padded garden chairs,

"Do make yourself comfortable. I fancy dry martinis. Will you join me?"

After a brief exchange of small talk, and commiseration over the death of her husband, he got smoothly down to business,

"I mentioned that we represent the major retail groups, who of course are always looking to expand in appropriate areas. Before I go any further, I wonder if you could just help me to confirm one or two important points? You are now the owner of Hawkins Timber Limited?"

"Part-owner. The other owners are my husband's . . . my late husband's two sons, Alan and George Hawkins."

"Ah, yes of course, the sons. Thank you. Now, if you could look at this plan with me."

He unfolded a large-scale map of Lynchester. The timber yard was roughly outlined in red, a four-acre site on the river bank, across the bridge from, and more or less opposite the town's Market Square.

"I am not at liberty to name my clients at the present time, but I give you my word they are extremely prestigious. Your site is currently zoned for light industrial and warehouse use. We believe that, if we were to offer the Council a package that included certain civic amenities – car-parks, gardens, another river walk perhaps – then in exchange, it should be possible to have the site re-zoned for an attractive Shopping Centre or Mall development. I'm being very frank with you, Mrs. Hawkins, in fact I'm probably saying more than I should. But my company and my clients most certainly want to co-operate with you in this project. We actually want to have your family as full partners in this venture, since your property is the initial asset, and your undoubted local prestige could be of great influence in winning local support. For instance, if you were interested, we could envisage commemorating your late husband, and the long history of family involvement in the site by naming the development 'The Hawkins Centre' or something similar. Would that be appropriate?"

He paused, and waited for an answer, like the practised salesman that he was. Jennifer took a long pull at her martini, and looked at her garden, the tall standard roses now just catching the last rays of the setting sun. A major retail development! A Mall! A Hawkins Centre! She tried to recall some of the ratios of area to useable space she had learned on a Woolworth Management Training course.. Something wasn't quite right, she thought.

"From memory, the site has a gross area of about four acres. Surely that would not be large enough for the kind of Shopping

Centre you're talking about? Wouldn't you want well over a hundred thousand square feet of rentable space? Then you'd need the internal courts and lanes, and the access roads, car-parks, gardens and so on. My guess would be that you'd need at least twice our acreage."

"I can see that you know your modern retailing, Mrs. Hawkins. Of course you're absolutely right, at least double. However, we do already have an option on these ten further acres next door to yours, right here."

He stabbed a bony finger into the map, indicating the area of the river bank immediately downstream, where the river started to bend to the east around the northern edges of Lynchester.

"Crabbe's Marsh? Now I know you're not serious. That's no use to anybody except as a summer pasture. It's under two feet of water every winter. I'm surprised that a professional property developer, if that's what you are, wouldn't have found that out before going to all this bother."

"It is indeed a winter marsh at this time. But if the money were there to dyke the banks properly, and build a retaining wall, we have been assured by our engineers that it would dry out quite quickly and permanently. Does that convince you that we are serious professionals?"

"How does it come about that you approach me now? To be totally frank, it looks as though you've been hovering around, just waiting for my husband to die?"

The hostility and challenge were apparent again as she leant forward in her chair. Layton responded smoothly,

"Nothing so calculating, really. We've been investigating possibilities in the area for a year or more, and this last week I have been in Lynchester to tie up the option on Crabbe's Marsh. I just happened to see the announcements about your husband's funeral in the local paper. I knew of course that Hawkins Timber was the adjacent site, and that set me thinking. I discussed it with my clients, and came up today to put our initial ideas to you. A mixture of pure chance and a little intelligence, you see."

He allowed a small, self-deprecating smile to flit across his saturnine features, which Jennifer thought made him look even more ghastly than when he was serious. She decided that she did not know how much to believe, but that it didn't matter very much at the moment.

"What sort of money would we be talking about? If the scheme went through, I mean."

Christopher Layton, who had experienced many bruising negotiations in his time, felt a warm certainty of victory to come. She hadn't said "If we were to sell," so he could take it for granted that the business with its land was for sale, if the price was right. The mouse was inside the trap – now to make her want the cheese!

"That's a difficult one at this early juncture, there are still so many unanswered questions. Will the planning permissions be forthcoming? Will the engineering works find any unexpected snags? You understand I'm sure."

"You must have some figure in mind."

"Well, I could indicate an idea of the potential return for you, based on our very preliminary assessment, and without commitment at this stage of course,"

"Another martini?"

"Thank you. Our approach would be to suggest that you might put the land into the Development Company in return for a combination of some cash up front, and a share of the profit when the completed development is sold on to a property company."

"Could you unwrap that a bit more? It sounds very complicated to me."

"Of course. We set up a limited company specifically to carry out this development, with a modest amount of shareholders' capital, and funding drawn in as loan capital as required in stages. The company would buy the land from you for a substantial cash sum plus, in return for your continuing support in the local community, an issue of shares which would entitle you to a proportion of the profit when the Hawkins Centre is finished and sold on to a property company, which has the skills to actually handle the letting and management and so on."

Jennifer found her head beginning to swim, under the combined effect of several large martinis and Layton's business logic,

"Mr. Layton, it's been a long hot day for me, and I am rather tired now. Could we get to the point, please? How much money for the land?"

"I think we'd be talking of a million . . ." He saw her frown, and continued quickly "A million each for yourself and your stepsons, assuming equal shares. So, three million up front, and say ten percent of the profit achieved when the mall is sold on."

"How firm is that million each, as a minimum?"

"Now, Mrs. Hawkins, you know quite well that I am in no position to negotiate directly at this time. I can only try, with your assistance, to put together a package that should be attractive to all sides. No doubt you will want to consult your own financial advisers and your stepsons also, but I can say, in all honesty, that if you had consulted me as your adviser, I would be recommending something along these lines, as the way to maximise your return and give you the best opportunity to minimise the tax payable."

"I'll accept that at face value for today, Mr. Layton. Of course I'll be taking professional advice as you suggested, and I must also consult my stepsons. They're likely to have strong views of their own, I should warn you. However it's fair to say that I'm interested in principle. Will you put something in writing?"

Millions! Millions! The prospect tumbled through Jennifer's mind in a whirl of excitement and trepidation. That smooth bag of bones, what was his first name? She found his card: Christopher Layton, Senior Property Consultant. Was he on the level? Could he be trusted? He seemed a very serious, professional sort, but then a good con-man would be just like that. Oh Joe, Joe! Why aren't you here to tell me what to do?

Jennifer's bedroom, which she had shared happily with Joe Hawkins for fourteen years, was huge, extending from front to back of the double-fronted Edwardian house, with a bay at each end. In the hot, velvety darkness of the summer night Jennifer paced up and down from end to end, trying to marshal her racing thoughts, and sipping now and again from the tumbler of dry martini and tinkling ice-cubes she had brought upstairs as a nightcap.

Millions! Freedom and security for all of them! She could travel, live abroad perhaps, meet new people. What would Alan and George say? No one, surely, would turn down an offer of millions? And a Hawkins Centre to commemorate Joe's family and the business? Perhaps there'd even be a statue of him? She giggled at the thought. At last, as though she had finally come to a decision, Jennifer drew together the thick plush curtains at the front, and opened the french doors at the back, with their little balcony that overlooked the rose garden. The air outside was a little cooler, and a crescent moon was just rising to lighten the dark landscape of formal garden and fields beyond. Enjoying the half-darkness still, she kicked off her white sandals and slowly unbuttoned the lacy blouse and the flower-print skirt that had so surprised the men that afternoon. Was it just a few hours ago? Everything seemed so changed now. Her fumbling fingers told her that the gin was working, and she sat down in front of the old-fashioned dressing table with its triple mirrors, and began unpinning and brushing her black hair, which fell heavily onto her bare shoulders. As always, the steady rhythm of the hairbrush served to slow down and soothe the tumult of her thoughts. She looked at herself in the mirror, it seemed for the first time in years. How well did she know the shadowy person that peered back so solemnly at her? The high forehead, the thick black eyebrows, the lustrous eyes, with more than a hint of dark rings beneath them – those were one side of the Jennifer she knew, intelligent, caring and compassionate. That was the woman Joe had loved, wasn't it? But the determined chin would have appealed to the Pre-Raphaelite painters. And that full, sensual mouth belonged to a different Jennifer, one that Joe hardly knew, one she hardly knew herself perhaps? Adolescent nonsense! That was the gin talking!

Nevertheless she stood up in her white bra and pants and turned this way and that before the mirrors, as though taking stock. *Tall, big eyes, long legs and a good-looking body. And now to be rich with it. You're a pretty desirable woman, Jennifer Hawkins!* She ran a hand over the gentle roundness of her belly. *Was it too late to think about having a baby? Could be riskier now, but not too late, surely? Have to find a man first!* Ten years or more ago she had tried to give Joe a child. The doctor had said there was nothing wrong with either of them, but there had been no baby.

She finished the last of the martini, and stretched out on top of the cool cotton duvet that covered the bed. Sleep was slow to come.

Chapter Five

The morning after his press conference, Tuesday July 17th. Detective Chief Inspector Jim Renton called his two principal assistants on the case into his makeshift office for 'a quick look at where we're at.' Jim was thirty five, promoted only a few months earlier to Chief Inspector rank, and seen in the force as a rising star. He had joined straight from school, after an unexpectedly poor set of A-level results had cost him his university place. He was well over six feet, lean, with a long, bony face, a marked widow's peak in the dark hair he kept carefully brushed back, and deep-set eyes of a pale watery blue, their colour strangely incongruous against his dark complexion. Proud of his promotion, he knew that a well-organised, cost-effective and above all successful murder hunt would establish him in the front rank of Chief Inspectors. He also knew that if, as the A.C.C. had hinted, this case proved to have a random or serial killer, the media pressure would become very intense, and any mistake or error of judgement could be magnified into a personal disaster.

"Alison, you first please. How's it going?"

"Early days of course. The incident room here is up and running. The biggest gamble was running that press conference before we were certain of the extra telephone lines, but we made it in the end. It looks as though the publicity is producing a strong response, the telephones have been ringing off the hook. Usual collection of nutters of course, but some interesting information too. We're concentrating on identifying first everyone who was at the Club on Saturday, and then lining up interviews."

"Anything that could be called a lead?"

"Not really. Mind you we've only talked to half a dozen people so far, and there must have been eighty or ninety there that evening."

"O.K. keep at it, and let me know at once if anything interesting turns up. I've got the local uniforms checking on hotels and boarding-houses to see if any visitor has a record that might fit. I've just had a fax from Birmingham on the enquiry there. Seems she has been living for a year now in a small, but very high-class rented apartment in Edgbaston, not far from the cricket ground. It's been sealed up, and I'm off there this afternoon. Local Estate Agent estimates the outgoings would be around £4,000 a year, so we have to wonder how that was affordable on her salary."

"Big-city boyfriend?"

"Could be, though none has been identified yet. Perhaps her fiance will offer an explanation when he comes in. Might be more than one, of course, in fact she might have been on the game I suppose, in a part-time sort of way. Her employers have given her a good reference, 'Quiet, efficient, reliable and discreet.' No men phoning her at the office, no one collecting her after work. I haven't dismissed the possibility that her boss might have a reason to say nice things about her, of course. There's a preliminary report from the autopsy, confirms the time of death as between ten p.m. and midnight."

"Can't they be more precise?"

"Apparently not. It was a warm night, and 'local microclimate could significantly affect body-cooling.' Best estimate is eleven p.m., but could be an hour either side. She was pregnant, by the way, about three months, and there had also been an abortion, about a year previously. So there's another couple of lines of enquiry. Perhaps there have been two serious lovers, one whose child was aborted, one kept. Might be more than one kind of motive there."

"I have another hypothesis, sir."

Alison had spent an hour that morning writing up her idea of a lesbian affair, and the possible sequence of cause and effect. Jim listened with keen attention. Alison was by way of being a protegee of his, and he was pleased to see her now taking responsibility for an independent approach.

He scanned her short script. "I like the argument about the absence of semen. And it fits well enough with the pregnancies too, I suppose. What do you think, Andrew?"

"Bit out of my line, sir. For what it's worth though, none of the people we've interviewed so far has mentioned any boyfriend. Not for either of the girls, so there could be something in it."

"I agree. How do you want to go about testing this idea? I suggest it is highly desirable that we confirm or eliminate Joyce as a suspect very quickly. If the Press get hold of it things could get . . . quite messy."

"I'd like to get Joyce back in and try a little pressure. I got the feeling she was very stressed, and she might crack."

"O.K., but be very careful. If she's a neurotic, she might even admit to being responsible, because she feels guilty and wants to be punished, if you see what I mean. Get that forensic psychiatrist lady at Stafford to give you a briefing. Record the interview, and have a reliable W.P.C. with you, all the time. Understood?"

"Yes sir. And I would also propose to have another very close look at the place where she was found."

"Go on."

"Knee-marks, sir. Susan apparently was not wearing a bra, and we've found the panties under the body. Her dress was carefully unbuttoned from top to bottom, suggesting a seduction or an act of love, rather than rape. If it was a man, we might expect to find marks of kneeling between her legs. If it was a woman, we might not."

Jim Renton nodded slowly, "Might is the operative word, I'd say. You'd best pick up a set of the location photos, and get over to Crabbe's Wood straight away. See if you can get Joyce back in later today. Now, can I have a look quickly at the numbers of P.C.s you're rostering to man the telephones? What means do we have of getting hold of any people who call, but don't get through? How rapidly can we get our data onto the computer?"

Chapter Six

As the D.C.I. was starting his review, Grace Hawkins was sitting down to tea and a piece of toast, having seen the children and Alan off as usual.

"I won't be back for lunch today, love. Jennifer phoned first thing, before you got down. Something about a possible buyer for the Yard, though with George in his present mood I can't believe it'll get very far. Anyway she wants to talk it over, and offered lunch, so who am I to argue?"

The Birmingham Post arrived just after they had left, and Grace opened it casually,

MIDLANDS GIRL STRANGLED IN BEAUTY SPOT

'Lynchester' leapt out of the first column, and 'Susan Stevens' – the name was not familiar, but the photograph had reproduced well, and Grace thought she recognised the face.

'Played tennis on Saturday at the Lynchester Tennis Club, and came back later for a meal and the disco . . . last seen around 9.30p.m.'

Grace read the story avidly, together with the appeal for witnesses. How terrible! They had actually been there, that night!

Grace and Alan had made up a four with Helen and George for dinner, and had stayed gossiping with friends and enjoying the disco. *Perhaps she had seen, or even spoken to the murderer?* Grace searched her memory. *Had she seen that girl, Susan, on Saturday night?* She could recall nothing definite, yet the face was familiar. Of course, if the girl was a member, she might have seen her anyway, perhaps lots of times. Deeply moved by the near approach of violent death, she went upstairs to dress. If Helen was home, she thought she might stroll round there for a cup of coffee and a chat. Maybe Helen would remind her where they had seen Susan, and they could offer to 'help the police with their inquiries'? The sun was warm, but Grace shivered a little as she dressed. *What must it be like, to be killed like that? And how does the murderer feel this morning, knowing what he has done, and knowing he's going to be hunted like an animal?*

"You're a thief! A bloody thief and a swindler!"

Alan Hawkins had been in a good mood when he arrived at Hawkins Timber, just before eight-thirty. The morning was already pleasantly warm, and his thoughts were still full of the excitement that Jennifer had conveyed over the telephone first thing. Jennifer really was an attractive woman, and lunch with her was something to look forward to. Perhaps there really might be a buyer who would pay millions for the business? In contrast, the verbal assault suddenly unleashed by his brother was hysterical in its intensity,

"All these years I've put up with your bullshit and your patronising. Dad noticed it too, but left you to get on with it as long as he was in charge. And don't think I've not spotted the way you acted, during his illness, as though you were going to take his place. I'll see you in hell first! All this time you've been swindling us, taking bribes behind our backs like a cheap little shyster. Cheating Dad, cheating Jenny and cheating me. But you won't be doing it any more, I'll see to that, you greedy, conniving bastard! Only yesterday you wanted to sell me out for a few measly quid. I'm not surprised now, it's all quite clear. You were already worried you might be found out, weren't you? Just how long has this been going on? And how many other little arrangements am I going to unearth when I start digging? Because, believe me, I am going to start *really* digging!"

Alan held up both hands to check George's torrent of accusations. Their small suite of offices was built on the outside wall of a mezzanine level of the warehouse, with a narrow corridor deck in front, and cast-iron railings inside extending across the width. Alan walked out of George's office to the railings, and looked out over the neat stacks of building materials, and the retail display area. There was no one in sight. He had seen Jeff Tindall, the foreman, and Bill Coates, the assistant, busy in the yard when he arrived, starting to unload a delivery of plasterboard. As he watched, he heard the key turn in the plate-glass front doors, as Jenny's manageress arrived to open up the retail side. Fortunately it's Jenny's day off, he thought. Alan went back into the small office, where George was still standing, his rage and aggression bursting out of every sweating pore, and closed the door. He drew a deep breath, and sat down on the little chair, looking calmly up at his brother.

"For God's sake, George, what's got into you? I'm hardly at the top of the stairs before you go off the deep end, ranting and raving at me and calling me all sorts of names. Sit down now. I've shut the door so we don't have to broadcast this silly mistake to all and sundry. Sit down, please, and tell me all about it from the beginning. SIT DOWN!"

The note of command in Alan's voice finally got through, and George subsided into his comfortable swivel-chair. Frantic animosity was succeeded by a dogged determination,

"There's no mistake, Alan. I only wish there was. Do you think I enjoy this?"

"Before we go any further, would you mind telling me what this is all about?"

"It's about a 'phone call I had, sharp at eight this morning. A man called Linden, Neil Linden of Armitage Brick. Name ring any bells?"

A hard, cold lump began to form at the pit of Alan's stomach, but he maintained his impatient expression,

"Of course I know him, he's the Sales Manager there."

"Not any longer, it seems. The company have decided to 'let him go', as the saying is. He seemed to think we owed him a favour, 'because of the special way he looked after us'. Something of the order of three thousand pounds in cash over the last twelve months in volume discounts, as he called it. He assumed it was simply a tax-fiddle for the two of us. I suppose that's how we just happened to drop Ibstock and Butterley, so that Armitage could become our sole suppliers? He wants us to write him a really good reference, so that he can get a job somewhere else. Can you imagine it? Oh Alan, how could you do it? To your own family, for God's sake, how could you?"

There was true pain as well as bitterness in the reproach, and Alan felt almost sorry for him. George has been like a lost soul without Dad, he thought, and noticed that George's half-open bottom drawer contained a bottle of Johnny Walker, with a good deal missing already. *He's been at the sauce already this morning! Just coming up to nine! A bit of Dutch courage, or is it a regular morning habit now? . . . This is not the moment to weaken . . .*

"George, this is all totally unjust. Of course Neil promised us a volume rebate. And I'll make sure we get it, even though he's moving on. Why else would Dad have dropped the other two, as you said? But I've had nothing out of it myself, I swear. No cash, no suitcase of old notes. Everything is above board."

"Have you got the terms on paper?"

George's voice was still hard with suspicion, but there was less certainty now. Alan had been thinking very quickly. Armitage had found a way to pay out the cash to himself, so no doubt they could find a way to accept it back, if he offered it, and then pay it out officially as a volume rebate, either in cash or, more likely, as a reduction against what Hawkins Timber owed them. It should work!

"Nothing on paper. Neil said that their customers had friends in his sales office, and if it was on paper it would soon get around, and everyone would be after a volume rebate. It was special for us, you see, because they hadn't been doing anything with us up to then. But they'll pay all right. It's not just Neil, you know. I met their M.D. Bill Theackston too, and he knows what was agreed."

"When is it due?"

Accusation was fading down to resignation in George's manner, and Alan stood up to assert his authority once more

"The first full year is up at the end of September. Give them a few weeks to do their arithmetic I suppose, and we should be looking at a nice early Christmas present."

George stood up also, ran a hand through the thinning strands of his hair, and then rubbed his face wearily,

"I suppose I owe you an apology, Alan. I'm sorry, really I am. I shouldn't have flown off the handle like that, but, well, these last few months, with Dad just hanging on, like an empty husk . . ."

His voice trailed away, and they stood facing one another for a long moment in the small, stuffy office. Alan put a hand on George's shoulder.

"Say no more, I know how it's been for you. It's easier for me, I'm out a lot, but you're here inside, carrying the burden of keeping things going, and being reminded of Dad at every turn. Look, if you feel like getting out for a couple of hours, I'll mind the fort. I've got some figures to work on anyway. Get yourself a breath of fresh air."

George just shook his head, and sat down with his elbows on the desk, his face buried in his hands as though in prayer. After Alan had left he sat looking at the half-open door for what seemed an age. From the floor below, he could hear cheerful voices, the whine of the fork-lift, the ring of the cash-register. Dad was gone, but the business went on. Life went on. With a small sigh he reached into the bottom drawer, took out the bottle and glass, and poured a stiff measure.

"Here's to life."

Alan let out a long breath as he closed behind him the door of his own office – the big one at the corner with windows on two sides, that had been his father's. For a moment his legs felt like jelly, and he leant back against the door.

"My God, that was a close one!"

He sat down at his desk and reached for his battered address-book, then picked up the telephone.

"Armitage Brick? Can I speak to Bill Theakston, please? Bill, hullo, it's Alan Hawkins. Yes, I've just heard about Neil. Look, the fact is, we need to talk Yes, it's important. Will you be there if I come in at the end of the afternoon, say five o'clock? No, I don't think it will take long. Thanks, Bill, see you at five."

So that could be sorted out. Make a nasty hole in the old bank-balance though. Still, it would be months before Armitage would want the cash, and in the meantime there were a few other arrangements due to mature. That's a problem for the future though, making sure George doesn't stumble across any more evidence. Damn George and his Puritan conscience, sticking his nose into things that don't concern him. Life would be a lot simpler if he weren't there. So what if I've used my intelligence to squeeze a couple of percent extra out of a few suppliers? The company hasn't suffered, in fact it's doing very nicely thank you. And where's the sense in making the tax-man richer? God help George if Jenny really has got something good going, and he tries to block that!

His train of thought was interrupted by the telephone ringing. The irritation was only to obvious in his voice when he answered.

"Yes? Who is it?"

"Mr. Hawkins? Mr. Alan Hawkins? I hope I'm not calling at an inconvenient time? This is Staffordshire Police, Detective Sergeant Andrew Wilson. We're enquiring into the murder of a young girl in Lynchester on Saturday evening last, and we'd like to ask you for your help. Had you heard about it?"

Coming immediately on top of the confrontation with George, Alan felt as though some evil Nemesis had chosen today to bring him down, and he sat for a long moment looking at the telephone receiver as though it possessed some terrible power of its own. What could possibly have led the police to call him?

"Murder? No, sorry, I haven't seen this morning's paper, if it's in there. What's it all about? What makes you think I can help?"

"Just routine, sir. The poor young lady had dinner at the Tennis Club on Saturday evening, and we are talking to everyone who might have seen her there. Your name was amongst the table-reservations, so I'd like to come in to see you as soon as possible. Say in half an hour?"

"That's a bit awkward, I've got some important business that won't wait. Look, I need to come into town anyway, can I come and find you at the police station, say ten-thirty?"

"Ten-thirty will be fine sir. We're at the T.A. Drill Hall by the way, not enough room for us in the police station."

"So, if I might sum up your statement, Mr. Hawkins? You've known Miss Stevens casually as a member of the Club, and you knew her friend Miss Clumber the same way. You remember seeing them at supper together, apparently in earnest conversation, but you have no recollection of either of them after that. You spent the entire evening, from seven-thirty to just after midnight, at the Club with your wife, your brother and his wife, and you did not leave the Club at all until you all left together. Is that everything?"

"It is."

"You've given us also this list of names of everyone else you can remember seeing. Is there anything at all you could add which could be useful to us?"

"Not really. I mean, it's so terrible isn't it? It's hard to think what could be helpful to you. Susan used to be around the Club a lot, in fact last year I remember she and Joyce were the losing finalists in the Ladies Doubles. They'd have won this year for sure, but I don't think I've seen Susan on a court this summer. Joyce has been around quite a lot, but she hasn't had a regular partner, so I can't see her making this year's final. I don't suppose that's of any help?"

"You never know, sir. I'll have this typed up, and if you drop by later in the week you can sign it for me. And perhaps when you speak to your wife you could ask her to give D.S. Alison Clarke a call to go through the same process for us? And thank you very much for your co-operation, sir."

As he came out of the Drill Hall, Alan felt altogether too sweaty and shaky to go back to the office, with the ever-present possibility of another run-in with his brother. Besides, Jenny was expecting him for lunch in an hour or so. He decided to go home to freshen up.

The house was cool and empty.

He felt in control again as he towelled dry after a long shower, buttoned up a clean white shirt, and climbed into his new fawn slacks. He used Grace's blow-drier as he combed the wave into his thick fair hair, and he grinned at his reflection in the dressing-table mirror. *Nice-looking chap that! How could anyone even think he might be involved in a murder? No fool that detective though, asked all the right questions. He got all the right answers too!*

Chapter Seven

Jennifer Hawkins had slept badly, but woke early nonetheless, and called Alan at home to tell him about the extraordinary proposition Christopher Layton had outlined,

"Alan, there could be enough money for all of us! Even if George wants to carry on with the Merchant business, there'd be enough for him to simply move it to another site. I hardly slept a wink last night, just thinking about it . . ."

"Steady on now Jenny love, there's a long way to go yet. But it's lovely to hear you so excited and full of life again. It's your day off today isn't it? All right for some, but I've got work to do. How about if I come over in the lunch hour and we talk it through calmly? All right? Look forward to that. Cheers for now."

Jenny was intensely fond of her rose-garden, and decide to spend the cool of the morning tidying it up. The old-fashioned climbers on the pergola were past their best, but it was still blissful as she pottered happily along its cool, richly-perfumed tunnel, weeding, pruning, tying-back, just enjoying the pleasant physical labour and proud of the beauty she had created. Her thoughts kept drifting back to the subject of Alan, and the expression of desire she was certain she had seen on his face,

"I wonder what he really thinks of me? Does he think about me at all, or was that look just an automatic reaction to any good-looking woman in a summer blouse? Of course I wouldn't really want to come between him and Grace. She's such a nice little thing. Still, you couldn't call them a devoted couple exactly. Everyone knows that Alan's got a roving eye, and if half the stories about him are true, he's long ago stopped worrying about his marriage vows. Perhaps they just have a convenient arrangement between them? She and the children are well taken care of, and he keeps his activities discreet? Surely she must know what goes on?"

After about an hour, the pergola was finished, and she stretched out on a grassy bank in the sun for a rest.

Just suppose, for a moment, that this deal goes through. I'm going to be a rich woman. Even after costs and taxes, I'd have to be left with well over a half-million, and this house of course. So, without lifting a finger, I could have, say, thirty thousand pounds a year coming in. How would I spend that? What do I want from my life now? God, these last few months have been hard, having to watch poor Joe just fade away. No wonder I've been a bit down. Mmm, this sun feels lovely on my face. I'm definitely not down now! I feel like a girl again, except that I know my way around. I'm still young, I'm attractive to men, I've built a successful business, and, with any luck, I'm going to be quite disgustingly well-off. I can do anything I want, I can get anything I put my mind to. So what do I want?

Her pleasant daydream was disrupted by the sound of the Town Hall clock, winding up to chime the hour.

"Nine, ten, eleven, twelve. Heavens, it's midday! Alan will be here in half an hour, and I'm covered in mud!"

Jennifer sprinted through the french windows and took the wide staircase two at a time. She thought longingly about a bath, decided there wasn't time, and settled for a stinging cold shower that made her gasp at first, and then was sheer bliss for two minutes. As she turned off the water and wrapped her body in a big soft bath towel, she came to a conclusion of sorts,

This is the first day of the rest of my life, and I'm going to enjoy whatever comes my way.

She flicked quickly through her wardrobe – she'd bought nothing except the black all year – *what would suit the occasion? Something summery and innocent, but maybe slightly encouraging* . . . she chose a simple white cotton dress, trimmed with bright orange piping at the hem, and an orange leather belt she used to cinch in her waist an extra notch. It had a high collar with a deep 'V' neckline that flattered her curving bosom. She brushed the shine back into her dark hair, and pinned it back neatly with two large combs that allowed a thick lustrous tress to curl down her back.

"Jenny, that was just great. Apple pie is the guaranteed route to my heart!"

Alan pushed away his plate with a sigh, and held up a hand to refuse a second helping. They were sitting around the scrubbed pine table in the old-fashioned kitchen, which was shaded and cool at this time of day.

"You've listened very patiently, Alan, while I've chattered on about this idea for a retail development. What do you really think of it? Could it really happen?"

Jennifer stood beside him as she refilled his glass with the last of the chilled, flowery German Spatlese. He felt the warmth of her arm as it brushed his cheek, and knew, with absolute certainty, that she had paused there on purpose. He raised a hand to steady hers as she tipped up the bottle, and felt the tension in her body. What made her so nervous? He kept his reply carefully matter-of-fact.

"As always, everything will depend on the Council's reaction to the application for outline planning consent. Dad knew a lot more about the ins and outs of it than I do, but I'd guess that the Council will want the extra tax revenue and the jobs that would follow, and there'd be opposition from the existing shopkeepers, who can put together a good deal of clout if they combine forces. And there'd be a protest from the Green brigade about the loss of Crabbe's Marsh, although it was actually excluded when the wood itself was made a protected area."

She moved away and busied herself at a worktop, making coffee. As though drawn by a magnetic force, Alan rose and stood behind her. As she poured the boiling water into the cafetiere, she tried to make casual conversation.

"What about that awful murder in Crabbe's Wood? It was on the local news at breakfast. I wonder if I'm safe here by myself?

Alan rested his hands on the worktop each side of her. Had his reading of the signs been correct? There was one way to find out.

"Do you know you've got a birthmark, just here behind your left ear?"

He touched her neck just below the ear, and she jerked her head away in a startled reaction. For a few long seconds she said nothing, slowly pressing down the plunger on the pot. Then she turned in slow silence, leaning back against the worktop and looking up full into his face. That arrogant bony nose, those blue eyes and that boyish wave of fair hair. It could be Joe fifteen years ago! But there was a hardness about Alan, a spoilt streak perhaps, that made him different from his father. She guessed that he was off-balance for the moment, even a little unsure of himself. A good opportunity to keep him that way . . .

On a sudden impulse she reached up to pull his head down, and kissed him. She felt the surprise on his lips, which warmed rapidly to enthusiasm as he wrapped his arms around her body, lifting her for a few moments onto tiptoe. She revelled in that glorious feeling of wanting and being wanted again, then pushed him away firmly with her hands flat on his chest.

"Oh Jenny, sweetheart, I've always wanted you, ever since that day when Dad first brought you into the Yard. But I could see then that he fancied you himself, perhaps before he did, and I never dared think even . . . you do like me don't you? Say that you feel it, the same as I do?"

Jennifer stood close to him, her eyes bright with the excitement of that kiss, the hardness of his body still imprinted on her,

"I don't know what I think or feel, Alan. It was just a sudden impulse, because you reminded me so of Joe when we first met. Coffee's ready now I think. Why don't you go out into the garden, and I'll bring it out to you."

Alan felt vaguely uncomfortable, aware that Jennifer had taken back the initiative, and uncertain what the result might be if he tried to renew the attack at this time. He walked out from the kitchen into the bright sunlight on the patio, and stretched out on the same padded lounger that Christopher Layton had occupied the previous evening. The unanswered question hung between them as Jennifer came out with the tray, and busied herself serving coffee.

"I do like you Alan, but I never thought . . . I didn't mean . . . Oh, you know what I'm trying to say. How is it between you and Grace?"

The sudden directness of the question took Alan by surprise again, just as her half-spoken apology was beginning to restore his wounded ego. How was it between Grace and himself?

"All right, I suppose. How's it supposed to be when you've been married a few years? We still share a bed, if that's what you mean. But, well, she's got the kids, the tennis, squash now in the winter, swimming too. And I've got the business to worry about. I know George thinks he does all the work, but who does he think brings in the work in the first place? And he's useless at any negotiation, whether it's buying or selling. Too soft-hearted I think. So it's me that has to earn the profit. You and me, Jenny, we're alike in lots of ways. We're that bit hungrier for more out of life. Together we could knock them all for six. Don't you feel it?"

Together! That was some kind of proposition. Did she want that? Was Alan prepared to walk out on Grace and the children? Or did he have something altogether more casual in mind?

"Alan, this is all going too fast. Just one kiss means I like you, but I don't know about anything else at this moment. Can we just slow down? Let's talk about George for a minute. He's not likely to come out against this deal, is he?"

Alan recognised, with a small inward sigh, that he was not going to make more progress that afternoon. *Those big, dark eyes under the arching eyebrows, the promise of those heavy breasts, and the long slim legs now so primly crossed, all that would have to wait for another time. If there was to be another time? He would have to try to be patient for once, Jenny was worth a wait. Maybe she would come to depend on him as this development got under way.*

"I don't know what got into George yesterday morning at Charles Harrison's. Most of the time he's too sozzled nowadays to care much about anything. He doesn't often seem tight, I know, But you try to keep a watch on the bottle of Scotch he keeps in his bottom drawer at the office. He's supping at it all day, I reckon. Little and often, that's his way. I'd guess he's up to a bottle a day now. Something's got to be done, it can't go on this way."

"I had no inkling, really I hadn't. How long has this been going on?"

"The drinking? Years, I suppose. But it's got serious over the last six months, since Dad . . ."

"I understand. George was always very close to your father wasn't he?"

They drank coffee together in the warm afternoon sunshine, and agreed in a relaxed, friendly way that 'something must be done' about George and his drinking, with Jennifer undertaking to see if it might be possible to get Helen to lead the attempt. Alan urged caution.

"Just be careful and diplomatic when you talk to Helen. She can be very prickly and protective where George is concerned. I'll lay odds that it was Helen that screwed up George's courage to make that speech yesterday."

Alan remembered his appointment to cover his tracks at Armitage Brick, and stood up to go. Jennifer shaded her eyes as she looked up at him, suddenly huge in the glare of the sunlight. He leaned down and kissed her on the forehead, determined not to try again until he detected more encouragement.

"Great lunch, Jenny. No point in getting too excited about the deal until you get something formal on paper that we can show to Charles. I do want you, more than I can say, but I'll wait while you make your mind up. You're worth a wait, I know."

There was a hint of a swagger in his walk as he left, raising a hand to say, "Don't get up." Jenny felt the tension draining out of her body. Alan was just a boy really, playing games that he enjoyed winning. So why did her stomach knot up with excitement each time he came near?

Chapter Eight

First thing in the morning, the old Drill Hall that had been pressed into use as the Incident Room for the murder investigation was reasonably cool, but by mid-afternoon it was oppressively hot and stuffy. The tall, lancet windows could not be opened, and the sun shone against one side or the other all day. Rows of constables sweated and answered the telephones at the trestle tables in the Hall itself, while Alison Clarke and Andrew Wilson used the two small offices for interviews. There were only two lavatories, and their use throughout the day added to the general miasma.

"Who was that pair?"

Alison looked up from the report of interview she was drafting, and smiled wearily as she accepted the mug of strong tea that Andrew had brought into her office.

"Pair? Oh, you mean the Mrs. Hawkins. Close to aristocracy in Lynchester, one might say. The pretty little one with curly dark hair is Grace, wife to Alan, and the tall bony one with the blonde hair shoulder-length is Helen, wife to George. They were at the Club on Saturday night with their husbands, so it saved time to interview them together. They were as keen as mustard to help. Helen claims that she knew Susan and Joyce casually, and thinks she remembers the two of them going out together at around ten o'clock. She remembers the time because that was when their foursome got up from dinner, and she and Grace went off to powder their noses while the men went for a game of snooker before the disco got going properly."

"When are you due to meet Joyce again?"

"In about an hour. It could be quite an interview."

Andrew turned to leave, then paused at the door,

"Be careful, won't you, Alison. Remember what the Chief said about having a W.P.C. present, and the video-recorder. By the way, any luck with the knee-prints you went out to look for?"

"No sign. I suppose it was always a long shot. The ground is hard there, and it seems to have been a popular area for picnics, so the grass is pretty well trampled. It was always a bit of wishful thinking when you look at it. Mind you, Joyce won't know that, so I might have a card to play. By the way, we have another line to follow up. The fiance says he didn't know about the baby, but thinks it could have been his. Susan told him she was on the pill of course. So we're doing the D.N.A. tests. If it turns out not to have been his, we could have another lead, perhaps."

"Provided the father was amongst the forty or so men we've identified already as having been at the Tennis Club on the night. Then all we've got to do is match the D.N.A., prove motive and opportunity, and ideally get a confession."

"Somehow, Andrew, I sense that you aren't feeling your usual cheerful, optimistic self."

"Joyce, you're very prompt. Thank you very much for coming in to see us again. Please do sit down, I know how very painful it must be for you to be reminded of Susan, but we do need all the help we can get. Can I get you a cup of tea?"

Joyce Clumber shook her head, and sat down, stiffly upright on the folding wooden chair in front of Alison's desk. Her smooth black hair was neatly bobbed, and held back from her face with a youthful alice-band. There was a just perceptible hook in her fine Roman nose, and her dark complexion might also have been an inheritance from some Moorish ancestor. She wore a plain, navy-blue cotton dress, cinched in at the waist with a wide matching belt, which emphasised her athletic figure. She looked around the tiny office with an expression of sullen hostility.

"What's that she's got in the corner?"

"It's a video-recorder. We've started using them routinely for interviews. This is W.P.C. Davies by the way. Apart from running the recorder for us, she's also sitting in as part of her training. You don't mind, I hope?"

"Why should I?"

Alison decided to go straight on to the attack.

"Now, Joyce, we have reason to believe that you were not completely frank with us when you gave us your statement. At this stage I'm prepared to be persuaded that you were very upset at the time and weren't really thinking about what you were saying. But I have to warn you now that if you persist in telling a story that we know to be untrue, or only partly true, you will very quickly find yourself in deep trouble. Do I make myself clear?"

Joyce glared fixedly at Alison, as if she wanted to drill into the mind of her accuser. Alison sensed that she was torn between stalking out of the room and attacking her, and was glad of the presence of the W.P.C. After a long, long pause Joyce spoke slowly and carefully, now in full control again,

"Am I to be accused of something? Because if I am, I should have a solicitor here now. I've told you everything I know, and tried to help you catch . . . She was my best friend, and now you're cutting her up on some marble slab somewhere, and accusing me of I don't know what."

"Did you know that she was pregnant?"

Joyce flinched visibly as though avoiding a blow.

"I'm waiting for your answer, Joyce. It's surely a simple enough question, did you know or didn't you?"

"Yes, I knew. She called to tell me last week, when we fixed up this weekend. Silly thing, she seemed quite pleased about it. I told her she was too young to tie herself down to a baby. She is . . . was a bit weak about men sometimes."

Alison got the impression that Joyce was not reluctant to talk about Susan's past, and decided to pursue that line, saving the harsher interrogation till later.

"Did you advise her to get rid of it, to have an abortion?"

"Like I said, I thought she was to young to tie herself down. Yes, I said she should get shot of it before it was too late."

"As she had done previously, the time before?"

There was another long pause,

"I don't want you to get the idea into your head that Susan was, well, some sort of loose woman."

Alison thought the choice of words had an old-fashioned sound,

"Go on, Joyce. What sort of girl was Susan, really?"

"She was nice, gentle, soft-hearted. She wanted people to like her. When her parents broke up she tried it here for a bit, then got this job in Birmingham, and went off there by herself. Naturally she needed friends and, well, I reckon she was taken advantage of, if you know what I mean."

"Who was the father?"

"Of the first one? I never did know, she wouldn't tell me. Said it was a proper gentleman who'd looked after her, and that was the end of it. I tried lots of times to get it out of her, but she wouldn't say."

"What about the second one?"

"Susan said it was her fiance's, Bob Heaton. Have you talked to him? He's a salesman, got good prospects, so she said. Apparently he just swept her off her feet. But they were planning to get married, so I suppose . . . suppose he must have loved her in his way."

"How did you feel about that?"

"About what?"

"About Susan getting married and having a baby?"

"I told you, didn't I? I thought she wasn't ready for babies yet."

"And marriage? How did you feel about Susan getting married?"

"I haven't met Bob, so why would I have any feelings about it either way?"

"Why indeed? It was her life wasn't it? But I think you did care about it, and very strongly indeed. I believe your relationship with Susan was much more intense, much more intimate than you've led us to believe so far. In fact I think that you and Susan were lovers, and have been for several years. Think carefully before you answer, Joyce. I can see a denial in your face, but I've got plenty of statements to support what I'm saying."

Alison tapped the pile of papers in front of her. In truth there wasn't much confirmation, just a couple of casual remarks about two attractive girls who spent a lot of time together, and the absence of boyfriends. Alison tried to look confident,

"Well, do you want to tell me the truth?"

Suddenly Joyce's shoulders slumped, and her dark eyes filled with tears,

"There's you, and her, and that video thing. How do I know that anything I say won't be all over town in an hour?"

"I give you a solemn promise, Joyce. If you are innocent, everything you say here will be as private as if you were talking to your doctor or vicar."

"Priest. Priest, not vicar. I'm Roman Catholic, you see. But I've never confessed . . . I just couldn't . . . I mean, what if he said I had to promise not to do it again?"

"Confess what, Joyce? I have to warn you that anything you say may be recorded, and may be used against you in a court of law, and . . ."

"Court? Law? It's not a crime, not a crime to love someone is it? I loved Susan, of course I did. I loved her. I loved her more than anything else in the world."

She was sobbing now, and Alison pulled out a tissue for Joyce to wipe her cheeks. Suddenly filled with pity she said,

"Look Joyce, I can see you're very upset. We don't have to go on now. We could break off and start again tomorrow."

Instantly she regretted her generous impulse. *Joyce was wide open now, and would surely tell the full story if pressed. Tomorrow she would have her defences rebuilt, might even have consulted a solicitor. The D.C.I. would be furious at such a stupid mistake, "That's the trouble with women, they let their emotion get in the way of the job. Too soft, and a murderer goes free."*

"No, no I want to go on now. You seem . . . kind. I feel that you understand, and now I've got to tell someone or I'll die."

Alison heaved a silent sigh of relief, and carefully avoided the eye of W.P.C. Davies. No doubt Davies had spotted the risk.

"All right then, Joyce. I do understand how you must be feeling. Let's take it slowly and calmly, shall we? Can we go back to the beginning? When did you first become lovers?"

"We were in the same class together, all through school. Susan was always the pretty one, but she was shy and a bit weedy, you know. The other kids would pick on her to bully her, but I took her side, stuck up for her, and we became friends. Do I have to go into the rest of it?"

Alison was concerned not to interrupt the flow of confession,

"We can skip the rest of the stuff about school. What happened after you left school?"

"I got a job teaching aerobics, you know physical fitness, diet for housewives, that sort of thing. I was always good at gym at school. Did you know I was the County junior champion at 400 metres? Susan did a secretarial course, then landed a job at Harrison's the accountants. She is . . . was always very neat and methodical, good at arithmetic too."

Joyce's voice trailed away, and her expression became abstracted, her thoughts locked away in some remembered past.

"Go on, please Joyce. There isn't much more to tell now is there?"

The pain Joyce was experiencing was only too apparent.

"It's so terrible isn't it, her being dead, I mean. She was so pretty . . . so helpless."

There was another pause, but this time Alison kept silent and waited. Eventually Joyce shook her head slowly, as though to dismiss further regrets, and continued quite firmly,

"Where was I?"

"Susan got a job as a secretary."

"That's right. But things became awful for her here, her mother and father were having rows all the time. I don't know what about, not for sure,. Susan thought there was another woman. She came to stay with us for a bit, that's when I was still living at home. Then she decided to get a job in Birmingham."

"Did you encourage her to do that?"

"Go off alone you mean? No, I certainly did not."

"You quarrelled about that?"

"Quarrelled? No, I wouldn't say quarrelled. We argued a bit. I was planning to get my own flat, and of course she could have lived there. But I think there was somebody, a man, who was offering to help her get set up in Birmingham."

"Do you have any idea who that was?"

"No, no idea at all really. I always thought it might be the same one that fixed up her abortion, but, like I said, she knew how to keep a secret. She never would say anything about him, except that he was a sweet lover."

"Did she tease you with that?"

"How do you mean?"

"Brag about her wonderful experiences with him, that sort of thing."

"No, absolutely not. She really loved me, see. She wouldn't do or say anything to hurt me."

"What happened after Susan moved away?"

"At the beginning she used to come back to stay at my new flat most weekends. We went on holiday together last summer, rented a boat on the Broads. We were really close."

"And then?"

"Well, these last few months, she's been really busy. Moved out of her furnished rooms and into an apartment in Edgbaston, two bedrooms and a lovely view across the whole city, especially at night."

"How could she afford that?"

"Renting, I suppose, like anyone else. She had a very good job, she'd been promoted to confidential secretary and personal assistant to one of the directors. I know she made a lot more than I did."

Alison could see that Joyce was becoming self-assured again. Her answers were less emotional, and she was volunteering fewer insights into her relationship with Susan. But she was reluctant to let up if there was a chance of a confession that afternoon. She decided to keep on with the 'softly, softly' approach that seemed to be paying dividends.

"This last Saturday afternoon, I imagine you and Susan had a wonderful day together?"

"It was lovely, just the way it used to be. I mean her fiance was off on this company shindig in Spain, and Susan was absolutely fed up because he'd gone off and left her. She came over in the morning, and we were so friendly again, just like always. We had lunch in the pub, then lots of tennis. Susan hadn't played for ages, but she got her forehand going ever so well, I was really proud of her. We talked about going in for the Ladies Doubles again. Afterwards we had a bath, and a bit of a rest . . ."

"I understand, Joyce, please go on."

"Then we put on our faces and glad-rags, and came back to the Club. We'd booked a table, being Saturday night, sort of celebration."

"But something went wrong?"

Joyce opened her mouth as if to reply, then suddenly stood up, her hands resting on Alison's desk, her face reddening with anger, and only inches from Alison's.

"You bitch! You bloody, bloody bitch!"

The W.P.C. moved forward, but Alison checked her with a hand movement, and rose quietly to confront Joyce, though she was half a head shorter.

"There's no need to get upset, Joyce. I am trying to be your friend, I really am. You said yourself you had to tell someone."

"That's what I mean. I thought you were my friend. But you're not. You're a conniving, cheating . . . You think I did it, don't you? You think I killed Susan! How could you think that? I loved her. Haven't I spent all this time to explain to you how much I loved her? If I find the bastard that killed her I'll . . . I'll . . . well, you'll see what I'll do. As for you, you're rubbish! You're not trying to help me at all, you're just hoping to pin it on me and get yourself a promotion or something. Well, I'm not saying another word, and you can turn that bloody machine off, miss. Can I go, if I want to? Or are you going to arrest me? You'll be sorry if you do, I can tell you that."

Joyce sat down as suddenly as she had stood up, and folded her arms in a gesture of defiance. Alison gestured to W.P.C. Davies to turn off the video-recorder, and made a last try to rescue the interview.

"Joyce, I do want to be your friend. I want to help you, really I do. Look I've turned off the video, just like you wanted, and if you want, I'll send the W.P.C. out of the room, so it will be just you and me, for a few minutes more. How would that suit?"

"I don't trust you now, no matter what you say. I'm not talking any more about it without a solicitor, and that's final."

Alison had to accept that there was no point in going on. The rapport that she had so carefully constructed was totally destroyed. Could she hold Joyce on suspicion? So far, there wasn't a shred of hard evidence, just the feeling she had that Joyce was holding something back. That last show of righteous indignation – had it been genuine surprise at being suspected, or could it have been an act put on for her benefit?

"All right, Joyce, you can go now if you want, but I'd like you back tomorrow, when you've finished work. Bring your solicitor if you feel it's necessary. O.K.?"

Joyce stood up in silence, as if dazed. Her dark eyes searched Alison's face to find some clue as to what was really happening.

"I liked you in the beginning you know. I thought . . . thought we might be friends. But you don't really want a friend like me, do you?"

Chapter Nine

Having convinced George that the suspect 'backhanders' were perfectly above board, Alan found it easy to get him to accept the proposed plan for the "Hawkins Centre", provided there was a clear promise that George would be allowed to have the merchant business to relocate. Despite this prospect, George continued to spiral more deeply into his world of private misery. Most weekdays he sipped his way through a bottle of whisky, without ever appearing drunk. In the evenings and at weekends he managed with much less, with Helen for company, and his beloved fishing to distract his thoughts.

Two days after the lunch with Alan, Jennifer arranged to visit Helen 'for a cup of coffee and a chat'. Helen was a woman of independent mind, and Jennifer knew that she would not take kindly to any approach that seemed to criticise George behind his back, or that could be construed as patronising. Aware that she was threading a path through a minefield, Jennifer began by admiring the way Helen had decorated and furnished their enlarged farm cottage, with its beautiful view down to the river and Lynchester in the background, then chose a practical issue to start,

"Helen, I wanted to ask your advice about this development project. What do you think about it? Should we be selling up and encouraging them to build the Hawkins Centre?"

Helen poured more coffee for both of them from her best bone-china service, and sat stirring her cup for what seemed an age. She was a gangling, bony woman, with blonde hair that she wore long, usually covering one side of her face, except when she pushed it back with a restless gesture. Ten years ago she had been quite handsome, Jennifer recalled, but her looks had faded as lines of discontent had become etched around her thin mouth. After what seemed to Jennifer an age, she seemed to come to a decision,

"I'd like to be rich, same as anyone else, I should think. Of course, it's George that has to decide, I mean the shares are in his name, aren't they? But he listens to me, if that's what you're after. We talked about it a lot when the old man died. I liked Joe Hawkins, did you know that? I reckon I went in to see him as often as you did."

"I know, I'm grateful. He . . . he needed love, especially at the end."

"Yes. Well, after he'd gone, George and me talked about the business. I knew Alan and you'd want to sell up, and I told George not to. Not unless he was going to clear half a million or so. I mean, it's not a matter of principle or anything, it's just that, you see, George has built his whole life around it. So if he sells up, he's got to get enough to start up again. I'm not having him mooning around here doing nothing, with me just scraping by, or having to go out to work full-time again."

"I don't know about mooning around, Helen. I can see that someone's done masses of painting and wallpapering around the house, and the garden is looking an absolute picture. I bet you've made sure that George does his bit. He always was a fair handyman, wasn't he?"

Helen allowed a rare smile to emerge, and looked momentarily much younger.

"Oh, I've kept him up to the mark, I suppose. But these last few weeks, I don't know, he's been under the weather or something. He misses his father, more than any of us knows, I think."

Jennifer was grateful for the opening to talk about George, and decided to plunge on,

"Alan said to me that he's more than a bit worried about George too. He thinks he's been drinking. A lot, and in the office."

Helen bristled defensively, sitting suddenly upright in her chair, and furiously pushing back her hair from her face,

"Oh, I see, so it's Alan and you now, is it? I wonder, does Grace know what's going on? And poor Joe barely cold in his grave. I should be careful if I was you."

"Helen, it's nothing like that, really it isn't."

Jennifer felt a moment of small surprise that the lie came so easily.

"Alan came to see me because he cares about his brother, and hopes we can do something to help him before it's too late. He really is worried. He told me he thought George might be getting through as much as a bottle a day. Like you, I've noticed that George has been a bit miserable recently, but I put it down to him missing his father, as you did. But it's more serious than that, believe me."

"I could believe that Alan would come to you, rather than have the guts to say something to George's face, or to me. He's a shifty piece of work is Alan, always has been. If he hasn't made a pass at you, it's only because he's biding his time. He will. He tried it on with me, a few years ago. I sent him packing with a flea in his ear, I can tell you."

Helen glared at Jennifer, who sat in silence and waited for the storm to subside. Eventually Helen sighed, stood up, and walked slowly over to the big new picture window that looked out over the garden and the river below.

"I'm sorry, Jenny, I shouldn't have gone for you like that. I suppose I've been worried too, without quite knowing why. Not seeing the wood for the trees, perhaps. He's no trouble, you know. Most evenings he eats his tea, then if it's fine he takes his rod across the field there to the river."

She looked suddenly alarmed,

"Do you think he's drinking there too? I know he likes a tot, I can smell the whisky on his breath. But he never seems to be what you'd call drunk. He talks quite steady, sensibly I'd say, most of the time. And yet . . ."

Helen stopped, came back to her chair, and busied herself collecting the cups back onto the tray. Jennifer tried to be supportive,

"You've noticed something different too, haven't you?"

"I suppose I have. He's changed, quite recently really. About bed, and all that. He used to be, well, very affectionate like. But this last month or so he's sort of lost interest. I didn't worry about it, though I must say I did give it a thought when I read about that girl being murdered. Well, any woman would, if you thought he was bottling it up somehow. But then Alan said George was with him at the time, so I just put it down to the grieving over his father. But the whisky is something else, isn't it?"

"It certainly is, especially if George is putting away anything like the amount Alan says. It's not just the problem in bed, it could kill him. You're a nurse, you know what happens better than me, I should think."

Helen sat down heavily into the armchair, covered her face with her hands, and then slowly pushed her long hair back again. There was a look of emptiness and of bleak despair, and her pale eyes brimmed with tears.

"Oh Jenny, what can I do? He's everything to me. I don't know what I'd do if I lost him."

Instinctively Jennifer crossed over the room to sit on the arm of Helen's chair, and comforted her with as much confidence in her tone as she could manage,

"There, there, don't take on, love. We'll sort something out, don't you worry. The first thing is to get him to recognise that he's got a problem, and then find him something to focus on, something important for the future. How about this new development? Surely he can take an interest in getting a million to set up afresh? How about looking around for a new site for the yard? And once he comes to realise how much we all care, that should pull him back, don't you think?"

Christopher Layton leaned back in his chair and looked out of the elegant Georgian window of his Mayfair office. The little Lynchester deal was coming together very nicely, he thought. He had the option on the Crabbe's Marsh plot, and the Hawkins site was available if the price was right, he felt sure. Tesco and Asda had expressed strong interest, Boots and W.H. Smith were near certainties, and he knew he could rely on one of the D.I.Y.

chains to round out his list of "anchors" for the new Mall. With those in place, the other shops would be easy to lease. Turiff had put together a very nice "design-and-build" package which he had used already to sound out the Chairman of the local Planning Committee, Councillor Rowlands. He had apparently been an old crony of Joe Hawkins, and was also a great admirer of the beautiful widow, so that looked very promising. As anticipated, there was some opposition over the use of Crabbe's Marsh, but it really was virtually a derelict site at present, because of the regular winter flooding, and it seemed unlikely that a big enough protest movement could be stirred up to make a costly and time-consuming public enquiry necessary. Unwise to count one's chickens of course, but with any luck they could be breaking ground before the year was out, and opening for business to catch the following Christmas. Very neat, and very profitable.

At the back of his 'Lynchester Mall' file was a collection of newspaper cuttings, including a two-page spread, with pictures from the Lynchester Herald. The banner headline said it all:

LOCAL GIRL FOUND MURDERED IN BEAUTY SPOT

The story also made the front page of the Birmingham Post and of the Evening Mail, and there was a half-column from the Daily Telegraph. The Sun had a story about Crabbe's Wood having been a noted meeting place for witches, and trailed the possibility that the girl had been killed in a ritual. More recently there was another appeal from the police for anyone who knew, or had seen Susan, to come forward. 'Baffled detectives seek new leads' the headline proclaimed.

A slight smile played across Christopher Layton's cadaverous features as he re-read this last item. *Really this stuff ought not to be in the open office file, not now that the project was so active . . .* He took out all the clippings, and looked through them again on his desk, tapping his long fingers abstractedly as he read. Coming to a sudden decision, he carefully tore each cutting into small pieces and swept the lot into his waste basket. "Poor Susan", he murmured softly.

Chapter Ten

"Let's be honest with ourselves, shall we? We don't have even one promising lead, do we?"

Detective Chief Inspector Jim Renton leaned back in the office chair of the T.A. Drill Hall that served as the Incident Room for the Lynchester murder inquiry, laced his fingers behind his head, and made a face at the ceiling. The Friday meeting with his two assistants to review the investigation was going nowhere, and his progress report to the A.C.C. would be doing him no good at all. He could hear the sneer in the A.C.C.'s clipped tones.

"Bit of a "No-Progress" report, wouldn't you say, Jim? Time for fresh minds perhaps? Cap in hand to New Scotland Yard, do you think?"

He sat forward, suddenly brisk and purposeful again,

"Somewhere out there is a man, or possibly a woman, who can persuade a pretty girl, engaged and expecting her fiance's baby, to lie down in the dark in a wood, take off her dress and her pants, and make love. And then can break her neck as easily as snapping a twig, and calmly walk away. What kind of person is that?"

"Are we sure it had to be in that order?"

"I don't think I quite get your gist, Andrew."

"It struck me, when you were spelling out the actions like that. The murderer could have broken her neck first, then undressed her and . . . and so on."

"I like the delicacy of the 'and so on' Andrew. O.K., at least it's an approach we had overlooked. Not common, literal necrophilia, I suppose. I mean the killer would be very weird, psychotic I'd say. Any obvious objections, Alison?"

"Struggle. I mean there were absolutely no signs of any struggle having taken place. We've assumed this was because Susan was taken by surprise in the act of making love. That's weird enough I agree, but it really would be frightening if our killer was capable of overwhelming a healthy young woman so suddenly that she was able to make no resistance at all."

"Not impossible, though. Any other thoughts?"

"Like Andrew, your catalogue of events got me thinking."

"Go on, please. We need new ideas. Badly."

"Well, I wonder if we're right to assume that lovemaking took place just before or just after the attack."

"The pathologist says so."

"Yes, but from what Joyce Clumber said, well, I wouldn't be surprised if they had a session in her flat late that afternoon, after the tennis, and before going back to the club for supper. Knowing that, the pathologist might agree that the physical signs could be explained that way, and that would also explain the absence of semen."

"I see . . . yes. We could also combine the two theories. Our killer breaks her neck, then undresses her. Why? Sexual curiosity? Or could it be that he wants us to believe that the motive was sexual?"

"Whereas the real motive could have been something quite different, you mean?"

"Exactly. I really think we may be getting somewhere. Maybe it's a stranger, who follows Susan when she leaves the club, chats her up, is turned down, perhaps very dismissively, and attacks her in a fit of rage. He breaks her neck before she can lift a finger in self-defence."

"We'd still have to explain why she would go up into the wood in the dark. Does it have to be a stranger?"

"Of course not, in fact our scenario is more plausible if it were someone she knew and trusted, some who perhaps had a real motive to kill her. Otherwise we have to assume that, alone or with a stranger, she walked up the lane and into the wood in the dark, or at least at dusk. Not many girls are that reckless these days. Trouble is, everyone at the club can account for their movements between say nine and eleven, isn't that so?"

Andrew put his hand onto the thick folder beside him, which held all the sworn statements,

"We've cross-tabbed them all, very smart little programme on the computer, and they seem to hang together. But it was a party, and people weren't really looking at their watches. We might eliminate the genuine couples for the moment, they're not likely to lose track of one another for more than a few minutes. But there were a fair number of singles, and groups of girls and men who were not strictly paired off. And there's always the possibility that we've not yet identified everyone who was there."

"I agree. Let's interview again every man who was not firmly paired off. Test the statements carefully, get them to recall each half-hour if we can, say who they were with, anyone else they saw nearby at the time and so on."

"Tall order, sir. There was a lot of drink, especially later on."

"Tall order or not, I think it's worth doing, and doing tomorrow please. How many might there be?"

Alison looked carefully through the computer printout,

"Ten, no twelve I'd say."

"Right, that's only four each. Give the list to that P.C. outside that looks bored out of his socks, and ask him to line them up for us. Allow a good hour for each."

D.C.I. Renton waited while Alison briefed the constable,

"This could produce the breakthrough we need, Andrew. Well done, lateral thinking they call it, I'm told."

"Thank you sir. Is it really a dead end in Birmingham?"

"I think so, at least until we can put up a suspect or two on an identity parade. Susan certainly had at least one regular male visitor, other than her fiance. The man in the ground-floor apartment, retired fellow named Moreni, says there's a man in a big saloon, colour uncertain, who kept using his parking space. He looked out for him more than once to tell him off, but kept missing him. He did however catch a glimpse of him late one evening, getting into his car. Too dark to see much – tall man, wearing a cap. He got the impression it wasn't an old man, but that's all we have."

"Not very promising sir, but I do have an idea that we could try. How about if I put together a little video show for this Mr. Moreni, made up of short clips from every one of the interviews with these men, the ones who were not paired off."

"I'm surprised at you Andrew, you know we undertake that the interviews will be kept absolutely secure."

"Quite. That would certainly make it hard to use any result in evidence. But if we just showed him the man coming into or getting up from the interview, just for elimination, with no sound of course, I wouldn't feel that was breaking our promise."

"O.K. But if we do get a lead from it, mum's the word, all right? If we found our murderer and the Judge threw our case out I would be very unhappy indeed. Now, Alison, how do we stand now with Joyce Clumber? Is she still your number one suspect? Surely if you think they had a steamy session before dinner, there is less likelihood that they would need to wander off in the dark later?"

Alison winced at the bluntness of the Chief Inspector's question. He was not one to respect her feminine sensitivity, she thought. *Which was just another way of saying that he treated her like a man, so she couldn't really complain, could she?*

"I'm undecided about Joyce, sir. I'm sure she's passionate by nature, very intense, certainly capable of murder if sufficiently provoked. I don't think that the pre-dinner love-making absolutely rules out a later session, no. Especially if there'd been a few drinks, a quarrel, a tentative reconciliation, then a final row. Or she could have led Susan out for a private talk, and then killed her in a cold fury and staged the undressing to put us off the scent."

"What does she say, exactly? I read the second interview, up to where she broke it off. Don't blame yourself over that, by the way, you were dealing with a pretty unstable package."

"She admits that there was a quarrel over dinner, because Susan wouldn't have the baby aborted. We know Susan believed that the fiance was the father, which may explain why she was being stubborn. Anyway it seems to give Joyce a motive – 'Hell hath no fury' – don't they say? She turned up next day escorted by her solicitor, and with the balance of her statement written out. He said it was to avoid uncertainty, and to eliminate the need for further distressing questioning."

Andrew thumbed quickly through the pile, and handed Alison a sheet of paper.

"After dinner the disco began about nine, but as usual it was a bit slow getting going. Susan and I had a dance with just a couple of other girls, but Susan said it wasn't much fun, and broke off. I thought she may have gone to the ladies room, but I never saw her again."

"That's the end of her statement. I asked Joyce if she left the Club at all. She said she hadn't. When I said we had a witness who would put her going out of the french windows at about 9.30, she said she had just gone outside for a breath of fresh air, but she had not actually left the club. After she came back in she spent quite a lot of time looking for Susan, and went to the ladies room herself, watched the dancing, and then she remembers buying herself a Cinzano at the bar before being asked to join the dancing. We have the barman who remembers selling her a drink, but thinks that was between 10.30 and 11.00. And we have one, two, no three men who actually danced with her between 11.00 and midnight, two of whom bought her drinks and had a friendly talk. They say she seemed a bit distant, but that wasn't anything unusual with Joyce."

"What about after the disco finished?"

"She says that she kept looking out for Susan throughout the evening, and at the end she hung on until the bar cleared and everyone seemed to have left, then she went home herself. She says there had been other occasions when Susan had strayed off with a man, and she had thought that was what had happened this time. She became very upset at that point, and her solicitor would not let me question her any more."

"And what's your opinion now?"

"I think we have to keep her on the list of possibles. I was right about the lesbian relationship, so Joyce seems to have had both motive and opportunity. By the way we've established that this aerobics-cum-keep fit class that Joyce runs has a men's karate and kung-fu section, run by a male instructor. He also lectures the ladies on self-defence. So Joyce could have had the opportunity to learn the skill or knack the killing might have required."

"It comes down to time, doesn't it? By Joyce's own admission, Susan went off about 9.30, perhaps a little before or after. And the barman puts Joyce buying a drink after 10.30. So there's that hour to account for. I think that in addition to tomorrow's interviews, we are going to have to go back to everyone else who was there, and ask them specifically if they can recall seeing Joyce Clumber during the evening, and try to nail down the time. Show them a picture of her in case they don't know her by name."

"Isn't that going to look as though she's a definite suspect?"

"Can't be helped, we've got to get this settled one way or the other. If she's guilty, she may well crack under the pressure, and we could get a confession."

"But if she's innocent it would be very hard on her, to lose a lover and be pilloried in the town as a suspected murderess also."

Renton looked in silence for a long minute at Alison. Was there now some bond of empathy between her and Joyce? He nodded,

"Your right, Alison, it's hard, but that's how it has to be."

Perhaps to avoid further discussion, he turned over a page on his notebook,

"Let's talk about strangers, by which I mean anyone not at the disco-night, and therefore not yet interviewed."

"That would include the mysterious boyfriend from Birmingham of course."

"It would, assuming he was not at the disco. But that's a dead-end for the moment, so I want to focus on any sightings of men anywhere near Crabbe's Wood. Let's go through every call we've had to see if there's a lead. Check again with the local police for any reports of vagrants. What about the Saturday market? Check the hotel and guest-house registers to see who stayed over. Who knows, perhaps our killer is a lonely salesman, going quietly off his trolley at the grim prospect of a weekend in Lynchester."

Both Andrew and Alison smiled as the D.C.I.'s change of mood relieved the tension of the meeting.

"We'll need to think again about manpower, sir. This lot could be really opening up the scale of the enquiry."

"Right, Alison. Frankly I don't think we are going to get much more from Joe Public unless and until we can wake up the Press with more news, so let's get all but one of the P.C.s out of the Incident Room and onto these new enquiries."

"I take it that we are fairly confident now that we do not have a serial killer on our hands?"

Jim Renton turned his gaze back towards the ceiling, and thought for several long seconds before he replied,

"We just don't have an answer to that one yet, Andrew. It seemed to me from the beginning that we would find motive and murderer in Susan's rather complex love-life, and I still incline to that line. But if it was some nutter, random or purposeful, I guess we won't be making much progress until . . ."

"Until he does another one?"

"Precisely."

Chapter Eleven

It would be an exaggeration to say that Alan Hawkins did not know the meaning of the word 'Love'. If pressed, he would say that he certainly loved his wife, Grace, and their three children – Sandra, fourteen, and already as pretty as her mother, Melanie, a tomboyish eleven, and Paul, who was five, and alternately spoiled and bullied by his sisters. Alan 'loved' his family as a man might love a house or a fine car; as possessions to be protected and treasured, without ever feeling the smallest obligation to put himself to any inconvenience on their behalf.

Alan's approach to life included certain well-structured priorities, in which the satisfaction of his pleasures came significantly higher than any notion of the duties of husband or father. Nor did Grace herself much object to this arrangement. Alan was reliable and affectionate in his way, and not usually mean with money, so the family was well-maintained. She was aware that he was less than totally faithful, but provided no particular affair impinged on herself or her circle of friends, she was not a very possessive woman physically. Grace put a lot of store by discretion and appearances.

Alan would have asserted very strongly that he had loved his mother. His understanding of what George was going through now was based on a still vivid recollection of the pain, the sense of loss, and the deep rage that he had felt when his mother had been killed. He had been engulfed for months in resentment and bitterness, because no one was ever found to be blamed for her death. Alan was eighteen at the time, and had always been his mother's favourite, perhaps because he was so like his father.

Alan's response to his mother's unthinking preference for him had been to learn to manipulate her to get his own way whenever the need arose. With her gone, he was truly lost in grief. But gradually he realised that there was a whole world of girls out there, any one of whom could be induced to take the place of his mother, at least for a few weeks or months, and to satisfy his strong sexual drive as well. If the truth was told, his feelings for Grace were not greatly different from his feelings for half a dozen other attractive girls around at the time, chiefly a desire to subdue, manipulate and possess. But it was Grace who got pregnant, Grace the daughter of Lynchester's biggest builder and Hawkins' best customer. To Joe Hawkins it seemed an ideal match, and Alan had seen no great necessity for argument.

Alan was not habitually an introspective man, but he sensed that his desire for Jennifer was of a different order from anything that he had felt before. Of course he wanted to subdue her, control her, possess her – what man wouldn't? But he knew it was more than that. When he had been with her he had wanted to bury his whole body in her. Upstairs at the yard he found himself leaning casually against the rail that bordered the deck, looking down into the aisles for a glimpse of her, elegant and business-like in white overalls. Sometimes he trembled like a schoolboy when she came upstairs, usually to chase George about some item that should have been in stock but wasn't.

For her part, having established that Alan was indeed anxious to add herself to his list of conquests, Jennifer found a strange pleasure in postponing the next steps. More than once she asked herself what she was doing, and why. *Surely there are plenty of attractive men in the world without borrowing Grace's husband? Alternatively, if you really fancy him, why are you putting it off?* And yet knew that she wanted him. Something deep and visceral drew her to him, a kind of hunger that would not be rationalised away.

About three weeks after Jennifer had visited Helen to talk about George and his drinking, the details of the proposal for the "Hawkins Mall" came through from Christopher Layton, addressed to Jennifer as the leading shareholder. It was a formidable bundle of plans, drawings and draft contracts, and Jennifer's immediate reaction was to seek the advice of the company's accountant, Charles Harrison. He was unusually enthusiastic.

"As you know, I made enquiries about Christopher Layton and his employers, Benson and Partners. They are indeed exactly what he said they were, well-known and respected property consultants, with an impeccable blue chip list of the top multiples as clients. No worries there, I think. And the Council Planning Committee are very favourably inclined, I hear, particularly after the undertaking to invite our local firms to tender for the construction contracts. That was an inspired move, if I may say so. So we're really getting down to the fine print aren't we?"

He looked with less enthusiasm at the thick pile of paper that Jennifer had brought in.

"I need to involve the solicitors at this stage, Jennifer, and they're going to need a little time to come to their valuable and no doubt expensive conclusions. Let me give this lot now to my secretary, and she'll make a copy for yourself and send them out also to Alan and George. And perhaps we can schedule a review meeting for the four of us in two weeks, that's Thursday, August 23rd. Say ten o'clock?"

George Hawkins received his copy in the next morning's post with mixed feelings. He could now see that the "Hawkins Mall" was no longer the fantasy that Jenny had chattered about, but almost a reality of brick, steel and glass. Site layouts, plans and elevations were things he understood well. He could envisage the progression from site clearance through foundations and construction to finishing, fitting out and official opening. It all made sense now. He could get a million out of it, enough to make him independent of Alan at last. But now it was necessary to start thinking about relocating the business. His head hurt, and he needed a drink, but he'd promised Helen not to have any, at least not before midday, and then only one. Where was the best place to relocate? He was determined that Hawkins Builders Merchants should continue, with himself at its head. This was his place in the world, this was where he stood. He didn't ask much from life – a bit of time to himself, preferably with a fishing-rod in his hand on a quiet stretch of the River Lynn; freedom to run the business in the way he understood best, without Alan everlastingly interfering, and without Jenny going on about how important the cash business was; and best of all, the companionship of the builders, tradesmen and suppliers he had grown up with. His share of the Hawkins Mall would buy all that, with money left over for a nice holiday and some improvements around the house for Helen. *Poor Helen, she'd had the dirty end of the stick recently. She'd always wanted kids, but they'd been unlucky that way. And she was right about the whisky, it was a killer.*

With a painful effort of will he kept his hand away from the bottom drawer of his desk where the bottle lay in wait. *Not a drop before midday. Ten o'clock, two hours to go. What about the Crabbe's Marsh? If they reinforced and built-up the river-bank as planned, might there be enough land released for a new warehouse as well? Could be a problem there if they brought in one of the big DIY multiples, like B&Q. On the other hand the Mall and its shops and parking would certainly increase the flow of customers for our D.I.Y. side. Who was there he knew on the Town Planning department? Perhaps they could suggest a good site? Only an hour and fifty minutes to go.* Usually he had taken his first drink by ten. For two weeks now he had stuck to his promise, after that long tearful evening with Helen. But today was special, he had so much to think about. *Surely if he waited until eleven that would be long enough?* George licked his lips. *Eleven then.* He began to sort out the week's out-of-stock items amongst the suppliers.

"Dear Alan,

Jennifer has today received the enclosed from Benson and Partners. As you will see, it is quite complex, and will involve consulting the solicitors as well as myself. She has therefore suggested that you should study it carefully, and I am arranging a review meeting at these offices at 10a.m. on August 23rd. Please give me a call if I can be of any assistance in the meantime. Best regards,

Yours sincerely, Charles Harrison."

Alan read and re-read the letter. "Jennifer . . . has suggested". Could this be the sign he had been waiting for? An invitation to meet again and give her the benefit of his advice? He poured out his second cup of breakfast tea and looked through the bulky papers. Maps, site plans, elevation of the 'Hawkins Centre'. That looked *very* handsome. Draft contracts, preliminary planning applications, lists of likely tenants – Tesco or Asda, Boots, W.H.Smith, what a list! Real class! He reached for the telephone.

"Morning, Jenny, it's me, Alan. Didn't wake you up I hope? Oh good. Look, I've just opened this parcel from Charles. Terrifying isn't it? What say we go over it together? I mean, I think I can follow all the site and construction stuff. The drawing of the Centre looks grand, don't you think? But I'm sure you'll be better at all the 'whereases' and 'heretofore', and especially at the money side. When would be a good time? Later today?"

Jennifer had expected that Alan would call, and was prepared for the immediate pressure he applied. She had decided to allow herself the luxury of one last postponement.

"That would be wonderful, Alan. I really do think it would be best if we worked together on it. But not today."

"Tomorrow then?"

"No, not tomorrow either. I'm already late on my promise to Charles to let him have the figures on the half-year stock take on my side, so that he can do the valuation. I'll be glad when we get the tills computerised, I really will. Anyway that's going to take all of today and most of tomorrow, and then I'll need the weekend to recover before I'll have the strength to focus on this lot. Would Monday evening suit you, Alan? Come round here after supper, say seven-thirty?"

Chapter Twelve

It was almost eight o'clock on a fine summer's evening when Alan Hawkins knocked solidly at the door of Jennifer's double-fronted Edwardian house. The sun was still warm on his back, and he felt almost a schoolboy's tremor of excitement as he saw her moving behind the old-fashioned stained glass, and heard the click of her heels on the oak floor.

"Sorry I'm late, Jenny. I was held up getting back from a sales call on a new builder in Brum, and it's been rush rush ever since".

The confidence which had served Jennifer so well up to now seemed to have deserted her, and she led the way into the big living-room with no more than a nervous smile. Alan noticed, with surprise, that she was wearing the same white dress with the orange piping that she had worn when he had come to the house before. Was that intentional, he wondered? A kind of signal that this occasion was a continuation of the last? But there was something different too. Jenny was, well, 'uneasy' was the best word he could think of. That cool, commanding poise was missing.

As she turned to face him he decided he had nothing to lose. He wrapped his arms around her and kissed her, a strong demanding pressure on her lips. He felt her stiffen momentarily as though to resist, then rising on tiptoe she put her arms around his neck and kissed him back in a long moment of total abandon. Then suddenly she was pushing him away,

"Not here, not here, Alan. Anyone could be walking past and see in. Upstairs . . . upstairs is better. Just give me a few minutes, then come up."

And she was gone, leaving him wondering how she could change so quickly. Certainly this was better than last time! He paced restlessly about the room, now bathed in a golden light, with its sunny bay window onto the street, and the french windows at the other end opening onto Jenny's rose-garden. He looked at his watch, and flopped down into a big armchair. He remembered it as a boy, covered in worn, dark green leather. Now it was a pretty chintz, with a floral pattern that echoed her roses. She was different this time . . . more like a young girl perhaps . . . yes, that was it. He relived the kiss in his imagination, feeling the warm weight of her body against him. He wondered if 'upstairs' implied what he hoped it did . . . he looked again at his watch . . . ten minutes since she had left. He walked quietly into the hall, and climbed the wide staircase with the polished mahogany balustrade. *George and I used to slide down that*, then he was pushing open the door of what he still thought of as his father's bedroom.

After the brilliant light of the hall and stairway, the bedroom was dark as he closed the door behind him. The broad bed was a few feet away, towards the curtained windows that opened onto the garden balcony.

"Over here, Alan. Over here."

Her voice was soft and inviting. Peering through the shadowy interior, he saw that Jennifer had thrown off the covers of the bed, and was indeed waiting for him under the sheet. He could make out the rounded outline of breast and hip beneath the cover, and her hair was a black mass on the pillow, partly covering her face. She sensed his uncertainty as he sat down on the bed beside her, and she reached out to touch his face,

"I told you I wouldn't go off the boil, didn't I? No ifs or buts Alan, I want you so much now."

His hand moved to stroke her throat and then her shoulder, and she sat up to let him cup her heavy pointed breasts. Eagerly she opened the buttons of his shirt, and pulled him down to her.

Once he was naked and in bed beside her she was impatient with his attempt at the rituals of foreplay,

"No, please Alan, not this time. I want you *now*."

She spread her legs wide, and stretched her arms down the length of his back to urge him into her. She felt herself jump with a sudden, sharp pain as though she was losing her virginity again, then her whole body was filled with his hardness, and at once hot waves of thundering contractions made her tighten her grip across his back until her nails scored and pierced the skin as she demanded his orgasm to satisfy her hunger.

Afterwards they lay side by side in silence, apparently staring up at the moulded patterns on the ceiling, but in reality registering nothing. Jennifer felt a relaxation of mind and body that was much deeper than anything she could remember with Joe. *So, she was a harlot, an adulteress! Did it matter? Could she get pregnant the first time? How long before Alan could do it again? 'Once more with feeling!' How many millions of his tiny sperms were even now struggling inside her, towards extinction or – or what?*

Alan was wrapped in stunned bewilderment. He had fantasised for weeks about seducing Jennifer. Even downstairs, just a few minutes ago, he had wondered what would happen when he came upstairs to find her. He had imagined long kisses which gradually melted her resistance, so that when he eased down the zip she responded at last to his touch, and as the white dress slid to the floor she would be standing before him, glorious and vulnerable. Perhaps a lace petticoat to slip off those wide shoulders . . .

Instead of all that proper seduction, as he saw it, she had simply taken him to bed and used him. It was almost like being raped! Perhaps this was how a girl felt, after yielding for the first time to the urgent excitement of a lover? He was conscious that she had turned to look at him. Her eyes were dark and mysterious – was that love, or was it triumph he saw there? She reached across to run her forefinger down his cheek, to caress his throat, and to rest her hand, now cool, on the muscle of his chest.

"Do you know you haven't said a word since you came upstairs? Was I such a surprise to you?"

Alan decided that he liked the playful smile on her lips, and the friendly warmth in her belated coquetry,

"You were a bit . . ."

"Yes?"

"A bit sudden, love. It's me really, I suppose. Apart from Grace, I've never gone with a woman my own age. Well, not since I was a kid. I just didn't know what to expect."

Jennifer smiled at the unintended compliment. She was nearly five years older than Alan, but it was nice to pretend it didn't show. She leaned over to kiss him, a warm loving sort of kiss, letting him feel the weight of her breast, with the nipple still hard. As he responded she ran an exploratory hand down his belly. 'Too soon', she thought, and kissed him lightly again,

"Don't you move an inch. Just relax there and get you breath back. I've got some bubbly chilling nicely in the fridge, and we can sip it while we go through this stuff about the Mall, can't we? Could you manage to eat a ham sandwich? I'm starving!"

Alan nodded, and watched her as she walked to the door and put on a pale silky robe that only emphasised the lines of her body. *She really is a marvellous woman. The others were just kids compared with her. And smart with it. What a team we're going to make'.*

A few minutes later she returned carrying a tray with a plateful of crusty sandwiches, two glasses and a bottle of Veuve Cliquot, beaded with condensation. He sat up and turned on the bedside lamp.

"You open the bubbly, please Alan, but don't get the bed wet. We may need it, don't you think?"

There was a gaiety about her that dissolved the last of his doubts. He was sure that she wasn't just using him, that she really liked being with him. Jennifer sat on the bed alongside him with her legs tucked underneath her, and the pale robe tied modestly around her. They giggled like children when the bubbles got up her nose and made her sneeze, and she ate most of the ham sandwiches.

Alan explained the site plan, the special drainage and bank-reinforcement for Crabbe's Marsh, and the meaning of the architect's annotations on the elevations that showed how the Centre would look, inside and out. He felt at home and comfortable as Jenny listened so attentively to his explanations, and in turn she went through the turgid prose of the draft contracts.

"Of course we will have some specialist advice from the accountants and solicitors, but it does all seem to be very much the way Mr. Layton outlined it to me. There are really three stages to the contracts, I think. At the first stage, which is now, we are offered £20,000 each, that's £60,000 altogether, for an option on the freehold of the land presently occupied by Hawkins Timber."

"£20,000 doesn't seem very much," Alan objected, trying hard to keep his thoughts on business.

"Well, it is just an option. The hook is that, if they haven't paid us the full price for the site within twelve months, the option lapses, we keep our £20,000, and we're free to do whatever we want with the land. "

"O.K. I've got that. It's the table stakes. To show they mean business. I suppose we could always suggest that thirty thou' would be more acceptable"

"Right. Why not? The second stage is that they exercise their option, and acquire the site from us. We have to give them vacant possession, they have to pay Hawkins Timber three million pounds in cash."

"The money is paid to the company? How do we get our hands on it?"

"Good point. We'll make that the key question for Charles. Obviously we want the cash in our control in the easiest way possible, preferably without handing over masses to the taxman."

"And the third stage is this offer of shares?"

As he spoke she was conscious of a gentle touch of his fingers on the inside of her thigh, and her voice shook slightly,

"That's it. And that's in the form of an option too. If we want, we can just walk away with our money. But to encourage us to sign up for stages one and two with this particular developer, we are each offered the opportunity to buy ten percent of the development, for one hundred thousand pounds each."

"Could be a gamble. I mean, if the Centre didn't let well, the company could be left with empty space and not enough income to cover the overheads and the borrowings. We've seen a few go down over the years."

"You're right to be cautious, Alan. I feel that way too. But we would be gambling with just a small part of the money. Either way, we'll have best part of a million each."

Alan ran his hand across her back, and pulled her to him for a long, slow kiss.

"Jenny, sweetheart, I love you."

He pulled at the knot of her robe, and she lay back on the bed with a sigh.

"Don't forget now, we've still got to get George to sign. Nothing can go forward without his agreement, you know."

She reached out and turned off the bedside lamp, and Alan looked up from kissing her breast,

"He'll be no problem. Just you leave George to me."

Chapter Thirteen

On Thursday August 16th D.C.I. Jim Renton had to go up to London to attend a dinner in honour of a former colleague who was retiring, so he took the opportunity to interview, without any great optimism, the three men who had signed in as visitors in local hotels on the Saturday night of the murder.

Two were easily disposed of, as they had been accompanied by their wives and had been guests at the same local wedding. The third was Christopher Layton, Retail Property Development Consultant. As the D.C.I. remarked to Detective Sergeant Alison Clarke the following day,

"If ever a bloke looked like a sex-murderer, Layton's the one. He's about six foot six, very thin, high cheekbones, deep-set dark eyes, black hair a bit lank, and a very dark complexion. Wouldn't be surprised if there's a touch of the tarbrush somewhere in his ancestry."

The interview had begun with the D.C.I. being shown into Layton's handsome Mayfair office by a pretty blonde secretary who was obviously bursting with curiosity, but too discreet to ask his business.

"I would like to express my appreciation of your kindness in agreeing to see me at such short notice, Mr. Layton."

Renton offered his card, which Layton took between a long finger and thumb,

"Well Inspector, sorry Chief Inspector, how may I help? I should say straight away that if it's a fraud enquiry I would not be allowed to say anything without the company solicitor being present. We have to be so careful to protect the legitimate commercial interests of our clients, you know."

"No sir, not fraud. My business today is murder."

The Chief Inspector was watching Layton's face closely as he spoke, and duly noted the quick sideways glance to the filing cabinet, and the little smile. Was that relief? Or just tension? He waited for Layton to speak. When no reaction came, he continued,

"Saturday 14th July a young girl was murdered in Lynchester, in a local beauty spot called Crabbe's Wood. I wonder if you could recall for me your movements that evening please?"

For several seconds Layton rested his dark, unblinking gaze on the D.C.I. in absolute stillness and silence. Was he about to fly into indignant protestation? Or just refuse to answer?

"I'm sorry, Chief Inspector, I was trying to recall the day. Yes, I have it now. We had – have – a project for a retail development in the town, and I had been in Lynchester for several days. On the Saturday I had actually concluded negotiations for an option on the Crabbe's Marsh site, by the river, and the vendors were kind enough to invite me to dinner. A kind of celebration. Very friendly gesture, I thought."

"A bit unusual isn't it sir, staying on in a small provincial town over the weekend?"

"Unusual? Yes, I suppose it must seem so. But I have no marital or family obligations, so I can please myself what I do. I had a second reason. Earlier in the week I had seen a report in the local paper of a funeral, a Mr. Hawkins. The name rang a bell with me, and I recalled that Mr. Hawkins had been the owner of the timber yard and builders merchant on the site alongside my Crabbe's Marsh site. So I stayed on, hoping to make contact with the new owners. There was an opportunity too good to miss."

"And did you sir?"

"Did I make contact? Yes, I finally tracked down the family Chartered Accountants, Charles Harrison. That would be late on the Monday afternoon. The Monday after your murder, that is. And I had a reasonably successful meeting with the widow, Mrs. Hawkins on that Monday evening."

"So you stayed on in Lynchester not only the Saturday night, but also the Sunday and Monday?"

"Not Monday night. I drove back down to London after meeting Mrs. Hawkins."

"I'm still puzzled that you would stay on Saturday night and Sunday?"

"Saturday I had no choice, really. There was a lot of champagne and so on at dinner, and I couldn't contemplate driving a hundred miles after that, could I? And Sunday? Well, as I said, I have no ties, and I take particular pleasure in looking into the history of our old towns and cities. Did you know that Lynchester was the site of a Roman legionary fort, protecting the ford-crossing of Watling Street over the Lynn? Watling Street itself has a fascinating history . . . But perhaps I bore you?"

Jim Renton realised that Layton had recovered from whatever shock the word 'murder' had induced. And he made careful note that Layton had avoided any reference whatsoever to Susan. Might that be significant?

"Could we come to Saturday evening, sir? The dinner party, where was it?"

"At the Crown Hotel. My hosts – do you want the names?"

Renton nodded, and Layton thumbed through his well-worn Filofax.

"There were six of them. Harry Cunliffe, the farmer who owns Crabbe's Marsh, his wife Becky, their two daughters and their husbands. It was Mr. Cunliffe who pointed me in the direction of the Hawkins' solicitors, but of course I had to wait for Monday to see them."

"You drank a lot?"

"A fair bit, I suppose. I am not often invited to such occasions actually. I would categorise it as friendly rather than riotous."

"What time did it break up?"

"Not late. Nine-thirty, no, say ten o'clock by the time we had said goodnight."

"And what did you do then?"

"I thought I might sleep better after a walk, so I went out. It was a pleasant, warm evening."

"Can you remember where you walked?"

"Oh yes. Across the square to the bridge, over the river, then I turned right along the towpath and back."

The D.C.I. reached into his briefcase and drew out a large-scale Ordnance Survey map of Lynchester.

Could you perhaps show me on the map?"

Layton pressed the map out flat with his large bony fingers,

"Here's the hotel, with the square in front of it. Very attractive square, with the river frontage on the west, and nearly all Georgian facades, though I would expect to find that many have original Tudor and Jacobean half-timber behind the stucco. Here's the bridge, and over the bridge I turned right along the towpath."

"In front of the builders merchants?"

"That's right. There's a high wire fence that separates their site from the towpath. I walked along there, then across the Crabbe's Marsh."

"Wet underfoot?

"Wet? No, not in July. It's only wet in winter, when the river level rises substantially and soaks through the bank. We'll be putting that right with our development."

"So you followed the towpath here across Crabbe's Marsh. Then what?"

"I just turned around and walked back the way I'd come, and went to bed."

"Did you speak to anyone during this walk?"

"No. The towpath side was deserted. Though there were people around by the bridge and in the square."

"How about back at the hotel?"

"No. The receptionist was off, and the porter wasn't there either. I just helped myself to my key and went up."

"What time was that?"

"I couldn't say exactly. Soon after eleven I suppose."

Renton paused, allowing the tension to rise again as he considered his next move,

"If you'll look at the map again, sir, you'll note that there's a footpath here, at the end of Crabbe's Marsh, where you turned back. It forks off left up into Crabbe's Wood, and comes out onto Crabbe's Lane here, just before the tennis club."

"It's marked as a footpath, yes, but it's really quite a steep scramble up through a lot of overgrown brambles."

"I see, sir. So you know the path?"

"Oh yes. I walked over the whole area during the week. It's my job, you know. Crabbe's Wood is a Site of Special Scientific Interest, mainly because of the butterflies there. We have to be able to show that the development of the marsh down here will not disturb them too much."

"But you didn't go into the wood on Saturday night?"

"Certainly not. Once you move away from the towpath, which is lit from the streetlights on the town side of the river, that path up is – would be – very dark and difficult. Wouldn't fancy that at all."

The D.C.I. concluded the interview soon afterwards. As he said to his two assistants the next day,

"Apart from calling him a liar and accusing him outright, there didn't seem much else to say."

"But he is a live suspect, isn't he?"

"Very much so. He's got form too."

"Violent?"

"No, but relevant. He lives in Bayswater, by himself. A girl in a flat opposite complained that she seen him watching her through binoculars. Local uniform called on him. He said that he was a keen birdwatcher, showed the P.C. a shelf full of books on birds. 'He might have looked casually across the road, but there was no intention to spy, and he apologised if the lady was upset'. The P.C. suggested he should be extra careful in future, and the matter was dropped."

"Nothing further?"

"Not so far. We're feeding his description into the main C.I.D. computer to see if it fits any other incidents. Right then, that's enough of Mr. Layton for the time being, we can come back to him later. What else is new?"

Andrew and Alison looked at one another.

"You tell him," Alison said. Andrew nodded, and took a deep breath,

"We may have a positive ID. of the mysterious boyfriend in Birmingham. You remember the idea we had to put together a video of all the unattached men at the disco, and show it to the irate neighbour, Mr. Moreni? You might have told us that he was Indian, by the way."

"What difference does it make?"

"He got very uptight because I sent a police car with a uniformed driver to collect him. Said we wouldn't have done that if he'd been white, and what were his neighbours going to think?"

Renton sighed. "So how did it go?"

"Once we got him here, and convinced him that it was not an intentional insult, he calmed down all right. I think he was rather flattered that he might be the key witness."

"So who did he pick out?"

"George Hawkins."

Andrew handed the D.C.I. a brown file with 'Lynchester – S.S. Inquiry' stamped on the front, and 'George Hawkins' written underneath. Renton scanned the statement.

"But this says that he was at the disco in a party of four, with his wife and brother and his brother's wife. At the time of the murder he was playing snooker with his brother. I remember now the brother says the same thing. And anyway, how come he was included in the video of unattached males?"

"An accident sir, my fault I suppose", said Alison, "I asked one of the young P.C.s to put together the video, and gave him the full print-out with the names of those we wanted marked in pencil. There was an accidental mark against George Hawkins' name on the paper, so his picture got included."

"A happy accident, if it stands up. Go on."

"Moreni was really very thorough. I showed him the whole set of people once. He made no comment, simply asked to go through them again, then said, 'Number Seven is the nearest'."

"Not a positive identification?"

"No, he said it was dark, the man had a cap on, and anyway he didn't get a proper look at his face. But Moreni seemed confident it was him, I'd say. I mean there were two or three others with what I thought were the same general look and build, and Moreni was quite firm that they were not right."

"Well, it's a starting point at least."

"There's more. We went through the records of that course in karate that was run by Joyce Clumber's colleague. Both George Hawkins and his brother Alan attended, about two years ago."

Alison had been urgently shuffling through a file while Andrew was talking,

"Got it! Harrison's. I thought I'd heard the name. You mentioned it just now sir, the accountants that Layton visited, because they were handling the Hawkins estate. There's another connection. Harrison's was where Susan started after leaving school. Interesting, don't you think?"

"Interesting, I agree. And what about this alibi of theirs? Either Alan would be covering for George, or George for Alan. Or indeed perhaps they're both in it together in some way."

"You're right sir to suggest that we should not exclude Alan at this stage. I had a look at his video too, and they really are quite similar. George is a bit thin on top, and seems to have the cares of the world on his shoulders, and Alan has a more confident look, and a lot of wavy hair."

"But our man was seen wearing a cap anyway."

"Indeed he was, sir. I feel we've had a tremendous piece of luck with this one, and we should ride it now to the utmost. May we pull them back in for questioning?"

The D.C.I. leaned back in his chair and rubbed his face wearily. He had promised to get back to Stafford early for his wife's birthday. Was there anything to be lost by waiting?

"Yes, but not immediately. We'll get just one chance of a confession, and without a confession we've got almost no case at all against either one. Let's give ourselves some breathing space, now we have some targets, to come up with something in the way of forensic. Any ideas for possible clinchers?"

"Both George and Alan admitted to knowing Susan casually at the Tennis Club. We could ask around, starting at Harrison's, to see if there was anything more tangible – phone calls to the office, obvious flirting, any gossip. It's a small place."

"Good start, Andrew, though I'd like you to let Alison take that on. No offence, but accountants can cut up very difficult if they think their discretion is under attack. Easier for Alison to chat informally to the girls in the office. Any more?"

"Fingerprints, sir. At the flat in Edgbaston. Most were Susan's of course and her fiance's. But there were some yet to be identified. There's just a chance that George or Alan might have left a dab – then we'd have him, wouldn't we?"

"We'd be close, I'd say. That's just the kind of thing to hit them with at interview."

"Whether we do or don't?"

"Could be, Andrew. But I'd rather play it straight if we can. So, your job is to find a way to get their prints for comparison, preferably without them finding out you're doing it. And the big task, of course, is to interview again everyone else who might be able to confirm or deny the story that they were playing snooker."

"That must include everyone at the disco, sir. I've been through the statements already, and no one mentions using the Snooker Room other than the Hawkins."

"Right, but quite a few might have looked in, and found it being used. No need to mention the Hawkins at this time, just 'We'd like to establish if the room was being used on Saturday night, and can you recall looking in to see?'

Andrew wondered briefly why the D.C.I. was being more circumspect in this enquiry than he had been in the similar one about Joyce Clumber, which had so far drawn a blank, but decided there was nothing to be gained by asking.

"How long should we hold off from pulling in the Hawkins, sir?"

"How long is that piece of string? It really depends on what we can come up with, doesn't it? If either of them is the murderer, the motive is likely to be . . ."

His voice trailed away thoughtfully, "Where was I?"

"Motive, sir."

"Yes, motive. Not obvious, you know. I mean it could be blackmail, but neither of them strikes me as particularly vulnerable. Nor does it seem likely that Susan, with a good job, a new fiance, and a baby on the way, would be issuing threats to shake them down for a few quid. I get the impression that there would be no great stigma attached to having been one of Susan's lovers. Probably quite the opposite in this town."

"Not impossible though, sir. I mean it could be a combination of things that produced a sudden explosion – a threat of exposure, a taunt about the new fiance, the baby even. And if our man had a few drinks inside him . . ."

"O.K., let's leave it for now. If you think about it, we're making extraordinary progress. A week ago we were stalled without a single serious suspect. Now we've got at least four, with Joyce, Layton, and the two Hawkins."

"Down to a lot of good police work, sir."

"I agree, Alison, and I'll leave out the bits of luck when I put in this week's report to the A.C.C. As they're a prominent local family, he may have an opinion about the timing of calling back the Hawkins, by the way. But I'll say we're proposing a delay of one week, until August 24th. And now I'm off home before my wife decides to murder me."

Chapter Fourteen

Monday August 20th was a red-letter day for Helen Hawkins. It was the day when her husband George came home at lunchtime in triumph,

"I've done it love, I've done it! Here's the bottle I bought yesterday, still unopened! That's yesterday evening and the whole morning without touching a drop!"

There was a fierce, almost feverish exultation in his voice, and Helen could only guess at the effort of will he had exerted to get through the morning. She matched her mood to his and hugged him tightly.

"Oh George, I'm so proud of you. I knew you could do it, I really did."

He stroked her long fair hair gently, and lifted her face to kiss her as she clung to him, a long tender kiss, as though they had only just met. For the first time in months he felt the stirrings of desire. Helen rubbed the tears from her eyes with the back of her hand, and giggled,

"Is that a stranger in our midst? Seems to me you need to save your strength after all that effort this morning! Tell you what, you deserve a half-day off, and I've got some steak in the fridge. Our bedroom is still lovely and cool, so why don't you slip upstairs and lie down. You have a little rest, then I'll bring lunch up to bed for us. Steak, new potatoes and garden peas. How's that for a reward?"

"No wine?"

"Definitely no wine, not now, not ever. But I could offer something interesting for afters, if you like?"

The mood of tenderness and strained gaiety lasted through the meal, taken on trays side by side in bed, and into the lovemaking that followed. It ended abruptly with George flinging himself, exhausted and sweating, onto the pillow beside Helen.

"It's no good, no good at all. I need a drink."

Helen didn't know what to say, so she leaned over him and stroked his cheeks and his forehead as though he were the child she never had. After a few minutes his harsh breathing slowed, and he reached up a hand to fondle her small breast. Her hair shadowed her face, and brushed against his chest, and she was so beautiful.

"Helen, love, I did so want to please you today."

And now she knew how to respond,

"You did, my sweet, you did. You pleased me by just wanting me again and loving me. The rest will come in time, of course it will. You've been soaking up that poison for months now, and you can't expect it all to have left your system just like that. Let's have a sleep now, and there's a good film on telly this evening."

She kissed him lightly, and continued stroking his face until he fell asleep.

Helen's mother and father still lived in the small terrace house in Lynchester where she had been born, and Helen had trained as a nurse at the Lynchester Hospital. After marrying George she had continued to work at the hospital for ten years, and they had been glad of the money she brought in. After a miscarriage she was off work for six months, and a second miscarriage a year later was decisive. As the doctor said,

"I can't guarantee that if you stop working you will have a baby. But I'm pretty sure that if you carry on with the nursing, you won't."

Helen loved nursing. She was proud of her expertise, and enjoyed intensely the satisfaction of seeing people in her care get well again. But she wanted a child more than anything else in the world, so she resigned. That was five years before, and no baby had come. She and George had submitted themselves to the long drawn out hopes and despairs of the Fertility Clinic, to no avail. They had begun to think about adopting, until George had been caught up in the agonies of his father's terminal illness, and his own surrender to the bottle.

The next day, Tuesday, Helen was late getting home. A few months before she had taken up hospital visiting, with occasional part-time work, as a first step towards a possible return to nursing, and that evening she had stayed on to chat to Sister and the Administrator about prospects. It seemed they would be glad to have her back to work any hours she wanted, and when she let herself into the cottage at seven-thirty she was rehearsing in her mind how to broach the subject with George. But the cottage was silent, and empty. Might he be working late? They had talked the previous evening about the draft contracts for the Hawkins Centre, and about what George's position should be at the family meeting, planned for the Thursday, with Charles Harrison. Perhaps he was going through it in advance with Alan? She telephoned his office at the yard, but there was no answer.

It was a bright sunny evening, and there were still a good two hours before dark. Could he have gone fishing? She looked in the tall cupboard under the stairs where he kept his tackle, but it was too much of a jumble to be sure whether a rod was missing. A cold shadow of foreboding went across her mind. *Might he have slipped back into the drinking, and be helpless in some ditch? People drowned in that river.* Almost eight o'clock. On an impulse she walked out of the cottage and down the path towards the river. There would for sure be some of his fishing cronies there, who could tell her if he had come that way.

Earlier that day Alan had again driven into Birmingham for a site meeting, and when he got back to Hawkins Timber just after six p.m. he was hot, tired and bad-tempered. He had got the business, but at prices that would leave precious little profit. And he had to be out all the next day at site meetings in Coventry, so he wanted to check the 'materials required' list against stocks that evening, and leave a requisition for George to order before the weekend. 'God knows if the stock records will be reliable anyway', he thought, as he turned his key in the Yale lock to let himself into the office door at the back of the building, and climbed the steep stairs. 'Perhaps the smartest thing would be to throw the lot onto George's desk, and leave a note for him to sort it out tomorrow.'

He was startled by a voice as he got to the top of the stairs,

"That you Alan? How did it go?"

"I didn't expect to find you here, George, it's after six. Yes, I got the contract for that new hotel. But they were vicious negotiators, quoted chapter and verse at me for the lowest prices on everything. We'll make something on the plumbing fittings, but that's all I'd say. Only consolation, they've agreed payment in seven days from invoicing, and we'll have our usual eight weeks credit from the suppliers, so we'll build up a nice cash balance at the bank. Two or three hundred thousand at the peak, so we'll come out all right. Might even wipe out the overdraft altogether for a few months. That'll annoy the bank. God, it's hot today! Fancy a cold beer? I've got a few in the fridge in my office. Come in, the sun's moved round now."

Alan did not notice the deep frown on George's face as they went in to his own slightly cooler office. The cold froth splashed over his fingers as he poured, and he licked it off and drank back most of his glass with a huge sigh of relief. He had sunk back into his swivel chair before he realised that George had not picked up the lager he had left for him on the corner of the desk. Instead he stood in the doorway, just looking at the glass as if it contained some fearful secret.

"What's the matter, George, had too much already?"

Alan saw the tension as George gripped the doorpost, his knuckles showing white through the tan, and realised immediately that he had said the wrong thing. There was no need to fall out with George, was there?

"I'm sorry, old man, I shouldn't have said that. I know you've been trying to cut down recently, and I'm proud of you, really I am."

George said nothing, but returned in silence to his own office, then came back holding something behind his back. Alarmed, Alan stood up quickly, and George grinned,

"Don't get worried, Alan, I'm not going to brain you. There, what do you think of that?"

With a flourish he brought from behind his back a bottle of Teacher's Scotch Whisky, and thumped it down onto Alan's desk, beside the glass of lager.

"I bought that on Saturday. I went all day yesterday without touching a drop, and took it home to show Helen. She's a wonderful wife, you know. She actually suggested I bring it in again today, to remind me that I could do it. I'm off the sauce, Alan, off it for good. That's a present for you, though if you'll take my advice you'll pour it down the sink. It's a killer."

Alan had told Jennifer about George's drinking on the spur of the moment, as a way of emphasising to her his own importance to the business. Now he regretted his stupidity, especially as it was apparent that Jennifer and Helen together were in the process of effecting some sort of cure. *A sober George, a reformed George could be a real danger. There were still several of those cash rebate schemes to come to fruition. And there was the snooker game . . .* Alan put his hands on George's shoulders.

"Like I said, George, I'm proud of you, and I'm sure Helen is too. By the way, what time is Helen expecting you home? I wouldn't want her telling me off for overworking you."

George looked at his watch, "No great hurry. She's doing her hospital visiting, could be another hour yet. That's why I was putting in a bit of overtime, catching up with the stock records. They're about up to date now."

"Well, if you can stay, that's just where I could do with some help. It's the material schedules for the hotel job. They've really gone to town with their critical path planning and just-in-time deliveries, like they were building a bloody battleship. Anyway time is of the essence, as it says in the contract, and we really need to go over what we've got in stock and identify anything on a long lead time. We could probably crack it in an hour together, and you could get stuck in to the ordering tomorrow, when I'm due out again."

Alan pulled up another chair for George at the desk, fished out the schedules from his briefcase, and spread them out on the desk. The papers rolled themselves up, so he spread them again with two hands and weighted them down at each side with the two glasses, George's still full, his own almost empty. Without a word he took another cold lager from the fridge, refilled his glass, and sank half of it with a huge sigh of appreciation,

"That's better, I feel almost human again. Sit down, George. It'll be nice to do a bit of work together again, instead of snapping one another's head off, won't it? Look, I really don't think one glass of cold beer is going to ruin you, but if it worries you I'll drink it for you, shall I?"

Alan's question had been all casual nonchalance, but he made no move towards the full glass, and almost held his breath as he waited for George's response. It was slow in coming, as though some enormous inner battle was being fought. Then his hand reached out and grasped the glass. Alan let his breath go very gently, and stood up.

"Start looking through the schedules, would you? I'll get your stock cards and bring them in here."

George kept his stock-and order records on an old-fashioned card-index system. Alan delayed deliberately in George's office for a couple of minutes before picking up the first of the heavy card trays to carry into his own room. When he got back George's glass was empty.

"You're right, Alan, that was bloody marvellous. 'Amber nectar', exactly!"

Alan smiled, and took two more bottles from the fridge to refill the glasses. They settled into a routine, with Alan calling out the item, quantities and delivery date required, and George flicking through his well-thumbed cards to check the stock and then making notes on his pad of orders to be raised. George kept sipping steadily at his glass, which Alan refilled regularly. Alan had noticed over the preceding weeks that George could sup whisky all day without appearing to get drunk. A couple of pints of lager had a marked effect however, and George suddenly sat back, blinking and shaking his head slowly,

"P'lice were here this morning. Did you know?"

Alan felt a hard knot of apprehension gripping his throat, and he struggled to keep his voice casual,

"No, you hadn't said. Been some pilferage again? Those damn kids?"

"Not pil-fer-age," George pronounced the word in careful syllables, "Not pilf'rage. Murder. You know, that girl, Sushan, a month ago in the wood."

"What did they want this time?"

"Very int'restin'. Joyce. You know, that friend of Susan? Had I seen Joyce during or after our game?"

"That is interesting. Sounds as though Joyce might be a suspect, doesn't it?"

"That'sh what I thought. But I couldn't remember anything. N'fac' I told them I couldn' remember anythin' about the snooker either."

Something very cold and hard wound its way into the pit of Alan's stomach. Did it matter if George could not remember their game of snooker? It might become very important indeed. But from the outset the bigger risk had been that George might remember too much about that evening. He had been right, once off the booze George was too much of a risk to have around. He shared the opened bottle between their two glasses, went to the fridge and came back with the ice-tray.

"That's the last of the beer. If we're to get this job finished I need another drink. How about you?"

Without waiting for an answer he twisted the plastic tray to release the cubes, and dropped three into each glass. "Time to open your present, I think."

He unscrewed the gold cap of the Teachers, and George held up his glass with a smile, "Jush a small one."

Alan poured in whisky until all the cubes were floating, and did the same for his own glass,

"Cheers. Your good health. Right, let's get back to work!"

And so they began again the familiar routine of Alan calling out the items required, and George making increasingly less legible notes on his pad. George drank thirstily from his glass, Alan more circumspectly from his. Every ten minutes, George's glass needed topping up with ice-cubes and another big slug of whisky, and Alan added a token amount to his own. The end came suddenly. George drained his glass, and raised one hand as though to proclaim some eternal verity, then his head fell forward onto the desk.

"Got you," Alan whispered.

He poured another tumbler of whisky and, cradling George's head like a baby, gently fed it to him. George took it down sip by sip without opening his eyes. Alan wiped the bottle, then pressed George's right hand around it and did the same to the beer bottles. He put the lot untidily onto Georges desk. Anything else? The stock-cards, of course! They got the same treatment, then he carried them back into George's office. He looked at his watch. Seven-twenty, time now to check and double check. There must be no sign that he had been there that evening . . . George's telephone had a direct outside line.

"Hi Grace, it's me. Everything all right? Good. Look, I'm just leaving Birmingham now. Yes, I know it's late. The traffic was seized up solid when I came to leave the site, so I stopped off to get a beer and let it die down. Then I had a job to get the car started. Something in the fuel line, I think. Anyway, I'm on my way now. Got the contract for the new hotel by the way, probably the biggest job we've ever had. Should keep George and the lads very busy. O.K. then, darling, see you in three-quarters of an hour."

He put down the telephone, and sat for a few moments, gazing into space. Had he thought of everything? Everything?

George was still sleeping peacefully, looking somehow younger. He suppressed a momentary feeling of pity. That innocent-looking child was a real threat.

At the back of George's office he found something he had noticed and tucked away in the back of his mind a few weeks ago, a sample reel of half-inch Terylene rope, left behind by a hopeful salesman. Alan used his handkerchief as a glove to pick it up, pulled the rope off, then pressed George's hands around the reel before dropping it on the floor in George's office. There were about ten metres of orange rope he estimated, plenty enough for the job. He tied a big loop with a clumsy slip-knot in one end.

From the railing that ran across the front of the small office deck it was easily possible to reach up to touch one of the steel frames that spanned the warehouse, supporting the roof. Alan pushed the looped end of the rope over this girder, then paid out the rope until the knot swung before him, level with the deck and about three metres above the floor below. He wound the other end of the rope several times around the railing, then finished off with a couple of half-hitches, being careful not to make it too neat. He used the handkerchief to wipe the knot for fingerprints, and pulled in the loop to do the same thing. George was still slumped with his face on Alan's desk, his mouth open and his breathing noisy but regular. Alan put his arms around him from behind and lifted. God, what a weight! But if he dragged him across the deck there would be a trail of scuff marks on the linotiles for sure. It would have to be a fireman's lift from the front. He took a deep breath, and stooped low to get the necessary purchase. Suddenly the telephone rang, and rang, and rang. Alan stood up in alarm. Who could be phoning at this hour? Then he realised that it was the phone in George's office. He looked at his watch – seven-forty. *Of course, Helen was back, and was wondering where George was. Might she come looking? Not likely, if the phone was not answered . . . should he abandon his plan? He could take down the rope, and just drive George home, no harm done. Except he had called Grace to say he was on his way from Birmingham . . .* the telephone stopped. He knelt low again in front of George, took hold of one limp hand to pull him over his shoulder, and stood up slowly. One arm through his legs and the weight was balanced, though he almost buckled beneath it. Step by slow step he crossed the deck until he could rest by sitting George onto the railing, while he reached out for the noose. Fingerprints? He wiped the knot again, and pressed George's fingers around the knot, before pulling the loop over his head. There was a moment when George's eyes fluttered, as though he might be about to wake up. Alan had a total recall of a day when he had been learning to ski for the first time, and had stood at the top of a long steep slope, willing himself to thrust off. He stood up straight, placed both hands quickly onto George's chest, and pushed hard.

There was a thud that shook the deck and the roof, and then he was looking down on his brother, spinning on the end of the orange rope. The head was distorted to one side, the body completely limp. It was done.

Alan's brain was racing, everything was crystal-clear, he felt in total control. He scanned the deck and the two offices for possible mistakes. The chairs – two side by side was a dead giveaway! He moved the spare one back against the wall. His office looked neat and tidy, as though he had been out for the day. Right. There were bottles and drink spilled on George's desk, the stock-files looked untidy. Could they work out how much George had drunk? He picked up two of the beer bottles just in case. One last look round then he was moving quickly down the steep concrete stairs to let himself out of the side door through which he had entered. As he left he tossed the two bottles into the rubbish skip. Because the evening sun had been so warm he had parked his car under the big sycamore that grew beside the compound. Once inside he glanced at the clock – ten minutes to eight. *He should not arrive home before eight-fifteen. Half an hour to kill . . . what a peculiar phrase that was!* He realised that he had left the warehouse and fled to the security of his car without once looking at his brother's face. No matter, he was dead for certain. The whole building shook, his neck was broken. Alan started the car, and headed off into the countryside.

Chapter Fifteen

Jennifer Hawkins was at home by herself, and grateful to have a few quiet hours. She needed to think about what she was doing.

Since that first passionate evening with Alan, there had been four other occasions when he had come to her – three times during the day, when she had taken afternoons off work to receive him in her bedroom, and one evening when he had collected her at six and driven out with her into the countryside, and they had made love on a rug like two teenagers. That part of the affair was fine. Alan was vigorous and enthusiastic, and surprisingly sensitive as a lover, with a delightful interest in finding out how best to please her. For her part she felt as though she had been released from some prison of the spirit, as she luxuriated in the simple animal pleasure of sexual gratification. Once, during that evening in the quiet wood, her sharp cry of delight as she climaxed had startled the roosting woodpigeons and sent them clattering overhead, leaving them both helpless with laughter. That part was good, she thought, very good. From the beginning she had wanted Alan partly because he reminded her so much of Joe when he was younger, and partly because, having endured all those months of Joe's decay, she was hungry for the narcotic of unthinking physical pleasure again. Now she felt a need to think about the future, a demand that was sharpened by having had to accept, that very morning, the fact that her period was a full week overdue. Of course it might be just a one-off irregularity, a combination of her age perhaps and the burst of sexual activity after a long abstinence. But just suppose . . .

She sat on her bedroom balcony overlooking the rose-garden, enjoying the last of the evening sun. On her lap was a book about travel in China, 'Behind The Wall'. She wondered vaguely if there was some symbolism in the title that had led her to pick it up at the bookshop. *Suppose Alan had fathered a child for her, did she actually want him to be a real father? Had she in fact ever wanted him for anything more than a pleasing companion in bed? Should she keep a child? The money would give her unlimited independence. Did she want to surrender that to Alan? Was he more deeply committed than she was? What if . . .*

Her reverie was interrupted by the bedside telephone. *A quarter to nine – perhaps it's Alan, wanting to come round for a couple of hours? I'll definitely be having a headache.*

"Hullo, is that you, Jenny? It's Helen. Jenny, I'm so worried, I don't know what to do. I hope I'm not calling at an awkward time?"

Jennifer suspected that this last question might be an oblique reference to Alan, but said reassuringly,

"Of course not, Helen, I was just dozing over a book in the garden. This summer seems to go on and on, doesn't it? How can I help?"

"It's George. He's . . . he's missing. I was a bit late getting back from the hospital this evening, and he's not home. I phoned his office, but there was no answer, so I went down to the river, where he usually goes fishing, but none of his friends had seen him today. Oh Jenny, he's been doing so well, but now I'm half out of my mind and can't seem to think straight."

"Now just you sit still there. Chances are he's had a bit of a lapse, and is sleeping it off somewhere, afraid to show his face. That's a good sign, if you think about it, it means he cares about what you might think of him. I'll jump in the car and pick you up, and we'll start at the Yard again. I've got some keys. If he's not there, we'll try the 'Feathers'. And then anywhere else we can think of. Don't worry, it'll come right. These things always take time to sort out."

Jennifer put the phone down, thought for a moment, then dialed Alan's number. Grace answered, and Jennifer thought she detected a slight edge of hostility in her voice. Perhaps she had heard what was going on, and was thinking this affair was one too many?

"Hullo Jenny, did you want Alan? He's just eating his supper. He only got back from Birmingham half an hour ago, and he's all in."

"No need to disturb him, Grace, it's about George. Helen is very upset because he's gone missing. Have you or Alan seen him at all?"

"I haven't seen him, and as I said Alan has only just got in from Birmingham. He got that big hotel contract, by the way. You tell Helen not to worry about George. That kind usually have a fairy godmother watching over them. He's probably trying to sober up before he shows his face."

When Jennifer got to Helen's cottage she found her even more distraught than she had expected.

"I've got this terrible feeling that something awful has happened. After yesterday, I mean. I didn't tell you about yesterday, did I? He came home at midday, absolutely cockahoop because he had gone the whole morning without opening the bottle. You know I've been nagging at him to cut down, and he really had been trying. And yesterday he had none at all, and he was so . . . so loving again, you know. This morning he didn't feel so good, but he went off quite determined to keep off it. I should have made him come home again for lunch, but I had a meeting with the new Hospital Administrator at one, and I thought he would be all right. He was so determined, you see. I think he really does want to make me happy, I really do."

Jennifer had only to murmur comfortingly while Helen poured all this out, and in a few minutes she was parking at the office door at the back of the warehouse.

"I don't often have to use a key, at least not the office one. This big one is the door to the showroom, but this one should be the office."

It was pitch dark at the foot of the stairs, and she found the light switch before climbing the stairs to the office deck, with Helen close behind. It was Helen who called out first,

"George? George, are you there?"

Jennifer put on the light in George's office, and took in at a glance the mess of bottles and spilt drink on his desk. She put her arm around Helen's shoulder,

"Never mind, love. Two steps forward, one step back, I'm sure that's only to be expected."

"What's that awful smell? Do you think he's passed out in the loo?"

Jennifer turned from George's office and was leading the way along the deck to the lavatories at the end when she saw the orange rope, taut and gleaming against the shadowed geometry of the roof trusses, and her eye followed it down to the knot around the railings and then below.

"Oh, dear God."

At that moment Helen saw it too, and pushed Jennifer aside in her anxiety to get to the railings.

"It's him, it's him, it's my George. Quick, quick undo that knot and let him down. I can do mouth to mouth."

Helen ran for the stairs as Jennifer untied the knot and lowered him to the ground. Her legs were trembling beneath her as she scrambled down the stairs. At the bottom she switched on the big lights that lit the showroom, expecting to see Helen in desperate mouth-to-mouth resuscitation. Instead she was kneeling beside the crumpled, stinking body, with the head in her lap.

"Poor George, my poor George. He's dead, Jenny, he's dead. We were too late."

Jennifer felt the bile rise and bite at the back of her throat, but resisted the pressure to be sick. She realised that nothing she could do would help George or Helen, and ran across the showroom floor to her desk. This time Alan answered the telephone himself.

"Hullo, Jenny, Have you found George yet?"

"Oh, Alan, it's so horrible. We're at the warehouse. We've found him, Alan, we've found him. He's dead. He's . . . he's hanged himself."

Alan allowed a few moments silence, as though digesting terrible news, then Jennifer heard him call out to Grace,

"It's Jenny. They've found George. Sounds as though he's committed suicide."

"Jenny, have you called the police?"

"No, I called you first."

"Right, you leave that to me. You concentrate on looking after Helen. Poor thing, she'll be in an awful state, I should think. I'll call the police and the ambulance, they'll be there in no time, and I'll come right over too. All right?"

Detective Sergeant Alison Clarke was working late that evening in her office at the Drill Hall that served as the Incident Room for the enquiry into the murder of Susan Stevens. She was wrestling with the mass of files, video interviews, computer print-outs, wall diagrams and the range of hypotheses, trying to write a summary in preparation for the review next day with D.C.I. Renton, in the knowledge that the summary review was likely to be presented straight on to the A.C.C. The D.C.I. had been brutally frank that morning,

"I'm sorry to drop this on you, Alison, but I can't see how else it's going to get done. I'm having to put more and more myself into this investigation into the West Midlands Crime Squad, so I'm going to be off the patch. And the A.C.C is starting to get restless about the amount of money this murder enquiry has cost, especially as it seems to be a one-off, not the first in a series as he originally thought. So it's down to you and Andrew. I want the basis for an arrest, or at least for a limited enquiry that isn't going to cost the earth. From what I've seen, I think you're very close. If you can pull it off it's promotion on a plate next year, if I have anything to say about it. That's a promise."

The telephone call came as a welcome relief,

"Detective Sergeant Clarke? This is the Station Sergeant here. Yes, Lynchester. Thought you'd be interested to hear, we've just had a phone call from Mr. Alan Hawkins. Seems his brother has just been found hanged. Yes, dead. In their warehouse. Hawkins Timber, you know where that is, just over the bridge? Ambulance is on its way, and the beat car."

Alison wondered about the phone call from uniform as she strapped herself into her car. How did the Station Sergeant know they were interested in the Hawkins? The D.C.I. had imposed tight security around that development. 'Sometimes a security leak can be quite useful,' she thought, as she drove through the now deserted Market Square and across the bridge to Hawkins Timber.

It was quite dark when she pulled into the small car park inside the chain link fence that surrounded the yard. The beat car was there already, its light still turning and flashing a cold blue glare onto the wall of the warehouse, now brightly lit from within. The ambulance arrived as she was getting out of her car. She showed her warrant card, and asked the crew to wait whilst she went inside first. She noticed two other cars parked already, both silver Ford Mondeos, with consecutive registration numbers.

She quickly found the open door at the back, and stepped through the dark passageway under the mezzanine deck into the showroom, momentarily dazzled by its array of bright overhead lights. As she took in the scene she was reminded of a long-forgotten school trip to Italy, and a particular painting that had impressed her. It was a Pieta, with the pathetic body of the dead Christ cradled in Mary's lap, surrounded by grieving disciples.

Just to her left was a tall, fair-headed man she recognised as Alan Hawkins. He had been deep in conversation with the uniformed constable taking notes next to him, but looked up expectantly as Alison entered. To her right, leaning back against a pillar, was a very good looking woman, tall, dark hair carefully pinned-up, wearing an elegant white silk dress. She stared straight ahead, and seemed still paralysed by shock. Alison made a mental note that she might require medical attention. In front of her, immediately beneath the balcony's edge, a woman with long blonde hair was sitting on the floor. In her lap she was nursing George Hawkins. The face was bloated and purple, the eyes popping out, the tongue protruding. Around his neck she could see the orange rope, with the length of rope piled on the floor beside the body. The head was at a peculiar angle to the neck, and he was obviously dead. The blonde woman was the first to speak,

"Hullo, are you the doctor? I'm Helen Hawkins, his wife. I was a nurse, so I know he's dead. There's nothing to be done. We were too late."

Her voice was calm, matter of fact. Alison looked at the constable,

"Would you call for the police doctor and the forensic team, please?"

He looked slightly surprised, but had met Alison before, and knew better than to ask questions. Alison became conscious of an acrid stench, and made a face,

"What's that awful stink?"

Alan answered. "It's George, my brother. He's . . . he'd crapped himself."

Whilst she waited in silence for the constable to return from his car, Alison took stock of the situation. Strictly speaking, this was none of her business. Lynchester Police had ample resources of uniform branch, and detectives if need be, and the constable could perfectly well carry on, summoning his superiors as required. On the other hand, George had been a prime suspect in a murder investigation. She turned to Alan Hawkins,

"Where's the telephone, please?"

Alan led her to Jennifer's desk at the retail end, as the constable returned.

"The doctor will be about ten minutes."

"Don't allow anything to be moved or touched in the meantime, please."

Alison called D.C.I. Renton at his home and summarised the situation quickly. He was very decisive,

"No doubt at all that we should treat this as part of our inquiry. Any chance that he was pushed?"

"Nothing obvious, sir. I've called for the doctor and forensic, just in case."

"Right, well you carry on and interview the witnesses. Go gently with the wife – sorry, I probably didn't need to say that. I'll come straight down, be with you in forty five minutes. I'll clear things with Lynchester police for you."

Alison returned to Alan Hawkins, who was now standing by Jennifer.

"Did you find the body, Mr. Hawkins?"

"No, it was Helen and Jennifer here. I'm sorry, I don't know your name."

"Detective Sergeant Clarke."

"This is Mrs. Jennifer Hawkins. My father died a few weeks ago. Mrs. Hawkins was . . . is my stepmother. Really Sergeant, I wouldn't want to interfere with your inquiry, but I don't think either of the ladies are in a fit state to answer questions now. I got here a few minutes after they found him, and I think I can tell you everything you need at this stage."

Alison was impressed by the calm authority in his manner, and the note of concern obvious in his voice. She looked at Helen, still sitting with that ghastly head pressed to her breast, and Jennifer still pale and silent against the pillar, which was clearly the only thing that prevented her falling to the ground.

"All right. There's an ambulance outside that could take them home I think. Would you lock up their car? Then I would be grateful if you could just go over what you know."

At that moment the police doctor arrived. Dr. Carr was Lynchester's senior G.P., and his practice included most of Lynchester's wealthier citizens. To add some variety, he enjoyed assisting with the earthier aspects of police business, which was the reason he made himself available to inspect the occasional victims of assault and rape, and the drunk drivers that made up the usual round. A suicide was rare. Particularly when it involved the Hawkins family, who were all on his list of patients. He was a lean, leathery man in his early sixties, used to getting his own way.

"Pronounced dead at nine-forty. He's been dead about a couple of hours. Helen, my dear, I'm so sorry about George. I did warn him, you know, when Joe went, that the whisky was a dangerous road."

Helen did not reply. His eye lighted on Alison, "You are . . .?"

"Detective Sergeant Clarke, sir. Chief Inspector Renton is on his way down from Stafford. He should be here in half an hour or so."

"Meantime I trust you're not proposing to question these two ladies at this time? They are known to me personally, and I can vouch for their reliability. They have had a terrible shock, and should be put to bed at once."

"I had just agreed that with Mr. Hawkins, sir, and suggested they might have the use of the ambulance to get home."

"I congratulate you on your good sense. Helen, dear, there's really nothing more you can do for poor George. If you will leave him in my care, I will ensure that he is well looked after."

As he spoke he reached down and gently unfolded the arms that held George so tightly, and Alison came forward to help Helen to her feet. The constable took this as a cue to approach Jennifer.

"Mrs. Hawkins, can I help you to the ambulance?"

Jennifer stared at him as though he had spoken in a foreign language.

"The ambulance, Mrs. Hawkins. It will take you home now."

He held out an arm, and Alan came across quickly to take the other side. She seemed to awaken suddenly, and shook off his hand from her elbow with some asperity,

"It's all right. I'm all right. There's no need, I can walk to my car."

"No, really, Jenny, you mustn't drive. I'll bring your car round to you tomorrow. You go with Helen now in the ambulance."

She stood for a moment as though to argue, then her shoulders slumped and she released a long sigh.

"Here's the key. Just stick it through the letter-box."

Dr. Carr had been kneeling beside the crumpled body, and stood up briskly,

"I heard that you've called for the forensic squad, so there's not much you'll be needing immediately from me, is there? He's been dead a couple of hours, cause of death almost certainly a broken neck as a result of hanging, presumably a drop from that balcony. There's a strong smell of whisky, if you've got the stomach to put your face down? I'm going home with these ladies, who are both patients of mine, to see them safely to bed with a sedative. I assume you have no objections?"

Alison opened her mouth to say it was very irregular to leave the scene so quickly, but thought better of it,

"May I ask you please, Doctor, to return afterwards and talk to my D.C.I.? Mr. Hawkins, when you've finished helping Mrs, Hawkins, is there somewhere quiet that we could sit and talk?"

"My office is upstairs, in that far corner."

"No, not upstairs. I think that's the forensic team arriving outside. They'll want the upstairs left exactly as it is."

"We could use Mrs. Hawkins desk, down the far end of the showroom, where you made your telephone call."

"Fine, if you wouldn't mind waiting for me there, whilst I brief forensic, please."

Chapter Sixteen

Alison had barely completed briefing the Forensic squad when D.C.I. Renton arrived.

"Evening, Alison. Need any help?"

She took a deep breath, and kept a tight grip on her temper,

"I don't think so, sir. Doctor's been and pronounced Mr. George Hawkins dead at twenty one-forty hours. Time of death – about two hours previously. Cause of death – broken neck, apparently by hanging."

Renton walked over to the body, and knelt to inspect the rope still around the neck. He wrinkled his nose in disgust.

"It's his excreta, sir. Presumably a reflex action when he dropped."

"Presumably. I thought I could smell something else. Whisky?"

"Doctor suggested the same thing, sir. The constable here was on the scene a few minutes after the body was found."

"P.C. Hughes, sir, Lynchester Police. There were two ladies when I arrived, both very distressed. One, Mrs. Helen Hawkins, the deceased's wife, was sitting on the floor here with the body, just rocking it, backwards and forwards. The other was standing against this pillar here. Mrs. Jennifer Hawkins, she was his late father's second wife. Both of them were very shocked, in fact I didn't really get a word out of either of them. Fortunately Mr. Alan Hawkins was here, sir. He'd arrived about five minutes before me, and he been able to get them to say what they'd found and done. He was starting to tell me when D.S. Clarke arrived."

"Right, Hughes, you seem to have coped admirably. I think if you would turn off your blue light outside it would make it less likely that we would gather a crowd, and perhaps you could close the gates also, and then stay there to ensure that we are not disturbed, please. Now Alison, Forensic?"

"Already briefed, sir. I suggested they should start upstairs."

"Good, the doctor then?

"He's not here, sir."

"He's left the body already? Rather unusual that isn't it, even for Lynchester?"

Alison privately agreed, but felt bound to defend him, as she had not objected.

"It was because of the ladies, sir, as they were both patients of his. He insisted they should not be questioned tonight, and he's gone home with them, about fifteen minutes ago, to sedate them and put them to bed, he said. He promised to come back to see you, sir."

"Very decent of him, I'm sure. So our remaining witness is hearsay only, and is also one of the suspects in the Susan Stevens case?"

"Mr. Alan Hawkins, sir. He's sitting over there, waiting for me to interview him."

"He's probably getting a bit impatient, and nervous too. That won't hurt him, will it?"

"Probably not, sir. May I just ask one question, please?"

The D.C.I. nodded, and edged a few yards away from the body,

"Times like this I wish I still smoked that pipe. What's the problem, Alison?"

"This morning you put me in charge of this case. Am I still in charge, or have you now taken over again?"

Jim Renton rubbed his eyes wearily, and looked down at D.S. Alison Clarke, short, fair, stockily built and standing four-square in front of him, signalling 'challenge' in the strongest possible body-language. It was after ten p.m. and he had spent a foul day interviewing detectives under suspension. He had hardly been home an hour when Alison had called.

"This is your case, Alison. I'm just around to be helpful if the need arises."

"Thank you sir, no problem then. I'll tell Mr. Hawkins that we'll be a few minutes still, and perhaps we should see how Forensic are progressing, sir."

At the top of the stairs they were confronted with the usual controlled chaos they expected from the crime-scene team.

"D.S. Williams, sir, in charge of the Forensic team tonight. Any particular reason for calling us out?"

"Very good reasons, Sergeant, though I'm afraid they have to remain confidential for the moment. Have you found anything at all that might suggest this was not a routine suicide?"

Williams, newly promoted from Cardiff, was a little disappointed not to be taken into the D.C.I.'s confidence, but not greatly surprised.

"Early days yet, sir. You can see the signs of a private binge in the office here. Only one person's dabs on the bottle and glass, and I bet those turn out to be the deceased's. You can see the shiny marks over there on the railings where the rope was tied, and a tall man could easily reach up to pass the rope over that roof-truss. I had a quick look at the body. There's no obvious sign of a blow to knock him out, or of the hands having been tied, nor of any sort of struggle."

"He was sozzled though. No sign of a suicide note?"

"Not found anything yet, sir, so I doubt if there is one. Unless it's on the body? You can smell whisky on the body, and there's three empty bottles of lager here, and a whisky bottle, freshly opened by the look of the cap, with about two-thirds gone. Post-mortem may say something different, sir, but it looks pretty open and shut to me."

At the foot of the stairs Renton paused. "Sorry to grab that off you, Alison, but I could see that he was prepared to give you a hard time for getting them out unnecessarily. What's your view of this business, just off the top of your head?"

"Suicide during a bout of depression induced or accompanied by heavy drinking. I don't think we knew that George was drinking that heavily, but I just got the feeling that our constable downstairs was not surprised. This is a small town."

"That's why I was so careful about pressing the investigation of the Hawkins – prominent citizens and all that. Might get very awkward if we've got it wrong. Where are we on that now?"

"All negative, or at least nil progress. I got a fingerprint of each of them off the statement sheets they signed – no match to those we found in Susan's apartment. Only one man from the Club recalls going into the Snooker Room. He just put his head round the door, saw Alan was setting up the frame, so he withdrew."

"Was George there?"

"He couldn't say for certain. The room was dark, except for the light over the table itself, but he assumed that Alan wasn't going to play by himself, and it was generally known that the brothers had a regular thing going at snooker."

"What time was that?"

"Fairly early, about nine-thirty, he thought."

"Damnation. I can see our whole inquiry grinding to a halt with no arrest. Come on then, let's hear what Mr. Hawkins has to say. He's all yours, I'll just listen."

"There's one other thing which may be relevant, sir. Andrew visited George this morning, part of the routine inquiry about the movements of Joyce Clumber. We thought it would look odd if we didn't include the Hawkins."

"Oh God, you don't think that had anything to do with the suicide?"

"I wouldn't go as far as to say that, sir. His report isn't typed yet, but Andrew said George was extremely vague, not to say evasive, about that game of snooker, in fact about the whole evening. He had a lot to drink before and during the dinner, and says he can't remember the game at all."

"We'd best go over the interview very carefully with Andrew tomorrow. One more thing. I know you were doing some discreet investigation of the brothers around the town. What's the general impression?"

"Not so much alike in character as they are in looks. George is the quiet, sensible one, very much under the father's thumb. Alan is 'Jack the Lad', with quite a reputation as a ladies man."

"So Alan is the more likely to have got involved with Susan?"

"That's the obvious inference, yes. But by the same token, it's harder to imagine that he would have motive to kill her, isn't it? Whereas if George was the straight one who had got in too deep . . . alternatively he might have become very intense about the forthcoming marriage and the baby, insanely jealous even, and he could have killed her in a sudden, or a drunken rage."

"A sort of male equivalent of Joyce Clumber's motive, you mean?"

"Could be, sir. Shall we see if the waiting has softened up Mr. Hawkins a bit? He might also be feeling vulnerable, after his brother's nasty death."

"Mr. Hawkins, thank you for being so patient with us. May I introduce Detective Chief Inspector Renton? The D.C.I. is my immediate superior in this investigation."

"Top brass is it now? Forgive my asking, Chief Inspector, but aren't there an awful lot of resources being applied to poor George's awful suicide?"

"Possibly, sir, but you'll have to allow me to be the best judge of that. In this case I'm just the interested observer, and

Detective Sergeant Clarke here is conducting the actual investigation."

Alison had decided to go straight onto the offensive,

"Mr. Hawkins, you have already taken note of the weight of resources we have involved this evening. In part this is due to the fact that the Chief Inspector and I are also working on a murder investigation, that of Susan Stevens, and we are convinced that you can be of more help to us than you have been. I hope I don't need to warn you that impeding a police inquiry is always a serious matter, but especially so when it is a murder inquiry."

Alan looked startled by the implied threat, and ran the fingers of his left hand nervously through the thick blonde wave on his forehead,

"Murder? Susan? I don't understand. I've been waiting here nearly half an hour to tell you what the girls had to say about finding poor George. Am I accused of something?"

"Not accused, sir, no. At least not at this time."

"What does that mean? I've already told you that I hardly knew her. She was just another member of the club. I mean, I've talked to her at the club, she was very pretty wasn't she? Poor kid. I'd really like to help catch the bastard that did it. But I didn't have anything to do with it."

"I never said you did. If you are to be accused of anything, it will be of not telling us everything you could have. I want you to be very clear in your mind how serious it is to withhold evidence. Very serious indeed."

Alison paused to allow this to sink in.

"I'm sorry, I don't know what you mean."

"For instance, sir, we are aware that you knew Susan outside of the mere acquaintance at the Tennis Club."

Alan continued to look fixedly straight at Alison, and said nothing. Was there apprehension in that concentrated gaze?

"Didn't you get Susan her job at your accountants, Harrison's?"

"That wasn't me, that was George."

"Are you sure, sir? We will check you know."

"Check away, it was George. Must be two years ago now. Apparently he'd been chatting to her one day at the club, and she said she needed a job. George's thought was to take her on her as a trainee, with one of those Government grant things. But I said I didn't think we had time for a trainee, and then I saw her next time I was at Harrison's. She said that George had put in a good word for her. I mentioned it to Charles Harrison, and he said she was quite bright, and he was well pleased."

"I see, yes. Do you think your brother had a soft spot for her?"

"Old George? For Susan? I wouldn't have thought so. I mean he's . . . he was very much the straight up and down husband, you know. And Helen would have killed him if . . . I'm sorry, can I stop for a bit, please?"

Alan rested his face on his hands for a minute or so, and when he finally looked up he knuckled away a tear.

"He was my only brother. We were twins you know, not identical of course. I was always, well, a bit more grown-up than him, and I helped him along after Mum was killed, even more so after Dad died. And Jenny, our stepmother helped a lot too. More like a big sister, she is."

"You were saying that you didn't think there was a relationship between George and Susan?"

"If there was, he kept it very secret. Mind you, something was bugging him."

"How do you mean?"

Alan paused and looked Alison in the face, then looked up at D.C.I. Renton, who was leaning against a gondola full of tins of paint, apparently reading a label with no great interest. Alan seemed to reflect for a moment or two, then sighed,

"It's all going to come out now anyway, so you might as well hear it properly from me. It's the drinking. I mean, he was putting away a good bit. We thought it was because of the way my father was going, they were very close, you know. And there was also the problem with Helen, they were so keen to have a baby, desperate you might say, but it wasn't happening. But it could have been something else, couldn't it? Or perhaps one thing on top of another. All I can say is that this last month, since Dad dying, and then that awful murder, he's been getting through up to a bottle a day. You ask Jenny, or Helen, they'll tell you. I said to Jenny 'Something has got to be done, or he's going to kill himself.' And he did, didn't he?"

"Do you mind if I come in with a question, Sergeant? Mr. Hawkins, I'd like you to be totally frank with us. Your confidence will be respected, I promise you. Do you think there is any possibility, any possibility at all, that your brother could have had anything to do with the death of Susan Stevens?"

Alan stiffened as though to make an instant denial, then sat back as though reflecting. He looked down at the desk, at his fingers tapping idly on the polished surface. He nodded slowly,

"It's possible, he could have, yes. He had the time. But he really wasn't that sort of man."

Go on, sir, please."

"That night, at the club. When we played snooker, he could have met her."

"Between points? He'd have needed more than a few minutes to go up to Crabbe's Wood and back. I've walked it. It takes eight to ten minutes each way."

"George was out for forty, forty-five minutes."

"Was he indeed? That's not what you told us previously."

Alison felt it was high time she took charge of her case again,

"If you remember what I said when we began, sir, I did warn you of the very serious consequences that might follow from withholding information. We now have two conflicting statements from you. One said that you were with your brother from nine-thirty to ten-thirty. Now this evening you are saying something quite different. I feel that I should warn you that you could face a charge of obstructing the police at least, and it would be perfectly proper for you to ask for your solicitor to be present."

"No, no that won't be necessary. I haven't really done anything wrong. I mean, I meant to be helpful. He was my brother, after all, I never thought for a moment that he could be involved. So we . . . so I thought there was no point in sending you off on a wild goose chase, was there?"

Could we get down to the detail, please? You went into the Snooker Room together?"

"Yes, the disco always takes a while to warm up, and the girls – that's Grace and Helen – wanted to powder their noses and chat with some of their cronies."

"But George didn't in fact play?"

"Well, to be precise, he hit a couple of shots, then said he had a bit of a headache and needed some fresh air. He said it would do me good to get in a bit of practice, and when he got back we could have a proper game. He was a good player, usually beat me easily."

"Did he leave through the bar?"

"Oh no, there's a door straight on to the terrace. He went out that way."

"And you stayed at the table?"

"Yes, more or less."

"More or less?"

"Well, I'd brought two pints of lager with us. George hardly touched his. Probably that was the problem, he'd had too much already. Anyway I drank mine while I was getting in a bit of practice, then as he hadn't come back I took his as well, and went out onto the terrace for a few minutes. It was a beautiful evening."

"Did anyone come into the room while you were there?"

"No. Oh, yes, wait a minute. When I was setting the balls up. Someone opened the door, said something, and then went out again. I didn't see who it was."

"And did you talk to anyone on the terrace?"

"No."

"Or see anyone else?"

"Yes, there was one person. But she was going back in through the main french doors farther along the terrace as I came out, so I couldn't speak to her. She may not even have seen me."

"Do you know who it was?"

"I think it was Susan's friend, Joyce."

"Could you be sure it was her?"

"Well, it was dark outside, but the lights were shining through the glass doors. I'm pretty sure it was her, yes."

"How long were you outside?"

"Not long, ten minutes or so. There's a grassy bank that slopes down from the terrace to the tennis courts. I just sat there, sipping my lager and looking at the stars. Then George just appeared. He said he'd been for a walk around the pond. There's a large pond in the grounds, stocked with those big goldfish."

"Koi."

"That's it. We had time for a few points, then Grace came in, said it was our turn to buy some drinks, so we packed it in."

"And afterwards, sir?"

"We had a few drinks and dances."

"No, I meant after you heard about the murder, Tuesday, or Wednesday. Did you discuss with George what to say to the police?"

"Not exactly. I mean, when he came back he asked me not to tell Helen he'd had to go out, I thought he was afraid she'd tell him off for the drinking. So naturally I said nothing to you either. Will I get into trouble, do you think?"

Alison looked quickly up at the D.C.I., who had withdrawn once more to his contemplation of the paint. He returned her glance without a hint of expression.

"I'm afraid that would not be my decision, sir. I can say that if you had told us the truth at the beginning, it would have saved a great deal of time and money, and . . . and . . ."

Her voice died away.

"And we might have saved my brother's life. Wasn't that what you were going to say?"

"It has to be a possibility, sir. May we go on now to this evening? Just tell me everything that happened, please."

At this point there was a discreet cough behind her. Alison looked round to see D.S. Williams.

"The Doctor's back, Sergeant. I believe the Chief Inspector wanted a word with him? And we're ready to remove the body, the ambulance is back, if that's all right?"

Alison turned enquiringly to the Chief Inspector, who nodded.

"Fine. You just carry on here with Mr. Hawkins, and I'll have a word with the Doctor, and a last look at the body in situ."

His steps and those of D.S. Williams echoed crisply across the floor of the brightly lit warehouse. Alison turned again to Alan Hawkins,

"You were saying, sir, about this evening?"

"I was late getting home from Birmingham, after eight, I'd say. Anyway Grace had tea ready, and I'd just finished when Jenny, that's my stepmother, telephoned. Grace took the call. Apparently Helen had just called Jenny, in a bit of a state, because George hadn't come home. Grace told her that neither of us had seen him, and Jenny said something about going off to help Helen look."

"And after that?"

"I couldn't swear to the time, but it was about half an hour later. I was sitting on the settee with Grace, watching the B.B.C. News I think, when the phone went again. I took the call, and it was Jenny, saying they had found George hanged here. Poor George, he always kept things bottled-up so. If only he'd confided in us, whatever the trouble, I'm sure we could have helped work it out. He was ever so fond of Dad, you know. I think he let his dying like that get on top of him somehow."

He sighed, and looked at Alison, as though for sympathy and understanding.

"Quite, sir, I do appreciate how very distressing this must be for you, and we've almost finished now. You were saying that

Mrs. Hawkins said they had found the body. He was definitely dead when they found him?"

"So she said. Helen was a nurse for a good number of years, so I think she would know. Anyway I said I would call you people, and then come right over. The constable arrived five minutes after me, and you came soon after that."

"Was the body still hanging when you arrived?"

"No, he was on the floor, with Helen nursing him like a baby. I wanted to get her up, but Jenny said to leave her. They were both sort of numb with shock I suppose. The Doctor did the right thing, packing them off to bed."

At that moment D.C.I. Renton returned, holding the noose in his left hand and the rest of the orange rope in his right. His voice was very quiet.

"Mr. Hawkins, I wonder if you can help me with a bit of a puzzle? This rope is Terylene, isn't it?"

Alan took the coil from him, and rolled it between thumb and forefinger.

"Yes, I'd say so. Could be polyprop. Man-made, anyway."

"If you look at the end, you'll see it's very neatly cut. This other end is the same. Do you think your brother did that here?"

"I don't know. I suppose he must have."

He looked more closely at the two ends. There was no sign of fraying or unravelling.

"I see what you mean. They're very neat, aren't they? But if you look carefully you can see that the fibres have been melted slightly, and fused together a bit. I remember once buying some of this stuff to make a garden swing, though mine was bright red. I bought it in a boat chandler, and he cut it with a blade that was fixed to the wall, and had some kind of electrical system that got it red hot."

"Do you have that sort of system here?"

"No, we don't sell rope at all."

"So we should assume that your brother, or somebody else, bought the rope specially?"

"I suppose so. No, wait a minute. About three months ago, we had one of our regular meetings to review the range. Jenny was there too. It's when we weed out things that don't sell, and look at suggestions for things to add. George had an offer from a salesman of a stand with a selection of different sizes of ropes and cords on reels. I think that would have needed a hot blade to cut off a measured length, and we put it off because we thought that would cause more work than it was worth. Jenny was quite interested though. George had a sample, I know, but I couldn't be certain that was it. Could be though, don't you think?"

"I suppose it could. As Mrs. Hawkins was there, she may be able to identify this rope for us, which would seem to explain where it came from. Thank you, Mr. Hawkins. Do you want to carry on now, Sergeant?"

"Actually, sir, I'm about done with Mr. Hawkins, he's been very helpful, this time. I do have to ask you to come into the Incident Room, that's the T.A. Drill Hall, tomorrow please, Mr. Hawkins, to sign a formal statement. Are you all right to drive home now, or would you like the constable to give you a lift?"

Alan stood up, his brain still racing. Had he really pulled it off? He moved slowly, as though treading on thin ice,

"I'll be all right. I'll go carefully, and it's no distance."

Chapter Seventeen

When Alan finally got home it was after eleven, and he was weary to the bone. The elation at having come through the ordeal safely was overtaken almost instantly by exhaustion. Anxiety and the concealed tension of the interview with the police had used up his reserves of nerve and confidence. As he let himself in through the front door he was thinking longingly of cool sheets, a cup of cocoa and sleep. Tomorrow's trip to that Coventry site would have to be cancelled. The customer would expect that anyway, when he heard about the sad death of his brother. *There would be funeral arrangements to be made – must ask Helen if she would like him to take that on. But would the police release the body? Probably not for a week or two. There would have to be a post-mortem, and an inquest. 'Tragic case of suicide whilst the balance of the mind was disturbed. Warning of the dangers of heavy drinking.' Life must go on.* He wondered if Jenny would want to carry on with the Thursday meeting at Harrison's? Helen would get George's share, but he thought she would not make any difficulties about going ahead with the Hawkins Centre. *Call Jenny tomorrow, and let her decide.*

Grace was watching television as he came in. *Grace looks at T.V., but Jenny reads books. That's one of the things that makes Jenny so much more interesting.*

Grace was thirty-four, and had been married to Alan for almost fifteen years. Her father was Lynchester's leading builder, and she was his only child. He had gone into local politics, as ambitious builders like to do, and was to be Mayor of Lynchester the following year. Grace's mother had been determined that her daughter should 'make something of herself,' so she had been sent, not altogether willingly, to a good boarding school in Worcestershire. For the first three years her school results were encouraging, and there was talk of university. But by the age of sixteen she had matured into a very attractive young woman, not unlike the young Elizabeth Taylor, at least in the eyes of her doting parents. Boys, and later young men, were drawn to her like bees to lavender, and she found it easy to respond. The surprise was not that she found herself at nineteen pregnant by Alan Hawkins, but that it had not happened previously.

"Oh, Alan, at last. You've been a hell of a long time. I suppose you've been taking Helen, then Jenny home, is that what happened?"

There was a sharpness in Grace's question which would normally have alerted Alan's well-honed antennae, but fatigue had dulled his perceptions,

"No, I offered to do that, but Doctor Carr came and insisted on taking them home himself and putting them to bed with a sedative. If you could have seen it, Grace, it was terrible. George had put a rope around his neck and gone off the balcony rail, I think. He looked really horrible, I can tell you. When I got there Helen was sitting on the floor with him, just nursing his dead body, and Jenny was just standing there, totally shell-shocked. And the police kept on asking questions. I couldn't tell them much, really, but they were quite sympathetic at the end. I tell you. Grace, I'm absolutely beat. And there'll be masses to do tomorrow, I expect. We'll close the yard, of course. I'm sure the customers would expect that. If I go on up to bed, do you think you could come up with a nice bedtime drink?"

As he spoke he moved to the foot of the stairs, and had climbed two stairs before he realised that Grace had not replied, but was standing in the doorway that led from the living room to the hall, hands on hips and ominously silent.

"Now what's up? Look, I wanted to ring you from the warehouse, but the police just went on and on, and there wasn't anything you could do. So what's the matter?"

"You. You're the problem, you cheap conniving bastard! My mother was against me marrying you, she said you weren't good enough, even though Sandra was on the way. And she was bloody right! All these years, I've watched you flirt with the girls at the club, and I've never said much, have I? I reckoned you'd grow out of it in time, and you weren't a bad father to the kids. That Susan was the latest one, wasn't she? You kept that very quiet, and then she went off to Birmingham, and I thought that's one less to worry about. Mind you I was worried when she was murdered, but I knew you were with George at the time, so that was all right. I liked George, you know. He was a bit soft, but straight as they come."

Alan listened to the tirade intently, all his senses alerted by the mention of Susan. Was she guessing? Or did she actually know something? What was all this about? He sat down wearily on the stair, and held up his hands.

"All right, Grace, I give in. I'm the wandering husband, and you're the dutiful wronged wife. What am I supposed to have done?"

"There's no supposed about it, you . . . you grave-robber. Jenny, it's Jenny I'm talking about. Mrs. High and bloody Mighty Hawkins. Your dead father's wife, your stepmother, for God's sake!"

"Grace, I swear, I never have. I mean, I've been round there, you know I have, to talk about this deal that's going to make us all rich. But that's all. There's nothing . . ."

"Don't you bother to lie to me, it's pathetic. Old Mrs. Harrison – you know, Charles' mother? – she lives in that big white house across the road from Jenny. I rang her this evening, because I was worried about you. There's a laugh! I asked her if she had seen Jenny come home, and she told me about the ambulance. Of course we got talking, and she asks me, all innocent, if Jenny has been poorly. I said not to my knowledge, what made her think that? "Oh, I've seen your Alan visiting two or three afternoons recently, and with the curtains drawn upstairs I thought she must be poorly." You bastard, you've even been taking her flowers, haven't you?"

Alan knew better than to admit anything, and summoned all his strength to attempt a dignified retreat.

"Grace you've got the wrong end of the stick, really you have. It's not a bit like you're imagining, and Mrs. Harrison's a wicked old bat to suggest such a thing. Look, I'll explain it all properly in the morning, but just now I'm at the end of my tether, and I've got to get my head down."

He stood up without waiting for a reply, and made to climb the stairs.

"Not in my bed you don't. This time you've gone too far. Mrs. Harrison is Chairwoman of the Wednesday Luncheon Club, so by the end of next week it'll be all over town. If you go up those stairs now, I'm leaving. It'll be Daddy or his solicitor talking to you tomorrow, and then we'll see how much you'll be left with when they've finished with the pair of you."

Alan could only stop and stare down at her. It had been a hard, sweltering hot day on the site in Birmingham, then there had been the 'problem' with George, then the police, and now this! For a moment he considered calling her bluff. 'No way,' he thought 'that's just the tiredness pulling me down.' There was determination and aggression in every inch of her pert body. If she as much as mentioned Susan in her complaint to her father it could well get back to the police. Giving in now was certainly the less risky way to go. Later, there could be another plan for maximum security . . .

"All right, you win. Let's talk about it now. But you've got it all wrong you know."

His head bowed, his shoulders slack, he came down the stairs and stood before her.

"Don't look so cross, sweetheart. You're the only woman I've ever loved, really you are. If I come in and sit down in the living room, will you make us some coffee? Please?"

Beneath his submissive demeanour, Alan was struggling to get his mind working again. The more he thought about it, the more danger there seemed to be in the situation. Just one word about Susan could start the police looking again at the assumptions about George that he had so carefully nurtured, and that could be fatal. Could Grace have an accident? He toyed with possibilities for a moment. A few days by the sea, and a swimming tragedy? He dismissed the thought, it was inconceivable that he could get away with it, so soon after poor George. *A break-in? 'Murderous Attack by Mugger?' Too many uncertainties. Best concentrate on what he did best, the old charm and the silver tongue. After all, Grace probably* wanted *to believe he was innocent, and that was half the battle. But what about Jenny? Would she deny everything? Grace was certainly going to be watching him closely from now on, but she probably had too much pride to challenge Jenny directly, particularly if she was persuaded that there might be nothing in it. For her part, Jenny must surely understand how deeply he was affected by his brother's awful death. 'I'm sorry, Jenny, I love you dearly, but I'm just numb inside now. Could we be just good friends for a month or two?' That would go down well. The police files would be closed after the inquest.* When Grace reappeared with the coffee he patted the seat beside him on the soft, chintz-covered settee.

"Come and sit down here, love."

He stood up to pull over the coffee-table, and took the tray from her. She sat down, still stiff with suppressed rage, but on the settee, and Alan breathed a quiet sigh of relief. He poured the coffee in silence, black, no sugar for Grace, white with four spoons of sugar for himself.

"Well? I'm waiting."

Alan kept his face serious, but felt instinctively that she wanted to be won over,

"Like I said, love, there's really nothing to tell. Old Mrs. Harrison was right in a way, Jenny has been poorly for weeks, but trying not to show it. I mean she bore up very well didn't she while Dad was ill, but after the funeral I reckon there was a sort of delayed reaction – headaches, dizziness, unable to concentrate at work. She's been taking one or two days a week off, and spending the morning just sleeping. I suppose when I came round in the afternoon she'd got up but left the curtains drawn upstairs."

"Did she see the Doctor?"

"I don't know, I told her she should, but she was worried he might insist she went off on holiday or something, and there was so much for her to do, what with the half-year, and this Hawkins Centre business. That's kept her going really, I mean she's got more business sense than George and me put together."

Alan could see that the tension was gradually leaving Grace's body, as the sheer ordinariness of his explanation sank in.

"So you were just soothing the fevered brow?"

"A bit of that, I suppose. Not literally of course. I mean, be honest now, have you ever known me fancy an older woman? I'm no saint, love, never have been, but what was it you said, a grave-robber? Definitely not my style."

Grace put down her coffee, and put her hand under Alan's chin. His pale blue eyes met hers unflinchingly.

"I'll say this for you Alan Hawkins, you tell a good tale. All right, I'll call Mrs. Harrison in the morning, and ask her not to say anything about Jenny being poorly. I'll think of some reason. As for you, I'll say no more about it. Just you remember this is a small town, and I'm not the only one watching you. So behave yourself."

Alan was quickly asleep. Grace lay awake much longer, looking at Alan's face illuminated by the streetlight that filtered in through the curtains. He looked peaceful, innocent, with that boyish fair curl that dropped irresistibly over his forehead. Had he really finished with Susan when she left town? Did she believe his story about Jenny? On reflection, she thought it was probably true as far as it went. Perhaps there had been something between them, but his taste had always been for young girls, and it seemed unlikely he had suddenly changed now. Still, he had been warned now, thus far and no farther! In truth, she had not wanted her challenge to be taken up. How embarrassing it would have been to have Jenny as a rival, after all these years! She was reminded of an historical play last week on T.V., about the 'droit de seigneur', that was it. The Hawkins were like the Seigneurs of Lynchester, and Alan was just keeping up the old tradition of deflowering all the village maidens, so that no one could complain that his bride was not a virgin. She giggled silently. He was a real man for all that, not like poor George. Helen would be heartbroken, though. What a bloody mess!

Might all this trouble affect the plan for the retail development? 'The Hawkins Centre' sounded good. She could imagine the family at the centre of everything on opening day, T.V. News there as well as the newspapers, and Daddy performing the opening ceremony, or more likely introducing some famous personality to cut the ribbon. That would prove she hadn't married beneath herself, wouldn't it? And it would be fun to wave that 'million or two' under her mother's nose. A bit of revenge for those remarks about 'Pity they didn't teach you at that school to keep your legs together until after the wedding.'

The night was warm, and Grace stirred restlessly. She considered the possibility of waking Alan, and being very forgiving and loving. He was still deeply asleep. *What a day he'd had! No wonder he hadn't put up much of a fight! Poor lad, best leave him be, he probably wouldn't be up to it anyway. 'Up to it' was a funny phrase, wasn't it?* She ran her hands over her body, enjoying the firm feel of her breasts, and the sudden hardness of her nipples. *No wonder men liked touching women!* She turned away from Alan, so as not to disturb him.

Chapter Eighteen

It is neither day nor night, but a grey twilight, and I must be forever looking over my shoulder. I am walking down a street, with houses terraced on either side. I've got to get somewhere, it's a matter of life and death, but I don't know why, or where it is I have to go. As I walk along, the houses become different, they get taller, and have no doors or windows. Now the houses have become tall grey walls on each side. Something behind me is getting closer, and I begin to run, faster and faster. As I run the walls draw closer together on each side of me, until there's only just room for me to pass. The ground begins to drop away beneath my feet, steeper and steeper, and I have to run faster and faster to avoid toppling over. I'm running faster than I can bear, I can't get my breath, there is a shadow overtaking me, and as I look ahead I see a great darkness like a pit, and I am falling, falling, falling . . .

Alan awoke with a sudden spasm. He was bathed in sweat and breathing hard, as though he had truly been on that merciless run. He lay quite still, and waited for his body to stop trembling. He wasn't running, or falling. He was in his own bed, and it was already light outside. Carefully he picked up his watch from the bedside table. Six-fifteen. Beside him, Grace was sleeping peacefully, curled up like a baby, with her back to him. Momentarily he felt a great longing to have her smooth away the horror of that dream with her brisk common-sense, but decided against it. *She might ask what he was so frightened of, and anyway he was a grown man, why should he need comforting after a silly nightmare? He could explain it for himself, and by explaining it take the horror out of it.*

Instead he moulded his body around hers, and held her to himself. She stirred drowsily,

"That's nice Alan. It's too early to wake up."

Not being used to the effect of sedatives, Jennifer Hawkins had slept heavily and late. It was ten-thirty by her bedside alarm clock when she finally struggled back to consciousness. Lord, she'd overslept! She sat up quickly, and the room spun around her. Recollection of the previous night flooded back. Helen cuddling that awful body. She shuddered, feeling cold through to her bones, despite the morning sunshine already warming the front windows. Poor Helen! Dr. Carr had suggested she should stay the night, and they had put her to bed in the second bedroom on the other side of the house. Jenny pulled on her red satin dressing-gown, and was brushing her hair more gently than usual when the telephone rang,

"Jennifer Hawkins."

"Mrs. Hawkins, this is Detective Sergeant Alison Clarke. You remember, perhaps, we met briefly last night. Your stepson introduced us."

"My stepson? Oh, yes, Alan, of course. I remember now, I'm afraid I wasn't thinking straight last night."

"I hope you are feeling better after your night's sleep?"

"Better? Yes, I suppose so. To tell you the truth, I have only just woken up. Doctor gave me some sort of knockout pill, and I'm still a bit woozy. Anyway, how can I help?"

"My Chief Inspector would like to come round with me, just to check a few details, if that would be convenient? I've called Mrs. Helen Hawkins by the way, but there was no answer."

"That's because she stayed the night here with me. I've not heard her moving around at all yet, but I suppose she'll be waking up too."

Jennifer peered at her clock again, and then at herself in the mirror. She thought she looked awful.

"Look, I can't speak for Helen. I mean the Doctor was quite concerned about her last night, and he said he would be around to see her after morning surgery. Do you think your Chief Inspector would mind leaving it until after lunch, say two o'clock?"

She put down the telephone. *What was there they could tell the police?*

We got there about nine-fifteen. We came upstairs first, to the office, found the bottles and the glass. We smelt something awful. Then I saw the rope tied to the railing and over the roof truss, with

George hanging below. Helen rushed down to try to revive him, and I undid the rope to let him down. She said it was too late, he was already dead, so I called his brother, and he called you.

Jennifer went over the words in her mind as she made coffee, and carried a tray up to Helen's room, where she put it down on the floor to knock at the door.

"Helen it's me, Jenny. I've got some lovely strong coffee."

There was no answer. She knocked again,

"Helen, are you awake?"

Still no reply. She tried the door. It was locked. Fear rushed into her mind, and there was panic in her voice as she pounded on the door.

"Helen, Helen, wake up, wake up. Oh please wake up."

She heard a slight sound behind the door, and felt a flood of relief as the key was turned and the door opened. Helen stood there in the curtained dimness, wearing one of Jennifer's white nightdresses, blonde hair dishevelled, her care-worn face still crumpled in sleep.

"Hullo, Jenny. Where . . . Oh God, I'd forgotten, George is . . ."

Jennifer saw her begin to sway, and half caught her as her knees buckled. She helped her back to the bed, where she sat silently for a few seconds. When she lifted her head the tears were trickling down her cheeks.

"Oh, Jenny, I've just thought that I'm never going to see him or talk to him again. Why? Why did he? He knew I loved him. And I was so proud of him."

Jennifer brought in the tray, switched on the bedside lamp, and poured out two mugs of strong sweet coffee. Only when Helen was holding hers in two hands and sipping obediently did Jennifer reply,

"Nobody knows why he did it, love. Why do we do most of the things we do?"

"I did give him a hard time. I mean after you'd been to see me, and we'd talked about the drinking, I really laid into him. I told him that if he didn't cut it out I'd walk out, and he'd never see me . . ."

The silent tears became great sobs, and then howls of animal pain as she fell back on the bed and buried her face in the pillow. Jennifer sat beside her, stroking her long fair hair and trying to think of something reassuring to say. She had never seen true grief before, and she could only follow her instinct, which told her that the more complete and overwhelming the surrender to the sense of loss, the better the chance of a full recovery. She was concerned though that Helen should not take more blame on herself than was absolutely necessary, and when the sobbing had subsided she tried to share the burden.

"There, there Helen, sweetheart, you mustn't blame yourself. We all of us laid into him, me and Alan as well as yourself. If we hadn't, the whisky was going to kill him anyway. I think he knew that we cared about him and was glad of it. It's just that . . ."

Her words died away. Soothing noises were all very well, but why had George killed himself? Of course it made no sense to look for a totally rational motive, but was there even an irrational one? Helen sensed her uncertainty, and sat up, pushing the tears from her cheeks with the backs of her hands.

"Thanks, Jenny, I'm over the worst now. I bet I look awful, don't I?"

Jennifer nodded in sympathy, "I've seen both of us look better, Helen. Would you like to have a soak in a bath and put your face on? Doctor said he'd be here late morning, and it's after eleven now. And the police will be here after lunch, just to take formal statements."

Jennifer retreated across the landing to her own room. Her mirror showed black rings under her eyes, and she felt unutterably weary. Had she also helped to make George kill himself? In fact, she had not attacked him directly about his drinking, but she had certainly spoken harshly to him on more than one occasion during the last month, when his inefficiencies in stock management had left her with empty spaces on her shelves. Could she have been kinder, more understanding, more helpful? Might that have made a difference?

She took a lingering, hot, relaxing shower, turning the temperature down to 'cold' for the last minute, and felt somewhat restored as she put on her makeup. No problem about deciding what to wear either, 'I never thought I'd be putting on this black dress so soon.'

The telephone rang as she was zipping it up,

"Hi, sweetheart, how are you feeling?"

"Not that marvellous, Alan, but I'll recover. It's Helen I'm really worried about."

"She's with you?"

"Yes, Doctor Carr thought it would be a good thing for her to stay over, and I certainly agreed. I tell you, Alan, I banged on her door to wake her this morning, about eleven. There was no answer, and it was locked, and I really thought something awful had happened to her as well. They say these things go in threes, don't they? First Joe, then George, I was so frightened. But it was just the effect of the sleeping pill. She's been crying fit to break your heart this morning, I've never seen anyone so broken up."

"That's a good thing, though, isn't it? I mean letting it all come out? I was worried last night, I can tell you, when she was just sitting there, with that awful head in her lap, not crying or anything, but sort of crooning over him like a baby."

"Yes, I'm sure it's better to get it out rather than bottle it up. It's just that she's so crushed. What's the word? 'Desolate', perhaps. You'd understand, I'm sure, if you saw her. She seems to be blaming herself, for going on at him about the whisky."

"Something in that, I suppose."

"Alan! How can you possibly say such a thing?"

"I don't mean that she should blame herself, of course not. But that could be part of the reason why he did it. You know, because he found himself drinking again, and felt he was letting everybody down, especially Helen."

"Yes, I see. I suppose I was beginning to work out something like that myself. But you be careful what you say now, to Helen or to anyone else. It's bad enough for her as it is, being left all alone now, without having to torture herself with guilt. Was there another reason, by the way?"

"How do you mean?"

"Well, you said that was part of the reason why he did it. What's the other reason?"

"I'd rather talk about it when I see you."

"Look, Alan, I've got to cope with Helen now. If there's another reason, I'd like to hear it now."

"Well, all right. But you must promise not to say anything to Helen about it. Promise now?"

"I swear. Let's have it then."

"Did you know that the police came to see George, yesterday morning?"

"No, I didn't. What about?"

"I phoned in, early afternoon, to say that the hotel contract was looking good, and it would be a good idea if he could get the stock records absolutely on the ball, as I was going to be out again today. George said that the police had been that morning to see him. He wouldn't say what they wanted, so I dropped it."

"What did they want?"

"It was pretty obvious from the questions they were asking me last night that it was to do with the murder of that girl, Susan Stevens. You remember?"

"Of course I do. But how could that have anything to do with George? I remember talking to Helen about it once. She said that you and George were together playing snooker at the time."

"I'm afraid that's not the whole story. We did start to play, then George said he needed some fresh air, and went out for three-quarters of an hour. When he came back he asked me not to tell Helen, as he'd had a bit too much again, so I didn't, and I didn't tell the police either."

Alan stopped, and waited carefully for Jennifer's reaction, knowing that if she worked it out for herself she would be more likely to accept it. So he made no attempt to fill a long silence. Finally she responded,

"Let me get this quite straight. You're saying that, because he went out to get some air, George is the murderer? And that's why he killed himself? What possible connection was there between George and this Susan, for God's sake? And why should he kill her? Are you sure you know what you're talking about?"

Alan was careful not to be too definite,

"Jenny, love, I know it's difficult to understand. That's why I wasn't keen to go into it over the telephone. But George knew and liked the girl, that's definite. He wanted to bring her into Hawkins as a trainee two or three years ago, and as I wasn't having it he fixed her up at Harrison's in the office there. Charles will tell you about it, if you ask him. Then she left Charles, apparently for a good job in Birmingham and I don't know what happened, but the police think there was something going on, I'm sure of it."

"Alan, I'll have to break off now, I can see Doctor Carr at the gate."

"All right, Jenny. One last thing, though. We've got a review meeting in the diary with Charles tomorrow. Shall I tell him it's off, at least for a few days?"

"Lord, I'd forgotten all about that. I think we ought to be having him tell us if George's death will make any difference to the plan. And I will have to ask Helen what she thinks, that's if she's up to it. Look, let's leave it as on, for the moment, and I'll get back to you if we have to change that. See you tomorrow then."

* * *

Jennifer poured a cup of coffee for Doctor Carr, and told him of the sickening panic she had felt when she had not been able to awaken Helen. He was sympathetic,

"Frankly, Jenny, I'm not a bit surprised that you had a job to wake her. I gave her a bit more than you had, and thought she might sleep until I came. Best thing really, sleep, you know, 'knits up the ravelled sleeve of care' and all that. How was she, once you got through to her?"

"Very, very upset. Devastated, and she blames herself, that's what's so awful."

"That really is nonsense. George was in a very depressed state, for months, because of his father. Do you know he once asked me if Joe's terminal condition might be hereditary? I got him to come in and see me just after the funeral. I'd heard about the drinking, and I warned him quite solemnly that the whisky would kill him. Of course Joe used to put away some himself, but it didn't seem to affect him the same way. Dear old Joe, we were good friends. I suppose you miss him a lot?"

"To be honest, not so much now. I feel that the Joe I loved left me a long, long time ago, and I've just got to get on with the rest of my life."

Doctor Carr drained his cup and stood up. He put a hand on Jennifer's shoulder,

"Good girl. I remember telling Joe you were the most sensible girl I had ever met. Believe me, George was carrying his doom around with him, like a bomb waiting to go off, and I'll tell Helen just that. She must not feel responsible, still less guilty. Probably no one could have saved him."

Chapter Nineteen

Jennifer had made a ham salad for lunch, but Helen could eat nothing.

"I'm all right, Jenny, or at least I will be. Just a few days, the Doctor said, to get used to the idea. And I'm not going to blame myself any more. Doctor made me see it was like a crack in

George's mind. I mean the weakness was there, and the whisky just undermined it until it split."

There was a note of fierce concentration in her voice, as though she had mastered a script and was determined to stick to it. Jennifer could feel that the tears were not far beneath the surface, and wondered whether it was best to encourage Helen to be workmanlike and rational, or whether there was more deep grieving in her that ought to come out. They sat in silence on the small lawn between the house and the rose-garden. Jennifer had poured drinks from a tall jug of her favourite dry martini. Helen's restraint quickly collapsed again,

"You know what hurts, what really hurts?"

Jennifer sipped her drink, but said nothing,

"What really hurts is the feeling of being rejected. It makes me so angry, though I don't know whether I'm angry with George or with myself. When you get down to it, he made a choice last night, if you follow me? He had a choice between death and living with me. And he chose death. That's what he did, he decided he'd rather die than live with me any more, and that hurts so much . . . so much."

As she spoke the tears welled up again and streaked down her makeup. Jennifer stood up as though to offer comfort, but Helen put up a hand to hold her off.

"Don't fuss yourself over me, Jenny, I'll get over it. I'm glad we're together, mind. God knows what I'd do if I was by myself. Probably go mad and bite somebody. A couple more of these martinis and I'll be feeling nothing, and no doubt halfway under the table. What time did you say the police were coming?"

"Two o'clock. But there's no need for you to talk to them today. I can tell them what happened."

"Oh, I want to. Get it over with, and get on with things. I'll just go upstairs now and repair the damage, and I'll be ready for them. You call me when they've finished with you."

At two o'clock sharp Chief Inspector Jim Renton and D.S. Alison Clarke were being shown into the big living room that went from front to back of Jennifer's house.

"Thank you for waiting till the afternoon, Chief Inspector. I'm afraid neither of us would have been much use to you this morning. Would you prefer to talk here, or we could sit in the garden if you'd rather?"

Renton looked wistfully through the open french windows at the warm sunshine and the roses. 'Best keep things formal at this stage', he thought.

"Thank you Mrs. Hawkins. This needn't take long, so here will do fine."

"Helen, that's George's wife, is resting at the moment, but she wants me to call her when we're finished. I hope you'll go gently with her, she's terribly upset."

"Of course. As we haven't met before, Mrs. Hawkins, I'd like to be sure I've got the background quite clear. You were Mr. Joseph Hawkins' second wife?"

"Yes, we were married for fourteen years, until he died a few weeks ago. His first wife was killed in a hit-and-run accident some years before, when the sons were only eighteen."

You couldn't have been much older than that yourself at that point."

Jennifer managed a blush. "You're very flattering, Chief Inspector. I suppose I have been more like an older sister to Alan and George."

"We believe the facts of this case are fairly self-evident, but we do have to understand and report to the Coroner about the reasons, if at all possible. Can you shed any light on that aspect?"

Jennifer paused, then rose from the armchair and stood by the fireplace. Her black silk dress swung about her long legs as she moved. Renton sensed a mood of almost sexual challenge that made him feel unusually uncomfortable as was forced to look up at her. His response was to take refuge in bureaucratic formality,

"Of course if you do not want to comment at the present time, you would be quite within your rights. The Coroner on the other hand . . ."

She cut him short, "Oh, I want to comment all right. I'm just trying to think of the best way to make my point. Quite simply, I believe that you and your colleagues must bear a major share of the responsibility in this terrible business."

The D.C.I. glanced quickly at Alison Clarke, and prevented her from intervening with an almost imperceptible frown.

"Go on, please."

"I believe I am right in saying that you interviewed George this morning. Do you mind telling me what about?"

"I'm sorry, that has to be totally confidential at this time."

"I'll bet it does. Well, this is the way we see it, and perhaps you will correct me if I go wrong? George was very close to my late husband, his father. You could almost say that he worshipped him, and was very badly affected by his death. Very badly indeed, so much so that he had taken to drinking quite heavily."

"Can you give us some indication of how much he was drinking?"

"I can't say from my own knowledge, but Alan guessed that he was up to a bottle of whisky a day."

"Thank you. I apologise for interrupting."

"Two or three weeks ago I talked to his wife Helen about this, and we all agreed on a campaign get George to stop before . . . before it killed him."

"And was the campaign successful?"

"Yes. Helen tells me that, two days ago, George came home absolutely triumphant, because he had gone the whole morning without touching a drop, and he went the rest of the day without it too. That was the day before yesterday. And then yesterday your people lean on him about whatever it was, with the result that, come the evening, when he's tired and alone late in the office, he starts drinking again. As a consequence of this he feels so depressed and guilty that he kills himself. That's how the family see it, and I think you have some explaining to do."

Renton had been fairly certain of the line he thought Jennifer might take, and had kept his eyes down throughout, in order not to reveal a reaction. 'High-heeled black patent shoes, nice ankles, long legs in very sheer black stockings, an expensive-looking black dress with a matching leather belt. Handsome figure, very demure high neckline.' His brain ticked off items in a description automatically, while consciously he wondered if she was quite as strong as she appeared. He raised his gaze to meet hers, and noted the two bright spots of pink on her cheeks. 'She's not as confident as she would have us believe', he thought. He kept his tone calm and formal,

"I'm sorry, I don't think I fully understand what you are driving at. As you know, as well as the death of George Hawkins now, my officers have been investigating for over a month the brutal murder of a young woman. We have a duty to follow up any and every line of enquiry that may lead us to the killer. I hope therefore you are not accusing us of driving Mr. Hawkins to kill himself? Because if you are, it would be my duty now to explain to you the official procedure for the investigation of such a complaint."

"No, no, I had nothing like that in mind. I just wanted you to be aware of how it might seem to some of us in the family. And I particularly do not want to fall out with you, Chief Inspector, definitely not. In fact I have a personal favour to ask."

"I will of course be happy to oblige, within reason."

"It's about Helen. I mean she's suffered dreadfully already. I think she's coming to terms with the idea that George killed himself in a fit of depression, brought on by the drink and by brooding about his father. So far she does not know you interviewed him yesterday. I shudder to think how she might react to the idea that George had anything to do with the death of that poor girl, and that the interview was part of the cause of his suicide. Do you see what I'm saying? It's not as though there's any definite proof, is there? So is there any point in dragging it up now?"

As she finished this last defiant question she sat down again into the big armchair, and leant her dark head back against the chintz cushion, suddenly exhausted and fragile. Alison thought the performance deserved a round of applause, but said nothing. She knew they were on very shaky ground, and was pleased to have the D.C.I. there to take the decisions.

"You say that Mrs. Hawkins does not know about our interview. Isn't it likely that she will find out? Won't that then make things worse?"

"Perhaps, yes. But we could face that when we come to it. Just for the moment, my concern is to get her through the inquest and the funeral and so on. Please say you'll help me?"

Jennifer leaned forward in her chair, and stretched out her hands to the Chief Inspector in a pleading gesture. It was obvious to him that she was under considerable strain, and he had no reason to deny her.

"Of course. There is no reason at all for yesterday's interview to be mentioned at the present time, in fact I agree it could well be counter-productive. I wonder if we could go forward now to your own description of the events of yesterday evening, please?"

"Thank you for your understanding, Chief Inspector. I left the showroom about six. I shouted 'Cheerio' to George as I left, but I'm not sure he heard me upstairs. I drove across the bridge into the town to do some shopping at Sainsbury's. I was there over an hour, so it must have been after seven when I drove back past the yard and on home. I noticed the light on upstairs and George's car outside, so I knew he was still there . . ."

She paused, then continued, her voice breaking.

"I've thought about it since. I remember feeling rather pleased he was still working, because the stock-records had been getting into a bad state . . . if only I'd thought to stop . . ."

Her dark eyes filled with tears, and Renton understood why she was so stressed.

"Please, Mrs. Hawkins, you must not torture yourself with useless speculation. Our experience is that, once the thought of suicide takes root, the victim will return and return to it. It really is very unlikely you could have made a difference. In fact it is more than possible that Mr. Hawkins was already dead by that time."

Despite her previous cynicism, Alison too was moved to sympathy, and offered a handkerchief.

"Thank you. I haven't mentioned this to Helen, and I'd be grateful if you didn't either. It's bad enough that I've got to live with it. Anyway I got home and had some supper, and sat watching the sun go down from my little balcony upstairs. Then Helen phoned to say she was worried because George hadn't come home, so I picked her up and we went to the warehouse and . . . and . . ."

"I think we know the rest from Mr. Alan Hawkins, so you need not distress yourself further. In fact if my colleague agrees, I don't think we need trouble the deceased's wife today. What do you think, Sergeant?"

Alison looked startled, but knew better than to argue,

"Perhaps you could ask her to give me a call next week sometime, and I'll come round to take a formal statement. Whenever she feels up to it will do. And do please give me a call, Mrs. Hawkins, if you think of anything else at all that could be useful."

The D.C.I. said nothing during the brief car ride back to the Drill Hall that was serving as the Incident Room. Once there Alison's suspicion about his mood was confirmed by the vicious way he slammed her car door.

"I'll want your office for a while. Get me some tea, if you please, and tell Andrew I want to talk to him. Alone."

Alison had only a minute to outline to Andrew the accusation of misconduct that Jennifer had hinted at, before he went in to the D.C.I.

"Sit down, Andrew. This is an informal discussion at this stage, with no minutes, but if you want to break off at any time and re-convene with your Police Federation representative present, I will quite understand. Now then, a week ago we reviewed the case, and decided that both the Hawkins brothers had to be seen as prime suspects. I said that we were short of hard evidence, and that the best prospect would be to bounce one of them into an admission of guilt. Before trying that, I said that I wanted one last effort to dig up some evidence, and we agreed to hold off from the brothers until after another review, scheduled for today. Is that accurate?"

"Yes sir."

"Despite that, I understand that you saw fit to interview George Hawkins yesterday morning. Is that correct?"

"Yes, sir, you see . . ."

"Save it, Andrew. Yesterday evening it appears that George Hawkins hanged himself, probably in a fit of drunken depression. This afternoon I met his stepmother, Mrs. Jennifer Hawkins. Do you know her?"

"No sir, she hasn't figured in any of our enquiries up to now."

"You've missed a very special experience, I assure you. Mrs. Hawkins suggested, obliquely but quite definitely, that there was a cause and effect connection between your interview and her stepson's suicide. So let's get the formalities out of the way, Andrew. If she does make a complaint, you could be in the direct line of fire, particularly as the Hawkins are a prominent, well-respected local family. So do you want to go on with this now, or should we adjourn until you can be appropriately represented?"

D.S. Andrew Wilson was not as quick-witted as Alison, and his career was likely to plateau, one or possibly two ranks higher. A lanky six-foot four, with a friendly, open expression, he was a man that people trusted instinctively, a hard-working professional, proud of his work, and without a mean bone in his body. Faced with a choice between loyalty and self-preservation, his reaction was to go for loyalty every time.

"No need for representation, sir. I'm quite sure I did the right thing, though I'm very sorry about Mr. Hawkins of course."

"All right, Andrew, if that's your decision, that's one thing we should minute, and I'll ask you to initial that later. So, let's forget for the time being that Mrs. Hawkins may make a complaint, and get to why you decided to jump the gun and interview George?"

"Well, it was essential, in my view, after you told Alison yesterday to take charge and prepare a review of where we were, with the objective of reducing the scale of the investigation. I knew we had nothing like enough for an arrest, so I decided to have a go at the two brothers, while she got on with the other leads and the written review."

"*You* decided? Did you consult D.S. Clarke?"

There was a barely perceptible pause,

"No sir. Though I summarised the outcome to her as soon as I got back at lunchtime."

The D.C.I. was experienced enough to spot the cover-up, but decided there was little to be gained by pressing the point further. No doubt Alison would assert it was her suggestion, and the probability was that, with no reason to anticipate the awful aftermath, they had simply agreed together to get on with it. Renton read through the interview report again.

"This all seems very innocuous. I mean, you didn't get much out of him, did you? Was that because there was nothing there, or was he keeping something back?"

"I've been asking myself that question, sir, especially since the suicide. To be perfectly frank, it could be either. I mean, he was very nervous and tense throughout, very fidgety and on edge. Smoked a lot, lighting one cigarette from another. Eyes bloodshot, hands a bit shaky. Of course we'd heard stories about the drinking previously, and I attributed the symptoms to that. But it could just as easily have been the nervous tension of a guilty man. I had intended to interview the two brothers, separately, and try to establish if one was covering-up for the other, or whether perhaps they were in it together in some way. Unfortunately the other brother, Alan, was out for the day in Birmingham, so I'd intended to see him this morning if possible. I'd like to be more positive, sir, but this suicide has upset everything."

"It has indeed. George says in your interview report that he passed out in the snooker room, and came to only a few minutes before the ladies called for them. If anything, he's pointing the finger at Alan. On the other hand Alan claimed last night that, far from passing out, George went outside, apparently for a breath of air, for anything up to three-quarters of an hour. Really, he was implying that his brother could have been the murderer."

"Did he actually accuse him, sir?"

"Not in so many words, no. All right, let's get Alison in, shall we? And some more tea would be very acceptable, please."

When all three were assembled in the stuffy office, the D.C.I. drank his tea with them in companionable silence, then rose to stand behind his chair, resting his hands on the back. He looked from one to the other with expressionless pale blue eyes, dark circles beneath showing up even on his dark complexion. His tone was blunt and uncompromising,

"If anyone is to be blamed in this matter, it's me. That's official, and for the record, Alison."

Alison looked up, startled, opened the pad on her lap, and made a note.

"I took my eye off the ball. I should have realised that we were getting to the sensitive point in the investigation, when the whole thing could blow open. Instead I listened to the A.C.C. and his damn budget restraint, got involved in this Crime Squad inquiry, and as a result a man has died, perhaps unnecessarily."

Renton resisted the urge to pace about the tiny office, blew out his cheeks and sat down heavily with a sigh.

"Let that be a lesson to us all. Ninety-nine percent of detective work is procedure, logic and hard graft. But there's always that one percent when you need intuition or insight, and I missed it when it came my way. All right then, let's go through the exercise of considering each of our leads, before we come to any decisions. Alison, what about Joyce Whatshername?"

"Clumber, sir. We can now definitely place her back in the bar at ten o'clock. Last night's statement from Alan Hawkins has her going back in from the veranda just before that, which confirms her own claim that she went out for a breath of air at about nine-thirty, and came back in a few minutes later."

"She was your favourite suspect, Alison. How do you feel about her now?"

"I think she's out of it"

"So do I. Agreed, Andrew? So let's move on to Christopher Layton, our property man. Andrew?"

"We circulated his description all over, and asked if he fitted any unsolved cases of sexual harassment, Peeping Toms, rape and murder. We've had no less than five strongly positive answers. I've suggested to the C.I.D. officers concerned that Layton could be a worthwhile suspect, particularly if they can place him at the scene through one of his retail development jobs. His diaries would be very revealing."

"What were the crimes?"

Andrew thumbed through his file,

"One indecent assault, four bedroom peepers."

"No rapes or murders. So what's your verdict on Mr. Layton?"

"He could have done it. He was there, and there is some form. But there's no evidence whatsoever. On the face of it, Susan lay down and took her clothes off in that wood for someone she knew and fancied. Layton does not fit that profile at all."

"Which brings us to the Hawkins. One is dead, and the other seems to want us to believe his brother was the culprit. So let's play devil's advocate for the moment, and assume that Alan is the guilty one. What follows, Alison?"

She wrinkled her snub nose as she puzzled over the Chief Inspector's question,

"I'm sorry, sir, I don't see what you're getting at."

"Andrew, your turn. If Alan Hawkins murdered Susan, what follows?"

"I think I've got it, sir. If Alan murdered the girl, he would have a strong motive to kill his brother, to protect his alibi."

"Exactly. So let's start from that end. Did Alan kill George? What do we have from Forensic?"

"Just a verbal report at the moment. There is no evidence of any kind to suggest that George's death was anything other than suicide. I phoned the people that produce the rope, and they confirm there was a sales drive to Builders' Merchants about eight months ago, and salesmen were encouraged to leave sample reels behind. I've no doubt we will find the reel is one of those. There was no trace of barbiturate, or any other drug, in George, and no signs of force. Just the remains of several beers and most of a bottle of whisky in the stomach. All very straightforward and regrettable."

"So Alan did not kill George?"

"I don't think so, no."

"Alison, time for another go. What follows if Alan did not kill George?"

"I could see that one coming, sir. It's not conclusive, but there has to be a strong possibility that he was not the killer of Susan, either."

"Fair enough. Who do we think did? Andrew, is it possible to construct a plausible scenario that takes in everything we already know?"

In his cautious way, Andrew did not offer the obvious answer at once, but took his time to re-read Alan Hawkins' statement of the previous evening.

"A lot depends on whether or not Alan accepts what Alison has written as a fair record of what he said. Assuming he does, I go along with the idea that the most likely killer is his brother, George.

"We can prove that he knew Susan, and was friendly enough to find a job for her after she left school. His interest might well have begun as elder-brotherly, and then progressed to something more intimate. When she was distressed by the break-up of her parents' marriage, and decided to move to Birmingham this interest could well have extended to help with the rent, and so on. By way of background, his wife is a rather strong-willed, domineering woman, who could not, or would not give him children. This gives him an incentive to look outside his marriage for affection, and also a powerful motive to keep his affair a secret."

"And Alan says 'Helen would have killed him if she had found out something like that'," Alison interjected.

"Right, thanks Alison. We have the report of a fairly frequent visitor to the Edgbaston flat, and a witness, Mr. Mureni, who identified George Hawkins as the best match. We know that Susan got engaged earlier this year, and presumably gave George the push at or about the same time. Also at that time George's father was terminally ill, and we might connect the combination of the two losses as trigger-factors for the start of heavy drinking. How does it sound so far?"

"Persuasive," said the D.C.I. thoughtfully, "But I could wish there were more hard facts and fewer suppositions."

"My feelings exactly, sir, but there isn't any more as far as we know. Coming now to the day of the murder, we know that Susan arranged a sort of farewell sex session with Joyce. She might well have offered something similar that evening to George."

"I like the parallel, it's convincing psychologically."

"Thanks Alison. Anyway she lays herself out for him, but before actual intercourse takes place something goes wrong. Maybe something is said about the fiancee – an unfortunate comparison, perhaps. Or something about the baby. Whatever the cause, he snaps and throttles her – no, perhaps he attacks her in a wild rage without meaning to actually kill her, and breaks her neck by mistake. Yes, I think that fits his profile better. After I interviewed him yesterday, he panics. Perhaps it's paranoia, the feeling that everyone is persecuting him, that things are closing in around him. His beloved father is gone, his girlfriend is gone, his business is to be sold up, his wife is giving him a hard time about the booze, perhaps the childlessness is down to him too. Gloomy enough to make a level-headed man look for a way out, and George was anything but that, especially after giving in to the whisky again."

"That reminds me. Alison, did you get any comment about George's ability to carry out the suicide after drinking that much?"

"Well, we know he'd had the rope for several months, so the idea doesn't have to be a sudden impulse. He could have been thinking about how to do it for days, even weeks. He could well have tied the knot and put the noose up before he got stoned."

"Yes, but could he have actually walked from the office to the rail, put the noose on, and dived over?"

"I asked the pathologist something like that. He said there was no reliable guide for predicting the effects of alchohol on an individual. Especially an habitual drinker. A good deal of what he'd drunk was still in his stomach and so had not yet had its full effect. Basically, there's no scientific answer to your question, sir."

"Well, that's all I've been able to come up with to challenge your hypothesis. It all seems only too plausible. Alison, Andrew, unless there's anything further, my conclusion is that we seem to have no reason not to accept the scenario just outlined as the most probable sequence of events, and I propose to make a recommendation to the A.C.C. to that effect."

"Would that mean the case was closed, sir?"

"No, not closed. But I feel certain he will agree to wind up the investigation, and allow us to indicate to the Coroner, in strictest confidence, our reasons for this, and for proposing a verdict of suicide on George Hawkins."

After his two Detective Sergeants had left, Jim Renton wrestled with his decision once more. *Had they carried out a full, competent and professional inquiry into the deaths of Susan Stevens and George Hawkins? Were there any leads left unfollowed, any awkward pieces of evidence left unexplained?*

'Yes' to the first question, 'No' to the second.

If we'd been able to prosecute George Hawkins, I'd have been eighty percent certain of getting a conviction, particularly if the brother's story had held up.

Chapter Twenty

The brass plate had been polished and re-polished every week for thirty years since it had first been put up, so that the old-fashioned italic of 'Charles Harrison F.C.A.' was barely legible. The big door beside it had a fine Georgian tracery fanlight above, and opened onto a wide, thickly carpeted staircase that led up to the reception area, furnished with well-worn leather settees. Behind a nice desk the secretary/receptionist sat with an electronic switchboard to one side, and a new computer in front of her. She had close-cropped curls of bright red hair, and wore saucer-size spectacles.

"My name is Hawkins, Mrs Helen Hawkins. I believe there's a meeting . . ."

The girl was instantly attentive.

"Of course, Mrs. Hawkins, if you would like to follow me."

She led Helen through the door on her right which opened directly into Charles' office. As before, he had shaded the room with blinds, and this time had installed a machine which hummed away quietly in on corner, cooling and filtering the air so that it was not necessary to let in the bustle of the Market Square outside. Alan and Jennifer were already seated on opposite sides of the table that butted up to Charles' desk, and the conversation ceased abruptly as he rose to greet Helen.

"Helen, you poor girl. I never expected . . . that is nobody said . . . do come and sit here beside Jennifer. The coffee is still ice-cold, if you'd like a glass?"

"It was Jenny's idea, really. She's been so kind. I made her take me home last night, though. I slept all right even without taking those damn pills the Doctor gave me. Jenny said you'd be having a meeting still this morning, just to review how things stood. I thought about it when I woke up, and realised that without me things would just be held up unnecessarily. So I just decided I had to snap out of it and come too."

She took a long pull at her glass of iced coffee. Like Jennifer she wore black, in her case a black suit with a pencil-thin straight skirt and a mannish jacket with high rolled collars, open at the throat. Her blonde hair had been set and expertly pinned up, and to Jenny's experienced eyes she wore enough make-up to hide the lines that were normally visible on her face. There was a bright nervousness in her manner, and perhaps a slight enlargement of her pale blue eyes, that made Jennifer wonder if she might have taken a different kind of pill to get through the day. Alan reached across to cover her hand with his on he table,

"We're very proud of you, love, and very glad you decided to come. Shall I ask Charles to take you through the mechanics of the deal?"

"That's not necessary, Alan, thank you very much. It's me that's been coaching George . . ." her voice cracked, and Jennifer could feel the desperate strength of the will-power that made her go on. "Coaching George so that he could understand about the money. It was me really that made sure you didn't go ahead with a sale at a daft price when the old man died. Did you know that? I told George what to say. Good job I did too, or we might not be sitting here now. You can take it that I've been all over the pile of stuff that Charles sent us, so the question is, where do we go from here?"

Charles Harrison reacted cautiously. For almost thirty years he had dispensed financial advice to Joe Hawkins, with little enough return. Indeed, it was only over the most recent few years, with the development of Jennifer's cash and carry showroom, that the business could be said to have prospered, in the sense of generating more cash than was immediately needed to fund the inevitable increases in stocks and debtors that accompanied the steady increase in sales to small builders. His had been the steady hand that had kept the bank off their backs during the inevitable downturns in trade, and had made sure that the Inland Revenue did not feel the need to enquire too deeply into their modest profits. Last year's sales had broken through one and a half million. Encouraging, but hardly wealth untold. Secretly he had sympathised with George when he had been so scathing about the original suggestion that they might sell out for a millon to be shared between them, less tax. What was a million, less tax, these days, especially when split three ways? Unknown to Lynchester generally, Charles owned a controlling interest in 'William Hartmann – the Estate Agent', which operated from the retail premises on the Square, beneath his offices. Last year William Hartmann had made more profit than Hawkins, and Charles had fended off buyout offers from most of the major chains. Now, if the Hawkins Centre project went through, he would expect to steer the commissions on the retail leases and rentals into Hartmanns, and then it really would be worth negotiating with those potential buyers. Meantime he needed to be seen to be looking after the best interests of the Hawkins family.

"That's wonderful, Helen, and if you are all agreed we can probably make some real progress this afternoon. I suppose though I have to ask you one important question, that is if it's not too distressing to talk about poor George?"

"I've done my crying, if that's what you mean."

"Quite. I mean, it's only been a couple of days, and I have heard nothing about the will . . . have the solicitors . . .?"

"There isn't one. Not to the best of my knowledge, anyway. After his father died, we did discuss it, but George was so upset he never got round to it, and I never pushed him. The house is in our joint names, so that's no problem. I just assumed that his shares would come to me. Isn't that right?"

Charles glanced at Alan and Jennifer, who both looked blank,

"Well, there was nothing in Joe's will that would prevent you inheriting from George, and obviously Jennifer and Alan would not object anyway. But Intestacy is a tricky legal area, and there are tax considerations too, so it might take a while to sort out. Your solicitors are Ryknilds too?"

Helen nodded. Ryknilds had been practising law in Lynchester for almost as long as Hawkins Timber had been in existence, well over a hundred years, and they had been both the family and the business solicitors for as long as anyone could remember.

"Mr. Parrish looks after us usually," she said. "He telephoned this morning to offer his condolences, and I'm to go in to see him next Wednesday."

"Fine. I'll talk to him in the meantime to see if we can speed things up a bit. May we proceed on the assumption that Helen can vote George's shareholding?"

"I'm sure that's what George would have wanted," said Jennifer quietly, and Alan nodded. In truth he had been taken aback by the strength and vehemence of Helen's assertion that George had always followed her lead. What if she was to come up now with some crackpot modification or objection to the project? The possibilities for delay and frustration were endless!

"Well then, unless anyone objects, I'm going to assume that you are all familiar enough now with the framework of the plan. The immediate object of our attention this afternoon is the 'Option Contract'."

He extracted one closely typed text from the pile on his desk.
"Are there any queries about this, or can we go ahead? Very briefly, it offers to pay each shareholder an immediate cash sum, in return for giving the Developer, called 'Mid-Court Properties', the exclusive right to acquire the Hawkins site within a twelve-month period, on the terms specified. So really there are a number of questions involved that I would like to make clear to you, and hopefully get answered. First, are you all willing in principle to sell the site? Alan?"
"Willing."
"Jennifer?"
"Me too."
"And Helen?"
"George and I . . . we discussed this quite a bit. Basically he was willing to sell if he could have the business and the right to set it up somewhere else."
"Did that mean as a gift? As a sort of sweetener to get his consent?"
Alan's voice was quiet, but there was no mistaking the challenge in his tone. Jennifer cut in quickly,
"If Helen still wants the business, and all the hassle of moving it and re-opening on another site, which has yet to be found, she can have my share as a gift, once the site has been sold."
Alan stared at her. Her dark eyes were firm, and the set of that chin would not be argued with. Where was last week's docile bedmate? He hastily adjusted his stance,
"You're absolutely right, Jenny, this is not something we should argue about. I certainly never had any intention of continuing in the business if the developer came up with the million each we were talking about, so I suppose that means I would have given my share to George. It's yours, Helen, if you want it. But I think it would only be fair, if you decide to sell out after all, that we should be entitled to our share of the proceeds."
"You don't change, do you Alan? Ever keen to grab the last penny, until someone stands up to you. Well, thanks for the offer, but I never meant to suggest that I wanted to take on the business. Let's put it up for sale, by all means. I just wanted you to understand how George felt about . . ."
She broke off, obviously close to tears again. Jennifer put a hand on her shoulder and squeezed encouragingly. She had never realised that anyone could be so attached to a business,

particularly not to something so prosaic and unromantic as a Builder's Merchant. A feeling of regret surfaced in her thoughts, as she recognised that she had known George all those years without understanding or sharing that side of his life.

"There, there love, we understand, really we do. I think Alan feels it's his job to keep us all businesslike. It's all that wheeling and dealing with customers and suppliers, isn't it Alan? Makes you hard and mean?"

She smiled to soften the teasing in her voice, and he melted appropriately,

"Quite right, Jenny. Sometimes it can be difficult to switch off. All right then, Charles, we are agreed that we are all willing sellers. What about the price? Is it a good one? I must say that a million each strikes me as superb. Or could we do better?"

It was definitely not in Charles Harrison's interest to have the Hawkins family shopping around for a higher bidder, with all the risk and uncertainty that would imply. Equally, he had to be sure to retain their trust. Anticipating Alan's style, he had discussed this possibility with Jennifer four weeks previously, soon after the initial approach from Layton.

"Better? Possibly, but in all probability not much better. I commissioned an independent valuation from a well-known and respected firm of Property Consultants, Hamilton and Co. Strictly speaking they would be competitors to Layton's firm, but in this matter they are totally impartial."

He thumbed through a thick file on his desk, and finally extracted a lengthy letter.

"It's a bit long-winded, but the gist of it is that, assuming planning approval, a fair price for the site with vacant possession would be between two and four million. You have been offered three, which is bang in the middle, together with some attractive sweeteners. As a starter, there's the Option Fee, which at Alan's suggestion I've managed to push up to thirty thousand cash, each."

"Good start, Charles."

"Thank you, Alan. In addition, when you put the business up for sale, it can be with the benefit of a contract to supply all materials in your price lists to the developers at a standard discount. Should make it very easy to sell at a good price. And finally you have the opportunity to take a shareholding in the Development Company on favourable terms."

"That's the part I found most difficult to assess. In fact I was inclined to pass it up."

"That has to be your decision, Jennifer. There is always a risk in business, but let me put it this way. I would personally be happy to buy your shares in the Development, and pay you double the one hundred thousand you are being invited to put up."

Jennifer looked hard at his chubby, round face, trying to determine if there was a twinkle in the eyes, or whether he was indeed serious.

"That good is it Charles? In that case I'd best hang on to it, thank you very much."

"I congratulate you on your good judgement, Jennifer. Are you all agreed, then?"

Alan looked at Helen,

"I'm game if you are, love."

She nodded, not trusting herself to speak.

"Splendid. And I actually have here the cheques, which I am to hand to each of you in return for the three signatures on the Option Contract. Helen, you may sign for George, but the cheque is made out to him, and has to go into his account and be part of his estate."

"It's a joint account. Either of us could draw a cheque on it."

"I leave that between you and Barclays. But I would recommend that you discuss the legal situation with Mr. Parrish before you rush out and spend it."

Copies of the contract were solemnly signed, and he handed over the cheques.

"I know it's only the middle of the afternoon, but I felt we should not let this occasion pass without marking it appropriately. My secretary has some champagne on ice, so I hope you will join me in a toast to The Hawkins Centre?"

Chapter Twenty-one

He could see her pale dress flickering a hundred yards up the lane ahead of him, seeming to beckon him up the hill in the gathering summer darkness. He had noticed the delicious way it rippled about her hips when she had been dancing and there was the same enticing movement again as he followed her into Crabbe's Wood.

Beneath the tall trees that grew right alongside the path it was suddenly much darker, and he stopped to allow his eyes to become accustomed to the gloom.

"Boo!"

She jumped out from behind a tree, and tumbled into his arms with a little squeal of delight.

"Oh Alan, I've missed you a lot. You were so good to me."

Her body was light and soft in his arms, and she turned up her pretty face to be kissed. He was restrained at first, but she had a way of wriggling against him and pushing her tongue into his mouth that broke down all resistance. He ran his hands down her spine, and reached over her flanks for the hem of her short dress. Suddenly she broke away.

"Not here, Alan, anyone might come by. Let's find our special place, you know, the one where we can look down on Lynchester."

He kissed her once more, and they walked along the path deeper into the wood, his arm tight about her waist so that he could caress her breast through the light fabric.

"I've missed you too, Susan. But it was you that broke it off, wasn't it? Are you really going to get married?"

They turned to the left off the path and climbed up a gentle rise onto a grassy knoll surrounded by small trees. She reached up on tiptoe to nuzzle his cheek,

"I am, Alan. He's a really nice man. You're not going to give up your Grace for me, are you, not ever? This is definitely the last time, so let's really enjoy it, shall we?"

They sat down as she spoke onto the soft, springy grass, and he began to kiss her more seriously.

"Mind my new dress, won't you?"

And to prove her concern she took his hands from her body, and, kneeling up, carefully undid the ten buttons down the front. In a moment she stood up to remove it, and peeled off her white pants to stand before him naked, her slim body gleaming against the dark background. He reached up a hand to take hers, and pulled her down beside him.

"You're so pretty, Susan, you really are the prettiest girl I ever met."

Delicately he traced the outline of her breast with his fingertips. He felt the nipple harden, and kissed her, still gently, as his hand moved down to her waist, around the hips and onto her belly. Her arms were tight about his neck as she spread her legs to encourage him, then she reached down to undo his belt. She pushed her body rhythmically against his fingers, and pulled down the zip of his trousers.

"That's lovely, Alan, that's really lovely. I want you now, Alan, I want you to stick your big one into me, like you used to. What's the matter Alan? Why isn't it really hard like it used to be? Are you getting old, Alan? Perhaps you've had too much dinner? Alan? Alan!!"

"Shut up, shut up, SHUT UP!"

And then she was silent, and still. His hands had been around her throat, but he could not for the life of him remember how they got there. He zipped up his trousers and looked down at her. Small, fragile, she looked like a sleeping child, except for the eyes, open and staring. Cautiously he stood up and listened. The wood was apparently empty, and undisturbed again. Peering down the slope he could see the shine of the river, and beyond that the lights of Lynchester, full of ordinary people going about their Saturday night business. He looked at his watch. Just after ten o'clock. He had been out barely half an hour. Probably George was still passed out in that chair in the snooker room.

"Daddy, Daddy! Mummy wants to know how much longer you're going to be leaning on that lawn-mower? Tea will be ready in five minutes, and if you don't come in at once and wash your hands you won't get any. Do you hear me, Daddy?"

He pulled off his boots at the patio door, and ran his fingers through the tousled hair of Paul, his five year old.

"Quite the little Sergeant-Major, aren't you? Tell Mummy I'll be there in one minute."

Oh Susan, my poor pretty Susan, I never meant to hurt you, really I didn't.

After tea and the six o'clock news on the T.V., Alan told Grace more about that afternoon's meeting at the accountants.

"Helen was really quite impressive. I mean I told you how she was that night with George, just sitting there on the floor, nursing the body. I really thought she gone round the bend or something, just sitting there, not crying, not saying anything, and rocking him like a baby. This afternoon you wouldn't have recognised her as the same woman. She had her hair pinned up, you know the way Jenny does hers, with a gold comb at the back. All those lines on her face had disappeared, she really looked quite young again. Well almost. And she had the black suit on, the one she got for Dad's funeral. She really did look smart."

At the beginning Grace had been interested to hear about Helen, but rapidly decided that Alan was sounding a good deal too enthusiastic,

"You sound as if you quite fancy her now. Bit of a comedown after Jenny, wouldn't you say?"

"Now, Grace, sweetheart we've been through all that. I swear to you the closest I've been to Jenny is a respectful peck on the cheek. Honestly."

"Honestly! That'll be the day! Well, just you watch, my lad. If you're going to be a man of substance you won't want any nasty skeletons popping out of the cupboard, will you?"

For a heart-stopping moment Alan wondered if Grace had really put two and two together, and was intending to hold something over him. Then as she turned away, distracted by an item about a new by-pass on the local T.V. News, he decided it was just her way of talking.

"So we all signed the contract for the option to sell, and Charles produced these cheques for thirty thousand pounds each. I've got ours in my wallet to bank."

"Wasn't it going to be twenty thousand?"

"It was, but Charles pushed them up, after I'd given him a bit of a push."

"Whether the scheme goes ahead or not? I mean, it's ours, it's not a loan?"

"It's ours to do what we like with. Any ideas?"

"Just save it for now, and we'll think about it. I told Daddy about the clause in the contract that requires the actual building work to be offered to local builders. He thought that might be difficult to get enforced."

"He's right, of course. There has to be competitive tendering, but the local builder should be in a preferred position. Your Dad will know how these things are done. He is on the Council, after all."

"And he says he's the only local builder big enough to do a proper job. Though he would share out the sub-contracts."

"Is that what he said? So it's all wrapped up before the tenders are even called for is it?"

She looked at him in silence for a few seconds, then kissed him on the cheek as she got up to start clearing the tea table. Their two daughters, Sandra and Melanie were away for the afternoon, having tea with a school friend who had a pony. Paul was in the garden striving to push his father's lawnmower.

"I had a long talk with Mummy and Daddy after lunch, while you were at Harrison's. They were always against me marrying you, even with Sandra on the way. Mummy thought I could have had the baby adopted, and looked around for somebody better. Daddy thought I was too young to marry anyway, and ought to have gone to university."

He put his arms around her waist from behind as she picked up the teapot, and kissed the nape of her neck beneath the dark curls. Her body felt warm and solid. *She was a pretty woman, competent, and fun in bed. A man could settle for that, why do I always have to be reaching out for something else?*

"I know they didn't think much of me, Grace, but I haven't done too badly for you, have I? And when this deal goes through you'll be able to buy and sell your father, and any of your mother's toffee-nosed friends twice over. The Hawkins Centre will be something to be proud of in Lynchester, I'm certain of it."

"It will. Daddy's very impressed, you know, in spite of the things he's said about you in the past. And that's what I want you to get into your head now. There mustn't be any slip-ups in this plan. It's very, very important for both of us, so no more messing around, is that clear?"

He continued to press his body affectionately against her back, kissing her neck and running his hands strongly now over her breasts. Despite the seriousness of her intention – she had been planning this speech most of the afternoon – she felt herself aroused by his persistence, and turned her face up for an affectionate kiss.

"Have you got something on your mind?"

"Why don't we settle Paul with his favourite video in front of the television? I don't think I need to collect the girls for an hour or so, do I?"

Chapter Twenty-two

Hawkins Timber re-opened on the Monday for business, and after the usual early morning rush had died down Alan made his way into the showroom, where Jennifer was teaching a new recruit the basics of plumbing and plumbing fittings, with a handful of samples.

"The copper tube and metal fittings are for bringing water into the building and distributing it to the various appliances. Good morning, Alan, have you met our new recruit, Dawn Hutchins? Dawn, this is Mr. Alan Hawkins, our Managing Director."

Dawn was blue-eyed and snub-nosed, with close-cropped fair hair and very long legs. Under her pristine white coat she wore a short black mini-skirt and a body-hugging red cotton tee-shirt. She was seventeen, and exuded sexual curiosity like a perfume. Alan was aware that Jennifer was watching him closely, with a sardonic little smile on her face as she made the formal introduction. He shook hands quite casually,

"Welcome to Hawkins Timber, Dawn, and I hope you'll be very happy with us. Just at the moment though I need to interrupt your training, as I have to borrow Mrs. Hawkins for half an hour upstairs."

He followed Jennifer back across the showroom, enjoying the movement of her legs and hips as she strode crisply across the tiled, polished floor, and enjoying even more the way her body swayed above him as they climbed the dim staircase to the office door.

Once inside his corner office he put his back against the door, pulled her roughly against himself and kissed her with a fierce intensity. Taken by surprise she found herself responding warmly, until eventually she pushed herself off him, gasping for breath.

"Oh Jenny, it seems ages. I could fancy you right here in the office. It must be that starched white coat that turns me on."

Jennifer felt the need to marshal some defences, and retreated across the office to sit down on the wide ledge of the window that overlooked the yard.

"I noticed that you were quite impressed with Dawn's white coat too. I think I'll advise her that trousers would be better than that mini-skirt. Better for blood-pressures all round I think."

She opened the casement window. A small pick-up was being loaded with a complete central-heating installation – boiler, electrics, copper tube, fittings and radiators.

"There's Hedley Walters collecting his stuff. Sixteen hundred pounds paid by cheque this morning against a two percent discount. And we know the cheque won't bounce, because he'll have collected at least that much as an advance on the job. That's the way to do business these days. If you add up all the costs of delivery, then waiting six months for the money, and then the bad debts from some of the small builders Joe and George were so friendly with, we probably made nothing at all. Any one of them could go bust at any time, and we were left to whistle for our money, umpteenth in line behind some bloody bank that has already creamed off all the cash."

It was obvious to Alan that Jennifer was deliberately leading him away from any thoughts of romance or intimacy, and he reacted accordingly,

"It was nice of you to introduce me as Managing Director. We haven't had chance to talk about anything – should I take that as official?"

"Up to you, I suppose Alan. There was never a right time to decide anything like that while George . . . while George was alive. Now, I feel it would be the sensible thing, give you more status in negotiations and so on."

"Great, I'm now M.D. And I agree entirely with you about Dawn's mini-skirt. My first executive decision on taking office is to get a young lady's skirt off!"

Jennifer laughed with him, and he was careful to keep his distance, sitting down on the edge of his desk,

"Next item on the agenda, how do we replace George? In business, that is."

"Actually I was thinking last night about finding a replacement for him as a husband for Helen, but no obvious candidate came to mind. She's going to be awfully lonely, and she deserves a bit of happiness, you know. Any thoughts?"

"Hmm, that's a tough one. She's not exactly love's young dream, is she? On the other hand, by the time the deal has gone through she'll likely be a very wealthy woman, so she'll probably be beating them off with a fly-swatter, on her world cruise. Can we concentrate for a few minutes on the business, Jenny? Until the ink is actually dry on the sale of the site, I think we should try to carry on running it as though nothing was happening. Agreed?"

"Agreed."

"I've just this last week sold us in as principal merchant supplier for the new hotel at the Birmingham Conference Centre, and I wouldn't like to see that one come unglued. We need someone in urgently to handle the stock and order system. It's not that difficult, but it's got to be done right."

"I'm going to do it. Myself"

"You? But what about the showroom? That's where the real profit is, so Charles keeps telling us."

"The showroom will look after itself for a bit. The girls know what to do, and it's not as though I'm far away if there's a problem, is it? We'll be putting in the new computer system in a couple of weeks, so I will need to be up here to be right on top of that anyway."

Alan thought about the little cash commission arrangements that had still to mature. Extreme caution would need to be the order of the day. Jennifer was as sharp as a tack, and would be very unforgiving if she found out. He made a mental note to see them all. Very soon.

"Right, love, I'll leave it to you with pleasure. I'll look after the supplier contacts, you just give me a shout if anyone needs a chase. You concentrate on getting the manual system up to date, and requisitioning what we need, then switching to the computer controls. You shouldn't have to worry about cash either, this hotel deal is set up to produce really prompt payment for us. But we must be able to supply. I'll take you through what they're calling for, and you make absolutely certain we don't run out of anything."

He paused, waiting for a response. Jennifer just sat quietly on the window-ledge, her legs crossed and one elegantly shod foot swinging idly. Once again he felt that old excitement that comes before a journey into unknown territory. With a small inward sigh of regret he suppressed it. 'No messing about' Grace had said, and Jenny was forbidden ground.

"Jenny love, can we talk? About us?"

Instinct warned her that he was planning to back off in some way, and her immediate reaction was to want to hang on. 'Damn him', she thought, 'if anyone is going to break it off, it should be me.'

She rose to her feet, put her hands up to his shoulders and kissed him lightly.

"You're right, Alan, I've been giving it a lot of thought, and we should talk. But not here, not now." She looked at her watch, "It's eleven now. Let's break for lunch at twelve-thirty. I'll get something brought in and we can go for a stroll along the towpath, O.K.?"

He nodded, and she did not resist as he kissed her again.

"O.K. then, sandwiches and sunshine at twelve thirty."

They walked along the towpath in friendly silence, enjoying the warmth of the sun, the sparkle of the river, and the Georgian backdrop of Lynchester on the other bank, dominated by the Gothic pinnacles and spire of All Saints Church, at the top of Market Square. Part of the towpath ran along the back fence of Hawkins Timber, and then the river bent to the right, away from them, on its way north to join the Trent. This bend was where Crabbe's Marsh lay. Autumn rains would raise the river-level by a foot or more, and the part of the path that led across Crabbe's Marsh would live up to the name, becoming too muddy for ordinary strollers, and sometimes actually under water. Today the path was hard and rutted, and a good few others were using it in both directions. Jennifer was the first to speak, choosing a suitably impersonal topic,

"It's hard to imagine how changed all this will be by, say, August next year."

"If they stick to the plan timetable, this will all be a building site, with the contractor under pressure to get it finished fitted out and open by early November, to catch the Christmas trade. Mind you, I'll believe it when I see it. Too many things would have to go exactly to plan. It'll be nice when it's done, though. Instead of this bumpy path, there'll be a raised walkway, nicely paved, with a terrace of flowers above us, and I suppose the car-park cut into the slope above that. You won't know the place."

Alan had a simple enthusiasm for 'progress' that Jennifer did not entirely share. She looked at the expanse of long grass, reeds and hawthorn scrub that made up the Marsh, and felt vaguely sorry that something old was going to be lost. She thought of her million pounds, and the freedom it would bring her, and decided that she could bear the loss without too much pain.

"What's happening about the planning permission?"

"Comes before the full committee for the first time next week. I hear on the grapevine that they are 'minded to approve' so the developers are getting ready to go out to tender. Might well be pouring concrete before the end of the year. As you can imagine, Grace's father has his eye on a very nice contract."

While Alan had been talking they had climbed over a stile, and then turned left from the towpath to walk up the rough path that led up into Crabbe's Wood. After a few minutes Jennifer put her hand on his arm. They were just inside the line of trees – mixed hazelnut, oak and ash. There was some shade now, and they had climbed up far enough to be able to look down across the river and into the busy streets of Lynchester.

"I've got high heels on Alan, and this path is getting rougher and steeper."

He slipped an arm around her waist,

"You're light enough for me to carry."

She disengaged herself, and stepped sideways off the path into a clearing lit with dappled sunshine.

"Here will do very nicely, I'd say. Help yourself to a roll."

She lay back on the soft grass, with her hands clasped behind her head, and closed her eyes. She wore a black cotton skirt with a plain white blouse, and a black lace fichu tucked into the neckline as a mark of respect. She had made up carefully before she came out, and she knew she looked young and vulnerable. The warmth of the August sun pressed against her closed eyelids, and there was something irresistibly schoolgirlish about waiting in pretended trepidation for Alan to make the first move. When it came it was in the form of a sudden pressure of his hand on her stomach, that made her gasp and open her eyes. He was grinning down at her, his face a few inches away from hers.

"Are you putting on weight, Jenny? Seems to me your tum's a bit rounder than it used to be!"

He undid the bottom button of her blouse, and brushed his fingertips across the soft skin,

"Jenny, you're not . . . not having . . . I mean you couldn't be . . . could you?"

"Don't be daft, of course not. And how would you feel about it if I were?"

"Having a baby? My baby?"

He pushed his hand under the elasticated waistband of her skirt, and smoothed her belly possessively,

"Proud, I should think. Proud as could be. I'd be like a dog with two tails, I wouldn't know which one to wag first."

She clamped a hand on his wrist and removed the probing fingers, pleased, despite herself, with his reply, and surprised at how easy it would have been to encourage him to go on. This wasn't how it was supposed to go! She sat up and brushed the dry grass from her shoulders.

"Well, I'm hungry if you're not. And you make absolutely certain I've got every speck of grass off before we go back. We wouldn't want to give young Dawn more ideas than she's got already."

Alan said nothing whilst they ate crusty rolls with cheese and tomato, but Jennifer could almost feel his mind working. She dusted the crumbs from her mouth,

"That was nice. Come on, out with it, Alan. What's on your mind?"

There was an openness in her gaze that Alan found difficult to match, so he kept looking at the sunlit panorama of the river and the town as he spoke,

"Do you realise that we are only a couple of hundred yards from the place where that girl was killed?"

Her mood of confidence and relaxation was destroyed in an instant. The sun was still bright, their picnic glade was still idyllic, but she felt suddenly cold.

"I suppose your right. Up near the top of the wood, wasn't it? What made you think of that?"

"Because it won't go away. It's the inquest tomorrow on George, and it's odds-on the police will bring the murder up when they offer an explanation for the suicide. I feel so awful, Jenny, for having pointed the finger at him. Mind you, I think they were getting there anyway."

He turned to look at her, and the remorse on his face was palpable. He lay back on the grass beside her,

"Oh, Jenny, what a mess! What a bloody, bloody mess! It'll kill Helen when it comes out."

Jennifer was touched to find that Alan seemed to care about Helen as much as she did.

"I don't think it will. Come out, I mean."

He shaded his eyes from the sun as he looked up at her,

"Not come out? Why ever not?"

"I think I may have been able to fix it, so that it doesn't need to."

She related the conversation she had engineered with Detective Chief Inspector Renton when he had come to the house, concluding,

"So at the end, he didn't think it necessary to talk to Helen at all, at least not at this time. It's the inquest tomorrow, and the cremation on Thursday, so presumably Helen will go in to make her statement some time after that, most likely next week now. My impression is that the police know already all they need to know about George. They will quietly wind up the murder inquiry without making a song and dance about any part George may have had in it. Like I said, they're never going to get absolute proof now, so why make Helen more miserable?"

She bent down to kiss his forehead, and he held her dark head down to his so that he could kiss her on the lips, a long gentle kiss that would prevent her seeing the truly seraphic smile that insisted on breaking through. Eventually she unlaced his hands from behind her head.

"I'm so glad about that, Jenny, I've been so worried about Helen. I mean she was incredibly strong at Harrison's but I couldn't help wondering if her spring wasn't wound up tight enough to bust?"

Jennifer stood up and began to pick off the grass,

"That's the trouble with black. Everything shows."

"I like that," said Alan enthusiastically, as he ran his hands down her back and thighs, "It could take me all day to get every speck off."

She pushed him off playfully, and they started off down the path, laughing like two schoolchildren.

'We're behaving like two people in love,' thought Jennifer as she stepped carefully down the slope behind him, 'and I really think he's in love with me. Or at least he thinks he is, which is nearly the same thing. But do I love him? Do I love him enough to break up his family, and ruin myself as far as Lynchester is concerned? That wasn't what I had in mind when I started this affair, was it? Let's face it, I just wanted a man. Almost any nice man would have served to bring me back to life again. I thought I would be safe with Alan. No commitments, no regrets, no awkward entanglements.'

At the stile he paused to help her over,

"We've got to talk about us too, Jenny."

Jennifer wanted nothing of the kind, fearing now some declaration that she didn't yet know how to handle, but she could see no way to stop him as he continued,

"It's Grace. I've got a problem with Grace."

Jennifer felt a huge surge of relief as he told the story of Mrs. Harrison's dangerous observations, leaving out his own ignominious climbdown.

"I explained that you had been poorly since Dad went, and I was in fact coming round just to talk business and get your advice and so on."

"Did she believe you? I wouldn't have."

"You're not Grace, thank the Lord. Yes, she believed me, or at least she said she did, which is good enough. I think she wants to believe me, because she knows it would be something quite different if I did go for you."

"How do you mean, 'different'?"

They had stopped by another stile, and Alan did not answer as he waited for three chattering children to scramble over and run on ahead,

"Shall we walk on? By 'different' I mean important, long-lasting, even permanent. Up to now, Grace has never taken that much notice if I've cast a glance in the direction of this girl or that girl. You know, she sort of expects a man to have a roving eye, and I've always put her and the family first."

It was Jennifer's turn to avoid his eyes, and she kept her gaze fixed on the ground, as though to avoid the risk of turning an ankle on the hardened ruts of the path.

"This path is definitely not meant for high heels. So what about Grace this time then, Alan?"

"You don't know Grace the way I do. When she thinks it matters, she can be very tough, proud too. And her father absolutely dotes on her. He could make a lot of waves in the town. What with this business with poor George, and Grace stirring it up because of you, the Hawkins name could be mud in Lynchester. For a long, long time, and neither of us would want that, for Dad's sake, if for no other reason."

Jennifer realised that Alan was softening her up for some sales pitch, and admired the delicacy – or was it deviousness – of his approach. She kept her face solemn,

"So what do you think we should do?"

"Nothing. That's the answer, do nothing, at least for a few months. Let's get Helen settled in some way, let's get the business sold, the building of the Hawkins Centre under way, and you and I will have the money to look after everyone else properly, and also to please ourselves about what we do. I love you, Jenny, but I don't want to spend the rest of my life feeling guilty."

Jennifer was sure that Alan had rehearsed the last speech, though it could still be an honest statement of his feelings. And all told it suited her very well. They were coming up to the gates of Hawkins Timber, and she adopted a bright smile,

"All right, Mr. Managing Director, you're the boss. This affair stops right here, as of now. Not so much as a nudge or a wink from now on. Perhaps you should chat up our Dawn, so that Grace continues to see the same Alan she's always known and loved."

The inquest on Tuesday was a formality. "Suicide whilst the balance of his mind was disturbed". The Coroner drew attention to the evils of strong drink, but chose not to comment on the reasons for George's death, and was quietly congratulated for his good sense by his old friend, Dr. Carr.

"Our concern should be primarily for the needs of the living, don't you agree? And poor Helen needs now our support and sympathy. Not a lot of pointless muckraking."

Nor did the police make difficulties about releasing the body, and the cremation took place on the Thursday. To judge by the crowds attending, most of the suppliers of Hawkins were represented, as well as many of the customers. Helen found herself surrounded by burly men who wanted to give her a card or a telephone number,

"He was a good man, your George. Absolutely straight, and there's not many you can say that for. You could always depend on him for help too, when you needed it. Just like 'is dad. We're going to miss him. Anything you need, anything at all mind, you give me a call, and I'll come running."

Helen was more moved than she had thought possible by this evidence of the warmth of feeling for George. Thinking about it later, she said to Jennifer,

"In a way it helps to know that he was appreciated by so many people. I mean, they're going to miss him too, and I'm sort of sharing it with them, not carrying it all by myself."

Jennifer did not pay much attention to the actual words at the time. Indeed they didn't seem to make a great deal of sense. But later they came back to her mind, and gave her an inkling of the weight of stress and grief that Helen was trying to bear.

Chapter Twenty-three

"Grace? It's me, Helen. I though I'd call you up to thank you for the lovely flowers. I've got them in a vase beside me now, they came first thing this morning. Cheered me up no end. I thought the funeral went off all right yesterday, didn't you? I meant to ask you this yesterday, but there was such a scrum of George's mates. I wonder if you and Alan would like to come to Sunday lunch? I'm going to ask Jenny, and I thought it could be a sort of family get-together. What do you think?"

"This Sunday?"

"Yes, if you could. The children too of course"

"Yes, fine, we'd really like that. The girls are off on their ponies for the day, and Mum and Dad have been dying to take Paul to Dudley Zoo, so we can come by ourselves anyway. Lunch would be lovely."

"See you about one then."

At Helen's suggestion, Jennifer came early on Sunday, in time for coffee. To mark the occasion, and to help set the mood, she wore a new dress, white linen, with a scoop neckline that showed off the sun-tanned skin of her shoulders. Two columns of small blue flowers were embroidered down the front, and she wore a matching blue belt and sandals.

"You look so nice and summery, Jenny, just what we need to cheer up the day. As soon as I've finished here with the vegetables I'll change into something nice myself. It's time to make a new start."

Helen was wearing jeans and a jumper, and Jennifer donned an apron to peel the potatoes. Helen chatted brightly,

"Getting back to nursing next month, more or less full-time. But I'm going to give myself a bit of a holiday first. I thought I'd go down to Torquay, and keep a look out for a nice bachelor."

She seemed confident and cheerful, but Jennifer felt there was a brittleness there, as though there was something seething beneath the surface that Helen was fighting to hold back.

"Come upstairs with me, and help me decide what to wear."

And there she found what Helen was holding back. Laid out on the dark green bedspread was the most exquisitely beautiful nightdress that Jennifer had ever seen. It was a soft, creamy white, high-necked, with long puff sleeves. The dress itself was made of alternate vertical bands each about two inches wide, of white silk and filmy white lace.

"Oh Helen, isn't that lovely! Where did you find that?"

"That's just it, I didn't find it. The police did. In George's desk drawer."

"I don't think I understand."

"I think I do. You know I went into that Drill Hall place yesterday, to make a statement? I don't think they were much interested really, they'd already heard it all from you, but the lady Detective Sergeant wrote it all down. Then just as I was leaving she produced the box with this in it. It had come by post, to the yard, and George must have kept it in his desk drawer until he could wrap it up properly."

Her voice trailed away. She sat on the bed and picked up the nightdress, running her fingers over the silk with a caressing motion. There were tears in her eyes when she looked up,

"Oh Jenny, don't you see? Last Sunday, it was my birthday."

"I'm sorry, love, I'd forgotten."

"He'd bought this for me, for my birthday. Can you imagine him, choosing this for me? He must have been so looking forward to giving it to me, to seeing my face . . . It was a sort of celebration. Jenny, I'm as sure as sure can be that my George couldn't have bought this for me and then killed himself just a day or two later. He couldn't, he couldn't, he couldn't . . ."

She dropped back on the bed and buried her face in the white silk. Jennifer sat beside her and stroked her long fair hair, but could think of nothing to say that would staunch the great heaving sobs that came from deep within Helen's body.

Eventually the storm of weeping subsided, and Helen sat up,

"He was trying so hard, you know. Once I'd got him going, he cut down each day on the amount he was drinking. I made him set himself little targets, each day a bit longer before the first drink, then a bit longer between drinks, then smaller measures and so on. I knew he couldn't just go teetotal, it was too much to ask. But it was working, he was getting off it. I told you didn't I, about the day before . . . before . . . And he was good in other ways too. After that first big row we had about the drinking he actually gave me his car keys, so that he wouldn't be tempted to drive. He said he'd walk to the yard every day. He really did try, didn't he? That's why it's so hard to accept that he did what he did. So hard."

Jennifer handed her a tissue, not trusting herself to speak.

"You're right, Jenny, there's no more to be said, is there? He did it, and we've just got to get on with living."

She stood up and walked over to the wardrobe,

"Come on then, let's see if we can find something that will surprise Grace and Alan."

Jennifer offered advice about the choice, and at Helen's suggestion went downstairs to get a drink, whilst Helen repaired the ravages of her outburst.

Armed with a large gin and tonic Jennifer stepped out through the french doors into the back garden. Helen's house was really two old cottages, knocked into one many years ago. Outside it was quite plain, painted white with diamond-leaded casements. Inside there were old beams revealed in both walls and ceilings, and a comfortable feel about the polished oak floors and chintz armchairs. Unlike the Edwardian formal style of Jennifer's garden, Helen had chosen to keep most of the old orchard that backed on to the original cottages, and had put in beds of marigolds, large daisies, hollyhocks and snapdragons, all now bursting with flowers.

Jennifer sipped her gin as she walked down the garden to the gate at the bottom, and looked down across the fields to the River Lynn and the town on the other bank. Crabbe's Wood filled the sky to her right, its tall oaks starting now to shade the garden from the pleasant warmth of the midday sun.

George had a nice walk to the office, along Crabbe's Lane and the wood, then down past the Tennis Club to get to . . .

And then the realisation struck. Helen had said that George had given up driving and had given her the keys!

Jennifer's legs felt suddenly too weak to bear her weight, and she put a hand against an old plum tree for support. It was hard to draw a breath, and she drank down the remainder of her gin and tonic in one convulsive gulp. She tried to think of other explanations that would fit the facts, but nothing else made sense. It had to be him, he must have been there! She turned back towards the cottage, her mind still spinning with the consequences.

Following Jennifer's advice, Helen had chosen a dress she hadn't worn for a couple of summers. High-necked and full-skirted, it was bright orange cotton, with a Greek-key motif in white appliqued around the hem and around the mandarin collar, and a wide gold belt. As Jennifer reached the house again, Helen came down the stairs with a youthful skip and a flourish. Her blonde hair was still down, but was now pinned back behind her ears with two black combs. It was obvious that she had gone through another complete mood-reversal.

"What do you think, Jenny, will I do?"

Her gaiety was checked when she saw the expression on Jennifer's face,

"What's the matter, Jenny, you look as if you've seen a ghost."

"Helen, could you get me another gin and tonic please? Make it a big one. And you'd better get one for yourself while you're at it, you're going to need it."

Mystified but obedient Helen poured two stiff drinks, and they sat down side by side on the big settee.

"Come on then, Jenny, what's the big surprise?"

"It's Alan, he's the big surprise, if that's the right thing to call it. You remember what you said to me about George not driving? What about on the day he died?"

"Tuesday? I definitely had the car that day, because I drove to the Hospital for my visiting, and I also had an appointment with the new Administrator. I put the car into the garage when I got back, and started looking for George down by the river. I could have got it out to go on looking, but I was starting to feel really shaky, and I was so grateful when you came."

"Helen, I've told this to the police already, but I didn't understand the significance, and I don't think they have. That evening I left the office about six and drove across the bridge to do my shopping at the supermarket. I had quite a bit to get, and there were the usual queues at the checkout, so it was well after seven when I drove back past the yard on my way home. I told the police that I knew George was still there because I saw a light in the office and noticed his car parked on the road outside, under the shadow of the big tree."

"But you couldn't have. I had it."

"I know that now. All three of us have identical silver Mondeos. It wasn't George's, and it wasn't mine."

"So it must have been Alan's. Oh, my God. That bastard, that cruel bastard. He was there. He was there, killing my George, wasn't he? That's what he was doing."

In her intense excitement Helen jumped up from the settee and began to stride about the room. She splashed half a tumblerful of gin into her glass and took a deep swallow. There was triumph as well as rage in her voice,

"I knew it, Jenny, I just knew it. Didn't I say so this morning? I knew George loved me too much to kill himself. Don't you see, that beautiful nightdress was the proof, the absolute proof! Alan butchered him, just when he was getting well again. But why,

Jenny, why? He knew we were in favour of selling out for the new Hawkins Centre. What reason could he have to kill his own brother?"

Jennifer looked up from the settee, and took another swallow from her own glass,

"Sit down, love, I think I know the answer."

Carefully she went over the story of the conflicting alibis,

"So you see in the beginning George had told the police that he and Alan were playing snooker together, at the time that the girl was murdered. Later he probably admitted that he was too fuddled to be certain of anything. Alan could see his alibi going out of the window, perhaps even being contradicted by George. So he staged the suicide, and told the police the story about it being George who had left the snooker room."

"Does that mean you think Alan murdered the girl as well?"

Jennifer paused. She conjured up Alan in her imagination – Alan the son Joe had loved, Alan who was so like her Joe, Alan the playful companion, Alan the passionate lover. And Alan who had deceived his wife for years, Alan the schemer and manipulator.

"I don't know, Helen, but I think it's more than possible, yes."

It was Helen's turn to fall silent. She was sitting in the armchair opposite Jennifer, nursing her glass in two hands against her breast, with her eyes closed. Her body began to rock slightly, back and forward, and Jennifer recalled with a shudder that awful night when they found George's body.

"Helen! Helen, do you hear me?"

She looked up slowly, seeming to be returning from a long journey,

"I'm sorry, Jenny, what were you saying?"

"It's almost twelve-thirty. They'll be on their way soon. Let me call Grace and say you're feeling poorly. They'll accept that, I'm sure. Then I'll call the police, and tell them about all this."

"No, NO. Definitely not. Don't stop them coming, and don't call the police yet."

Jennifer was startled by the vehemence of Helen's demand.

"I'm sorry, Jenny, I didn't mean to shout at you. That's what I was thinking about just then. I want Alan to come. I want us to sit down to lunch just like we planned, and then we'll spring it on him. I want to see his face when I accuse him of murdering his own brother, like Cain and Abel. I want to hear him squirm.

I wonder if he's got a conscience about it? Say you'll help me in this Jenny, please say you will. It's not much to ask, after all I've been through, is it?"

Commonsense told Jennifer that it was wrong to lead Alan on, to torture him in this way. But Helen pleaded so much she hadn't the heart to refuse her.

"All right, I'll leave calling the police for now. But don't expect me to join in baiting Alan, it's not my style. And he is Joe's son, after all."

"So was George."

Usually on a Sunday morning Grace received breakfast in bed, particularly if the previous night's lovemaking had been good. It had indeed been good. Alan had been exceptionally loving and attentive, and, for once, she had not needed to fake her pleasure and her enjoyment of his body. However this Sunday both were up early, Grace to get Paul ready to be collected by his grandparents for the long-promised day out at the Zoo, and Alan to make sure that Sandra and Melanie had proper breakfasts before he drove them, chattering excitedly, to their school friends, for a day at a Pony Show.

After they had left, Grace luxuriated in a long hot bath, and was dressing by the time Alan returned. A pair of expensive dark blue tights; lace knickers and dark blue court shoes, new and with very high heels. She tried a few tentative steps in front of the bedroom mirror. Higher than she'd been used to, but they did make her ankles look slimmer. She was stepping into a slim silk waist slip, also in blue, when Alan came upstairs.

He opened the bedroom door, and threw an arm across his eyes as though dazzled,

"Oh Grace, you really are something. Let's go out just like that, and I promise I'll never even so much as look at another woman."

Grace blushed, "Get off you daft bugger, you'll get me arrested."

She pirouetted before the mirror, "Not bad though, for an old woman with three children."

"Not so much of the old, either. You're six months younger than me, and I'm in my prime."

He put his arms around her from behind, and kissed the nape of her neck gently, enfolding her breasts in his big hands,

"I'll prove it to you now", he murmured, rubbing himself against her back, "With pleasure, with the greatest of pleasure."

She leaned back to kiss his cheek, then jabbed him in the ribs with a playful elbow,

"That's enough seduction for one morning, thank you Mr. Hawkins. If I arrive late with puffy lips, and you with hollow eyes, what kind of an impression do you think that will make? Your turn for the bath now. I'm going to fix my face and put on my new suit."

"Without a bra?"

"Yes, without a bra. I think it improves the line, don't you?"

"Definitely."

Alan opened the front garden gate of Helen's cottage, and waved Grace through with a flourish. 'That new two-piece in dark blue really suits her', he thought. She had tucked a white scarf into the deep cleavage, at his suggestion,

"Just for respect today. If Helen and Jenny are wearing something cheerful, you can let the sun in."

Jennifer opened the door and greeted them both with a peck,

"You are just in time for a quick drink. Helen is busy in the kitchen, and I've just made a pitcher of dry martinis, if that's all right?"

Alan was conscious of a certain restraint or formality in her manner, which he attributed to their recent discussion. For her part, Grace had never been very close to Jennifer. Joe Hawkins had always kept the boys under his thumb, and Jennifer was perceived by Grace as a part of that authority, even though she was only a few years older than herself. She appraised, as though seeing her for the first time, Jennifer's dark eyes, fine figure, and the expensive white dress with its embroidered flowers.

"You do look so bright and summery, Jenny, I think I'll take this scarf out. I wore it really because Alan wasn't too sure how cheerful Helen would be feeling. How's she bearing up now.?"

Jennifer struggled for an answer that would be truthful, without breaking her promise not to warn Alan,

"Quite well, I suppose, all things considered. I helped her chose the orange dress this morning, as a sort of sign that she is returning to the business of living."

"What's she going to be doing, do you know?"

"I think she's going to get away for a bit of a holiday, then she's planning to start again nursing at the hospital. I do like your suit, Grace, where did you get it?"

"I looked all over for ages, and found it eventually at Rackhams."

She stood up and smoothed the skirt over her hips, and covertly admired herself in the antique gilt mirror over the fireplace. Helen called from the kitchen,

"If you'd all like to sit down now, I'm just about ready for you."

The ground floor of one side of the cottage had been opened right through, so that the kitchen looked out onto the front garden, and the dining area onto the orchard at the back.

"Alan, you sit at this end, and I'll bring you the roast to carve. Grace, if you could carry in the vegetable dishes and sit at the other end? Jennifer, you're here on Alan's left, and I'm on his right. I'll just sharpen this for you."

Grace picked up an old-fashioned cook's knife, the blade very broad at the handle, and tapering to a sharp point. There was a nerve-jangling screech as she pulled it four times through the sharpener on the worktop, then she moved towards the table with it. For a thunderous moment Jennifer watched as Helen paused behind Alan, with the blade flashing in the sunlight.

Then she sat down beside him, and handed him the knife,

"I'm sorry, Alan, we don't run to one of those electric carvers, but this one will do the job all right."

Jennifer let her breath out as slowly and unobtrusively as possible, and raised a little smile of encouragement. Alan stood to carve the roast rib of beef with no sign that he had noticed anything unusual. As he was finishing he said,

"I almost forgot. I brought a bit of a present for the occasion."

He left the table, and returned with a coolbox, which he opened to reveal two bottles of sparkling Saumer. Jennifer found the wineglasses, and Alan popped a cork.

"I give you a toast. To Helen. May she soon find happiness again!"

Grace stood up, and Jennifer followed,

"Helen. May she soon find happiness again!"

Jennifer watched Helen closely as they sat down to begin the meal, but there was no hint of the turmoil she must be feeling. Alan and Grace had arrived only a few minutes after Helen had made her promise to keep quiet, and Jennifer had no idea what she planned. Perhaps she had no plan? She found herself drawn into a conversation with Grace about the difficulty of shopping for clothes in the Midlands, whilst listening at the same time to Alan, describing to Helen the likely stages of the Hawkins

Centre project. He seemed oblivious to the fact that Helen's responses were minimal. Jennifer could see that Helen kept her eyes fixed on his face, as though to consume him, and she guessed that he found this interesting, and was probably flattered to have her total attention. He broke off to open the second bottle, and fill the four glasses. Suddenly Helen stood up, and raised her glass, keeping her gaze fixed on Alan,

"I'd like to propose a toast to George, my husband and Alan's brother. May he rest in peace."

With only a slight hesitation the other three rose,

"To George, God bless him. May he rest in peace."

All four sat down in silence. Jennifer could sense that the dam was breaking, and Helen continued, almost in a hiss.

"And may his murderer roast in Hell!"

Jennifer reached across the table to put a restraining hand on Helen's, but she shook it off irritably. Grace was the first to speak,

"Now Helen, love, you've been through so much, but George wasn't murdered, was he? He was ill, what with his father dying and everything, and he took his own life. You know that really, don't you?"

"I know no such thing. He was murdered. And murdered by this cruel bastard here, your wonderful husband."

Alan opened his mouth, and then said nothing. He stared at his accuser, who was drawing breath in deep gasps, as though coming up from a long dive. Her eyes were wide with excitement, and beads of perspiration were visible on her forehead.

"Now, Helen, that's a wicked thing to say," said Grace, still quite calm, as though admonishing a naughty child, "You know that Alan has been as upset as anyone about George. It was Alan who first brought up about George's drinking, wasn't it? Wasn't that trying to save George's life? How can you be so ungrateful?"

"He did it, I tell you he killed my poor George. He was there, that evening when it happened. Jenny can tell you, she saw his car outside, didn't you Jenny? Tell them, tell them."

Jennifer looked down at her plate as she spoke in a tense monotone,

"It's true. I wanted to phone and tell you not to come today, but Helen insisted on having it out. I drove back past the yard around seven-thirty that evening, and saw one of our cars parked under the big tree. I took no notice at the time nor afterwards until today, because I thought it was George's. You know they all look alike. But now I know it was Alan's, because Helen had George's.

She raised her eyes to look at Alan, and saw the panic in his face, "Oh, Alan, how could you? Your own brother?"

"I didn't, Jenny, I didn't, you must believe me. I was there, I admit that, but he was already dead. There was nothing I could do for him. I was so upset I just came out and drove home . . ."

"Liar!"

This time the accuser was Grace, facing him down the table,

"You phoned me. You said you'd been delayed in Birmingham, and were just going to leave the city. You must have been there, phoning from his office. Oh Alan, were you arranging for it to look like suicide at that very moment?"

The noise that came from Helen was more an animal growl than anything recognisably human. In a crashing flurry of movement she picked up the big knife and launched herself at Alan. Jennifer saw the point buried into his throat as he went over backwards in his chair, with Helen on top of him. A fountain of bright scarlet sprayed blood into Helen's distorted face and onto Jennifer's white dress. There was a flash of steel in the air as Helen withdrew the blade, then she pulled it with a vicious, controlled backhand slash across his throat, so that the sound of metal grating on bone was distinctly heard.

There was a moment of total silence before Grace began to scream, a thin, high-pitched squeal of pain that rose and fell with each breath. Alan was clearly dead, his body had a huge gaping wound making a second open mouth in his throat. Blood was dripping from the white folds of Jennifer's dress and falling with a distinct noise onto the polished wood floor. She looked up to see Helen standing over her, still holding the knife, her face and chest ghastly with Alan's blood. Her voice seemed to come from far away,

"I'm so sorry, Jenny. I know you fancied him, but he was bad, really he was."

She made no resistance as Jennifer took the knife and sat her down in her own chair. Grace continued her scream, but more weakly now as Jennifer dialled 999.

"Police, please. And an ambulance. There's been a terrible accident."

FAMILY BUSINESS

Prologue

Lloyd Teller, Executive Chairman of American Cereal Products, was a big man, well over six feet tall and solidly built, without being fat, with a thick mane of dark hair and a prominent nose that proclaimed his Armenian ancestry. He was seated in his favourite position, with his jacket draped over the back of his black leather chair, and his feet up on the low ledge of the window that looked out onto Chicago, almost twenty miles away. He was browsing impatiently through the morning's post. He had risen to his present position just eighteen months previously, after thirty five years with the company, mainly in Manufacturing and Engineering Management, and was very proud to have made it to the fiercely coveted top floor without the benefit of a fancy degree or friends in high places. In its turn the company, still with a substantial representation from the founding families on its Board of Directors, was happy to have found reliable management without having to go outside. Lloyd's attention had been caught by the letter now in his hand, from a British merchant bank. He read it carefully for a second time, felt the thickness of the fine paper, and ran a big thumb over the embossed crest alongside the name, 'De Boissy'. He scratched his chin thoughtfully, and stood up to walk through his PA's office.

"Betsie, I'm going along to Ben with this letter from England. Try not to disturb us unless you have to."

By Chicago standards, the modern fifteen-storey office tower was simple and functional, but it stood out as a landmark on the lakeshore, because of the bold red neon sign which revolved on the top – 'A.C.P. Inc' – in letters ten feet high. The lower floors held the general sales and accounting offices of the group, behind a fine facade of stone-cladding and smoked-glass windows. Management occupied the upper floors, in a nicely ascending pecking-order of seniority. Immediately below the shining red sign was the Executive Suite, a handsomely panelled set of personal offices arranged around the perimeter, each with a wide and deep picture-window view over the lake or the land, and each insulated from the inner corridor by a P.A.'s office. Naturally Lloyd had the best suite in the south-east corner, allowing him one window with an immense view eastward across the blue expanse of Lake Michigan, and a second with a stunning panorama of the skyscraper towers of Chicago, glittering now in the low-angled sunlight of the early December morning.

Ben Camina was ACP's Chief Operating Officer. Small, slim, dark and quick-moving, he too had climbed the long slow ladder through ACP's management, where his background had been in Accounting. The son of poor Mexican immigrants, he had won on merit an assisted-place scholarship to Stanford University, California, when such an entry was exceedingly hard to come by. He and Lloyd were seen as a good team by the Board, and their working relationship was easy-going and comfortable. Ben was reading the Wall Street Journal when he heard Lloyd's booming tones in the outer office.

"Come in, come in. I suppose you want to remind yourself what a factory looks like?"

It was a standing joke between them. One window of Ben's office on the south-west corner did indeed look down onto the sprawling sheds, silos and steaming chimneys of the plant, though if you raised your eyes a fraction there was also a view inland, over the broad flat acres of Illinois to a blue line of hills probably thirty miles away, and he too had a fine view of Chicago from the other window. Lloyd ignored the jibe and held out the letter.

"This came in the morning's post from England. What do you think? Do we know these guys at De Boysey?"

"It's pronounced 'De Boissy', just as it's spelt. Yes we know them, or know of them at least. They are one of the merchant bank contacts suggested to us by our brokers . . . you remember the circular we put around last month, looking for possible acquisitions or joint ventures in the European cereal business?" He scanned the letter, "Interesting. I don't think we knew that a bank had as much as a twenty percent shareholding in an English breakfast cereal business. Must be through a nominee account. Let's get Vince in, and see if he can throw any more light on this 'Strongwheat Ltd.'

Vince O'Hanlon had previously had ten years experience in New York wheeler-dealing, which included being one of the researchers in the notorious Reynolds Tobacco-Nabisco merger. He was proud to have been one of what the Press called "The Barbarians at the Gate" at that time. Just over a year ago he had been recruited into ACP straight out of putting himself through a Harvard MBA, when the Board had belatedly come to the conclusion that it was necessary to play catch-up in the race to achieve 'global domination' of its market sector. His job-specification, as V.P. International Business Development, was, "*To identify and open negotiations with potential targets for acquisition in Consumer and Industrial Foods, with particular emphasis on ACP's core competencies in Cereals and Cereal Derivatives. At the present time priority is to be given to establishing a company presence within the EU.*"

Potentially, his salary and stock-incentive package was almost as big as that of his boss, Ben Camina. By the same token he needed to perform, and perform quickly now. He read through the letter. Vince was in his early thirties, tall, lean and dark-suited, with black hair cut short and brushed back, sharp blue eyes deep-set in bony features, and an expression of keen intelligence. He handed the letter back to Ben, who glanced through it again.

"So, Vince, what d'you think we should do?"

"I've got their financials in my files, I believe. I would probably have put them low down in my opportunity grading, because of the family control. That's turning out to be the major issue in Europe, all over. If the business ain't American-controlled already, it's because there's some ancient patriarch hanging on until a son, or a grandson, or even some distant cousin is ready to take the reins. Anything to keep it in the family."

He took the letter up again, and continued. "This guy, Alex Hampshire, sure knows how to trail the bait. The company is '*highly respected in the industry*'. Ain't they all! '*It has a five percent share of the U.K. market for breakfast cereals*' – that's more than we have of the U.S. market, so we'd sure as hell want to see some proof of that. '*The business has been held back of late by the prolonged illness of the Chairman, who is also the principal shareholder, and the Bank feels that an international partner would strengthen the management situation*'. In other words, 'Come over and use your fingers to pull our chestnuts out of the fire, and then we'll sell them to you at a very fancy multiple of future earnings.' Still, I've gotta admit, it's the best lead into a potential acquisition in breakfast cereals we've seen so far. Let me have a look through my files, and I'll likely suggest a trip over to London. There's another possibility coming up in Essen, Germany, that's a cooking oil business that looks promising, and the olive-oil processor in Parma, Italy you already know about. Could be a really fruitful visit."

ACP had recently celebrated its centenary, and the row of jetties extending into the lake, with their grain silos and tall cranes, bore witness still to the company's origins as buyers and shippers of the Mid-West's abundant harvests of maize – the corn that was the principal cereal in 'Cereal Products'. A natural progression had over the years led them into adding value by processing the grain that flowed in, so that now shipping raw corn was only a minor part of the business, and the real profits were earned in derivatives – corn flour, corn oil, corn margarine, and corn breakfast cereals. With sales totalling well over a thousand million dollars a year, ACP was a well-respected, if rather humdrum component of the American industrial scene.

After Vince had left the two men stood side by side, looking westwards to the distant horizon. Lloyd had come under some pressure at the last Board Meeting to produce some tangible results for their new 'Global Dominance' strategy, and was the first to break the silence.

"I sure hope we've backed the right horse."

"Vince? He's as hungry as they come. Smart too. If there's a way to do a deal, he'll find it. Nobody had the guts to say it to the Board, but we're trying to do now what Kellogg and Quaker did sixty years ago. Hell, you and I were both pushing that way, when was it? Certainly ten, more like fifteen years ago. But they were all too happy then getting fat running the business they knew in the States, with a bit of activity for amusement in Mexico and South America. 'Who needs to be chasing after a bunch of Frogs or Brits?' Now the word is that Wall Street is going to look down its nose at you if you're not 'global'. So we've got to start piling up those frequent-flyer miles."

Lloyd nodded and sighed, "It's sure as hell goin' to get tougher and tougher."

Chapter One

Just before 8.30 a.m. on that same crisp morning in early December, Dick Routledge manoeuvred his company Rover expertly through the narrow pillared gates that separated the small forecourt of Sceptre Mill – 'Home of Strongwheat' – from the busy road that ran alongside the river Lyn, on the north side of the small English Midlands town of Lynchester. He scarcely noticed the Mill's handsome, but soot-blackened stone exterior as he crunched to a halt in the space marked 'Managing Director', levered his large frame from behind the wheel, and walked vigorously, though with a perceptible limp, up the four broad steps. The polished brass on the mahogany swing doors flashed brightly as he pushed through, acknowledged with a cheerful wave the respectful "Good morning, sir" of the receptionist-cum-switchboard operator, and made his way through another pair of fine doors into the panelled and carpeted corridor of the management offices of Strongwheat plc.

Dick was a broad shouldered, powerfully built man in his early forties, with fair bushy eyebrows and thinning hair. He had played wing forward for the R.A.F. for three good seasons before a knee injury had cut short his career as a player, and also led to his being grounded. Elizabeth Boyd, his secretary, took the fleecy car-coat from him as he passed through her office into his own.

"Good morning, sir. Today's correspondence is on your desk. Nothing urgent, except that Mr. Helvin was particularly concerned that you should sign those cheques before you go in to the Board Meeting, and I am to post them off."

Elizabeth was in her fifties, at least ten years older than Dick. She was also secretary to his father, James Routledge, Chairman and principal shareholder in the business. After thirty-four years with the company she knew she was invaluable, and was immensely proud of her discreet efficiency. Dick dutifully signed the cheques, glanced at the post, and stood up.

"If anyone needs me desperately I'm in the Board Room. I'd like a little peace and quiet to go over my Board papers before the others arrive. Ask the kitchen to organise some coffee for me, would you please?"

The Board Room at Sceptre Mill was known by various names amongst the two hundred employees who saw it every working day. 'The Greenhouse' and 'The Funny Farm' were two of the more friendly; the less well-disposed referred to it as 'The Tropical Paradise', or even 'The Fuhrerbunker'. It was a remarkable structure under any name. It was built in the form of an island – or rather a peninsula, because of its connecting covered corridor extending from the outer wall towards the centre of the main factory floor. The nicknames arose from the fact that its Victorian designer had created it in the form of a fine gentleman's conservatory. Externally it was tiled to waist-height, with clear glass walls above on all four sides, and an elegantly curved glass roof which was crowned with a carved and curlicued ridge-top. All around packets and cases of the company's product, Strongwheat Breakfast Cereal, surged in an incongruous roar and rattle of automated packaging lines, which approached but never quite touched its graceful shape.

Inside the contrast was absolute. Double-glazing shut out the din of the factory. When, as today, it was to be used for a meeting, it was the practice to draw the thick cream velvet curtains that extended from the suspended ceiling to the floor, and so transform the interior into a haven of calm. A walnut boardroom table, with a virgin blotter in front of each of the seven red leather chairs, occupied the end of the room immediately opening from the corridor. At the far end was a matching sideboard and two deep and comfortable leather sofas, one each side of a low coffee table.

There was over an hour to go before the scheduled 10 a.m. start to the Board Meeting which, on this occasion, was expected to be mainly concerned with the consideration of the company's results for the year ending 30th September. For an hour Dick was the room's only occupant, sunk deeply into a sofa and humming contentedly to himself as he leafed through his Board papers, made an occasional note or underlining, and finished a second cup of strong coffee. Now and again he ran his fingers through the thinning strands of his fair hair.

His thoughts drifted back to the time – was it only eighteen months ago? – when the family doctor had telephoned him at his office in R.A.F. Wenford.

"I think you should come home urgently, Richard." He could still hear Doctor Carr's thin, precise tones, "Your father has suffered two strokes this morning, and I am concerned that the prognosis may not be good for a third."

And that decided things really. When he arrived home two hours later his father had not had that third seizure. But he seemed palpably to have shrunk as he lay asleep, or perhaps unconscious in the big bed. There was a greenish pallor in his cheeks, and he was breathing in short, shallow gasps. That evening he opened his eyes, but was obviously without control of the left side of his body, and his face had a curious lop-sided look. Against the doctor's advice he insisted on talking to Dick, "Alone. Now. *Please.*"

"Sit close here on the bed, Dick, and just listen. They've given me another of those damn blue pills, and I must talk to you before I drift off again."

Dick was aware of the fierce willpower his father was exerting to hold off the combined effects of the strokes and the medication, and took his hand in silent support.

"It's the company, Dick . . . Strongwheat . . . I'm frightened."

He paused to draw a deep shuddering breath, and seemed to be fading away before he looked sharply up into Dick's face.

"It's too soon . . . We've . . . I've made mistakes . . . I'm not ready to let go yet. Things to be done . . . I need you. Your grandfather made me take it on, though he knew I wanted . . . really wanted to be a lawyer." The memory of past struggles seemed to lend him strength, "When I came in it wasn't much. We didn't have Sceptre Mill then, just an old warehouse where we brought in sacks of milled oats and flour, and broke bulk to sell in packets. It was me that brought in the rusk-making. And Strongwheat was my idea, mine . . . he wouldn't have it, but I made him. Said I'd walk out if he didn't back me . . ."

The left side of his face turned down more sharply as he recalled old battles fought and won.

"Dick . . . I can't talk more . . . that damned pill . . . Please, help me, won't you?"

Dick felt the grip of his father's hand slacken as his head sank back into the pillow. He called in the doctor.

"No need to worry for the moment. James is a remarkably tough old man," said Doctor Carr, "He'll sleep now until the morning, I'd say. Call me at once if there's any problem, otherwise I'll look in after morning surgery."

Dick protested, "Surely he should be in hospital, in intensive care or something?"

"Of course he should, but he won't," was the laconic reply, "Your mother, Ellen, is an excellent nurse though, and I dare say he'll do as well here as anywhere, as long as there are no complications. Trying to overrule your father is likely to do more harm than good."

From that moment, Dick Routledge was committed to Strongwheat Ltd. The R.A.F. put no obstacle in the way of his application to resign his commission on compassionate grounds. In fact 'ground-bound' Squadron-Leaders were in substantial surplus at the time, so that his early retirement was processed with unexpected despatch.

He came into the company as a 'mature executive trainee'. Dick recalled, sometimes with pleasure, sometimes with acute embarrassment, the months of 'sitting-with-Nelly' that had constituted his training programme. Well, a long succession of 'Nellies' really. Solid English Midlanders with lifetimes of experience at Strongwheat, who mostly took a special delight in making sure that Dick learned the things that each thought were important. Bill Bowman for example, who had joined as a labourer in the warehouse when packing flour and oats was the whole business, and who was now Distribution Manager. Cereals were bulky and relatively low value, so the cost of distribution needed to be tightly controlled. Bill could yarn for hours about the wiles of transport contractors and how to spot them. Walter Hurd, who had been the company's first professional salesman, taken on for the launch of Strongwheat, and who was now Sales Director. "Twenty-five years ago you could take your pick of a hundred and fifty thousand independent grocers to sell to. Now, three-quarters of the business goes through about ten buyers." And so many more – there was so much to learn. Important customers to be met and reassured about the long term continuity of the business. Cost-of-Sales accounts to be analysed and re-analysed until he was confident that he understood the workings of what Chief Accountant Jim Helvin called 'The levers of profit. That painfully small difference between two very large numbers – sales revenue and costs.' A trip to Australia with the Buyer, Tom McMurtry, to renegotiate a long-term contract for Australian Hard Wheat, 'A few coppers per tonne either way could halve – or double – the year's net profit. And we have to pay in US dollars.' Pleasant hours – Dick smiled at the memory – alongside Jean Carey, Personnel Manager, newly-divorced and appointed just about the time he arrived. They had pored over the reports of local and national wage rates, and prepared together for the annual round of wage negotiations, and reviewed the possible challenges from the Health and Safety Executive over the dangers of high-speed food production in a building that was over a hundred and fifty years old. And, most vivid of all, the meetings with his father. Initially the old man had tired quickly, and wanted only to hear and enjoy Dick's reaction to this or that character or event, as though reliving, through Dick's eyes, his own well-worn familiarity. Later, after about six months, the discussions became purposeful and more demanding, as his father clawed back his powers of concentration, and Dick's opinions became the more valuable.

"What will happen to the market for Breakfast Cereals over the next three years?"

Dick thought it would keep on growing.

"Every section of it? Which parts will do best? Why?"

"Can the whole production line be speeded up?"

Dick thought there was a practical limit, set by the amount of time the product needed to be baked in the long continuous-baking oven.

"How about getting more through by doubling the band-width? Or doubling the oven-length and going twice as fast?"

And so the probing and the challenging continued. Early on, Dick realised that his father was using him as a substitute for the daily cut and thrust of the office. While James was still enfeebled, Ellen Routledge and Dr. Carr had combined forces to extract a solemn promise that he would not set foot in Sceptre Mill for a full year. But, as his father said to Dick with a conspiratorial grin, "I didn't promise anything about not bringing Sceptre Mill back here, did I?"

So, nine months after the strokes, his father's willpower was sufficient to require a regular flow of managers to be arranging appointments at the house. At first this form of 'consultation' was more of form than of substance, since James was still dutifully taking his medication, and his strength was not adequate for much debate. But steadily the rituals became less of a formality. The turning point came when Jean Carey came out with her immediate boss, Phil Wythe, then newly-promoted to be Director of Manufacturing, to go over their suggested approach to the annual wage review, with Dick sitting in as an observer. His father seemed to have decided that this was an ideal opportunity to give Dick a lesson in the rougher skills of management.

"Why the bloody hell do we have to have this farce of an annual review at all? Why can't we just pay each of the buggers what we think they're worth?"

The challenge was merely the opening salvo in an increasingly vehement exchange. Jean was rash enough to suggest there was no need for bad language.

"Don't you come the lady with me. I gave you this job because I thought you could do it, not because I thought we needed a token woman. So you can take me as you find me, or else shove off to some politically-correct conglomerate where you can be politically-correct too, and sit on your arse in front of some bloody computer all day."

Phil Wythe felt bound to intervene in Jean's defence, but was astute enough to avoid confrontation when the old man was so obviously in the mood for it.

"Come on, Chairman, let's skip the battle of the sexes for now. Mightn't we just leave it to Kellogg's or someone else to experiment with some daring new system of remuneration, and we just concentrate on finding the way to carry the workforce along with us into another profitable year?"

And so the row subsided into a routine discussion, but it was the last managerial visit to the house. A week later 'Mr. James', as he had been called to distinguish him from Dick's grandfather, William Routledge, appeared without warning on a Monday morning, and asked acidly how long it had been since his office had been dusted. He came in one day a week for a couple of months, and for the last six months, with Dick duly appointed Managing Director, he had been coming in for two days most weeks, and was once again chairing the Board Meetings.

Dick made a few last notes against the draft figures for the past year, then closed his file with a quiet nod to himself. He was quite looking forward to presenting the results to the Board, particularly to the outside non-executive directors. *It had been a good year!*

Chapter Two

The other members of the Board of Strongwheat plc arrived in the final few minutes before ten o'clock, when the meeting was due to begin. Each made a beeline for the hot coffee, now kept regularly refreshed.

The two non-executive directors had come up together on the train from London, and had been collected from Lynchester station by the company driver. Oliver Sedburgh greeted Dick warmly. Short, bald and pudgy, Oliver was a contemporary and lifelong friend of Dick's father, and had started as a trainee with a local firm of accountants some forty years before. That firm was still the official auditor for Strongwheat plc., but Oliver was now a partner at Bell's, in the City of London, one of the 'Big Six' international accountancy and consulting groups.

"Dick, I don't think you've met John Savage from De Boissy before? Your father asked me to look out for him at Euston, and we've entertained one another over breakfast."

John was tall and lean, with a shock of blond hair. In his mid-thirties, he was quick and attentive, but made a habit of concealing his sharp intelligence beneath a warm and genial manner. Five years ago James Routledge had sold 20% of Strongwheat Ltd. to De Boissy. The merchant bank had also more recently arranged the loan that had funded the new automatic packing line that now rattled unheard and unseen around the exterior of the boardroom. John now had a portfolio of De Boissy's industrial investments to monitor. The Strongwheat investment had been added to this just a month previously, on the retirement of a senior partner, so today was his first Board Meeting at Lynchester.

"Good morning Mr. Routledge. I can't tell you how much I've been looking forward to coming up to Strongwheat."

"It's Dick, do call me Dick. Everyone else does. Can I introduce Jim Helvin, Company Secretary and Chief Accountant?"

Jim put down a hefty pile of papers on the table in order to shake hands, and introduced in turn Walter Hurd, the Sales Director, and Phil Wythe, the youngest Board member. The conversation turned to the quarter-point increase in Bank Rate announced that week, and the likely cost of money over the next few months, but was cut short as James stomped in, still leaning quite heavily on a cane, but noticeably brisk as he took the chair at the head of the table.

"I've already had my coffee, so shall we get started? I'd like to welcome John Savage for his first meeting, and thank him for making an early morning start to be with us. John speaks for our big money friends in the City, who are dying for us to go public."

John looked slightly startled, and murmured, "When you judge the time is right of course, Mr. Chairman."

James allowed himself a small smile, and continued, "I would also like to thank Oliver for the same early rising, and perhaps to welcome Mr. Wythe to his first formal year-end. And this is Dick's first year-end as Managing Director. Now, can I take the minutes you have received of our last meeting in September as an accurate record?"

No one demurred, and Jim Helvin passed the Minute Book to James for signature.

"Any matters arising not likely to be covered in the Agenda? Right, can we go straight into the financial results for the year ending September 30th please? Mr. Helvin, you have our undivided attention."

Jim Helvin was a Scot, stockily-built with close-cropped white hair and rimless glasses. He took the Board crisply through the pages of financial analysis, and concluded, "Summing up then, we have a seven percent increase in volume which, with good control of overheads and the benefit of a price increase earlier in the year has come through as a twenty percent increase in the Trading Profit, making that just over the half million. Loan Interest and provision for Tax take £140,000, leaving £361,000 as the bottom line profit. On the balance sheet, our customers took a couple of days longer to pay, as seems inevitable these days. But we offset that by trimming our stocks and taking a little longer to pay our suppliers. Capital expense was nicely controlled over the year, so we have been able to use the profit as earned to pay down some of the loan and reduce the overdraft slightly. In my opinion, a tidy result."

"Any points for Mr. Helvin?"

As the executive directors had already gone through the results individually and collectively earlier in the week, the question was aimed at John and Oliver. John decided to bide his time, and shook his head.

"No problems at this time," said Oliver, "I'd like to hear Jim's opinion on the possibility of a dividend being affordable when we reach that item on the agenda."

"No doubt he will be happy to oblige. Now Dick, what would you like to add by way of a Managing Director's report?"

"Just a few points Mr. Chairman. This result looks very smooth and satisfactory, but there was a heck of a lot of paddling beneath the surface to make it happen. In particular I would like to record some good achievements, not in any particular order of merit. For instance:

"Every two months we receive from A.C.Neilsen Research a presentation on their sample audit of retailers' sales of Breakfast Cereals. Walter has some copies of a summary chart which he'll pass round. You'll see that eighteen months ago, after we had reduced our spend on advertising, our share of the market had drifted down slowly but relentlessly from our normal six percent to barely four, threatening, I would suggest, our very existence. The market was growing, but we were just about standing still in volume terms. Since that low point we restored the advertising budget and pushed our share back up to four and a half percent a year ago, and an average of five percent over the last twelve months. Perhaps a bit more in the most recent periods, so that we are certainly at least growing in line with the market again. Bear in mind that we are the little man in a business that is dominated here by the American multinationals, who can dig as deep as necessary into their pockets to develop and protect their volumes here in the UK. I think that a vote of congratulations to Walter and his sales and advertising teams would be appropriate."

There was a murmur of polite agreement, and Jim made a note for an 'Extract from the Minutes' to be sent to those concerned.

"We did make a gain from the price increase. But don't forget we were only following the market up, when the pound fell and the price of Australian Hard Wheat in dollars rocketed. We made a gain because our buyer, Tom McMurtry, had forecast that the government would make a mess of the balance of payments, which would put downward pressure on the pound, and so had cannily bought well forward and exceptionally, John, with good advice from De Boissy, we had borrowed dollars through a hedge fund. I have to admit that the Chairman and Jim and myself were very concerned about the gamble, but it has worked out well for us."

John sensed that there was a point to be made, "Hardly a gamble though, Mr. Chairman, with the advice and backing of De Boissy."

"Fair enough. What else, Dick?"

Dick caught sight of an anxious look on Phil Wythe's face. "We should also take especial note of the major achievement on the Operations front, which was to get the Automated Packing Line working. That was the big commitment for us at the end of the last financial year you may remember, when Phil here was the Plant Engineer responsible for recommending that we invest the equivalent of that year's whole profit on it. He and his boys sweated blood and worked all the hours God sends to get it set up, trialed and into regular production."

Dick recalled the days and nights when the new line seemed perversely determined to turn into crumbs all the cereal they could produce, and was eventually found to have an intermittent computer fault that was wrapping 13 or occasionally even 14 packets into a one dozen outer, crushing each packet just enough to make room.

"We had some difficult times, because no one had ever done it with a product like ours before. But Phil led us bravely through it, and here he is on our Board as a result."

There were appropriate congratulatory noises.

"Thank you, Dick. Are there questions for Dick or his team?"

Oliver's firm of accountants acted for some of the largest retailers and food manufacturers, and his approach was not inhibited by politeness, "This new packing line, Dick. What sort of return on investment is it giving? I seem to recall that Phil's proposal promised a three-year payback, is that right? That means a saving of over fifty thousand pounds a year will be required."

Dick looked quickly at Phil, and they both began shuffling through papers. They were saved from embarrassment by Jim Helvin.

"If I might come in here, Mr. Chairman? I have of course been collecting and analysing the data all year. On the up side, we have the direct savings on the cost of labour. Previously the forewoman had 3 semi-skilled and 35 girls on average to pack the Strongwheat 'biscuits' as we call them into cartons, and the cartons into outers. Now she has just 5 semi-skilled and the occasional labourer. On the down side, we have the extra costs for maintenance and depreciation for the line, extra power consumed, and increased packaging material for the new method. I have of course identified separately the one-off costs due to trialing and installation, and it's really only over the last two months that we have anything like a stable cost-base to compare with last year's."

James was reluctant to allow Jim to develop his lecture further. "So, what's the answer to Oliver's question?"

"Bottom line, it's 20% cheaper to pack Strongwheat now than it was a year ago."

Seeing the Chairman's eyebrows rising, Phil Wythe broke in hastily. "There's more to it than that of course. Today's costs include absorbing per-hour rate increases for labour of 8% compared with last year, and 12% for packaging materials, right Jim?

Jim nodded and sat back, so Phil continued, "And I reckon we're still climbing the learning curve, working now at about 70% efficiency. So there's plenty of improvement still to come, as we work the bugs out of the system. You see the servo-motor complex . . ."

Phil was cut short by the motion of the Chairman's hand, "All right, Phil, we'll agree it looks promising, and suspend judgement for three months, if you're happy Oliver?"

"Agreed, James. Were you about to propose lunch?"

James pushed the bell that alerted the canteen staff to bring in the buffet meal, and Dick acted as barman at the sideboard drinks cabinet. By long tradition senior managers reporting to executive directors were invited to attend this lunch, so that within a few minutes the room was filled with an animated buzz of conversation. Tom McMurtry was being quizzed about his last Australia trip, especially about hotels in Sydney and Melbourne, as Oliver was anticipating a visit himself, to include Fiji if possible. John Savage seemed to have struck up an immediate rapport with Jean Carey, the Personnel Manager. Jean was about thirty, a tall, slim brunette in a tailored pinstripe grey jacket and skirt, with a plain white blouse caught at the neck with a brooch of red stones. Her high forehead and prominent cheekbones made her handsome rather than pretty, but men were immediately attracted by her large dark eyes and a disconcertingly friendly way of smiling. Dick felt a little possessive about Jean, as they had started at Strongwheat within two weeks of one another, eighteen months previously. So he was amused to catch the small flicker of irritation that crossed John Savage's face when Walter came over to introduce his Advertising Manager, Paul Williams.

"Paul was in charge of our advertising at Crofton's, our Advertising Agents in London. We thought he was pretty good, bit of a thinker, very knowledgeable about Marketing and Market Research, and of course he knew us and our business well enough. So when Dick began to press me to put more time personally into cultivating the big supermarket chains, it seemed altogether natural to invite Paul to come in here and lend us his brains."

Paul was short and square, with dark curly hair and a cheerful snub nose. John guessed that there was Welsh parentage was not too far below the surface, despite his polished London manners.

"You seem to have settled in well at Strongwheat. One of these days I'm going to have to ask you to teach me the basics of marketing consumer products, if you wouldn't find that too tedious?"

Paul looked down modestly, "I'd like that very much. And if I can teach you, it's because I've had Walter here as a very good mentor for myself over the last year or so."

Dick thought, not for the first time, that Paul was a young man who would go far.

After lunch, when the managers had left and the Board had reassembled around the table, James set about deliberately changing the atmosphere of the meeting.

"Well now, this morning's session was quite painless, and lunch was amusing too, wasn't it?" He looked pointedly at John Savage, who had maintained a spirited conversation throughout with Jean Carey, and to a lesser extent Paul Williams, about the London theatre scene, and how to become an 'angel'.

"You all seem very satisfied with the results so far, and to be fair, I believe that Dick and his people have made a good beginning. But it's just that, a good beginning. So let's get a couple of the outstanding items cleared away. First, I am not yet ready to talk about going public. John, I know your people will be disappointed in this, but believe me, it's much too soon. When we sell our company, or another piece of it, I want it to be a much, much bigger business, so that even ten percent of it will be worth what fifty percent is worth now. Will you support me in this?"

Oliver shrugged, "It's your company, James, and if you think it can be grown that much, I'm certainly interested."

John Savage however had a Chairman of his own to report to, with a shareholding that had produced no tangible benefit so far, and was less relaxed about the issue.

"With respect, I'm not sure the Bank will be entirely happy about what sounds like an indefinite postponement, Mr. Chairman. I mean, there's a nice growth in profit this year, and

I can see the trend continuing, given good fortune. But things would need to accelerate out of all proportion over the next few years for the value of the business to increase fivefold, say. Is there really a plan to do that, something that I can take back to De Boissy with confidence?"

James was undeterred, "Fair comment, John, and I'll answer you in a minute. My second recommendation to the Board is that we do indeed pay a dividend, the first in the company's history. Can I have your views? Do you agree? If so, how much?"

Oliver took it upon himself to answer. "Presumably you will intend to waive your personal entitlement, James? Otherwise the tax consequences will be quite painful, and no doubt the company can make better use of the cash."

James nodded, "I feel we owe De Boissy a gesture, a promise of bigger things to come. And it makes a start in demonstrating to the City that we are a serious business. Something to be built on year by year."

Oliver turned his attention to John Savage, "I seem to recall – do correct me if I'm mistaken – that De Boissy put up £200,000 for its twenty percent stake in Strongwheat five years ago? So with this year's result I would guess that you will be looking at a four or fivefold increase in the value of your investment. Not that you'd consider selling out at this time, but the gain in capital value must be quite comforting, wouldn't you say?"

John stayed silent, knowing he was being softened up. Oliver continued, "Still I'm sure the natives back in Mayfair are getting restless to see some spendable return on their investment. I propose therefore, Mr. Chairman, that we allocate £100,000 to dividend, but that you waive your entitlement, so that the actual outgoing is just the £20,000 to De Boissy, less tax. Ten percent on the investment, as a start."

John knew when to accept gracefully, "I'm quite sure my Board will be delighted with this token of greater things to come. Merchant Banks are accustomed to taking the long view, you know. Is it possible for me to take back also some idea of this new strategy for the future?"

James nodded, "Yes . . . indeed. Well, an exciting project, I think, something for Dick here to really get his teeth into, win his spurs as it were."

Dick tried, without much success, not to look totally bewildered. Nothing at all had been said during the week about an 'exciting project'. He bristled too at the suggestion that he had still to 'win his spurs'. What more was there still for him to prove?

James began to speak again, this time obviously from notes in front of him. "I think we are too small and too vulnerable to survive. We are just a tiddler in a sea full of sharks. Great big American and multinational sharks at that. Of course we can go on tweaking up our performance, indeed we must, and it's comforting to be in a growing market. But basically we are a one-product business. What would happen to us if one of our competitors, with their infinitely deep purses, decides to go for us with a product similar to Strongwheat, perhaps even better? We might get lucky and beat them off. But what are the chances that the costs of doing that cripple us, wipe us out even? We must have a broader base, do you see?"

He looked up from his notes, but there was silence around the table, as much in response to the almost evangelical tone of his voice as in reaction to the content. Oliver was the first to speak.

"But there's no one in the market for sale, and diversification outside of Breakfast Cereals would really be a case of out of the frying pan and into the burning fiery furnace."

James nodded, "I agree. Instead we are going to develop and launch a new cereal product, perhaps a range of new products. I don't need to tell you, if we could push up our share of the market to 10% say, we would have enough market power not to have to worry about security. We could fortify our position with a much stronger marketing budget, and have the potential to push our profits up out of sight."

The silence that followed around the table was evidence enough of the reaction to the proposal. Dick, Walter and Phil could see hard-won progress being put at risk, gambled away even at the whim of an old man who was still recovering from a debilitating illness. Jim Helvin, with only five years to go to retirement, and his pension already secure, was less worried for himself, but voiced the concern they all felt.

"Mr. Chairman, the costs of getting into this market are known to be exceptionally high. And the odds against success are very high also. Indeed I believe that Strongwheat itself was one of the last entries to achieve reasonable viability. What if we were to fail, how could we protect ourselves?"

"Then we'd better not fail, had we? Believe me, I've had a lot of time to think about this, and I'm convinced it's the only way for us. Without a successful new product, this company is going nowhere. And I'm not having that. I took on a ramshackle business from my father, and I've made it into something of real value in the world. Now Dick has given up his R.A.F. career to back me, and this is his chance to make a difference."

After that there was no more opposition, and the discussion was about ways and means to progress the project. Dick was to lead a team, with members co-opted as required. Walter made the suggestion, "Let's involve those bright brains in the Advertising Agency to see if they can come up with a good idea or two." And within another half hour the meeting concluded.

The cheerful bonhomie of lunchtime was now quite forgotten. Instead they walked in silence, each preoccupied with his own thoughts, down the short corridor that connected the insulated world of the Board Room to the offices and the factory outside, full of its special warm baking smell and the rattling reality of the process lines.

Chapter Three

"Rage, rage against the dying of the light."

"And what, pray, is that supposed to signify?" Jean Carey put down her gin and tonic, "Don't tell me you're coming over all poetic on me?"

Paul Williams was sitting beside her in the bay-windowed alcove of the 'Feathers', a cosy old pub on the outskirts of Lynchester, with new houses beginning to infill amongst the cottages that surrounded it, but with open farmland still at its back door.

"Not exactly, I guess it was that gorgeous sunset that filled my office this afternoon." He waved his hand toward the window. "And now it's all swallowed up in the darkness. I suppose I was thinking that Lynchester could do with a little brightening up. Or perhaps it's just me that could do with a little excitement."

Jean glanced at him sharply, to see if there was a hint of innuendo in this last remark, but decided that it was innocently meant. She had joined Strongwheat eighteen months ago, a few weeks before Paul, and both of them had lived in the Station Hotel for a time She was still nursing the wounds of a recent divorce, he was trying to find a house and commuting back to Richmond to his wife Jacky and their small daughter at weekends. As the only recruits to have come in at management level they were naturally thrown together, indeed one of Jean's first responsibilities as Personnel Manager was to take formal charge of his familiarisation programme. Like most males who met her, he was very conscious of that hint of wounded sexuality that made her very attractive. After a couple of pleasant dinners together, he had impulsively suggested that they might get more closely acquainted – and had been rejected – kindly, delicately, but quite firmly.

"Paul, you're an attractive man, and definitely fun to be with. And I suppose I'm classed as 'available'. But you have a wife and daughter at home, and I'm just trying to recover from . . . from being married. And we've got to work together, hopefully for a good long while. So could we keep sex out of it, and just stay good friends? Even better, could we stay, 'allies against the unloveable,' to quote your description of some of our stuffier colleagues?"

She smiled at him, and he couldn't feel hurt. In fact instead of rejection he felt a strange relief that their relationship had been simplified. She was a woman that men wanted to please, and Paul knew that he could do that now without needing to make a pass. That hadn't stopped him fantasising sometimes about her slim body and those great dark eyes, but they had remained friends and allies ever since. Jean had eventually rented a cottage in a small terrace a few doors along from the 'Feathers', where Paul regularly stopped off for a pint and a gossip on his way home to the new house that he and Jacky had bought in a village a few miles away.

Jean decided to take Paul's remark about needing excitement literally.

"From what I've heard about this afternoon's Board, you're going to be up to your neck in excitement and stress with this new product thing, and in no time flat. Seriously though, Walter is the only one on the Board with much understanding of the market out there. And I suspect he'll lean pretty heavily on you in this case. Which means that, if the project should go pear-shaped, you could be very exposed."

"Don't I know it. Don't get me wrong, he's gone to endless trouble to help me fit in, and I'm very grateful to him. And he's really taken notice of some of my textbook stuff about concentrating on getting Strongwheat fully distributed and promoted in the big multiples, and continuing to cut back on the time the salesmen spend in the smaller shops. But if push comes to shove, and they need a scapegoat, he'll look after Number One, for sure. But, I suppose I left the agency in the first place because I wanted to be up in the firing line – sorry, joke in very bad taste."

"Apology duly noted and accepted. Let's just hope it all goes well."

"I'll drink to that."

James Routledge often complained to his wife Ellen that they rattled around like 'two ha'pennies in an empty tin' in the big old house he had inherited from his father, along with the company.

"Now that the children have flown the coop, we ought to have somewhere more modern, more convenient to run. We could have a bungalow, built to measure, for instance."

But they did not move. Ellen felt comfortable with the solicitors, accountants and local businessmen that were their neighbours, mostly of long standing. And she had put in too many hours getting the garden just the way she liked it to be bothered with starting again amongst some builder's rubble. "I manage just fine here," she would reply, "As long as you don't go out of your way to make a mess all over the place."

That evening Dick and Rosemary came round for supper, as happened about once a week, and Ellen had laid on a roast beef dinner with all the trimmings.

"I had a call from Ruth today," Ellen had said as they came through the door. Ruth was Dick's younger sister, who had trained as a paediatrician, and married Dr. Andrew Wilson the previous year.

"She says she almost certain she's pregnant. Baby would be due in late July or early August sometime."

"That will be really marvellous for her," said Dick, who thought privately that Ruth had already invested too many years in her career, "Perhaps there's some kind of psychic connection between her starting a baby, and Dad going for a new product."

Dick had not said much when he came home from the Board Meeting, but had told Rosemary the gist of what his father had said.

"I know which one I think is the more important," said Rosemary, and followed Ellen into the kitchen to give what help she was allowed.

After supper James settled down in his armchair beside the fire, with Dick opposite.

"Your Rosemary's right, of course. A new baby is more important, to me at any rate. But I remember when I was working on Strongwheat first, the excitement. It was like giving birth, I can tell you. Terrifying, and painful, and great once it was out! Did you get any feedback from the managers about the project, after we wrapped up the meeting?"

"Some. I talked with Walter and young Paul. We see him as a sort of project co-ordinator. Nervous, I'd say at this stage, very nervous."

"Just like me, when your mother told me you were on the way."

Dick liked to sleep on his right side, with his big body curled around Rosemary's back, and could usually rely on drifting off in a few minutes. That night however was different. Rosemary had listened, but said little whilst they enjoyed supper with his parents, and Dick had been relaxed enough afterwards to be able to give her a fairly full report on the Board, especially the second half. Once or twice she had wound her fingers thoughtfully into a strand of her long auburn hair, and said, "I'm glad they were pleased," and, "Your father almost ruined the business with that cutback in the advertising. They don't begin to understand how much work you've put in to get things moving again."

Much to his surprise, she had made hardly any comment about the decision to go for a new product. Dick had tried to report the discussion as coolly as possible, in particular trying not to expose his instinctive resentment, because he knew he would not be able to avoid communicating as well his own deep apprehension.

Some peculiar tension transmitted in the angle of Rosemary's spine warned him that he might not have been entirely successful.

"All right, sweetheart, something is niggling you, I can feel it. Let's have it out."

There was a perceptible pause, as Rosemary, for once, weighed her words before she spoke. Then she sat upright in bed, and switched on the bedside lamp.

"You know, Dick, I was really quite pleased when you came out of the Air Force. I mean, I was worried at first, the R.A.F. had been most of my grown-up life, and all our married life too. But when I thought about it, I realised I was getting fed up with only having a married quarter, never a home of our own, and having to keep moving the boys from school to school. And having to be nice to senior officers who made my skin crawl. Lynchester is a nice friendly town, isn't it, and the boys have really settled in well at the Grammar School."

Dick looked up cautiously at Rosemary. Still slender in a close-fitting white nightdress, with pale blue eyes and an aristocratically elegant nose, only the crinkles around her generous mouth betrayed her age.

"Right. And civvy life seems to suit you too. Not so many late nights at mess parties, and no night-flying for me either. Y'know, I could fancy you."

"You can just cut that out. You asked me to talk, and I'm trying to be serious. You're the Managing Director now, and obviously the old man intends for you to take over altogether in due course. We've got settled in this nice house with a lovely garden and green fields behind. And now he wants to stir things up, change things, risk things. And for what? I mean, he's got as much money as they're ever likely to want to spend, hasn't he? I don't think I really believe all that stuff about share of the market. And being vulnerable, wasn't it? Is it truly that, or is it something else, something you haven't told me? Do we have to do what he says? I mean, what if he's going ga-ga, you know, those strokes affecting his judgement?"

Dick lay quiet for a long time before answering, "That's been going through my mind too. But it is still his company. Well, the company is his life really. That's what brought him back from the brink, the urge not to let go yet. And if you'd heard him at the meeting, you'd know it wasn't some wild fancy. Not a casual thing at all. He'd prepared most of what he had to say, thought it all through, in fact written most of it down. I didn't tell you, but I drove John Savage and Oliver to the station myself so that I could ask them for their candid opinions. Oliver is just about Dad's oldest friend you know, and he said something like,

'Dick, I don't know whether your father is right or wrong. And I don't suppose John here does either. But I can tell you one thing that is absolutely certain, and that's that he means every word of what he said. I think it would be terribly serious if you were to set out to oppose him in this. The one thing I would recommend is that you should learn to go cunningly into this. Try to find ways of minimising the risks as you go forward. Take things one step at a time, keep testing and retesting the water. Keep asking yourself, 'What is being assumed here?' And try to find ways then to test the assumptions properly.'

"What did John Savage have to say? He sounds quite bright."

"Nothing much. I think he was a bit surprised, well shell-shocked."

"I like that word of Oliver's," said Rosemary, almost to herself, "Cunningly. Go into it cunningly. Right then, Dick, we're just going to have to learn cunning. And learn to be careful. That's enough for one night, so you can go to sleep now."

She reached out of bed to turn off the table-lamp. As she leant out, Dick rested his hand on the white silk that covered the smooth curve of her hip.

"I'm wide awake now."

Chapter Four

On the Saturday following the little office meeting about the English company, Strongwheat Ltd., Lloyd Teller, Executive Chairman of American Cereal Products Inc. took his wife Rose out to dinner at the Midwest Country Club, which occupied a few hundred choice acres about halfway between his office and the sprawling Chicago conurbation. In summer the club was full of families enjoying the pool, the tennis or the two Championship golf courses. In December the outside temperature that evening had already dropped to ten degrees below zero, and that was before taking into account the wind-chill factor contributed by the thirty knot wind that seemed to be blowing unchecked all the way from the Rockies. There was squash, curling, bridge of course, but Lloyd missed his golf – the occasional weekend in Florida or Puerto Rico were no substitute for the familiar bonhomie of his own club. Over their pre-dinner martinis Lloyd mentioned the letter from England,

and floated the possibility that he might have to be doing a lot of foreign travel in the future. Much to his surprise, Rose did not raise an objection. She was a Junoesque lady with long blond hair tightly coiled, an imperious eye and an occasionally severe temper that Lloyd had learned over thirty years of marriage to be wary of. She could also be exceptionally kind-hearted, when her sympathies were aroused.

"Gee, Lloyd, I've always wanted to go to England. Do you realise that neither of us has ever been farther east than New York? I think it would be nice to have a passport and see a bit more of the world. We really should get some compensation for all the hours you put in at that office, all those phone calls and e-mails you take at home and at the weekend."

Lloyd had not of course envisaged that Rose would be accompanying him on business trips, but, after all, why not? He'd talk to Ben about it on Monday, see what Ben thought about bringing the lovely Juanita, his second wife. Could be a lot of fun!

"OK, good, I'll think about it seriously. So, what do you fancy? Steak, or how about duck tonight?"

Following Walter Hurd's suggestion, Paul had talked in general terms about the need for a new product to Roger Daniels, the Director responsible for the Strongwheat business at their London advertising agency, Crofton's, and in turn Roger had briefed the copywriter on the account, Jill Lister. A week later, just a few days before Christmas, the two of them drove up to Lynchester for a first meeting on the project.

Roger liked Lynchester, at least as a place to visit. It was at least as old as the Romans, who had built a fortified town where Watling Street, their road from London to Chester, crossed the River Lynn. It had remained small but prosperous until the coming of the railways, when its fine coaching inns, now no longer required, had sunk into a hundred and fifty years of quiet, genteel decline. As compensation for this neglect, Lynchester had avoided the excesses of Victorian development, and had kept most of its old centre intact, with classical Georgian facades that, in many instances, masked much older half-timbered interiors. Within an hour of leaving the northern outskirts of London he was driving around the handsome Market Square, with the old church on the east side, Georgian buildings north and south, and with the river and its promenade and bridge on the west. It was just a few hundred yards north along the river to Sceptre Mill. The M1 motorway had been unusually clear, and for forty minutes of the journey Roger had revelled in being able to let his Maserati accelerate effortlessly above a hundred miles an hour, with Jill keeping a conspiratorial watch for any police presence. The exhilaration had been marred by a vague feeling that all might not be well with their relationship. A couple of months earlier she had entered enthusiastically, as it had seemed, into an affair. This was the first time they had been together in over a week, and he sensed that a cooling-down was imminent. Jill was petite and pretty, with short fair hair and large blue eyes, usually hidden behind enormous spectacles. She had an acerbic wit that made her dangerously entertaining as a mistress. "All good things . . ." he thought, as he parked in front of the Mill, beside Dick Routledge's Rover.

Their arrival was signalled to Paul Williams by a sudden movement of office staff to the front window, and a buzz of simple envy of the scarlet Maserati from which they emerged. They were led to Operations Director Phil Wythe's office, and Paul gave them a potted history of the Mill while they were served coffee.

"This place is a piece of industrial history," he began, "It was built almost two hundred years ago as a woollen mill, using the river to provide power as well as for washing the wool. It was abandoned and empty when the Chairman's father, William Routledge, took a long lease of it for nothing much in the early sixties. They had a small business then pre-packing oats and flour, and it was the Chairman who got his father to set up the Number One baking line to make rusk. Not baby-rusk of course, but the kind that butchers use to put in sausages. That made good money, so they quickly put in a flaking line to make a wheat flake."

"Any good?" Roger was determined to show he was alert.

"Terrible. More nourishing than Corn Flakes of course, which are made from maize, but they didn't have the expertise at that time to make it light and crisp – so it came out tough and chewy. That's when the Chairman had the idea of combining the wheat flakes with crumbled rusk, adding flour, salt and a thin sugar solution, baking it like a thick biscuit, and found he'd invented Strongwheat."

"I'll bet it wasn't as easy as that," said Jill.

"Probably not, but if you're ready we should have a quick look around the factory, so that you can go away with an idea of what we can do."

Afterwards, Jill had two vivid memories of the factory. The first was when Paul stopped at the beginning of the great black oven, twice as tall as themselves and extending away from them the length of two cricket pitches. She felt the blast of red heat where the continuous metal band carried the flood of raw Strongwheat biscuits into the fiery maw. And the second was at the other end of the oven, where the golden baked product poured out to be carried into the packing lines. She felt that she had witnessed a piece of modern civilisation, which transformed raw power into a breakfast treat for children, and wondered if the idea might be worked up into a commercial.

"Here, taste one. But don't burn your mouth." Phil had let Paul do most of the talking, but could not resist the moment, like a master chef presenting his favourite dish.

"But that's much nicer than when I've had a packet at home," said Jill, nibbling and blowing at the same time, "Have you improved the recipe?"

" 'Fraid not. It's the same with everything that's baked. Straight from the oven is best, like French bread. After that it loses flavour by the minute. Well, that's the bones of the process. Paul, I wonder if you'd like to alert Walter and Dick that we're ready, and could they join us for lunch in the Board Room? Jill, Roger, I expect you'd like to freshen up?"

Lunch in the Board Room was more informal than on a Board Meeting day – ham sandwiches and hot sausage rolls washed down with fresh coffee. Dick had met Roger Daniels previously at a presentation of advertising plans, and appreciated the shrewd business brain that Roger normally kept hidden behind a chubby persona, but he was very intrigued by Jill Lister. Petite, blonde and pretty, she had dressed for the occasion in a dark blue trouser suit, and wore saucer-size spectacles.

"I liked the latest commercial for Strongwheat, the one with the boy lifting huge weights. Is it one of yours?"

Jill nodded, "It's a fun product to work on. Always room for a bit of creative fantasy. Now, about this new product project. Could you help us to understand where you're coming from? I mean, clients often ask us to help evaluate an idea, or identify a target market. But it's not very common to be in right at the beginning, actually inventing it. Interesting of course."

Walter, who had been listening with half an ear whilst talking to Phil about the sales forecast for the Spring, put down his coffee to intervene.

"As you can tell, Dick, I've been quite guarded in what's been said up to now."

"Fair enough. But now we have to move forward together. Strictest security, Roger, 'need-to-know' basis only within the agency, and no typed minutes of this or any subsequent meeting. Paul will act as secretary-cum progress-chaser, as required."

Roger nodded, and the meeting got going around the table, with Dick taking the chair. He began by summarising his father's analysis.

"Any comments on the thoughts of our beloved Chairman?"

Roger smiled and raised a finger, "I'd like to be sure that everyone understands the size of the project we're undertaking, especially the scale of the effort and resources that will be required, I mean in relation to the size of this business. First, we have to find a product that we can make, and which will have more appeal to the consumer than any of the last ten or a dozen attempts by some of the largest and smartest food companies in the world. But that won't be enough by itself. In addition you have to be prepared to support it adequately with marketing effort and money, perhaps through several years of losses. To put some numbers to that, I'd say that you have to be looking at an extra investment, on advertising alone, of two million pounds a year."

There was silence around the table, then he continued.

"That's as much as we spent in total last year on Strongwheat. I haven't been privy to your last year's profit result yet, but I'll be astonished if that isn't a hell of a lot more than you made. My point is this. If the company is prepared to undertake that kind of investment on a product that doesn't exist yet, should we not also be considering the potential benefit from just doubling the amount of money we put behind Strongwheat?"

Walter was immediately dismissive, "Oh come on now, Roger, we've had all this out before. The Board simply refuses to believe that there's that much potential in Strongwheat after all these years. We'll be very satisfied if we can claw back one more point of market-share, from five percent back up to six. Don't forget that will increase our volumes by a fifth."

"Well, with respect, chairman." Paul came into the discussion with studied diffidence.

"Yes, Paul, we'd like to hear from you. You must be sitting on both sides of this particular fence."

Paul smiled at the reference to his Agency background, "I've been worrying at this problem since you and Walter briefed me last week. We don't necessarily have to choose between increasing support for Strongwheat, and backing the new product. Suppose the new product could be related to Strongwheat, in the family as it were, then the money we put behind it would also rub off on Strongwheat."

"For example, both products might appear in the same commercial," said Jill, carefully avoiding Roger's glare of disapproval.

"Something like that." Paul was delighted to find a supporter, "I think we should move forward simultaneously on two fronts. The first should be a new market-research study, talking to carefully-drawn samples of both users and non-users, asking them how they see the strengths and weaknesses of Strongwheat. The idea is to try to identify a new niche that we could occupy. And the second should be right here, to explore what we can do with the plant – basically to play tunes on the Strongwheat theme."

There was a silence around the table. It all seemed too straightforward . . .

"If I could come in here," said Phil, "I think we need to go very gingerly on that last point, I mean playing around with the process. You will all agree that the situation here at Sceptre Mill is not ideal by any means. This is an old building, becoming quite expensive to maintain for food production. The plant layout has more or less grown like Topsy over the years. Any management consultant would have a field day telling us how good a return we would get from investing in a purpose-built new factory."

"All right, Phil, we get the message. If the Agency want to double the advertising, you'd like to stake your claim for a new factory. How about you, Walter, will you need to double the size of the sales force?"

"Actually no, Dick. Quite the opposite in fact. A new product would give our lads quite a lift, especially if it could be said to be in the Strongwheat family. One thing though, I'd need a lot of convincing if the target required us to double our current volumes."

"Well, you remember, that's the target the Chairman has set us." Dick was unwilling to back off too soon, "But we all know it takes time and a lot of fuel to get up to operational height. Just off the cuff, I'd say the Board would look favourably at investing that extra two million on the new product year by year if it brought us, say, a fifty percent volume increase. Paul would you take that on? Get together with Jim Helvin, and get a paper written projecting the cost and profit factors at a range of extra volumes, allowing for a range of increases in the Marketing spend. And that brings us neatly back to you, Phil. What about plant capacity? Assuming the new product can be made on the existing plant, are there any insuperable bottlenecks?"

Phil knew from bitter past experience that casual forecasts have a nasty habit of coming back to hang around your neck, like the Ancient Mariner's albatross, so he decided to play for time.

"I've done some basic analysis, but I'd like to put something together against what we're now saying. Would you like to break for tea while I do that?"

The unwritten rules of business meetings require that nothing serious be discussed during a break for tea, and this one was no exception. Jill Lister concealed a mischievous streak behind those innocent blue eyes, and much enjoyed an opportunity to tease a client, especially an ex-agency client.

"What's it like, Paul, living up here after – what was it? – ten years altogether with Crofton's in London?"

The question seemed amiable enough, but Paul was fairly sure Jill's idea was to provoke some kind of discussion about the sacrifices involved in leaving London. He was relieved therefore when Dick joined in.

"I'd be interested to compare notes with you, Paul. I must say I found the first few months out of the R.A.F. quite difficult."

"Depends what you want, I suppose, but to my mind for sheer quality of life, Lynchester wins hands down. Jenny and I have a modern sort of house that we could comfortably afford, in a pretty village about eight miles out. I don't even have to go through the town centre, so it's about fifteen minutes country drive to the office, where it used to take a good hour to get into London from Richmond. Our daughter loves it at the primary school, and Jenny teaches there part-time too."

"Sounds positively idyllic," said Jill, obviously far from impressed, "But what about the culture shock? Or the lack of it?"

"That's a myth, put about by Londoners to keep up the prices of their houses, I should think. We're on a main line here, so it's only an hour and a quarter up to London. Once you've got a family, you don't go out casually anyway, because of the babysitter problem, but I'd say that we're in London for a theatre or something more often than when we lived there. And there's theatres at Stratford on Avon, there's Birmingham with theatres and a top-rate Concert Hall, there's Nottingham and Leicester. And we've certainly made more friends. I think people here are more open, less pressure to keep yourself to yourself . . ."

"Right, sorry to cut you off in full flow, Paul, but I can see Phil has crunched his numbers for us."

Phil pulled from a corner of the room an easel which carried a large pad of blank paper, used for informal meetings. He flipped over a few used pages until he came to a blank sheet, and listed his points in large print as he spoke.

"As we don't know yet what form the new product will take, I've worked on the assumption that we are looking at a fifty percent increase in the volumes of current Strongwheat. Going through the production process stage by stage,

"1. Raw Wheat. We receive the husked raw wheat in irregular trainloads directly into our silos for cleaning. I would expect no problem in simply increasing the frequency of deliveries.

"2. Making wheat flake. The line runs for only two hours a day, so again no problem – in fact higher volumes might justify spending some money to improve quality.

"3. Rusk. We buy it in now. I would hope we could actually negotiate a better price for a volume increase. There might come a point when we could justify making it again, but I doubt if we would have the space in Sceptre Mill.

"4. Mixing and baking – could be a bottleneck. Not in absolute terms, because the line only runs for forty hours a week on average. But the work force is exceedingly attached to our system of four ten-hour days per week. There'll be a rough old negotiation probably, and we might end up having to buy it out.

"5. Lastly, packing. We've got masses of capacity in the new automated line. But once again we will have to face the four-day week problem.

"Taking it all together then, it's doable – provided only that the product fits the plant. I'm going to give some thought to Paul's suggestion about variations on the formula."

Dick thought back to last week's Board Meeting, when his father had thrown down the challenge, which had seemed so terrifying at the time to all of them. And now here they were, calmly contemplating spending an extra two million – four times last year's hard-earned profit, and using words like 'doable'. *Was this Oliver's 'Go cunningly'?* He hoped so.

"All right then, we seem to have accepted the Chairman's challenge. Paul, as I said earlier, no minutes as such, but I'd like you to draw up lists of who's doing what and by when. Go over it with each of us, and prepare some sort of progress chart. Keep that locked up too. Should we have a codename, do you think?"

Jill kept a straight face. "How about 'Pipedream'?"

"I'll buy that. As far as I'm concerned, keep me posted if there are any snags I can help to resolve. Once again I'd like to say a special 'thank you' to Jill and Roger for venturing so far north of Watford to be with us today, and also to say how much we look forward to seeing your creative input early in the New Year. Walter, will you schedule the next meeting when there's a reasonable amount of progress to consider?"

Not much was said as the Maserati purred down the M1 towards London, more or less obeying the speed limit, with Jill preferring to lie back and enjoy that special 'new car' smell, and the sensation of power and purpose as Roger used the gearbox to weave through the thickening traffic. By the time they were passing Luton the sheer volume of cars and lorries forced him to slow down in the gathering dusk. He settled reluctantly for moving only at the same speed as the lorries and homeward-bound salesmen in their Mondeos and Volvos that filled the road in front of him.

"I wonder why they assume that going at seventy-five entitles them to hog the outside lane?"

"Oh, relax now," said Jill, "How much difference can it make over the last twenty miles anyway? So what did you think of today then?"

"Good, really. I'm left with the impression that they really will go for it, if we can come up with a half-decent product idea. An extra million or two from this client should certainly fatten the bonus a bit. And looking at it strategically, I think that their Chairman may well be right when he says they're vulnerable. Mind you . . . Damnation!"

Roger broke off to tread hard on the brakes and bring the car to a halt.

"Looks like another bloody traffic jam. Where do they all come from? What was I saying? Oh yes, I was going to tell you off for not following my lead about doubling the spend behind Strongwheat. It would certainly be safer for them if they put more money behind it, you know. But on reflection, I think we left them with a better impression by not being too single-minded. Gives them the idea that our eventual recommendation will have considered every commercial alternative."

"And will it?" Jill enjoyed pricking Roger's bubble of self-justification.

"Probably not," he said with a small grin, "We have to live too, don't we?"

By now the traffic was opening up again as they came into London against the outgoing tide, and soon he was pulling up outside Jill's Hampstead apartment.

"Shall I come in for an hour?"

She had drifted into the affair with him a few weeks previously, partly as a deliberate step to protect her position within the agency, and had been having second thoughts. Roger was clever, but he could be pompous, and was certainly no great shakes as a lover. "Not this evening, Roger, if you don't mind. All that Midlands fresh air has left me ready to put my feet up." She pecked his cheek, and clambered quickly out of the car before he could object. "See you in the morning."

Chapter Five

Banks are not charities. For all their promises to listen, to respond when you press for action, and all their encouragement to you to put your money on that black horse, retail banks have to give priority consideration to their depositors, their shareholders and (of course) their employees. Commercial customers matter, but usually they come next. The High Street banks suffer especially from the inescapable conflict between those strong images of dedicated service projected by their advertising, and the brutally competitive financial disciplines that press daily upon them. This is the source of the vicious cynicism of the public's judgements, particularly those of the million small businesses that depend on the million overdrafts. 'Pawnbrokers in striped suits, that's all they are.' 'They'll offer you a ten thousand loan, as long as you've got fifty thousand in assets to pledge as guarantee.' 'They'll lend you an umbrella, then demand it back if it rains.'

Merchant Banks, by contrast, are more favourably regarded by those who use them. Not because they are kinder, or more indulgent, far from it. But because they have less need to practise hypocrisy or image making. They use their capital and their skills to offer a service which has to be costly, so small or naive customers need not apply. De Boissy and Co., where John Savage was employed, was very much in this mould. Having founded his business in mid-eighteenth century Paris to find and channel capital to the lucrative but dangerous triangular trade in cocoa, slaves and sugar, Lucien De Boissy had seen the French Revolution's long shadow somewhat sooner than his less fortunate competitors. He moved his capital and his company to England, to a handsome newly-built house just off Curzon Street, in London's Mayfair district. Very quickly the De Boissy's became English, by marriage and assimilation. In fact the direct male line had died out a hundred years ago, due to a surfeit of daughters and a devastating absence of sons. But the current Managing Director, the Alex Hampshire who had written to American Cereal Products, was indeed a lineal descendant of the original Lucien, and his very considerable personal fortune was locked up in the bank. He was a slim, saturnine man, about sixty years old, habitually quietly-spoken, and seldom seen to be excited.

Three days before Christmas John Savage was called down to Alex's palatial first-floor office. A pair of tall Georgian windows looked out onto a corner of Shepherd's Market. A profusion of exquisite plasterwork, painted and gilded, strung an elegant Greek-key pattern around the cornice, and the high ceiling itself was decorated in a delicate star motif that recalled Robert Adam's best work. Alex's desk had come from the Palace of Versailles, and was marked, inside the secret drawer, with the Queen Marie Antoinette's cipher. The paintings too were from the best French artists, including a Boucher and a deliciously erotic Fragonard. One wall featured a Gobelin tapestry, which had been intended, before the Revolution struck, for the King's bedroom. The story was that Lucien had smuggled it into England himself, so evading the penal customs duty of the day.

Alex's mood was however far removed from those images of idyllic shepherds and shepherdesses.

"Just remind me, would you John, how did we happen to get involved in the first place with these people at Strongwheat?"

John had no doubt that Alex knew the history better than he did, and recognised a storm signal.

"I believe it was some years ago, before I came in, anyway. It was at the time that the Bank's strategy was to take a significant equity interest in its own portfolio of venture capital projects. Exactly how or why we came to choose Strongwheat, I'm not too sure. The original memos in the file were from your cousin, Lionel, who was a friend at the time of Oliver Sedbergh at Bell and Co., you remember? He's the other non-executive director, and it may be that Lionel hoped to cement our relationship with Bell?"

Having established that, whatever the problem, he was not personally the cause, John felt bound to offer a comment.

"I know we're only just starting to see a return on the investment, but they haven't given us any cause for concern about the security of our capital either. That loan last year for the new packing line was repaid ahead of time, with our interest."

"I'm sure I don't need to tell you that our margin on that loan would hardly buy a decent weekend in Paris."

John thought it was typical of Alex to bring up this waspish reference to his long weekend last month with a very presentable young Research Analyst, just to make him feel uncomfortable, but wisely he said nothing. Alex, satisfied to have scored a hit, continued.

"I was anticipating a flotation from them in this coming year, something to provide us with a little fun and profit from a dim little business. Now that the son – what's his name? – Richard? Yes, well now he's got the profits moving up to half a million, I could see it being easy to forecast a million, which would make our twenty percent worth two, even three million, say. Add in the fees, and the right to subscribe for, say, ten percent at a discount, and we'd have something quite worthwhile. Would be a feather in your cap, too, John. Grocery manufacturers have a nice image in the market, because everyone thinks they can understand what they do, so you'd get the pension funds wanting a piece."

"I don't see the need for all this gloom, Alex. He's only said he wants to postpone the float, not cancel it."

"You're being unusually naive, if I may say so. I see from the file that James Routledge has just reached sixty. One imagines that he now sees a flotation as a fine exit for himself. When? In five years' time of course. Meantime, he's to have this new product to keep himself amused. But what if it's a flop? Could bring the company down. We might end up having to sell the shares to some asset-stripper, just to get our money out. And where's the joy in that?"

John sensed that, beneath the professional veneer, Alex was very piqued indeed not to have been consulted.

"Right, Alex, I've got the message. I did have a long talk with Oliver Sedbergh on the train coming back. His relationship with James Routledge apparently goes back to their schooldays, fifty years ago. He was sure that James would not back off this thing unless there's some serious hitch in the development. He did say that James was not so stupid as to throw money away if his new product did not look promising, but that's about the only thing that could stop him now, assuming his health holds up, of course."

"Well, I wouldn't wish a disaster on him, not of any kind. I just don't like the idea of us waiting another five years whilst they gamble with our money. He should have asked our opinion before committing the company to this, you know. I want you to stay very close to this one, John. See if you can't find a way to be kept fully informed of the state of play on a week-to-week basis, and give me regular reports."

They moved on to review the rest of the portfolio that John looked after, and a few minutes later John left. Alex called in his very efficient, very discreet, very well paid Personal Assistant.

"Elaine, we had an e-mail in last week from a Mr. O'Hanlon at American Cereal Products, responding to the letter we sent. I believe he wants to come over in the new year to visit Strongwheat. Would you e-mail him back to say that a direct visit to our client might be premature at this time, but that we would be more than pleased to welcome him to London for what we are sure will be fruitful discussions and so on. Lots of warm noises. Offer some vacant dates in the diary, say mid-January onwards. If he takes the bait, book a room for him at the Ritz, send a car to collect him at Heathrow, see if he would like to go with me to the opera or the ballet at Covent Garden, you know the sort of thing. I have a feeling that this Mr. O'Hanlon will respond well to the red carpet and a little TLC. And just for now, I don't think there is any need at all for our Mr. Savage to know anything about this. We don't need to make the natives restless, do we?"

John Savage climbed thoughtfully up the narrow staircase to his own office on the second floor. It was a quarter the size of Alex's, but was still nicely decorated and furnished with a mahogany desk, a matching upholstered chair and settle on a fine blue Persian carpet, and featured a tall Georgian window that also looked out onto the lively street scene in Shepherds Market. John's father was a successful London stockbroker, and John could readily have joined him in the family firm when he came down from Oxford. Instead he had chosen to strike out independently, and had joined one of the leading management consultancy groups as a trainee. He had loved the continuing mental challenges that consultancy offered, and had only given it up when his new young wife had objected to the eighty-hour weeks, and the endless travelling and nights away it demanded. Now they were divorced anyway, but at least he owed his current job to an introduction from her Daddy, three years ago.

He reviewed in his mind the less than satisfactory meeting with Alex Hampshire, and also the events of the Strongwheat Board Meeting. What a peculiar place that was! Outside was the tall smoke-blackened stone and brickwork and the lofty chimney of a typical 'Satanic Mill', while inside was that extraordinary greenhouse place, with the pale curtains that turned it into a kind of Bedouin tent. And the people, so *committed* to their little business, as though their lives depended on it. Even that sexy Personnel girl, Jean Carey, seemed quite happy with her existence out there in the sticks. Though she had seemed to want to catch up a bit with the London shows. John suddenly toyed with the exciting idea of inviting her up to London for dinner and a theatre . . . for the weekend . . . too soon? Think about her again tomorrow!

His thoughts returned again to Strongwheat. Was Alex right to want to interfere in the old man's plans? Because the business was his very life, that much was obvious. Wouldn't it be simpler, and kinder, to say, 'Look, we're not happy with the direction you're taking. How about buying back the shares from us, and we can part as friends?' He knew from experience that was not Alex's style. He looked around his comfortable office. *A hundred thou' a year plus bonus buys an awful lot of conscience. Now, how can I ensure a regular supply of progress reports without seeming too nosey? Well, it will keep until after Christmas, there won't be much progress to report until, say, late January. Might it be possible to glean enough information from the lovely Jean? Combining business with pleasure?* He guessed her involvement with the new product would likely be only peripheral, and reluctantly put aside a tempting fantasy of Jean Carey as Mata Hari. Who else? Of course, that advertising chap who had insisted on joining the conversation at lunch. What was his name? John had been well-trained in the importance of remembering people, and turned to the pocket diary in which he carefully recorded names and a short note about everyone he met. Yes, there it was. 'Paul Williams, Ad-man. Young, bright, very ambitious.' He reached for the telephone.

"Paul, hullo, this is John Savage. I hope you remember me from the last Board Room lunch, from the merchant bank, De Boissy?"

Paul was astonished to be called out of the blue by a non-executive director of the company, but tried to keep the surprise out of his voice. "John, yes, how nice to hear from you. How can I help?"

"Well, as I mentioned, I am in dire need of education. I mean I've had a lot of involvement with industrial business over the years, but Strongwheat is my first exposure to a consumer product business. I have to admit that I found myself treading water at the Board to follow the significance of Nielsen brand shares, costs-per-thou-rating-points and all that sort of thing. And just the sheer amount of money that's spent on marketing. I really need some help to get up to speed on this stuff, and you did sort of volunteer, if I remember aright?"

"Of course, I'd be delighted. Did you have any particular time in mind?"

"No great hurry. Why don't we leave it like this; next time in the new year that you're due to come up to the smoke, give me a call in advance, and I'll try to fit in around your meeting. Perhaps we can combine the lesson with a spot of lunch, we're quite close to the Ritz here."

Paul could hardly contain his excitement, and bustled along to the open door of Jean Carey's office.

"Come in then," she said with a measure of relief, as she closed a weighty pamphlet about Industrial Tribunals, "Doesn't Walter give you enough work to do?"

Paul ignored the friendly assault, and told her about John Savage's call.

"The cautionary tale of the innocent Marketing Man and the wicked Merchant Banker," said Jean, trying to hide the fact that she was more than a little piqued that John had not yet called her, after she had given him her home number, "Just be careful it has a happy ending. Seriously though, he's a director of the company, so there's no reason why he shouldn't avail himself of your invaluable advice. And bankers do know lots of useful people, which could well come in handy at some time. Knowing a grateful banker never did anyone any harm."

Later that evening, Paul told the story to his wife, after they had tucked up their daughter for the night. Jacky said much the same thing, but added, "It wouldn't hurt to mention it to Walter when you get the chance. Then you'd be in the clear."

Later that same day Vince O'Hanlon at American Cereal Products was scrolling idly through his e-mails, and stopped suddenly when he came to the message from England:

Re; Your visit to London

We were delighted to receive your expression of interest in our client, Strongwheat. At the present time, however, we feel certain that a direct approach to our client would, for personality reasons, be certain to meet with rejection. We need some time to prepare the ground on your behalf.

None the less, we would very much welcome you to London early in the New Year for preliminary discussions which could help us to clarify your views on a possible valuation, and hopefully answer any questions you may have.

At present, I am free for the Monday and Tuesday, January 17th. and 18th. Would that be convenient? Just confirm your flight detail, and how long you would like to stay, and I will look after all the arrangements this side for you.

Vince read and re-read the message, seeking for every nuance of meaning. It all seemed straightforward. De Boissy's original letter had merely expressed an interest in selling their twenty percent holding. Now they were taking it for granted that ACP wanted to buy the whole company, and offering to broker the deal if he would put himself in their hands. Why not? Vince's experience so far of trawling for acquisitions in Europe had taught him that time spent on reconnaissance was likely to help him to locate and avoid some of the minefields that awaited the unwary. A common problem, he had found already, was the conflicting ambitions of the shareholders in what was usually a family business.

He logged on to the Internet to look for business-class seats from Chicago to London. Allow a weekend in London to get over the jet-lag . . . so travel on the Friday. Leave London on the Wednesday morning for a day in Essen, then pick up a flight from Dusseldorf to Florence that evening. Rent a car, and drive to Parma the next day, no . . . Friday. Afternoon meeting there, then some skiing perhaps . . . Or grab the chance to see Venice? This job could actually be quite interesting at times!

Chapter Six

Courtship is a fine old-fashioned word, and John Savage was not a particularly old-fashioned man. But he had decided that Jean Carey was worth courting, and planned his campaign with diligence and care.

First he needed to know more about her. The opportunity came early in the January, at a reception for some visiting Japanese given at London's Mansion House. He spotted Oliver Sedbergh, his fellow non-executive director at Strongwheat, sipping champagne by himself.

"Can I keep you company?" John asked, approaching with a glass in each hand.

"As you are bearing my refill you are most welcome to join me. May I ask, how did De Boissy take your report of that meeting at Strongwheat?"

John wrinkled his nose. He was experienced enough to guess that Oliver already knew the answer, since the City's channels for gossip were all-pervading. A bout of moderate honesty would not do any harm, he thought.

"Alex Hampshire was not best pleased. Think of a tiger, being made to wait for his supper? And he seemed to think it was all my fault that his nice flotation has been postponed. Though I'm damned if I can see what I could have said or done that would have made any difference whatsoever. As you said yourself, James is a very determined character."

"Dear Alex was probably just letting his temper get the better of him. De Boissy's are seriously addicted to getting their own way, you know. Still, the day wasn't a total loss for you, was it?"

James did not reply, but instead skilfully fielded another two glasses of champagne as a waiter glided past them. The large room, with its Persian carpets strewn across polished floors and its elegant gilded plasterwork was filling up now, and was getting hot and noisy.

"I was thinking of that good-looking Personnel lady, Jean Carey. You two seemed to be hitting it off famously."

"Was it that obvious?" James came close to a blush.

"I'd say so. I seem to recall James teasing you a little too. Have you seen her since?"

" 'Fraid not, I've been desperately busy these last few weeks, including working through most of the Christmas break. Do you know anything about her?"

The studied casualness of John's question did not escape Oliver, who tucked it away as another piece of information that might come in useful at some time.

"Only what James told me, must be nearly two years ago now, when he was thinking of recruiting her. She's a graduate, redbrick university I think, but no doubt none the worse for that. Came up through Personnel in G.E.C. as it was then, at Rugby. She met her husband there, he was an accountant, they had no children. He started playing around with a secretary to one of the directors, very messy, so Jean left him and got out of G.E.C. at the same time. We do some work for them, you know, so I was able to check out with my contact there the background to her departure. Strictly as a favour for James. She was very highly thought of, very highly indeed. In fact I got the impression that they would rather have let the husband go and kept her. But the secretary apparently had some leverage with the director – no doubt she knows where the bodies are buried, or something similar. Does that tell you everything you need to know?"

John grinned, "Oliver, you are an absolute wonder. I suppose we should be following the rest next door now, no doubt to hear something momentous. I do just hope that it's nothing to do with the Internet."

John telephoned Jean Carey at her home in Lynchester the next evening. "Hullo, Jean, it's John Savage. I hope you remember we met at the Board lunch last month?"

Jean sat down quickly on the leather stool beside the telephone in the hallway of her cosy terraced cottage, and took several long slow breaths to keep her voice steady. "John, yes, of course. How have you been? Good Christmas?"

John duly noted the subtle reminder that several weeks had passed since the lunch. "Fine, just fine. Look Jean, I've been meaning to call you, but each day when I got round to thinking of it there was some crisis or other coming up that made it impossible to plan to get away at the weekend. I actually worked through most of Christmas too. But I didn't call to moan, I wanted to say that I've got my time more or less under control now, and I do very much want to see you again. In fact I've got two tickets for Stratford on Saturday week, and I wondered if you could possibly be free then and would like to come? I mean, I could drive up to collect you, and take you home again of course. What do you think?"

By now Jean was in full control of her wits again. Wild horses would not have kept her from accepting John's invitation, but she felt that a little uncertainty would serve him right, as penance for his having made her wait a month since they had met.

"John, I really would love that, but . . . I see from my diary that I've got an invitation to a party that night here in Lynchester. Look, let me find out how many are expected, and perhaps I won't be greatly missed. Would you like to call me again, tomorrow?"

Jean's neighbours were suitably impressed when John called for her on the Saturday in a lovingly maintained silver Triumph saloon, the 1952 Renown model, which was openly admired by three small boys.

"That's a nice car, mister. Is it a Rolls Royce? It looks like one."

"No, it's a Triumph, and she's about fifty years old. I suppose she was meant to resemble a smaller version of the Rolls Royce of the day, so you're nearly right."

He ushered Jean onto the polished leather upholstery. "I thought you'd enjoy a ride in this. She's a bit stately and she's called 'Bessie'. The bank gives me a Citroen, French of course, with all the bells and whistles for work and so on, but Bessie's my pet. She comes out in fine weather, and for special occasions."

Jean decided she was quite pleased to find that John had a schoolboy passion for a vintage car – it seemed that bit more human than an all-consuming interest in money, which she had expected to find in bankers. She asked about the evening's play.

"All I can tell you is that it's a revival of a trilogy about the Wars of the Roses, and it's had pretty good reviews."

Jean had pinned her glossy dark brown hair high for the evening, emphasising her high cheekbones and the exquisite lines of her profile. In the theatre she threw off her warm red coat to reveal a white wool dress that she knew clung nicely to the shape of her body. After the show they stayed in Stratford for dinner at a Greek restaurant that Jean had recommended.

They settled quickly for the Mezes and a bottle of Retsina. "What did you think of it?" John asked.

"Absolutely exhausting. I mean, I'm tired out, and I've just been watching it. It must be murder for the cast."

"In more senses than one. I lost count of the number of secret, black and midnight deeds. That was our noble ancestors at work!"

"That Margaret of Anjou came across as one very strong lady, the forerunner of all of us determined and emancipated females. After Clytemnestra, of course. How would you fancy either of them as the next Prime Minister?"

"Scary thought, I'd prefer King Log to King Stork at any time. More wine?"

There were few awkward pauses, and conversation flowed easily between them as they got to know one another's minds through the multiplicity of courses, with the gentle melodies of the bouzouki in the background. With a show of confidence, Jean took charge of the evening when the coffee was brought.

"John, it's going to be well after midnight when you get me home, and I have to think of my job and my reputation in Lynchester. This means I won't be able to ask you in for coffee at this time, so fill up now please. I'd hate to think of you falling asleep on the motorway."

John had been calculating differently, but had come to a similar conclusion. In his case, he had decided he was seriously interested in Jean, and was worried that a premature pass could go wrong. On the other hand she might feel it unflattering if he didn't try. Even so, her firmness was slightly disconcerting. He put it down to her experience as a manager among men, and the drive back to Lynchester together was warm and cosy. He felt like a teenager again as he opened the car door for her to swivel out, and she thanked him for a lovely evening as she stood up, brushed his cheek with a soft, perfumed kiss, and was waving goodnight as she turned the key in the door of her cottage.

Jean too felt surprisingly and suddenly uncertain as she leant against the inside of the door as it closed behind her.

"Oh God, I hope I played it right this time!"

Chapter Seven

On January 26th Vince O'Hanlon was back at ACP, still somewhat jet-lagged from his trip to Europe, but constrained nevertheless to provide a verbal report to his Chairman. Lloyd Teller had been brutally frank.

"Vince, I'll level with you. You've been with us just over a year now, and so far the Board have seen sweet diddly in the way of results, unless you count some mighty fancy expense claims. I can keep them off your back for a mite longer perhaps, but you've gotta give me some ammunition to shoot back with."

"I appreciate your support and your frankness, Lloyd. To be equally frank, I'm disappointed not to have made a tad more progress by now."

"For Christ's sake then, what's the big problem? Hell, we're champing at the bit, and there's wall-to-wall money just waiting for you to find a home for it."

"I'll lay it out for you. Nothin' I've seen so far says it can't be done, nothin'. But it takes time and patience to find the right deal for us. If you remember the direction you gave me at the beginning, your view was that we were doing O.K. in South America and around the Pacific generally with the packers we'd found for our corn oils and margarines, but the big gap was Europe, where we have zilch. And yet Europe is where our U.S.competitors have been digging in for years, to say nothing of some real smart local players like Unilever and Nestle, to name just two. The other problem is ourselves."

"Come again? I warn you, Vince, I'm not in the mood for some smartass lecture about our style of management, especially not from you. You knew all about us when we joined."

"Lloyd, I'm on your side. The problem for ACP, as I see it, is our very success. We turn over well over a billion dollars, right?"

"I've just had the flash summaries for December this morning. Last calendar year . . . one point four seven billion, total sales. Bottom line should come in at about 9% of that. Damn good year."

"So, I figure any business we put together in Europe should be capable of getting to, say, a hundred million sales within five years for us, or it will just eat us alive for management time with peanuts effect on the corporate bottom line."

"O.K. then, are we getting there?"

Which, as Vince would be the first to admit in private, was indeed the sixty-four thousand (or million) dollar question. All the way back on the flight from Zurich he had been asking himself the same question. The olive-oil in Parma was as good as a done deal, and the margarine/vegetable oil business in Essen looked straightforward and not too expensive. Together they would take ACP half way to its one hundred million dollar target. On the face of it, Strongwheat would provide the other half, and just as importantly take ACP into another section of the food industry that fitted well with its U.S. operations. But could Alex Hampshire really deliver it? Just as important, could he be trusted to deliver it to ACP exclusively, and resist the temptation to stage an auction? He sensed that he was sitting across the table from a hungry, maybe desperate beast, and now was not the time for temporising.

"If you'd asked me that a month ago I'd have been pushed to give you a straight answer, or at least to come up with much more than a lot of maybes. But now I think I can see the way clear. Parma Olive you know all about, and the draft contracts should be on your desk by Monday. They're real bright people, eager to start marketing our products too. The German business, Dornfeld in Essen, looks good, and I should have their final terms in another week. But the big breakthrough is going to be the Strongwheat breakfast cereal business, you remember the letter from the London merchant bank? I think it's for real."

"So they do have five percent of the market there?"

"You obviously remember the letter. Yes, they do. I've seen the actual A.C.Nielsen retail research charts, and they don't lie.

Four years ago they had six percent, then they were foolish enough to cut back on their advertising and slid down to the fours. But they've got their act back together, and they're clawing their way back up again. My guess would be that they'll get it all back within a year or two."

"How did you rate that bank, De-something or other? Are they straight?"

"De Boissy. Absolutely straight." Vince's answer was confident and immediate, because he had anticipated the question and decided already how he would respond. In reality he was still anything but sure of Alex Hampshire, and was still casting around to find a way to bind De Boissy to ACP.

"What they wrote turns out to be the truth, but not the whole truth. You remember they said that the Chairman and CEO there had been incapacitated by a stroke, and we thought that meant we would be picking up the pieces? Turns out the old guy has in fact made a miraculous recovery, and has double-banked himself by getting his son to come out of the British Air Force and come on board. Bottom line is that they made a big jump up to about eight hundred thousand bucks last fiscal, before taxes, on a turnover of forty million, and seems like they're on the way to being in pretty good shape."

"Don't tell me, this is one of those momma and poppa businesses you talked about, and they don't want to sell out to the wicked Yanks?"

"That was my fear. But this guy Alex Hampshire at De Boissy's – that's one smooth operator you should certainly meet, by the way – anyway Alex thinks he can swing it for us."

"Go on, surprise me. He wants the keys to our cashbox, right?"

"This one is not going to come cheap, that's for sure. But Alex suggests we have something to offer that he can persaude them to want more than money, and it's something the competition won't match."

"You have my full attention."

"I know it'll sound a bit weird, but it's because we're so far behind the other U.S. companies in getting into Europe that we actually may have something to offer that they can't have. We're going to need a European H.Q., and experienced top management to go with it, since there's not a snowball's chance in hell that we could optimise a string of European subsidiaries from here. Alex knows these people at Strongwheat, and would rate this Chairman – he's called Routledge, Jim Routledge – very highly as our European front man, let's call him Chairman of ACP Europe. Of course we'd need to get the health issue checked out thoroughly. But we both know that there's plenty of CEO's in the States managing perfectly well after their first stroke. And if the son comes out well, he could manage the Strongwheat business for us, and perhaps go on to lead a breakfast cereal business for us across Europe. That's the bait in the trap, Lloyd. Our U.S. competitors could just absorb their company into their existing European operations, and spit out the pips. But we have something interesting to offer – power, influence, status. Make sense so far?"

Lloyd Teller had supported Ben Camina some years before to advocate a policy of global expansion, but he had known it would not get past the Board of the time, and his taking that stance had really been part of a long-term plan to put down a marker as a thinker, with an eye out for the top job in due course. Now, despite his deep-seated nervousness about getting involved in Europe, Lloyd felt the stirrings of a visceral excitement at the picture Vince was painting. Goddam, this globalisation stuff might just be bearable! Vince's stock rose a few points in his estimation.

"Ben will be back from his trip to Hawaii on Monday, and the Board will be looking at our draft year-end fiscals in three weeks . . . this globalisation thing is bound to be on the agenda . . . so, where do we go from here?"

"I was aware of the date of the Board, so I've undertaken to get back to De Boissy within four weeks. I'd like to try to get a short document to you and Ben early next week. It will cover the U.K.market data, up-to-date financials for Strongwheat, and an approach to structuring the offer. Anything else required?"

"Strikes me this Hampshire fellow is the key. Any thoughts on how to tie him real tight to us?"

"I was going to propose that he be invited to act for us now in Parma and Essen?"

"Good thinking. Gives him an extra reason not to twist our tail too much. O.K. put that in. I'll kick the whole package around with Ben, and we'll get something out to the Board at the end of next week."

"Perhaps I could liaise with Betsy to pencil in a date in your diary for us to go over and press some flesh?"

"Done deal. And let me say 'Well done', too. I always knew you had it in you. Now, I've got this wonderful work of fiction in front of me, laughingly called your expense claim. Thinking of going for the Pulitzer this year? Enough snow for the skiing was there?"

Chapter Eight

Summarising the above therefore, we are able, with some changes to working practices, but without significant capital investment, to increase the production of Strongwheat, or a broadly similar product, by fifty percent or more. Such a substantial increase in volumes would enable us to double our annual expenditure on Advertising and Sales Promotion, whilst still increasing annual operating profits from five hundred thousand to between two and a half and three millions.

Just before the end of January, Dick Routledge read out the concluding paragraph of Jim Helvin's paper to his New Product Committee – Walter Hurd, Sales Director, Phil Wythe, Manufacturing Director, Paul Williams, Advertising Manager. As before, Roger Daniels and Jill Lister had come up from Crofton's, their London advertising agency.

Dick continued, "Well, that's the value of the prize we are working for, and I have to admit it has some appeal! So, Phil, would you like to start by telling us where you're at with the experiments on varying the formulation of Strongwheat?"

Phil had been promoted to the Board only six months previously, having joined the company five years ago as Engineering and Packaging Manager. Still only in his late thirties, but already balding, he had a nervous, diffident manner that belied his real ability. He cleared his throat, and mostly read from the notes he had sat up half the night to prepare.

"Jim has the financial details in the Appendix to his paper. Briefly, our standard Strongwheat is made up from four parts of crumbled Rusk and one part Wheat Flakes with the addition of a little flour, salt, malt, vitamins, and bound together with a weak sugar solution. I've concentrated on playing around with the aspect that I thought would make most difference – varying the Rusk/Flake ratio. We tried going from four-to-one to three-to-two, then equal parts, then two-to-three, and finally the complete reversal, one part Rusk to four parts Flake. Straight away we ruled out this last one as impractical without huge losses due to the product breaking up when we came to pack it. In fact it wouldn't even travel safely along the production line. But the first three variants seemed to go through the plant all right, so I gave some of each to Walter to have a look at. By the way, as Jim's paper shows, there is a nice benefit in going down this route, inasmuch as the higher the Flake content, the lower the packed weight in a given volume, so the lower the cost. Jim estimates, I guess conservatively as usual, that the two-to three version would be fifteen, maybe twenty percent cheaper to make."

"I suppose that we have to find the right product first. Walter, do we have a runner amongst the variants?"

Walter's usual air of rotund affability dropped away, to be replaced by a crisp authority that helped to explain how he had risen to become Sales Director.

"We all know, Dick, that because of its make-up, our Strongwheat is seen as a relatively 'adult' breakfast cereal, towards the Shredded Wheat and All Bran end of the scale. On the other hand we also know that most of the volume in the market is driven by the presence of children in the household, and it's the kids that get their mothers to buy the Corn Flakes, the Rice Krispies and the flavoured, sugar-coated products that occupy the opposite end of the scale to us. So Paul and I thought that the best opportunity for us would be if we could find a version that appealed more to children, as that would give us an entry into the main volume end of the market, without necessarily hitting sales of our current product. When we tried Phil's variants here, we thought they were all promising. One thing we noticed right away was that all three were palatable in cold milk, whereas I always think our current Strongwheat needs hot milk. Anyway, we sent down to the agency 100 packets of each of the three new versions and 300 packs of the current product, all in plain white boxes coded with an identifying letter. And we asked them to arrange a little 'in-home' trial in households with young children."

"Your cue, Roger?"

"And very exciting too, Dick. We got the hand-written report rather late yesterday from the Market-Research people, so I've only had time to put together this simple summary at home last night." He handed around copies of a single sheet, containing a table of figures. "This shows the result of the comparison of each variant with Standard Strongwheat. The outcome is clear-cut. All the new versions are preferred to Standard Strongwheat. And reading down the table, you can see that, as the proportion of Flake increases, so the rate of preference rises, so that for the version with two parts Rusk to three parts Flake, we have a very impressive two to one preference for the new product."

Roger had exerted a lot of pressure on his Research Manager to get the results through before the meeting, and had called Paul at home the previous night to take him through the findings. Paul had used the advance warning to reflect a little on the situation.

"It's difficult to believe that all these years the company has simply been ignoring a potential goldmine. I mean, was there some reason why the Chairman chose this particular formulation when he first launched Strongwheat? Were these pretty obvious variations just ignored?"

None of those present had been involved in the original work on the creation of Strongwheat, and Dick made a mental note to talk to his father about it when the time was right. Walter had joined the company as its first full time salesman specifically to assist in the launch of Strongwheat, and he ventured an answer.

"They'd had a pretty expensive disaster, you know, with the launch of a Wheat Flake, which was a straightforward attempt to go after Corn Flakes and the children's market. I think the Chairman may have deliberately decided to go for the other end of the market. Perhaps he wanted a product which would be a bit tough. Mind you, things were a lot less scientific then with the consumer research, and it was a lot simpler and cheaper just to have a go."

"Whatever the reason, we've got a good prospect now," said Roger, "And Jill has something important she wants to add."

"The thing that caught my attention as I sat in on a couple of the trials was that none of the children thought the products were sweet enough."

"They said that?" Phil looked doubtful, "I've got a six-year old myself, and I think he's pretty bright. But I couldn't imagine him coming out with something like that. Not spontaneously."

"You're quite right, they didn't. But they didn't need to, you could judge what they thought from the amount of sugar they ladled on. That's what set me thinking. There was this little girl, about four or five. She poured cold milk onto the cereal in the bowl, tasted it, and then added a heaped spoonful of sugar. Her mother said to me, "She's got a sweet tooth, and no mistake. Like most kids her age, I suppose. Her father and me try to set her a good example, but it doesn't seem to have much affect. We want her to eat the cereal for breakfast, so we have to let her have the sugar." I wrote that down, with a lot of other stuff at the time. Afterwards I read through my notes, and that phrase 'sweet tooth' sort of jumped out at me. I wondered if that might be a clue to something else that's been bugging me, namely the problem of making our product so different, so uniquely interesting that the big retailers will have to give us the shelf space. Let's face it, Walter here will be the first to agree that getting the product onto the shelf in the first place will be make or break."

Walter nodded, "There must be simply hundreds of new products offered every year, all no doubt worthy in their way. Retailers have to guess which will be the winners, and an awful lot just fade away because they don't get to that first base – a place on the shelf. And the cereal market is tougher than most, because the packs are so large and take so much shelf-space, compared with their value."

"Exactly what I've been thinking. So ideally we need to persuade them that our product is so special that it will actually increase the total market, not fragment it further. I thought that, no matter what we might do to make the product sweeter, the kids will still ladle the sugar on out of habit. So why not do something directly about that 'sweet tooth'?

"You know that, before we start writing a commercial, we try to agree with the client a basic story, a sort of summary of the message we would like to leave behind in the consumer's mind. Here's a story for the new product."

There were only two sentences on the sheets of paper she circulated, but she and Roger had argued for hours over the words already. Paul had been shown the final draft two days before, and had expressed cautious interest.

New 'Strongwheat For Kids' is the ideal breakfast cereal for growing children. Made of whole-wheat, it is lighter than regular Strongwheat, and includes added vitamins for health, and also fluoride to protect young teeth.

There was a long silence. Roger was an experienced salesman, and knew when to sit still and allow the customer to react. At last, it was Paul who got things moving again.

"I know lots of people have reservations about putting fluoride in the water. But I don't think there's ever been any campaign against the fluoride in toothpaste. I'd say that's because people think that if you don't want the fluoride you don't have to have it – you can get a toothpaste without it, so it's voluntary. At least that's the theory. In a kid's breakfast cereal it could get an endorsement from the dental profession, which could set us up for a runaway success. Everyone will agree that it's easier to get kids to eat new Strongwheat for breakfast than to brush their teeth. It's an idea that's well worth researching further."

There was a murmur of approval around the table. As Roger had forecast to Jill, "It's not going to be difficult to get the client to research the idea. The difficulty comes when someone has to decide to act on, or to ignore the result."

"Where do we go from here, then?" asked Dick.

Walter moved smoothly back into control, "Let's all remember that so far we've just tested the new versions against our own product. To succeed in the market, it's got to score well against the competition, which for my money means Corn Flakes and Weetabix. So that's the next step. Phil needs to produce for us a couple of hundred plain packs of the best variant, that's the one with two parts Rusk and three parts Flake. Then the agency will arrange a rigorous trial against the competitors in the homes of people with young children. At the same time they can be exploring people's attitudes to the fluoride idea. Frankly, I hope it scores well, we're going to need any edge we can find, I promise you."

Dick could feel a surge of momentum building behind the new product. Were they going cunningly enough? "Paul, is there anything else we should be doing?"

Paul looked carefully through his lists of 'Activities required for the launch, and time needed'.

"The research into consumer opinions about Strongwheat and other breakfast cereals is in the field now, and we should have the results in a couple of weeks. That should help us with decisions about how to present a new product effectively. There is one thing. If we're feeling sufficiently encouraged to spend some more money now, it could make things a lot easier later on. We are tight for time, if we're hoping for a launch early in September, as Walter has suggested. Going back from there, we'd need to start packing the new product two months before that, say July first, so the new cartons must be here by then. That means the printer has to have the carton artwork by June 1st., latest. It's almost the end of January now, and Roger must have eight clear weeks for the in-home trials of the new product. We've got to make it and get it out to him, so we'd best not expect the results before mid-April. Analysis and recommendations go out soon after that to the Board, so we could be calling a Board meeting to decide 'go' or 'no-go' for, say, May tenth. In my judgement that's getting a lot too close for comfort to the June first deadline for the carton artwork. If you would agree, I'd like to be spending a couple of thou' now on preliminary designs, so that we have lots of time to consider them, and we're not stressed out in May."

"Agreed in principle. Sounds too as though you're getting a good handle on the timing, so I'd like you to take me through that next week, and also to review all the spending we're committing to on development, research and now design. In fact, I think the right thing to be doing now is to schedule a meeting with the Chairman in four weeks time to kick around a first draft of a business plan for the new product. Walter, would you take that on, please? It would be good if we could be showing him our ideas for advertising and packaging at the same time. And he's bound to have an opinion about changing the four-day week too."

After the meeting had broken up, Dick went on one of his favourite walkabouts, around the Sceptre Mill factory. Partly, it was the simple need to walk off the stiffness in his knee, and partly he needed to try to clear his mind of the torrent of excitement that now worried him a lot. *Was he letting the sheer momentum of the development process cloud his judgement? How could one stay cool and in control?*

As he moved around the sections he exchanged a wave or a friendly 'How's it going?' with each supervisor, and stopped to listen to the answers. His R.A.F. training had been that a commander should know personally every N.C.O., as well as every officer, and Dick conscientiously tried to follow the precept. He had begun to comprehend the deep visceral excitement that his father had forecast. "*All right, he had to push me into it in the first place. But it's me that's making it happen now, and this new product is going to change everything at Strongwheat.*"

Chapter Nine

John Savage had motored back from his evening with Jean Carey at Stratford in a thoroughly confused state of mind. His original judgement, that Jean would need a bit of old-fashioned courting, had been fully confirmed. He had never been with a woman so relaxed, so confident, so *detached* on a first date. At dinner the conversation had ranged over the play, the effects of tourism on the economy in general and on the theatre in particular, the prospects for business and employment over the coming year, what John had been doing at the Bank recently, and what effect a new product might have on Strongwheat and the people who worked there. Jean appeared to have sturdy left-of-centre views on most things, but was strongly in favour of small companies, and cynical about the built-in inefficiencies of large corporations and state-run organisations. John thought longingly about her slim firm figure, the shining dark hair, and those great dark eyes – were they black? Dark brown, definitely dark brown – that had flashed and mocked his staid 'City' political positions more than once during the evening. As he slowed down at the southern end of the M1 for the London traffic, still busy even though it was past two a.m., he suddenly realised what had been so unusual about the whole evening . . . it had been just like a theatre evening with another man. A sensitive, intelligent, charming man, but there was definitely a masculine cast to her mind. She had volunteered almost nothing about her personal life. Even stranger, she had asked nothing about his. Apart from that soft, glancing kiss at the end, there had been no hint of sex. And yet he was acutely conscious of her as a woman. As he carefully parked Bessie, under cover in his reserved space in the public car park near Covent Garden, he suddenly thought, 'What if she's really one of *those*? Perhaps that's why her husband went walkabout?' He dismissed the thought as soon as it came. *There's a very special woman in there somewhere.*

Jean at least had no such worry. John Savage was only too clearly an alpha male in full pursuit, trying to keep it from seeming to obvious by paying her the compliment of taking as much interest in her mind as in her more superficial attractions.

'Cunning devil,' she thought, as she kicked off the heels that made her only an inch or so shorter than John's six feet, and curled up in her favourite armchair in the bedroom, by the flaring warmth of the gas fire. As she sipped her hot cocoa she heard the rattle of the cat-flap downstairs, and she was joined by Peanuts, her tabby tom, just returned from his own evening's prospecting.

"What do you think, Peanuts?" she asked, scratching the top of his head as he burrowed into her warm lap and set up a rhythmic purring, "Have we got a hook into him? Or is he still sniffing at the bait? He needs someone like me, you know. I could really make something of him."

John had not raised any overt objection to being packed off down the motorway without so much as a cup of coffee, but what if he was really quite angry, and didn't call again? Jean put the cat on the floor, and undressed for bed. She looked at herself in the mirror as she took the pins from her hair, which shone with coppery tones in the firelight as it fell, and reached for her nightdress. Of course he would call!

Sunday was busy for John, as he was invited out to Surrey for early morning golf with an old school friend, then they went back to a late lunch with his parents. Bridge in the afternoon, because it rained, and when he eventually got back to his Covent Garden flat he fell asleep as soon as his head touched the pillow.

Jean was only too insistently in his thoughts again as he tried to pick up the threads of Monday morning in the office, and he started visibly when the telephone rang to drag him sharply back from a pleasant reverie.

"John, good morning, it's Alex. Look, I have to go out almost immediately, but I would very much appreciate the benefit of taking your mind once more today about the situation at Strongwheat. Something quite interesting has come up. Could you be free for lunch? I'm in the City this morning, but a short walk will no doubt do us both good. Suppose you book a table at Simpson's, and I'll meet you there as soon after one as I can make it?"

John had often thought that the best thing about Simpson's, in London's Strand, was that it had maintained the tradition of keeping one of its dining rooms for men only. No ladies. The seating was in upright pews, set in small private cubicles. The food was strictly English Traditional, roast joints of mutton or beef carved at the table from a silver trolley, treacle pudding, pints of excellent bitter. Alex was svelte of figure, and tucked into his ample lunch with almost schoolboy enthusiasm, washed it down with the beer, and talked about a new private client who had sold his business and had been recommended to De Boissy's for help in managing the investment of the two million he had netted. John was more circumspect with the size of the portion that he ate, asked intelligent questions, and waited patiently for Alex to get down to the reason for the meeting. Alex was in no hurry, composing his thoughts carefully while he chatted, but eventually he broached the subject of Strongwheat as the plates from the main course were clattering away.

"John, you remember our talk about Strongwheat? I seem to recall that I was rather ill-tempered at the time, and I do beg your indulgence. It's just that I like to feel that our clients are doing the best for themselves, and in my experience that usually means following our advice. I hear you've been keeping in touch?"

John mentally cursed Oliver Sedburgh for an old gossip, "You did ask me to keep a close eye on them, Alex. So I've been developing some useful connections at several levels."

"Quite. But you've yet to give me a report?"

"So far there's precious little to report. The development of the new product seems to be under tight control, but we shan't be presented with any proposals for several months yet. Then there's likely to be a special Board Meeting called, probably mid-May, which I would expect will also have the October to March half-year to consider. That's the time I would expect James to be looking for a Go/No-go decision."

Alex kept his eyes down as he scraped the last of his treacle pudding from the dish, "What's your gut feel at this time?"

"It's likely to be well planned, well controlled, and James Routledge has given it a fair old shove. I'd say it's more likely than not."

They both fell silent while they moved back to the comfortable lounge, with its ancient leather settees, and the coffee was brought.

"Right then, John, I'll tell you the tale, and you say what you think."

As Alex told the story, he glossed expertly over his own original approach to American Cereal Products back in December, and gave the impression that Vince O'Hanlon had himself made the first contact with De Boissy's.

"They're based on the western shores of Lake Michigan, 'in sight of the towers of Chicago', as Mr. O'Hanlon rather picturesquely puts it. Turnover is equivalent to one thousand million pounds a year, decently profitable. Core business is as corn-brokers – that's maize, I believe. But they're well diversified into cornflour, corn-oil, margarine and of course corn breakfast cereals. They have only a small share of the American market for that product, but that still gives them a volume of sales considerably larger than our friends at Strongwheat. Interesting so far?"

John nodded, but remained silent.

"They came in to see me last Monday, this chap O'Hanlon, together with a pair of accountants he'd picked up from Price Waterhouse. I wonder what the collective name should be for an assembly of accountants? A Quibble perhaps? Or a Niggle?"

"How about a Depression of Accountants?"

"Excellent, thank you. I'll make a note of that. Anyway O'Hanlon is here to look for acquisitions – 'partnerships' I think they'd prefer to call them. Suddenly woken up to the glories of commercial imperialism, or perhaps it's the threat of Fortress Europe. They'd heard of our investment, and came in for a general chat, and to sound out the possibility that we might be interested in selling our holding. Pleasant lunch, though they do insist on talking business right from the moment you sit down. Fact is, we have a powerful hand to play, having both a shareholding and a seat on the Board of the only company in the market not already controlled by a major international player. They had already gone over the published accounts of course, and suggested the company was looking vulnerable."

"Last year's accounts are not filed yet."

"Indeed, so they were not aware of the recovery situation you've described to me. The upshot was that O'Hanlon got rather excited, and proposed to head off up to the Midlands to talk terms with James at once."

"I'd be prepared to bet a year's pay that James would send them packing with a hefty flea in the ear. That's if he even agreed to see them."

"My thoughts exactly. Which could sour things for years to come. You can rest assured that I put that to them quite forcibly, and I'm happy to say they saw the force of my argument. More coffee?"

Alex used the interlude to finalise his thoughts. "John, I would like you to agree that, in this instance, I should approach James myself to sound out his feelings. I believe I can persuade ACP to offer an interesting future to James pere et fils, if they wish to continue in the world of business, and I might use that to overcome any initial reluctance he might have to opening negotiations. What do you think?"

The simple reality was that Alex did not need John's approval to approach a client of the Bank, but John realised that Alex's subtle flattery was intended to keep him on side. Still, he saw no reason not to ask the obvious question.

"You've been round the track a good few times, Alex, so you must have a good reason to want to do it yourself, rather than send me?"

"Two good reasons. One, I can foresee immense long term potential benefit for the Bank in having a friendly working relationship with an ambitious American corporation, and I want to be seen to be maintaining a personal commitment at this stage. Two, what if it all goes wrong? What if James becomes seriously hostile? I would not want you to be personally compromised. You could reasonably say you've had no part in it, and so continue your good work on the Strongwheat Board, ready for next time. Do you see my reasoning?"

In fact Alex had a third reason, which he hardly recognised himself at the time. Delegating, and managing his bright young men was all very fine, and was good banking practice. But it was nowhere near as much fun as pulling the strings of a big deal 'hands on'. And Alex was feeling a craving for a little more excitement in his life.

Lloyd Teller felt that, on the whole, ACP's Board Meeting at the end of January had gone well. The fourth quarter draft fiscals had confirmed that the business was still growing steadily. He had been able to report that turnover for the year had actually exceeded the budgeted one point four thousand million dollars by no less than seven percent, and as a result profits were likely to be up twenty percent on the previous year. A nice increase in the dividend had been agreed, which would undoubtedly go down well on the NYSE. Most satisfyingly of all, he had been able to silence his immediate predecessor as Chairman of the Board, that smug bastard Simcox, with the announcement of the potential acquisitions in Italy, Germany and England. Imagine the cheek of that guy! He'd sat on his fat fanny in the top job for twelve years, and done sweet diddly about developing international business. And now here he was, glorying in the fancy title of' 'President Emeritus' and enjoying a cosy sinecure as a 'consultant to the Board', and leading the pack of non-executive directors who'd been climbing all over Ben and himself over the lack of progress in this new frenzy for globalisation. Of course they'd still howled at the potential price – one banker had sneered that 'anyone can build a global business if you're prepared to pay a hundred times last year's profits for the privilege'. But Lloyd had sensed they were hungry, and had beaten down the opposition by showing that the cost would be spread over three years, and would in any case be dependent on some very ambitious growth in the profit numbers. In the end he'd actually been congratulated. The same banker had said that 'The market would certainly be impressed by the move, and that now could be the time to pick up a few shares'. No doubt he was well aware of his fiduciary responsibility to avoid insider dealing, and was just joking . . . Time to tell Vince that his dream was about to become a reality!

"Paul? Is that Paul Williams? It's John Savage from De Boissy's. Look, I'm sorry not to have been available the last two times you've come down, but I wonder if we could try to fix up something definite now? I made a note that you were coming down tomorrow, but you remember I couldn't make it because I was expecting some visitors from Germany? Well, they've just cried off, so I wonder if you might still be available for tomorrow morning? And lunch? You can? That's absolutely first class. About ten here then? Let me give you some directions to find us."

Paul came down to Euston on the morning Pullman from Birmingham International. When asked, Walter had encouraged him to improve John Savage's understanding of consumer products marketing, so Paul felt justified in travelling first class and enjoying a good breakfast en route. After queuing for a taxi, it was just before ten o'clock when he pushed open the walnut front door of the grand Mayfair house that was De Boissy's offices, and stepped nervously into the marble-floored reception. Immediately in front of him a fine cantilevered staircase spiralled around the hall, with two delicate settees on his right, upholstered in pale blue satin with profuse gold trim. To his left he found the elegant blonde receptionist, sitting behind a gilded Boule table that was inlaid with tortoiseshell. Her appraisal was polite, almost gracious, but Paul felt that she had instantly classified him as a fellow worker, rather than a client. He was amused to see the way her sculptured eyebrows rose at the warmth of John's welcome as he came down the stairs at the run.

"Hullo there, Paul. I'm so glad you were able to come in. Come on up now to my humble abode."

He saw that Paul was distinctly impressed by the Georgian sumptuousness of the house, with its tall, mahogany doors, blue Persian carpet, and the serried ranks of portraits up the staircase. Halfway up, on the landing outside Alex's office, he stopped and leant back against the brass handrail. He waved a casual hand towards the De Boissy ancestors.

"Don't be taken in by this bunch. Most of them would have found themselves in the dock at the Old Bailey if they'd been operating today. Standards of banking ethics in their time would have made Dick Turpin blush. Mind you, those were good times for making serious money. Slave-trading, sugar plantations, privateering, new colonies, South Sea Bubbles – all a lot more fun than scraping a living in Asian currency derivatives! We're all a bit cabinned, cribbed and confined now."

This last was said as he ushered Paul into his office on the second floor.

"This is gorgeous!" Paul compared it in his mind with the functional plastic and steel of his own dark and poky office at Strongwheat.

"Glad you like it. We usually receive clients in a meeting room, but as we're sort of colleagues I thought we'd be more relaxed here. Ah, here's the coffee. Instant, I'm afraid, but at least Bill's made a good pot, so we shan't go short. Paul, may I introduce my assistant, Bill Fernleigh. Bill joined us only last autumn from Cambridge – Philosophy, wasn't it, Bill? We're very democratic here about the coffee-making, as the partners do not believe in sprinkling idle secretaries around the place. And typing likewise. Unless it's a major document, we're expected to two-finger it ourselves on the PC. Would you be happy if Bill sat in too, as part of his education?"

The next two hours passed quickly, with Paul outlining the theory and practice of marketing a product through the grocers to the consumer. In John's mind, Paul's dissertation was distinctly secondary to the real purpose of the invitation, but he was intrigued by what he perceived to be the unusual financial demands of the business.

"But be honest now, is it absolutely necessary to spend so much money? Last year I believe the spend on Advertising was about a tenth of your total sales, that's four or five times what you made as operating profit. Can that really be justified?"

"In part, it's a problem of scale for a business like Strongwheat. We're just a minnow swimming in a sea full of big fish like Kellogg's, who can afford to spend ten times as much as we do. But an advertisement in the newspaper, or a commercial on TV costs us just the same as it costs them. In fact they can usually buy cheaper than us, because of sheer weight of their buying power. Four years ago Strongwheat actually took the decision to cut its advertising budget by a third. That was while I was still at Crofton's. We fought the decision, but you've met the Chairman, and he usually gets his own way. Within a year they'd lost *a quarter* of their share of the market, from six percent down to four and a half. That policy was reversed just before Dick joined, and it's taken all this time to recover some momentum against competitive pressures, and get back up above five percent. I haven't done the sums, but I'd be pretty sure that the loss of past and future profit will far exceed what was saved at the time. Think of it as like feeding fuel into a steam engine – a steady input is a lot more economical in the long run than letting it slow down, then having to get it going again."

Paul kept his tone cool and objective, but beneath the surface the passionate recollection of old battles was very apparent.

"Point made, point taken. Very salutary. Which seems like a good time to be breaking for a spot of lunch. Regrettably, Bill has had his time out for the day, as he has an urgent report to draft. But we could just stroll across to the Ritz now and beat the crush."

"Super to meet you, Paul," said Bill, bearing the loss of lunch with good grace, "It was great to get a whiff of the real world. Hope to see you again soon."

Following Alex's earlier example, John made pleasant conversation through a lunch of Dover sole and Chablis, and only raised the real topic of his interest over the coffee.

"I suppose this new product has got you pretty wound up? It must be like a good war for the cavalry."

"You mean a few casualties are good for promotion prospects? Sorry, bad joke. Yes, it's making us all concentrate very hard. There isn't much room for error, is there?"

"I suppose you're all really committed to it? I mean, is it really going ahead?

"Committed at this time to giving it the best possible try, yes. But the real crunch time will come in May, when we'll be seeing how well the product idea we've come up with compares with the competition in the market. I expect Elizabeth will be ringing around any time now to book a date in your diary."

He went through the plan for the consumer trials, but left out the idea for adding fluoride. Paul regarded that part of the development as speculative, even frivolous, and felt instinctively that John's perception of the quality of his judgement would not be enhanced if he talked about it. Time enough to support it if it researched well! John was signing the bill when Paul mentioned the scale of the potential improvement in profit that Jim Helvin had referred to in his paper, and looked up sharply.

"Did you say two and a half million? That's five times last year's result?"

"And that's after doubling the spend on advertising and sales promotion. It would put us in a different league. The three-year plan envisages a hefty jump in the investment behind the Strongwheat brand in the first year, and that absorbs all the margin generated by the sales of new product. Then in the next two years we should maintain that level of spend, but the volumes should keep growing, so by the end of year three the total volumes are fifty percent more than this year's, and the margin increase thumps through to the bottom line."

They crossed Piccadilly through the underpass, and came out on the north side, into wan sunshine.

"If you could excuse me now, John, I'm due at Crofton's in Holborn in twenty minutes."

"I'm very grateful, Paul, for the trouble you've taken to help me to understand what you do. I promise to defend your Advertising and Marketing Budget to the death at the next Board! Seriously though, I rather envy you. You've climbed on the back of a tiger, I'd say, and you seem to be enjoying the ride."

Paul grinned, "Let's hope I don't end up inside it. But it is fun."

Back in De Boissy's, Bill Fernleigh took notes from John for a report to Alex Hampshire. "I liked Paul," he said, "I mean that enthusiasm and dedication came across as absolutely genuine."

John thought of Jean Carey, "It's a funny old business they've got up there. Yet somehow they're all committed to it, just like Paul. It's their living, of course, but it's something more to them than making money. It's as thought they all feel they are a part of something worthwhile. I told Paul that I envied him, and I meant it."

When Bill had left his office to draft the minute for Alex, John put his feet up on the desk and took stock. Alex would be keen to hear the precise timetable of Paul's plan, and any future negotiations with those American people would definitely be coloured by the scale of that projected increase in profit. Two and a half million! He felt a small twinge of discomfort that Alex had used him – no, he had allowed himself to be used – as a sort of spy, on behalf of ACP. He stifled the pang of conscience with the thought that Alex would surely use the information to drive up the potential price when the time came. *What would Jean say if she found out? It was easy for her to take moral positions, she didn't have to earn her living in the City. Flowers would be good. Get some delivered to her tomorrow, then call her at home and fix another date. If only my diary wasn't so damn crowded!*"

Chapter Ten

Rosemary was a good wife for Dick Routledge. When they had first met, he had been a young Flying Officer, newly posted onto one of the Tornado squadrons at R.A.F. Bruggen, West Germany. Rosemary held the same rank, and was the Assistant Station Adjutant. In Dick's case it was a matter of love – or at least total, overwhelming lust – at first sight. She was tall, lean, and had large bright blue eyes which were set off by a mane of coppery red hair, kept severely pinned up during working hours. From most angles she was a very pretty, attractive young woman, though a purist might have cavilled that her fine Roman nose was a little too prominent for the perfect profile. Germany was full of opportunities and temptations for a bachelor fighter-pilot with money in his pocket – especially one who was well-built, good-looking with a mop of fair hair, played wing-forward for the RAF, and who had an uninhibited smattering of delightfully incorrect schoolboy German. Dick however met Rosemary on his first arrival, when he reported to the Adjutant's office. Immediately he asked her 'to help him find his way around' by partnering him at that weekend's Station Dance, and he was totally smitten from that moment on. Rosemary had never been short of admirers, but she had never been pursued by anyone with Dick's all-consuming energy and enthusiasm. He reminded her of her father's Golden Retriever, a dog that probably had some wolf in its immediate ancestry, which had grown to the size of a young horse in no time at all, and would knock you flat on your back with affection if he took a liking to you. She loved it.

She thought of those days as she dusted around the framed photographs one bright morning in early February – Dick trying to look invincible in the R.A.F. Rugby Union team, but succeeding only in producing a sickly grin; Dick shaking hands with a Marshal of the Royal Air Force before a big game at Twickenham; Dick with herself and half a dozen of their friends, tankards raised in celebration of some triumph. Good times! Had he, had they both given up too much for Strongwheat? They had friends now in Lynchester, pleasant company for a dinner party or a summer picnic. But when compared with the gaiety and excitement of those days in Germany, weren't they all grey-haired, grey lives, grey souls?

Rosemary shook her head to dismiss the mood. Romantic nonsense! They had all been young and carefree then, so of course life had been one long summer's evening party. What about those three miserable years in the wilds of Linconshire, poisoned by that Wing Commander, Dick's immediate superior, who had taken a fancy to Rosemary, now a civilian wife with a small baby. He had made their lives a misery, because she would have nothing to do with him. And that grim posting to the Air Ministry in London, when Dick had been trying to come to terms with having to give up flying, and they'd had two young boys and not enough money? Lynchester was paradise compared with that. Best of all, they had some control over their lives, and a really bright future to look forward to. She scolded herself. "*Here you are, a capable, intelligent woman, the wife of the man who runs the biggest employer in the town. And what do you do with yourself? Coffee mornings, and looking after three male animals who should be learning some self-reliance!*"

Perhaps she should get involved in local politics? 'Lady Mayoress' sounded nice. "*It's been a long winter, I'm sure we could both do with a break.*" She searched under the cushions of the settee for Sunday's paper – hadn't there been an article about South Devon? Yes, Salcombe looked nice – that Marine Hotel, right on the water's edge. She put the paper to one side, to remind her to talk to Dick that evening. Early May would be good, just before that Board Meeting that was going to be so important, something to look forward to for both of them.

After the delicate manoeuvrings of his lunch with John Savage, Alex had been in no great hurry to call James Routledge and start the negotiations on behalf of ACP. He recognised the importance of negotiating from the best possible position however, and John Savage's report on his meeting with Paul Williams provided him with just the information he thought would get the Americans adequately excited. A new product in the pipeline, a plan to increase profits by a factor of five over the next three years – they would surely feel the pressure to get on board now, before their American competitors noticed the moves, and the price rose out of sight. So now was the time to involve James Routledge in the proceedings.

In fact Alex was prompted to make his move by Vince O'Hanlon calling him on February 2nd, to say that ACP had approved his proposal for the acquisition, in principle at least. Alex was at pains to make Vince understand that the process could not be rushed, and so, he hoped, make the Americans the more eager, and the more dependent on the good offices of De Boissy. There were several long transatlantic telephone calls, followed in each case by carefully drafted e-mail confirmations, as Alex made quite certain of the deal that ACP were prepared to offer. He took a professional's pride in driving the terms to the absolute limit – even though he was by no means certain that the client would accept, or even be grateful. Finally he felt he was ready, and called James Routledge on February 25th, only for James' secretary to inform him that 'the Chairman was working at home this morning'. He decided to push on, even at the risk of annoying his client with a call to the house.

"Good morning, is that you James? It must be three or four years since we met, but I hope you may remember me, Alex Hampshire at De Boissy?"

James had been getting ready to take Ellen down to the Golf Club for lunch with some friends, and was caught somewhat off guard.

"Alex, yes, how are you? I've been meaning to write to you about that postponed flotation business. I didn't want you to feel that we are not grateful for your interest. I know we're not a grand investment for you yet, and you've been patient for a few years already. But I'm very serious about involving Dick in a major development, and so making us a lot more profitable and a lot more valuable, before we sell off any more."

Alex was relieved, and a little surprised, to find James less than his usual hard-nosed aggressive self, in fact just a little on the defensive. Perhaps that illness had softened him up?

"Not at all, James. I do most certainly sympathise with the personal as well as the commercial considerations concerned. And from what John Savage has said, it is clear that your son is doing a really first-class job, and I'm sure your right to want to do everything you can for him. Actually, I was calling on a different matter really, though it is certainly related. We have had an interesting approach from a major multinational in your field, looking to invest for the first time in the UK. Now I know you will feel that the timing is not yet right for that either, but they are in no hurry, no hurry whatsoever. I mean we are looking at the kind of deal that would leave you in control, with a huge incentive geared to results, over the next three to five years. A most unusual, even enlightened approach, if I may say so. I was sure you would be interested to hear about their ideas, and I was wondering when it might be convenient for me to come up for a bit of a chat? No great urgency, as I said, I'm looking in my diary now a month or two ahead. How about soon after Easter? Or down here if you'd prefer that, we're quite convenient for the Ritz, if you remember?"

The pause before James replied was so long that Alex thought for a moment that the telephone connection had been lost, but James answered at last in a tone that was perceptibly firmer.

"Alex, I'd be delighted to meet you again, though I'm sure John Savage will have left you in no doubt about our plans for the future. On reflection, I think it would be sensible to get through the special Board Meeting we're setting up in May first, so that we know where we are going. And I think Dick should be with us, as I would not like him to feel that I have been negotiating behind his back. You know, I have a suspicion that he has yet to forgive me for pitching him into this new product project quite so abruptly. How about the following month, say early June?"

Alex cursed quietly to himself over the inclusion of Dick Routledge. In his experience, having two people on the other side of a negotiation meant four times the problems. He turned the pages of his diary. On the other hand . . .

"June looks good. As I said, the Americans are prepared to wait until we're ready, for once. In fact I see in my diary that I have a box at Ascot, third week of June. Ladies Day is already promised, but how about the Thursday, Gold Cup Day? With ladies, of course. We could meet for dinner and our discussion the previous evening, if that would suit? Or perhaps better, you could just enjoy the Wednesday evening in London, and we could get together for an hour or two in the morning, before we relax at the races?"

"Sounds delightful, Alex. Let me check with Dick, and I'll get my girl to confirm."

Alex leaned back from his chair, and gazed with unseeing eyes at the Gobelin tapestry on the wall opposite. So far, so good. He calculated that the nuisance of having to negotiate with both father and son would be counterbalanced by the charm and excitement of the Ascot occasion. He would be at ease and in control in his Ascot box, a few yards away from the Royal Terrace. And the ladies would help to keep the day civilised too. He walked next door.

"Elaine dear, we need to spread a red carpet or two for a get-together with our friends at Strongwheat. Would you see if you can book two rooms – no, a suite with two bedrooms – at the Ritz please? On the De Boissy account, of course. That's the Wednesday night, June 21st. Mr. and Mrs James Routledge, and Mr and Mrs. Richard Routledge. And we'll need a car to take the six of us to Ascot on the Thursday. And of course an extra driver to bring their car."

"Might you think of inviting Mr. O'Hanlon from America?"

"Clever girl . . . but no, not on this occasion, it could be too much of a risk. If anything came adrift with the Routledges we might have no place to hide. But get me a call to him when I get back from lunch. I'm sure he will appreciate being kept informed personally."

Jean Carey's self-confidence had been badly bruised by the trauma of her divorce. John Savage had reflected on the intelligent, competent, controlled persona that she projected, but had yet to understand that it was in part created by her own vulnerability. Like the growls of a wounded animal, it was designed to prevent people getting close enough to wound her again. John had in fact partly penetrated her defences by accepting her on her own terms, and treating her like a friend. So by the Wednesday after that Saturday evening at Stratford she was becoming seriously anxious for him to call again. Relief flooded through her that evening as she was locking up her Mini outside the cottage, and her next-door neighbour bustled out holding the fat bunch of red roses.

"Delivery boy arrived with these an hour ago, so I took them in for you. Aren't they lovely! Is this the chap who came for you on Saturday in the little Rolls-Royce my Jerry was talking about?"

There was a card inside.

Got home – safe but lonely. Talk to you soon, Love, John.

He telephoned later that evening. Still maintaining his 'softly softly' strategy, the next date was also arranged on neutral ground, this time for a Sunday in Oxford near the end of February.

"I'd give anything to be able to see you sooner, Jean, but I've got meetings piling up with clients in Germany and France, and I've now been landed with a new client to visit in Mexico. I'll meet you off the train from Birmingham International, it's due in to Oxford at 12.03, so you won't have to get up too early to catch it. We'll have lunch at the Randolph, haven't done that for years. Then we'll just be tourists for the day, catch up on some of the things I loved about Oxford. But I have to be at Heathrow by seven, to meet a client coming in from Hamburg."

John enjoyed the little drop in the noise level as he ushered Jean into the dining room at the Randolph, but was hugely disappointed to find that the fondly-remembered traditional Sunday lunch there had moved markedly towards the 'nouvelle cuisine' style for the day, and Jean laughed aloud at the expression on his face when the main course was served.

"It's all right for you." he said in pretended misery, "You're slim and beautiful, and no doubt that pretty plate is adequate for your needs. But I'm a growing lad, and I need to keep my strength up."

Indeed the special feel of a bright Sunday afternoon at Oxford during term time seemed to Jean to have had a Peter Pan effect on John Savage. They walked down the newly-pedestrianised High Street hand in hand. 'They say it's one of the most beautiful streets in the world, and today I believe it.' He seemed to lose the inhibitions of his City gravitas with every step, and regress to being a carefree undergraduate once again. With huge enjoyment he showed her his old rooms, overlooking the Deer Park in Magdalen College, and used his whispered charm to persuade the Porter to allow him to escort 'my new lady' up the narrow spiral staircases to the very top of Magdalen Tower.

"On May Morning, the choir comes up here and sings to greet the dawn," he said, with more than a touch of owner's pride in his voice. "People dance till then at the Summer Balls in various colleges, then come out again in punts on the river Charwell down there for a champagne breakfast and to hear the singing. It's absolutely magic, as long as the sun does shine. And just look at the view the choir have!"

The bright sunshine was casting golden highlights onto the turrets and roofs below. University and Town, interlocking but separate, were spread out below them like a map.

"That big dome there is the Radcliffe Camera, it's a library and reading room. Popular as a place to work with people whose lodgings are a way out of town. The gothic church next to it is St Mary's, that's the University church. That's Brasenose College on the far side, and the one this side with all the pinnacles is All Souls. Down there below us is the Cherwell. It flows under the Magdalen Bridge, past the Botanical Gardens and St. Hilda's, and joins the Isis over there – that's the name for the Thames within the city of Oxford."

Jean was filled with a longing to hold on to the magic a little longer. "Those punts tied up there by the bridge – do you think we could rent one? You can punt, of course?"

"Me? Punt? Just sit back and admire!"

Impulsively Jean hugged him in the simple joy of the moment. Just as quickly John's lips sought hers in a kiss, which began delicately and tentatively, and when she did not pull away became stronger and more demanding.

"Steady on there," she whispered as the towers whirled around her, "I've got to make it in high heels down those little winding stairs."

In fact John was no expert with a punt pole, but he summoned up enough of his old skill to propel them safely a few hundred yards up the waters of the Cherwell, still shallow, but made the more awkward by the brisk current from the rains of February. Jean stretched herself out luxuriously on the big green leatherette cushions in the bow, with the sun on her face giving warming hints of the summer to come. Her long orange skirt picked up the appliquéd motif of orange flames that rose in graceful curves from the waistline of her white polo-necked sweater. Like so many girls before her, she trailed her fingers in the cool water, crinkled up her eyes to look at John as he concentrated at his task and ducked his head beneath the overhanging willows, and wondered if it was safe to feel as happy as she did at that moment.

John felt distinctly less secure. Partly this was the result of the conflict between wanting to look nonchalantly competent, and the need to maintain total concentration on the pole, the punt, and the river. More importantly, the recollection of her impulsive response to his kiss on Magdalen Tower reminded him that this lovely creature, now spread carelessly before him like a living Renoir, really was a living, breathing woman, vulnerable as well as capable. Suddenly, it was no longer a game, and it seemed desperately important that he should not be the cause of further pain for her. He felt the need to lower the romantic temperature for the present, to allow him time to think. Just below the graceful arch of the Parks Bridge he saw a shelving section of riverbank that allowed him to bump ashore, and he sat down beside her, grateful for the rest.

"How are things at Strongwheat? What's happening with the new product?"

Jean had been daydreaming and was startled by the abrupt change of mood, but responded cheerfully to his obvious interest.

"Mmm, business has been good, in fact we've been working quite a bit of overtime. Did I tell you about the Great Fluoride Crisis?"

"Fluoride? As in water supply?"

"Yes, there's a possibility that we'll be adding a small amount into the new product. Very hush-hush, of course. Could allow us to find a niche that will appeal to modern mothers with young children. Helps to offset the guilt about them piling in the sugar. Anyway this rumour got out, and caused a full-scale protest in the factory. I had an official Union delegation at my office last week, 'Wishing to communicate their concern formally' about any possible change to their beloved Strongwheat. To be perfectly frank, I hadn't heard about it myself, so I had to ask my boss – you know, Phil Wythe, the Director of Operations – to see them himself. He swore them all to absolute secrecy, then explained that the idea was being researched as a part of the plan for the new product, but that there was no intention whatsoever to add or take anything away from regular Strongwheat. That calmed them down, and they went away quite happy. But it reminded me just how strongly they identify with the company and the product. It's almost like an article of religion, with the workforce as the guardians of the true faith."

John smiled at her story, and touched her cheek affectionately, as he wondered casually to himself why Paul had made no mention of fluoride when they'd been talking about the new product. What other secrets might he be keeping?

"Jean, it's just lovely here with you, but I'm thinking I've got to propel this beast back to Magdalen Bridge, and then it's a walk to the station."

They strolled back along Holywell and Broad Street, window-shopped at Blackwell's book store, and discovered that they both liked Zola and Mickey Spillane. It was obvious that John's light-hearted mood had deserted him for the moment, but Jean was content with the companionable silence, confident that she had seen something of the real man for a few hours, and liking what she had seen. They stood on the platform as the last couple of minutes ticked by before her train back to Lynchester was due. John seemed to come to an important decision.

"Jean, I think we need to invest a lot more time to get to know one another. How does a weekend in London sound? Say two weeks time?"

He saw the beautiful arches of her eyebrows rising in silent question, and continued hastily, "I mean, I have a spare room in the flat. It's just off Covent Garden, so it's really convenient for whatever you want to do. If you'd like to come down on the Saturday morning, we could organise things from there."

Jean thought for a moment, before replying, "I'd love the time together. But I've got another priority too, which I've been putting off till my next visit to London. Spring is just about here, in case you hadn't noticed. Last year I was too miserable to buy myself anything new to wear, so now I'm ready to splash out. May I come in first thing Saturday just to drop off my bag, and have the day to myself at the shops? You could meet me for tea, and carry home the booty like a proper gentleman."

As she finished the little two-coach train rumbled in. There was a quick, tender kiss, the sweeter because it was a kind of public declaration, and she was gone in a swirl of orange and white.

"I'm going to have to think very seriously about what I'm doing," John said to himself as he slipped into the seat of the big Citroen provided by De Boissy. He began rearranging his mind to think in German, as he trundled with the Sunday evening traffic eastwards towards Heathrow Airport.

Chapter Eleven

"Corporate man producing corporate fuck-all and getting in the way of everyone with an ounce of creativity. Little grey man in his little grey suit with a little grey mind. What the hell are you doing in advertising? Why don't you go off and do something better fitted to your qualifications and personality – could I suggest a nice safe job with your local Council, collecting the bloody Council Tax? And make room for the people here who actually want to make a difference, and aren't shit-scared to stick their necks out in the attempt. For God's sake, don't you ever ask yourself what it's all for?"

In the world of Crofton's, the London advertising agency, Roger Daniels was considered a good politician as well as a good manager. But the quarrel with Jill Lister was the sharper because of their shattered affair, and was now escalating to the point of becoming a real disaster. The issue was her proposal that the client should add fluoride to the new version of Strongwheat. Given the timescale, they had to get on with producing ideas for the launch commercial in advance of knowing the results of the consumer research which was now in the field. Trying to appear objective, Roger had been prepared to concede that the new product lacked glamour. 'Worthy but dull' was a fair assessment. Fluoride would certainly produce some controversy, and could well be the key to getting space in the big supermarket chains that controlled the market. But was it sensible to go ahead on the assumption that the client would buy it? Even supposing that they accepted fluoride, was it automatic therefore that it should dominate the commercial?

"Look, Jill, I think you're right," he said, trying to stem the flood of invective, "But what would you suggest we say if they have reservations? Fluoride or nothing? Paul won't stick his neck out for you, so it would be us versus them. A split like that could cost us the account."

Jill, sensing weakness, was pitiless. "Cost you your job, too. So you'd better exert all your famous selling skills to ensure they do buy it, wouldn't you agree?"

"I don't think my job comes into this at all. You may feel it is desirable that the client adapts his product to make it easier for us to produce a memorable commercial. A bit of a platform for you to stand on and crow to the world 'I did this'. On the other hand the client may feel, not unreasonably, that he's paying us sell his product, and if the product was bursting with intrinsic interest and unique appeal he wouldn't need to employ expensive people like us and chuck in a cool two million to sell it. Do you see my point?"

"I hear you. You haven't said anything yet."

"You understand me well enough. I'm the Agency's Director on this account, and one of my functions is to decide how much effort we should commit to this campaign. In my judgement we'd be foolhardy to go to them with just one campaign idea, based on fluoride. I want an alternative campaign, without fluoride, as a back-up. I suggest you aim to appeal to the kids as well as the mums. It should be lively, vigorous and memorable."

"In short, just like every other commercial for every other breakfast cereal," Jill sneered.

"Oh for God's sake snap out of it, Jill, and grow up." Roger dropped all pretence of appeasement, now that she was on the defensive. "They expect us to be clever and different. I know you can do it if you want to, but, make no mistake, it's going to be done, with or without you. Now, do you want some time to think things over, or can you tell me now that you want to stay with it? Or must I ask another writer to take over from you?"

"You're a pompous, chicken-hearted prig, Roger Daniels, and I ought to leave you to stew in your own bile. But I want this success, and I'm damned if I'll walk away now and let you make a mess of it. You'll get your alternative, and it will be bloody brilliant too. But there's one condition. You have to promise me that you'll try very, very hard to sell them on the fluoride idea and the fluoride commercial, as the Agency's preferred approach. Harder than you've ever tried to sell anything before."

"It's a promise. So, we have a deal?"

"We have a deal. Now bugger off and let me do some thinking. That's what they pay us for, remember? And don't think I've forgotten about the pleasure of having a bit of girl-chat with your darling wife, because I haven't."

As Jean Carey had forecast on Sunday afternoon on the banks of the Cherwell, George Thomas and the members of his Union at Strongwheat quickly lost interest in fluoride, once it was confirmed that Strongwheat itself was not to be changed. But the prospect of a significant increase in the volume of production concerned them all directly. Jean had found George sitting in the small office where he ran Engineering Stores, when he was not being active on his Union work. She tried to get him to focus on the potential scale of the increase.

"Of course nothing is definite yet, George," she began, "First of all the Directors have got to approve the investment, and that can't happen for a couple of months yet, say mid-May. As you've heard, the plan is for a second variety of Strongwheat, aimed more at the kids. The target is to increase volumes by fifty percent, that's half as much again as we make now. More jobs, more security, better prospects for promotion."

"And what's the catch?"

"Now George, there's no need for cynicism. The company will likely be investing a lot of money in this, much more than they've ever risked before. There is no catch. It's just that, to enable us to go for this prize, we've got to have a commitment from our people to flexible shift patterns. Sales are bound to be lumpy at first, which makes them very hard to predict. So the numbers employed will have to be increased, and in turn everyone will have to become more flexible in the ways they work."

"How flexible is flexible, exac'ly?"

"Five-day week flexible."

A few years earlier, under Phil Wythe's predecessor, the company had followed a local trend and replaced the traditional five eight-hour day shifts on the factory floor with four shifts of ten hours. After the usual doubts, the system had become very popular with the workers, who found the three-day weekend very appealing. A whole sub-culture had grown up to exploit the long weekend. Camping, caravanning, building a holiday home, commercial horticulture and running a chain of market-stalls were just a few of the activities. Management and staff worked a five-day week still, and there was a certain amount of latent envy of what was seen as the privileged arrangement enjoyed by production workers. George knew that the situation was further complicated by the fact that the majority of the women employed were part-timers. In some cases they were only working part-time out of necessity, because their family commitments would not allow more hours to be put in. Just as often it was a convenient way to get out of the house and earn the money for a new kitchen or that holiday abroad – with earnings kept below the tax-threshold if possible.

George was well aware of the variety of attitudes to the job, and of the problems that changing things would stir up. Of course a bigger workforce would improve his standing, provided he could recruit the additions into the Union. He guessed that management were well aware that the present system was hugely popular, which meant that he was being set up as 'piggy-in-the-middle'.

"*It's a political move,*" he thought gloomily, as he bought a pint of bitter and retreated to the Snug Bar to await the arrival of a few cronies who were joining him that evening for an unofficial Union meeting, "*They're setting me up. She knows I've got to be in favour of expansion and more jobs, and she's hoping I'm going to solve the four-day week problem for them.*"

George's approach was not exactly a text-book consultation of the membership. Rather he was intending to talk to a group of old friends who would understand the problems, and maybe suggest a few solutions.

Maisie Carver arrived first, a large, handsome woman in her late forties, who had successfully brought up four sons, after her husband had been killed in a car crash fifteen years before. She had never remarried, though the boys had never been short of an 'uncle' who could help with the homework or a game of football. Maisie was the forewoman on the packing line, and she came in carrying a large gin and a bitter lemon.

"I've got supper in the oven, George," she said, sipping her gin with an expansive sigh of appreciation, "I hope this isn't going to go on too long."

"Don't you worry, Maisie, he'll wait for you." They clinked glasses in a friendly toast.

The two other members of George's unofficial caucus arrived together – Jeff Wilkes, now Engineering Manager, following the promotion of Phil Wythe to the Board the previous year, and Bill Bowman, Warehouse and Distribution Manager. Strictly speaking, both were part of 'management' now, but both had been Union members since they had joined Strongwheat as apprentices, and George was comfortable with their ability to understand how his people might react.

"Right then. Maisie 'ere is anxious to get away, so let's get started. You all knows about the new product. Jean Carey 'as been doing some figgurin', an' she reckons we've got to be plannin' for an increase in production of fifty percent. Not a straight-line increase she says, which means they don't have a clue really. Anyway, as I sees it, that means fifty or sixty more people altogether. That's going to mean trainin' an' promotion for quite a few, some of the part-timers bein' offered full-time, an' a fair crop of new recruits. So that's extra money for a lot that's already workin', extra jobs, an' the company genrally bein' more secure an' so a better place to work in for all on us."

"Where's the catch then?" asked Maisie.

"That's exactly what I said to Jean Carey. An' the catch is bloody obvious. We can't possibly find that amount of extra production an' still keep the four-day week. It can't be done. An' management knows it."

"Well, I'm not so sure about that," said Jeff Wilkes, "I mean, I've been lookin' at ways to tweak up the Flakin' line, an' I'd bet we could do the same with the Strongwheat line. Or it might be best to 'ave a second line altogether. That would do it."

"Pigs might fly, too," said Bill Bowman, returning with a second round of drinks, "Sorry, Jeff, I didn't hear everything you said, but you've got to be talking of spending millions. To start with, where could you put a second line inside Sceptre Mill? Look, there's an 'undred and sixty eight hours in a week, right? The Strongwheat line runs for thirty eight, say forty-five with a bit of overtime like we've 'ad these past two months. Don't make sense to even think about a second line. George is right, it's the four-day week that's got to go."

Maisie raised her glass in thanks for her second gin, "It's all right for you to talk, Bill, you've got to work the five days anyway. I 'aven't got as many to worry about as I used to, before they brought in the Automatic Packing, but some of my girls 'as other commitments, I know. Could be very awkward to give up their Fridays. I mean, why should they? Money isn't everything."

"But it 'elps," said Bill, "I've got a sign up in my office. It says, '*The only reason for needing money is in case you don't die tomorrow*'. I reckon that sums it up nicely. What do you think, George, will they spring any extra cash? Compensation like, for sacrificin' their Fridays?"

George sighed. The discussion was following exactly the lines he had anticipated. He was being set up, by his own side now, to go back to management and negotiate for a buy-out of the four-day system. Stiffened in advance by a stern briefing from Phil Wythe, Jean had been adamant that no new money was available, "But get your members to think about the extra money from promotion, extra money for part-timers going full-time, extra overtime that's sure to come up."

George knew that the 'pie-in-the-sky' stuff about future prospects would not go down well. On the other hand if he could be seen to be negotiating hard for some extra money up front, it might well be useful as a lever to get more of the workforce to join the Union, in order to add more weight to the negotiating position. He decided to play it very cautiously.

"I wouldn't be too optimistic about extra money up front. You can all remember when the four-day week was first proposed. There was a lot of talk about demandin' more money, and a lot was against it for one reason or another, but Mr. James just pushed it through, and there weren't no more money then."

"I don't think Mr. Dick or Phil Wythe is as 'ard as Mr. James," said Maisie thoughtfully, "I mean, any time they's in the factory they stops by to ask 'ow things is, an' that's somethin' Mr. James never did. Liz Boyd can tell you, she's bin secretary to Mr. James an' to Mr Dick, an' she says Mr. Dick is a real softie to 'andle compared with 'is father."

George was not persuaded. "That may be so. But Mr. James ain't dead yet, not by a long chalk, an' he's still goin' to be in charge with somethin' like this, you mark my words. Getting anythin' extra is not going to be easy."

As so often at their meetings, it was Bill Bowman who suggested a solution. He was gifted with a powerful natural intelligence which might well have taken him to the top of some business, if education and opportunity had come his way early in life. As it was he was happy with his comfortable situation at Strongwheat, but just occasionally enjoyed the chance to demonstrate his insight.

He held out his empty glass to Jeff Wilkes, "I think you should just play it a bit crafty, George. Start by paintin' a picture for them of 'ow much of a sacrifice it'd be to go back now to the five-day week. For instance, I know there's a couple that makes more on their two days at the markets than they does in their four days 'ere. And that's cash, self-employed, an' tell the tax man only what you 'as to. Then you asks for a thumping increase in the hourly rate in compensation, say twenty percent."

"Twenty? They'll never wear that. Mr. James would rather shut the gates than pay that much."

George's rejection of Bill's approach was the more scathing, because of his disappointment that Bill seemed to be no more realistic than Jeff had been.

"I knows that as well as you do. But you've got to make them think it's really serious. There must be best part of an 'undred that are on four days or are part-time tied to four days. Management pushed them into it, an' there's got to be a price to get them off it. Now, where was I? Oh yes, we'd got you fightin' real 'ard for us, right George? As soon as they're convinced it's serious, you can get down to a proper negotiation. I wouldn't be surprised if you needed an overtime ban or somethin' to convince 'em of just 'ow serious this is, an' that you've got the shopfloor solidly be'ind you. Get the idea?"

George nodded, without any great enthusiasm. His was essentially a simple straightforward nature, and the wiles of the professional negotiator did not come easily. "So, what sort of deal do you think they'll go for?"

Surprisingly, the answer did not come from Bill Bowman, but from Maisie, who had been listening closely. "Cash. They'll pay one-off cash, a lump-sum payment of some kind to buy out the four-day week. Or it could be an extra week's 'oliday with pay. That'd do it, cash on the table and an extra week's paid 'oliday as well. Let's face it, those of us with 'alf a brain always knew this four-day week lark was too good to last."

There was silence around the little bar, as the other three sipped their drinks. Trust Maisie to hit the nail on the head! And her proposal carried the more weight, as she was the only one amongst them who actually had the four-day week to give up.

"Well, if that's all then, I'd like you gentlemen to excuse me. I've got my dinner to see to. Thanks for the drinks."

Maisie left to a chorus of 'Cheers, love' and the meeting broke up a few minutes later. George knew his wife was out at Bingo with her sister, so his dinner would keep warm in the oven for a few minutes longer. He settled down with another pint and the Birmingham evening paper. He made a mental note to call his Area Secretary in the morning, and turned hopefully to the racing results.

Vince O'Hanlon wanted to be a player. Not a football or baseball player, but a player in the big league of money and power. At thirty-five, he was only too aware that many of his contemporaries on the Harvard MBA course were now living it up in San Francisco having floated their Internet company, and were already on their way to their first billion. Of course some had come messily unstuck, but it was the winners that he remembered. Whilst he was stuck in this antique food business called American Cereal Products, twenty miles away from even that smidgeon of civilisation he had managed to dig up in Chicago. As compensation, he had a salary of $250,000, and the prospect of doubling that with bonus and stock options – if he stayed in favour. Which was OK for a first job following the self-financed twelve-month MBA course he had taken after ten hard years working as a researcher for some of New York's best wheeler-dealers. But Vince's appetite for the grand style had been whetted by his trip to Europe. That English merchant bank, for instance, De Boissy, with their fancy office in an old house in London's Mayfair – that was the way to live! Quietly impressive, without becoming too vulgar or ostentatious. These Mid-Westerners thought that if you weren't shouting about how rich you were, you must be poor. Vince wanted to live amongst people who could recognise your worth, without having it branded on your rump.

Early in March he had just finished a detailed report for his boss, Ben Camina, and the company Chairman, Lloyd Teller, confirming the outcome of the long and tortuous negotiation he had just completed for the acquisition in England he was recommending, Strongwheat plc. It was a good prospect – "*Let's be totally frank, it's the only really worthwhile prospect I've dug up in the whole year.*" It was not going to come cheap, but that was not necessarily a disadvantage. Corporations like ACP tended to the view that, if something seemed to good to be true, it probably was just that. He wondered idly if this deal might throw some real dough in his personal direction. Not just the hundred thou' or so he might look forward to as his year-end bonus, but real money, seven-figure money. Who could be the provider? Those smart people at De Boissy were going to get ten, maybe even twenty million dollars for their twenty percent. Plus a handsome finder's fee from ACP, which had yet to be negotiated. Could there be an angle there for himself? The latest e-mail from Alex Hampshire had expanded at length on the plan they had at Strongwheat to push up volumes by fifty percent with a new product. The projected profit numbers looked very tasty! He wondered if the product would find a place in the US – what a prospect that would be! Would one of ACP's competitors maybe pay more? A premium to keep ACP out of Europe? On the other hand, they might be taking some real risks with that clever idea of adding fluoride . . . the papers were always carrying 'scientific' stories about the possible dangers from modern food-additives. Perhaps the reason it hadn't been done already was because it was just too smart? Too dangerous? Vince recalled a friend he had made during his Harvard year, who was now something big in the Government's Food and Drug Agency. The FDA was responsible. among other things, for testing and licensing everything that went on the shelf. Impulsively, he found the number in his little book and picked up the telephone.

"Is that Gerry Masters? Gerry, Hi! It's Vince, Vince O'Hanlon. How'ya doin'? Me, I'm doin' just fine, working in a great food business here, ACP, I guess you know us? Gerry, I'd like at this time to ask for your help on an informal basis, just some research, really. Do you know what's going on at the moment in the field of fluoride? You know, fluoride as an additive to water or toothpaste. Is it totally safe? Right, right, then can you point me in the direction of the top FDA expert? I'll owe you one."

Chapter Twelve

It was just after nine on a crisp sunny Saturday morning towards the end of March when Jean Carey paid off her taxi and rang the doorbell of John Savage's London flat, near the Covent Garden Opera House. The door opened as though he had been waiting behind it.

"Good morning, my man. Is this hotel open for business?"

John took her small suitcase and ushered her up the stairs ahead of himself. "We are extremely selective about our clientele, modom. Do you come with a personal recommendation, from our owner, perhaps?"

Jean was wearing a full-skirted white cotton dress, cinched in with a thin blue leather belt that accentuated her slim waist, and she carried a navy blue worsted topcoat. John's flat was above a dusty, but highly-respected bookstore that specialised in military history. His street-level front door opened onto a steep and narrow staircase, expensively carpeted. At the top of the stairs she stepped through an open door straight into an airy, handsome living room, with a wide bay window at the front and another at the rear, so that the room was flooded with light. The pale Berber carpet that covered the floor throughout was complemented by the big soft settee and armchair, arranged each side of a Victorian fireplace and upholstered in fawn velvet. There was a small dining table and two chairs in the rear bay. Jean formed a quick impression of a comfortable, uncluttered room. The only decoration was the floor-to-ceiling bookshelves, and five rather nice water-colour seascapes, which looked like eighteenth-century originals.

"It's a beautiful room, John. How do you keep it so neat? Is that coffee I can smell?"

John did not reveal that he had been playing housekeeper since seven, taking particular care to ensure that there were no embarrassing 'souvenirs' under the beds or tucked down the sides of cushions. "It's just a bachelor pied-a-terre really. I'm away a lot, especially at weekends, so it doesn't get used that much. Coffee's just about ready. Make yourself at home. I'll just put your case in the spare room here, then I'll bring in the tray."

When he returned from the kitchen he saw Jean standing beside a bookcase by the east window, with the morning sunlight haloing her profile and the dark mass of her hair, which she wore loose but neatly bobbed. Her face was in deep shadow as she leafed through Kissinger's 'White House Years'. *If she can excite me this much, this early in the morning, it must be love, or something equally serious.*

"I enjoyed the Kissinger," he said as he poured the coffee, "You can learn a lot about negotiating from him, he's a real master. Would you like to borrow it?"

Jean shook her head, "It's the sort of book to enjoy when you've got two weeks on a Greek island to look forward to. I've been puzzling though over the arrangement, if you can call it that, of your books. You don't strike me as a random sort of man, but you've got Graham Green here next to 'Zulu', and Frederick Forsyth next to 'Interim Management'. Is there a Zen logic to it?"

John grinned at her happily as they sat down to large cups of strong black coffee. "There's a logic to it. You just have to look."

Jean sipped her coffee and gazed at the serried ranks of books, punctuated with a few nice pieces of porcelain – Meissen? Bow?

"Oh yes, yes of course. They make a design. Blocks of colour."

"That's it. I've just put together books of roughly the same size and colour, once I've finished reading them. So they help to decorate the room. And it's always a bit of fun to look for something I'm sure I've got, but can't remember where. That way I'm always coming across something I've forgotten I had . . . more coffee?"

Jean finished hers with a gulp. "No, no thanks, that was a real life-saver, but now I'd just like to hang up my stuff and be getting along to Oxford Street."

She gratefully accepted his offer of a lift to Oxford Circus, and he took the opportunity to kiss her, gently but proprietarily before she got out. "Don't wear yourself out, I've got seats at the English National Opera for tonight. I'll meet you for tea at four o'clock at the Tea Centre, Lower Regent Street. Have a great day!"

John had endured a heavy evening the night before, giving a celebration dinner to his client from Hamburg and the Chairman of a Newcastle-upon-Tyne manufacturer of speciality chemicals who had that day agreed on a merger, with De Boissy as the lead advisers. Getting up by seven had been a true test of his commitment, so his first thought after dropping Jean off was to get back to bed.

He fell asleep immediately, and was only awakened at two-thirty by the sun falling full on his face through the casually pulled curtains. He wondered if it might be hubris – or bad luck – to change his sheets? He decided to do it anyway. He guessed that Jean would probably be late getting to the Tea Centre, but decided to leave plenty of time in case it was hard to find a place to park. *Lord, he was as nervous as a teenager on a first date!*

As luck would have it, he found a parking meter in the first place he looked, in Saville Row, which left him with half an hour to kill before four o'clock. It was now a brilliant Spring afternoon, and he decided a brisk walk would help to blow away the last of the night's cobwebs. Not for the first time, he noticed the number of foreign faces that thronged London's West End. Sometimes it seemed that everyone he could see was a tourist. Fortunately he was dressed casually himself in fawn slacks and a brown lightweight polo-neck, so he was able to mingle unobtrusively with the crowds, and was not called upon to rack his brains to recall the quickest way to the Abbey or the Tower of London. He dodged the traffic across Piccadilly Circus, and walked down to the bottom of Lower Regent Street and into Pall Mall. On the Duke of York Steps he stopped to admire the panorama, from Admiralty Arch on his left across the Mall and St. James' Park and round to Buckingham Palace. *Visitors to London got good value on a day like this. That's if they're able to stand still long enough to let it soak into them.*

He knew he had some serious thinking still to do about Jean. Just those few minutes together that morning had been enough to restart that bumping excitement inside. So, in a way, that was the easy decision – he wanted her, he would pursue her with all the skill and persistence he could assemble, and some fate would decide the outcome. That was simple enough, and he felt instinctively that Jean was travelling in the same general direction. Which left unresolved a nagging uncertainty. What if they got together, and it didn't work out . . . as it had not worked out with his ex-wife, Isabel? Not necessarily the physical thing, but just not working out – how could he avoid hurting Jean, perhaps really seriously? And there was the other problem getting closer now with Alex starting to knit together his plan to sell Strongwheat to ACP. Of course John could swear he had no role in the negotiations, and he would be able to maintain an acceptable fiction of ignorance, so that his position on the Board should not be compromised. But he knew already that Jean was too perceptive to be deceived by polite fictions. For her it would be up close and personal, and she would judge him for what he was, an informer for De Boissy. Worse still, her very vulnerability might lead her instinctively to assume the worst, and to believe that he had set out deliberately to make himself agreeable to her, as part of the De Boissy master-plan. So he had to say something that weekend, because his very soul rebelled at the thought of the scorn she would feel for him if he were caught out apparently in a deception. But how to say what had to be said?

It was just four o'clock when he got to the Ceylon Tea Centre, and he was surprised to see her already sitting at a window table. "Hi there," he said, basking in the warm glow of her smile of welcome, "I'd expected to have to wait another hour for you."

"I remembered your warning about not wearing myself out. And I've spent more than I planned to anyway. There is a well-known Law of Shopping for us wage-slaves. It says, 'If you really want it, you can't afford it'."

"I see you managed to afford one or two things," he said, glancing at the pile of handsome carrier-bags beside her seat, "Bet you're glad you've got this porter to give you a hand. Shall we get some of their tea? I'm told Nuwara Eliya is the smart thing to order."

As they returned to the flat Jean wondered why it was she felt so comfortable with this man – almost like an old married couple. She suppressed the thought. Looking beyond the moment was a guarantee of future pain. But it was lovely to be pampered, as John insisted she relax in the armchair while he produced some more tea, and apologised that the shortbread was slightly aged.

"I don't often have anyone here for tea," he said, with absolute truth but less than total frankness.

"So what's the plan for this evening?"

"Simple enough. I've got tickets for 'Don Giovanni' at the Coliseum in St Martin's Lane. That starts early, at seven, so we'll eat afterwards. It's just after five now. We can walk there comfortably in ten minutes, so you've an hour and a half to relax, take a bath, dress, put your hair up or whatever."

It was apparent that, secure in the familiar environment of his flat, John was revealing another side to his personality – the domesticated, friendly, capable organiser – *Mr. Ideal Husband? Stop It! How real was this John Savage? Did that matter?* She refocused her thoughts firmly. "Right then. I'll have a quick bath first, then I'll get my head down for a nap. Bang on the door at six, please?"

John stretched out a hand to help her uncoil from the depths of the armchair, and in a moment he was kissing her, a long, thunderous exploring kiss that imprinted their bodies on one another, and left her breathless and trembling. She took a pace back, lifted a nervous hand to push back her dark hair from her forehead, and smiled sweetly.

"That was nice. Bath now. Don't forget please, wake me at six."

As Jean walked calmly from the living room, John abstractedly collected the cups and carried the tray into the kitchen. *This was a fine romance! When he was passive and domestic she was warm, friendly and encouraging. But when he made any kind of positive advance she immediately became the sophisticated lady. 'That was nice'! She had spoken so coolly, like an aunt thanking a small boy for a kiss! She was certainly bright, she was a psychology graduate for God's sake, divorced and definitely no bimbo. Is she playing a game? Every instinct tells me she's as honest and straightforward as anyone could be. There's a padlock somewhere. I just hope she hasn't thrown away the damn key.*

Promptly at six John was knocking at her bedroom door. Jean had been dozing on the big soft bed with only a bathrobe for covering, and she sat up in momentary alarm that he might walk in. But she need not have worried – whilst he was bathing and shaving, John had made a decision about the evening. He had concluded that the right tactic was to relax the sexual pressure, enjoy her company, and wait for her to provide some sign that she wanted him to move forward.

He had dressed in a mohair dark blue suit with a faint pin-stripe, a white shirt and a plain red tie. Usually his weekend style was less formal, but he guessed that Jean would be wearing something special for an evening at the opera, and wanted to be discreetly supportive. He was not disappointed.

He was reading the Evening Standard, and looked up as the room seemed suddenly to fill with her perfume and her presence. She whirled her skirts and made a deep curtsey.

"There, sir. Will I do?"

She rose to stand before him. She wore a long, tailored jacket in a rich saffron satin, and a billowing skirt to match. She had pinned her dark hair up tightly, with a small sparkling comb on one side. He was reminded irresistibly of the head of Queen Nefertiti, consort of Akhenaton. The severity of the style was immediately denied by her soft, dark eyes, a loose string of pearls in the deep bare neckline, and the widely-set lapels of the jacket that gave emphasis to the delicate curves of the cleavage.

John could only think of how much he wanted simply to possess this woman. "You look absolutely gorgeous. I think you are the most beautiful, exciting woman I have ever met. God, that sounds so trite. But you knock all the clever words out of my head."

And Jean, whose wounded soul longed perversely to be admired for her looks as well as her brains, actually managed a blush of sheer pleasure and exhilaration.

"Come on then, let's go and flaunt it down St. Martin's Lane, and see if there's some competition we can make miserable."

In the few minutes it took for them to walk from the flat to the Coliseum, John was delighted to have his judgement confirmed every few yards by the envious eyes, both male and female, that turned to follow their progress. At the theatre the foyer was already thronged with opera-goers. The English National Opera did not pretend to be as grand as the Covent Garden Opera, but it was a Saturday night, and there was plenty of competition for Jean. In John's eyes none of them came even near her for sheer quality that evening. For her part, Jean simply abandoned herself to the romance of an evening at the opera. From their seats in the red plush stalls the gilded and decorated tiers and boxes rose in layers on three sides, giving the theatre a truly Edwardian sense of pomp and occasion. She knew the music from recordings, but the sumptuous sets and costumes, the immediacy of the music, and the vibrant realism of the acting added a new dimension of meaning to the drama. John had chosen the Mozart more because he thought it would impress and delight Jean than because he was a great fan of opera itself. But that evening he too found himself swept up by the power of the music, and by the excitement and pleasure that Jean communicated.

Afterwards they had only to walk a few yards up St. Martin's Lane to find 'Il Nettuno', an Italian Restaurant where John was a well-known customer.

"Good evening Mr. Savage, sir. I have kept a quiet table for you, where you may enjoy your dinner, I hope."

'Il Nettuno' is below street level, and has live music for dancing on Saturday nights. Jean had been very quiet since the curtain came down after the last encores, and John had not interrupted the mood. After they had ordered dinner, she pecked his cheek affectionately.

"Thank you for a wonderful evening. I know it's not over yet, but I can't begin to tell you how much I've enjoyed it already."

John guessed that there might be something quite significant behind the gesture of the little kiss, and the simple words of appreciation. Perhaps she was saying that the barriers were coming down, and handing him some sort of initiative? Rather than respond at once he turned instinctively to action.

"Would you like to dance? They'll hold our first course until we sit down."

Vince O'Hanlon closed the door of his office, which was next to Ben Camina's and only slightly smaller. He had been exceptionally active the night before, having recently made the acquaintance of a tall, blonde Texan girl from Austin. Anna was working for a Chicago stockbroker, managing their on-line Internet service. She was bright, had an amusingly acid turn of phrase, and was very presentable. But she also worked out with weights, and swam half a mile before going to the office each morning, and seemed to value making love as a useful form of horizontal jogging. Vince was not sure if he was going to be able to stand the pace. He drank deeply from his large mug of strong black coffee, and tried to concentrate on writing down his action plan for the Strongwheat deal:

1. Make Ben and Lloyd nervous about the price to be paid. Get them to fix a maximum. Get them pissed off and ready to bale out.

2. Line up an alternative buyer. Preferably more than one.

3. Get a watertight commission arrangement for my help.

4. Ensure that Alex Hampshire will support, or at least not oppose the switch.

5. Destabilise the ACP/Strongwheat deal. Fluoride?

He tore the sheet from his pad, and folded it carefully into his wallet. Then he tore off the blank sheet underneath and carefully shredded it into his waste-basket. He'd need to sleep on the problem of how to calculate the best order to roll out these elements. That's if he could get some sleep tonight! Why had he promised to join Anna and a couple of her friends for ice-skating that evening? He decided to duck out, and called Anna, to find that she was out for a business lunch. He remembered she'd said something about a bank as a potential big new advertiser for their web-site.

"May I leave a message for her, please? It's Mr. O Hanlon. I think I may be coming down with some bug, and I'm going home now to bed. I'll call her, hopefully in a day or two."

The 'Nettuno's' little dance floor was two steps down from their table, and was already crowded. Fortunately the music was relaxed and undemanding, a sophisticated night-club trio of piano, rhythm and alto sax. There being no practical alternative, Jean enjoyed dancing very close, allowing the pressure of John's hand and body to direct her around the other couples.

"It's been ages," she breathed, as the trio came to a suitably enigmatic conclusion, and they came apart to join in the ripple of applause. Over dinner they drank a bottle of Verdiccio – fresh, fragrant and cold on the palate as the enjoyed the house special for the evening – a hearty rib-sticking lasagne and a simple grilled sea-bass with salad. When the laden sweet-trolley arrived John admitted defeat, but watched enviously as she tucked into pears in red wine with clotted Devon cream.

"You'll get fat," he prophesied, proud of his own display of willpower.

"No I won't. I'm trotting around the factory all day long, while you spend the week chained to a desk or slumped in an aeroplane. That's when you're not forcing down another expense-account lunch."

Over coffee he judged the moment was right for some confession. "I wonder, Jean, how much you know about De Boissy and the sort of things we do? Don't worry, I'm not going to talk shop tonight, at least not for long, but I do want to ask your advice about something." He could see that he had her full attention, and squeezed her hand gently, "This has to be totally confidential – just between us two."

He explained succinctly the story of De Boissy's investment in Strongwheat, "And now we've had this approach from ACP, which is a pretty large American food business. They'd like to buy Strongwheat, and use it as their toehold for a programme of investment in Europe." He paused, waiting for Jean to protest.

"But that's marvellous."

John blinked. "Do you really think so? What about the loss of independence, and the intimacy of a small company? I thought you'd tried a big company, and decided you preferred a small one?"

"Well, yes, I do. At least, I like this small company. But I couldn't be so selfish as to want to keep it small, not if there's a nice American sugar-daddy that wants to make us big. Besides, I'm good at my job, so they'll need me. I might even get promoted, or sent to America to learn how they do things there."

She saw the mingled relief and uncertainty on his face, and asked, "Is it definite? Or just one of those business propositions?"

"The Americans are very serious, not at all casual. Of course it all depends on what James and Dick Routledge want to do."

"They'll say 'Yes'. Eventually."

"How can you be so sure?"

"Because you and your Alex Hampshire will find out what they want more than their independence, and offer it to them in exchange for their company."

"I suppose you've no idea what that could be?"

"I can guess. Money, of course. Power. Security. Prestige, most likely. You'll find it."

Whilst Jean was talking, almost to herself, John caught the eye of the wine-waiter. "Fancy some champagne to see us through some more dancing?"

"Lovely."

As they clasped one another closely on the small dance floor, John reflected that he had once again totally failed to anticipate her reactions correctly. He kissed her ear softly as they moved, and was rewarded with a tightening of her hand on his shoulder. They turned and turned around the floor, and it was difficult to know where his body ended and hers began.

They walked back to Covent Garden at one a.m. like a couple of teenagers, his arm locked tightly around her waist so that he could feel the soft pressure of her breast on his wrist. He led the way upstairs into the living room, now dimly lit through the half-closed curtains from the street lamps outside. Jean looked at John quizzically, his face dark in the shadows. The saffron satin seemed to glow in the darkness. He leaned back against the door as it closed, and said nothing.

"Damn you, John Savage", she murmured, and stepping forward put her hands up to his cheeks and kissed him, gently at first, then opening her lips in a fiercer pressure as she tightened her arms around his neck. She trembled a little as she felt him fumble with the buttons of her long jacket, and she gave a small gasp as he found that she was naked beneath it. She felt a surge of desire breaking through as his left hand caressed her shoulders, and pressed against the small of her back, and his right cupped her full rounded breast. He broke away from her lips to kiss the hollow of her neck, and then the hardening nipple.

"Softly, softly, John. It's been such a long time."

Chapter Thirteen

On March 20th Vince O'Hanlon finished, with a sigh of relief, a long telephone conversation with Mike Mantara. Mike was a colleague of Vince's friend at the FDA, Gerry Masters, and a man who seemed to know everything anyone could possibly want to know about fluoride. Out of habit Vince had taken copious notes as Mike talked, and now he sat back to browse through them. Mike said that there had been precious few problems that could be attributed with any scientific credibility to the fluoridation of the water supplies, and there had been significant gains in the reduction of dental caries. However governments world-wide were currently reluctant to extend the process, largely to avoid being pilloried by one sect or other of the environmental lobby – 'I guess it's seen as anti-libertarian'. Vince had been as frank as he dared, and Mike was quite taken with the possibility of fluoride being added to a children's food product. 'I could see that catching on, like fluoride in toothpaste, better perhaps'. He could think of no reason why it had not been tried in the States. There were some current concerns about the possible side-effects of food additives in combinations, but fluoride had not come up in that context. No obvious prospect there . . .

He pulled out his copy of the document he had put together for the ACP Board at the end of February, after the long negotiations with Alex Hampshire. Vince was comfortable with the concept of 'stretch'. This is roughly defined as the spread between the value of a company, looked at objectively as an investment comparable with other investments, and the price the owner was prepared to accept. In all honesty, it had to be admitted that Alex had tried to extend the 'stretch' in the case of Strongwheat to a point where it might be said to be at the outer reaches of the most elastic commercial logic. The Board had bought into his concept – well, Alex Hampshire's concept to be exact – that payment should be in two sections. There should be a reasonable lump sum up front, and then a further payment, or series of payments, dependent on results over the following three years. Alex had spent most of the month of February pushing and pushing against the limits that Vince tried to impose, until there was no more to be got.

Looked at as a simple investment, Vince had judged the present value of Strongwheat to be of the order of $20,000,000. Alex was asking ACP to take his estimate of the profits three years out, (assuming the new product was a success), to consider the extra value of the business as an entry-point into the EU, and then to add another premium because it was the only breakfast-cereal business in Europe that was likely to become available – all the rest being locked up inside multi-national competitors. The result of all this salesman's jiggery-pokery was an asking price that could total $100,000,000! Of course a large chunk would be contingent on the actual results, but would the Board really go along with such an open-ended commitment? Did he want them to? Suppose he could get the Strongwheat people and Alex lined up to do the deal, and then turn off ACP somehow and immediately come in with an alternative buyer? A buyer who would be grateful enough to Vince to give him in return the kind of entry-stake he wanted to become a player in his own right. He estimated he needed a stake of two million minimum to get off the ground, three would be better. And especially, indeed essentially he needed a clean reputation, to allow the usual leveraging techniques with bank money to become available to him. Not too much to look for, peanuts really, in the context of a deal this size. Dangerous waters though, full of sharks and shoals . . . he began to thumb through his little book of contacts.

* * *

Jean Carey was finding it difficult to concentrate on her calculations of the likely cost of alternative shift-patterns, because John Savage kept intruding into her thoughts. He had made love to her on Saturday night in London with delightful, concentrated enthusiasm, and impressive stamina, and on Sunday morning he had brought coffee and hot buttered toast for them to enjoy in bed together like an old married couple. She had finally plucked up courage to ask about his wife.

"Ex-wife," he corrected. "We've been divorced now for almost ten years. In fact it only lasted six months."

"John, if it's still painful, you don't have to say anything. I know it's over, and it's not really any of my business."

"But it is. Or at least, I'd like it to be. I want you to know everything there is to know about me, warts and all. Isabel came from a very good family, big farmers and landowners in Suffolk from way back. Her father was a private client of my father from way back also – same school, you know how it goes – I think I told you my father is a stockbroker? I went down with the old man to Suffolk one weekend. He was working on setting up a trust arrangement for Isabel's father, so they wouldn't be wiped out by inheritance tax, and I was helping with some informal advice on investment selection. I met Isabel at lunch, and that was it. 'Love at first sight', and all that sort of thing. She seemed to feel the same way, and we had a slap-up wedding the following year. Even had her engagement picture in 'Country Life', complete with the family pearls".

It was clear that there was still some pain in the recollection. Jean kissed his forehead, and lay down quietly beside him. After a minute he continued. "Didn't work out, didn't work out at all. The physical side, she just didn't want it. Didn't like it. Of course we'd had a bit of a kiss and cuddle, but she'd been very strictly brought up, convent-school in the country somewhere. Virgo-bloody-intacta when she walked up the aisle, and only technically different when we split up. Her father came on a bit heavy with me, said I must be an inconsiderate brute and all that. I mean, I was quite young and inexperienced, and she could have made anything she wanted of me."

There was another long pause. "Since then, I've kept it light. No serious entanglements, nothing that lasted longer than a few weeks. Of course the word went around, 'There must be something wrong with John Savage if darling Isabel could only stick him for six months'. But gradually other girls found out that there was nothing wrong with dear old John. I was quite pleased to find that out too."

He slid down the bed, and turned to her for a long kiss, which seemed to Jean to be a cue for her to offer more reassurance, and that had occupied another blissful hour. He really was a very satisfying lover. Not tremendously skilful perhaps – Jean guessed that his liaisons since the divorce had probably been with a series of quite young girls – but he offered a total absorption that was irresistibly flattering.

Afterwards he got 'Bessie' from the garage, and they had lingered over lunch at a pub in Aston Clinton. She had not allowed him to drive her back to Lynchester, foreseeing the impossibility of sending him away this time, so he had put her on a train at Watford.

"I'll call you this evening, just to be sure you got home safely."

Jean still felt out of her depth with John Savage. Intellectually, there wasn't much in it. Magdalen College, Oxford was a good deal grander than her University of Exeter, but she guessed that a stockbroker father who could afford to send him to Eton would account for that difference. But their backgrounds were so far apart that they might have been born in different continents. Her father had just retired after thirty years as branch and for the last seven years area manager of a Building Society. When her marriage had come unglued, her family had rallied round with support and sympathy, but she knew that in private they thought she was partly to blame, because she had postponed having children. The move from Rugby to Lynchester, though no great distance in terms of miles, had been important psychologically for Jean. It had represented a physical break from her family, and more importantly a move to an environment where, being alone, she had been forced to make a new life for herself. And simple economics had required her to commit herself afresh to building a career, and not just having a job that contributed to the family income.

And now this man had elbowed his way in, and disrupted all the quiet patterns she had so carefully built up around her life. A man who didn't fit into any pigeonhole she was familiar with. He reminded her of the actor, James Fox, with his casual elegance, and a certain ruthless style about him. Perhaps that was why it was so difficult to pin him down, because he was always playing some role? A human chameleon? At that first lunch in the boardroom, he had been the perfect pin-striped City gent, doing his best not to appear condescending. Then at Stratford he was a warm, intelligent companion for a theatre and dinner evening. For the day at Oxford he had become a light-hearted teenager. And this latest weekend in London? Was he again playing a part? Or was he just a man falling in love, really in love, for the first time in his life?

Objective analysis of this relationship is going to get you precisely nowhere, Jean Carey. You've fallen for this man, and no ifs or buts. It's like whooshing down the helter-skelter – trying to get off now would be extremely painful, if not downright impossible.

She smiled ruefully at the perverseness of her own mind. Most girls would be delighted to have a relationship with a man like John Savage, no matter what the terms. And here she was worrying, because she might no longer be in control?

"*Now, if we double-shift the four-day week, but only half a crew on the second shift, how many auxiliaries do we need? What do Health and Safety Regulations require? When will he call again . . .?*"

Alex Hampshire dropped his old-fashioned telephone back into its elegantly enamelled cradle, and sat back with his fingers laced behind his head. One of the things he most enjoyed about running De Boissy was the cut and thrust of negotiating a good deal, and 'this dim little Strongwheat business', as he had once labelled it, was turning out to provide surprisingly good entertainment. The call had been from Vince O'Hanlon at American Cereal Products. Alex looked through his notes, and wondered if there might be advantage in having a recording arrangement for such calls.

O'Hanlon had begun by being quite conspiratorial, and had asked Alex for 'an absolute guarantee of confidentiality – what I have to say is for your ears only, Alex'. Intrigued, Alex had given the promise, reasoning that, if it became necessary to break it, O'Hanlon would be in no position to impose penalties. It appeared that O'Hanlon had established a connection with 'another multi-national who already have a business in the UK'. That narrowed the field considerably, but not by enough to make speculation worthwhile.

'He feared that his masters were going to jib at the asking price, and had been looking around on Alex's behalf to find an alternative buyer. Would De Boissy go along and support such a move?'

'Would we pay O'Hanlon commission on the sale of our 20% stake? If so, what rate was fair?'

Alex wondered briefly if such activities were normal for an employed VP of an American corporation – he was certain the English ones he knew would take an extremely dim view – but decided that it was no business of De Boissy to enquire. On the other hand, V.O'H had gone a long way out on a very thin branch, and in effect had put his reputation, if not his very freedom into Alex's hands. He must believe that he was playing for big stakes . . .

Alex had undertaken 'to consider the position fairly and sympathetically, and get back within a couple of days.' He considered the possibility that the call might be a piece of play-acting, a thinly disguised threat to get Alex to drop his asking price in order not to lose ACP as a buyer. Possible, but not very likely. Alex thought that, on the whole, he would prefer that De Boissy maintained the connection with ACP if possible. They were much more likely to have a long-term use for his services than a multi-national already established in the UK. So was there any truth at all in the suggestion that ACP might not accept the price? Alex recalled his own words at the conclusion of their negotiations, 'I would suggest that you need to be thinking of a total cost somewhere in the region of $100,000,000, based on the assumption that they do achieve the growth in profits forecast for the next three years.' That was indicative, but not an absolute demand. It left enough room for negotiation, surely? It seemed therefore to follow that O'Hanlon was being economical with the truth in some way. What game was he playing?

Vince O'Hanlon leaned back in his seat at the Chicago Symphony and let the Mendlesohnn Violin Concerto wash over him like a soothing balm. He sneaked a look at Anna beside him. The concert had been her idea, and she seemed to be totally absorbed. *Funny that, in the beginning I'd taken her to be a kind of female jock with a gift for arithmetic, but there was more going on inside that pretty head than you might think. Theatre, ballet, music, books, she had made me feel that my horizons were badly in need of widening. I've put in a lot of years of grinding work to get to this point, where I can almost smell some serious money.*

Just one more good push, and I'd be able to do something about my own education in the finer things of life. And she's calmed down a bit on the sex front, too. All in all, this was a girl a man could invest a lot of time in, and be confident of a good return. And her body is truly sensational.

That Alex Hampshire fellow at De Boissy had been cautious yesterday, but he was interested in the prospect of some 'action'. Could he be trusted? Definitely not. But he would keep his mouth shut until he could see which way the cat was going to jump. And by then the deal would be in the bag. Next step is to find the right deal, and then to wind Lloyd and Ben up a little . . .

Chapter Fourteen

As the Tornado moved off from the apron and taxied around the perimeter, it was traditional to keep the cockpit roof open, for a last breath of fresh air before the take-off. Even with the headset and bonedome the roar and whistle of the twin Rolls-Royce engines was deafening. Then came the staccato clearance from the control tower, the roof was slammed shut and the throttles were opened. The kick of acceleration in the spine was indescribably exhilarating as the fighter-bomber was hurled down the runway and lifted off up, up, up into the air. A glimpse of the tidy countryside of North Germany far below, then a furry darkness enveloped them as they thrust upwards through ten thousand feet of cloud. At last came the brilliant moment as they burst into the glorious glare of the sunshine, and were looking down onto the billowing acres of white cloud tops. In sheer joy of living the Tornado was eased through a huge, climbing barrel-roll, and continued climbing, climbing . . .

Dick Routledge wasn't really asleep. He had sailed the hotel's 'Enterprise' dinghy into The Bag, at the northern end of Salcombe harbour, then dropped the sails, splashed an anchor over the side, and just leaned back in the warm sunshine of early May to watch the white cumulus drift overhead, changing shape and shrinking as it moved inland towards Dartmoor. He missed his flying. Of course his last posting before the Air Ministry as

Station Admin. Officer had been strictly a ground job. Five years ago the Doc had been depressingly firm, "I'm very sorry, Squadron Leader, we've done everything we can for that knee, but the consultant's of the opinion that it's not going to get any better than it is now. Frankly, it might get worse. What are you, thirty six now? That's it for flying as far as you are concerned, except as a passenger."

At the time it felt as though he had been sentenced to death, but the pain receded gradually. Rosemary had helped, in fact she had been wonderful in getting him to snap out of his black moods, "You're a great baby," she'd said affectionately. "You're just cross because you can't play with your toys any more. But you'd have had to give them up in a few more years anyway, so what have you really lost?"

Although Rosemary had herself been an R.A.F. officer until they had decided to get married, Dick found it very hard to explain to her what he had lost – indeed he found it hard to explain to himself. He asked her once to imagine she had just found she couldn't have children. The feeling of lost potency was at least as great for himself. She tried not to seem to be denying his feelings, but instead put herself out to make up for the loss. She became more loving, more appreciative, more sympathetic. She pushed him to go well beyond his routine duties to make an exceptional success of the Station's functions and entertainments, and he discovered he had a natural flair for leading teams and getting people to enjoy working with him. And she encouraged him to invest hours in getting to know his young sons.

In a way, the summons to his father's bedside had been a real blessing. When he had been a teenager, twenty-odd years before, he had learned from his mother something of the barely repressed resentment his father had felt at being forced to go into the family business, when his ambition was to become a lawyer, so it had been natural for Dick to seek an escape also, to the R.A.F. College at Cranwell, and his father had not opposed him then. Now he was pleased, as Rosemary was, that he had been able to escape again, from the R.A.F. into the excitement of learning to make Strongwheat go better than it had ever gone before – and into something he found deeply satisfying, being responsible for the leadership of the biggest employer in Lynchester, and for the well-being of over two hundred people and their families.

Suddenly he felt the boat tip, and then right itself, and then tip again. Strange, there was only a light breeze, and those small ripples didn't look sufficient to tip his boat . . . Oh Lord, the tide! The Enterprise drew only a few inches with the centreboard raised, but the tide was running out fast now, and in five minutes he would be stuck on the mud, a hundred yards from the shore. With a frantic lunge Dick heaved in the anchor, now black and smelly, and used a paddle desperately to propel the dinghy into deeper water, where he could raise the sails again. Thankful to have been spared embarrassment, he sheeted in the mainsail and jib for a long tack down Salcombe Harbour towards the Marine Hotel, which overhung the water on his right like a stranded liner. On his left the East Portlemouth shore was largely undeveloped, with steep rolling green fields and a sprinkling of summer villas. On the right Salcombe Town cascaded down its own hillside in a profusion of shapes and colours, Devon's nearest approximation to a Riviera fishing port. After four blissful days, and some fortunate weather, Dick decided he liked Salcombe very much, and that Rosemary had been absolutely right to make him take this holiday. He wondered, not for the first time, if the preparations for next week's Board Meeting were going smoothly, especially the new product. He had still not heard any results from the vital consumer research. Then, again not for the first time, he decided he had every reason to trust his team. '*My team*'. *I like the sound of that!*

Deftly he brought the dinghy up into wind, and leant over the side to pick up the mooring, then waved to call the hotel launch. The sun was dropping low behind the craggy pinnacles of Bolt Head at the mouth of the harbour – just time for a drink with Rosemary and a bath before dinner.

When Dick let himself into their second-floor room, the curtains had been drawn cutting out the handsome view down the estuary, and he could hear water running out in the bathroom. 'Good, Rosemary's getting ready for dinner', he thought. He was peeling off his comfortable old sailing shorts and shirt when she came into the room, naked herself except for a shower-cap and a big fluffy towel wrapped around her. She looked relaxed and happy as she peeled off the shower-cap, and let her auburn hair tumble around her shoulders, which were now showing a pleasing tan.

"How was the sailing?"

"Blissful. Just enough wind to move the boat, not enough to make it too exciting."

She sat casually to dry her feet on the edge of the bed, and was suddenly aware of Dick standing close to her. "Would you like some help with that?"

She leaned back on her elbows and smiled, "Mmm, that would be nice."

Her smile widened to a grin, as she giggled, "I can see the holiday is doing you good, now."

It was almost nine when they came down to dinner. Dick had a schoolboy grin on his face, and Rosemary was feeling pleased with herself too, like a new bride at a honeymoon hotel. She wore a bottle-green sheath dress, scooped low at the back, with a halter neck and a deep plunge that accentuated the contrast between her lean body and the generous swell of her breasts. They made a handsome couple as the head waiter eased them to their table by the window, overlooking the estuary now beginning to sparkle with lights.

"You can wipe that lecherous smirk off your face," she hissed, after they had ordered Salcombe Crab Bake and a bottle of Sauvignon, "I spoke to your mother this afternoon on the 'phone. She's loving having the boys with her this week. Says they're no trouble at all, and we can stay away as long as we like."

"They're no trouble because she spoils them rotten."

"She wants me to go shopping next week, you know for the evening at the Ritz next month and then the next day at Ascot. We don't want to let the side down do we?"

"I'm sure you don't, and no doubt I'll look suitably ridiculous in topper and tails from Moss Bros. Just remember, I'm only a poor working man."

"You like me in this dress, don't you?"

"Yes. And even better out of it."

Outside, the warm sunshine of early May glittered invitingly on the wind-ruffled Lake Michigan, and the white sails of the first of the morning's pleasure sailors could be seen emerging from Chicago's yacht-marina. However inside the corner office of ACP's chairman, Lloyd Teller, the atmosphere was distinctly chilly.

"Jesus wept, Vince, how many more times are we goin' to get jerked around by these damn limeys? When we started, it was supposed to be a sick business that needed rescuin'. Fair enough, we've done that a few times here and overseas, an' it's somethin' we know how to do. Then it's all going great, an we're going to have to pay through the nose for the privilege of getting into bed with the finest company since Coca Cola. So I sell that to the Board for you, an' now you tell me they're gettin' even greedier? Is it really worth spendin' any more of your very valuable time on this can of worms? 'Cos I tell you, there ain't no more money. Not another nickel. Top dollar is top dollar, an' that's what's on the table. Are they goin' to pick it up, or no?"

Vince winced a little at the threat that he felt was implicit in that 'valuable time'. He knew only too well that his continuing existence in ACP hung on the not very substantial thread of Lloyd's and Ben's continuing goodwill and trust. He was courting disaster by baiting this particular tiger, but he had a strong motive. He needed to set up an escape route, an excuse to walk away, with justification, if his plan went wrong and he then wanted to hang on still to reputation and the job at ACP, at least until the next opportunity came along to make a bundle.

"I couldn't agree more. Ben here gave me a good steer through the financials, and I really thought all that was behind us. Those bankers, De Boissy, promised to soften up the owners for us next month at some horse-racing do the people in England are very fond of, and it's all pencilled-in now for you and Ben to go over in July to check out the plant and the people, press the flesh, and progress those corporate development ideas we talked about. But now I've had this Alex Hampshire guy on first thing, saying he might need a little more room to negotiate with, because the business is going so well now. I felt I had to keep you informed."

Ben Camina was Vince's direct boss, and liked to see himself as the real brains behind ACP, though he was always careful to defer to Lloyd's authority in public.

"If you recall the detail of the deal, Lloyd, these guys are to get thirty million bucks up front for their company, and then we've proposed a three-year pay-out arrangement in addition. Locks the management into the handover, with a powerful incentive to keep it sweet for us. At the end of each of those three years they get paid a further four times their pre-tax for the year, converted to dollars at the going rate and paid out as ACP shares. We've taken their own growth projections, and told the Board we could end up paying an additional seventy million, making a total of one hundred million for a growing business making, say, eight to ten million pre-tax profit a year. Steep, very steep, but bearable if it gets us up and running in Europe. Getting that agreed by the Board was like milking an alligator, and there's no way I'd consider even raising the possibility of a five-times multiple, which is what De Boissy are now proposing."

"All right then, we're resolved. It's put up or shut up time, Vince. Not a red cent more. What do you want to do?"

"Call their bluff, that's what. I know Alex is off on holiday next week, so I'll let him sweat till he gets back early in June. He'll find a letter on his desk confirming the terms of our offer, subject to due diligence and contract, and saying the money is non-negotiable."

After Vince had left, Ben and Lloyd quietly shared a fresh pot of coffee. It was Ben who broke the silence.

"We're right to stick on the price Lloyd, I'm sure. But if they do walk away, we're really goin' to have some deep egg-stains to worry about. Still worse if they go with one of our competitors. The Board are seein' this English deal as some kind of a flag to wave at Wall Street, to prove that ACP is not the moribund heap of shit they seem to think it is. I reckon some of 'em have been talkin' it up already in their little get-togethers. 'Confidential briefings' – damn insider-dealin' if you ask me. Probably they'll have added to their holdings somewhat, so now it's personal if it goes down. There's a lot ridin' on it now, and if it goes wrong, we could find the market unloadin' our paper big time, or even lookin' for someone to take us over and create 'shareholder value', or some such crap."

"I know, Ben, I know. And I'm dependin' on you to keep Vince up to the mark. God help him if he lets us down."

"And God help us too."

De Boissy had of course made no such demand for improved terms, in fact Alex felt that he had negotiated exceptionally well to get ACP to go as far as they had. But Vince was content now to have his bosses believing that the deal was not yet secure. He had two important telephone calls to make. The first was to his former employers, one of New York's most noted wheeler-dealer investment banks. Vince had been a fairly humble cog in their machine, a confidential researcher. Every day, people came into the bank with suggestions for takeover deals and clever stock market manoeuvres. Vince's job had been to dig deeper than anyone else to find the truth behind published figures and statements, and sometimes to identify weaknesses behind the public persona of a top manager or investor. He had actually played a significant but secret role in the very public dog-fight for the merger/acquisition of Reynolds-Nabisco, and now was the time, he thought, to collect on a personal favour he was owed. His former boss, Bill Shavely, was now running the Chicago office, and Vince had heard from his girlfriend, Anna, that Bill was getting ready to move to London to open the bank's first European office. Anna had suggested that Bill would surely be hungry for a deal in England to set things up. Arranging a lunch in Chicago for the next day with Bill proved to be as easy as she had forecast.

The second call, to the Food and Drugs Agency in Washington, was more difficult, because Vince deemed it dangerous to hint to his Harvard buddy, Gerry Masters, that there might be an opportunity for him to fill his boots with money – at least not before he had tested the temperature of the water with a face-to-face meeting. But Gerry seemed to see no need to question Vince's statement that he needed a confidential talk, and they agreed to meet in Washington for dinner on Tuesday, May 23rd.

Vince sat back at his desk with a sigh of relief. All the pieces of his plan were moving along very nicely. He looked down at the scrap-pad on his desk. The top page was covered with telephone numbers, cryptic notes and question-marks, names with circles around and arrows joining them. He tore it off, together with the blank page beneath, and stuffed both into his pocket for safe disposal later. He knew from experience that, where big money was concerned, it was impossible to be too careful. He grinned to himself as he recalled a Wall Street saying,

'*Just because you're paranoid, it doesn't mean they're not out to get you.*'

Chapter Fifteen

"Hullo, hullo, This is Ellen Routledge here. May I speak with the Chairman please?"

"I'm sorry, Mrs Routledge, but the Board meeting has just started, and I ought not to interrupt them. Can I take a message? They're expected to break for coffee in an hour, about eleven."

"Yes, it's very important. No, on second thoughts, put me through to his secretary, Liz Boyd please."

"Elizabeth? Is that you? It's Ellen. How are you dear? Good, now listen please, this is very important. Could you give the Chairman a message, as soon as there's a break? It's about our daughter, Ruth. You know she's expecting a baby in about three months' time? The doctor is afraid she may be losing it, and she's been taken to the hospital. I'm expecting my taxi any minute now, and I'm taking the first train. Tell him I'll be stopping there at least for tonight, but I'll call him when there's any news."

"Oh, Mrs. Routledge, I'm so sorry. The Chairman only said to me yesterday that he was hoping for a granddaughter this time. Hospitals can do marvels you know, and of course her husband is a doctor himself, isn't he? I'll say a little prayer too."

"Bless you, Elizabeth. There's my taxi at the door. 'Bye now."

As Ellen had been told, the special Board Meeting on Wednesday May 17th had begun at ten in what John Savage continued to think of as Strongwheat's 'Bedouin Tent'. It was planned that, for the first hour, the meeting would consider the results for the October–March first half of the year. After the break for coffee they would be joined by Paul Williams, the Advertising Manager, together with Roger Daniels and Jill Lister from their advertising agency, Crofton's, for a meeting devoted exclusively to consideration of the projected new product.

By ten-fifteen Jim Helvin was in full flow with his financial review.

"Volume for the half-year was excellent, no less than twelve percent up on the same period last year. With the full benefit of the price increase, turnover was fifteen percent higher. On the Manufacturing side, there has been a good deal of quite expensive overtime worked, which has eroded some of the benefit of the new Automated Packing Line. As was agreed at the last Board, I have done a detail study of the last four weeks' performance on the line. This shows that, on a per-case basis, our overall cost to pack is a full one-third lower than last year. My analysis shows that performance was improving throughout the period."

"I would like to propose that we put on record a note of congratulations to Mr. Wythe and his team for a brave job, well done."

Oliver Sedburgh's request, and the unusual warmth of his tone were duly noted, and Jim Helvin continued.

"Probably because of the increasing volumes, our wheat and bought-in rusk actually cost a little less per tonne than last year. Overheads, mainly sales and marketing costs, were virtually unchanged, and the end result, unaudited of course, is that our profit for the half-year comes out at £490,000. That's just about what we made in the whole of last year."

"Any questions for Mr. Helvin?"

John Savage recalled Alex Hampshire's forecast, during that rather querulous meeting in his office at De Boissy's, that profits might reach a million in two years. This suggested that things were going even faster! "Only the obvious one, Mr. Chairman, how do we see the second half now?"

"Dick, would you like to stick your neck out?"

"Forecasts are made to be proved wrong of course, but we do seem to have a bit of a tail-wind at the moment. April and the first two weeks of May are bang on trend, indeed we've been worrying a little about how we'll be able to maintain supply, as we come up to the holiday period, especially if we want to build stock to launch a new product in September. Barring accidents, I'd say we're on course for £900,000 for the full year, before interest and tax. If we do go ahead with a new product, we might want to reduce that total by taking some of the launch costs into this financial year."

"I must say, James, I am extremely relieved to see the business getting some momentum behind it again." Oliver's pleasure came through in the warmth of his tone again, "I feel that it suffered very considerably as a result of your unfortunate illness, and the inevitable hiatus before Dick could 'get his hands on the controls', as he might put it. I'm waiting to hear about the new product, but there is no doubt at all that you are vulnerable, as you argued in December. I don't think I am breaching any confidentiality if I tell you that the major supermarket retailers that we service as auditors and financial advisers are certainly going to be pruning out their weaker suppliers. They have to, in order to release the space for the private-label versions they want to bring in to compete with the major brands. I have heard as much said at a board meeting elsewhere."

"Thank you Oliver. If you will agree, I would like to postpone further discussion until we've decided what to do about the new product. You will find in your Board papers a proposal from Mr. Wythe for a further substantial investment on our manufacturing, this time to improve the quality and efficiency of Flake production. We could take that as part of the consideration of the new product. Shall we break for coffee?"

As soon as the buzzer from the Boardroom sounded Liz Boyd came in, to find James standing by one of the chesterfield settees, in conversation with John Savage. "Your master has invited us to be his guests at the Ritz and Ascot next month. I thought that was a remarkably generous response to our paying a modest first dividend . . ."

"Mrs. Routledge telephoned earlier, Mr. James. I've typed her message exactly as I took it down."

He stopped speaking, and stared at the paper. No sound came from his open mouth, but there was a clatter as he suddenly sat down on the arm of the settee, and his stick fell from his hand to the floor. The room became silent.

"Dad? Dad, what is it? Are you all right?"

For a long moment James looked at his son as though he did not know him, then he drew a deep breath. "I must make a call, Dick. Could you give me an arm please, this damned leg seems to have frozen up."

Dick picked up the cane, took his father's arm and helped him to move laboriously from the room. He read the note himself as they went, and Liz Boyd fluttered behind.

"Are you all right, Mr. James? Should I call Dr. Carr? Would you like one of your tablets? Shall I bring in some coffee?"

"For God's sake, don't fuss, woman. Dr. Andrew Wilson, Ruth's husband, you'll find the number for his practice in my address book. Would you get him for me, in my office please? You stay, Dick, and we'll have coffee here please, Elizabeth."

James' telephone call to Andrew was brief. Ruth had woken up in the night in considerable pain, and Andrew had taken her to the hospital himself. They had confirmed his diagnosis of a potential miscarriage. She was barely six months, so survival for the baby was problematical. Andrew kept his tone very cool and matter-of-fact

"They've confirmed that Ruth is very fit in herself, so you should not worry yourself unduly, James. She is under the personal care of one of the best gynaecologists in the country. Everything that can be done will be done."

"Ellen is on the way down to you already."

"I know, we spoke earlier. That's fine, Ruth will be relieved to know that I'll be well looked after. Just try not to worry now, James, for all our sakes. They'll tell me if there's any development, and I'll keep you posted with any news."

James put down the telephone and rubbed his eyes. Dick saw the anxiety in his father's face. Ruth had always been the favourite.

"I think we should suspend the meeting, don't you Dad? Neither of us is likely to be able to concentrate, and . . ."

"NO!"

The fierceness of the interruption took Dick by surprise, and brought Liz Boyd scurrying in from next door.

"I want to go on now. We must go on, please Dick. Andrew said there's nothing we can do for Ruth. She's in good hands, the best possible, he said. I couldn't bear just to sit around thinking about it. I'm going on with the Board. You can stay or go as you think fit. No, I didn't mean that, please stay, Dick."

Dick nodded, and handed the cane to his father. Back in the Boardroom, Roger Daniels and Jill Lister had arrived from London, and been introduced by Paul Williams to Oliver and John, and then to James as he returned, still ashen-faced, but walking firmly with his stick.

"Welcome to Strongwheat. We are most appreciative of the contribution you've been making, aren't we Walter?" He took his place at the head of the table, "I can see you are all concerned about the little excitement we had a few minutes ago. Let me put your minds at rest, so that we can all concentrate properly on the business in hand. Dick's younger sister, Ruth, is expecting her first baby, and her husband, who is himself a doctor, is naturally very protective. He arranged for her to go into hospital this morning as a precaution, and we all got a bit carried away. I am most appreciative of your interest and concern, but I have been assured that there is nothing for us to worry about, so can we just get on, please? Dick, would you like to start by outlining the programme for the rest of the day?"

Dick was nervous at first, but his voice projected more confidence as he got into the flow of his presentation.

"As a first step to finding a new product, which we have already completed, Phil Wythe set out to establish what could reasonably be done with our existing plant, assuming minimal modification. Basically we found that this involved varying the proportions of the two major ingredients, Rusk and Wheat Flakes. One version, with a much higher proportion of Flake, and therefore much lighter, was liked very much by consumers in a trial against regular Strongwheat. So we've put that into another consumer trial, this time against our major competitors, Corn Flakes and Weetabix, both of whom sell a lot more than we do. Walter and Paul are going to give us some background on the market, and then the results of this comparison, which is of course crucial to our decision today. Phil will outline the costings for the new product, and some capacity considerations, and our friends from the agency here are ready with their proposals for a launch, if we decide to go ahead. Finally I will be showing the Board a three-year profit plan, with and without a successful new product. That's a lot to get through, so I've laid on a buffet lunch to allow us to break any time we like. Walter, would you kick-off please?"

"Thank you, Dick. As you saw this morning, our sales have been quite buoyant." He passed around copies of a single sheet of paper, containing a series of bar-charts, headed, 'Volume sales of Strongwheat in cases'. "This shows our quarterly sales, in cases of product, over the last five years. We are bang up to date, as I've made the five twelve-month periods end with April. You can see volumes rising for the first two years, then falling quite sharply in year three – that's when the advertising was reduced – and recovering nicely since. The last quarter's volume is about ten percent above the previous peak three years ago. Then we had six percent of the market, and our latest Nielsen Research puts us at five and a half, with the market growing steadily and ourselves still recovering share."

"And will the market keep expanding at that rate?"

Oliver's question was not unexpected, and indeed Walter and Paul and the team of Area Managers had debated it at length, when Dick had put them under pressure for a three-year forecast a few weeks before.

"We fall into the 'more substantial' end of the market, which includes us among the currently fashionable bran and fibre-rich products that appeal to adults for health reasons. This is the strongest growth section, so we're fairly confident the trend will continue for a good few years still." He looked around the table, "Right, if there are no questions, I'll hand over to Paul, who has some interesting results to present."

Paul sat at the end of the table, opposite the Chairman, James Routledge. For what seemed a long time he said nothing, while he looked around the table, at Roger and Jill on each side of him, at his boss, Walter Hurd, at Jim Helvin and Dick Routledge. Then he began in a quiet voice that crackled with barely suppressed excitement.

"I've been in advertising and marketing for ten years now, and in that time I've seen a lot of consumer research. I can honestly say this is the most satisfying of the lot. Let me give you this sheet of paper, which summarises in two lines what I've got to say."

Result of a Trial in 500 households with young Children
Overall Preference

Cornflakes 48%	New Strongwheat 52%
Weetabix 55%	New Strongwheat 45%

Paul had only gone through the figures with the agency the previous afternoon, and Walter and Dick had been shown them that morning. Paul tried to keep his tone cool and objective as he described how they had chosen the new product for the test, and how the trials had been run by a professional research organisation, but at the end he could restrain his enthusiasm no longer. "These competitors' products have been on the market many years, and although we put all the products into plain packs for the trials, you can be sure they were recognised for what they were. And yet they preferred our product to Corn Flakes, and we are only marginally worse off against Weetabix. These two are the leaders of the UK market."

"Does that mean you'll sell more than them?"

The note of incredulity in John Savage's voice was plainly discernible.

"Definitely not," Walter was very firm, "As Paul said, they've got years of advertising and sales momentum behind them, and we're not going to threaten them seriously overnight. Nor in ten years, if you want my honest opinion. But it does mean that we're in with a fair chance that, once someone has tried our product, they'll like it enough to speak well of it, and come back for more. Over time we'll build up the numbers of users by advertising and sales promotion, and that will give us more shops stocking, and that will build the volume, and so on. We're in it for the long haul, and I feel very confident that we can reach the target we've set for ourselves at this time, which is to reach a volume, for the new product, of roughly half the sale of regular Strongwheat, within three years. That will see us reaching a total market share of say nine percent, with more to come, we might hope."

James was triumphant. "I knew it! I said in December that there was a lot more mileage in this little business, do you remember, Oliver? And now you see a glimpse of the real potential. I tell you, John, when we decide to sell a piece of our company on your precious Stock Exchange, they'll have to dig very deep into their piggy-banks to afford us!"

"I'm happy for you, James," Oliver's tone was cool, "But there's many a slip, as they say. Mr. Daniels, I'd be most grateful for some comment on the reliability of this research, please."

Roger was prepared for a challenge. "Delighted. The first thing to note is that the study was managed for us by one of the most reputable names in the industry, MSR. In our experience, a typical study of this kind – an in-home comparison of two products – specifies a sample of eighty to a hundred, because they are very expensive to carry out. Paul however felt that the step was so significant for the company that we specified a sample of five hundred homes each with at least one young child, the heart of our target market. MSR found the sample and conducted the research, and we worked together on the questions to be asked. Of course any sampling technique is subject to the possibility of statistical error, but I have a note on that subject from MSR, as I felt you would want reassurance on that issue. If I may quote what they say? 'There is only one chance in a hundred that your product is not at least as well-liked as Cornflakes'. Put that round the other way, it's a hundred to one on that it is at least as acceptable."

"A hundred to one," James murmured, "I like the odds, especially as we'd be betting with my money." There was a ripple of laughter around the table. "How do we interpret the Weetabix result?"

Roger sensed they were ready for some hard-nosed realism, "As a warning. Weetabix has flake but no rusk content, so it's fairly close to that version of Strongwheat which we knew the kids would like, but which we did not put out because we were told it could not be packed without unacceptable damages. Weetabix seem to have solved that problem. The result tells us that there is a natural barrier in the marketplace to the development of the new Strongwheat, represented by the entrenched presence of Weetabix. Equally, looking into the future, we might expect Weetabix to feel threatened by our progress, and respond with a variant of their own to attack us."

"Which they could do anytime now", James interjected, "And that's exactly why I said we were vulnerable last December. A good moment to break for lunch, I think." He stood up, "Dick, I don't want Andrew to think I'm fussing unduly. Would you like to give him a call yourself, and see if there's any news about Ruth?"

John Savage was gratefully sipping a cool lager and congratulating Roger on the professionalism of the research work, when he caught the sound of her voice. It brought with it a memory of the darkened room in his flat, and the way her jacket glowed saffron in the lamplight, in that time when each had waited for the other. Since then she had been down to London four or five times, and he knew they were close to an important decision for themselves. He turned quickly to find her standing behind him, cool and executive-crisp in a white shirt and black slacks, which served to emphasise rather than reduce her femininity. Her voice was casual as she held out her hand. "Good afternoon, it's John Savage, isn't it? I hope you may remember we met before Christmas, Jean Carey?"

There was an electric moment of contact as he took her hand, then Paul arrived to bring Jean a large gin and tonic, clinking with ice. "You won't have heard yet, Jean, but I've just finished telling the Board that our new product knocks spots off the competition in the research. I think it's blown their minds. At least, nobody's said much so far. What do you think, John?"

"I was just saying as much to Roger when Jean came in. I'm no expert at consumer product marketing, despite your excellent tuition, Paul, but I'd say your new product looks good enough to make a useful dent in the competition. I'm very pleased of course."

His eyes were on Jean as he spoke, and Paul, who was gifted with good intuition, sensed a hint of conspiracy between them. He turned away to pour a beer for Dick, who had just come back in. *I wonder . . . I just wonder if there's something going on between those two? That might explain the odd mood she's been in over the last few weeks.* He was self-analytical enough to recognise a spasm of jealousy, which he could rationalise as protectiveness. *Brotherly concern, that's what it is. If there is something between them, I just hope he treats her properly. She deserves a good man.*

Dick helped himself to a plate of cold meat and salad, and made his way through to where his father was sitting on a settee, chatting to Oliver. "Andrew says that Ruth has responded well so far to the treatment, Dad. It's too soon yet to be certain the baby's all right, but the first crisis is over."

The lines of deep concern that were etched around James' mouth broke up into a smile that was almost boyish. "That's just the best news, Dick, the very best news! What was I saying to you, Oliver, we Routledges are as tough as old bootleather. Good old Ruth, I was sure she'd be all right." His relief was as exhilarating as his previous anxiety had been crushing, "I can see it coming. We'll be launching the new product on the same day that our new grandchild is born. We must ask Andrew to give us a forecast date for the new arrival, and I'll get Walter to fix the Sales Conference for the same day. The salesmen could run a sweepstake to guess the weight of the baby . . ."

James pulled up abruptly. "I suppose you're thinking the old man's gone soft," he growled, then defiantly, "Well, perhaps I have. All those months sitting at home, being treated like a helpless infant myself, you get to sort out in your mind what's important. Family, friends, making a difference in the world before it's too late . . ." He realised the room had fallen silent, listening to his soliloquy, "If you've had sufficient, I'd like to get back to our presentations and discussions." He turned to Jean and Tom McMurtry, the buyer. "If you two are not too busy this afternoon, you'd be very welcome to join us. I can guarantee you'll find it interesting."

Paul introduced Jill Lister. Accepting the desirability of reassuring a nervous client, Jill was wearing a severe dark blue tailored suit with a high-necked white blouse, and black horn-rims instead of her usual saucer-size spectacles. She spoke quietly, in a tone of calm authority. She reviewed the agency's argument for wanting to develop a unique point of difference for the new product.

"We considered that it would be more effective, and longer lasting, if the difference could be built into the formulation of the product, rather than be just a copywriter's phrase or slogan." She explained again the idea for a cereal with added Fluoride, "So this 'concept', as we call it, is the image of the product that we want the advertising to leave behind in the mind of the consumer, to be reinforced, we hope, by actually trying it. We showed this concept to each of the sample of five hundred housewives that had already tried the products, and asked for their opinion. Of course there were a whole raft of different reactions, but I have summarised the results like this."

She handed round her own sheet of paper,

Housewife reactions to adding Fluoride to a children's Cereal
(Sample – 500 homes with young children)

Strongly in favour	25%
More or less indifferent	55%
Hostile to some degree	20%

"Frankly, we feel that this result is extremely encouraging for us. We have a quarter of the potential market who really like the idea, and in total over three-quarters who are not against it. That's before there's been any publicity to support it, no endorsements for instance from the dentists. Bear in mind that we'll be very pleased to get just a few percent of the market for our new product. I will allow that fluoride itself is a controversial and emotive subject, and adding fluoride is a radically new departure for your company, indeed for any company. However I venture to suggest that the controversial heat has been generated over the years by the practice of *forcing* it onto the public through the water-supply. That is condemned as anti-liberal, big-brother stuff. Our drinking water is seen as something that comes down from the sky to us totally pure, and it should stay that way. As far as I am aware, there is no campaign against fluoride in toothpaste. Indeed one might hypothesise that if a range of children's foods containing a trace of fluoride had been available, the practice of fluoridating the water to stop their teeth going rotten would never have got started. Look at it another way, nearly all cereals feature added vitamins, and I've yet to hear of any proposal to add the vitamins to the water. I think my colleague has a word or two to add, Roger?"

Roger Daniels would in fact much have preferred to sit on the fence until he could see which way the client was inclining, but he knew there was no way to escape Jill's determination. "We think it comes down to brushing away the cobwebs of what you might call knee-jerk reactions, and trying to assess honestly where the balance of advantage lies for us. For instance, Walter thought that a point of difference such as this could be absolutely crucial in getting the retailers to provide shelf-space for the product from the beginning, so that decent availability allows the advertising to get to work to get the product tried. We think too that a little effort directed towards a skilful Public Relations campaign could be expected to get us a lot of favourable comment in the press, just because our new product would be news itself, and that will also encourage the retailers to support us. How does it strike you now, Walter? Are we on the right track, do you think?"

Walter responded without hesitation. "I like it." Roger breathed a quiet sigh of relief. "Mind you, I don't think it's necessary to have fluoride dominate the pack or the advertising. As Jill pointed out, most consumers are not that excited about it, at least not yet. But I have taken the opportunity to try out the fluoride idea on a couple of the major multiples, and it's fair to say that the buyers were extremely encouraging. Of course these things always have to go through the Buying Committee, but I'd say those two will be recommending it on our behalf, and that's half the battle. Interestingly, both thought that putting fluoride in the water was wrong, and that we had a better approach."

Paul caught the Chairman's eye with a raised finger.

"There is also a downside risk. I mean a possibility of total catastrophe." He spoke in a quiet, almost throwaway tone, but slowly and distinctly, so that it was obvious that he had measured in his mind the possible significance of his words. "I hope you will bear with me, because I haven't any balanced or reasoned considerations to offer, and I don't have a different set of research figures to quote to you. But I have read the verbatim reports of what the housewives actually said, and I paid particular attention to the ones that were hostile, because I thought those were the ones that we might need to be worried about. The thing that struck me was that they mostly were unreasoned, you know, the kind of 'knee-jerk' response that Roger referred to. 'I am absolutely against putting chemicals into food', and 'Fluoride is a poison', that sort of thing. I thought to myself, 'what if our product gets caught up in some new campaign'? Suppose it becomes the focal point of a witch-hunt against food additives, or food manipulation? Suppose the anti-fluoride brigade calculate that we look a softer target than the water companies? Suppose we become a target for vandalism against our retailers? I know this may all sound a bit far-fetched, but you could have been very optimistic a few years ago if you were working on genetically modified grain, and look how that has blown up in their faces – and we're just a small, vulnerable business. Do we actually need to stick our necks out in this way? Walter, I'm sorry not to have raised this before, but I've had this vague, uneasy feeling about the fluoride idea for weeks, and it's only now, having sat up half of last night reading the material, that I've felt able to put it into words. Does that make sense?"

Walter nodded. He was honest enough to admit that he himself had felt a similar indefinite hesitation, but he had been unable to think of any specific objection, so he had preferred to rely on the relative certainties of the reactions of his major customers. He wondered too if Paul might not be using this public occasion to show the Board that his judgement might be maturing to the point that he should be seen as Walter's natural successor when the time came.

James broke the long silence, "Dick, this is obviously a critical issue. Do you want to press on for a decision now?"

"No, not if we can put it off for a bit, Mr. Chairman. I can see both sides. It would be wonderful if we could hit the market with an interesting, a really irresistible product. But that makes me remember the old Chinese curse, 'May you live in interesting times'. Do you think we could just break for some tea, please?"

Chapter Sixteen

"Mr. Savage? There's been a call for you from Mr. Hampshire at your office. Could you call him back, preferably before four o'clock please?"

John had been approached by Liz Boyd with the message, just as he was wondering how to renew his enjoyable conversation with Jean, without making it too obvious. No such luck! Was their relationship still a secret from the people here? Why did Jean think it important to keep it secret?

"If you would like to follow me, you could use the Chairman's office. I'll get your call for you, and bring you in a cup of tea."

John enjoyed her calm efficiency, and wondered idly how much she was paid. Probably about half what she could have got in London, he guessed, and then his speculation was interrupted by the telephone.

"Alex, hullo, yes it's John. Something urgent come up?"

"Well, yes, slightly pressing. I hope this is a convenient time to break? Good. I had call an hour ago from our friend O'Hanlon at A.C.P. He is very keen to know today if Strongwheat will definitely be going ahead with their new product. And he also wants to know if the fluoride additive will be included. I asked him why he needed to know these things today, but he was evasive, and I felt it would not be politic to press too hard, after all they are the potential buyer. I said that you might have a decision today, and I would get back to him. My problem, as you know, is that I am being dragged off kicking and screaming by Marie-Louise for a holiday in Gaudeloupe this evening, so I must get away by four-thirty at the latest. Of course if there is no decision yet, I will have to tell him just that."

"Well, we are still going through the various presentations by the people who've been working on it, so presumably James will look for some kind of consensus at the end, I'd say in a couple of hours from now."

"Too late for me. How's the mood of the meeting so far?"

"Very positive, very optimistic, I'd say, definitely bullish. James got distinctly excited when they produced some quite favourable results from a trial of the new product by a panel of five hundred housewives and children, compared to its competitors. I'd be prepared to bet serious money that there will be a 'go' decision at the end of today, launch-date around September 1st."

"Good enough. What about fluoride?"

"Much more problematic, I'd say. There are good arguments for, and some deep concerns also. Could go either way. Have you any idea why A.C.P. are interested? You've structured their proposed deal on the basis that the price is essentially a multiple of the next three years' profits, so they pay more for a more successful business, and less if the business runs into difficulties. So where's the problem for them with fluoride, one way or another?"

"Search me, old boy, I'm just the humble messenger here. Anyway, you'd say that fluoride is definitely in the running still?"

"Definitely."

"Fair enough, and O'Hanlon will have to be content with that. I'll get an e-mail off to him now. If he needs to know more, I'll leave a note with Elaine here, and perhaps you would call him tomorrow if necessary? I'll let you get back now to what sounds like an interesting meeting. My regards to James Routledge."

John made his way back to the Board Room to find the meeting reassembling around the table. There was some sort of argument going on in whispers between the two people from the Advertising Agency, but it stopped as Phil Wythe began. To judge from John's face, he was listening attentively whilst Phil was explaining the costings,

"The new product has, as you know, a lower content of rusk, which is bought-in, and a higher content of flake, which is manufactured in house. It is also coming out slightly lighter in weight for our standard biscuit volume, so even allowing for some additional loss of product due to fragility, it's going to be between five and ten percent cheaper per box to manufacture than regular Strongwheat, and so more profitable if sold at the same price".

Inwardly however John was seething with a fierce resentment, all the stronger because he was not quite sure what it was that was making him so angry. He rationalised his animosity as being due to the way Alex had so calmly assumed that he would keep on providing whatever inside information he asked for. In his heart he knew that it was due also to a sense of guilt and helplessness, closely connected to his growing feelings for Jean Carey, and a recognition that he was becoming desperately concerned not to endanger her good opinion of himself. She was sitting just back from the Board table, a yard behind Phil. For no good reason he tried to catch her eye, but she kept her eyes resolutely on something she was writing in a notebook on her knee. John realised that his concentration had wandered, and focussed his attention on Phil Wythe.

"It's for this reason, Mr. Chairman, that we are proposing the investment in a 'state of the art' flake line, complete with a new oven. We have tested our flake on a similar oven at the premises of the oven manufacturer, and there is no doubt there is a startling improvement in both speed of production and quality. We get a significantly greater 'lift' or expansion when the heat hits the flake and makes it 'puff', and this in turn will save more cost by reducing the weight of flake needed in the product. On regular Strongwheat alone, we would recover our investment in two years. But if we add in the extra flake tonnage required for the new product, the payback period is reduced to not much over a year. And we improve the quality of the product as well."

"Any questions?"

Here I am, casually conspiring with Alex Hampshire to hand over confidential plans for future development to a potential bidder. And for what? So that De Boissy – which meant Alex – could realise some dream of global influence. But what should I do about it?

"Right then, thank you very much, Phil. The Flake Line is approved in principle, but I would like to sit down later with you and Dick to review the plan to install it over the Christmas break. Who's next, Dick?"

"Mr. Daniels from the advertising agency would like us to have a look at the ideas for the pack, the advertising, and the introductory promotion to the Trade."

Commonsense suggests that any direct challenge to Alex about commercial ethics will get very short shrift. Alex would 'Very reluctantly have to let you move on, old boy'. And I would be condemned across the City by rumour and innuendo, 'Nice enough chap, but not really sound, you know.'

"So the new product should be called 'STRONGWHEAT LIGHT', and the pack should be similar in basic design to the regular pack, but with a change to the background colour, red instead of blue." Roger passed around a mock-up of the pack, "In keeping with the target market, the back will be used for games and promotions aimed at youngish children – for instance animal masks to cut out, or Space Adventure scenes to be coloured. The fluoride story is contained in a panel here on the side, headed 'Healthy Young Teeth'. It's there as a talking point for the salesman, which can become an advertising story when the time is right."

Should I talk frankly to James Routledge? That's a stupid idea! James had already been informed by Alex about the approach from a potential buyer, so what do I have to add? Only that I might myself be a potential liability on the Strongwheat board for reasons of security – and how would that help?

Roger and Jill presented the advertising with the ease and skill of professionals. Knowing that the Board would be more interested in the TV commercial itself, Roger went through the plan for the TV expenditure first. "So we would propose dividing the two million budgeted for advertising the new product simply into two equal halves. The first burst begins November 1st, which allows two months from September 1st for the selling-in process, followed by physically distributing product into retail outlets and getting the necessary shelf-space established."

"It's always a tough compromise," said Walter, "The salesmen want TV running right from the beginning, when they're doing their selling, because it helps the sale. But realistically, the money spent on TV can't work for us until there's a reasonable build-up of availability. Eight weeks is about right."

"Thanks, Walter. The second half of the campaign is scheduled to begin early in February, but we would recommend that we do not book that until say, mid-December, when we get together with you to review progress. That way you have some control left if things do not go to plan."

Jill's TV commercial was the version that did not mention fluoride. It was a clever mix of real-life children with fantasy cartoon sequences that suggested the tremendous strength they got from eating Strongwheat Light. She played a sound-track with a catchy jingle on a small tape-recorder, and the smiles around the table told her she had made the sale. Roger finished with the launch promotion, which involved giving away a free sample of Strongwheat Light.

"Paul has talked this through with Walter and Phil, and it can be done. Each regular Strongwheat box now contains four individually wrapped stacks of product. We propose to make the box bigger to allow you to increase that to five stacks, with the fifth of course being Strongwheat Light. And a big flash on the box to announce the offer of the free sample."

O'Hanlon has some strong motive to want to know about our plan for the new product, right down to a detail like the fluoride idea. He's not likely to want to increase the cost to ACP of buying the business. Therefore I should assume he has some scheme afoot to get it cheaper. Anything like that is likely to involve some grief for James here, and Jean is going to find herself caught up in that and could blame me. Rightly too, if there was something I could have done and didn't. But what? I wonder if they've got their heads around the size of the risk they're proposing to take?

"Any questions? John, you're looking thoughtful?"

"Yes, Mr. Chairman, I'm trying to do some rough arithmetic. We've got the build-up of stock of the new product, must be best part of a million, plus the sales to the trade, which won't be paid for until a couple of months later – another million? Then there's the two million for advertising, and a half-million for the free samples and so on. Altogether, not much change from five million to be invested for this project – that's an extra cash requirement of five year's profits, even at our current improved rate. And we shouldn't overlook the half-million for the flake line. Not that I'm concerned about profitability at this stage, because I'm sure Dick is going to blow our minds with some exciting figures in a minute. But I have to be concerned about the sheer scale of the risk we are considering. Even if it goes to plan – and things hardly ever do, in my experience – can it be funded? Will the Bank increase the overdraft facility by that much? Or will you be looking to De Boissy for funds? I suppose I'm asking if the company might just be getting out of its depth?"

"Dick, that sounds like your cue?"

"Indeed it is, Mr. Chairman. John is right to be concerned about the scale of the investment, though fortunately it's not quite so terrifying as his rough figures suggest. I'm going to offer the Board two alternative sets of figures, showing quarter by quarter our forecasts for sales, profit and cash-flow for the next three years."

He passed copies of two sheets of paper around the table.

"The first one is for Strongwheat without the new product. The basic assumption is that we keep going with the recovery of our share up to 6% of the market, and the market itself keeps on growing at a cautious three percent a year. Advertising stays at the current two million. You can see sales of twenty-seven million this year, rising to thirty-one after three years, and profits moving from just under a million this year to almost two and a half millions. Cash-flow is positive throughout, even whilst we're paying for the new Flake line."

"I have to congratulate you, James," said Oliver, "The transformation in the business would really be complete with results like that."

"And the transformation in the value of the business, as I told you before Christmas. Three and a half years from now the profit we are forecasting is no less than five times last year's."

"Thank you, Chairman, but if you look at my second sheet now, which shows the effect of adding in Strongwheat Light, you'll see something even more exciting. The cost of launching Strongwheat Light will consume all the margin from the extra sales in the first year, so there is no gain to the bottom line, and a reduction in our cash-flow. But in the second and third years, assuming that by then we are reaching our target of selling at half the rate of Strongwheat Regular, we are forecasting sales of fifteen million and sixteen million for the new product alone. The resulting extra margin comes through to the bottom line, producing a total profit for the company of FIVE millions in the third year, even allowing for our continuing to spend at *double* our current rate on advertising and sales promotion. However I agree with John that we should draw the Board's attention to the effect on cash-flow. It's not quite as devastating as John calculated, but Mr. Helvin and I have been through this most carefully, and there's no doubt that the various factors John has referred to do accumulate together. By this coming Christmas we would expect to be between one and a half and two million worse off as far as cash is concerned. This is principally because of the advertising, the extra funds tied up in stocks, and trade sales not yet paid for."

It's not enough to stop them. They'll find a way to finesse that much. And the reality is that, if the new product does not sell quite as well as the plan, they'll actually need to hold lower stocks, and the customers will owe them less, so the cash position will probably be not much worse. It's going to go ahead. Which still leaves me with the problem – do I say anything about Vince's questions?

"Any comments? Oliver?"

"On the straightforward issue of cash-flow, I'd say it looks eminently doable. John might care to have De Boissy quote for a short-term loan, but equally I'd say you have such a blue-chip customer list, so it should be no problem at all to set up some form of short-term invoice discounting. This is where the bank credits you as soon as you issue the invoice – could be cheaper too, because the loan is flexing with your sales and cash receipts, and is secured on the trade debt. But I am much more concerned about the absolute size of the risk. I must say, until I saw Dick's figures I had no real feel for the scale of risk you were contemplating."

Oliver paused, and looked at James, but there was no reaction. James was his oldest friend. He knew that Dick's vision of the future for the company had rekindled the fire of ambition that he had thought had died out long ago. Perhaps it was the revived ambition, the new partnership with his son, that had saved James' life after the strokes, or had at least rescued him from an enfeebled old age? He kept his tone cool.

"As I see it, the key assumption in all these plans is that Strongwheat Light can produce a fifty-percent increase in the business, which means an increase in share of market from five percent to seven and a half percent, or from six percent to nine. Over the last ten years to my knowledge, we've seen a dozen entries into the market, from clever, powerful companies like Kellogg, Quaker, and Nestle. I doubt if more than two have reached that threshold of three per cent of the market, and the rest have disappeared without trace after a short, inglorious and no doubt financially painful life. I would suggest that the kind of momentum Walter has forecast is the minimum necessary to stay in. If for any reason the sales fall short, there must be a serious possibility that, after say six or nine months, you will find retail outlets discontinuing your product, the launch stalling, and so on. One could construct a variety of scenarios, corresponding to various types of disaster, but I would say it is terrifyingly easy to lose a million, and even two millions is not impossible. I don't think I need to tell you, James, that the company would in all probability go under."

For a few seconds after Oliver had finished James looked at him in silence. Did he believe that a disaster was to be expected? Oliver was like the chart of a rocky coastline – a necessary indicator of where the dangers were, but silent as to the advisability of attempting the passage.

He's going to ask for my opinion next. Can I find a way to suggest to them that some mischief is afoot? Perhaps I can get a message to them privately?

"Thank you very much for the warning signal, Oliver. John, I wonder if you can offer any flashes of light?"

"Just one thought, Chairman. The new product is, in a way, an improved version of the current product. So launching it is really a dramatic way to do what the Agency have been recommending, that is doubling the advertising support behind the Strongwheat brand. I think you need to be super-careful with your planning, but the chance is there to establish the brand really well. On the fluoride issue, there seems to be agreement that the value, at least at the beginning, will be in helping the salesmen to get the product into the shops. I wonder if Walter might not agree to forego that particular benefit, in the interest of minimising our risk?"

"Thank you John. It's after five now. I wonder if there is any other useful contribution anyone would like to make? If not, then it only remains for me to thank you all for everything you have done so far. I'm going to 'think on't', as they say, and I'll also be talking things through with each of you as the opportunity arises. Dick, shall we see how Ruth is getting on?"

As they filed out of the Board Room, John caught up with Phil Wythe, "Last time I came I had to rush straight off afterwards for an evening meeting in London, so I couldn't fit in a look at the manufacturing process. This time I'm all right as long as I catch a late train, so I wonder if you could arrange a little tour, please?"

"Gladly, John. You're in luck really; usually we're shutting down by now, but tonight there's some overtime being worked, until eight, I think. Look, I'd love to do the honours myself, but I've promised my wife I'll be home today before the end of my daughter's birthday party. She's six today, and this is the first party with all her new school friends."

Like Paul, he had noticed the interest in Jean Carey, and a mischievous thought crossed his mind as they caught up with her. "But here's a ready-made solution – Jean, we need a chaperone for John here, who wants to see the glories of our production line. Do you think you could oblige, please? Make sure he sees only the good bits."

Chapter Seventeen

Jean giggled, "Did you enjoy the five-shilling tour?"

John looked up from the soft curves of Jean's left breast, and smiled that slow friendly smile she loved so much, "Very much. Especially the good bits." He moved up in the bed and kissed her, the gentle reassuring kiss of a sated lover.

"How long can you stay?"

John response was to nibble her ear, and marvel at how much the world had changed. Just a few weeks ago, Jean had been concerned at what the neighbours would say if he as much as set foot in her house. She had seemed to feel that she should be seen as some sort of paragon of respectability. But that evening, after the factory tour, she had led him into her cosy terraced cottage with hardly a word said. The bedroom curtains were quickly drawn, though it was still bright evening sunshine outside, and they had made love as though it was impossible ever to have enough of one another. And now her question was, 'How long can you stay?'

"I'd love to stay for breakfast, but I'm due in Southampton for a meeting at ten tomorrow morning, and I doubt if even the milk train would let me do that. That's if they still have milk trains? Anyway I think I ought to catch the late train from Lynchester back to Euston. It goes at nine-twenty. Could you give me a lift to the station?"

"I'll do better than that. The nine-twenty stops all over the place, doesn't get into London till well after midnight. Instead I'll cook you a good steak, then put you on the ten o'clock from Birmingham International that gets in before eleven-thirty. Of course you have to pay my price."

John groaned in mock horror, "Not again?"

There are friendly silences, dignified silences, and the deafening silence of resentment, pique and wild rage. It was this last that was maintained as Roger Daniels drove back to London that evening with Jill. He made a couple of attempts to start a light conversation, but got only the stoniest of glares as a response. After the second withering rebuff he thought, 'Why bother? We've got a good campaign commercial, and the client is happy. She's not the only copywriter in London. There must be fifty just as good, and less likely to throw temper tantrums too.'

Jill waited until the Maserati pulled up outside her Hampstead apartment, then spoke in a flat monotone, looking fixedly ahead through the windscreen. "I won't be in the office tomorrow morning. I've got a meeting to finalise terms with the creative director at J. Walter Thompson. They seem to value what I can do rather more highly than you do."

Roger had been half-expecting something of the kind, but was in no mood to make things easy for her. The mention of JWT rang a particular alarm bell. "Jill, you're a free agent, and you must decide for yourself how best to advance your career. But I would recommend that you read very carefully the terms of your contract of employment. You will find that it requires you to give us three months' notice of leaving. You will also find that for the three months after that we can continue to pay you, but legally require you not to work in any capacity for an agency with clients that compete with ours. That's until six months from now. I'm sure I do not need to remind you that JWT have most of Kellogg's breakfast cereal business. To protect the legitimate interests of our client, Strongwheat, we would have to insist on the letter of that contract."

"Bullshit! Everyone knows those contracts cannot be enforced. Do you think the law exists to enable petty bullies like you to make slaves of employees? I don't believe you'd dare go to court. You'd be the laughing stock of the industry if you tried it, and who'd work for you after that?"

"You are being unusually naive. I know most of the directors at JWT. In fact I believe I sat next to their MD at the Advertising Awards dinner last year. If I give him a call to explain our little problem, he's not about to go to war over you, I promise you. After all, he might have the same problem next week with one of his people. So why don't we try to find a reasonable compromise while that's still possible? I did my best with that fluoride thing, you know I did."

"Your best? A damn feeble best, if you ask me! Will they put fluoride into the product? Who knows! Will it feature in the advertising? No fucking way! You just went through the motions and waited for the client to decide, or rather not decide. I think that's typical of your whole spineless approach to the business. I want to work for an agency that really backs its creative people, not one that just uses them as bait to suck in the money."

There was a long pause as Jill continued to stare straight ahead, then she said, "All right, Mr. Great Politician, what's the compromise then? I'm going to leave, no matter what you say."

"The compromise is just what I've said. You have to help us to be seen to be protecting the client's security. Assuming JWT offer you the job, you can agree to start with them on September 1st. That's just about the time that the new product will be launched. We'll pay your salary until then, but you have to promise not to say anything to anyone about the new product. Not to anyone, mind. So you'll have your new job, and a nice long paid summer holiday between now and then. And I'll be able to look Paul and Walter in the eye and swear that the plans are safely locked away in that pretty bosom. Is it agreed?"

Roger held out his hand in anticipation, but Jill ignored it as she levered herself out of the car. "I'm glad I kicked you out of my bed, you conniving, sexist bastard. Perhaps I really will call your wife one of these fine days, and have a good old woman-to-woman chat. We could even compare notes on your performance, if you can call it that. That should give you something to worry about, wouldn't you say?"

She stood at the door for another minute, but Roger said nothing. "OK you've got your deal. Mind you don't slip under a slug on your way home."

She slammed the car door with a venomous energy that rattled the padded interior to the last nut and bolt, and took the steps up from the pavement and into her Edwardian apartment block two at a time, in a swirl of high heels, slim calves and tailored pleats. Roger watched her go, with a mixture of regret and relief. *She wouldn't call his wife . . . would she?*

"I hope your sister and the baby are all right," said Rosemary, as she and Dick companionably did the washing-up together – not a very arduous task, as supper had been cold smoked mackerel, brought back from Salcombe, fresh bread and butter and a salad. "Ellen called me this morning to say she was rushing off down to Harlow, and she really was in a state. Are they as fond of you, I wonder, as they are of Ruth? I suppose that, being the younger, she was always spoiled a bit, especially by your father. Though I must say that in my family it was always the boys who were fussed over. Girls were expected to fend for themselves, mostly."

Dick was half listening, but mainly he was reviewing the board meeting in his mind, and waiting for Rosemary to make some comment. Like a dutiful Managing Director's wife, she had read the drafts of his board papers as they were circulated, and had listened to Dick's summary when he came in, but had not given him much of a response. He wondered if he had spelled out the implications of Oliver's warning too specifically, and now he felt quite uncertain how she would react.

After they had finished they walked out into the garden to enjoy the last of the evening sunshine. Rosemary was wearing a scoop-necked cotton summer dress, plain dark green with a short full skirt, that showed off her Salcombe tan. She sat on the wooden bench in a favourite sunny corner of the lawn. Dick, his shirtsleeves rolled up and his tie loose, lay on the grass with his head against her feet, and closed his eyes.

"Now, don't you dare go to sleep. I want to hear more about what we've got at risk with this new product thing. I suppose your father's as determined as ever?"

Dick sat up, and clasped his arms around his knees. "I think so, yes. I mean, I didn't say much after we'd talked about Ruth. I think he was exhausted, really, he'd had a tough old day you know. He just said he thought it had gone well, and we'd get together tomorrow to sort out the details."

"What do you want to do?"

Strangely, that was the one question Dick had never asked himself. He had concentrated his thoughts and effort on finding ways to reduce the risks – 'going cunningly', as Oliver had recommended. Perhaps he had thought that, if he was careful enough with the preparations, the decision would surface without any more ado, of its own volition. Perhaps, at least at the beginning, he had subconsciously expected, even hoped, that a clear negative would emerge. Then he could have said to his father, 'We tried, but . . .' That would have eliminated the need to consider the risks. But once the work had got under way he had been caught up and carried along by its very momentum. And now 'Strongwheat Light' could be said to have an independent life, a personality of its own almost. He guessed his father felt that way. *Perhaps the other managers did too? But what do I really want?*

"You haven't answered my question, Dick. I'd be pretty sure that your father would not ride roughshod over you now, not if you wanted to pull back, that is. Aren't there more things that you can do to reduce the risks? What about the idea I read in one of those papers – was it from Paul Williams? – to start by selling into a limited area, say a quarter of the country? Was that discussed at all?

"I talked that paper through with Walter and Paul. Walter said it was right to consider it, but he was basically against it. A sales campaign limited to an area is a nuisance to the big chains, who are geared up for national distribution, and it makes it easier and cheaper for the competition to clobber us really hard. And it sends a message that we're not really very confident about our product. I know I mentioned that thing Oliver said, about the danger that a failure could wipe us out. He's right, at least in theory. But we are a good deal stronger than we were a year ago. And the new product is really an improved version of regular Strongwheat, which itself is doing very nicely again. So

I come down to the view that, while Oliver is right to remind us that failure could be very painful, I don't think it's likely to produce a total disaster. It's not as though we've got lots of hungry shareholders to appease. And there is just a chance, a fair chance, that we could have a smash-hit on our hands."

He turned to look up at her.

"I was reading a book last week about the glider pilots, training for the D-Day landings in 1944. They all knew it was going to be incredibly dangerous, and that a lot of them were certain to be killed. But they still really longed for the day to come, and none of them would have missed it for the world. Our new product seems ready to have a life of its own now, and I really want to see it come into the world and make a mark for us."

Rosemary had never heard that almost mystical tone of heartfelt commitment before from her husband, and despite her private misgivings about the cost of failure, she was deeply touched.

"You and your father, when you get down to it you're two of a kind, aren't you? Romantics, dreamers of dreams, that's the pair of you. It's a good job you've got Ellen and me to stop you floating off into the wild blue yonder! Just remember, success will have many fathers, but failure is just a poor lonely bastard. Come on then, hero, let's see if you can get your sons to turn off the television and do their homework. And tomorrow, you tell James you're going at it full-throttle. That's the safest way to take off, isn't it?"

Dick pushed himself upright and bent to kiss her forehead affectionately, "Absolutely. Full throttle it is, skipper. It's just coming up to seven-thirty, and I promised Dad I would call the hospital one last time. Funny, he doesn't want Ruth to know how concerned he is."

Dick came back into the garden five minutes later to find Rosemary kneeling over a flower-bed. She was tugging at a dandelion as he approached, "This time of the year you've only got to turn your back on the garden for a day and . . . Dick? Dick, you look awful. It's not Ruth? Dear God, say she's all right. Dick?"

"I spoke to Mum, she was on the ward. She was just screwing up her courage . . . just going to call Dad. The sister put her on, rather than tell me herself. The baby . . . the baby's dead. Ruth had some sort of crisis, and they decided to do an emergency caesarean. Ruth is poorly, but not on the danger-list. But they couldn't save the baby. It . . . she was a little girl, just like Dad hoped for. And Mum is sobbing, and so upset she wants me to tell Dad. Oh Ros, how am I going to tell him?"

Chapter Eighteen

As John Savage climbed into the London train, he had impressed Jean yet again with the importance of the task he had explained to her over their steaks. So she spoke to Liz Boyd first thing the following morning, and at ten she was hovering outside Dick Routledge's office.

"Morning, Jean, is it me you want? I'm just finishing with Elizabeth. I don't know about you, but yesterday's meeting left me feeling punch-drunk. And now . . . I'm sure you've heard already about Ruth's baby?"

Jean nodded. "I think everyone in the factory has heard. Of course they all knew the Chairman was looking forward to being a grandfather again. I've seen any number of girls on the shop-floor wiping away the tears, as though they'd lost one of their own. Perhaps . . . perhaps it might help Mr. James if you could tell him that?"

"I will, thanks Jean. Won't you sit down? Just now I'm trying to pin down exactly what was decided yesterday, and what was left to be finalised later. Before I talk to the Chairman I decided I'd best go and sit down quietly with Jim Helvin, and go through his notes. I can see you've got something important on your mind, but can it be quick, please?"

Elizabeth gathered up the morning's post and withdrew, closing the door behind her. Jean was wearing her severest navy-blue suit with trousers and a plain white shirt, but even so Dick was intensely conscious of her femininity. *Why do I feel so guilty to be alone in my own office with her, with Elizabeth just outside? Dammit all, I am a happily married man with a lovely wife, and I've no intention at all of making any kind of pass at her. At least, she would have to send out a lot of unmistakable signals . . . But there was no denying she was very attractive, and just recently I've seen a new air of confidence radiating from her. A new man perhaps? Lucky fellow . . .*

"Do sit down please, Jean. Not that fluoride business again, is it?"

"No, well yes, partly, but not the same as before."

Dick sensed that she was not quite ready to go on, and continued, "By the way, I got another bit of an update from Ruth's husband first thing this morning. She had a comfortable night and is off the danger list. He thinks she'll make a full recovery in due course. I know everyone is concerned and we're all grateful. It brought me up a bit short last night I can tell you, and made me think a bit about what's really important. Made me understand too this morning that the people here are . . . are more than just employees. Could you put the news around on the grapevine please? And if you can let people know just how grateful we are for their sympathy?"

Before coming to Dick's office Jean had carefully rehearsed in her mind what she wanted to say, but suddenly the expression of honest concern on Dick's face made her speech seem trite and irrelevant.

"Of course. Dick, what I actually came in to talk about . . . it's about John Savage, or rather myself and John Savage. We've been seeing one another quite a lot over the last few weeks. Getting on very well, I think."

"Jean, that's marvellous for you. If it's still a secret, I swear it's safe with me. I don't know John very well of course, but Paul told me he had got on well with him, and I've been impressed with what I've seen so far. But presumably you haven't come in to ask my blessing?"

"Not exactly, no. But I did want you to understand how things are between us, because I'm acting as a kind of messenger for John. It's about a couple of things he wanted me to put to you on a personal basis. He thought that, if I said them, you'd be clear that he wasn't speaking for De Boissy now.

"Now you've got me really intrigued."

"The first is simply about the fluoride. He says that he's got a reason, but it's only a bit of a suspicion. He couldn't, or wouldn't even tell me what it's about. Unless you are convinced that it's absolutely essential, he advises against it."

"Message received and understood, I think. I'll be talking to Paul and Walter about it anyway. What's the other thing?"

"He hopes you won't feel that he's breached a confidence, but he's told me a little about the enquiry from De Boissy about the possibility of selling the company. I mean, I couldn't really be a useful messenger for him unless I knew something of the background, and you can be absolutely certain, Dick, that my lips are sealed outside this office."

"I'll have to judge the confidentiality thing when I've heard the message, Jean, but you know I trust you absolutely. So what's it all about?"

"He suggests that, before your Ascot occasion with Alex Hampshire, you or your father could do worse than seek some advice about the potential valuation of Strongwheat. He suggests that Oliver Sedburgh could probably suggest which U.K. companies might be interested. He said that some companies might be willing to pay a very handsome premium for Strongwheat, and especially to stop another US company getting into the UK market via the acquisition of Strongwheat. Does that make sense to you?"

"Very much so, thank you Jean. I can see that John must be pulled every which way, between De Boissy, Strongwheat and yourself. Would you say to him that his consideration for us is much appreciated, and I'll be as silent as the grave about our conversation today. I can raise the second issue with the Chairman as though it were my idea, I'm sure John won't mind. And you tell him he's got to look after you properly, or he'll have me to reckon with."

Jean left his office with a smile on her face and a spring in her step, and Dick leaned back in his chair and thought, not for the first time, 'It's the people that make life interesting.'

He wondered what John's special reason was for not having fluoride. Some sort of suspicion . . .? Something to raise with Walter, but it could wait until after he'd talked to Jim Helvin. Now, they'd agreed the new Flake line in principle, but Dad wanted to be persuaded that it could be put in during the Christmas break . . .

On June 15th, Vince O'Hanlon was going over his plan for what he thought might be the last time. Were there any gaps or weaknesses? Suppose it went totally adrift, was he safe from prosecution for criminal fraud? Safe from dismissal for apparent incompetence? As safe as could be, given the scale of the reward he was playing for?

The lunch with Bill Shavely, his one-time colleague in KKR, had been a partial success. Bill was currently head of KKR's office in Chicago, and while they were lunching in the discreet recesses of Chicago's Drake Hotel, Bill was regularly raising a hand to acknowledge friends and business acquaintances. More than once their talk was interrupted by a friend coming up to congratulate Bill on his recently announced promotion to KKR's main board, and on the imminent move to London to be Head of European Operations. Vince had found it difficult in this atmosphere to get Bill to concentrate on the scheme he was trying to sell, and indeed it was soon only too obvious that it wasn't going to fly. Bill had turned respectable. The old spirit of marauding commercial piracy that had characterised their former relationship had been replaced by something closer to bankers' caution.

"I can see you've got a great deal there," he had said over the coffee, "But it's not for KKR. At least, not at this time. We've done our research in England, France and Germany, and they're not ready for our American view that 'all's fair in love and business'. At least, not so obviously. The English are closer to us, but they're all running scared of the possibility of some Europe-wide regulatory control over mergers and acquisitions, and no one wants to take a chance on being accused of rocking the boat. They're nervous especially of anything which could result in the rules being drawn more tightly. Brussels is heavily into regulation and state control, and you bend the rules at your peril. A newcomer is going to be watched even more closely than an established player. I'm not saying that we're going soft, not at all. But we've taken a strategic decision that we're going to tag along quietly for the first two years or so. Try to strike up a few alliances with the big players, avoid making enemies unnecessarily, show them we're not the ogres they might think we are. Do you get my drift?"

Vince nodded, unwilling to let go completely, "So what would your advice be?"

"Advice? I'm suitably flattered that you should ask, Vince. Well, the obvious advice is to suggest that you drop your hook in the place where the fish are feeding. In this case . . . do you know a guy called Aaron Kaminsky?" Vince shook his head. "He's the new kid on the block in Chicago, eager, hungry, he's where KKR was ten years ago. He's pulled off a couple of deals in the forty to sixty-million bracket, and he's getting the reputation of being a cool operator." He lifted a finger to attract the attention of their waiter, "This one's on me, Vince. And I still owe you for the way you covered my back that time when the Reynolds thing was going wrong, so I'll tell you what I'll do. I'll call Aaron, tell him you're a friend of mine, and that you'll be calling him and you want to come in with a proposition that he should listen to. After that it's up to you, but I'd say he's likely to bite, provided he hasn't gotten sucked into something bigger already. Aaron will want to do me a favour, you understand? Will that do?"

Privately Vince was less than happy at the prospect of having to lay out his beloved scheme to another potential player, but there was no alternative, as far as he could see. To say 'no thanks' to Bill would be to turn a friend into an enemy, which was not Vince's way. He had already put out some cautious feelers to three multi-national U.S. companies where he had personal contacts, to discover only that their bureaucracy was as stifling and slow-moving as ACP's. There was no chance that any of them would respond on the kind of timescale his plan required, even if they did not balk at some ethical consideration.

"Gee, Bill, I'd really appreciate that. And next time we meet, in London I hope, let's make it roast beef and pink champagne on me!"

Vince had now had two meetings with Aaron, a tough, hard-nosed Midwesterner who looked like Harry Truman, and was equally unresponsive to sales patter. At their first meeting, in a bleak office suite high up in the John Hancock Tower, he had sat impassively through Vince's enthusiastic presentation, and at the end had said,

"Is that it?"

Vince nodded.

"So, exactly what do you want us to do? And how much do you expect to get out of it?"

Even Vince's thick skin was dented by Aaron's brutal style, but he recognised some hint of real interest in the body-language. He explained the plan again. Aaron steepled his thick fingers, and pressed them flat on his desk, as though he might leap to his feet. He fixed his gaze on Vince.

"Let me be sure I understand you. You put some kind of spoke in the wheels of this take-over deal in the UK, give us the nod when to step in and what to offer, and in return you want twenty percent of our gross profit after we sell it on? Is that the deal?"

"Yes".

"I'll say this for you, Mr. O'Hanlon, you've got balls." He pushed out his thin lips. "And I'm going to surprise you. I'm not going to kick your arse out of here, not yet at least. I'm going to say I want you to come back one week from now, with a plan that thinks of everything. You know better than me all the things that could go wrong – so show me how my money will be protected, no matter what. Got it?"

Vince got it. For the next week he went over and over the plan. There were two ways he had thought of to put that 'spoke' in. The 'fluoride scare' was the nicer one, because the FDA would provide the perfect cut-out to ensure that he would not be suspected. But it was the weaker line, partly because he could not be sure it would happen, or if it did on what exact timetable, and partly because it was difficult to be certain how ACP would react. So, as a fallback position, the 'demand' for a higher price was to be kept in reserve. ACP's reaction to that was totally predictable, because Vince had already tested the water. The problem was going to be making it plausible, and ensuring he was not found out in the lie.

Compared with his own scheme, the proposal for Aaron Kaminsky was simplicity itself:

1. Arrange a line of instantly available cash – $50,000,000 should do it.

2. Be prepared to move in with a fair offer the moment the rift appeared.

3. Organise a sale of the Strongwheat business, probably some sort of auction amongst US companies already operating in Europe, who could be expected to bid high to keep the competition out, and who could also anticipate the savings from rationalisations of some kind, which could be used in turn to lever up the price. Aaron could run this on his own timetable – the only limiting factor would be how long he was prepared to keep his money locked up.

4. Pay Vince his cut.

At the second meeting in Aaron Kaminsky's grey, functional office on the twenty-fifth floor, Vince had handed over the document he had laboured so long over, and had been surprised to find Aaron almost genial,

"Sit down, Vince, make yourself comfortable. Enjoy the view while I look through this. Want some of this coffee?"

He pushed on his thick horn-rims, and sat in silence for fifteen long minutes, frowning in intense concentration over Vince's draft, and making the occasional note in the margin. Vince had seen the enormous view over downtown Chicago many times already, from this and from other towers, and he stared into space through the big window without being conscious of seeing anything. *This is the big one. This is my chance to make the three to five million I need as table stakes to begin to be able to insert myself into the world of KKR and Kaminsky. Of course I'll have to start small, putting together one or two itsy-bitsy ten million dollar deals to prove my skills to the bankers. But then I could begin to be able to use bank money to multiply the power of my deals, so that my four million say would become eight, then sixteen, then . . .*

"O.K, I'm impressed, Vince. You certainly know your business, and you know what we need. Just one thing, there's a mention here of drawing up a contract of some kind between us. I don't do that. If we shake hands on a deal today, that's it. Nothing else on paper between us. That way I'm protected, you're protected, you know what I mean. Take it or leave it."

"But you agree to my share?"

"I agree. We take the risk. If we make a profit on the deal, you'll see the audited figures of our total return and our costs, and I'll pay you the twenty percent of our profit. If we make a loss, I'll pick up the tab and no hard feelings. Do we have a deal?"

He held out his hand, and Vince found himself taking it without further hesitation. On his way down in the elevator he recognised that he had encountered a great salesman, and felt oddly proud.

By contrast, the dinner in Washington with Gerry Masters had gone smoothly to plan, and was delightfully above board. Vince actually told Gerry something quite close to the truth,

"We're looking fairly closely, Gerry, at a foreign food manufacturer that is proposing to put out a children's food product with fluoride included. The intention is that the fluoride should support a healthy, 'builds strong teeth' platform. As you know already, we're not opposed to the idea, and in fact we think it could have a relevance in the US, as a way of appealing to concerned parents and bypassing the environmentalists lobbying against the fluoridation of the water supply. But I talked to the expert you recommended, and he gave me copies of a couple of Policy Statements from the American Academy of Paediatrics. Reading between the lines, I got the impression that fluoride is still a pretty hot potato, politically speaking. So that's why I wanted us to meet again today, Gerry. I know you'll appreciate that all this has to be in the strictest confidence, and it could really be damaging to my company's interest if it got out that we were talking ahead of any acquisition. But do you think it would be advisable for the FDA or one of its offshoots to be taking a look at the idea? I know we would be giving up the advantage of being ahead of the game, but I've learned from experience that our people at ACP would prefer to come along second and be safe rather than get in first and then have to face an embarrassing climb down."

Gerry Masters was no soft touch. His Harvard MBA year had been paid for out of his own savings and a family legacy, and was part of a calculated plan to help him get to the very top of US Government service. He had made a 'note for file' of Vince's original call, and had come prepared for the meeting by having read up himself on some of the literature on fluoridation, including the papers Vince had referred to. He was not unwilling to be helpful, provided the game was to be played under his rules.

"You're right about fluoridation being a delicate subject. Basically the medics are all for it, but there's been the usual opposition from the Greens and the 'right to God's pure water' people, and the whole thing is pretty well stalled now. A product of the kind you've been talking about could certainly be expected to stir things up again, especially if an American corporation was involved. There could be real advantages, as one would expect it to be seen as a voluntary medication, like the fluoride in toothpaste. On the other hand there could be medical worries about the quantities to be ingested, in areas where the water is already fluoridated for instance, and especially where very small infants are concerned. Can you tell me more about the product?"

"More than my job's worth, I know you understand. But we're talking about a product aimed at children, not a baby food."

"Fair enough. By the same token, there's only a limited amount of help that I can offer at this stage. So how would you ideally want this to be played?"

"It's the beginning of June now. Is it feasible that, say in August/September time, the FDA might say that it is proposing to recommend that a number of actual and potential food-additives, including fluoride, should be evaluated for possible interaction and toxicity?"

Gerry chewed the last of his grilled sea-bream in silence, and finished the excellent Chablis. He was square and powerfully built, with his fair hair cut aggressively short in a brush. He looked quizzically at Vince,

"There's something going down here, isn't there? Have you got some sort of fix in? Am I being played for a sucker? Because if that's what it is, you're in for a nasty surprise, I promise you."

Vince lifted his gaze to look straight into Gerry's blue eyes, which had lost their friendly twinkle and were suddenly cold and suspicious.

"Gerry, I'm going to tell it to you exactly as my boss told it to me. We like this business I mentioned, and we're prepared to pay a very fair price for it. But the guys who run it at this moment have a bee in their bonnet about fluoride. They think that, by being first in, they'll be able to put one over their competitors, who are in fact mainly overseas branches of US corporations. We see things rather differently. We are concerned that they may be stirring up a hornets' nest, and if we become the owners we'll be right in the hot seat. So we'd like to deter them from launching the product, at least until a lot more research has been done, and, most importantly, until we are clear about what the attitude of the regulatory authorities here will be. We know that their decision time is around mid-August, so that would be the ideal time for the FDA to announce its proposed enquiry. And that's the honest truth."

There was a fierce note of commitment in Vince's tone that made Gerry Masters believe him. "O.K., Vince, I'll give it a go for you. No promises mind. I can give the ball a push, but the decision about what happens next is my boss's, and he's got to go through committee as well. And even then it will only be a recommendation for a study. There are committees and sub-committees to decide whether it's worthwhile, whether it's affordable, and even if it's doable. And let me warn you again – no games, right?"

"I understand only too well, Gerry, and I'm in your debt. A brandy to go with the coffee?"

Vince sat back from this last review of his meetings with Aaron and Gerry, and thought his plan was simple, and had the great merit that, if the wheels came off, he should still be safe. The dice were rolling!

Chapter Nineteen

"Come in, come in, and welcome to De Boissy! James, it's a great pleasure to meet you again, and Richard, I've heard a lot about you from John Savage, all of it impressive, I'm happy to say. I hope you were comfortable at the Ritz last night? I really do appreciate your taking the time to come here today."

Alex Hampshire was only too well aware that the initial impact of the splendour of his Mayfair office could be somewhat inhibiting, and he always made a great effort to put visitors at their ease.

"We don't maintain this office in order to intimidate or dazzle potential clients," he had once said to John Savage, "The idea is to make them feel that, with us by their side, they too can aspire to similar privileges."

James had been through the process years before, but Dick was happy to be charmed, "The Ritz was fine, thank you Mr. Hampshire."

"Alex, do please call me Alex – everyone does."

"Thank you, Alex. I've left Rosemary and my mother preparing to do a little window-shopping in Bond Street. We've suggested they should be back at the Ritz and ready to go soon after twelve?"

"That should do nicely. I have asked my wife, Marie-Louise, to meet me here about the same time, so if we aim to finish this morning's discussions by midday we will all be on schedule for the car to Ascot. We have my box there with a buffet lunch laid on."

James was intending to be studiously polite, but felt that it was important to lay down some markers early on,

"It's a while since we met, Alex, but I'm sure John has kept you closely informed of our progress. Last year was a year of recovery for us, almost a half-million profit, and as you will recall, our first dividend payment."

"A most encouraging precedent."

"Just so. This year we are on track to double that. Dick here is still being cautious, but I think you will see the million. And now we have this most exciting new product coming out, which we believe can lead the way to as much as five million profit in three years from now. I'm the first to admit too that much of the credit will go to Dick for his skill in unlocking the potential from Strongwheat and also from its people. The fact remains that without the assistance – if they do assist – of any of those expensive multi-national consultants and bean-counters, we are managing to make something quite worthwhile out of our little business. I'll be totally frank with you, Alex. We enjoy doing what we do, but we're not wedded to it. For us, Strongwheat is a business, not a religion, so there's no need for you to think that you have to sell us off some deep emotional commitment to the company that Dick's grandfather started. That's not the position, not at all. You're the one living here in the trappings of two centuries of tradition. We're just simple chaps from the provinces, interested to turn an honest penny where we can."

Alex respectfully acknowledged the quality of James Routledge as a businessman and as a negotiator. With a few words he had demolished Alex's selling plan – there was a capability there that his cousin Lionel had recognised when De Boissy had made its original investment. *What a pity it had been locked away in Lynchester! Perhaps there was still time for James, under Alex's tutelage, to perform on a wider stage? I like to think of myself as an impresario of business talents – but it was undoubtedly desirable to land one's fish before designing its showcase.*

"James, I do so much welcome and appreciate your direct approach to things. If I may say so, you will find that ACP, which is the American company I mentioned to you, is managed by kindred spirits. Very direct, very down-to earth. I understand that the principal managers have all come up through the business; and that aspect of management policy is very much a matter of corporate pride for them and for their Board. My position, James, is that De Boissy are minority shareholders in your company, which enables us to identify your interests as identical to ours. We would like you to accept us as being on your side in this matter, a specialised extension of your team, if you will."

James nodded, "Willingly, Alex. As I said to Dick, you won't have invited us here just to sell us something, but so that the three of us together can decide if we are interested in buying into what the Americans have to offer."

Alex wondered fleetingly if there was more than a hint of irony in this last remark, then decided it was best to take it at face-value.

"That seems to be my cue to unwrap what we know about our friends in American Cereal Products Incorporated."

He opened a capacious drawer in his desk, and drew out three copies of a thick, ring-bound document, whose red leather covers were embossed with the De Boissy crest in gold.

"It's not as formidable as it looks. The thickest part, at the front, is a potted history of the company and copies of the last two annual reports to shareholders. I think it would make sense though if you would just glance through it."

There was silence for about ten minutes, during which Dick read about the company's various activities, and James, who already knew a considerable amount about every company in the cereal industry, concentrated on the latest accounts and balance sheets.

"Of course you never know quite where you are with a set of U.S. accounts, but I get the general impression that they can well afford to pay quite a lot for us, without breaking the piggy-bank."

"Indeed they can, James. And the other favourable factor is that they are really quite anxious to get themselves established inside the EU, as soon as possible. There is a fairly new executive team emerging, and the Board seems to be more aggressive, more expansionist than previously, when they were notably isolationist. The new team have set their sights, as you might have read in the last report, on 'building a global business in cereals and cereal products'. The man I have met, Mr. O'Hanlon, has the title of V.P. for Business Development, which means, I think, that he has been recruited with the specific job of making it all happen."

"And Strongwheat is his target for tonight," said Dick, looking up from his reading, "I see that they already have a biggish division in America producing breakfast cereals. Is that what makes us attractive?"

Alex did not answer immediately. Instead he got up from behind his carved and gilded desk, and stood for a moment looking out of the tall Georgian window. His face was in shadow as he turned to speak,

"Of course the business attracts them. It's in a field they understand, it's well-respected and growing well, by all accounts. It could provide an excellent springboard for them. But they want something even more important."

"And what more could there be?" said James, caught up despite himself.

"You, James. You and Richard here. The Routledges, that's what they want. You've been hiding yourself away for years in Lynchester, but you've not passed unnoticed. They've watched Strongwheat over the years, seen how you've kept pushing it up, despite the enormous pressure exerted in the market by competition like Kellogg, Quaker and Nestle. Those are the very same people who have severely limited ACP's own penetration of the US market. So they know what you can do. Do you remember, a few years ago, attending an international convention in Toronto for major grain buyers? I believe you had quite a lot to say on the subject of retail price maintenance – were you for or against? Doesn't matter now. Point is, American Cereal had a representative there, who wrote a confidential report on the various delegates. I saw a copy, James, of what he wrote about you. Very flattering, I can assure you.

"And now there's an extra bonus for them, in the shape of Richard here. Two years ago he was, if you'll forgive the phrase, an unknown quantity. But now it is perfectly obvious that he has the business under excellent control, and indeed is showing some of his father's old nose for an opportunity. James, it's this fortunate combination, a good business with good potential and, most importantly, good management, that ACP are excited about."

Alex returned to his chair, and waited in stillness for a response. Had he said too much, had he gone over the top? Would the fish rise to take the bait, or flick away because the lure was too bright?

"What did they have in mind as a price?"

A bite! A bite! A veritable thumping bite! Alex kept his voice calm and slow. *Make sure the hook is well and truly down before you strike . . .*

"Of course I've been negotiating that issue very hard on our behalf, James. I've said that you and Strongwheat together represent an absolutely unique opportunity for ACP. There is nothing comparable in the U.K., still less in Continental Europe. Of course all this is subject to due diligence and final Board approval, but I think we can be confident of a handsome sum up front, and then a three-year earn-out formula which should add up to several times the initial payment. And there would also be extremely attractive contracts for yourself and Richard."

"Would you like to unwrap some of that into a form that us simple manufacturers can understand?"

"In the most general way, I explained to them the tremendous momentum for growth you were building up, and we agreed that the proposed terms should reflect that. For instance, the lump-sum to be paid up front should represent something like the present value of the business . . .

"How much do they suggest that is, exactly?"

James' question came across flat and hard, disturbing even Alex's well-honed professional urbanity. He liked to persuade a client like James to be willing to accept a little less than he actually expected to get, so that a subsequent improvement produced appropriate feelings of respect and gratitude.

"Well, I've indicated to them that this year's operating profit should be around double last year's at, say, one million, so there is obviously a surge in current performance, without at this time taking any account of the new product. I think you could expect to see an offer of twelve to fifteen million pounds, as a kind of immediate down payment."

James pursed his lips to express his dissatisfaction, "I can't say that I find that very appealing. Dick, you've been doing some work on this, would you like to take it from here? I wouldn't like Alex here to think that I'm just a miserly old has-been, standing in the way of progress."

"With pleasure. As you know, Alex, we do have Oliver Sedburgh from the accountants Bell & Co. on the Board, so I asked him to give us some advice on valuing the business. He called me back only yesterday with some pointers." Dick read from his notes,

"1. The value of any company is absolutely in the eye of the buyer – I think that's his way of disclaiming responsibility.

"2. Strongwheat isn't a Cadbury-Schweppes or a Weetabix even, not yet at any rate, but we are what the market calls 'a nice little earner', with some potential. There aren't that many U.K. businesses available to be bought in the Food/Grocery area.

"3. Oliver thought it would be fairly easy to get one of the American manufacturers already here to pay twenty times our pre-tax profits, particularly with a view to making it harder for a potential competitor like ACP to get their toehold in the EU.

"4. Knowing that, ACP should be prepared to offer twenty-five times, in order to pre-empt the development of a public auction. So a price in the region of twenty-five to thirty million pounds would be about right."

Alex winced slightly at the mention of the word 'auction'. He could see his fish breaking away and sinking into the depths.

"James, I would not wish to appear to be disagreeing with Oliver, but I wonder if the sale of a U.K. business to an American multi-national is entirely within the field of his competence? Whereas De Boissy has much experience over the years, and a track-record of highly satisfactory achievements for both sides."

He saw James' eyes widen a fraction at these last words, and realised too late that he had made a tactical error.

"Oliver and I go back a long way, Alex, and I trust him absolutely. If he's offered Dick the benefit of his advice and judgement, it will be after he has consulted people who know about these things. And really, you know, I'm not here to help you to come up with a deal that will be highly satisfactory to you or to ACP. If they want in, I'm for squeezing them until the pips squeak, and they've just enough strength left to sign the contract. So which is it, Alex, are you on our side, as you said at the beginning, or are you just going through the motions?"

Now was the time to give the fish some more line and let him run, "On your side, James, absolutely on your side. I was only anxious that you should understand that there are limits to what ACP can offer without losing the confidence of their shareholders, which include some of the most prestigious institutions in the US. Equally I do see the force of Dick's argument – ACP will be anxious to avoid alerting their competitors, who might be very tempted to start or join some kind of auction, even if it's just a spoiling activity. These are early days in the negotiation, and I really wanted only to give their ideas an airing, and of course play back to them our reactions, as you feel appropriate. So, what would you suggest I should be saying to Mr. O' Hanlon at this time?"

"Dick, suppose you carry on."

"Alex, I suggest you could say that we are not opposed to their proposal for an earn-out over three years. But the initial payment would need to be more attractive than your twelve to fifteen million. I would ask for something in excess of twenty five, and we might settle for a bit less. Then the earn-out could be a multiple of each of the next three year's operating profit. That way, if the business doesn't grow much after this year, and they agree to pay a factor of, say, four times the profit, that's four times a million, times three years – an extra twelve million, making thirty-two altogether. On the other hand if the next three years produce the kind of growth we are hoping for, the total could be nearer fifty, even sixty millions. That sounds like a lot now, but they'll only be paying that if we're pushing the profit through five million in the third year, and then they'll be highly satisfied, wouldn't you say?"

Alex recognised that Dick and his father between them, no doubt with some assistance from Oliver Sedburgh, had in fact come to the kind of total that O'Hanlon had already prepared his board for, so there should be no great worries there. *Still, this was no time to let the client think these things were easy . . .*

"That's a very difficult question for me to answer, Richard. On the one hand, a total cost that comes to so large a multiple of current profits is unheard of, in my experience, particularly as there are no significant assets to be disposed of, which might have helped to reduce the overall cost to them. On the other hand we may be able to get them to take a view that all the excess is dependent on future growth, so the deal can be presented to the New York Stock Exchange as highly contingent, and so not too over-generous. The sticking-point is likely to be what multiple of future profits should be used in the calculations. Richard said four times, but perhaps that was just to illustrate your thinking? They may come back with, say, three times, and we can be negotiating upwards from there."

He paused, and looked thoughtfully through his notes. *Really, the discussions had gone far enough. Any more, and the client might start forming firm ideas, which might be difficult to shift if the need arose.*

"James, Richard, I think I have everything I need in order to be able to respond to ACP with some authority. After all, they have sought you out, not the other way around. Your position is that you are not actively seeking a buyer for your company, but neither are you opposed in principle to considering an attractive offer. And you have given me some parameters to help to determine what 'attractive' means in this context. We have not discussed what for ACP will no doubt be a major consideration, namely your willingness to continue to manage the business, perhaps with expanded roles, but it seems to me that a discussion of that kind might best be held on a face-to-face basis. I have a note that two or three of their senior executives are able to come over to England next month sometime for that purpose, so if you are content I will invite them formally after our secretaries have compared diaries, and get back to you in due course."

"That'll suit," said James, and Dick nodded.

"As it is coming up to midday now, I think we should break off, so that you may walk across to the Ritz and change. Marie-Louise and I will call for you with the car at the front entrance in forty minutes, say?"

After they had left, Alex closed the mahogany door to his office and swore out loud a few fine English swear-words, and then for good luck added a few of Marie-Louise's French ones. Damn, damn, DAMN Strongwheat plc. It had seemed a convenient, easy vehicle to use to ride triumphantly into De Boissy's first significant American client – with who knows what prospects of money and reputation to follow. Now, it might be going wrong. They had taken away all his negotiating slack. He was going to have to insist on terms which invited ACP to pay perhaps in excess of *fifty* million pounds for a company that had struggled to make five hundred thousand last year. If he presented the terms cold, he could be laughed at. If he made a big pitch about 'Strongwheat's wonderful prospects' he might well appear to be talking up the value of his own holding. Still worse, he might look less like the wise, even-handed counsellor he wanted ACP to trust and believe in, and more like one of those stock-market hucksters he so despised.

I wonder if I was right, if it was entirely fair of me to deny John Savage the opportunity to bring this one off? After all, he's on the Strongwheat Board, so he should be able to be the more convincing about their prospects. He's the one who has sat through all the deliberations and planning on this new product of theirs, so he is certainly best-placed to take on this next stage, now that I've laid the groundwork with each side.

He took an ice-cold shower in his private bathroom, and was wrestling with his grey silk tie when Marie-Louise arrived. Blonde, slender, elegant in what Alex always thought to be a very French way, she wore a slim knee-length sheath of dark-blue chiffon that flattered her long legs and slim ankles, and a neat cloche of white straw. She was a few years younger than Alex, and her bright blue eyes sparkled as she stood very close to take control of the tie for him,

"Will I like zees people, Alex?"

"I can't speak for the wives, but I think you'll find James Routledge and his son Richard amusing enough for a few hours in the sunshine at Ascot. I mean they are provincial, of course, but quite sharp. Quite sharp. The father is self-made, and no doubt the Almighty is very pleased to have been relieved of that responsibility. And the son was a pilot in the R.A.F. until fairly recently. Quite a good-looking chap. Eager to please, I'd say. Right, if you're ready, let's go and be entertaining."

Chapter Twenty

Vince O'Hanlon was not entirely satisfied with the information Alex had provided about Strongwheat's new product, but reflected that his plans were flexible enough for him to be able to wait a few weeks for details. He had barely got in to his office, a few days later, when his telephone rang.

"Vince? Hi, it's Gerry Masters at the FDA. How are you?"

"Well, thanks. And it's good to hear from you, Gerry. What's the news?

"News is that my boss likes the idea of that study we were talking about. The likelihood is that we will be looking a lot wider than just the fluoride thing we discussed, so your particular scheme will be one amongst many. Can't be too precise about the timing. Best guess would be late August for a public announcement that we are planning the study, which should suit you."

"I owe you."

"You do. By the way, you probably don't know that sodium fluoride is technically listed as a poison, and we have a section here that gets reports from the U.S. producers on all sales. Goes back to the Cold War days, when we were all shit-scared that the Russkies were about to poison New York's water supply. Turns out we have a recent report on file of an English food manufacturer starting to buy. Just a small quantity. Breakfast cereals?"

"My lips are sealed."

"Just remember, Vince, Big Brother at the FDA is watching you!"

The afternoon at Ascot had passed in a kind of dream-state. Gold Cup Day – the Thursday of Royal Ascot Week – is not quite as glamorous as the Wednesday, which is the Ladies Day immortalised in the film, 'My Fair Lady'. But it is in some ways the favourite of the racing crowd, because of the special format of the Gold Cup race, being a hard two and a quarter miles, with a big cash prize as well as the old cup itself, competed for by the best stayers in the world. Alex had established that Dick and Rosemary had never been to a racecourse before, and set out his stall to impress.

The big white Rolls-Royce was waiting for them outside the Ritz Hotel promptly at 12.30p.m. Alex ushered Rosemary into the front, alongside himself and his uniformed chauffeur. A second chauffeur was on hand to bring James' Daimler on to Ascot.

"James, Ellen, why don't you join Marie-Louise on the back seat? Dick, if you would like just to drop down that fold-up seat, I'm sure you'll be very comfortable for a short journey."

In not much over 30 minutes they were stepping down outside the members' gates of Ascot Racecourse, and being led into the big lift that took them smoothly up to the second floor of the Grandstand. The De Boissy box was a long through room, painted white, with a door at the rear onto the corridor, and french doors onto a balcony at the other end that looked out onto the course itself. They were positioned about twenty yards short of the finish line. A snowy white tablecloth down the centre of the room was laid with a cold buffet of lobster, roast beef, salads and strawberries with clotted cream. Four silver ice-buckets held the champagne, and the waiter opened the first with a ceremonial 'pop' as they came in. Once everyone had a glass Alex led them out onto the balcony.

"First race is at 2.15. You'll find race cards and some copies of *Sporting Life* on the table. The Queen and her party will come out of the gates of Windsor Great Park over there," he pointed away to the right, "And they'll drive in three or four open horse-drawn carriages all the way up the course, to pass in front of us and get out to go up onto the Royal Terrace, which is the fenced green lawn area immediately below us to the left. I think I'm right in saying that they've been doing that drive since Queen Anne's time. If you will agree, I would like to have the pleasure of looking after Ellen and Rosemary this afternoon, and Marie-Louise will be delighted I know to entertain James and Dick. There is a race roughly every half-hour, which perhaps sounds like quite a long, leisurely process. But between each race I know you'll love going down to see the horses and the people parade in the paddock ring, and by the time you've counted their legs to be sure they've each got four, and been thoroughly confused by studying the form in the *Sporting Life*, and then got a bet on with the Tote or a bookmaker, and then got back up here to watch your money running – after all that you'll think that 30 minutes is barely enough. Of course there will be champagne or anything else you fancy available here all afternoon, and you might like to stay to have some tea at the end of the racing, to allow the crowds to thin out before you go down to your car."

He led them back inside for an instant refill of the champagne glasses, "As I'm sure you'll want to see the royal procession, I suggest we should help ourselves to a snack now. Marie-Louise, by the way, is something of an aficionado of racing, so she is certainly better qualified than myself to take you through the form, and to point you in the direction of a profitable bet or two."

John Savage called Jean from his hotel room in Dusseldorf. "Hi darling. I miss you."

"Miss you too. I've just come in from a stroll along the river bank and a soothing gin and tonic in the 'Feathers'. Where are you?"

"Hotel called the 'Breidenbacherhof'. Big, old fashioned place, rather like the Grosvenor House. Full of antiques, and that goes for the furniture too. Any news?"

"Not much. Oh yes, you know you were so concerned about the fluoride thing? Well, they've decided to go ahead with it nonetheless. The Sales Director, you remember Walter? He came out very strongly in favour, so Dick has gone along with it."

"Oh well, we shall just have to see what happens. Now, about this next weekend, what do you think about coming over here? I know there's a direct flight from Birmingham to Dusseldorf Friday evening about six. I could order your ticket for you from here. We could rent a car and spend a couple of days looking at some of the old towns on what they call the 'Romantisches-trasse', that's the road up the Rhine that used to be part of the spice-route in mediaeval times, from Venice and Munich to the Baltic?"

"Sounds wonderful."

There was a long silence, whilst each waited for the other to ring off. Then John whispered, “I love you.”

“I’m glad.”

“So what did you like best about Ascot?”

“Collecting my winnings.”

James Routledge was riding in the front passenger seat of his Daimler, alongside Dick, who was concentrating on driving and navigating from Ascot to the crowded M25 and then onto the M1. motorway. James’ laconic reply to Ellen’s question made everyone smile. His wife persisted,

“Rosemary, take no notice of him, he enjoys being a professional sourpuss sometimes. Did you have a good time?”

“Absolutely, though I didn’t actually have to spend very long collecting my winnings. I thought it was lovely just to be part of the event. I mean that feeling of participating in it, not just being a spectator. I’ve watched Royal Ascot before, and the Derby too, on television. But it’s just so much more involving when you’re there. I walked right behind the Queen when she went down to the paddock. And aren’t the horses beautiful? Watching those thoroughbreds strut their stuff before the races, with the jockeys standing like bright little jewels on the dark green turf, that was the best part for me.”

“Not the parade of posh frocks?” asked Dick.

“Not really. I could tell you enjoyed ogling the pretty girls, but you can see that part definitely better on television. And it puts me off once they open their mouths and let out those awful tortured vowels. One question though, James, how come you got four winners and didn’t let Dick here in on one of them?”

“I did, I did tell him what to back,” James protested, “So of course he had to go off and do something quite different.”

“And where, may I ask, did your information come from?”

There was an icy edge to Ellen’s question that warned James he might be on delicate ground,

“Now, love, it was a business occasion, so of course Marie-Louise had been told to look after me.”

“Well, she certainly did that. I don’t think you spoke two words to me the whole afternoon. Every time I saw you, you had your heads together over another glass of champagne, or you were giggling like schoolgirls while you counted your winnings. And I thought it was really quite extraordinary when she changed her hat for that ridiculous great floppy red thing when the sun came out in the middle of the afternoon.”

"My grandmother used to say, 'red hat, no bloomers' ", said Rosemary, being helpful.

James maintained his dignity, "I think you misjudge the lady. As I said, she was only doing her job."

"What job was that?"

"Helping Alex to soften us up. Giving us humble provincials a glimpse of the gracious life we could aspire to, if only we'd let De Boissy's guide us. I'll say this for her, she really knows her way around the paddock. Owners, trainers, jockeys, bookmakers, she chatted up all of them. It's that French accent of hers that turns them on".

"And the long legs, and the blonde hair, and the bright, bright blue eyes," Dick added encouragingly.

"I think that's quite enough of the Marie-Louise fan club", said Ellen with a certain waspish severity, "If it was a business occasion, I'd certainly like to hear something about the business of the morning. All you said was that it had 'been interesting'. What did Mr. Hampshire propose? Do you think you might really sell up?"

"Dick, you're making the running now. Why don't you tell the girls where we stand?"

Dick, now safely on the M1 and through the bulk of the traffic, flicked the big car expertly past a line of lorries, then settled back into the middle lane.

"Fine, Dad. Well, the first thing that needs to be said is that nothing is finally settled yet. Alex has had some talks with this company, American Cereal Products, and frankly I think he's got them on the hook. So he's been asked to float a couple of ideas in our direction. He's the go-between. He would like us to see him as the honest broker."

"And is he?"

"Is he what?"

"Is he honest?"

"I think so, but it's hard to be sure. I mean, I've never met anyone quite like him before. He's very grand, if you know what I mean. Beautiful manners, very thoughtful, very attentive. Well, you saw for yourself this afternoon. But you're left feeling it's all a bit of an act, a show that's been put on for your benefit. Will the real Alex Hampshire please stand up? What did you think, Dad?"

"He's a salesman, and a very good one, and I don't hold that against him. Nothing happens in business until someone makes a sale. He works very subtly and carefully to find out what you want, then offers you just that, dressed up slightly differently of course. Is he honest? There's a question. 'What is Truth?' asked Pilate, and didn't wait around to be told. I would say that, by the standards of the City, he's scrupulously honest. Perhaps more so than most, because he's truly proud of the history of his business, through all those generations of his ancestors. But it's important to bear in mind that the City exists to make money out of people like us, so we have to look out for ourselves too."

"And how do we do that? You seem to be saying that we can't simply depend on Alex for unbiased advice."

"Right, we should not. But we're lucky in having Oliver Sedburgh who has been a friend for fifty years, and he marked Dick's card for him. Dick, why don't you tell them how we left it with Alex?"

Dick had to slow down and concentrate on his driving again, as he negotiated a lane-closure, then they were accelerating in the three-lane section once more.

"Oliver told us a few useful things about valuing Strongwheat. Apparently English manufacturers are flavour of the month in America now, as they're waking up to the importance of being represented inside the EU. Or perhaps they're afraid that Wall Street will classify them as secondraters if they don't operate on a fully global scale. Whatever the reason, we've got something they really want. And they'll pay a premium to stop their competitors getting it."

"How much, then?"

It was typical of Rosemary to want to get down to price immediately. Dick responded accordingly, "Fifty million."

"Dollars?"

"Pounds."

"That is quite ridiculous," said Ellen firmly, "I remember just before Christmas your father showed me last year's result. We made about five hundred thousand, and that was before paying interest and taxes. No one could possibly want to pay a hundred times the year's profits for Strongwheat. I'm surprised at you, Jim, encouraging Dick this way. He's bound to be badly disappointed. Tell him, Jim. A million would be nice though. You've worked so hard, both of you. It would be nice to be millionaires, wouldn't it?"

"Of course it would," said Dick testily, intensely irritated that his mother thought he was still an idiot child. "But the business is worth more than that, much more than that. To start with, we are near enough to the end of this year now to be fairly sure that we'll come close to doubling last year's result. We could make a million before interest and tax this year. The market is still growing, and we're clawing back the share of it that we used to have. There are cost-saving investments still to pay off, and then there's the new product. Dad and I figured that, if you look say three years ahead, we'll be making between three and five million a year in profit. That's what the Americans would be buying, as well as our position in the industry, to use as the springboard for their ambitions in Europe. At fifty million, we could even be a great bargain for them. And Oliver said something quite interesting, he said that the bigger the price, the more likely the Americans were to treat it seriously. We've asked Alex to put a kind of formula to them. They pay a lump sum up front, then in addition a multiple of each year's profits over the next three years. Actually, if we did climb to the five million level, they could end up paying as much as sixty million for us, but Dad thinks that forty to fifty is more realistic."

Ellen and Rosemary were reduced to total silence. Ellen knew that her house was now worth between five and six hundred thousand pounds, so with a stretch of the imagination it was possible to imagine the buying power of a million pounds. But fifty million, or more perhaps? What sort of people had control of that much money? What sort of people would they become? Finally Rosemary found a down-to earth rejoinder,

"I'll bet the tax man would take most of it."

Ellen thought of Ruth, and the baby she had lost, "That wouldn't be so bad if they did something useful with it. Could we build a hospital or something, Jim? I was talking last week to one of our neighbours, Jennifer Hawkins. One of the three 'rich widow Hawkins', as the town calls them. Her husband died last year, and then there was that awful business with her two stepsons being killed, do you remember? She's using her money from selling up the builders' merchants to build the new shopping centre, and it's going to be called 'The Hawkins Mall'. I think 'The Routledge Infirmary' sounds very good. Or perhaps we could endow a wing at Great Ormonde Street Hospital for Sick Children, in London?"

"Hang on, woman, we haven't got sixpence yet. And anyway Dick has this idea of taking most of the payment in the form of shares in their company. Then we needn't pay tax until we want to sell them. And we'd be important shareholders, which could be useful in the future."

Dick was concentrating on his driving again as they slowed for the exit from the motorway to Lynchester, so James undertook the task of explaining to Ellen and Rosemary that, far from planning retirement, he was considering taking on the responsibilities of being ACP's chief executive for Europe. As Dick dropped his parents off at their house his mother was beginning what would undoubtedly be a long protest campaign.

"We are going to have to have a serious talk about this, Jim. What do you think Dr. Carr will say if you start gallivanting all over, just when we've got you well again? I could lose my temper with you, really I could . . ."

Chapter Twenty-one

After the Ascot day with the Routledges, Alex wasted no time before handing over to John Savage the responsibility for the negotiations between ACP and Strongwheat.

"First of all things are very amicable between us and the Routledges, so there's precious little chance that the business of negotiating could damage your position on the Board. Secondly, I can see any amount of to and fro across the Atlantic, old boy, and quite frankly Marie-Louise has put her pretty foot down, and very firmly. She says she does not want me to become permanently jet-lagged, so I am commanded to delegate. And in this instance I feel I can do so with complete confidence in a brilliant outcome. ACP are very keen to buy, and James and Son – there's a chip off the old block if ever I saw one – I say James and Son are willing to sell if you can lever the price a little, and perhaps construct attractive contracts for their future employment. Elaine will give you a copy of the minute I wrote of the meeting I had with them on the morning of Gold Cup Day last week. You will see we have an excellent fit between what the Routledges want and what ACP have been persuaded to offer. I'll give James a quick call to tell him about the handover, and

I'll call O'Hanlon too after lunch, to put him in the picture, and then you're off and running."

John had mixed feelings about the task. He was pleased to have control again of the dealings on behalf of the business where he was, after all, the assigned director from De Boissy. And there would undoubtedly be more opportunities to spend time up in Lynchester with Jean Carey, and that had become a significant priority in his life. But he was suspicious of Alex's reasons for handing over – common sense told him that gift horses from Alex were just as likely to be white elephants with very bad teeth.

His first action the following afternoon, having checked with Elaine that Alex had already made his promised call to ACP, was to call Vince O'Hanlon. There had been a mention in Alex's minute of a planned visit to the UK in July by a top team from ACP. Was that still on?

"Gee, John, it's good to know that your Mr. Hampshire feels there has been sufficient progress to hand the work on down to us humble labourers. Yes, I've had the e-mail from Alex with the results of his meeting with the people at Strongwheat, and he seems to have done a fair job for us. Of course the price looks potentially very full, but not so far out as to be beyond reasonable negotiation. I know that my two bosses here, that's Lloyd Teller, our Chairman, and Ben Camina, our Chief Operating Officer, have pencilled in a visit to England in late July, assuming the omens look favourable. Knowing them as I do, you might expect wives on the trip as well. If you agree, I'd like to tell them that things look promising enough, and I'll get back to you with a suggested schedule. I hope I may be allowed to come along, in which case I look forward very much to us meeting."

John liked the sound of Mr. O'Hanlon. He thought he had a nice, laid-back style, intelligent and practical, but not too pushy. His second call was more fun,

"Hi, Jean. It's John. I hope your flight back from Cologne was OK? Can you come down this weekend? Or shall we shock your neighbours again?"

John's third call was to Dick Routledge, and Dick hardly hesitated before consulting Liz Boyd, the Very Senior Secretary he shared with his father,

"Elizabeth, I expect you're the world's expert on this sort of thing. We are to receive a state visit from probably three very important Americans, plus probably a couple of company wives. You know of course about the possibility the Chairman has been negotiating. Towards the end of next month sometime. How do we entertain them?"

"Belfry', if you can get the rooms."

"Belfry? As in ding-dong?"

"I'm sorry, Mr. Dick, I keep forgetting you are still a stranger round here really. The Belfry Hotel is actually on the course where the Ryder Cup, the golf match between Europe and the Americans, is usually held. Between Tamworth and Coleshill, quiet and secluded, but very convenient for the airport. Nice modern comfortable hotel, and we can even arrange for your very special visitors to play the Ryder Cup course, as long as there's not a tournament going on. Americans usually play golf, don't they? It's less than half an hour from here. You can take them to Stratford on Avon one evening, and a concert at the lovely new hall in Birmingham another, and the ladies will love to see Warwick Castle and shop for antiques while the men look over the factory and negotiate or whatever. They'll all have a lovely time. Do let me know how many, and when, as soon as you can, and I'll arrange everything."

The visitors from ACP came at the end of July – Lloyd Teller accompanied by his wife Rose, a large but very well groomed lady, with a delightfully infectious giggle, and Ben Camina with his second wife Juanita, a dark attractive girl twenty years younger than himself, with huge eyes and a charming Mexican accent. Vince had been left behind – "It's important that Ben and me can tell the Board that we looked at this independently, and so our decision is our own. Take it as a vote of confidence that you've done a good job laying the groundwork on the numbers, Vince, and we're just going over to press the flesh a bit, try to suss these guys out and see what kind of plant they have. That Alex Hampshire guy is pressing us to include meeting with him in our itinerary, but I've told him that you are his contact in ACP, and he'll just have to do without us on this trip."

Their American Airlines flight from Chicago came into Heathrow, and Dick met them with two cars for the drive north to the Belfry. Liz Boyd and James' wife Ellen had put together their programme with military precision:

Day 1. Arrive at Belfry Hotel late morning after overnight flight. Allow time for a rest. Collect at 3p.m. for informal visit to

Lynchester (riverside walk and mediaeval church). Tea with Ellen and James at their house. Chauffeured car back to the Belfry. Meet at 7p.m. for dinner in hotel with Ellen, Rosemary, James, John Savage and Dick. Mr. Savage has arranged his own accommodation.

Day 2. Lloyd and Ben to join Dick and John Savage for a round on the Ryder Cup course, tee-off booked at 9a.m. Ladies all together at 10a.m. for visit to Warwick Castle and shopping, including lunch. Men to lunch at the Belfry, then to Strongwheat for short factory tour and business presentation by Dick, James and John. Collect from Belfry at 7p.m. for visit to Royal Shakespeare Theatre, Stratford on Avon (10 × best stalls at 'Henry V'. Mr. Savage to be accompanied by Miss Carey), and supper afterwards in Stratford.

Day 3. Ellen and Rosemary to collect Mrs. Teller and Mrs. Camina at 10a.m. for free day – shopping, a National Trust property, a visit to Coventry Cathedral, a picnic in Shropshire – are possible ideas, depending on the weather. Gentlemen at Strongwheat for business meeting. Collect from Belfry at 6.30p.m. for concert (Beethoven) at Birmingham Symphony Hall. 10 seats reserved. Supper at the Jazz Club.

Day 4. Car at Belfry at 10a.m. to take guests to Birmingham International for flight to Paris.

At the end of the week Dick looked in to his father's office after he had checked his post.

"I don't know about you, Dad, but I'm absolutely exhausted. And I didn't have to fly the Atlantic before we started. God knows what state our American friends will be in – I know they're intending to spend the rest of their two-week trip touring from city to city across Europe."

James nodded. He had even got up early himself that morning to see his guests onto their flight.

"One of the odd things about them is that none of the four had ever been to Europe before. Rose told me that she felt quite adventurous, because only about one American in twenty has a passport. I suppose if you've got all America to visit, plus Mexico, Canada, Puerto Rico and Hawaii, Europe must seem a long way off, and not very important. I imagine they'll travel for ten days now on pure adrenaline then pass out when they get home."

Dick poured a second cup for himself and his father, who then quietly asked,

"What did you think of Lloyd and Ben?"

Dick knew that his father's question was not a casual one. It was clear from the tone of their talks with the Americans that Alex Hampshire had been right when he said that ACP was as interested in the management of Strongwheat as they were in the business itself. So the personal chemistry between them was going to be very important, especially at the beginning, when so much had to be taken on trust.

"Two solid citizens, I thought. I liked the way they listened and asked questions, and didn't talk too much. They've clawed their way up over a good number of years, through a pretty tough business, and neither of them is the slick salesman type. If we go along with the idea of joining them, we're going to be pretty dependent on those two for support when the going gets rough – as it's bound to, sooner or later."

"You're going to need them for longer than me, I would say. I think they're men you could depend on, as long as they believe you're honest."

"What's Mum saying now about you taking on the Obergruppenfuhrer Europe job?"

"Not that much. I had a quiet chat with Dr. Carr, and he's told her that there's every reason to believe that having a new interest, as long as it's not too strenuous or stressful, could help keep me going. Prolongs active life, you know. She may have looked at Ben's beautiful Juanita, and decided I'd be safer with a new business interest to keep me out of mischief. I've told her that I'll be strictly non-executive, part-time and doing lots of delegating and all that. I don't think she believes me altogether, but she's probably worked out that starting a fight could be bad for my health. At least I hope so. Will you be comfortable reporting to Lloyd?"

"He reminds me of a Wing-Co I knew – a big, shambling easy-going bear as long as you did what you'd said you would do, but a snarling monster if you crossed him. Lloyd really loves his golf though, and playing the Ryder Cup course was like an advance visit to Valhalla for him. He shot a net eighty for the Championship course, which has to be brilliant twenty four hours after you've just flown the Atlantic. He practically did a war-dance after he pulled off that hairy 4-iron shortcut across the water and onto the green at the seventeenth. I've talked it over with Ros last night, and we're going to give it a go, as long as the contract makes sense."

"It will, it will. They've too much at stake to mess that up now."

"I was surprised at how easily they accepted the terms for buying us, pretty well exactly as John spelled them out. From what Alex had said, I'd thought we were in for a couple of days of haggling. I suppose we've just got to sit still now and wait for the paperwork to come through."

"And make absolutely certain that our new product is as right as it can possibly be, – manufacture, packaging, promotion, advertising, sales conference, everything."

A holiday is important, but American senior executives like to keep in touch with the office, and Ben Camina was no exception. On the day he arrived in Paris he called ACP from the 'George Cinq' early in the evening, Paris time.

"Lucy my dear, you have a very lovely way of saying 'ACP, may I help you?' Now, as you know, I am calling from Paris, France, on the other side of the Atlantic Ocean. Would you see if our Mr. O'Hanlon can take my call now, please?"

"Good afternoon, Vince, it's Ben Camina. All OK back at the ranch?"

"All goin' smoothly without you, Ben."

"Thanks for the compliment. Now about this Strongwheat business, I am very pleased to be able to tell you that you've done a great job for us. They're good people, very good people. The plant is like something out of Charles Dickens, all smoke-blackened stone and a tall chimney. And the weirdest boardroom you ever saw. Still, if their Health and Safety pass it, who are we to complain? Some very smart new packaging machinery though, and we'll be making a little diversion, extending the trip by a couple of days to talk to the makers on our way through Italy, that's providing they're not all on fuckin' shutdown already for the rest of the summer, like most of Europe. How do these guys ever make a living? Anyway we've agreed terms, and we'll be faxing details over to you from this fancy George Cinq place in Paris. That's if they ever send up the typist they promised. Would you put it in hand with the lawyers for drafting, and crank up the due diligence bullshit from the accountants? Tell both of them we don't need to try to boiler-plate every last damn comma – just follow my instructions as per this fax, got it? They could do worse than use those model acquisition contracts we slaved over last year for the Mexico deal. And you remember we talked about a press release? Lloyd thinks it will play better if you just talk personally to one or two of the top financial reporters, you know the ones. Off-the-record briefing, not for attribution, 'little-bird-told-me' stuff. We'd like to see the stock market reaction before we go formal. OK?"

"Got it, boss. Have a *great* holiday – it's all in safe hands here."

Vince replaced the old-fashioned telephone onto its cradle slowly and softly, as though it were made of finest eggshell porcelain. Really, he did not want to break the spell that seemed to be delivering everything so beautifully into his hands. He looked down at his notes. *Everything was agreed!* And the timing and wording and placement of the press release were his to determine also . . . *Magic!*

Chapter Twenty-two

Vince O'Hanlon had contacts established already at the *Chicago Herald Tribune* and the *Wall Street Journal*, and had no difficulty in getting them interested in the possibility that ACP was about to pull off a significant acquisition in England. "Two of our directors are in Europe at this time," he said, "And I should have more news for you in a week or two. Of course the deal will be subject to due diligence and shareholders' approval." He also called Aaron Kaminsky, to ensure that he was still ready to act when Vince gave the word.

Two stories appeared the next day. The *Herald Tribune* ran the story in its business gossip column:

Cereal Shopping

We hear that Lloyd Teller, Executive Chairman, and Ben Camina, C.O.O. of ACP are 'holidaying' in Europe. The likelihood is that their souvenir purchases will be just a tad heavy this year. Could be a nice present for their shareholders.

The Wall Street Journal treated it more formally:

ACP Looks to Europe

Unconfirmed reports indicate that Illinois corn brokers American Cereal Products are joining the flood of U.S. companies seeking their fortunes inside the E.U. Asked about an imminent acquisition, an ACP insider said, 'no comment at this time.'

There were no follow-ups, and, surprisingly, no calls from other papers or the TV asking for more information. But Vince noted an immediate effect on the ACP share price. For years ACP had been one of the steadiest shares on the Big Board, gaining ground when the market rose, (but not as much as the market,) and easing back down when the market fell. Rated in the NYSE as a typically safe Pension Fund recommendation, yielding a rock-solid 4%. He had noticed some weakness in the last week in July, resulting in a daily fall of one or two percent. *Someone feeding in a regular hefty 'sell' order?* But in early August it jumped 8% in a day immediately after the press stories, and from there on just kept moving up day by day. It was obvious that someone was in the market with some weight, mopping up all sellers. By August 14th he reckoned the company was standing 15–20% above its normal level. Experience told him that such a rise usually indicated an imminent bid on the way. He thought of Aaron Kaminsky. Might he . . .? Impossible! ACP could not be bought for less than a billion dollars, perhaps a lot more. Kaminsky was not in that league – yet. Vince knew by the smell of it that something big was going down, and wondered about taking a plunge on ACP futures. Then he realised that he could not forecast accurately when the FDA story would break, nor even if it would have any effect on a possible buyer or the share price. There were just too many uncertainties, he thought. And he liked to deal with certainty. '*Mugs gamble. Investors use information*'.

Walter Hurd, Sales Director at Strongwheat, had personally been very taken with Jill Lister's idea to introduce fluoride into the new product, and had gone to considerable trouble to pre-sell the idea to three of his four largest supermarket customers, with a very satisfactory response. At nine o'clock in the morning he was drafting his presentation for the sales conference to launch Strongwheat Light, just two weeks before the scheduled September 1st launch date, when his secretary rang to say she had the cereal buyer from his favourite customer, Binbury's, on the line. His heart skipped a beat.

"Walter, I'm really sorry to have to say this, but I've got some very serious news to do with that new version of Strongwheat you discussed with me. Is the launch still on for next month?"

"It most certainly is, Geoff. The consumer research has come in with a terrific preference in our favour, the TV commercial is the best we've ever done, and we've already had your opening stock order for the 'Free Trial' promotion pack of regular Strongwheat, and the allocations for the new product into all the larger branches, delivery week-commencing September 21st. Is there a problem?"

"Well, the problem is in America at the moment, but we have to respond to it here, just to be safe. The Food and Drug Administration people there have just put out a press release, saying that they are proposing to start a study of a wide range of food additives again, looking at potential toxicities, and sodium fluoride is one of the things mentioned as under suspicion. We picked it up early because we routinely monitor their web-site. Have you seen it?"

"Not yet, no."

"I'll fax a copy to you. Frankly Walter, Binbury's could not offer its customers a food that was suspect."

"Geoff, there must be some mistake. Half the civilised world is drinking fluoridated water. Most toothpastes, including your own brand, contain it. All the dental authorities and paediatricians are for it. How could there be a problem after all these years?"

His buyer was firm. "According to the release, the problem may not be fluoride or any other individual ingredient as such, but fluoride, and indeed any other additive, in combinations, for example vitamins and artificial sweeteners, and other kinds of combinations too. It says:

'There is an hypothetical possibility that combinations of such additives may be potential carcinogens, even where the additive by itself presents no risk.'

The FDA is proposing a study programme that is going to take two or three years at least. Walter, I thought it was a really good idea, and I'm so very sorry to have to tell you that we must withdraw our order. Personally I've no doubt that the outcome will show that there's nothing in the hypothesis, but I'm sure you understand my hands are tied. What do you think you will do?"

Walter had been thinking very hard about what he should say, and had come to the conclusion that nothing was more important immediately than to make the customer feel valued and important.

"Geoff, I'm really grateful you've thought to call me this morning, and I understand your position perfectly. I'm going straight in to see our MD now, and I'm certain he will take my advice about the new product. I see in my diary, Geoff, that I've got an appointment booked with you for September 4th at ten. I'll be there, with the new Strongwheat Light, and without the fluoride. That's a promise. In the meantime, can you hold back on issuing the cancellation of our orders until I get back to you? I'll call by four o'clock today."

Walter put the telephone down, laced his fingers in a favourite gesture behind his bald head, and leant back in his padded office chair, breathing deeply. He would *not* go scuttling in to Dick with the problem. He had already discussed a fallback idea with Paul and Phil. Now was the time to present Dick with answers, not questions.

Dick Routledge had been working, as he often did when his father was out, at the Chairman's desk in his corner office with its tall window that gave a lovely view of the sunlit waters of the River Lyn and, on its far bank, a stretch of rough pasture still called Crabbe's Marsh, although the winter flooding that gave it the name had been cured by the building over the last year of Hawkins Mall, just out of Dick's line of sight to his left as he looked out. He listened without interrupting, but felt sick with a foreboding of total catastrophe, and his face was grim. He looked up at Walter, Paul Williams, Jim Helvin and Phil Wythe, who were sitting at the oak table that butted up to the desk.

"Before we go on to what we should do, could we run over the likely unavoidable costs? Phil?"

"First of all we've got all the stock for the regular Strongwheat with the 'Free Trial' promotion already packed. We've got to break open every pack, recover the four stacks of Regular, and scrap as pig-food the fifth stack of Light, containing fluoride." He tapped at his pocket calculator, "Assuming we don't lose more than ten percent of the Regular to damages in the process, I'd say we're looking at the thick end of £600,000. Assuming again that we still want to go ahead with the promotion, we've got another £500,000 for that. Plus writing-off stocks of packaging for Strongwheat Light that feature fluoride, say another £50,000. Fortunately, if you can say that, we were only starting this morning to make Strongwheat Light for stock, so I've been able to stop that. In total, allowing for contingencies, say £1.2 million."

Dick had written down the figures as Phil enumerated the arithmetic of the potential disaster. His voice was almost inaudible as he spoke. "More . . . more than we've made in the whole year. Jim?"

"I think Phil's estimates are reasonable. We were expecting a launch on September 1st, so a month's sales from the promotion pack and from the introduction of Strongwheat Light would have fallen into this current financial year, ending September 30th. I know Phil will be pulling out all the stops for us, but it's only sensible to assume that the launch goes back to October 1st, so all the sales will fall into the next financial year. You may want to reconsider your original intention to take some of the launch costs for the new product into the current year And we probably need to talk to Oliver and the auditors as to the best way to show these write-offs in the accounts."

"Walter? What would your advice be? Should we press on, or cut our losses?"

A loss of over a million. Twice as much as last year's operating profit before interest and taxes, and more even than this year's wonderfully improved result. Could the company survive? What would Dad say? What about ACP and the deal? Would they want to renegotiate? Have I been stupidly arrogant to go ahead with the new product? Should I have stood up to my father after all? First there had been that awful business with Ruth losing her baby, and now this. What if . . .

"Dick?"

"Sorry, Walter. You were saying?"

"As you know we delayed the decision about fluoride, so we had the printer proof up both the 'Free Trial' pack and the Strongwheat Light packs in two versions, with and without the panel on the side about fluoride and healthy teeth. Phil's already been in touch with the printer and told him we have an emergency. He's making ready now, and if we give him the go ahead before 1p.m. we will get some cartons in here tomorrow morning, so we can start straight in to pack the 'Free Trial' promotion again. Phil has already got the girls started at breaking down the 'Free Trial' packs. So we *can* do it. Do we want to? I've spoken already to three of my top customers and told them about the FDA announcement – I thought we might as well get what credit we could from not hiding the bad news. Because it's the Yanks who've sprung this on us, I think we're going to get a kind of sympathy vote. Of course if Strongwheat Light doesn't sell they'll throw it out just the same, but I believe they will give us a chance. To be brutally frank, Dick, if we don't press on now I'd say we'd have a damn hard time of it if we came out with a new product at some later date. It might even weigh against us if the crunch comes with some of the supermarkets' range rationalisation programmes, as Oliver was warning us about."

"Jim, could you assemble all this information from Phil and Walter please, and I'd like you to come with me – I'm going to call the Chairman now to say we're coming over to see him at home."

Vince had learned from his girl friend Anna that Aaron Kaminsky preferred to be known as 'Harry', and made a point of using the name this time.

"Harry? It's Vince O'Hanlon. How are you? Good. Look, Harry, about that UK acquisition we talked about? Now would be the time to have the funds available. Things are going down as planned at the FDA. I'll call you again when I think it's time to move in."

"Thanks Vince, I'll look forward to hearing from you."

Vince looked at his watch. Ten o'clock Chicago time, that would be four in the afternoon in London. He put in a call to De Boissy.

"Is that John Savage? John, it's Vince O'Hanlon at ACP. I hope you are well? Good. Look, John, I've just seen a press release from our US Food and Drugs Administration people. Have you seen it?"

"No. What's it about?"

"You can find it on the FDA website. It's about fluoride. I'll e-mail you a copy anyway, but briefly it says that there's to be an investigation of the effects of certain food additives in combination, as potential carcinogens. And fluoride is to be included. It may take a little while to reach your food industry in the UK, but it's got to be a sure bet that the new product from Strongwheat will be hit. I've just had the signed preliminary contracts back from the Routledge people, and I guess they're going to be very unhappy with this. I mean they've got a lot riding on the next three years, and this investigation is sure to end up smashing their fancy new product, and digging a hole into their profits, big time. I know for a certain fact, John, that ACP will not budge on the deal, and I feel real bad about it. I'd like you to know that, if your friends at Strongwheat are as pissed off as I'd expect them to be, it's more than possible that I could find them an alternative buyer here in the States. At a very fair price too. My reading of the legal situation is that nothing is set in stone yet – I mean they just could walk away. What do you think?"

John thought furiously. There had to be some connection between Vince having been so anxious to know about the fluoride back in May, and this bombshell from the FDA. But what? John found it hard to believe that even a company as large as ACP could make a US federal agency like the FDA jump through hoops for their commercial advantage . . .

"Vince, I'm really grateful for your call. I'll talk to Alex, and then no doubt he'll want me to talk to the client. We'll just have to await their reaction, but if it's what you expect, your offer could be very helpful indeed. I'll get back to you as soon as there's some news, and meantime I'll look forward to getting that e-mail from you."

James Routledge went carefully through the FDA story and Dick's figures, and his face gave no hint of emotion as he turned to Jim Helvin.

"Jim, we've got a cost of over £600,000 which is unavoidable now, and a further cost of as much again if we push on. My approach is a simple one. We can stand these costs, I mean we're strong enough to get over it, in time. But are we sure that there are no more bear-traps waiting for us?"

"The cost figures that Dick has quoted to you are basically those that Phil Wythe had me work out with him, Mr. Chairman. I'd say they are 'full and reliable'. There is one other effect, and that's the effect on total business over this year and the future of launching one month later than we had planned, and of course not having the benefit of the fluoride idea. I do not know how to evaluate either of those."

"Nor does anyone else, Jim, least of all me. From what you've said, Dick, I take it you want to press on regardless?"

"Two reasons, Dad. Firstly, in the consumer trial they liked our product before they knew anything about the fluoride, so that hasn't changed. And Walter thinks he can keep the backing of his big customers, perhaps even with a bit of sympathy to add momentum so that hasn't changed either. I say we go, on October 1st, earlier if Phil can do it in the factory"

His father nodded slowly. *If we don't go now, will I be here to see another attempt?*

"I agree. Right then, Dick, you get back to Sceptre Mill and wind up all the people. Call some kind of factory meeting and tell everyone what has happened, in simple terms, and what we're going to be doing. Ask for maximum cooperation. We're going to need full support now for the double shifting and lots of overtime. Jim, would you stay here with me and let's work out some rough cash-flow numbers, then we'll talk to Oliver before we put the wind up the bankers."

On consideration, John Savage decided not to involve Alex until after he had discussed the new situation with his client. He felt more personally involved than ever, and wanted every scrap of information to be available before he made what was likely to be a momentous decision for himself.

"Dick, it's John Savage. Are you free to talk for a moment? Good. Dick, I've heard a report about an FDA study into the possible effects of fluoride in foods. In fact I have a copy of their press release in front of me. Have you had this report? Is it going to affect you?"

There was a pause before Dick replied. *De Boissy was a shareholder. Was John asking on behalf of Alex?* John sensed the hesitation.

"Dick, I'm calling as a friend. I want to help, if you'll let me."

"As a friend, John, we owe you a vote of thanks. If you had not warned us that there might be a special risk involved in this fluoride thing, we might have been even worse off than we are. Yes, we've been working at it all morning, and it's going to hurt us, badly. I've just got back from a meeting with the Chairman, and I'm just getting ready to talk to the entire workforce. We are going to hang in with the product launch, without the fluoride of course. The launch will be around one month later, October 1st."

"And the cost?"

"Difficult to calculate, because of the long-term effect of changing the product, and the delay. Not less than a million, could go up to two perhaps, over the three-year plan."

"Can the company survive that level of loss?"

"We think so, John. We may need to look for some help from De Boissy, I just don't know yet. Dad is working on some cash-flow forecasts, and then he's intending to talk to Oliver."

"Tell him we'd like to help if you need us. Off the cuff, I'd say that idea of Oliver's, you know, about getting credit from the bank against your customer invoices as soon as they're issued, rather than having to wait until they're paid? Could be a godsend. Look, Dick, I know you're under the cosh for time at the moment. But there is something else that we must talk about. Could you give me a call as soon as you're free?"

It was late afternoon when Dick finally found time to call back to John Savage.

"Sorry it's taken so long, John, but I guessed it was something you had on your mind that would not be settled in a five-minute break."

John had made some careful notes of his recollection of the call from Vince, and he went through them with Dick Routledge, with meticulous care.

"Looking at the situation as coldly and as objectively as possible, Dick, I'd say that Vince is offering you a deal that may well be better for you and James than going on with the present arrangement with ACP. I mean, they're not likely to turn round and say,

'We're sorry to hear that your plans have gone adrift. Let us get together and renegotiate the deal to give you as much money as before, as though nothing had happened.' They'll insist on the original deal."

"But somehow I get the feeling that you're not exactly recommending that we should reach out to grab Vince's lifeline?"

In fact John had reported the call from Vince to Alex Hampshire, together with Dick's estimate of the cost, and the decision to press ahead anyway. Alex had been furious at the likelihood that his longed-for connection with an aggressive US company could be lost, but overtly had been typically cool.

"We are just humble players in the game, dear boy. Consider the downside. Strongwheat could well go under as a result of this debacle, and then where would our profit come from? Tell them to reach out to whomsoever offers the best deal, and we will follow their lead."

John tried to be more helpful in his answer to Dick's question.

"I would not want to influence you and James unduly either way, Dick. But my calculation is that all this loss can reasonably be buried in this current financial year, which ends in six weeks' time on September 30th. Remember the old saying, 'If you're going to make a loss, make it as big as possible.' Pile provision on provision, then, if things turn out a bit better than you thought, you can bring some of this year's provisions back as a profit into next year. You are the shareholders, so within reason you can do what you like with your accounts. And you can set the loss against taxes too."

"You're saying that under the agreed terms of the sale, this year's profit or loss does not affect the eventual total price, because the multiplier of earnings starts with next year?"

"I wouldn't say this year has no effect. We've given ACP to understand that this year you expect to make close to a million pounds profit, and that's the basis for the twenty million up front. Clearly it's not going to be that now, in fact you will probably want to show a loss in the accounts. That's a big hole, and buyers do not like surprises like that. If I might make another suggestion?"

"You have my total attention, John,"

"I remember you got on particularly well with Lloyd Teller last month."

"Yes, I did. Nice bloke, I thought, as long as you were on the same side. Wouldn't want him for an enemy, though. What's on your mind?"

"Well, this acquisition is a biggish step for ACP. I mean the price is going to add up to something like ten percent of their Stock Exchange capitalisation, and I believe their broker has been whispering it about amongst their major shareholders, perhaps also to some of the big institutions that were not shareholders yet, ahead of the official announcement. Certainly I've seen their share-price ticking up over the last few days, quite a nice cumulative rise. Uncertainty is always a bad thing in markets, so it occurred to me that a call to Lloyd would be very much appreciated, just to say that you'd noticed the story about the FDA and fluoride. Then tell him, exactly as you told me, how it's going to affect your business."

"He's going to be horrified."

"Perhaps. But you should also point out that this crash has been brought about by the Yanks themselves. Suggest that you and your father even suspect that someone over there may have pulled a string or two to make it happen. He'll deny that, of course, and you'll gladly accept his assurances. You'll point out that the sale price is a function of the next three years' profits . . ."

"Is there in fact any evidence of something nasty on their side?"

John thought quickly, and decided to keep his suspicions to himself, at least for the time being.

"Not exactly evidence, no. But you're entitled to ask the question, very carefully of course."

"So it's just this little matter of £20 million up front."

"Exactly, a little matter. That's what you should think of as table-stakes, and definitely not negotiable. Overall he's got a good deal to present to his board, because any long-term damage done by this crisis is going to reduce the eventual cost for ACP to acquire Strongwheat. And he does have some explaining to do, believe me, about the FDA's intervention. If ACP were to get really sticky, at least we know from Vince that there are alternatives out there. What do you think?"

"Sounds sense to me, John. We had an e-mail yesterday from Vince acknowledging receipt of the preliminary contracts, and confirming that 'due diligence would begin immediately, with finalisation after the expected Board approval at the end of September'. Right, John, thank you for your advice. I'll call Lloyd as soon as I can, and I'll call you back tomorrow with a report on the reaction I get."

John Savage had, by instinct and long training, suppressed his personal feelings while he was calculating how to deal with the call from Vince O'Hanlon. But now his temper boiled over. *That slimy bastard Alex has set me up! My role in the game has been to get James Routledge and Dick to put their signatures to a deal to sell their company on an apparently attractive multiple of future profits, while all the time Alex and that O'Hanlon man were conniving together to bring those profits crashing down with the fluoride scare. And I would have been piggy-in-the-middle! No doubt they had anticipated a forced withdrawal of the new product, with God knows what impact on the business, so that ACP could acquire its new European base for peanuts.* John speculated briefly what the quid-pro-quo had been for Alex to be persuaded to lower his expectations on the price to be paid for De Boissy's twenty percent. *Or perhaps this new buyer that O'Hanlon has turned up was all part of the plot? And how had O'Hanlon been able to influence the FDA?* Then he decided that it was probably impossible to trace that now. But he had no doubts about what had been done. The facts spoke for themselves. *And it would not be long before the people at Strongwheat came to the same conclusion. Including Jean Carey? God, what a mess! Would she decide he was a rogue? Or just a fool? She would trust me still, wouldn't she? But could I do anything myself now? The deal between ACP and Strongwheat might well go through, with nice contracts for Dick and James. Certainly I could claim most of the credit, and that would enhance my personal status in the city. A good time then to be looking for a better job? Or the deal might fall through . . . Oh, to hell with it all!* He knew that he just wanted out, whatever happened. *Time to start dusting off my address book! Oliver Sedburgh is a fellow director . . . I've got to trust somebody. Perhaps if I explained frankly why I was not happy to stay on at De Boissy, Oliver might poke around amongst his contacts for me? And Oliver would certainly be appalled by Alex's deceit . . .* John thumbed through his diary to identify in advance a few possible lunch dates, and reached once more for the telephone.

Chapter Twenty-three

Although it was already late afternoon in England, Dick Routledge realised he could take advantage of the six-hour time shift between England and the US mid-west to get down on paper a statement of the way the FDA/fluoride problem had arisen, what actions they were taking, and what the effect on volumes and profit was expected to be. He checked and double-checked his wording, trying to read it as Lloyd Teller would. After Elizabeth had produced a fair copy he asked her to keep it ready to be e-mailed. Then he called Lloyd, whose friendly response immediately calmed Dick's nerves.

"Dick! It's great to talk to you again. D'ya know since we got back last week I've done nothing but bore the pants off everyone I can get to listen to me about that shot at the seventeenth, you know, 'Sevvy's Shortcut'? Big problem, though, they're threatening to drop my handicap at the Country Club, so I'm having to do some fancy double-shuffles, I can tell you. I hear from Vince that the preliminary contracts are all done and dusted. Is there something on your mind?"

"Lloyd, we have had a serious problem here. And the strange thing is that the source of our problem is right over there, in the US. I want to send an e-mail report securely and direct to yourself, and then perhaps you could call me back to discuss it? I'll be staying on late at the office here. Could you give me your personal address for e-mail?"

"Sure, Dick. It's 'lloydteller@acp.com' – comes straight into my desk PC. And don't worry, Dick, there's nothin' so tough that a couple of friends can't fix it if we put our heads together."

Despite his optimistic style, Lloyd was seriously perturbed when he read Dick's report. He printed off two copies and walked round to see Ben Camina.

"Don't tell me, I can see it in your face. They've dropped your handicap by two shots, and you want me to instruct our corporate lawyers to fight it for you. Up to the Supreme Court, no doubt?"

"This is serious, Ben. Cast an eye would you over this report they've just sent over from England. I can see the whole fucking thing coming to pieces in our hands."

Ben was immediately serious and attentive, and read through Dick's report without a word. Then he pulled out his copy of the three-year plan for Strongwheat, together with Vince's recommendation for the acquisition, and read the report for a second time, making notes, and occasionally punching his desk calculator.

"You're right, Lloyd, it is serious for them. This disaster effectively wipes out this year's profits, as he says . . . but I can see why they've decided to go on. Takes guts, but then we thought they had plenty of balls didn't we? I can see a nasty hole coming up in the cash-flow . . . do you want to have a try at renegotiating that upfront $35 million?"

"I don't, no. He says in this paragraph here that 'If ACP are prepared to stand by the deal *as a whole*, we are prepared to accept the possibility that the overall total price may eventually be reduced as a result of this situation'. I take that as a pretty clear warning that they will not take kindly to any shenanigans on our part. Hell, it's not your money nor mine. I just want this one to fly now."

"You will have to tell them at the Board that we think Strongwheat's three-year plan is doable. Show the impact of this stuff as a one-off exceptional, and on that basis they're buying a good business at a full and fair price. It's our call now, Lloyd. Tell the Board to put up, or shut up about globalisation."

"I'll go along with that. There is one thing that's sticking in my throat. It's this part towards the end, when he says, 'It is very unfortunate that the challenge re Fluoride should have come from your side of the Atlantic, and at just the point to do us maximum damage'. What do you make of that?"

Ben was silent for a minute, while he re-read the comment, and turned it over in his sharp mind. "Those words, 'your side of the Atlantic'. I'd say we're meant to take that as a polite way of saying 'your company'. I'd say they're as good as accusing us of trying to trash their business."

"Ben, that kind of accusation gets me very pissed-off, very pissed-off indeed. I mean we've met and talked with the guy, played some golf. I even danced with his wife for Chris'sake. And now he calls me a cheat?"

"Now just come down off the ceiling a minute, Lloyd. How would you feel if some foreigner had just pulled a scam that wiped out the whole of our year's profits? I said 'as good as accusing'. He hasn't actually accused you personally."

"And he'd better not."

"Right, right. But let's just ask ourselves another question, Lloyd. Is there something going down over here?"

"Like what?"

"Like, why has our share price climbed twenty percent while we've been away? That's enough to pay for this acquisition twice over, even if they did make their whole damn three-year plan. Is some bastard stalking us? Let me call it up on the screen here . . . Jesus, will you look at that? Next question, why has our share price just fallen off a cliff? And it's still falling. Share prices rise when there's a lot of buyin', and fall when there's a lot of sellin'. The bigger the company, the more money it takes to shift the price. I tell you, Lloyd, something very big has been going on, and we'd better get after whatever it is before we get the S.E.C. climbing all over us."

"What'll you do?"

"Start by waking up our fucking broker in New York. He should have been on to this for us, days ago. You go and call your Brit pal back and tell him everything's hunky-dory, and we're all still pallsywallsy. Leave the Dick Tracy stuff to me. Somebody's been screwing us around, and I'll get to the bottom of it, if it kills me."

* * *

Jean Carey lay on her face in the king-size double bed that came as standard at the Bruges Hilton, and enjoyed the simple pleasure of having her back stroked. Long, soft, delightful strokes that moved from her shoulders to the small diamond near the base of her spine where a wisp of dark hair grew, and then back to the nape of her neck. Saturday had been spent doing the tourist things in Amsterdam – the Van Gogh Museum in the morning, the afternoon on a canal boat trip, and the evening at the Concertgebouw. John had driven the hired car to the hotel in Bruges that Sunday morning, and after a walk around the mediaeval city they had enjoyed a late lunch on the terrace of an old restaurant that overlooked a shaded canal, and had retired happily to bed an hour before.

"Jean, sweetheart, I have a question for you to answer."

John's tone was so serious that Jean reluctantly gave up being stroked, and turned over to look up. His face was inscrutable in the darkened bedroom.

"Jean, darling, I love you very much, very much indeed. I think I want to go on doing this, or something similar, for the rest of my life. Will you marry me?"

"When?"

An English Shuffle, by God, a good old English Shuffle. Ben Camina had devoted most of four working days to unravelling, with the assistance of the company's New York brokers, the strange patterns created by the movements in the price of ACP shares. Now he had the full picture in front of him. In the 1860s enormous fortunes were made and lost in the silver mines of Virginia City. But most of the money was made not from producing silver, but from speculating in the shares of mining companies. By far the most prevalent swindle was known as the 'English Shuffle', probably because the leading exponents were plausible 'gentry' from England. The trick was to buy up a bankrupt or low-value mine, salt it with false indications of a rich ore body, leak the news of a big strike, watch the share price rocket up and then of course sell out before the truth was discovered. Some mines were sold over and over again, often under different names, some operators pulled off the same operation with elegant variations several times, and thus the survivors laid the foundations of the great fortunes that in turn were used to build San Francisco. This was the activity that Ben had identified in the shares of ACP. The 'salting' they had unwittingly done themselves, by leaking the news about a forthcoming acquisition in Europe. The unknown dealer – or dealers – had simply taken advantage of the attention drawn to the company by their own press story. He noted too that downward movement in the shares in late July. *Which meant that someone had been selling to depress the price ahead of the announcement, someone therefore who knew what he and Lloyd were going to be doing before they did it* . . . As a modern improvement, he noted that the dealing had been mainly in three-month ACP futures, both short and long. The very professional operator had been able to work at an upfront cost of just the ten percent margin call, so hugely leveraging the effect of his manoeuvres. Ben calculated that, at the peak, as much as a third of the total value of ACP had been moving across the electronic dealings simultaneously. Some smart dealer – or a syndicate? – had put up 30 to 40 million dollars, and had probably at least doubled their money. But who? The stockbrokers could not (or would not) identify the culprits. Nor was it really clear yet if any significant crime had been committed. *Would we want to blow the whistle if we found a crime?* All they would say was 'a lot of the money came from Chicago'. That had led Ben to suspect that there might be an insider in ACP, and he had conducted a personal study of the telephone logs of senior managers, looking for evidence of calls to stockbrokers. There were none – most senior managers being on vacation over the relevant two weeks. But he was startled to identify Vince's calls to the FDA in Washington, and also to the offices of a certain Aaron Kaminsky in Chicago. Two and two made four in Ben's mind. He carefully closed the door of Lloyd's office behind him before he sat down and started talking.

"Lloyd, we've been screwed. I told you I thought somethin' big was goin' down. I was right. One of our own people here has been wired in to the FDA, and the very same man has been tippin' off some lowlife moneybroker downtown. Guess who?"

"John, my dear boy, I think you are being unkind. Unkind and unjust."

It was the end of August, two weeks to the day after John Savage had heard from Vince about the FDA investigation into fluoride. He was sitting in front of Alex Hampshire, and had just handed to Alex a letter which contained formal notice of his intention to resign, and, perhaps unwisely, had told him his reasons,

"To be honest, Alex, I do not understand at all why you thought it necessary to enter into such a shoddy transaction with ACP. They were grateful enough to us anyway for the introduction to Strongwheat, and would have been willing, in my judgement, to renegotiate if necessary. As it is, this is a thoroughly nasty little plot you and O'Hanlon hatched, to destroy Strongwheat's profitability. And that was after sticking me out in front to arrange, in all innocence, a selling price based on a multiple of those future profits. Frankly, even if it had worked, I think you would have seriously prejudiced your credibility, but no doubt I would have been the sacrificial goat as well. I'm the one who's been leading the final rounds of hard talking about terms, and everyone would assume that I had been corrupted in some way. Well, I'm not having it. I'm fed up with being used as a moving target, and this is the last bloody time."

Alex had stood up from his desk at these last furious words, as though he feared a personal assault, and had moved to his favourite position, standing with his back to one of the tall Georgian windows that flooded the beautiful room with late afternoon sunshine, but also set his face in deep shade, so that his expression was unreadable.

"Unkind and unjust. I admit to you quite freely that I placed great value on this opportunity to be of service to American Cereal. De Boissy has never done any serious business with an American corporation, and who knows where this could lead? But I assure you, I never conspired with O'Hanlon or anyone else to ruin Strongwheat. Never. It would not be in my interest to do so, you must see that. If there was a plot, I say *if* there was a plot, it's his and his alone. I recall that he asked me whether or not this fluoride idea was going to fly, and I got what information I could from you and passed it on. Then I simply went on holiday. John, we've known one another a good few years now. You know how deeply I treasure the De Boissy reputation for honesty and fair dealing. You cannot seriously think that I would put two hundred years of history at risk over so trifling a matter. I believe I am entitled to ask you to accept my word in this."

John paused before replying. He knew Alex's trick with the window from previous meetings in that office, and there was nothing to be read in his face. *But could I perhaps have been mistaken? Could Alex just have been an innocent pawn, tricked by Vince, like myself?* Doubt trickled in, where previously he had been filled with high moral certainties.

"Alex, I don't want to pick an unnecessary quarrel, not with you. Of course, now that you've given me your word, that is the end of the matter. However . . ." John paused, trying to sort out in his mind how much he should say, and how much was better left unsaid. Alex relaxed visibly, and moved back into his chair behind the great gilded desk.

"Go on John, I'm not going to hold anything against you."

"However I do have to tell you that we have a serious problem to face. On the one hand, our friends at Strongwheat have dropped the fluoride idea as you know, and I hear that the major supermarkets for once are supporting a British manufacturer. So ACP will likely find themselves, in due course, paying what we would call 'a full but fair price' for the company and their springboard into Europe."

"And on the other hand?"

"The problem, Alex, is that James and Dick Routledge are not stupid. From now on they're going to be working more and more closely with O'Hanlon and the rest. They're bound to follow up this FDA investigation into fluoride. How can they not smell a rat eventually?"

"You may be right, John, but I think you are being oversensitive. Even if they do make some connection, we are, still, innocent – well, guilty at the most of a minor breach of security in our zeal to impress a potential buyer with the value of a client's company. But where's the harm? Particularly if, as you say, the company concerned is coming through their ordeal with flying colours. Come now, John, I haven't had an opportunity till now to congratulate you on a first-class achievement with the completion of the negotiations between ACP and Strongwheat. If you are right about their prospects now, our finder's fee will be a very nice sum, and we shall realise as well a truly princely profit on the sale of our 20% holding. We may also reasonably hope to be retained by the Americans to act for them as they seek to develop further in Europe, where we certainly have a great deal to offer them, not least your own connections and undoubted skills. All in all, we owe a great deal to you, John, and you'll agree that I have never been backward in rewarding achievement."

He placed the middle finger of his right hand delicately on the sheet of paper that lay on the desk between them,

"We all get a little too close to events now and again, and minor problems can seem to loom very large. Believe me, I value very highly your sense of honour and propriety. It is one of your greatest assets. I have heard on the grapevine that you are to be married next month – a charming lady from within Strongwheat I believe? My most sincere congratulations, dear boy. Take your well-deserved leave of absence, and have a wonderful honeymoon. I think you might reasonably find a way to charge the first-class airfares and the hotel to De Boissy, as long as you don't frighten the tax man too much. And when you return, you will find a Director's office prepared for you on this floor, and some interesting new responsibilities to get your teeth into."

Alex's finger pushed the letter of resignation back across the desk, but John did not pick it up.

"I'm sorry, Alex, truly I am. I can see now that I have not been as fair to you as you deserve, and I can only apologise for the harsh things I said. But I cannot withdraw the resignation, I'm afraid. If you agree, I'll stay on until Christmas to tidy up the loose ends, and to hand over, but I must go."

"Must go? John, this is quixotic nonsense. You can't have another job in the City, or I would have heard about it. Why on earth 'must' you go? I do not believe you would find it so easy to explain to another banking house why you found it necessary to leave us."

If John had been entertaining a sliver of uncertainty about leaving De Boissy, the hint of a threat in Alex's last remark resolved the situation instantly. *I will* not *be dependent any longer on this man's goodwill.*

"I must go, Alex, because I have been offered, and have accepted, another position. Not with a bank, in fact not in the City at all."

Alex waited a few seconds to see if John would say more. Then he stood up with a small inclination of the head and sighed,

"Fair enough, dear boy, you obviously feel committed, and I shall not pester you further. I would still feel it proper for you to enjoy your honeymoon as a farewell present from us, and perhaps we could discuss your period of notice when you return. I would not wish to keep you a moment longer than necessary."

He held out his hand, and pressed John's hand warmly as they parted. He paced restlessly for a minute beneath the frolicking shepherdesses of his tapestries, and then walked next door to his secretary,

"Elaine, dear, what are my movements for the rest of the day?"

"You're free now until the dinner this evening, at the Mansion House."

"Would you see if you can raise Mr. O'Hanlon at ACP please? And some of your blackest coffee would be most acceptable."

Time to tell O'Hanlon that the helpful little scheme – 'plot' was definitely too harsh a word – had not worked, and that Strongwheat were apparently going to be doing well with the new product. Vince might be slightly aggrieved, he thought, at the likely cost of the acquisition, but a few extra millions, spread over three years, and payable in ACP shares, would hardly impact on his company. Of course O'Hanlon would not benefit from that personal introduction of an alternative buyer, but . . . win some, lose some. De Boissy would certainly benefit, quite substantially.

Which would make it doubly unfortunate if the Routledges were to come across any evidence of 'the-scheme-that-went-wrong'. The City here was such a village when it came to gossip. Oliver Sedburgh, for one, was no friend to De Boissy, and he could be desperately indiscreet when the mood took him. Alex was quite sure that Vince O'Hanlon, VP for Corporate Development, would see things in the same light as himself. They had a common interest in discretion, and in working together. And that could be *very* useful in the years ahead.

Vince O'Hanlon felt unusually nervous as he stepped into the express lift at the John Hancock Tower. Kaminsky had said that he would pick up the costs if the deal went down, but Vince was anxious not to make an enemy of a man who could well be a source of future opportunities. And on the other hand there was the extraordinary evidence of the aberrations in the ACP share price, which must point to some heavy dealing, most likely by Kaminsky. Had he made a profit? A big profit, perhaps?

"Gee, Vince, It's a great pleasure to see you again. Have you got something else for me to look at? I was real sorry about that English deal. We had the money all lined up and ready, you know."

Aaron Kaminsky kept the air-conditioning in his spartan office down to what seemed to be Arctic Winter Standard, and Vince shivered slightly. This was not going to be easy.

"Just one of those things, I guess, Harry. Our ACP people got on only too well with the English when they went over, so when that little local difficulty came up, as I had arranged, this English guy just picks up the telephone to my Chairman, and tells him not to worry. Gives him some more sweet talk, and I'm left with nowhere to go."

"So?"

Kaminsky was as reserved as ever, and Vince could see no easy way to raise the subject on his mind. Still, nothing venture . . .

"Harry, this is a bit awkward for me, but I wonder if you may have made some money from the ACP situation after all?"

Kaminsky's eyes became grey stone pebbles, and he began to drum quietly with two fingers on his desk,

"Come again?"

"Well, as you might suppose, I monitor the ACP share-price on the Big Board daily, sometimes hourly if there's a lot of activity. After we talked, I noticed that there was an unusual fall, as though there was a big seller in the market goin' short on the shares, and then a steady rise, not strong, but steady. As though someone was feeding money in on a regular basis, enough money to mop up the profit-takers. Are you with me so far?"

Aaron said nothing, but a sharp observer might have noticed that the finger-drumming had become a fraction louder. Vince continued,

"Then, just about a week after the time of the FDA press release, there were big volumes sold quickly. The price held for an hour or two, then dropped real sharp, as though the buying had been replaced by selling. I wondered in fact if there wasn't some short selling going on, to push the price down. The price ran down very quickly to eight or nine percent below the level before the rises started, and has just begun to pick up strongly again. I've been involved in ACP for over a year now, and there has never been this kind of volatility before. ACP has always been the typical 'widows and orphans' share, one to buy and lock safely away for ten or twenty years. Clearly there was a big operator in the market making waves, perhaps more than one."

"So?"

Vince drew a deep breath. "So if you've been in the market, and have made some money, it must be due in part to my having drawn your attention to the opportunities in ACP. Simple fairness would suggest that you could strengthen our relationship for the future by sharing some of that gain with me."

Vince had been nervous at the beginning, but by the end his tone was firm and determined. He sat back and waited for the outburst. Instead a strange wheezing sound was coming from Kaminsky. At first he thought he might be experiencing some sort of seizure. But then he realised that Aaron was laughing. He had been prepared for expostulating innocence, or cold rage, or hurt indignation. He had even thought he might be thrown out on his butt. But, for Christ's sake, what was so funny? Eventually Aaron stopped wheezing, and seemed to wipe a tear from the comer of one eye,

"Gee, Vince, that's the best laugh I've had in years. I ought to pay you for entertainment value. You come here with this weird scheme to rip off your own employer, let me down at the last minute, and then having accused me of participatin' in a strictly illegal market-rigging scam, you want me to slip you a share of the illegal imaginary profits. What's that Jewish word? . . . Chutzpah, that's it. You've got chutzpah, in spades. But I like you, I really do, and I'd like to put something your way. Tell you what I'll do. There are no profits from ACP for you to get a piece of anyway. But I did hear a little market rumour that I'll share with you for free. The story is that early next week there's going to be a big sell-off of IBM. Big Blue is going to get a black eye, OK? It's not for me to tell you how to take advantage, so I'll leave you to work something out. Just keep it to yourself, won't you? And don't come knocking on my door for a share of my profits."

He smiled as he slapped Vince on the shoulder, and sent him on his way. His mood changed suddenly as he closed the door, and picked up the phone.

"Artie, you old bastard, how's things? Listen, I've just had someone in here actually showin' me the evidence of that last little bit of fun we had with the ACP shares. Yes, it was a good use of the fifty million for a couple of weeks, but we're gonna have to find ways of smoothin' over our tracks a bit better. We don't need the S.E.C. crawlin' all over us now, do we? Now next week, this is how I think you should handle things . . .

Chapter Twenty-four

Since the beginning of August, Vince O'Hanlon had virtually given up using his own apartment, which was in a warehouse conversion just behind Chicago's Lyric Opera House, in favour of staying with Anna at hers, which was on the fourteenth floor of one of the spectacular circular towers that stood on the lake shore. When his alarm buzzed quietly at 7a.m he reached out to stop it and sat up. She slumbered on beside him, her blonde hair tousled over the pillow, her shoulders and back bare and tanned down to the white edge at her waist. Their routine on weekdays that summer was for Vince to shower, dress and make the coffee and toast, before waking her to share breakfast on the terrace overlooking the lake, with the morning sun by now half way up from the horizon. Weekends was his time for a lie-in, with his favourite eggs Benedict in bed.

That morning of August 31st there was a stiff easterly breeze off the lake, so they opted to eat indoors.

"Are you goin' to do anything about yesterday's IBM tip from our friend Kaminsky?"

Vince sank his second cup of black coffee and stood up, "That's top of my agenda for today. I need to study the trend on any 'put' options over the last few weeks, and figure out what the chances are of coming out with a profit. I have to assume that Aaron is on board already, big time. But there should be room for little old me. If I go for it, do you want a piece of the action?"

She rose and put her arms around his neck and kissed him. His lips drifted from hers down to her throat, and he pulled at the belt of her white silk housecoat as he kissed the warm cleft between her breasts.

"Mmm. Nice. Why don't you decide for me? But not more than fifty K at the margin, all right? Now I must get off to the Health Club, and you're going to be late at ACP."

Vince drove north as usual from downtown Chicago, travelling easily against the rush hour traffic flow, and arrived at his office just on 8.30a.m. to find his inner door locked still, and Ella, his P.A., in tears.

"Gee, Vince, they say I'm not to let you into your office, and I'm not to go in there myself. I'm to tell you to go straight round to Mr. Camina."

A hard knot of apprehension gripped Vince in the belly, and he felt the sweat on his palms. What had gone wrong?

He found Ben Camina sitting grim-faced behind his desk, with Lloyd standing at the window behind him.

"Siddown. This ain't gonna take long, you ungrateful two-timing bastard."

"Ben, Lloyd, for Chris'sake, what's the matter?"

Lloyd was equally abrupt, "Shut the door, Vince, and sit down. You're goin' to need to be sittin' down. That way you know I won't hit you."

"I've been workin' at your stuff an' nothing else for a whole week and more," said Ben, deliberately fixing his eyes down onto the pieces of paper in front of him, "And I'm sick, sick to my stomach. We thought we were doin' you a good turn when we took you on straight out of smart old Harvard business school. First job in industry, we thought you'd likely be raw, but eager to please, keen to make a name for yourself. Well, you've done that all right, but it's not a name I'd care to use in polite company, if you take my meaning. What the hell got into you? Are you in debt to some loan shark? Have you got mixed up with the mob? Or are you just so obsessed with your own greed that you think the rest of us are all a bunch of total fuckin' idiots?"

Vince blinked under this verbal onslaught. *Ben seemed so certain of his ground. But how could he know?*

"You've lost me, lost me altogether. What is it I'm supposed to have done?"

"There's no supposed about it. I'll tell you what you've done," Lloyd burst in, resting his big hands on Ben's desk to bring his face close to Vince's, "You've tried to unzip the only worthwhile deal you've pulled off for us, and damn near succeeded in ruining that little company in England. You made them think that Ben and me are a pair of fuckin' shysters. And you've fed inside information to some grubby dealer in Chicago, who's clipped our shareholders for God knows how many millions, thanks to you. Is that enough to be goin' on with?"

Kaminsky! They had followed up on the movements in the share price, and somehow stumbled across the rest. That greedy shit had ruined him! But I would certainly have heard from Gerry Masters already if they had got direct proof of the FDA connection. And Aaron had said nothing of any enquiry yesterday. Was there a bluff going down, in an effort to get me to confess everything?

"I tell ya', Ben, Lloyd, I don't know what the fuck you're talkin' about. If you've got something to accuse me of, spell it out, chapter and verse."

"It's all here, in your phone records." Ben tapped the paper on his desk. "We started lookin' at everybody's, when we came back from Europe and found the share price goin' fuckin' apeshit. New York told me the money was comin' out of Chicago, I mean millions. And what do I find, but calls from you to some creep called Kaminsky, who we discover is known as a would-be big-shot in finance. So we look back farther, and find his number comes up again and again in your calls. You tipped him off, didn't you? How much did you get paid? More than the regulation thirty pieces?"

Vince was getting his brain back into gear. *That's all they've got! Some miserable phone records! Not enough, buster, not enough by a long fuckin' way.*

"Go on, please Ben. For the record, I want to hear everything." His face was calm, his voice almost menacing. For the first time Ben felt a twinge of uncertainty.

"We've also got the records of your calls to the FDA in Washington. I've even established that three of them were direct to the office of the FDA's expert in that fluoride stuff. You're caught, Vince, you're caught like the monkey with your fingers in the fuckin' cookie jar, an' it gives me no fuckin' pleasure to say it."

"Thanks, Ben. Thanks for not giving me the benefit of the doubt. For not even askin' me if there might just perhaps be some other explanation of your 'facts' and your phone records."

"We're listening. So tell us," Lloyd growled.

"I will. Listen, and weep. First of all Kaminsky. I'll admit it, I've been talkin' to him. Why not? We talked first over a year ago, when I was comin' to the end of my time at Harvard, and I was lookin' hard for a way to earn a living. I talked to Kaminsky. I was talkin' to you guys, and you were progressing things with your usual lightning speed. I was talkin' to six or seven other corporations. At the time Kaminsky was keen to have me, but he wasn't sure he could afford me, I guess. So eventually you came up with an offer, and I joined ACP. Months later, Aaron comes on to me, 'he's got the info' about my new position from the Harvard Business School, and might I now be interested in joining him, as his business is doin' real well?' I don't say 'no' right off – this Business Development stuff is goin' so slowly, you guys are, not unreasonably, leanin' on me a little, who can say when you might lose patience? I suppose I was stringing him along, but a few days ago Ben calls from Paris to say everything's OK, and I called Aaron one last time to tell him that this is a great business to be in, at least for me, and I'm staying."

"So what's been goin' on with our fuckin' share price?" Lloyd's question came out flat and hard.

"How should I know? I'll show you my fuckin' bank-account if you want. There hasn't been a red cent in or out on ACP shares. Not now, not anytime. It's not my millions that's moving the share price, and I'm just living on my salary. Perhaps talkin' to me, and me sayin' this was a good business might have put it into Aaron's head to take a punt. That's what he does."

"And I suppose you were just passing the time of day with the FDA?"

"Not really, no. I was checking out with them what their attitude might be to the use of fluoride in a food product, without saying up front that it was to be a children's breakfast cereal. Wouldn't that be a sensible part of a due diligence program? Anybody else in this tower of geniuses beside Lake Michigan here think to do that? I thought not. Of course I tried to be discreet, but they had actually got a routine report from the US supplier of sodium fluoride when he made a sale to a new customer in England, so they knew who I was talkin' about. Perhaps the study they're gonna do was triggered by me asking, but I guarantee they would have got on to it sooner or later, and done the same damn thing. It's what they're there for. Might even have cost those Brits more in the long run."

Lloyd Teller came around Ben's desk to loom over Vince, "I'll say this for you, Vince, you can spin a good yarn. I'm not goin' to dignify that heap of horseshit by pointin' out to you the holes in the story. I'm just goin' to say, in a nice, friendly, gentlemanly way, that we've lost that vital element of mutual confidence that is so important in business. Put it simply, Vince, we don't fuckin' trust you no more. So we'd like your resignation in the post. Thank you. Goodbye and good fuckin' riddance."

Vince stood up, outwardly calm, but longing to throw a punch at Lloyd's beak of a nose.

"OK, you're the boss. I know when I'm not wanted. What's the proverb about 'pearls before swine'? My two-year contract has eleven months to run. What did you have in mind in the way of a severance settlement?"

"How about that you get your ass out'a here and never come back, and we agree not to prosecute you for fraud and mal-fuckin'-feasance or whatever?"

"You must be mistaking me for one of those hicks from Illinois here that you hire and fire from day to day, Lloyd. But I'm from New York, and the guy who drafted my contract eats blowhards like you for breakfast and spits out the pips. I suggest you consult quietly for a few minutes with Ben here, who, I notice, has been sitting very silent since I told you the truth about the fuckin' phone records you're so fond of. Talk to Ben, do it now, Lloyd. I'm going to tell Ella that I'm allowed back into my office, if that's all right with you, and I'll be there havin' a cup of coffee and clearing my desk, ready for you when you're ready to make some sense."

At Vince's suggestion, Ella scurried across to Ben's office, and returned with the key to his. He leant against the door as it closed behind him, and let out a huge sigh of relief. He knew from the expression on Ben's face as he left that they were not going to fight him over the principle of a severance payment. How much, he wondered, how much? If they held out though, could he really face taking ACP to court?

Ben almost sidled into Vince's office a few minutes later, and closed the door quietly behind him.

"Lloyd said that if it was his own business, Vince, I tell ya', he'd see hell freeze over before you got a busted nickel out of him. But I persuaded him to be realistic. We don't want to spend the next two years in some fuckin' court, and I don't suppose you do either. So we're gonna give you fifty thousand. That's it, no ifs, buts or argument. I assume you'll take it?"

"I've worked all year without a holiday. I take it you'll pay me two weeks' holiday pay."

"Two weeks, agreed."

Vince smelt weakness, "And I take it you'll want me to sign some sort of confidentiality agreement?"

"Naturally, total non-disclosure."

"That would probably include not talking to anyone about the 'business trip' you and Lloyd have just enjoyed with Rose and the lovely Juanita – first-class air travel, five-star hotels and so on. You remember that you had me and Ella make all the arrangements? Strangely enough, we came across the records of something very similar last year. Hawaii, wasn't it? I'm not suggesting that you've done anything wrong of course, but I'm just wondering what your immediate past chairman, Charles Simcox, might have to say about it all. He's gone holier than thou, you may have noticed? Been mouthin' off a lot in the press recently too about corporate governance and 'fat cats livin' on the backs of poor hard-working employees and shareholders'. But I expect you've seen all that?"

"Meaning what?"

"Meaning that we should try to part like gentlemen. To be very precise, Ben, I want a reference, a good one, signed by Lloyd and yourself, which I shall dictate. And I want you to be very aware that winks and nods and damning by innuendo over the telephone is a game that two can play at. If I find out that you've been doin' it, and be very sure, I will know if you have, well, like I said, that's a game that two can play at. And if I start to play hard ball, you can be very certain that you've got more to lose than I have. So, a nice, regretful reference, if you please."

"Just dictate it now to Ella, and you'll have it back signed with your cheque before midday. And just a piece of advice for yourself, Vince. Don't ever get another job with a manufacturer like us. We tend to assume that our people are straight. Naive, perhaps, but the downside is that we get very, very angry if some bastard lets us down."

A few days later James Routledge received the following letter:

September 7th
James Routledge Esq,. Chairman, Strongwheat plc. Lynchester

Dear James,

Thank you very much for giving me some time yesterday, and for such a helpful discussion. Confirming the main points arising:

1. I will be leaving De Boissy by Christmas at the latest, and intend to set up as a self-employed consultant, specialising in advising medium-size companies on mergers and acquisitions.

2. I was delighted therefore with your suggestion that I should make myself available to you to help with the programme of Europe-wide expansion planned for ACP. This is exactly the kind of work I had in mind and I can see no obstacle to my making it my immediate top priority as soon as I am released by De Boissy.

3. In addition I could advise on the eventual sale of all or part of what will be your very substantial holding in ACP, and on the investment of funds arising, to protect your capital and to minimise tax.

4. When De Boissy have sold their shareholding in Strongwheat to ACP, there will no longer be a requirement for them to have a non-executive director on your Board. If ACP are agreeable, I would be happy to offer myself in that role again. This could be particularly useful if you decide to proceed with the employee-incentive scheme we discussed.

4. I can be flexible about fees. We discussed a retainer of £5,000 per month, which would cover up to ten days per month, or a daily rate of £750 per day, plus VAT.

Please let me know what you think. I appreciate that you will have to await the final decision of ACP's Board at the end of September. Warmest personal regards,

Yours sincerely,

John Savage.

James tapped the letter a couple of times with his forefinger, then folded it carefully and put it in the inside pocket of his jacket. *That'll come in very handy this evening, when I have to explain to Ellen how I'm going to be able to operate as Chairman of ACP Europe without knocking myself out.*

Epilogue

Strongwheat Ltd. – Company Announcement – December 10th

As you will all be aware, the Directors of Strongwheat plc announced at the beginning of October that agreement had been reached in principle to sell our company to American Cereal Products Inc., of Illinois, USA.

The terms of this acquisition have now been approved by the shareholders of ACP. It is likely that this will be the first in a series of moves by ACP to strengthen its position in Europe, using Strongwheat as its springboard, so we regard the future prospects for all employees as improved and more secure.

There will be no cash element in the sale. Instead the shares in Strongwheat plc will be exchanged for shares in ACP, which by then will have a quotation on the London Stock Exchange. An initial payment will be made next April, and the balance of the total purchase price will be paid annually over a three-year period after that. The magnitude of these three subsequent payments will depend on the profitability of the Company over these three years, so that every employee will have the opportunity to influence those payments directly.

It is the intention of the Board to arrange that 4% of the total proceeds of both the initial and subsequent payments (i.e. one-twenty-fifth of the shares paid over by ACP) should be made available for division between all the employees of Strongwheat, full-time and part-time, on an equitable formula. A great deal of work has to be done on this plan, and a further announcement is expected to be made at the end of January. Individual entitlements will be announced at that time.

The Directors are absolutely confident that this step will lead to greater security and broader opportunities for every employee.

At four o'clock on the afternoon of Christmas Eve, Sceptre Mill was dark and deserted. The safety lights set at regulation intervals around the old whitewashed walls struggled without much success to resist the gathering gloom of the winter evening, and the silence was interrupted only by an occasional muffled metallic 'clank', as the fast cooling ovens contracted.

But the Mill was not quite empty. There was a light on in the Boardroom, and Dick Routledge stood silhouetted in one of the windows that surrounded the Boardroom peninsula, its heavy cream curtains drawn back, as was the practice when there was no meeting taking place. By midday, work had finished, except for cleaning up, and the usual friendly Christmas lunch had been held in the works canteen. This year it had been a touch more cheerful than before, and speculation was rampant about the size of the payouts to be expected as a result of the Chairman's decision to share the proceeds of the sale of the company with the workforce. Jean Carey, now Mrs. John Savage, was to be responsible for working out the details, and she had found herself almost under siege at one point in the festivities. George Thomas had rescued her by proposing a very sincere and heartfelt vote of appreciation, which had been taken up with much clinking of glasses, table-banging, and a loud 'Three cheers for the Chairman', followed by 'For he's a Jolly Good Fellow'.

Afterwards Dick had found himself strangely reluctant to leave, and had slipped away to the boardroom just to be alone for a while. With a gesture of sudden decision Dick tossed back the last of the single-malt whisky that he had been nursing whilst he heard the last of the cheery goodbyes, and watched his factory melt slowly into the darkness. He had been there for almost an hour, going over in his mind the events of the past year, and hardly appreciating the splendours of that twenty-year-old 'Glengoyne', kept for very special visitors.

He walked slowly through the darkened factory, pausing to caress here the great black side of number one oven, there the polished electronic control panel of the automated packing line. For almost three years now Strongwheat had been his life, or at least the most important thing in his life after Rosemary and the boys. The ink was hardly dry on the draft contracts for the sale, and for his new responsibility as 'Director for Cereals, Europe', but already he could sense the beginnings of a subtle change in his feelings toward the Strongwheat company – the start of an emotional divorce? Having Ben Camina come over last week to sit in at the Board had signalled somehow that changes really were going to happen. The irresistible urge to touch the inanimate machinery was some kind of response to a sense of uncertainty, of loss even, a longing to be reassured that things would go on as before. Periods of calm, of tedium sometimes, interlaced with moments of acute anxiety and times of glorious exultation. And all shared with people he had grown to like, and trust. People who seemed to like and depend on him too.

Last week his elder son James had brought home from school a list of 'Paradoxes', each of which had to be explained in one sentence. One in particular had stuck in Dick's mind,

No man can step twice into the same river.

Next year they would all be different people, stepping into different waters. Dick pulled on his sheepskin coat, slammed shut behind him the small side door into Sceptre Mill, and walked round to the front to climb into his car to drive home, his thoughts suddenly bright with the anticipation of Christmas.

FAMILY MATTERS

Chapter One

The 8a.m. flight from Birmingham, England to Dusseldorf was always full, and that Thursday morning in early July was no exception. Dick Routledge would have preferred to travel Business Class, but his employers, American Cereal Products of Illinois, had a strict rule that only intercontinental flights warranted the expense, and England to Germany definitely did not qualify. Still, as ACP's European Director for Breakfast Cereals, he certainly counted as a 'frequent flier', and his secretary had been able to reserve for him his usual window seat alongside the emergency exit, which guaranteed him those valuable extra few inches of leg room to stretch his long legs. He habitually travelled light, with just a change of clothes and his toilet gear tucked underneath a divider in his slightly battered leather briefcase, and he waited patiently for the other passengers to board before coming forward with his boarding card, as the last of the queue disappeared into the Boeing 737.

"Thank you, Mr. Routledge. Seat 13B, just over the wing on the right."

And there she sat – in his seat! Blue handbag, dark blue coat and silk scarf on the seat beside her, calmly reading *The Times*, sitting in *his* seat. He loomed over her, and was trying to decide whether to be cross or conciliatory when she looked up. Blonde hair, cut almost boyishly short with a small curl falling over a high forehead; brilliant blue eyes and a wide smile that completed the devastation. Conciliation, definitely.

"I'm so sorry, my coat is on your seat. Would you put it up in the locker for me, please? And the scarf too, if you don't mind. I will keep the handbag."

There was that sing-song lilt in her accent that said 'Scandinavia'. Sweden, Norway, Denmark? He forgot his indignation, took the seat beside her and buckled his seatbelt.

"I'm Dick Routledge."

She took the proferred hand with another of those smiles, "I am glad to meet you, Mr. Routledge."

"Make it Dick, please, everbody does."

"Dick then, of course. My name is Brit, Brit Carlsohn." She reached down inside her capacious leather handbag and produced an engraved card –

Brit Carlsohn

Senior Buyer, Steen & Strom, Stockholm.

The senior stewardess was going through the ritual of the 'Safety on Board' lecture.

"Do you have a card, please?"

Dick fumbled for the inner ticket pocket of his grey pinstripe, and found a slightly dog-eared business card. "I'm sorry if it's a bit battered. I got through a lot of cards when I first started this job, two years ago, but I hardly use them at all now."

The aircraft's engines roared to a crescendo, and in a few seconds they were climbing steeply away from the neatly ordered fields of the English Midlands and up through a thick layer of cloud. Dick noticed that she gripped the armrests of her seat very tightly, and only relaxed when they emerged into bright sunshine and were looking down on a level plain of white cloud that glittered as it receded in the morning sunshine. She let out a little sigh, and turned to him again.

"I was in an accident last year. In Milan. Not a real crash, you understand, but the aeroplane was landing too fast I think and went off the end of the runway in the rain. We were all very frightened."

"I was a Squadron Leader in the RAF before coming out about five years ago to join the family business. But I've never lost that nervous feeling when someone else is doing the flying for me."

"My father was a pilot too, in the Swedish Air Force."

Dick, who was forty-two, wondered with a touch of chagrin if she was putting him into her father's generation. How old was she? Her white tailored skirt was short enough to show her knees, the t-bar strappy high-heeled sandals and bare tanned legs, and the blue and white horizontally striped tee-shirt all said 'late twenties' – but there were those little creases around the eyes and beneath the elegant jawline that suggested she might be nearer his own age.

"What does Steen and Strom do?"

"It is a little complicated. Steen and Strom is a very good department store in Oslo, which has an arrangement with a number of other stores across Europe to manage together the buying of certain things, especially fashion goods. They have a small office in Stockholm, where I live, which has to manage the accounting of this buying, for all the stores. It can get a little complicated when an order is divided for delivery between several stores, and the Stockholm office has to collect the money from each store for its share, and then pay the supplier. I just have a desk there, but I travel a great deal."

"What sort of things do you buy? I'm sorry, perhaps I'm being too nosy?"

"Nosy?"

"Inquisitive. Asking too many questions. Sticking my nose in."

"Nosy. I love the English way with words. No, not nosy at all. It is very nice to talk with a man who makes such interest. I specialise in the small things of fashion – things like handbags, gloves, scarves, belts, stockings. Individually even the bigger stores are not buying so much of these things, but I try to encourage them to buy together, so that the price and the delivery can be better, and we can arrange to have some things made especially for us. Yesterday, for instance, I was visiting our two English associates in Wolverhampton and Birmingham who will lead the deciding about what the group will have for leather handbags this year. They listen to my advice, but the decision is theirs, and the other stores in the group will share the stock orders when they buy. And I went to a manufacturer of buckles for the belt in Tipton to negotiate prices and quantities for a range that will be enamelled exclusively for us in twenty different colours, which we have had designed in Denmark. And now you must tell me all about yourself." She looked again at the card in her hand, "What does a 'European Director' do?"

All the time Brit had been talking, Dick had been listening with half an ear, whilst he enjoyed the animation in her voice and features, the way she looked at him, and the way her hands moved to emphasise a point. He waited now during the arrival of trays with hot croissants and coffee, and noted that she wore a wedding ring.

"Don't you find that all this travel makes family life very difficult?"

For a long moment he thought he had spoiled everything, as she sipped her coffee before answering, but her voice still held that friendly warmth.

"I was married, for nearly ten years, but now my son Stefan and I have my mother to live with us, in her house actually, and it works very well. You have a family too?"

"I married Rosemary when we were both in the RAF, and we get along pretty well still. We have just the two boys, they're both doing nicely now at the local Grammar School in Lynchester, where we live. That's where Dad's factory is, a few miles north-east from Birmingham, where you've just been. We make a breakfast cereal that's quite well known in England, called 'Strongwheat'."

"Strongwheat. I'm sure I saw it on the big table at the hotel this morning. So that's your business?"

"Not exactly. Dad and I agreed to sell Strongwheat to American Cereal Products almost three years back, and since then it's really been very exciting. Dad has moved on to be Chairman of all their European businesses, and they're quite ambitious, so we seem to be putting on two or three a year. And I concentrate on the breakfast cereal side. There's the original factory at Lynchester – that's a nice little town about twenty miles northeast of Birmingham. There's a second up and running now, down near Bordeaux in France, and there's the one I'm going out to see today on the outskirts of Wuppertal. That's a former garment factory that we've taken on, and we're putting in the new plant and services to make a Corn Flake. Come to think of it, I shouldn't have said that, it's supposed to be secret still."

She turned to look him in the eyes, and put a hand on his. "Don't worry," she said solemnly, "Your secrets are safe with me. Always." And she kept her face straight for several seconds until they both burst out with laughter that had the other passengers turning their heads. And Dick wondered if she had sent him some sort of coded message.

"Ladies and gentlemen we are about to commence our descent to Dusseldorf, and the captain has switched on the seatbelt sign. Please return to your seats and fasten your seatbelts."

"Brit?"

"Yes?"

"I wondered what your arrangements were when you get to Dusseldorf. Where are you staying? Can I drop you off somewhere? There'll be a car with a driver to meet me."

She looked quietly at him, as though making some sort of calculation, "No, thank you. I am to stay at the Dom Hotel in Cologne. I have a meeting at the Europa Hotel at Dusseldorf airport this morning, then a taxi will take me to an afternoon meeting at the department store in Cologne. And I have to fly back from Dusseldorf to Stockholm early tomorrow."

She saw the disappointment in his expression, and reached across with her hand to touch his again. "But perhaps we could meet this evening for dinner?"

Dick found himself suddenly brimming with confidence.

"I'll come over to Cologne and pick you up, say seven-thirty?"

"No, that would not be the best thing. There will be many buyers from other stores meeting there tonight, and we cannot be just us together I think . . . I will come to your hotel in Dusseldorf. Which one is that?"

"The Breidenbacherhof. But . . ."

"No problem, Dick." The aircraft landed with a thump, that seemed to put a full stop to their conversation. "I must rush now to my meetings. Until seven-thirty at your Breidenbacherhof, Dick."

The Breidenbacherhof is one of the great business hotels of the world. It sits in a wide, tree-lined avenue, set back from the road and exuding an air of solid North German respectability. Broad steps lead up to an impressive Doric portico, and inside every corner and angle breathes – or perhaps whispers – quiet wealth. If you needed to ask the price of a room, this is probably not the right hotel for you. Dick's single room was not very large, but the carpet was two-hundred years old, from Persia, and the furniture was English Geogian.

Dick's afternoon at the Wuppertal site had passed in a kind of dream-state. The engineering work was on schedule, the formal permissions had been arranged, and tomorrow he was to sit in with his newly recruited German Managing Director on the interviews for Plant Manager in the morning, and Marketing Director in the afternoon. Out of deference to himself and the American owners, managerial meetings were supposed to be conducted in English, but in fact drifted in and out of German, particularly when technicians became involved. Dick found that, because the subject-matter was usually so familiar, he was able to resurrect the schoolboy German he'd polished up on an RAF posting to fly Tornados in Germany years before, and so he could follow most of the little aside conversations as well. First manufacturing trials were about eight weeks away. None of that seemed very important now as he bathed and shaved and dressed and waited for seven-thirty.

Would she really come? Did he want her to come? Really? He put on his jacket and looked critically at himself in the mirror.

He was tall and strongly built, still pretty fit from his years in the RAF, when he had played wing-forward for the RAF rugby team, until an unlucky tackle during the match against the Navy had damaged the cartilage of his left knee, putting an end to both his rugby-playing and his flying. His sandy hair was receding more rapidly now, emphasising the bushy eyebrows and the beaky nose. Was it possible that Brit actually fancied him? After fifteen years of pleasant unquestioned fidelity, was he actually contemplating an affair with a woman he'd just chatted to for an hour on a plane? Might she . . . a shrill jangle of the old-fashioned black telephone burst into his thoughts.

"Herr Routledge? Frau Carlsohn waits for you in Reception."

There were a pair of old-fashioned lifts a few yards from his room, the kind where you stepped in, closed the outer doors, then pulled across the brass gate before pressing the button to go down. The process calmed his racing thoughts, and by the time he emerged into the lobby he was sure he was just going to have a pleasant talk over dinner with an interesting businesswoman, one of the new breed of European executives.

"Hullo, Dick. It's lovely to see you again."

The polished teak curve of the reception desk ended just by the lift from which Dick emerged, to find Brit waiting, no more than a couple of yards away. She wore the dark blue coat slung around her shoulders, and he could see underneath a strapless dress of some burgundy-red satin material, with a short full skirt that distinctly rustled as she stepped towards him for the ritual cheek-pecking. There was a hint of perfume; was it violets? Something light and summery, to match the evening sunshine which reached in behind her through the revolving glass doors. There was that lovely smile again, and those soft blue eyes. He knew, for sure, that he wanted more than a pleasant dinner with a business executive.

"I've booked us a table at a restaurant I've been taken to before, called the Bateau Ivre."

"Is it French? 'Bateau' means 'boat', I know, but 'Ivre'?"

"I'd say its classification would be 'International, fairly dark, good food, high-class pianist.' I had to look up 'Ivre' myself. It means 'drunken'.

"Sounds fun."

And so it was. When they arrived the tables were already crowded, testifying to the appeal of the restaurant to its prosperous, mainly German clientele, with subdued up-lighting on the walls, and candles in silver candelabras to light the table. Brit liked it at once.

"It's the kind of restaurant you take a new client to or your wife for an important anniversary."

"Or a new girlfriend?"

"That too. The pianist has a very good style. That's 'Moon River', isn't it?" She hummed a few bars, "*Moon River, wider than a mile, I'm crossin' you in style, some day . . .*"

"Your English is exceptionally good."

"Thank you. Did I tell you my father was a member of the Swedish parliament? He spoke very good English, and he made sure my brother and I did too. Every time we meet to discuss the buying for the season, the meetings have to be held in English – it's the only language we have in common. And films or TV from America or England are usually not dubbed for us in Stockholm."

The waiter came with the menus, and they ordered vichyssoise, venison and cold salmon, with a dry Reisling.

"Was it a difficult thing to decide to sell your family business?"

Dick was just sampling the Reisling, and nodded to the sommelier.

"Not very. I mean it wasn't some ancient inheritance. My grandfather started it up after the war, and my father really made something of it with the Strongwheat breakfast cereal. I came into it about four, no five years ago, when Dad gave us all a scare when he had a bit of a stroke. He pulled through all right, and pushed me to launch a new product, well, a new variant of Strongwheat. We put a lot of money into it, and it's doing very well now, but at the time it all got a bit fraught."

"Sorry Dick, what is 'fraught'?"

"Um, worrying, stressful, dangerous. I mean we were sticking our heads above the parapet, trying to take some share of market away from some of the biggest and smartest companies in the world. Bit like a terrier stealing a bone from a tiger."

"So really you were glad to get out of it?"

It struck Dick Routledge that he had never had a conversation like this with his wife, Rosemary. Not that she wasn't concerned. She had been, passionately. But once the decision was taken, she'd simply got on with the rest of her life with the boys and the house and some good causes in Lynchester. She'd never asked what he felt now about being an employee of a multi-national, instead of being personally responsible for the lives of a couple of hundred people and their families, at Strongwheat. Was he 'glad to be out of it'? He looked across at Brit, her blonde head slightly tilted as she waited for his answer, white shoulders gleaming in the candlelight, the little notch in the centre of her neckline emphasising the deep shadow between the curves of her breasts. His mouth was suddenly dry, and he took a long pull of the Reisling. It was cool and fragrant.

"Well, it was Dad's business really, though I'm sure I would have inherited his shares in due course. As it is, there are trusts set up for the boys, and we don't have to worry too much about money any more, and I've just been enjoying the fun of creating a business that works, first in France and now in Germany. What about you? Do you have an ambition to go into politics, like your father?"

Brit found it very easy to talk to this big, friendly Englishman. She loved the way he seemed to be interested in everything that was going on, including herself. Politics? She'd never really thought about it.

"These days Brussels seems to be the only place where anything that matters is decided, and the Stockholm parliament is becoming more and more like a local council. Is it not the same in England?"

Their waiter came by to clear the dinner plates, and they both asked for coffee, without dessert. It was nine-thirty, and Dick did not want the evening to end.

"I don't know Dusseldorf that well, but I bet if we asked the head waiter he could find us somewhere we could go on to, perhaps somewhere we could dance. What do you think? I'll get you safely back to Cologne, of course."

Brit guessed that Dick had come to some sort of decision about their relationship, and was glad. "I'd like to stay longer too. Let's see what he can suggest."

The head waiter at the Bateau Ivre was well used to solving such problems, indeed he had an extensive network of appropriate contacts.

"You will like der 'Pfederstall', mein herr. It is a private club in the Altstadt, zat is the oldest part of the town. I will call a taxi for you, and perhaps ven you get there you will say zat Jurgen at the Bateau Ivre sent you. I vill telephone ahead."

Dick's German did not extend to the meaning of 'Pfederstall', but once they had been admitted he worked out from the cartoon on the front of the menu that it meant 'Donkey's

Home'. It was in a cellar, dimly lit and crowded, with a jazz trio playing music for (not too energetic) dancing. Brit tucked her head onto his shoulder and murmured, "Perhaps people end up in the hay?"

They drank a dry sparkling wine from Mosel, and turned and turned on the dance floor until they felt joined together. Dick discovered that Brit's son Stefan was almost eleven, which confirmed his calculation that she was in her late thirties. She was philosophic about her marriage.

"My husband Per was, still is a teacher. He was happy when he had the status, and I was working at a counter in the big store. But when I was promoted he found it difficult to accept that I was still growing, and he was standing still. So he began to drink, every evening the same, and I stayed with him when little Stefan was small, but a year ago we split, and I took Stefan back to live with my mother. My father died three years before, so she has a big house right by the sea at Djursholm, which is a nice part of Stockholm. We live very quietly."

"But you must have lots of men who want you."

She touched his cheek. "You are the first, I think. Perhaps I have not been very welcoming."

Soon after midnight the jazz group took a break, and it seemed natural that they should leave. As they waited outside for the taxi he dropped her coat around her shoulders, and kissed her cheek. She turned her face, and the kiss on his lips was long and warm.

"Where shall I tell the taxi to go?"

"To the Breidenbackerhof, yes?"

The lobby of the Breidenbackerhof was still busy, and Dick had to wait a couple of minutes for his room key. He led Brit to one of the old-fashioned lifts in the corner, and demonstrated his expertise as he closed the doors and pulled over the brass gate. She turned to him for another long kiss, harder and more urgent and then broke away to press the button to go up.

Dick was nuzzling her neck as they came out of the lift, drowning in her perfume and loving the way she seemed to melt into him. "It's just around to the right . . ."

They stopped abruptly. The corridor was filled by a formidably large blue-uniformed shape that Dick recognised as the senior porter from Reception downstairs.

"Mein herr? A t'ousan' apologies, but I must point out to you, with ze very great respect, zat ze young fraulein cannot go into your room."

Dick pulled himself away from Brit, feeling an urge to get very angry, and at the same time trying hard not to.

"I don't think I understand?"

"It is your room, mein herr. It is a single room, so you may not entertain a guest, if you understand me? It is ze rule of der hotel. A double room, or a suite, there is no problem. Single room, verboten."

"So if I changed my room for a suite . . .?"

"No problem of course, mein herr. Please to ask at Reception. But I do t'ink zat we are ver' full this night."

Dick felt his cheeks flaming with embarrassment, and they were out on the front steps and climbing into a taxi before either said a word. It was Brit who directed the taxi-driver.

"We want to go to Cologne, bitte. The Dom Hotel, it's near the cathedral. And then my friend will be coming back to Dusseldorf with you."

It is about twenty-five miles up the Rhine from Dusseldorf to Cologne, and their taxi had covered half the distance before Dick, who had been looking out of his window in gloomy silence became aware of a suppressed hissing noise coming from his companion. She was laughing.

"Oh Dick, I understand how you must feel so embarrassed and cross, but you must admit that it really was so funny. That German porter trying to be so polite and correct and dignified, and you . . . you looked like that tiger who finds his dinner has been taken away. I truly thought you might hit him."

She collapsed again with helpless giggles. Dick just glowered at first, but then he thought that she looked so pretty and appealing when she was smiling that he couldn't help grinning a sickly grin himself, and then their laughter melted into another long, long kiss. She ran her hand up his thigh, and he felt her lips smile again beneath his.

"I'm so glad that your enthusiasm has not altogether been destroyed."

The taxi was slowing down now in the shadow of the old Dom, Cologne's famous cathedral with its tall spire pointing to heaven.

"Shall I come in with you?"

Brit was refreshing her lipstick and checking her hair in the mirror of a gold powder compact, as the taxi came to a halt outside the Dom Hotel.

"Dick, I'm so sorry, but I can see Herr Mitel, the senior buyer from Kaufhof and two of his assistants talking there by the front door, on the steps of the hotel. My reputation . . . is important to me . . . do you understand?"

"Will I ever see you again?"

"I would like that, very much. I am visiting to England or France or Germany every few weeks, or perhaps you may come to Stockholm? Perhaps you could call me in my office next week, when I have my next journey-plan worked out?"

She held his face between her hands and kissed him again, a soft, loving kiss that seemed to promise so much, and climbed out of the taxi. Dick held her hand until the last moment.

"I'll call you, next week."

Brit pulled the coat across her bare shoulders, and her red skirts swirled about her legs as she hurried up the hotel steps, and disappeared through the revolving door.

"Dusseldorf, mein herr?"

"Dusseldorf, danke."

Chapter Two

There was a persistent tapping at his office door, and Charles Harrison raised his head with mixed irritation and relief from the pile of memos and correspondence he had been leafing through. Three weeks on holiday all at once was always going to be a problem in his small Chartered Accountant's office, and he had returned on this Friday morning so that he could pick up any urgent items and make some inroads over the weekend. It was already obvious that most of the awkward issues seemed to have been saved up for his return.

"Come in, come in. Rachel, how are you? If you're looking for my input on the likelihood of Colin Goodrich facing prosecution on charges of tax-evasion, I've noted the letter from learned counsel, but I haven't got my brain in gear yet. Still trying to get the Majorca sand out, I shouldn't wonder. Have you had coffee?"

Charles was sixty two, but had a full head of greying hair which he kept well-trimmed and brushed back, and with his newly-acquired tan he could pass for fifty. Rachel had come in holding a file, and Charles rose quickly to move towards the tray of fresh coffee on the sideboard in front of the Georgian window. He waved her to the leather chair in front of his desk, and helped himself to a chocolate biscuit as he poured their coffee.

His window, already open at the bottom, looked out onto a sunlit view of Lynchester's Market Square. To the left was its Gothic church, towering over a neat row of stuccoed Georgian houses and shops, and opposite stood the handsome classical facade of the Crown Hotel, with its pillared entrance surmounted by a large gilded crown. To the right the square sloped gently down to an open promenade along the River Lyn. Rachel Goldman was his secret pride, his first junior partner, recruited by means of personal contacts from the Birmingham office of one of the bigger national partnerships, Grant Thornton. She was just thirty, slim with close-cropped dark hair, well-groomed but not conventionally pretty, with thick black eyebrows and a strong chin. She had determination and a fierce intelligence, and there was, he thought, an irresistible charm in her lop-sided smile.

She sipped her coffee – black of course, no sugar – and opened her file of papers.

"Nice to have you back, Charles, but I haven't come to chase you about Colin. At least, not yet. It's one of your personal clients I wanted to talk about, Jennifer Hawkins, one of the 'Three Rich Widow Hawkins', as I believe they are called. She came in two weeks ago, with her little boy, Billy. I said you were away, but she didn't seem to mind. She wants us to look into ways of setting up some sort of protected trust for the boy, something that will pay his school fees and university, and be tax-efficient for them both. She's got her head screwed on, I'd say."

Charles leant back in his chair and laced his fingers behind his head. "Mmm, yes, Jenny probably knows as much as you or I about looking after the pennies and the pounds. Do you know the background to her money?"

"Only that there are three Hawkins widows, all very well-off. The money comes from the Hawkins Shopping Mall of course, but that's about the limit of what I know, me not being a local. I mean, they're your personal clients, and there's only the working papers and tax-returns in the files."

He glanced guiltily at his sideboard, where he kept a lot of information about his clients that his staff did not need to know.

"Let me tell you about the Hawkins."

Rachel refused a second cup of coffee as he got up again to help himself, and he remained standing by the window.

"As you said, there are three Hawkins widows, and they're all comfortably provided for. Jennifer is the widow of old Joe Hawkins. She was his second wife, a lot younger of course. He owned Hawkins Builders Merchants, which stood on the site where the Mall is now. She ran the retail side of the business, with some success, I might add. He died just over three years ago, and left the business to be divided equal thirds between Jenny and his two sons, Alan and George. Did I say that Jenny was his second wife?"

"But the little boy, Billy, he can't be more than three, I'd say?"

"Yes, must be three now. And before you ask, he's certainly not Joe's son. Joe was very ill for months before he died. The fact is, Jenny has always refused to say who the father is. Plenty of wagging tongues of course, but she's the only one who knows for sure, and she's not telling."

"Right, and really we don't need to know, do we? The other widows?"

"Helen Hawkins was George's wife. George was fond of the bottle, and was found one night hanging from a beam in the Builders Merchants. Everyone thought he'd committed suicide in a fit of alcoholic grief over the loss of his father, but then it turned out that he'd probably been murdered by Alan, his brother."

"I don't remember seeing any of this in the paper."

"Well, you were living in Solihull at the time, and I'd guess that it would have made just a paragraph in the Birmingham evening paper. Anyway it all came into the open when Helen found out what had really happened, and she took it out on Alan with the carving knife."

"Killed him, you mean?"

"Very very dead. They got a smart London barrister for her, she pleaded guilty to 'manslaughter when the balance of her mind was disturbed' and got five years, but suspended. She'd been a nurse previously, and she's been heavily into good works at the Hospital ever since."

"But she kept her inheritance? Oh yes, of course, she didn't get the benefit from her crime."

"Exactly. But she'd already got George's share. The beneficiary of her crime, if you put it that way, was the third of the Hawkins widows, Alan's wife, Grace."

"I think I've met her. Dark curly hair, quite pretty, three children? She's at the swimming pool a lot, and we got chatting only last week. Very friendly and nice. I'd no idea the background was so lurid."

"Lurid? Let's say 'tragic', shall we? Right then, that's enough background to be going on with." He opened his sideboard, and found a thick file. "There's all the stuff about Jenny's holdings and investments. It's a while since I looked at it, so the valuations will need careful review now, especially her holdings in the Mall. How much did she suggest putting into this Trust Fund?"

"We're to advise on how much and exactly what to transfer. She thought something between five hundred thousand and a million would be needed."

"Young Billy's to lack for nothing, I can see. But she'll not want him to have too much access, let alone control until he's ready for it. I'll leave it to you then to draft the Deed of Trust, which we'll have to have her solicitor look over of course, and to propose how much goes into it in the way of funding, and where the funds should come from. There is a sister in Birmingham, I believe, and Jennifer might want her as a trustee. And there should be something in the way of commissions for us to earn from re-investing the funds with appropriate flexibility for young Billy's requirements. All right?"

"No problem. And thanks for the briefing."

"My pleasure. And I'll get up to speed on poor dear Colin tonight, and we can see tomorrow if there's any way out for him, short of paying up and throwing himself on the tender mercies of the Inland Revenue."

"There's no way the IR can criticise us?"

"I believe we are in the clear on that one. Colin has been a naughty boy, piling up profits by trading in undeclared off-shore assets, and bringing the cash back into England in a suitcase. But I'm sure we can safely maintain we did not even know the assets existed. He's not going to contradict us."

After Rachel had left Charles sat down to browse through another file, which contained copies of everything he had given her, plus a few other items about Jennifer's tax planning. He knew that, after old Joe had died, Jennifer had been having an affair with Alan, and that Billy was Alan's son, born seven months after he had been killed. In those days the size of the gain to be made from selling the Builders Merchant site to build the Hawkins Mall was by no means assured, and Jennifer had asked for his very confidential advice about the possibility of making a claim, on behalf of her unborn child, against Alan's share of the business, which Grace had inherited. Fortunately there had been enough money for all three widows not to have to worry, so Jennifer had been easily persuaded to drop that idea. He read through his handwritten notes, thought for a moment, and then carefully tore the sheet of paper into small pieces. No need for that now! He was reminded that Jennifer and Helen and Grace had all been substantial contributors to the now almost-completed Hawkins-Routledge Childrens' Wing of the Lynchester hospital, which in turn led him to check his diary – next week of course, Wednesday afternoon, quarterly meeting of the Trustees. No doubt he would see them there. Together with the charming and very respectable Mrs. Ellen Routledge, whose husband James had contributed substantially, using some of the money he'd made from selling the Strongwheat cereal business to the Americans. He'd always felt there was an element of irony in his solemnly presiding over a charitable foundation whose funds came from such 'interesting' family sources.

Chapter Three

Dick Routledge's return flight from Dusseldorf to Birmingham arrived on time for once at 6.30p.m. on Friday evening, and he was pleased to see that his father's chauffeur was waiting with the old Jaguar. He threw his bag onto the back seat and climbed in beside the driver, Jack Walters. Jack was used to ferrying around the company's directors and VIP visitors, and confident of his place after long service with 'Strongwheat', most of the time as a heavy goods delivery driver.

"Good trip, sir?"

"Very good, Jack. I really think this German factory will start up on time. And we've been lucky with finding some good people. Though no doubt Mrs Savage, our esteemed Director of Personnel, would say that luck is not what it's all about when it comes to finding the right people. Anything special happening in Lynchester?"

"Not much this week so far. Though I did see in this week's paper that the new Children's Wing at the Hospital is nearly ready for opening. Didn't I hear somewhere that the Chairman has a stake in that?"

"He put in a big chunk from the money we got for selling Strongwheat to the Yanks. Some sort of 'thank you', I think, for the way they looked after him when he had that stroke, five years ago."

Later that evening, just after supper, the topic of the Children's Wing came up again. Dick's wife, Rosemary, had just brought their after-supper coffee into the living room, and Dick was thumbing through the television programmes. Rosemary was a year older than Dick, and had been the Station Adjutant when he had met her in Germany. She was tall and lean, with a beautiful head of red hair, starting to fade a little now, a generously wide mouth, and large blue eyes that usually held a smile, but could go startlingly cold if she felt challenged. She had joined the RAF originally to get away from a drunken father, and was in consequence enormously protective of her own family now.

"Your mother rang me this morning, Dick. Said your father was expecting to be tied up later next week with the visiting Americans, so she wondered if you would go with her to the quarterly meeting of the Board of Trustees of the Childrens' Hospital. You know, building the new wing. It's Wednesday afternoon. She said she wouldn't have bothered you, but this meeting is going to decide some important things about the official opening, and she wants the family to be properly represented."

Dick could think of many better ways of spending the Wednesday afternoon, and grunted non-committally.

"I called the office and asked Elizabeth if your diary was clear. She said 'yes', so I've told your mother that it should be all right for you."

Dick cursed Elizabeth Boyd silently. She worked as P.A. to both his father and himself, and after thirty years in 'Strongwheat' was a formidable lady in her own right. More than likely his mother had checked with Elizabeth before she'd even called Rosemary. He resigned himself to giving up the Wednesday afternoon.

"Seems like you've got it all nicely sorted out between you. I'll call mother tomorrow, and talk to Dad as well to see what he wants me to say. Do you know who else is on this Board?"

"I don't know all of them, but the Chairman is Charles Harrison, the accountant in the Square."

"I've met him a few times. Quite sharp, as I recall."

"And of course two of the famous three Lynchester widows . . ."

"Widows? Oh, of course the three Widow Hawkins. Haven't heard anything about them for ages. Look love, there's absolutely nothing on the box, and I'm beat anyway. What do you say to an early night?"

"Suits me, I've got a new Alan Furst to read. Real atmospheric story about spies in Europe in1940. You can hear the sound of jackboots on wet cobbled streets. Hard to put down once you get going."

"Well . . . I mightn't be all that tired . . . But I'll probably let you get through one chapter, as long as you don't wear that black nightdress."

On Monday morning Dick was in the office at 8.30, riffling through his in-tray and sipping tea – Rosemary had made him promise to cut down on the coffee, so now Elizabeth dutifully brought tea, whatever he had asked for. His attention was caught by a header-sheet of an e-mail printout:

ACP France – Unaudited results for the month of June

There was a scribbled note pinned to it:

Dick – I think something is going wrong in France. Have a good look, then call me in if I can help. Jim.

Jim Helvin was the company's long-serving accountant, now Director of Finance, with 'dotted line' responsibilities for the accountancy functions in the new European subsidiaries. In practice this meant that the local accountants reported to their local managing directors, but Jim was supposed to supervise the technical quality of their work, and in particular he made himself available as an informal counterweight, in case a local managing director leaned unreasonably on his accountant to massage the figures which were being reported monthly by e-mail to England and simultaneously to ACP in Illinois.

The new cornflake business near Bordeaux had been operational for eighteen months, and was expected to become profitable on a month to month basis by the end of the year. Having a cereal with milk for breakfast was anything but traditional in France, but there was a good potential market that research had identified amongst 'modern mothers of young children', and ACP was chasing Kelloggs to get a share. Dick looked with a newly-practised eye through the figures. Jim was right. Quite simply, the sales values were rising well above the expectations of the 3-year plan, but the bottom-line losses were increasing sharply, instead of decreasing. Dick tapped his fingers on the papers thoughtfully for a moment, then pushed back his chair.

"If anyone needs me desperately, I'm with Jim Helvin."

Dick found Jim Helvin in his small office, behind a desk covered in paper. Jim was coming up for retirement in a year or so, and the 'Director' title had been in part a reward for his years of loyal service. Somewhat to the surprise of his colleagues, he had responded with considerable enthusiasm to the challenges presented by the recent growth of Strongwheat, and the added responsibilities of supervising the Accounting function in new businesses on the continent of Europe. He had that sharp eye for a telling detail, as though he were still the accountant of a small family business. He was a lean, friendly man with bright blue eyes behind rimless spectacles and a brush of close-cropped white hair.

"Morning, Dick. How was Der Fatherland?"

Dick thought briefly about the frustrations of the evening with Brit Carlsohn and felt guiltily for her business card in his jacket pocket. He replied, "Coming along all right I'd say. Plant installation is on schedule, and we're finding some impressive people. Start-up in about eight weeks. In a way the recession there is good for us when we're recruiting, there's less competition for talent. But you wanted to bend my ear about France? I can see we've got a problem. Do we know the cause?"

"Headcount."

Jim was noted for the laconic concision of his answers to questions, and Dick waited patiently for the follow-on.

"I reckon your friend Jean-Paul reached what should have been more or less a plateau in the number of employees there about four months ago, when he got to seventy. Production there is pretty well automated, so the increasing volume since then should have needed at most one or two more, to handle stuff through the warehouse perhaps. But he's up to eighty-five now, in fact he's put on seven more in this last month. And that's after I sent a polite enquiry last month, when it first looked as if something might be adrift. He hasn't replied to that, by the way. So overheads are running way over budget. And there's something just as weird going on with the revenue statement too. The volumes in cases are just about on plan, but the revenue is nearly half a million Euros over plan, all absorbed and more by this bloated overhead factor. And of course the bottom line is looking sicker by the month."

"Any guesses as to what might be going on?"

"Guessing comes cheap, Dick. But the whole thing could blow up in our faces at year-end, especially if the internal auditors from ACP get nasty. We could all look very foolish if we haven't cracked it before then. I can think of some questions to ask, but they could stall us for weeks, months even, if we just sit around here sending and, if we're lucky, receiving e-mails."

"Message received and understood. 'For immediate action this day', as Winston used to say." Dick pulled his pocket diary out, "I could probably go over later this week. Fancy holding my hand in this French lion's den?"

Jim shook his head, "Sorry, Dick, I'm already spoken for. Your father has asked me to stand by when the Yanks are here, in case they want some figures tweaked. They're arriving Thursday lunchtime. You'll just have to dare to be a Daniel all alone. But I'll give you some notes and analysis to take with you. Try to get a quiet chat with the factory accountant, M'sieur Robarte, out of earshot of Jean-Paul. He's a solid citizen, but of course he wants to keep his job too."

Dick returned to his office, his thoughts racing with speculations about the French company. The local M.D., Jean-Paul de Clavignon, had been head-hunted two years ago from the French subsidiary of Colgate-Palmolive, where he had been a high-flying Director of Sales and Marketing, with a French MBA in his background. ACP itself had provided a team of advisers to accelerate him through the learning curve on manufacturing and finance, and his skill and enthusiasm had driven the business through to an effective product launch and a good first year. Dick knew that Jean-Paul was well-regarded back at corporate office, and if now something serious was amiss his own judgement might also be criticised. He guessed that Jim's suggested questions would be towards the brutal end of frank. And that was without the added complication of either speaking in French, when he could not be sure of picking the right words, or speaking English, when he could not be sure that he was being understood. *Perhaps I should have a chat with Dad too. He's bound to have come across something similar before.* He double-checked his pocket diary against the bigger one that Elizabeth maintained on his desk, and walked next door to her office. She was now coming up to sixty, but exceptionally well-preserved – tall, slim with short iron-grey hair and a disconcerting habit of looking up over the top of her gold-rimmed glasses with a slightly disapproving expression that reminded Dick of the old headmistress of his primary school. In addition to being PA to both Dick and his father, she had, over the years, assumed vague but unchallenged supervisory power over the other management secretaries in the office. Her husband had recently taken a generous redundancy package from his well-paid job in the County Planning Office, and her two grown-up sons were 'something in the City' down in London. No one had yet dared to ask her if she was considering retirement.

"Elizabeth, would you check with Jean-Paul's PA in France, see how he's fixed for a couple of days with me if I come over say Thursday/Friday this week? If that's O.K., book me onto the Bordeaux flight Thursday first thing. No, make that Wednesday evening if possible."

"You're not forgetting the Hospital Trustees' meeting on Wednesday afternoon, Mr. Dick?"

Dick had indeed forgotten the meeting until he had looked at the big diary, but answered quickly, "No, it's in the diary all right. That will finish by five I'm sure, and the evening flight goes at seven, if I remember."

Back in his office Dick took out Brit's card,

Brit Carlsohn, Senior Buyer, Steen and Strom, Stockholm.

Memories flooded back of the animation in her face as they talked on the flight, the shadowed notch between her breasts in that red dress, the feel of her body moulded to his as they danced. Suddenly he wanted to hear again that pretty lilt in her voice. She'd said that she had a trip coming soon to France – perhaps this week even? His hand moved to the telephone, but rested there. *This was stupidity! Here he was, a senior international executive, happily married with a lovely wife and two fine sons. Was all that to be put at risk for an affair with a woman he'd met casually on a business trip? Besides, it was only eleven*

o'clock on Monday morning, she couldn't possibly have fixed her travel-plan yet. He pushed her card into an inside ticket pocket.
"Any chance of some coffee, please Elizabeth?"

Jennifer Hawkins was bored. Her son Billy had recently started three half-days a week at Lynchester's best play school, which was hardly fifty yards away from her own home, in another of the handsome double-fronted Edwardian houses that lined both sides of her quiet, leafy street, across the river from the old town. He had been born seven months after the awful death of her lover and stepson, Alan Hawkins, and for over three years now she had allowed herself to become totally absorbed, obsessed even, with looking after him. It had been Helen, George Hawkins' widow, who had made her see the truth.

"You fuss around Billy too much. He's three now, and you've got to let go a bit. Get a life for yourself again. I was wrong to do what I did to Alan, and you know I regret it. Especially when I see how unhappy it's made you. But he was bad, you know, and he did deliberately kill my George, and nothing we say or do is going to bring either of them back. But Billy is a person too, and he deserves to be let out of your sight for an hour or two, if you see what I mean."

Billy would be returning in an hour, and Greta, his Dutch nanny, was busy in the kitchen preparing lunch for the three of them, before she collected him. Meanwhile Jennifer sat under the awning of a softly-padded seat in the garden, kicking her heels to make it swing and wishing for something, anything to happen. Jennifer was forty now, her hair very dark and pinned up to reveal her fine profile, enhanced by her soft brown, lustrous eyes and a generous mouth. She frowned over an article in the *Financial Times* which forecast that the Government would need to raise an extra fifteen thousand million pounds a year from taxes to fund state services, and, no doubt inspired by the Treasury, trailed a proposal to increase income taxes for the better-off from forty to sixty percent. Jennifer was, at least by the provincial standards of Lynchester, a rich woman. After the terrible events of three years ago, the Builders Merchant business they had inherited had been sold to a property development company, and was now the Hawkins Shoppers' Mall. She had agreed with Helen and Grace that they would each put half a million into the new Children's Wing for the hospital. Jennifer had worked, before she became Joe Hawkins' second wife, as a departmental manager for Woolworth's, and had herself developed an increasingly successful DIY retail side to the family business. So it had been natural for her to take up the opportunity to re-invest a good part of the remainder of her share of the money from the sale of the site back into the company that had built and now ran the Hawkins Mall itself. The first year had shown a small loss, but trading was now picking up strongly, the Mall was at last fully-let, and Jennifer was looking forward to the arrival of a nice dividend, which itself could be expected to make her shareholding substantially more valuable. That was why she had approached her accountants, Charles Harrison, for advice about setting up a trust fund for Billy's education. *Sixty percent tax would change all the arithmetic – horribly! Perhaps I should sell my share of the Mall, and invest in some tax-free haven off-shore? Why not move, and set up somewhere with a nice, warm climate? The south of France for instance. Of course, that would not necessarily be tax-free. Might even be worse. Still, it would be interesting. My house was one of the best in Lynchester, so if I sold up I could certainly get something very nice in France for the money. My schoolgirl French would soon improve, and Billy was young enough to become bi-lingual in no time. After all, what was there to keep me in Lynchester? Joe was dead, and Alan too.*

She thought of the hours she had spent with Alan. Grace had been quite forgiving – well, Jennifer had never actually admitted to her that Alan had been her lover and Billy's father, and Grace now had the children and Alan's share of the money, and had probably seen nothing to be gained from waving the family's dirty linen in front of the population of Lynchester, especially with her father coming up for Mayor. Alan had implied that things had been pretty cool anyway between himself and Grace. *How much might I get from selling my shares? The Mall company was not listed itself, but there were plenty of comparable property companies.* She turned the pages of her *Financial Times* to find the listings, but was interrupted by Greta emerging into the garden, plump, blonde and pretty, dusting flour from her fingers.

"Mrs. Hawkins, please? There is Mrs. Routledge on telephone. She wants to talk about the meeting for the 'ospital on Wednesday."

Jennifer had been introduced to Ellen Routledge at the first meeting of what was to become the Board of Trustees for the new Children's Wing, when it was announced that her husband, James Routledge, was offering to match the Hawkins' donation and put up one and a half million pounds himself, "By way of saying 'thank-you' for saving my life". Apparently the money was coming from the sale of his cereal business to an American company. There had been some polite but very determined discussion about possible names for the Wing – 'The Hawkins-Routledge Wing' was cumbersome but saved further unprofitable discussion, and was already being shortened to 'The H-R'. Jennifer had found Ellen Routledge pleasant enough, but inclined to expect to get her own way. She had never previously called Jennifer before a meeting.

"Jennifer dear, how are you? Good. Now I'm calling because the most important item on the agenda on Wednesday is to be the arrangements for the opening of the H-R, which I am told is likely to be in about three months' time. My husband knows the mayor – well of course you must know him too, he's Grace's father isn't he? Anyway we hear that the council wants some celebrity to do the opening, a pop star or a TV person, or even a footballer. If you ask me, they just want to see their picture in the paper or on the TV. Really of course it's got nothing to do with them. It's a decision for the Trustees, which means that if you and I agree, we can decide. James and I think that someone more dignified would be better, a minor Royal, or the Lord Lieutenant, or perhaps one of the top consultant surgeons from Great Ormonde Street Hospital for Sick Children. Preferably one who's been knighted, I'm sure you see my point of view? Of course I don't want to press you now, but could you think about it dear, please? I shall be having a quiet word to Charles as well. Give me a call if you want to discuss it some more, otherwise I'll see you on Wednesday afternoon. By the way I don't think you've met my son Dick? He's a senior international executive in the American company now. James is going to be tied up all day Wednesday, getting ready for their visiting firemen, as he puts it. Anyway Dick is going to be standing in for his father, so I shall look forward to introducing him to you. 'Bye then."

Jennifer had hardly said a word while Ellen was on the telephone – not many people did – and was trying to say something non-committal when she found that Ellen had put the phone down already. Uncertain whether to be flattered or indignant, she was interrupted by Greta coming out to the kitchen steps, untying her apron.

"The pie is on the oven already, Mrs. Hawkins, so I will go to collect Billy."

Jennifer nodded, picked up her FT and walked thoughtfully into the house to lay the table for lunch in the kitchen. *It's nearly two weeks now since I asked that bright girl in Charles' office to look at the idea of an educational trust for Billy, so there should be some progress on that now. And no doubt Charles would have something interesting to say about the possibility of selling the house, liquidating my holdings in the Mall and moving abroad. Of course it's just a casual idea at the moment, but it would do Charles no harm to invest a little time exploring the pros and cons for her, especially any potential pitfalls on the tax side. Time to set up a visit. Perhaps we could have a chat after the Trustees meeting?*

Chapter Four

Five years ago James Routledge suffered a stroke and had persuaded his son Dick to resign his commission in the RAF and come into the 'Strongwheat' business. James had been kept away from the company for almost a year, thanks to the determination of his wife Ellen, who nursed him through a slow recovery. Eventually he had become strong enough to insist on coming back and he had then pushed Dick to lead the development of a new variety for Strongwheat, which had led indirectly to the takeover bid in shares from ACP. As a result he was now a substantial shareholder in the American company ; part of the deal had been the offer of his present position as Chairman of ACP Europe. His particular responsibility was to manage the expansion of ACP into continental Europe, using Strongwheat as a base. As well as the Cornflake business in France, and the new plant in Germany, there was now a olive-oil company in Parma, Italy, which was just starting to market ACP's corn-oil, and a corn-margarine business in Rotterdam, Holland.

James had, late in life, learned the art of delegating, so that his duties were not too onerous, and he played a good deal of weekday golf. But once a quarter he could expect a more or less formal visit from an ACP team, sometimes grandly referred to as 'The International Cadre'. ACP's head office, being on the shores of Lake Michigan and about twenty miles north of Chicago, was pleasant, even attractive during good weather, but not the most exciting place in the world to work, and so competition was keen for a place amongst what James called the 'visiting firemen'. The constant element for these visitations was provided by Ben Camina, ACP's Chief Financial Officer, who had been one of the protagonists of the international expansion policy that had led to the sequence of acquisitions and start-ups in Europe. Supporting Ben, it was ACP policy to use membership of the Cadre as a way of combining reward for good work with providing a training ground for wider responsibilities. So the three or four younger ACP executives who came over with Ben every three months could expect to be given an international consultancy role for a year or so, with a good deal of transatlantic or transpacific travel. After that they would move back into a line job, hopefully with enhanced career prospects. In practice the European side of this system had usually resulted in Ben and James being able to cement transatlantic good relations around English golf-courses for a few days, while the Cadre's team of eager beavers visited factories, pored over figures and plans, and prepared a summary presentation of their findings and suggestions for action – to be given initially to James and Ben, and later, with suitable modifications, to a committee of the main board. This cadre, led by Ben Camina, was expected on Thursday.

James was at his desk by ten o'clock on Tuesday morning, going over the latest reports from Strongwheat and the continental companies with Jim Helvin, when Dick put his head round his office door.

"Morning, Dad. I imagine Jim's already filled you in about the peculiar numbers coming out of France?"

"He has. It's a pity you couldn't have got over there a week ago, so that I could have had a proper answer ready for Ben and his people. As it is, you're going to be over there looking for the explanation, when they're here asking the questions. This'll be the first time we've been caught with our pants down, and I blame you for it."

James was notorious for his 'call a spade a bloody shovel' manner, and Dick was not intimidated by the accusation that he had taken his eye off the ball. Instead he sat down opposite his father.

"Point taken, and you can be sure I'll be in touch as soon as I've got something sorted. In fact I'm going over Wednesday evening, and Ben isn't due here until Thursday lunchtime, so there's a fair chance I could get something to you by 'phone or e-mail before the proverbial rises up and hits the fan." He turned to Jim, "I was wondering if you'd had any more thoughts about what I should expect?"

Jim Helvin pushed his reading glasses up onto his forehead. "Not a clue. Except that they'll try to hide whatever it is under a load of flannel. I've looked at the raw grain usage, and that squares quite nicely with the reported sales in cases. But if the case quantities are right, then the turnover numbers are saying that they've had a price increase of twenty percent or more over the last two months, which seems unlikely, as they'd surely have mentioned it in some report. And then there's the strange increase in the overhead which wipes out the benefit of the extra turnover, and then some. I'll prepare some notes for you as soon as I'm done here."

James intervened, "So, Dick, if you've quite finished interrupting us, I'd like to get on?"

Back in his own office Dick looked at the report he'd started to put together about his visit to Dusseldorf. He found it difficult to concentrate, and eventually felt for the card that Brit Carlsohn had given him. *Tuesday, nearly midday now in Stockholm* . . . he looked up to check that the mahogany office door was securely closed. *Dial now, or for ever hold your peace.* 0046 8 254 2118. *There, that was easy, wasn't it?* He listened to the long continental ringing tones. *Still time to put the phone down* . . .

"Hullo, Steen und Strom, Stockholm?"

It was Brit! No switchboard to go through, it was her voice! Dick felt dizzy, as though he were diving for the first time from a very high board.

"Brit, hullo, this is Dick Routledge, I hope you remember me from Dusseldorf last Friday?"

There was a long pause, and Dick thought for a moment that the connection had been broken.

"Dick, yes, of course. Forgive me, I was expecting a call from Berlin. You surprised me. A very nice surprise of course." Her tone was becoming perceptibly warmer. "I didn't think . . . I didn't expect that you would call . . . so soon. It's lovely that you have. Does it mean that we can meet again? I would like that so much."

"Yes, I hope so. I have to go to France later this week. I wondered if that could fit in with your plans? You said that you would need to go soon. I'm going to be in Bordeaux, staying at the Hotel Amarys, that's right in the centre. Could you come?"

There it was, plain, unadorned, out in the open. An invitation to adultery! Dick could feel his heart thumping in his chest.

"Well . . . I have to visit Paris as I told you, and perhaps I could do that on Friday and come straight on to Bordeaux for the weekend. Unless you would rather come to Paris?"

Dick thought quickly. Paris would be great – but how could he be sure how long it might take to dig into whatever it was that was going on at the French plant?

"I think I have to stay in Bordeaux. I'm going over to investigate a problem, and I won't know till I get there how long it will take to solve. Could we plan for just Friday evening? I will probably have to get back on Saturday, but you could stay on of course."

"I remember that English saying about 'half a loaf' ". She giggled, "Don't forget to reserve a double room for us this time."

Dick was glad she couldn't see the blush that warmed his cheeks, "So you'll come then?"

"Unless some problem stops me." Dick noticed that her voice was suddenly very businesslike again, as she continued, "Do you have the phone number for the hotel? What was it called again please?"

"The Hotel Amarys Royal St. Jean is the full name. Rue Charles Domerq. Telephone . . . um . . . well the dialling code for France from England is 0033, then 5 24 291 5839. Any idea what time I should expect you?"

"Depends on the flights, I've never been to Bordeaux before. Shall we plan for seven in the evening? I will leave a message for you at the hotel on Friday when I know the flight for sure. Does it take long from the airport?"

"It's an internal flight of course, and the airport at Merignac is about half an hour in a taxi from the hotel. Or if you are in the centre of Paris it could be just as quick to come on the high-speed train, and you can walk to the hotel from the station."

"Dick, I would love to talk some more now, but I hear that my call from Berlin is waiting. It's the Head of Buying from a new store to join our association, and I want to make a good impression. Till Friday then, see you in Bordeaux."

A click, and Dick found himself once again listening to the burr of the dialling tone. *This is a side of Brit I haven't seen before, all brisk and cool. Business come first. Perhaps I can understand something of what happened with her husband!* He put her card away carefully in the inside ticket pocket of his jacket that hung as usual on the back of his padded leather chair, and returned to the not unimportant matter of summarising the CVs of the senior management team that he was now putting together for the German venture. The total salary bill was going to be a bit more than he had forecast, so they had better look exceptionally impressive to the Americans . . .

On Wednesday afternoon Charles Harrison's large sunny office overlooking the Square had been turned into a boardroom for the Trustees meeting by the addition of a table pushed up to the middle of his desk. As Chairman of the Hawkins-Routledge Trust he occupied his usual seat behind the mahogany desk, with Jennifer and Helen Hawkins at the table to his right, Dick and his mother Ellen Routledge on his left, and Dan Gundry, Lynchester's mayor, facing him at the end of the table. Strictly speaking Grace Hawkins, Alan's widow, could also have sat in, as she had contributed equally with Jennifer and Helen to the fund, but Dan Gundry was her father, so after the first meeting she had declared that 'One bored member of the Gundry family was quite enough for any committee', and had asked merely to be kept informed of progress. Charles had for many years been responsible for the audit of Dan Gundry's company, 'Gundry Construction', and knew him to be a successful local builder, who had done exceptionally well over recent years. He had been a principal sub-contractor for the Hawkins Mall, built on the site of the Hawkins family builders merchants, and his company had also got most of the work for the new Children's Wing that this Trust was funding. He was a friendly, good-looking man in his early sixties, with a mop of dark, curly hair turning iron-grey, and a way of smiling as he spoke that was very disarming. Sitting next to him, Helen could see in his profile a strong resemblance to his daughter, her sister-in-law, Grace.

Charles led them through the progress reports. The construction phase itself was complete, and fitting out would start in a week or two. "And, mirabile dictu, you can see we are within budget as well as on time."

"One of the benefits of using a local builder with local workers."

"Thank you Dan, I'm sure we all agree. Now the fitting out and staffing are the responsibility of the Warwick NHS Trust, spending our money of course, and I made a point of talking to the Project Manager there this morning. He seems very confident that the first patients can be admitted within ten weeks."

Dick spoke for the first time, mindful of his seven o'clock flight to Bordeaux, and so anxious to push the meeting along.

"So we could pick an official opening date in mid-October, to be safe?" He opened his pocket diary. "How about Saturday, October 12th? Or the 19th?"

Dan Grundy was suddenly attentive. "No, not a Saturday, Mr. Chairman. Interferes with the weekend for the people that matter. A weekday is better. If we go for a Tuesday morning, that suits the local weeklies best, they go to bed Thursday and publish Friday. Gives them time to do a nice spread with pictures and come out for the weekend immediately following the opening. I'm sure that's ideal, wouldn't you agree?"

Charles looked at the others, who nodded. "Right then, shall we go for Tuesday 15th. October? Obviously we need a name to cut the tape. I believe there are some suggestions?" He looked first at Dan.

"Not exactly suggestions, Mr. Chairman. More just a few thoughts from my Council about the principles that we should adopt in choosing the person to do the opening." He paused, looking around the table to ensure he had their attention. "The opening of the new wing is quite simply the first real news story for the town of Lynchester in donkey's years. I mean, with all due respect to those present, it's much more likely to be picked up by the national press and TV than say the opening of the Hawkins Mall, or even the sale of Strongwheat, which were both really what you might call strictly local business stories. But a new hospital wing for children, with the money raised from local subscription, that combines politics with human interest, and people all over the country will be intrigued in it, and arguing about it too. For instance, 'Is this a step towards privatising the NHS?' 'Is this one of those public-private partnerships the government is supposed to be so keen on?' You can imagine the kind of story I'm talking about, and Lynchester is to be right at the centre of the debate. I'm sure you can see that we need someone that will automatically be recognised by the media and the general public."

"A pop-star, for instance?"

Jennifer Hawkins spoke quietly, but there was no mistaking the distaste in her voice. Dick had already admired the way she filled out a high-necked white lace blouse, and now the sudden animation in her dark eyes as she spoke made her very attractive. They had been introduced before the meeting started by Charles Harrison, and Dick had wondered about her life now. Of course he had read all about the 'Hawkins Murder Sensation', as the local press had headlined. She was certainly a beautiful woman, but he had sensed a cautiousness about meeting people, and she had scarcely seemed to look at him when they shook hands. Dan was speaking again.

"Well no, I wasn't thinking of a pop-star as such. I mean only the younger element would recognise them, and they're probably not the ones we want to reach, if we're looking to interest people in setting up a business in the town, for instance. I was thinking more of a television personality, such as one of the main news-readers, Jeremy Paxman say, or an interviewer like Jonathan Dimbleby."

Dick felt a little prod in his ribs from his mother. She was happy to manipulate events from behind the scenes, but she disliked making herself too prominent by talking very much at meetings, and had made him promise to take the lead on her behalf.

"Our feeling was for someone with a bit more status, more – what do you call it? – more gravitas than a television personality. Perhaps the Lord Lieutenant of the county? Or could we expect a minor royal to take an interest?"

Helen Hawkins was also usually too shy to contribute much to the meetings, but she too had been approached by Dick's mother. There was a fierceness about the expression on her thin, bony features as she spoke, as though she felt very strongly about the issue.

"I think we should bear in mind that this is a hospital we're talking about. And we're going to be closely associated with the Hospital for Sick Children at Great Ormonde Street, almost a Midlands branch, I've heard them say. Perhaps we could ask the

Director there to come up – the media would be sure to want to hear what he had to say about the NHS and so on. Or there are some very distinguished consultants there, world-class experts on paediatrics, several with knighthoods too."

Charles looked around the table, but there were no more contributions forthcoming.

"Well, it's just after four now, and I know that Dick has a flight to catch. I wonder if we could agree on a little sub-committee to take this issue on? I think the task should be to identify three or four possibilities, put them in order of preference, make the initial approaches and let us know the possibilities before finally committing the Board of Trustees. Dan, you know how to handle these things, would you like to lead?"

"Happily, Mr. Chairman, if that's all right with everyone?" There were no dissenters. "And I think I should have a member from each side of the table. Dick?"

"OK by me, but my diary gets quite crowded."

Dan knew from experience that Helen was the more easily influenced of the two Mrs. Hawkins, and would have therefore preferred to have her on his sub-committee. He wasn't surprised though when she demurred.

"Honestly, no thank you, Dan. I'm busy almost every day at the hospital as it is, there are so many people who need advice and so on. I think this is more up Jenny's street, I mean she had a lot of experience with the development of the Mall. And you know my feelings already."

Jennifer smiled at the two men, and just nodded, and Dick felt a small stir of excitement at the thought of meeting her again. *First Brit, and now Jennifer Hawkins. And this time on my own doorstep! What would Rosemary say if she found out? Fat chance of keeping that a secret. She is a very interesting woman, though.* The meeting broke up as some tea was brought in, and he found himself standing close to Jennifer as they conferred with Dan about a date for their sub-committee to meet. She had put on a pair of horn-rimmed reading glasses which somehow made her eyes even larger and darker. He was aware that she was almost as tall as himself, and very feminine in a pencil-slim skirt in some silky green fabric. Dan was saying that he was anxious there should be no delay.

"Three months isn't very far in advance if we're to get anyone worthwhile, so we need to move quite quickly I think. How about if we aim to get together next Monday afternoon and agree our shortlist?"

Dick was suddenly conscious of the delicately sweet perfume that Jennifer was wearing. Lily of the Valley? "Monday's all right with me, but not before, say, four o'clock?"

Jennifer made a note in her diary and closed her handbag with a snap. "Monday at four then, and we could meet at my house, if that would suit everyone? Tea and a fruitcake?"

Dan laughed, "There's an offer no man can refuse."

In the small Stockholm office of Steen & Strom, Brit Carlsohn had just finalised the planning for her trip to France. She had tried to persuade her French contacts to come out to Charles de Gaulle airport for their meeting, but without success. So she would have to go by taxi in to the store on Boulevard Haussman, which would have made it very tedious to get out again to Charles de Gaulle or Orly for an internal flight to Bordeaux. But she had followed up on Dick's suggestion about the Train Grande Vitesse from Paris Montparnasse to Bordeaux, and thought that there should be no difficulty about getting there before seven. Coming back would be simpler, just taking a flight from Bordeaux to Charles de Gaulle, and then changing for the connection to Stockholm. She arranged for her return flights to be left open, and noted down a full list of all the flights on Saturday and Sunday. *Now, what should I pack? Should I be ready to stay more than one night? I think Dick will have a problem if he is too much away from his wife. Of course he has seen my favourite red dress in Dusseldorf. Shall I take the blue? I wonder if we will go dancing again? Or perhaps he will prefer to make an early night of it?*

Chapter Five

Charles Harrison liked to believe that he had reached an age when he was unaffected by being alone with a good-looking woman, but he admitted to feeling a small sexual frisson after he had closed his office door behind the other three trustees after the Wednesday meeting, and he was left with Jennifer. She was sitting with her hands spread out against the window ledge, her fine figure silhouetted by the afternoon sun from the square, with her long legs demurely crossed beneath the green silk skirt and idly kicking one elegantly shod foot.

"Good meeting, Charles. Interesting to meet the younger Mr. Routledge, too. Lot more amiable than his father, isn't he?"

Charles was tidying away the papers on his desk, and pulled out of his drawer the file that Rachel Goldman had left with him that morning containing the proposed investment plan for Jennifer's son, Billy. He paused momentarily to try to assess how serious Jennifer's last remark was, and decided *not very*, and so no answer was necessary. But she did seem to be in an exceptionally good mood, and he hoped that was a good omen for their discussions. Shifting around a million or so of Jennifer's money could be quite rewarding, he thought, and pulled his chair noisily up to his desk again.

"Well, I think I'm about ready to get down to it." Jennifer obediently left the open window and sat at the table again, next to his desk. "When you came in you briefed Rachel Goldman, as I was on holiday of course, and she's done most of the preliminary work. Would you prefer to carry on without her, or shall I ask her to join us?"

Jennifer pursed her lips. "Perhaps not, please Charles. I mean, I'm sure she is discretion personified, but I've got used to having you as my counsellor on matters financial, especially matters financial and personal. So could we carry on for now with just the two of us, if it's not too much trouble?"

Charles was suitably flattered, and not too displeased to have the delectable Jennifer to himself for a while longer.

"No trouble, no trouble at all. In fact I very much enjoy our meetings. Right then, the question of providing for Billy's education, preferably without arousing the interest of the dreaded tax man, and bearing in mind that we should realistically be looking ahead over a period of twenty years say, to take him through primary school, preparatory and public school – and you'll need to tell me in due course if we should anticipate the possibility of boarding – and finally university. And over that timescale we have to expect that the price of private education will continue to rise faster than general inflation, say seven percent a year. I'm sure you won't be surprised to hear that I'm recommending we set up a Trust for

Billy, so that technically the capital and the income becomes his, though you and I, as the Trustees, in fact have absolute control over how the money can be spent until he is twenty-five, say. I estimate that you will need to start by transferring into the Trust up to a quarter of your holdings in the Hawkins Mall Company. That will have an immediate benefit from the inheritance tax point of view, as that proportion of your estate is then a potentially exempt transfer, which means that as long as you live at least seven more years it is placed immediately out of the grasp of the Chancellor's Inheritance Tax . . ."

Charles continued with several pages of figures and charts to illustrate the anticipated requirements for cash each year, and how the forecast dividends and the progressive liquidation of the new Trust's shares in the Mall could be expected to cover the need.

"Of course we are assuming that the Mall continues to make the excellent progress we have been seeing, and so the shares continue to increase in value. I regard that as likely, but not perhaps certain, so I am recommending that we set up a regular review process, say every three months, and consider the desirability of diversifying Billy's holdings, and yours too for that matter, so as to spread the risk somewhat."

Jennifer found her thoughts wandering while Charles talked. *That man, Dick Routledge, he's quite interesting. I suppose one could call him the rugged type. Presumably he's done well too out of the sale of his father's company. And Charles said that they'd kept him on to manage some of their new European investments, so he must be quite bright. There aren't many like that in Lynchester. Let's face it, since I lost Alan I haven't met one. Not that I've really been looking I suppose, in fact I've probably been putting people off, being so tied up with Billy. I wonder how he gets on with his wife, what's she called? Rosemary, that's it. Tall woman, with a lot of red hair.* She became aware that Charles had asked a question.

"Sorry, Charles, I was miles away for a moment. What were you saying?"

"I was just asking how you wanted to proceed now? Shall I start the work to set up the Trust and transfer the shares into it? And would you like us to put together some initial recommendations about diversification?"

Jennifer looked down at the not inconsiderable pile of paper in front of her, the evidence of Charles' presentation of Rachel's painstaking work.

"I can see you've done a tremendous amount of work for me, and it all seems fine. Would you convey my thanks and appreciation to Miss Goldman, please? I think I should take the weekend to absorb this lot, as far as I can, and perhaps we could get together again next week?" She reached into her small green leather clutch handbag for a pocket diary. "How does Thursday or Friday suit? And by all means, if you would like to involve Miss Goldman, perhaps she could sit in too?"

Charles nodded, and began to gather up his working papers. "I've got an important property completion coming up. Can I call you to confirm a time tomorrow morning?"

"Just before we finish, Charles, there is one other thing I wanted to raise with you. I mean, it's just the glimmer of an idea at the moment, but do you know anything about the ins and outs of buying property abroad? In France, for instance?"

Dick Routledge had tried on Tuesday and on Wednesday to telephone the Managing Director of his French subsidiary, but without success. Each time Lisa, Jean-Paul's charming and very pretty PA, had apologised profusely,

"Monsieur de Clavignon is most regrettably not 'ere, 'e is visiting important clients in Lille and Amiens and Angers and Nantes, but I 'ave told him that you will come 'ere on Thursday, and 'e will certainement be 'ere then to welcome you again to France."

He was surprised therefore to find Jean-Paul waiting for him as he came through the arrivals hall at Marignac, Bordeaux's smart little airport, just after ten thirty French time on Wednesday evening.

"Good evening, Dick. 'Ow was your flight, confortable, I 'ope?"

"No problem, thank you Jean-Paul. I came on Air France via Paris. It's good to see you here, but I thought you were away in Normandy?"

"I was, and I came from Nantes today, you know my flight arrived just forty minutes ago. Of course Lisa 'as sent your flight times to me already, so I decided it would be good to wait a few minutes more to say 'bienvenu'. I must get 'ome soon though to see ma femme and per'aps she keeps our little Henri awake to say goodnight to papa, but we 'ave time for one drink I t'ink."

Jean-Paul led the way towards the airport bar, with Dick beside him, now even more curious to find out what was going on. Jean-Paul was about five years younger than Dick, – lean, with dark hair brushed straight back from a wide brow, prominent cheekbones and a rather saturnine complexion. His long legs made him the taller by half a head. There were dark rings visible under his eyes, and something indefinably tense about his manner. It was charming of Jean-Paul to meet him, but it was hardly logical, being so late in the evening, and Dick knew Jean-Paul to be an intensely logical man. Jean-Paul ordered two whiskies and some water, and they retreated to a quiet table. Dick guessed that this was not the best time to start an inquisition about the reported results, and instead asked,

"How was your trip? Any special reason for going?"

"The visite was excellent. You know we appointed a new representative for the area six weeks ago, and I wanted to see for myself 'ow she will perform?"

"She? Isn't this your first appointment of a woman in the sales force? How's she doing?"

"Merveilleuse. She knows the customers already of course, because she was trained by Nestle. Within the last month we 'ave new accounts already with a multiple from Nantes with twelve shops, and a cash and carry with five branches in Normandie and Picardie. Comme toujours they start very cautiously, just one or two cases for each outlet. But they like us because we manufacture in France, and I think our discounts are a little better than they get from Kellogg's. I tell them that our business grows ver'quickly, and we expect to start again on the TV next Spring, and that helps too. I know we must discuss these things together also, Dick, but I believe our business can go well, as long as we invest the right money now."

There was an urgency in his tone, a look of almost pleading in his eyes, as though he was willing Dick to think about the future, and not to start probing the present. Dick finished his drink and stood up.

"Fine, Jean-Paul, very encouraging. Now you want to see your family, that's out at Arcachon isn't it? So I'm going to just take a taxi into town. I'll give you time to catch up with things in the office tomorrow – could you send the car for me at the Amarys at ten please?"

Elizabeth had booked a single room for Dick at the Amarys as usual, but he had no problem in getting instead *une chambre au grand lit* when he checked in, though he did feel his cheeks redden when he asked for it. He ordered a ham sandwich and coffee to be brought up. "But I'll come down for breakfast." The hotel was a former eighteenth century gentleman's residence, just a few yards from the River Garonne and the Pont Saint Jean, and his room was spacious and airy, with two windows looking out over Rue Charles Domerq. He guessed that Brit would be tired after an early morning start from Stockholm on Friday. *Perhaps we should plan to eat in the room? Then again, perhaps not, unless she's very late arriving. It would seem like bed is the only objective on my mind. And I am actually looking forward to seeing her, and talking to her, and enjoying that feeling of envy from the other men who see me with her.* He thumbed through the Bordeaux guide provided by the hotel, and found a nice-looking restaurant called 'Le Chapon Fin'. It seemed to be decently expensive, about fifteen minutes stroll along the river and then just left into the old town, Rue Montesquieu. He dialled the local number.

"Je veux reserver une table pour diner, s'il vous plais. Non, non, pas ce soir, vendredi soir, vers huit heures, deux personnes, M'sieur Routledge. C'est bon? Je vous remercis." Dick was rather proud of his improving schoolboy French, and had vowed to try to practise it as often as possible. The waiter came with his supper, and he got into bed to eat it. Afterwards he tried with mixed success to follow the late night news on a French TV station, then decided he was really very tired, and he drifted off to sleep, wondering idly if perhaps Jean-Paul had something going with his new saleslady, and what the morning would bring.

His room faced away from the morning sunlight, but he woke up as usual and looked at his watch. Seven o'clock. No, he'd forgotten to put it forward an hour, it was eight here really. Just time to shower and shave, and have a quick constitutional along the quais before breakfast. He liked Bordeaux – it was proudly provincial, and seemed to let you know that it quietly despised the fancy bureaucrats and slick businessmen of Paris. He hoped there might be time during this trip to go into a few of the 'caves' of the big shippers for some wine-tasting.

The car was outside waiting for him after breakfast at ten, and within a few minutes they had crossed the river and left behind the suburbs of Bordeaux, and were headed south-west on the old main road, towards the little town of Belin. ACP had chosen the site, in a new industrial park, with some care, to be near the port of Bordeaux and with a railway line close by, so that, when the sales volumes justified the expense, a link could be built to bring the raw maize in bulk by rail instead of by road. The plant was just a large modern shed, with offices to one side, but distinguished already by its tall silo. As the car swung in through the security gates Dick noted with approval that poplars they had planted in a long line along the western edge of the site to provide a windbreak were already nearly two metres high, and looking very healthy. Jean-Paul had been expecting the car to arrive, and was at the front desk to welcome Dick warmly and usher him into his office immediately inside the doors. The managing director's corner office was plainly furnished with a modest desk of pale wood, and two settees in a light-coloured hide, one each side of a large glass-topped coffee table which stood on the only hint of luxury, a traditional hand-knotted Persian carpet in tones of rust and dark blue. Dick sat on one side of the table, and Jean Paul collected some papers from his desk before joining him on the other.

"I thought that per'aps we should talk a little first, and then I want you to see 'ow we make progress with the factory. Nothing ver' big changed yet, but lots of small . . ."

He was interrupted by a knock at the door, and Lisa came in with a tray of coffee, which Dick knew from experience would be very strong and black. Lisa was petite and dark, with huge black eyes and her hair cut very stylishly short to curve around her face. She was wearing a short sleeveless summer dress in some stiff yellow fabric that made the skirt swing a little provocatively around her hips as she bent to pour coffee into the small red cups. Dick was duly appreciative.

"Merci et bonjour Lisa. Comment allez-vous?"

"I am ver' well, t'ank you M'sieur Routledge. An' we all look forward to les vacances at the end of the month."

As she closed the door behind her, Dick decided that there was nothing to be gained from further polite conversation, so he opened his file on the table and dived straight in.

"Jean-Paul, I've come over for a general look-see of course, but specifically to find out what is happening here." He pulled out from the file the first two pages of the June monthly return, and turned them for Jean-Paul to read while he stabbed the relevant numbers with a thick finger. "I'm sure you are as familiar with these numbers as me. Your overhead costs are going through the roof, your head-count is way up, something very strange seems to have occurred with your sales price, and altogether the business is looking distinctly unstable. And very different from the good start that was made last year, and which seemed to be continuing during the first quarter of this year. Is there some simple explanation?"

He sat back, sipping the hot black coffee. Jean-Paul rested his outspread hands on the offending pages, as though they were a keyboard for him to play, then looked up.

"Dick, my good frien', I am so sorry that you 'ave 'ad all this trouble to come over to France in such an 'urry. Though it is of course alway' a pleasure to see you. The figures are just wrong. A silly mistake with the computer, so that the wrong file was selected to attach to the e-mail. You know that I 'ave been away all this week until last night, and I only saw the mistake myself this morning. Alain, that is M'sieur Robarte you know, our chief accountant, Alain 'as already sent the new figures to England and to ACP with a big apology."

Dick's whole being told him that there was more to it than this calm explanation. *Why else would Jean-Paul have gone to the bother of waiting for him to arrive at the airport last night? Of course he was worried then, desperately worried. Alain must already have discovered his mistake, if mistake it was, and telephoned Jean-Paul to tell him about it. And he must have been hugely relieved not to have been pressed for a response last night. So what had happened this morning to enable him to offer such a story, with such assurance?* Dick decided to play along for the time being.

"Jean-Paul, I'm just pleased to hear that there's nothing badly amiss. You know the chairman, my father of course, he's expecting the usual quarterly visit from the ACP people today, so I'll call him with the good news at lunch time, after we've had a look through the correct figures together. But I'd like to know how the wrong numbers could be sent in the first place? I mean, where did these numbers come from?"

"Comme j'ai explique, Alain sent the wrong attachment. I 'ad asked him la semaine derniere to do some calculation of possibilities, you call it 'what if', I think?" Dick nodded. "So these numbers were in 'is computer, 'e presses a wrong key when 'e send the e-mail attachement, we are alway' under pressure at the end of the month, et voila – une betise."

Dick sat in silence. 'Betise' meant 'a silly mistake'. He was certain he was not hearing the truth, at least not the whole truth. But he could hardly call Jean-Paul a liar to his face without precipitating the most ghastly crisis. And what would be the point? He'd need an audit, or at least a confession from someone.

"Fair enough then. I'm very relieved, I can tell you. Can we look at the new figures, then I'll call Dad. I know he will be relieved too."

Jean-Paul extracted two pages from a file on his desk, and sat beside Dick as he spread them on the coffee-table.

"I 'ave written in last month's figures too, so you can make a comparison, and of course this month is compared with the budget wc agreed last year. You can see that our sales in June were down from last month, as we expected, but still a little bigger than the budget. For the year to date we are still three percent below budget, but per'aps now we are beginning to catch up. M'sieur 'Elvin complain last month that we 'ave too many people an' so our cost is too 'igh. You can see that in June we 'ave corrected this, so the cost is below the budget again, an' we even make a little profit as we 'ave no advertising to pay. If you 'ave any questions, I could bring in M'sieur Robarte?"

Dick could feel the confidence flowing in Jean-Paul's manner now, and decided to play along for the time being.

"No, no that's fine. I'm so glad to see you are continuing to make such fine progress. I wonder if I could use your office please to call my father, just to check that they have no outstanding queries?"

"Of course. I will tell Lisa to call England for you, and leave you in peace. Help yourself to some more coffee."

As soon as the door had closed behind him, Dick sat down at the desk and pulled a sheet of paper from a stack in Jean-Paul's printer. He scrawled a few words and sealed the note in an envelope just as Lisa came through on the intercom.

"I 'ave M'sieur Routledge pere for you."

Dick wondered momentarily if she or Jean-Paul might listen in, but decided he was becoming paranoid.

"Dad? I presume you've seen the revised figures for June?"

James Routledge was seldom genial, and there was something about the telephone that brought out the curmudgeonly worst in him.

"Of course I've seen them. We're not swanning around in some French bar or bistro here you know, we're trying to get some bloody work done. The question is, do we believe them? What's the answer to that? Mr. Robarte apologises most profoundly for the unfortunate error, sending the wrong file attachment or something, and implies ever so politely that if we hadn't insisted on an impossibly tight timetable for producing monthly figures this kind of thing wouldn't have happened. Load of bullshit of course. Anyway, what do you think is going on?"

Dick had not had long to decide what to tell his father, and knew better than to suggest otherwise.

"Frankly dad, I haven't a clue. I'm pretty sure there's more to this than Jean-Paul would have us believe, but I need to be a bit cautious. Could you ask Jim Helvin if it's possible for us to get a copy of the current bank statements without alerting the French company? That should give us a clue. I mean if the bank's cash figures can be reconciled with this new report then I suppose we have to accept it."

"As you say, it could be a lead. But if there is something fishy going on, whoever's organising it will likely have thought of that, and set up more than one bank account. Probably a whole series of accounts. Any other bright ideas?"

"Jim's advice was to try to get a word with Robarte on his own, and I've just done a little note to ask him to come and talk to me this evening."

"Bear in mind that he's got to be in it up to his neck, that's if there is something. And the Americans won't want anything to come out publicly. Makes them look foolish, or soft, or both, definitely not the impression they want to give to the world, especially as their global expansion project is just getting under way. I get along fine with Ben Camina, but I get the feeling that he wouldn't let a beautiful friendship divert him from bottoming this. Anyway, they're with us until Friday lunchtime, so do your best to come up with some good news before then. I'll tell them that you're out there looking into it. That'll fill them with confidence, won't it?"

His father's closing words had not been unfriendly, but Dick felt suddenly very alone. Jean-Paul was a seasoned corporate operator, and would not be taking risks with his career unnecessarily. He habitually walked a fine line between confidence and arrogance, but that was no doubt the norm for a managing director in France. Dick sensed that a false step now could lead to a very nasty confrontation, which he could well lose. The team from ACP would almost certainly have seen the original figures for June before they left, but would not see the revised numbers until they arrived at Strongwheat – Dick looked at his watch, still on English time – in an hour or so. *It'll be this evening at the earliest before I know anything more. Dad will just have to stall them.*

Of course, he and his father didn't really need to work, there was plenty of money from the sale of the company. But Dick, like his father, had long ago come to the conclusion that the money was just a way of keeping score, not the game itself. And he really wanted to stay in the game – preferably to win. He wrote Alain Robarte's name on the envelope, and had just tucked it into his inside pocket when Jean-Paul came back in.

"Ca va? I 'ope your father is well? 'E understand about the mistake now?"

"The mistake? Oh yes, we'd both got a bit excited, but that's behind us now. What did you have in mind for the rest of the day?"

Jean-Paul looked out of the window, then fixed his dark eyes on Dick for a moment. He smiled and suddenly his serious expression softened.

"The sun is shining and the sea is warm. Per'aps we deserve a little vacance pour l'apres-midi? You could come back to Arcachon and meet Arlette, ma femme. We could take a little picnique sur la plage, if that would be acceptable. Of course we could continue to talk some business too."

"Great idea, as long as you can lend me a pair of swimming trunks."

"I will telephone Arlette to explain that we are coming. Vous m'excuserez, s'il vous plais?"

"Fine. I'll meet you outside, by your car."

Dick closed the office door as he left, and found Lisa at her desk. He pulled out the sealed envelope.

"Lisa, M'sieur de Clavignon and I will be out for the rest of the day, but I will need a few more figures from M'sieur Robarte. Would you give him this note please?"

At six o'clock Dick was back in his hotel room, pacing nervously from one side to the other and waiting for Alain Robarte to arrive. The afternoon on the beach had been delightful. Arlette had been better company than her husband, and had produced an instant picnic with fresh baguettes, Ardennes pate, apples and some cold beer. They lived in an old cottage just outside the pretty seaside resort of Arcachon. Jean-Paul had driven Dick through the town, so that he could see its fantastic variety of nineteenth century villas – Moorish, Gothic, English Classical, French Baroque – all built when Arcachon was developed as a summer playground for the Paris elite, including Napoleon III himself. From the cottage it was a short but steep walk, over the shoulder of a massive three-hundred foot high sand dune, to a favourite beach near the mouth of the Arcachon Bassin, a small tidal lake. Arlette, who was a tall, slim brunette with close-cropped hair, had looked very elegant in a black one-piece costume. She insisted on practising her English on Dick, and kept her face politely straight as he struggled to respond in French. The sea was warm, and the sun hot enough for Dick to borrow both her Ambre Solaire and her spare sunhat, which reduced all three of them to tears of laughter. She had left mid-afternoon to collect little Henri, and Dick and Jean-Paul had maintained a desultory conversation about the future of the EU and whether the UK should join the Euro currency block. Dick found himself arguing against it, although the potential advantages were patently obvious from the narrow point of view of his growing European businesses.

"Cold commercial logic is on your side, Jean-Paul. The majority of our UK trade is with our EU partners now, so it makes sense not to have separate currencies. Mind you, the present exchange rate couldn't possibly be acceptable as the basis for giving up the pound. The UK would be frozen for all time at a competitive disadvantage, with low or no growth, just because the value of the Euro collapsed almost as soon as it started. But would the other countries allow us to devalue on joining by, say, fifteen or twenty percent? And even if they did, what would that do to our inflation rate? Or will the Euro come back up against the US dollar again? That would be helpful to us, but terrible for France and Germany. But it's what our Conservatives call the 'democratic deficit' that worries us most. We don't like faceless bureaucracies that cannot be held to account. When you look at how the EU works, or doesn't work, I get the impression that it's actually been deliberately designed to bypass the inconveniences of democracy, if you see what I mean? Just look at what happens to anyone who blows the whistle and says 'this emperor or commissioner has no clothes on'.He or she is immediately jumped on from a great height and told that the real crime is not to be 'communitaire', whatever that means. It's like the EU is a new kind of religion, and the faith must not be challenged."

Jean-Paul had been very patient, rehearsing again the grand vision of an association of federated states stretching from the Atlantic to Poland and even perhaps to the Urals, and how this would enable them to meet the 'defi Americain' and survive the challenge of Chinese productivity, and of how these things were in the long run going to be so much more important to European peace and prosperity than petty considerations of sovereignty and even freedom. After a last swim the subject had been abandoned as 'too difficult', and Jean Paul had driven Dick back to his hotel. He had invited Dick to come out to Arcachon again that evening to sample Arlette's cooking, but had not pressed the invitation after Dick had suggested that Jean-Paul had been away long enough from his family, and Arlette deserved some time alone with him.

His reflections were interrupted by the sound of his telephone.

"M'sieur Robarte est arrive."

"Bien. Qu'il ascende, s'il vous plais."

Alain Robarte was a small, shy man in his early forties, with rimless spectacles and pale, thinning hair over a high dome of a forehead. He accepted Dick's offer of a drink from the mini-bar.

"Whisky-soda con glace, merci."

Jean-Paul had told Dick that he had got to know and respect Alain as a middle-rank accountant at Colgate, and had recruited him into ACP France soon after he had joined himself. Dick had sat in at a couple of management meetings when Alain had been present, and he had seemed competent, without perhaps the strength of personality that might take him further in the corporate structure. Dick was already on the lookout for a potential replacement for Jim Helvin, who was due to retire in a year's time, and Alain did not figure highly in his list of possibilities.

Dick knew that Alain understood English very well, and decided that there were too many possibilities of ambiguity and error for him to attempt to conduct this particular conversation in French.

"Alain, I am very grateful that you were able to accept my invitation this evening."

Alain said nothing, but inclined his head in acknowledgement, and fixed his pale blue eyes on Dick's face.

"Do you enjoy your work at ACP France?"

The pale eyes widened noticeably in alarm. *Was his position at risk?*

"Ver' much M'sieur."

"Not 'M'sieur', Alain, please call me Dick, everyone does."

He relaxed a little, and took a long pull at his drink. "Ver' much, Dick. Jean-Paul is a good man to work for, and it is most interesting to be part of a new company."

"Most interesting, yes, I agree. And I know that your salary now is about one third more than you received at Colgate, all your expenses were paid to relocate to a very beautiful part of France here, and there must be prospects that you will earn a seat on the Board, and the possibility of further promotion within ACP itself. What, I wonder, would persuade you to put all that at risk?"

"M'sieur! Dick, je vous assure . . ."

"Don't Alain, don't say anything that you will later regret." Dick opened his brief case and put on the table the original report for June. "Jean-Paul says this was sent by mistake, a simple 'betise'. I believe him. I am sure that it should not have been sent. What I want you to tell me, is exactly what these figures represent. And don't say they were just part of a hypothetical exercise, because that doesn't make sense. Why would anyone want to imagine it would be possible to put through a huge increase in the price per case, for instance? Even as an hypothesis? Why do the figures look like a continuation, an extension of the trend that was seen emerging the month previous?"

Alain was staring at Dick without speaking, without movement, as though he were hypnotised. Tiny beads of sweat appeared on that high forehead, and then suddenly the spell was broken. He stood up, and with some attempt at dignity picked up his briefcase and walked to the door.

"My deepest apologies, M'sieur Routledge, but I cannot answer your inquisition without the presence of M'sieur de Clavignon. I can comprehend zat you 'ave the suspicions, but you must accept my word that everyt'ing will come right for ACP. No one is stealing your money. You ask in your letter zat I should tell no one about this meeting. I must ask also you tell no one, especial not M'sieur de Clavignon, zat I 'ave come. An' so bon soir, M'sieur."

The door closed behind him, and Dick was left more certain than ever that something was seriously amiss with his French company, and absolutely at a loss as to what it might be, or what to do about it. He thought of calling his father, but hated the implication that he was not competent to solve his first real problem. He felt a headache coming on, and guessed he had got a bit too much sun during the afternoon. *A rest now would do me good, then a bite to eat and an early night. Tomorrow it may all look different. Jean-Paul is collecting me at eight, we'll look at the factory improvements and finish by mid-morning. Perhaps I'll find an opportunity to tackle him again, before I have to call Dad.* He stretched out on the big bed, and began to puzzle his way through a copy of that morning's *Le Monde*, provided by the hotel. An illustrated feature on a recent Paris fashion show reminded him of Brit, and he smiled, a smile that seemed to start at his toes and spread right through his body. *Brit Carlsohn was definitely something to look forward to.*

Chapter Six

Ben Camina was in his mid-fifties, a small lean man whose dark hair and swarthy complexion bore witness to his Mexican descent. Being the Chief Financial and Operating Officer of ACP, he was the corporation's number two executive. He arrived at Heathrow Airport with his 'cadre' of three eager acolytes on the overnight flight from Chicago, soon after eleven on Thursday morning. None of the three had visited Strongwheat before, so Ben had talked to them during the flight, to ensure they were prepared.

"I want you to put out of your heads altogether everything you've learned about how a cereal factory should look – nice big sheds, shiny plant, cost-effective layouts. These guys did it the other way. They got hold of a run-down former woollen or cotton-mill – and by 'run-down', think of Charles Dickens, blackened satanic mills and all that stuff. Probably driven originally by water wheel with the river right alongside, and no doubt 'modernised' afterwards with a new-fangled steam engine. Something that would have been state-of-the-art say one hundred and fifty years ago. Anyway the owner's father William Routledge gets this place for peanuts just after the Second World War, and puts in some cheap equipment. They start pre-packing flour, then they go into making rusk for sausage meat. Next, thanks to the present owner, James, they get into breakfast cereals with this Strongwheat product just over thirty years ago. By the way any of you guys tried it?"

Walt Collins raised a finger. He was bullet-headed, forty-ish, nearly as wide as he was high, and had shown promise as Manufacturing Manager of the breakfast cereals section back in Illinois.

"I got a pack from the product labs last week and had a go. Thought it was a bit chewy with cold milk, but very palatable with hot. I believe our Marketing people are seriously thinking about a test market of some kind in the States."

"Right, they are. In fact it's still very hush-hush, but they've pencilled in a date for next Spring. One thing I want you to do, Walt, during your days here is to get real close to the local managing director, that's a guy called Phil Wythe. He's bright and quick, came up through the Manufacturing side, just like yourself. Talk to him in absolute confidence about the possibility of this test market, and ask about the feasibility of them making a quantity for us. Establish how much spare capacity there is, and ask him to look into container-load quantities, and the costs and shipping time to Illinois. We sure as hell don't want to be investing a couple of million or more in plant until we've proven the demand. By the way, the previous owners launched a second variety a couple of years back, just before we bought in, lighter and softer in the mouth to appeal to the kids. Maybe that's going to be the way to go for us. Believe it or not these guys have got nine percent of the UK market with the two varieties, and I don't need to tell you that we only have four and a half percent of the US market, and that's against the same competition that they have here in the UK. So although the plant will likely give you the shudders, don't knock it. We're paying a damn fortune for the business, and it's showing us a fair return already. And it's our launch-pad into the EU."

The car that had brought them at high speed up the motorway from the airport carried them around Lynchester's handsome Market Square, allowing them just a fleeting glimpse of its mediaeval church at one end, an attractive river promenade at the other, and rows of Georgian houses, shops and offices on each side. A couple of hundred yards north along the bank of the River Lyn brought them to the pillared gates of the Strongwheat factory and offices. Despite Ben's admonition, his team gaped in amazement at the tall smoke-blackened mill building with its brick chimney and an incongruous modern steel silo on one end.

"I guess the Health and Safety people here take a different view from our guys in Illinois."

Walt was scheduled to stay with Ben in the Belfry Hotel, the regular UK site for the US versus Europe golf tournament for the Ryder Cup, whilst the other two members of the cadre were to come to Strongwheat just for lunch and to meet James Routledge, and were then to be returned to Birmingham airport to catch onward flights to Dusseldorf and Parma respectively, to study and report on ACP's new German and Italian businesses, returning to England on Friday evening. Saturday was supposed to be a free day for them, but they were all expected back at London's Heathrow airport on Sunday afternoon to take the eight hour homeward flight to Chicago, during which time they were to prepare their reports for submission to Ben on Monday morning.

James Routledge had the corner office at the front of the old building, and he was standing at the front door to greet them as they climbed stiffly out of his Daimler. Ben's PA had e-mailed over the details of the punishing schedule planned for the cadre, and he led them directly through the offices and into the company boardroom, where a modest lunch of beef sandwiches and cold beer was laid out.

"Welcome to England again, Ben, and you too, gentlemen. How was the flight?"

"Not bad. You've heard that American Airlines have extended the leg room in Economy? So we gave it a go. Comfortable enough. I took a sleeping pill and slept four or five hours. Bit hard on the backside though, so I'll probably let'em take the upgrade for the return."

Walt introduced himself, "Great honour to meet you sir. I guess me and the boys here were not smart enough to think of getting a pill, so we watched a lot of movies instead. I can confirm what Ben said about the butt-ache. Can I introduce Peter Mathan, one of our top Marketing people? Pete's going on to Parma, Italy. And this is Henry Borowski, corporate analyst and statistician, who'll be looking into the plans for Germany."

James and Ben had made plans to renew their long-standing rivalry on the Belfry's Championship Course on Friday afternoon and again on Saturday if business allowed, so they talked golf whilst they ate, and the three younger men stared in wonder out of the windows of the boardroom. The room was built like a glass greenhouse, a peninsular jutting out into the factory floor with windows on three sides, insulated from the sounds of production but giving an irresistible view of long black ovens and the intricate convolutions of fast-moving automated packing lines. Within a few minutes they were joined by Phil Wythe, who had been promoted from Director of Operations to Managing Director two years previously, after ACP had taken over the company and after Dick Routledge had moved up to become European Director. Phil was just forty, but looked older because he had already lost most of his hair. His bright blue eyes and lean mobile features radiated nervous energy, and he ate quickly as he talked about his beloved factory.

"I understand that you two have to be off in an hour, but you're very welcome to join us while I take Walt on a quick walk-through. You'll see a lot of things that you'll be certain could be done better, and you'd be right, but you have to bear in mind that the business here has grown like Topsy, in fact we've had to increase production almost double over the last three years, and this site is hardly ideal, as you've no doubt already discerned. If we offered public access we could probably apply for a subsidy or a grant as part of Britain's industrial history. But my Chairman here is a hard man to convince, and we're not going to get a new factory yet awhile. Still, we've found some quite clever ways to do things. If you're ready?"

The three younger Americans followed him out of a side door to the factory, whose rattling din intruded only momentarily into the boardroom as the door swung open and closed again. Ben took a long pull of his beer and sat back in the dark green leather settee, one of two arranged each side of a mahogany coffee table at one end of the long boardroom.

"So James, what the heck is going on in France? The damn numbers came in on Monday, and they're all over the place. Do you want Walt to go over tomorrow and sort them out for us?"

"I'm hoping that's not going to be necessary, Ben. We got the numbers at the same time as you of course, and Dick went over last night. And there are some new, revised numbers that came in this morning. Shall we adjourn to my office to look at them? Dick says that the French are claiming that the previous numbers were sent in error, accessed a wrong file on the computer or something. Anyway he's going over the whole thing in detail with Jean-Paul there and the accountant, and he'll call us tomorrow morning if there's anything to report. But he seemed fairly confident that there's nothing for us to worry about."

When Dick came down to breakfast in his Bordeaux hotel at seven-thirty he found a fax waiting for him, which Jim Helvin seemed to have sent the previous evening. As he walked through to the dining room he wondered briefly why no one had bothered to bring it up to him, and then coffee, warm milk, croissants and apricot jam came as he read it.

"Bank in Bordeaux can only release statements to England with approval from Paris head office, which may take a while to come through. Do you want me to chase it?"

He reflected philosophically that getting it last night would probably only have spoilt his dinner, wrote 'Yes please' underneath, and handed it in to the receptionist to send back as he left the hotel to enter the waiting car.

Jean-Paul was scrupulously polite and attentive, but Dick sensed that the rapport built between them during the previous afternoon on the beach had now been dissipated. *Had Alain decided after all to confess last night's visit?* He nodded in automatic approval as they inspected first a new system for handling raw grain, then an improved electronic temperature control for the oven and finally an automatic case-packer that was still being assembled, but his mind was elsewhere, on those 'erroneous' figures for last month. By ten o'clock they were sipping coffee again in Jean-Paul's office, and Dick decided that frontal assault was the only possibility.

"So tell me, Jean-Paul, getting back to these 'what-if?' numbers that got us so unnecessarily excited, what were the possibilities were you exploring?"

The Frenchman finished his coffee, and put down his cup with a little sigh. When he spoke it was in the tone of a weary schoolteacher, explaining yet again a perfectly simple theorem to a particularly slow pupil.

"Dick, this was just one set of figures amongst ver' many that Alain set up for us. You know we 'ave our three-year plan, but it is not made of stone, I think. We want to be sure that it will still be the best way for us to go, so we 'ave a thinking day wiz all the managers, an' Alain's work is to turn the ideas into Euros, so zat we can compare them wiz the plan. I think we were interested to increase the size of our Sales Force, so the numbers of peoples goes up. Then 'e looks at 'ow much the price must go up to cover the cost, and there are other figures which increase the volume but keep the price the same, an' so on. Like I said, zese numbers are just fiction, not real money, an' zere is no reason for you or ACP to worry, no reason at all."

Jean-Paul was so logical, so believable, but Dick felt a little warning bell go off in his mind when he heard 'real money'. It reminded him of Alain's words the previous evening, 'No one is stealing your money'. No doubt about it, he thought, Alain had told Jean-Paul what had been said, and Jean-Paul was, perhaps unconsciously, repeating the same thoughts. But was that simply because that was the truth of the matter? Or were they sticking to an agreed lie? He could think of no way to take the investigation any further, and decided to make the best of a bad job by showing his trust, as a way of attempting a repair of their damaged relationship.

"It's been great to see you again, Jean-Paul, and especially to meet your beautiful Arlette and to sample your beach. If I scribble a short e-mail for Dad, could you have Lisa send it please?"

The e-mail was intended as much for Jean-Paul's consumption as for his father. It read:

Jean-Paul and I have gone over last month's revised figures together, and everything is fine. Tell Jim Helvin that his comments on the previous month were duly noted and appropriate corrective action has been taken. Best regards to Ben and his team – Dick.

Jean-Paul was smiling warmly when he returned from Lisa's office.

"So, Dick, what will you do now? Would you like us to get you on this afternoon's flights to Paris and Birmingham?"

"That's very kind, but I've been meaning ever since we started down here to find time to visit some of the wine merchants in Bordeaux, perhaps to invest in a little Claret en primeur, and also to buy a few bottles to take home just like any other tourist. So I'm going to stick to my original plan, and go home tomorrow morning."

Jean-Paul's smile became wider.

"Zen I can definitely be of assistance. I play tennis most weeks with my frien' Henri Tratignant, you know 'e is the sales director of one of the very best negociants. They are the merchants who buy the wine from the makers. If you will allow me to telephone 'im now, 'e will certainement arrange for you to taste their best vendages, perhaps arrange a little discount for my ver' good frien' from England?"

Dick grinned and nodded, and Jean-Paul made his call, speaking now in rapid French that Dick found harder to follow, except for a phrase or two about 'un homme des affaires tres important'.

"Henri wants to know if he can offer you a little lunch?"

Dick thought of his hopes for the evening. A Bordeaux lunch could be very counter-productive!

"Thank him, but not today. Say I'm worried about my waistline."

"Bien. 'E will collect you at your 'otel at two o'clock. 'E asks you to remember that today is Friday, an' they must close at trois heures et demi."

Henri had arrived promptly at two. He was about the same age as Dick, a large friendly man with a splendid handlebar moustache to offset his rapidly thinning dark hair. They walked to Henri's office above a fine old warehouse in the Quartier des Chartrons. Dick was expertly led through a sampling during which they compared some vins ordinaires with a dozen different house clarets – traditional Bordeaux blends of cabernet sauvignon, merlot and cabernet franc. The oldest had been chateau-bottled some fifteen years before, the youngest was from the previous year's harvest, and so was still in the barrel. He chose two, and asked Henri if he could have three bottles of each. Henri pursed his lips.

"Je regrette, M'sieur, I cannot offer you 'alf a case. We could make you special price for a case to take wiz you, zat would be six bottles of each of ze two wines you 'ave chose. Or if you will order six cases I could arrange delivery to England wiz no charge?"

Dick could see that Henri had already come to the conclusion that his afternoon's work was probably wasted, but he was not so used to having access to money that he was ready to spend almost a thousand pounds on six cases just so that Henri would not feel disappointed. So they shook hands politely on the mixed dozen case, paid for by credit-card, and Dick walked out into a warm afternoon carrying his case of wine tied with thick, rough string, and feeling vaguely embarrassed. Still, he had learned to recognise the way a good claret started out as tough on the palate as a vin ordinaire, but with certain depths that hinted to an expert of the glories to come, and how over the years the tannin receded, and the *gout de terroir* took over, adding progressively more and more smoothness and complexity. He wondered what Henri would be saying to Jean-Paul next time they met. Something not very flattering, no doubt. Walking back to the Hotel Amarys in the warm sunshine he reflected that he had not been quite as punctilious as he ought to have been about spitting out the mouthfuls of wine, and certainly several of the best ones had been swallowed. He wondered whether an hour spent looking around Bordeaux's famous Musee du Vin would clear his head, then decided to continue straight back to the hotel, and have a rest instead. He drew the thick linen curtains in his room, hung his jacket over the back of a chair, pulled off his shoes and sank back onto the big bed with a sigh. As he drifted off to sleep his last thoughts were of the soft pressure and the warmth of Brit's lips as she kissed him goodbye in Cologne after that exciting but ultimately frustrating evening. Tonight would be different!

Rosemary Routledge had been to lunch on Friday with Dick's mother, Ellen. She had heard all about the meeting of the Trustees, especially of the way Ellen had manoeuvred things so that the Council's preference for a pop-star or celebrity for the opening had been sidelined, in favour of someone with more dignity.

"So there's to be a little sub-committee meeting on Monday at four at Jennifer Hawkins' house; Jennifer to represent the Hawkins, Dick for us, and Dan Grundy for the Town Council."

Dick had gone straight from the committee meeting to catch his flight to Bordeaux, so this was the first Rosemary had heard of the sub-committee. *Why does it have to meet at Jennifer's house? Why not here, or in a room at the Town Hall?*

"What's Jennifer like? I mean, I remember she was pointed out to me at some function, I think it was probably the official opening of their Mall, but I've never actually spoken to her."

"Well, you've seen her, so you know she's a very good-looking woman. Fading a little now perhaps, but aren't we all? She's actually very quiet, thoughtful, I'd say. Didn't say much at the meeting, but she made it pretty obvious that she supported our position. She's got this little lad, and she's never told anyone who the father is, though there's plenty of gossip of course. I get the impression she just wants all that dreadful business with the Hawkins boys to be forgotten."

In her bedroom Rosemary took off the cream suit she had worn for lunch with Ellen, and noticed with some annoyance that there were some spots on the left lapel. *Looks like gravy. That'll have to go to the cleaners.* She pulled on an old pair of jeans and buttoned up a favourite pale green blouse. She looked in the mirror, and ran a comb through her thick mane of auburn hair. *I wonder if Dick thinks of me as 'fading'? Of course I'm a year older than him. How old is that Jennifer anyway? When I saw her at the Mall affair I'd have guessed early thirties, but that was from a distance. And she must be older than that, I mean she was married to old man Hawkins for years. Well-preserved though – well, with her money so she ought to be.*

She looked at her watch – ample time to get to the cleaners before the boys came home from school. In fact it would do her good to walk into town. She looked out another skirt to take in, and opened Dick's wardrobe. There was that blue pinstripe suit of his that he wore most days to the office, that was well overdue for a clean! She pulled it out, and began to go carefully through the pockets.

Dick was awakened in the shaded darkness of his room by a tapping at the door. He looked at his watch. *Five-thirty – I wonder if it's Alain? Perhaps he's worked out which side his bread is really buttered?* The tapping was repeated more firmly, as he pulled back a curtain, pushed his fingers through his hair and put on his shoes and jacket. "Coming, coming."

It was Brit. Brit in a pale green business suit, with a short skirt and a long jacket over a white lacy blouse. Brit standing there beside a small suitcase, with her head tilted quizzically to one side, and that beautiful smile that seemed to fill the corridor. Dick opened his mouth to speak, but no words came out. Brit filled the hiatus with a rush of words.

"Are you pleased to see me, Dick? I meant to call ahead, but I only just managed to catch the TGV in Paris at two o'clock, and my mobile does not work on the train. I hope I am not too early? I told the nice girl in reception that I am Madame Routledge, so she said I could come straight up."

The only thing Dick could think to do was to reach for her and kiss her, a kiss that began as a shy welcome, with his hands resting gently on her shoulders, and was becoming more serious when Brit broke away with a gasp.

"Dick, we're still in the corridor. Someone may see us. I'm sure this is a very respectable hotel, just like the one in Dusseldorf."

Dick picked up her bag, ushered her into the shadowed room and closed the door. She looked around, noting the half-drawn curtains and the rumpled bedcover.

"Oh Dick, I'm so sorry, I woke you up, didn't I?"

"Guilty as charged, madame. It's just lovely to see you, Brit. For some reason I'd guessed that you wouldn't be here for ages, in fact I've booked dinner in town for eight, but I could change that of course. How was your day? Long, I suppose. Shall I ring down for some tea? Would you like a b . . ."

She stopped him with a finger on his lips. She unfastened the three buttons on the front of her jacket, kicked off her shoes and reached her arms around his neck. This time the kiss went on and on until she felt herself melting into him, and she clung trembling a little with her head on his chest. He found the zip at the back of her skirt, and the five pearl buttons down the front of her blouse, and she was kissing him again in white bra and panties, then pushing his jacket off his shoulders as he buried his face in her neck.

"Let's go to bed."

Chapter Seven

Dick's two sons, one called James after Dick's father, and the other Peter after Rosemary's grandfather, were aged eleven and nine, and were at the same school in Lynchester. As usual they had been ravenously hungry when Rosemary brought them home, and bickered ritually until they had been fed and settled down, James with some homework and Peter to watch a favourite TV programme. Rosemary sat with Peter, but the intricacies of the space-fiction adventure story that he was watching passed over her head. Instead she sat in a lonely world of introspection, fingering in the pocket of her jeans the business card she had found in Dick's suit. She had no need to take it out in order to remember perfectly the printed words:

Brit Carlsohn, Senior Buyer, Steen & Strom, Stockholm

She had been married to Dick just over thirteen years now, and in all that time there had never been the slightest doubt in her mind about his faithfulness. From that first date, when she had been the Assistant Squadron Adjutant on the RAF Tornado base in Germany, and he had been posted in as a newly promoted Flight Lieutenant, his intentions had been only too plain. Rosemary was the at first bemused, then delighted, and finally overwhelmed target of a single-minded campaign. Dick was an attractive man, good-looking, very athletic and already a regular member of the RAF rugby team. He was intelligent, and could be charming if he wanted, but in the end it was the sheer force of his desire for her that burst through the defences that Rosemary had so carefully accumulated during her time in the RAF. After they were married he had been very understanding and supportive during the hard times when the boys had come along, and she had of necessity given up her own career. Later, when a rugby injury had put a premature end to his flying, he had turned to her for help, and she knew she had lifted him then out of a pit of black despair. In a way the stroke that had threatened his father's life and had led to him leaving the RAF had been a blessing for them both, and she had loved the way Dick had thrown himself unreservedly into making a success of Strongwheat, and also into their new life in Lynchester. In bed he still seemed to her to be the same enthusiastic, playful partner she had married – *was it really possible that he was bored or restless enough to start an affair with some foreigner? Possible, of course, but hardly likely. Surely she would have sensed something amiss, perceived some clue to his discontent? Of course a single business card proved nothing anyway. It was part of Dick's job to meet all sorts of people. There could be a dozen perfectly reasonable explanations for its presence in the inside ticket pocket of Dick's jacket. And what could she possibly hope to gain by challenging him about it? Nothing but indignant denials and accusations of her own lack of trust; probably some sort of furious scene whose memory could poison their relationship for months to come, perhaps even permanently.* She breathed deeply and crushed the card in her jeans pocket, then got up to check on James' progress with long division.

Thank heavens I still understand the maths he's learning – not for much longer now, she thought, with a small sigh of regret.

Jennifer Hawkins's conversation with her accountant, Charles Harrison about buying property abroad had been useful, but had not filled her with any confidence that he could be of much help directly. But he did come up with the telephone numbers of a couple of UK-based estate agents who claimed to specialise in the field, one for Spain and one for France.

"I'll be perfectly frank with you, Jennifer, we've not been asked before to assist any of our clients to relocate totally to a European country, though we have done Australia, Canada and the USA. Those were all corporate moves anyway, so the circumstances were very different from your own."

He thought for a minute or two, and then continued.

"Once you've chosen a country, I'll assemble a file with all the information you need about managing your funds, and especially about the tax implications. But it seems to me that there is no need really for you to commit to a formal relocation at this stage. Why not decide where you'd like to live, then use an agent to find you a place to rent for a year, say. Billy is young enough to fit in easily to a local school, you can see if you can learn the language and get on with the neighbours and so on. It's a big step for a woman alone, if you will forgive me saying so. A foreign country can be a very lonely place until you make some friends. And as your friend myself I would say that making new friends is something you've got out of the habit of doing ever since . . . ever since the troubles with Alan and George. I'm not doubting your ability to do it, just urging a little care and caution, as I'm sure you'd expect me to."

She called the two agents the same day, and the expected thick envelopes of dream homes to rent in France and Spain arrived on Friday morning. Not having much idea about prices, she had suggested 'up to £1000 per month', and was duly overwhelmed with the quality on offer, from a two-bedroom apartment in what appeared to be a smart Parisian arrondissement to a country estate in the Pyrenees, complete with swimming pool and stables. She sat on her favourite garden swing for an hour, browsing through the brochures, and made one decision – there was enough that she liked in France to allow her to eliminate the Spanish alternative. 'I did learn some French at school, and I'm sure I could pick it up quickly enough. So why go to the bother of starting from scratch in Spanish?' Beyond that, it seemed too difficult to even think about where in France she wanted to live. *Should it be town or village, country or seaside? Might it even be fun to try three months in each?*

Instead she returned to the house and rummaged around in a kitchen drawer to find her cookbook. She looked up her favourite recipe for a spiced fruit cake which she planned to bake for the meeting on Monday. Something told her that Dick Routledge would respond well to a home-made cake . . . *Now then, Jennifer, why does that matter to you? Just common sense really – Dick was a well-travelled executive, in fact I think he said he was going straight off to France when we met. So I'm sure he'll be well able to advise me. And willing?*

Brit Carlsohn awoke with a start, and for a moment wondered where she was. Then memories came flooding back. Knocking nervously on the door of Dick's hotel room, and loving the way astonishment on his face had changed to delight. Loving the way he kissed her, as though she were the most precious thing in the world. Once into the big bed they had made love with an intensity that reminded Brit that it had been ages since she had had a man. Indeed, the first time he entered her she climaxed immediately in a great arching spasm that left her gasping for breath, and murmuring how sorry she was not to have waited for him. But he had been very gentle and persistent, and when it happened again half an hour later she felt him swell and follow her, and in the shadowy half-light she looked up to see his eyes shut tight with passion and pleasure as he thrust into her. She could hear him breathing softly on the pillow behind her now, but as she reached out her hand to look at her watch he awoke. A muscular arm came around her body, and his hand cupped her breast as he nuzzled her neck. She pressed back against him, and felt his hardness returning.

"Dick, it would be wonderful to make love again, but I have had nothing to eat since breakfast on the flight from Stockholm. It is after seven now – did you say you had a table for dinner at eight? Then we could come back and get to know one another all over again."

Dick rolled onto his back with a sigh. "Fair enough, but be warned, I'll be twice as demanding after a good dinner. I wonder if they have oysters? Would you like to use the bathroom first then?"

She got out of bed and walked round the bed to the bathroom, which was on Dick's side, pleasantly conscious of the way his eyes followed every movement of her naked body. He noticed that her breasts were fuller than he had expected, and smiled when he realised that she was not a natural blond.

It was a warm evening, and Brit dressed casually in a plain white summer dress with a low, square neck and a full skirt with a narrow black belt that showed off her waist. A pair of silver filigree earrings added a touch of glamour. Taking his cue from her, Dick wore a favourite pair of fawn slacks with a white shirt and slung his green sports jacket over his shoulder, having carefully tucked a plain red tie into a pocket, in case the restaurant was more formal than he expected. They walked out of the hotel to a murmured 'Bon soir M'sieur, Madame' from the receptionist. As they joined the crowds of Bordelais that thronged the Quai de Paludate and the Quai Richelieu beside the slow-flowing river, it seemed the most natural thing for his arm to go around her waist, and for her to lean her bobbed head against his shoulder, for all the world like two young lovers enjoying the evening sunlight.

Dick had memorised part of the Bordeaux streetplan, and at the old Pont de Pierre they turned left into the oldest part of Bordeaux, with its narrow twisting streets and the ancient facades, some half-timbered, some classical, of houses, wine cellars and expensive shops. Despite his confidence, Dick was somewhat relieved when they found the Rue Montesquieux, and the elegant front of the Chapon Fin beneath its white awning, just as eight o'clock was striking from a nearby church tower.

Tables well spread, crystal chandeliers, white linen tablecloths and napkins, a quiet hum of conversation, the Chapon Fin was everything Dick had hoped for. Being July there were no oysters on the menu, but the 'Fruits de Mer' was recommended for two people, and they shared the huge dish, together with a bottle of Pouilly Fuisse and a large pot of coffee. Brit thought that there was something delightfully sensual about tearing apart a crab and digging out the meat with fingers and a spiked fork, and as they fed one another particular delicacies she knew that the sexual temperature between them was rising again. There was a pleasure too in slowing down that familiar momentum, and over coffee she asked Dick about his day.

"When we were walking by the river you said something about a financial problem in the French business. Is it secret, Dick, or do you want to talk about it?"

Not for the first time Dick reflected on the difference in attitude between Brit and Rosemary. His wife actually avoided enquiring about business matters unless she thought they were personally affected. She perhaps felt that she did not have a lot to contribute, and anyway Dick needed his home to be a haven of refuge from the pressures of the job. Whereas Brit was an experienced businesswoman, she was interested in his work, and she wanted to share whatever concerned him. *Which approach was the better recipe for a marriage?* Certainly he knew that he wanted to tell her about his work. He went over the facts about the disturbing monthly report, the strange interview with Alain Robarte, and Jean-Paul's less than totally convincing explanation.

"Frankly, I don't know what to do next. If there's something going wrong and they're hiding it, by the end of the year there could be a very nasty hole in the accounts."

She tipped her head quizzically. "A hole?"

"A gap, where a large sum of my parent company's money should be. And I could be held responsible. On the other hand if it really was just a silly mistake, I could make a complete fool of myself by charging in and accusing people. D'you see the problem?"

She nodded, and rested a cool hand on his. "I can't think of anything either, so I suppose that means that you should wait and hope that you get some more information. You mentioned that the people in America have been sent the same information, so I am sure they will be worried also. Why don't you report what has happened so far, and ask them for their recommendations? I have found that management is not so criticising when they have to share the problem too."

Dick squeezed her fingers in appreciation of her contribution. *She really is something special.* He called for the bill, and was careful to pay in cash. He asked the waiter to call a taxi for them. "We don't want to get too tired, do we?"

Chapter Eight

On Saturday morning Dick Routledge awoke and lay on his back, keeping quite still in the big hotel bed as Brit slept beside him, nestling her blonde head on his shoulder. *His flight left at eleven, so he should be getting a taxi by nine-thirty . . . was there time to make love once more?* He tried to guess the time by the angle of the sunlight coming in through the edge of the curtains, but without much confidence. He felt her stir and stretch her slim body against his. She looked up to see if he was awake too, and smiled a long slow smile as their eyes met.

"Good morning, Dick. Did you sleep well?"

He grinned back and sat up. "Very well, darling Brit. That's when I was allowed to."

She blushed, because in truth she had probably persuaded him to make love just one more time than he had intended or expected. A long abstinence had certainly sharpened her appetite, and he was a very nice lover, an unusual mix of sensitivity and passion. *He must have a good wife, so why are we here? Perhaps she has forgotten how to look after him . . .*

"What time is it?"

He reached onto the bedside table and picked up his gold watch. He felt a little jolt of conscience as he recalled the birthday when Rosemary had given it to him, and put it down again.

"Damn. It's just nine, and I must get my taxi for the airport in half an hour."

She stretched up and pulled him down for a kiss, a soft, lingering kiss that was guaranteed to make him want to stay – then she stopped the hand that had pressed her breast and was now sliding around her waist.

"Enough, Dick, enough. You have to shower and shave and dress and settle the bill. As we agreed, I will stay on one more night to see a little of Bordeaux today, but you must let me pay for tonight myself."

Because of the time lost changing planes in Paris it was three in the afternoon by the time his flight landed in Birmingham. Fortunately Dick had driven himself and parked at the airport on Wednesday evening, and he sank with a sigh into the womb-like security of the Jaguar's well-worn leather seat. He had never deceived Rosemary before, and throughout the flight his mind had been busy trying to think what she might ask about his trip, and ensuring that he had innocent answers ready. Did he feel guilty? Not really. After all, there was no threat to Rosemary or the family, was there?. It had just been a time of harmless pleasure, a night in a foreign country with a very pretty, very charming woman. Of course he might see her again – to be honest, he very much wanted to. They had promised to talk over the telephone next week, and exchange travel plans for the coming month, with the possibility of trying to ensure that trips coincided. But Brit was quite delightfully undemanding and unthreatening, really a perfect mistress, he thought. Something was niggling at the back of his mind about today though, and he pulled out his pocket diary before he started the car. Jamie's cricket match, of course! Thank heavens he'd told Rosemary that he would most likely be coming back late on Saturday afternoon. Just three-thirty . . . if he drove straight to the school sports field now he would arrive in time for the tea interval. Maybe in time to see Jamie bat or bowl. Anyway, the important thing was for him to turn up. It was a fine summer afternoon, the Jaguar positively purred up the M42, and all was right with his world.

The rest of the weekend passed for Dick in a kind of warm haze of pleasure. He found Rosemary and Peter sitting in deckchairs on the boundary of the prep school's cricket pitch, while Jamie was just padding up to go into bat at number six. Rosemary was looking every inch the parent in a summery pastel blue and pink paisley print with an enormous straw hat, which she carefully removed to greet Dick with a warm but decorous kiss, while Peter bustled off officiously into the pavilion to find a ham sandwich and a glass of cold squash for his father. James went in to bat a few minutes later, and was unbeaten at the end with ten runs, while his captain, who was two years older, knocked off the winning runs just before five o'clock. Somehow he had expected to sense a difference in his relations with his wife, but that night she was her usual friendly self as they undressed early for bed, soon after ten. Rosemary brushed her long red hair at the dressing table as Dick found the half-read P.D. James thriller that he had forgotten to take with him and slipped into bed.

"I'm sorry, Dick, I haven't asked you how your trip went. Did you manage to find out what was going on?"

A more perceptive man than Dick Routledge might have noted that his wife did not usually initiate an enquiry about the business, especially in the bedroom, and might therefore have wondered what lay behind this sudden show if interest. But Dick was just pleased to share his problems.

"Well, they've come up with an explanation. The trouble is that I don't believe it. And I'm damned if I know what to do about it."

He went over the strange meeting at the airport with Jean-Paul, the events at the factory and Robarte's visit to his hotel. Rosemary pursed her lips thoughtfully.

"Your father or Jim Helvin may have an idea. It might also be useful to talk to John Savage. I remember him telling us once how he'd learned the hard way not to trust company directors."

John had been the representative on Strongwheat's board of De Boissy, their London merchant bankers, but now he was a self-employed merger and acquisition consultant, who had been doing a lot of work for Dick's father and ACP over the last two years, and was, incidentally, now married to Jean Carey, Strongwheat's Director of Personnel. Dick had not thought of asking his advice, but he was certainly experienced in the field of detecting corporate swindles and fiddles, and very bright too. Perhaps he should try to consult Rosemary more often?

She finished her hair and slipped off her dressing gown, to reveal the black lace nightdress that Dick so liked. He pulled back the bed cover to let her in, suddenly conscious that his exertions in Bordeaux had not tired him at all, in fact he actually looked forward very much to making love to Rosemary. As she knelt on the bed to arrange her pillows he pulled at the ribbon to open the little bow at the front of her nightdress and cupped her firm pointed breasts.

"I've missed you a lot."

She allowed herself to subside onto his chest, and twined her arms about his neck as she kissed him.

"I've missed you too."

It was just after eight o'clock when Dick arrived at Strongwheat on Monday, to be greeted in reception by a very worried Elizabeth, the secretary that he shared with his father.

"I have just this minute checked through your e-mails, Mr. Dick, and there's some terrible news. I've printed it off for you."

He slung his jacket around the back of his office chair and sat down to read the message on his desk.

I very much regret to have to inform you that our company accountant, M. Alain Robarte, was attacked in Bordeaux on Saturday night and severely injured. The police think it was an attempt to murder. He is in hospital, but has not yet recovered his sensing. The surgeons will most probably operate today. I will send more information when we know. Jean-Paul

Dick checked the time on the e-mail – sent at eight fourteen – an hour ago in France. His hand rested momentarily on the telephone, then he decided against making a call. Jean-Paul would no doubt be frantically busy with the hospital and the police. Did Alain have a family? Should he send flowers, a 'Get Well' card? Suddenly a terrifying thought leapt into his mind. What if this attack was connected in some way to whatever it was that was going on at the factory? Perhaps Dick had unwittingly been the actual cause of it, by persuading Alain to come secretly to the hotel? Should he go back to France and tell the police what he knew? A horrifying gulf seemed to open in front of him, full of endless ever-widening enquiries and endless French bureaucracy. He shook his head like a man awaking from a bad dream, and walked down the corridor to the office of the company's European Director of Personnel, Jean Savage. As Jean Carey she had joined the company five years earlier, just before Dick, and he had been partly responsible for her recent promotion to the board. He found her hunched over her desk with a distinctly aggrieved frown that rather spoilt her usually very agreeable features. Her dark hair was tightly coiled and pinned for the office, and her huge brown eyes were almost hidden by old-fashioned horn-rimmed spectacles. It was a cool morning, and she was wearing a V-necked dark green dress in a knitted wool fabric. She slapped an elegant finger on the document she was reading, apparently glad of an audience.

"Honestly, these people in Brussels get dafter every day. More regulations, more earnest meddling every day. None of them could run a sweetie shop. And then they're surprised that they've got growing unemployment, which they're trying to export to us. Who'd want to employ anybody over there if you could avoid it? It all comes from the big German and French trade unions, and people can't seem to see that every added protection for their members only disadvantages the poor blokes that haven't got a job."

She recognised the worried expression on Dick's face, and was immediately contrite.

"I'm sorry, Dick, I was letting my bad temper get the better of me. Can we start again? Good morning, Dick, how are you?"

The warmth of her smile was infectious, and he sat down on the hard chair in front of her steel desk with a small sigh.

"Good morning Jean, I'm fine. How's the young miss or mister?"

Jean had informed the board two weeks ago that she was expecting a baby in early November, although like most confidential matters at Strongwheat it was already general knowledge. There was even a sweepstake running on the baby's weight at birth.

"The baby's fine, kicking for England last night." She removed her glasses and sat back. "So that's the civilised decencies over and done with. What's up, Doc.?"

Dick liked the way that Jean had grown in confidence since her promotion. "Well, I think I need to consult your beloved husband on a fairly tricky matter. Can I do that without it costing an arm and a leg?"

"By 'consult', is that half a day with you in the office and a week's research for him, or is it half an hour on the telephone?"

"Half an hour on the 'phone should do it".

"Then I'm sure it would be covered under the retainer your father pays him. Anything I can help with at all?"

Her great eyes were all sympathy and concern, and Dick was strongly tempted to unburden himself. After all, she was a director, and the possible disaster in France was sure to be reviewed at the next board meeting. He decided to temporise.

"Well, this isn't exactly what I want to talk to John about, but you could do something really helpful for me. Do you remember the accountant for our company in France, Alain Robarte?"

"Yes, of course. Jean-Paul wanted to bring him in from Colgate without any formal recruitment exercise, and you got me to do some digging about him and his previous career. Came up smelling of roses, as I recall. Why, has something cropped up?"

"Poor chap's got himself bashed up in Bordeaux over the weekend. Haven't got much detail at the moment, but he's in a bad way for sure. Now, this is definitely not the time for that business to be without a qualified accountant for several months. Can you get someone in there A.S.A.P.? No infants, this needs a heavyweight, someone who's been around the block a few times in a manufacturing business in France."

Suddenly purposeful, Jean stood up and reached for a box file on the shelf beside her desk. Dick smiled for no very good reason as he noted for the first time the gentle rounding of her stomach beneath the close-fitting dress, but his expression was serious again as she sat down and opened the file.

"I've been keeping these for ages, without ever really believing that we would have a need."

She fanned one of the brochures from the box. "These are agencies who write in, in fact there's a reasonably local one that came in to see me. They sell what they call 'Interim Management'. Could be just what we need. An interim manager is an independent, like a consultant, except that instead of dispensing advice they actually come in for a few weeks or months and do the job. Sort of executive temp. So we'll want a Finance Director sort of chap – could be a woman of course, but not very likely, I'd say. Must have worked in manufacturing industry in France, and of course fluent French-speaking. How long might we need him?"

"Heaven only knows. I'd say we'll have a better idea in a week or so, assuming poor Alain survives of course. I'd guess three months minimum, could be six."

"Leave it to me, then. If the guy who came in is as smart as he claimed, we'll be interviewing by Friday and have a man in place next week. Be warned though, Dick, this is not a cheap solution. I'd guess ten to twelve thousand a month."

Dick blew out his cheeks, and then thought about the amount of money they had at stake in France. *And perhaps this interim manager fellow would be able to get to the bottom of the funny numbers too!*

"Let's do it. You start the ball rolling with the agency, I'll clear things with Jean-Paul. I suppose it's just possible that ACP might have a French-speaking financial guy they'd want to put up, so I'll run it past Ben Camina at ACP as well."

Back in his office Dick woke up his desk PC and started to draft an e-mail to Ben. Really, he would much prefer to have someone from England that he and Jean would control, but this was no time to fall foul of Ben and his cadre, especially after they had been alerted to the possible problems about last month's figures. His final version read:

Dear Ben, Just for your information, I have learned this morning that our accountant in France, Alain Robarte, was criminally attacked over the weekend and is seriously ill in hospital. We are recruiting a temporary financial executive to start next week, but do let me know please if you have a suitable internal candidate to put up. Best regards, Dick Routledge.

Dick leant back in his chair and read the message through a couple more times. Did it strike the right balance between corporate commitment and 'trust us, we'll get on with it'? He nodded, and pressed 'send'.

"Elizabeth, I could do with a cup of coffee and some biscuits, please."

She came in five minutes later with a tray of tea. "If you remember, Mr. Dick, I promised Rosemary that you would stick to tea instead of coffee. And no biscuits."

He thanked her with as good a grace as he could manage, and showed her the e-mail he had sent to Ben Camina. "I don't want to worry Jean-Paul just yet, so could you call Lisa, his PA, yourself please? Be very concerned, and ask if there is any news this morning about M'sieur Robarte? And say that I've seen the report he sent, and will call him this afternoon."

A moment later Jean put her head around his door. "I've spoken to the local agency about finding an interim. They sounded very confident, and ask if we can schedule Thursday afternoon for interviews, two people, possibly three?"

Dick opened his desk diary and pencilled into Thursday afternoon. "No problem. Do we get to see any particulars of these people before they arrive? And the price?"

"He's coming in to see me with the CV's and costs late Wednesday. I'll give you a shout when he comes."

After she had gone Dick flicked back his diary to Monday, and cursed silently when he noted the entry for that afternoon, in Elizabeth's handwriting:

4 pm. Meeting at Mrs. J. Hawkins re HR Wing Opening.

He wanted to talk to John Savage, and then he should write a report on his visit to France and his conclusions about the explanation for the curious figures for last month. He ought to show that to his father before it went off to ACP . . . were there enough hours in the day? He looked at his watch – ten-thirty – and was instantly reminded of that moment when he picked up the watch from beside the bed in Bordeaux, with Brit lying beside him naked to the waist and beautiful . . . And after all there was the elegant and delightful Jennifer to look forward to, with the promised fruit cake as well.

"Elizabeth, I wonder if you'd be kind enough to raise Mr. John Savage for me please? Mrs. Savage thought he would most probably be working at home today."

Chapter Nine

A few minutes before four o'clock on Monday afternoon Dick drove in warm sunshine across Lynchester's Town Bridge from the Market Square and turned into the avenue of fine detached houses that ran parallel to the river, about a hundred yards up from the bridge. Jennifer Hawkins lived in the big double-fronted Edwardian house she had inherited from her husband, and the front door with its gleaming brass knocker and letterbox was opened immediately even as Dick was climbing out of his car. Jennifer smiled as she came out, and offered a cool hand for Dick to shake. Her demurely v-necked cotton dress was pale lemon, with a print of tiny blue violets scattered all over it. A blue leather belt accentuated her slim waist and the swell of her full bosom; her dark hair was tied back in a girlish ponytail that was pinned with a silver comb.

"Hullo, and welcome, Dick. You're the first to arrive, but I'm sure Dan will be along shortly, provided the Council have let him off the leash. Come in. Go straight through the dining room here and out through the french doors. It's such a lovely day now, I thought we'd sit out in the rose garden for our chat. Make yourself comfortable out there and I'll leave the door open for Dan while I make the tea."

Dick followed her instructions, seeing no need to do more than murmur 'Hullo' as he thankfully peeled off the jacket of his grey suit. As he walked through the dining room, which was wainscoted in wood that had been painted a soft white, he admired the handsome antique mahogany dining table with its large vase of tall yellow roses, and ten, no, twelve matching chairs padded in green leather. Outside there was a large flagstone patio with three cushioned loungers, and a swing seat beneath a young oak, in front of which was a rectangular garden table in black filigree cast iron. Beyond the patio the garden climbed in a gentle slope for about fifty yards to the boundary hedge. Most of the space seemed to be devoted to a magnificent display of roses – beds of bush and standards near the house, giving way higher up to curving paths that connected pergolas and arbours loaded with ramblers and climbers.

The swing seat was sprinkled with some glossy colour brochures, and Dick was just starting to read one when Jennifer came through with a tray of tea and the promised dark fruit cake.

"I see you've found my guilty secret. I want a house in France. Not to buy, at least not yet. But Billy is three, so he'll be old enough to enjoy a foreign country, and I just feel . . . restless, I suppose. I think I need a change, perhaps a bit of a challenge again. Do you ever feel like that, Dick?"

Her eyes were soft, almost guileless, but Dick got a distinct impression that the conversation was about more than just a holiday in France. She seemed to be longing to talk about her plans, and he felt drawn into sharing the moment with her.

"I suppose so, yes. I mean, since we sold Strongwheat one couldn't say that my father and I have really needed to work, but there's never been any question of either of us just giving up. Sometimes the new business we're developing for the Americans presses hard on one or both of us, you know, even keeps us awake at night, but I don't think we'd have it any other way. Mind you, my mother is often telling Dad he's doing too much. But I know for certain that it was the commitment to the Strongwheat business that kept him alive when he had that stroke a few years ago, virtually dragged him back from death's door, so there's definitely a lot to be said for having a challenge, something to worry about."

She sat down beside him on the big swing seat, and a hint of that sweet perfume again made him very conscious of her femininity as she reached out to pour two cups of tea and cut the cake. *The average man thinks of sex every two minutes of the day. Now where did I read that? Until I met Brit I just enjoyed making love to Rosemary, and I don't think I really looked at other women. Have I changed so much, so quickly?*

"I suppose Dan must be held up on some important Council business, but he's almost fifteen minutes late now, so we might as well enjoy our tea and make a start. I hope you like my cake, it's spiced with cinnamon and nutmeg. It's from a recipe my mother taught me. The secret is to soak the fruit first, would you believe in cold tea?"

"It's very good indeed." Dick had given no thought to the subject of the meeting, and cast around for another topic to sustain the conversation.

"Where's Billy? Our boys were all over us, all the time, when they were three, I remember."

"He's upstairs with Greta, my au pair, probably watching a video. This is his first term at the nursery school, and he's quite tired when he comes back in. Greta's Dutch, a bit on the chubby side of sturdy, but very nice, and genuinely fond of Billy, I think. One thing that really worries me if we were to go to France is Greta's reaction. I know she came over here mainly to learn English, and she may not be that keen to be thrown into a French community, even if we speak English at home. I'd really hate to lose her, and Billy would miss her terribly. She's even taught him to sing Dutch nursery rhymes."

There was a ring at the front door, and they heard Dan call, 'Hullo the house?'

"Come through the dining room, Dan, we're in the garden, digging into the cake."

Dan Grundy bustled out to them, full of apologies for being late.

"It was a site meeting for a new housing development, eighteen or twenty what they call 'affordable homes' out by the motorway. Of course the affordability or otherwise is determined by the density they will let us build, and they now want a good size earth bank put in to cut down the traffic noise, so there's a lot of negotiating going on, and I couldn't just walk away. And to cap it all we'd done some preliminary digging to test the suitability of the ground, and we may have unearthed the edge of some Roman fort or a villa or whatever, so God knows what effect that's going to have on the building schedules. It would probably pay us to get that TV archaeology lot to come in and uncover the whole site in three days. As it is, we'll be lucky if we're only delayed three months."

He sat in one of the loungers and sipped his tea with a grateful sigh. "That's better. Been looking forward to this for the last hour." He looked around. "You've done wonders with the garden, Jennie. I remember when Joe first got this place, it was all plain lawn and a few shrubs around the edge. Fabulous site though, and guaranteed green belt beyond your hedge. Must be nearly half an acre. Very good cake too. D'you mind me asking where you got it? It's something I'm very fond of."

Dick thought there was a very appealing blush on Jennifer's cheeks as she poured Dan a second cup. "Flattery will get you everywhere, as you no doubt know already. I have to admit I made it myself, and I'm very pleased you like it. Another slice?"

Dan held up his hand. "Love to, Jennie, but I'm under strict orders to watch my waistline." He burrowed into the slim black briefcase he had brought with him, and pulled out a single sheet.

"Now then, I've taken on board the committee's preference for someone for the opening of the HR Wing with a bit of dignity and status. To be honest, my friends on the Council would still prefer a celeb – a footballer or a TV face that would get the town into the national press. But I told them that the Hawkins and the Routledges are paying the piper, so they should certainly be allowed to call the tune. But you'll be glad to hear that I've extracted a budget out of a little reserve in the rate fund to pay for some professional PR for us. Looking at it from the town's point of view, we want above all to attract in more employment, and a new children's wing to the hospital, under the general supervision of Great Ormond Street, has a chance of appealing to the kind of service industry we're definitely short of, something like an insurance company or a call centre. Suppose for instance that we find ourselves in competition with Tamworth, or Lichfield, or Nuneaton. Other things being equal, I told the Council, the 'HR' could just make the difference for us. Anyway, the Council are one hundred percent behind us, so we've virtually got a free hand for the opening. And they'll put out the flags, I can promise you."

He looked down at his sheet, "And now for the good news. I've had my girl do some telephoning last Thursday and Friday, and the answers have come back this morning. Obviously the kind of people we're talking about can only give us conditional promises, but I'd say we're in good shape so far. Top of the list is no less than HRH Princess Anne. Her PA says she has the afternoon of Tuesday October 15th. free at the moment. More importantly, she already has an engagement in Birmingham in the morning, and she likes children's hospitals, so we've actually been pencilled in. The PA has a diary review with the Princess on Thursday, so we should get a fairly definite yea or nay then. The good thing about this is that the Princess would usually be accompanied by the Lord Lieutenant of the county, so if she had to drop out for some reason there's a good chance he would stand in for her."

"I take my hat off to you, Dan," said Dick, "And your girl of course. Tell her if she ever needs a job . . ."

"Not a chance. The Council would scalp me with blunt scissors if I ever let her get away from us."

Jennifer was more cautious, "Helen was particularly keen there should be some medical representation. It is a hospital after all."

Dan remained determinedly upbeat, "I think we can cover that off too. I've spoken myself to the Chairman of North Warwicks Health Trust, and he's definitely committed to come. And we have a promise too from Great Ormond Street that at least one of their consultant Knights or Dames will come, so Helen should be well pleased. All in all it promises to be a great occasion for the town as well as for the benefactors, wouldn't you agree?"

Jennifer and Dick could only nod. "Right then, so if you'll forgive me I'll be on my way. There's a Council meeting at five-thirty, and before then I've promised to drop in to see our Grace. Apparently my granddaughter has something she particularly wants to tell me about. I think it might just have something to do with it being her birthday next month."

After Jennifer had seen Dan off, she returned to the patio doorway to find Dick leafing through one of the brochures again. She was longing to ask his advice, perhaps to get him involved in some way in her plans, but some instinct told her to hold back. It was a minute or two before he looked up and saw her there. And there was something about the way he looked at her that made her glad that she that she had not taken the initiative this time.

"I can't remember if I told you on Wednesday at the last meeting, but I was going straight off to quite a nice part of France, where we've got a new factory making corn flakes. If you've not got any particular part already picked out, you might like to consider Arcachon. In fact I was looking through the brochures to see if there were any places there to rent, and in fact there are several. It's a very stylish resort."

She sat beside him, and he showed her the pages he had found about Arcachon. "It's on the Atlantic coast, a few miles down from Bordeaux. Huge sand dunes, like hills really. And a tidal lagoon with the fishing port and village inside. Apparently the place was largely developed from scratch as a seaside resort in the second half of the nineteenth century. Lots of extraordinary Victorian villas. But there's a good road up to Bordeaux, and I should think quite a few French people live there permanently and commute, like the MD of our French business, for instance."

He studied her profile covertly while she read the pages in the brochure. Strong jaw, full lips, high cheekbones, huge dark eyes, fine skin with just a few crinkles around the eyes. No man could help being drawn to her. Interesting past too! He'd known the husband, Joe Hawkins, he must have been twenty, no twenty five years older than her. But apparently they'd been very happy together, and she'd built up the retail DIY side of the business, and made a real packet when the site was sold off after Joe's death to build the Mall. And there was Billy . . . who was his father, Dick wondered? *Not that it matters now, I suppose. Anyway, why am I getting involved and advising her to come and live in exactly the part of France that I have to visit? Except of course that if she's living in France she'd no longer be on my own doorstep, as it were. So it wouldn't be quite so risky . . .*

Jennifer too was wondering if there might be some hidden agenda behind Dick's choice of place to recommend. *On the other hand he could hardly recommend a place he didn't know, could he? But he was interested, she could feel it in the air, sense the way he was looking at her now, when he thought she was busy reading.* She looked at her watch.

"It's just after five, but I expect the agents will still be there. Why don't you help yourself to another cup of tea and a piece of cake, while I give them a call?"

She hurried back a few minutes later, clearly very excited. "Well, that's all in hand. I've told them I'm interested in a six-month let in Arcachon, starting September, say. I'd need a decent-size house, three or four bedrooms. They were sure there'd be a lot of availability at good prices, and they're going to get back to me in a couple of days with all the stuff, including some background material on the town itself."

Dick felt that this might be the right time to leave, and got up, to find himself standing very close to her. She backed away to let him through, very conscious of his solid maleness.

"I'll tell my mother and Charles Harrison about the Princess. They're bound to be pleased. Perhaps I could come by some time soon, when you've got all the details about Arcachon, and look through them with you. I was thinking, if you wanted, I could ask our MD there, Jean-Paul de Clavignon, to show you around. Come to think of it, his wife Arlette and you would probably get along very well. They've got a little boy too, a year or two older than Billy. Though you would have to get down there before the end of this month, as he'll be off somewhere for the whole of August, I expect. Which reminds me, we have a bit of a crisis down there at the moment, and I need to get back to the office to give him a call. Of course it's after six now in France, but he might be working late."

She ushered him ahead of her through the dining room. "It would be great to have the benefit of Arlette's advice, Dick." She paused at the front door. "You've been really kind. I'll have a talk with Greta this evening, and if she's not too anti we might get the plane this weekend."

He shook the proffered hand, noticing that it was not so cool as when he had first arrived.

Chapter Ten

The drive back from Jennifer Hawkins' house to the Strongwheat offices was not long enough for Dick Routledge to sort out his thoughts about Jennifer. In fact the only conclusion he had come to as he walked through the quiet hallway and pushed open the door of his office was that he didn't understand himself any more. An hour in Jennifer's company had confirmed last week's first impression – she was an exceptional, very desirable woman. But Dick saw himself as a happily married man, with now the added benefit of a delightful Swedish mistress. *So why has it seemed so necessary to develop my relationship with Jennifer? Am I unable now to resist the temptation to pursue any attractive woman that comes into view?* He blew out his lips in mock irritation with himself as he sat down, checked the messages lined up on his desk to ensure there was nothing urgent, took a couple of deep breaths, and dialled the direct line to Jean-Paul in Belin.

He listened for what seemed to be an age to the long rings being repeated, and decided that everyone at the French factory must have gone home. Determined not to let the moment pass, he called up the e-mail facility on his PC and composed a message.

Dear Jean-Paul,

We were all very shocked to hear the terrible news about M. Robarte, and we hope soon to have some better reports from the hospital. I tried to call you a few minutes ago, and am sorry not to have been able to speak with you personally.

Naturally we were concerned too that you should not be without a good financial manager at this critical time in the development of our business. In agreement with ACP therefore I am arranging for a very experienced executive to join you on a temporary basis next Monday morning. He will report to you, and can stay with you as long as required – I will carry the cost in my budget. Please telephone me tomorrow. Best regards, Dick

Dick read the message through twice. Of course there had not yet been any feed-back from Ben Camina about a temporary financial manager, but there was no way that Jean-Paul was likely to find that out. He concluded that it conveyed the right mix of concern and decisive authority, and pressed 'send'. In a way he felt relieved that Jean-Paul had not answered the telephone. *He would almost certainly have wanted to debate the decision to send in an English interim manager, and in all probability would want to put up an alternative candidate of his own. Now he is going to be faced with a simple fait accompli. He can express his worries about the wisdom of the appointment, but he is going to have to make the best of it. The important thing to try to get from Jean-Paul tomorrow was the motive for the attack on Alain Robarte. Of course, there might not actually be a motive, as such. It might be a casual mugging, a drunken brawl, or mistaken identity, or any one of a dozen silly things, other than some calculated connection with those funny numbers and with me.* His thoughts wandered back to the afternoon's meeting. *Jennifer seems to like me. She's beautiful, rich, a widow, with a son of unconfirmed parentage. Should I worry about it?* He thought of Rosemary. *You bet I should!*

As he was clearing his desk Dick looked again through the notes he had made before lunch of his telephone conversation with John Savage. Elizabeth had faxed the two sets of monthly figures through to John before their conversation had started, so that they could both have the same information in front of them. Dick's worries had been eased in a way, when he found that John was as distrustful as himself.

"Frankly, I don't believe that experienced accountants make silly mistakes like this. Particularly not when the boss is away and they've been told to get on with it. If anything that usually makes a man twice as careful. So I'd suggest that what you received first was *not* sent by mistake. Your M'sieur Robarte *wanted* you to see those numbers and start an enquiry about them. The question is, of course, what do they mean? And why was he so anxious that you see them?"

"It's odd, though, isn't it that when I got him to my hotel room, and gave him the chance to come clean in private, he backed off?"

"Odd, yes, but perhaps not inexplicable. Especially in the light of what's happened to him now. Perhaps the scenario is that when Jean-Paul was away and he sent the first figures he did intend to engage in a bit of honest whistle blowing, but then after Jean-Paul had returned and perhaps put the fear of God into him, he chickened out."

"Do you think I should go to the French police with what I know?"

There was a long pause.

"No . . . at least not immediately. I think you should press very hard for those bank statements. It seems to me that there are going to be two possibilities. Either there is a cash discrepancy, or there isn't. If there is, you've got no choice – you must involve Ben Camina at ACP, and it's then their decision whether or not the police are called in. And if they are called in you can bet your boots they will make the connection all by themselves between the money problem and M. Robarte's problems, and the chances are that you won't have to come into it at all. On the other hand if there isn't a discrepancy, it doesn't necessarily mean that nothing fishy is going on, because there could well be other sets of bank accounts in existence through which the funny stuff is still being hidden. You know it's always been a tradition, in France especially, to keep several sets of books, basically one for the owners and another for the taxman, but with variations on the theme. Jim Helvin will be familiar with this, but a typical place to find a difference is under the heading called 'Depreciation'. This is where an owner would reduce the declared profits in the official accounts by writing down the value of stock or plant or work in progress or some other asset, so there's a charge created against the earnings and they pay less tax. But it's not actually a cash transaction, just a write-down in the books, so there's still the money there to be siphoned out in some way or other. Anyway, let's suppose there's no obvious discrepancy between the monthly trading reports and the statements of cash movements from the bank. Then you're stuck, I'd say. But what I would do is maintain the connection with the bank, and get them to copy the statements to you or Jim Helvin on a weekly basis. Let Jean-Paul know what you're doing, and most likely it will all go quiet, at least for a while. People who are embezzling money from a company don't usually have to do it all the time, especially if they're given some reason to believe there's an investigation imminent."

" 'Embezzling' is a nasty word, John. Do you actually think that Jean-Paul may be robbing us and intimidating Alain Robarte?"

"Do you?"

Dick thought hard. "I suppose that's what has been at the back of my mind. But Jean-Paul is a man I helped to recruit. I've been working with him for two years now, with no worries whatsoever. Putting things at the most basic personal level, my standing with ACP would be horribly damaged, if not ruined, if Jean-Paul turns out to be a villain. And your beloved wife might pick up the odd brickbat too, since she was heavily involved in checking out Jean-Paul's CV and reputation for me."

"As Shakespeare says, "There is no art to tell the mind's construction in the face." All the more reason to sit tight and keep your powder dry until you're absolutely certain of your facts."

As he was leaving, Dick checked Elizabeth's big desk diary, in which she maintained the programme for both Dick and his father. He noted that his father was on the golf course today, but was due in the office tomorrow. *Best to tell him everything, including what John has said. And we'll get Jim Helvin chasing those damn French bankers too. I wonder what Mum's going to say when I tell her about the Princess?*

The next day, Tuesday, Dick was at his desk by eight o'clock, and heard Elizabeth take the call.

"Good morning M'sieur de Clavignon, we were all so worried to hear about the dreadful attack on poor M. Robarte. Is there any news? I see, yes . . ., yes of course. I'll put you straight through to Mr. Dick."

"It's Jean-Paul. He says that M. Robarte is stable but still unconscious."

"Good morning Jean-Paul. So there's no progress yet for poor Alain? Perhaps this is a case where no news is good news?"

"Bonjour, Dick. We are very worried, bien sur. The doctor says that 'e 'as taken several 'eavy strikes on the 'ead, and there is a breaking of the bone and swelling on the brain. But 'e is a strong 'ealthy man – did you know that five year ago 'e was champion swimmer of all Paris? I think the plan is to wait a day or two to see 'ow the swelling is less, and zen they will make an operation."

"Can you tell me anything about how he came to be attacked?"

"Nutting, nutting at all." Dick could almost see the open palms and the Gallic shrug as Jean-Paul spoke. "The police will send a ver' senior inspecteur to see me in one hour, but really I can tell them nutting. Alain lives in a quiet part of Bordeaux, you know? According to 'is femme, Viola, it was a custom for 'im to take a little walk by the river before bed. On Saturday soir 'e go out at about eleven o'clock, but Viola does not go because she wants to see a film on the TV. When this film 'as ended and Alain 'as not come back she is ver' worried, and call the police. They find Alain an hour later, nearly dead, at the side of La Garonne."

"Had he been robbed?"

"Non, 'e 'ad 'is monnaie and 'is plastique still."

"Any other ideas as to why he was attacked?"

"Pas de tout. Per'aps the police will be able to tell somet'ing. But I want also to talk wit you, Dick, about the temporary financial man to take the place of Alain. I am sure that we must 'ave someone, because sans doute Alain can not come back for many months. But it is not a good idea to send in a man from England or America. We 'ave many special lois and regulations, which must be followed exactly. And if 'e is to do good work the man must be able to talk with ordinary workers with no English at all. Did you know two of my supervisors and twelve, no quinze now of my workers are Arabes? I 'ave many contacts already in the region, and certainement I can find a French accountant to work exactement to the needs of ACP. Just allow me one or two days to make some searching and . . ."

"No, Jean-Paul, I must ask that you go along with myself and ACP in this. I will send the CV of the man we have selected in a couple of days, when we have completed our own checks, and he should be able to join you at the beginning of next week. From what I have been promised already by Mrs. Savage, our Director of Personnel, he will be very experienced in working in French industry, and perfectly competent to operate in French. Having said that, if you have a personal problem in working with our man we could of course discuss that in due course."

There was a pause, while Jean-Paul tried to see through the English nuances of what Dick had said. *Was there some sort of threat involved – 'do as I say or else'?* He decided this was not the right time to make a stand.

"Naturellement, Dick, I 'ave confiance in your judgement. I will await the information about your man, and you can be sure we will all do our best to work well with 'im next week."

"I am very grateful for your support, Jean-Paul. By the way, I don't think I thanked you for the introduction to your friend Henri, the negociant. He gave me a very educational afternoon tasting his wines. It's possible that he was a bit disappointed that I only bought one dozen, but next time I come I will definitely buy some more. Will you thank him again for me when you see him, please? There is perhaps one other thing you could do for me?"

"A votre service, M'sieur."

Was there a hint of irony in Jean-Paul's tone? Dick decided to ignore it.

"A lady here in Lynchester, a Mrs Hawkins, she's a friend of the family I suppose. She is a widow, but our age and quite wealthy, with a young son. She tells me that she's been thinking of going to live in France for a few months, so I suggested she should look in Arcachon, which I thought was very attractive. If she comes, could you or perhaps Arlette be kind enough to show her around and so on?"

Jean-Paul's response was immediate.

"Of course, Dick. There are some English people here in Arcachon you know, although they are older than us, retired I think. Anyway Arlette will be so pleased, and per'aps the little boy will like to play with mon fils. You will send me the information when Madame 'Awkins is coming, please?"

After Dick had left Jennifer dug out her old school atlas and went back to the garden seat, enjoying the evening sunshine and looking again through the two pages about villas in Arcachon. *'A onetime whaling port. Now a very substantial supplier of oysters.'* It certainly seemed an interesting place. Probably very quiet in the winter – she found the map of the southern half of France – but quite near Bordeaux. And not much over a hundred miles to Biarritz and the Spanish border. She looked at her watch – just five thirty – and walked upstairs to the computer she had set up in the small bedroom next to her own that served as a study. She logged on to the internet and found the Ryanair web-site. It seemed that from Birmingham their only connection was to Dublin, and they didn't fly to Bordeaux anyway. But they did go from Stansted to Biarritz, – comfortable flight time at ten to three every day . . . she kept on browsing . . . couple of nights in the Hotel du Palais, *built as a summer residence for the wife of Napoleon III* . . . then rent a car, say two hours to Arcachon. *Dick will be impressed by my executive style, no doubt. I wonder if some important business will drag him to France while I'm there? Silly nonsense, Jennifer. Can you imagine one of Lynchester's great and good having an affair with one of the 'rich widow Hawkins'? And in France to boot? Well, yes, I can actually. I may be a bit out of practice, but I wasn't mistaken about the way he was stealing a look at me this afternoon. He fancies me, I'm certain of it. And how do I feel about that? He's definitely an interesting man* . . . She abandoned the train of thought as too difficult for now. She guessed that Dick was the kind of man who would decide for himself what the next step might be, with just the slightest encouragement from her. Jennifer was old-fashioned enough to believe that was how it should be. At least for the moment.

She could hear Greta playing with Billy in his bedroom. *Time to discover what Greta thinks about France.* She found her spare credit card in the desk drawer. *There's only this week left of the school term. If she's all right about it, we could all three fly over on Sunday, say.*

Chapter Eleven

That Monday morning, back in her office in Stockholm, Brit Carlsohn had written up the results of her meeting in Paris – about gloves, belts and handbags for the winter season – with as much enthusiasm as she could muster. But somehow she was finding it difficult to stay focussed on business. Instead her thoughts kept drifting back to Bordeaux and Dick Routledge. After Dick had left she had luxuriated for half an hour in a warm bath, and then called down for cafe complet to be served in her room. She walked out of the hotel into the mid-morning sunlight, fully intending to spend Saturday and most of Sunday in the city. But somehow without Dick it hardly seemed worthwhile to stay on, and she had ended up by checking out after lunch and catching the afternoon flight back to Stockholm. She was home in time to read a bedtime story to her son, Stefan, and to enjoy her mother's meatballs in pepper sauce, sitting with her in front of the television.

On the face of it, there was no possible justification for her to be getting serious about him. They'd talked for an hour or so on that flight, and then enjoyed an amusing evening in Dusseldorf. She smiled at the irresistible recollection of his face when that hotel porter had stopped them in the corridor – like a small boy being told his birthday treat was to be cancelled. And now another dinner and one night together in Bordeaux. A very nice night, but just a few hours after all. Add up all their time together, and it came to less than twenty four hours. *And here I am, mooning over him as though I'd found her soul mate. Perhaps it was a sex thing?* She had not been entirely truthful when she had implied to Dick Routledge that he was her first lover since the break from her husband. There had been lovers before the final break, when she had sought refuge from the escalating jealous arguments at home, and a couple of affairs afterwards, neither lasting longer than a month. For several months now though she been living like a dedicated nun, simply concentrating on work and young Stefan, and ignoring the opportunities around her. *And then along came this big Englishman, obviously with a good marriage, who seemed to be really interested in me and my life, and I just fell into his arms – and into his bed. Did we truly made love four times? I've never done that before, even when I was an eager teenager, twenty years ago.* He wasn't the world's greatest lover, but he knew how to please a woman, and he made up in enthusiasm and sheer power whatever he might lack in finesse.

What could the future hold for us? Supposing, just supposing I wanted it, might he give up his family to be with me? Not very likely, she thought. He would possibly even back off if she hinted at the idea.

On the other hand, there is that standing invitation from the Buying Director of Baines Department Stores, based in London.

"I think you're very good at your work, Brit. Any time you feel like making a complete break from Sweden, just give me a call. I'm quite certain I could find you a good job in England, with a lot more money too."

She remembered that he had been talking quietly as he covered her hand with his, towards the end of a very good dinner at a buyers' conference in Amalfi. And he had suggested not much later that she might like to come up for a nightcap . . . Still, the offer had been there. *How might Dick react if I were living in London, instead of Stockholm?* He had talked over dinner about the plans he was making to set up breakfast cereal companies all over Europe, and how much he was looking forward to arranging meetings with her in each country. *Perhaps a mistress living in London would be uncomfortably close to home? Less international glamour, even a little threatening perhaps?* He had promised to call her later in the week, to see if they could make another date. Northern Italy was a possibility, she was due a visit to some of the fashion houses in Milan, and Dick had said something about him making a trip to Parma. She looked up at the big map of Europe that decorated the wall of her office, opposite her desk. *Stop thinking like a lovesick baby, and enjoy him while you've got him.* Milan was over a hundred kilometres from Parma, so there would be some travelling required for them to be together. *Unless Dick stays with me, in Milan? That would make sense, there are good flight connections to Milan from Stockholm, and no doubt from England too. Then how would he get from Milan to Parma? Was there a train?* She reflected that Dick was a senior executive in his corporation, and an experienced traveller too. No doubt he could find a way if he wanted to. *Will he want to? How much does it matter to me if he does or does not?* She could see his lop-sided boyish grin, feel that slight limp from the old rugby injury to his knee as he walked with his arm around her beside the Garonne, and she knew that Dick was already a large and important factor in her life. *It matters a lot.*

On Monday evening, after Billy had been tucked up, Jennifer shared a pizza in the kitchen with her Dutch au pair Greta, and was agreeably surprised to find her quite enthusiastic and down-to-earth about France.

"You are very kind to consult with me about your plans, Mrs. Hawkins. I think it would be most interesting to live in France for a while. Will I have an increase in my wages?"

She had no difficulty in booking their flights to Biarritz via the internet for the following Sunday, but the hotel was more complicated. The web site for the Hotel du Palais came up 'fully booked for these dates', so rather than look for another hotel she decided to telephone.

"I would like two double rooms for two nights, this coming Sunday and Monday, please"

"Je regrette, Madame, there are no rooms available. On Saturday we commence the annual Congres du Surf. You understand this famous competition brings in clients from all over the world. Our rooms were reserved from last year already."

Jennifer persisted. "I want so much for my young son to see the surfing. Really, money is not a problem if you can help me at this time."

There was a short silence. "Per'aps Madame could give me a number to call, and I will speak wit' the manager."

The telephone rang within ten minutes. "I am ver' content to be able to offer Madame a fine solution. The manager keeps always one of our best suites, in case we 'ave a request from an important homme d'affaires or perhaps, as last year, a prince. As we are now just a few days before the Congres, he thinks to offer this to you. You 'ave a balcon sur le mer, two chambres avec salles de bain et une tres jolie salle. Mais certainement Madame, it is not inexpensive, vous comprenez?"

"How expensive is that?"

"For two nights, that will be three t'ousand two 'undred euros, tax et petit dejeuner compris."

Jennifer did the arithmetic in her head – just over two thousand pounds for two nights! On the other hand, her income was just accruing now in the bank, not really doing anything . . .

"That will be fine, I'll take it"

"Bien, Madame, I wonder per'aps if you 'ave there a credit card, and we could complete the reservation. Will I also reserve for you a place for dinner?"

It was just six-thirty when Dick got home, to find Rosemary dressed in a new pale grey linen suit with a dark green blouse, obviously getting impatient.

"You're late, Dick," she said accusingly, "Was it so difficult to get away from Jennifer Hawkins?"

Dick was all injured innocence. "I promise you, I left the Hawkins' house over an hour ago. I've been back to the office to tidy up a few loose ends. Anyway, what am I supposed to be late for?"

"You know very well, we're due at the school for seven o'clock. We're supposed to have a little chat with the Head about how the boys have been getting on, then it's the end of term concert at eight. James is in the choir, remember? And Peter is acting as usher. They're both there already."

"Damn, I thought that was tomorrow." He looked at his watch, "I'm really sorry, darling. I'll take ten minutes to shave and change, then we'll make seven all right. Chances are they'll be running late anyway."

Rosemary sat down and took several slow deep breaths, which was her sovereign cure for bad temper. *Dick had apologised nicely, and it was easy enough to get the days mixed up . . . but why did it have to happen on the day he was visiting Jennifer Hawkins? You're getting paranoid, Rosemary. Dick is a good husband and father, and you've no possible reason to think otherwise.* Sure enough at ten to seven he was clattering down the staircase, looking very spruce in a dark blue pinstripe suit.

"Will I do? I like your new suit, by the way. Has your waist got slimmer?"

She kissed him lightly on the cheek. "Thanks for the compliment. You look fine, very much the executive husband. Let's go and intimidate that headmaster."

Chapter Twelve

Dick had intended to call his father at home on Monday evening, but it was after ten by the time he got home from the school concert, with Rosemary and the boys still chattering excitedly, and he decided he was just too tired for a serious business discussion – and he guessed that James would probably be having an early night anyway, after his game of golf. On Tuesday morning was at his desk by a quarter to eight. He was feeling unusually lethargic, and wondered if the exertions of his trip to Bordeaux might be catching up with him. He made himself concentrate.

"Elizabeth, I'd like a word with the Chairman as soon as he arrives, please."

"Very good, Mr. Dick, I'll tell him. It's usually just before ten on Tuesdays, if that's all right?"

"Fine. I'll probably be with Jim Helvin. And come and get me if Jean Paul calls."

For a few minutes Dick sat quietly at his desk and leafed through the contents of his in-tray. There were three brochures from property agents about factories for sale in various European countries – there seemed to be more of those every month. Requests from other ACP divisions or from head office for his comments on this magazine or that newspaper report about trends and prospects in Europe. A syndicated research report on the history and future growth possibilities of the market for breakfast cereals in each member country of the EU. Two commentaries about the future of the Euro currency – from the headline summaries they seemed to be totally conflicting. Confirmation from his Managing Director in Germany that all the contracts were now in place for the senior staff. A special and private study that John Savage had prepared, about the real problems of operating in Italy. Elizabeth had pinned that together with an e-mail received overnight from Ben Camina, ACP's deputy Chief Executive and Chief Operating and Financial Officer:

Sorry to hear about Alain Robarte. Please carry on with the temporary finance manager appointment as you propose. If Alain is seriously incapacitated for the future, remember that we do have a very generous insurance plan for senior managers which could kick in for him.

On another subject, our people in Parma, Italy have done well with our corn oil, and have now suggested that they could be ready by next Spring to market a Cornflake, to be made for them in France, (or Germany?). Assuming you and James are still in favour, may I suggest you make an early call to our MD there, Pietro Cavalli, with a view to working up a plan together for board approval please? regards, Ben.

Dick's thoughts immediately switched to Brit Carlsohn. Resting in the Bordeaux hotel bedroom after one strenuous session of making love, they had talked about meeting elsewhere in Europe, and Italy had been mentioned. Brit had said that she did not buy very much there, but the big Italian fashion houses like Armani, Gucci and Ferragamo would like to be better represented in her store group, and so were always pleased to see her in Milan. To maintain contact she made a practice of going once or twice a year. He had mentioned the possibility of a trip to Parma – and then the subject had been abandoned as they had slipped down the bed, into another voyage of discovery. Dick smiled at the vivid recollection of Brit's slim, agile body. *I'll do something about Italy this afternoon. Just now I need to focus on France.*

He found Jim Helvin with a pile of faxes spread all over his table. He was not very cheerful.

"Well, the French bank has come through with the last six months' statements. I had to ask for six months because there will be quite long lags between invoices out and payments received, and ditto for payments out of course."

"Anything meaningful?"

"I'll need a day or two to load the detail onto my computer and compare the totals in with the totals out. Then I'll need to analyse monthly trends and so on. Fortunately we've got just the one monthly payment going out to the payroll account, but it's still going to be fiendish difficult. It's not as though I've got one of their people on hand here to identify who's what. But I'll get there, don't worry. And just to be on the safe side, I've asked the French bank to send me the payroll account, and confirm that there are no other related or connected accounts."

Dick went over what John Savage had said. Jim Helvin's reaction was non-committal.

"It's not so difficult for Mr. Savage to say, 'If there's a discrepancy do this, if there's not, do that.' The problem's goin' to be deciding' whether or no' there *is* a hole. And I'm not makin' any progress chatting with yersel', Mr. Dick"

Dick raised a hand to signify that he understood Jim's message, and retreated towards his own office. Elizabeth came in before he had sat down.

"The Chairman arrived a few minutes ago, Mr. Dick, and he's expecting you when you're ready." Anticipating Dick's next request she added, "Don't worry, I'll bring the tea into you."

When Dick walked into his father's big corner office he found him standing at one of the two windows that looked out onto the tranquil sunlit waters of the River Lyn, and the bright green of the grassy slopes known as 'Crabbe's Marsh' on the far bank.

"Morning like this, Dick, sun shining and birds singing, I wonder what the hell I'm doing in the office. Why do we bother?"

Dick pulled up a leather-seated chair and sat down in front of his desk.

"Because within a month we'd be climbing up the walls at home, and we actually enjoy what we do. Mostly."

James sighed and sat down himself, "You're right, of course. So how are things? Anything new from France? Elizabeth told me about Alain Robarte. Bad business, bad business. How badly hurt is he?"

"He was clubbed around the head, so it's not good. Jean Paul says they think he's stable, and they'll operate to relieve the pressure on the brain in a few days' time. Meantime he's unconscious of course, and the Bordeaux police are digging around."

James was instantly alert. "What about you? Do you think there's any connection to be made? Will the police want to question you?

Dick went over his conversation with John Savage. "John was pretty clear that I have nothing to contribute at the moment, so I'm quite justified in keeping quiet unless I'm actually asked for information. Jim Helvin is going through the bank statements now, and if he comes up with anything we'll have to think of consulting Ben."

"Hell's teeth, I just hope we don't have to involve the Yanks. If Ben gets dragged in, he'll have to bring in their corporate accountants and lawyers, and we'll be snowed under with damned position statements and depositions and responsibility analyses and heaven knows what else."

Suddenly multinational business seemed to have lost some of its charm. Dick went over the plan to bring in an Interim Finance manager. "Jean's idea – strikes me as very smart."

"Nice to hear she's still earning her corn. Let's hope you can find a real tiger, but it sounds promising. Did you say that the CVs would be available today?"

"No, I'm pretty sure Jean said she was expecting them Wednesday, that's tomorrow afternoon. Do I take it that you'd like to have a look at them? We're planning to do the interviewing on Thursday."

James made a point of consulting his diary before answering. "No, no, I'll trust Jean to stop you getting the wrong man. But I'm planning to be in all day on Friday, so if you find your man on Thursday you could ask him back on Friday if you like, just to say 'hullo', if you know what I mean? And perhaps you and

Jean should be giving some thought to how much you're going to tell him about Alain's injury and this funny number business."

"Fair enough." He passed over the e-mail from Ben. "I take it you're still in favour of me making a start in Italy?"

"Especially as we don't have to build a factory there, at least not yet. You'll find it gets a bit fraught when you start to negotiate for the plant, and we have to promise to buy ludicrous quantities of Italian maize of uncertain quality in order to get planning permissions, and grease palms left right and centre for every other damn thing. Mind you, the compensation is that nobody seems to bother much with paying taxes, so it may even out in the long run."

"I take it you've been reading John Savage's report about doing business in Italy."

"I have. I get the impression that not a lot has changed since the Borgias were arranging things. And it gets nastier as you go south of Rome. There the bandits may nail you to the wall, whereas in the north they just strip you to your underpants. Anyway, I can see you're keen to conquer another country and extend the Routledge empire, so good luck in Parma. You'll like Pietro, by the way. Just don't introduce Rosemary to him."

As Dick left his father was still smirking at this parting remark, and he worked out the implications as he crossed the reception area to his own office in the other corner. *I suppose Pietro must be a bit of a lad for the ladies. We should definitely get on well, but I don't quite see us comparing notes. So, time to call Brit. Who knows, France last week, Italy next. It's a tough job, but somebody's got to do it.*

His jacket was on the back of his chair as usual, and he felt in the little inside ticket pocket for her card. *Damn, it's in the other suit, of course.* A momentary feeling of panic went through him, as he imagined Rosemary finding it.

'So, who's this Brit Carlsohn then? And why have you kept her card tucked away like this?'

'Just a lady I sat next to on a flight, my love. I chatted about the business, and she said that, if we were looking at starting up in Sweden, she knew a lot of people in the Government, because her father had been a Member of Parliament. So of course when she offered her card I kept it.'

'Pretty, was she?'

'Dunno, handsome, I'd say. Slightly hard-bitten, perhaps. Close-cropped grey hair, tall, lean, about ten years older than me.'

That should go down all right, he thought. The chances of Rosemary ever meeting Brit must be pretty close to zero. He tried to remember her Stockholm telephone number, but could get no farther than 0046 8. He dialled International Directory Enquiries, scribbled the full number on a scrap of paper, and within a few seconds his heart was beating faster as he listened to the long continental ringing tones.

"Good afternoon, Steen und Strom."

Not Brit's voice! He spoke slowly, "Good afternoon, I am calling from England. May I speak with Brit Carlsohn. please?"

There was a long pause, then another woman's voice, with an accent he thought might be German rather than Swedish. "You vant spik wit' Brit? I regret, she is not here for one hour more. Will I say to her you call? Or some message to give?"

"Yes, thank you. Mr. Routledge called. That's R.O.U.T . . ."

"Zank you, Herr Routledge. I vill tell her."

Dick was left holding the receiver as the phone was abruptly cut off. Perhaps he had offended the woman by offering to spell his name? He looked at his watch. Half-past eleven. Of course, it would be lunchtime already in Stockholm. Probably he had interrupted the woman's smorgasbrod or something. He looked up as Elizabeth came in carrying a tray.

"I thought you might like another cup of tea. And while you were on the phone Mrs Hawkins called. She would be most grateful if you would call her back before lunch."

Dick kept his face straight, as a couple of lines from a song floated into his head.

'*How happy could I be with either,*
were t' other dear charmer away.'

. . . *was that Gilbert and Sullivan? Or something else?*

"Thank you, Elizabeth. Perhaps you could try Mrs. Hawkins now for me. I expect it's to do with opening the HR Wing in October. Did you hear that we might be getting Princess Anne?"

He was carefully tearing up the scrap of paper he had used to note down Brit's phone number when the call came through.

Jennifer's voice was deep and warm. "Dick! Thank you so much for getting back to me. It's about France. You remember we talked about the place on the coast near Bordeaux, Arcachon?"

"Mmmm. Any progress?"

"Quite a lot, I'd say. I've got particulars of some properties available now, and also the names of the local agents. They say there'll be masses on offer once August is over. Greta is surprisingly amenable, and we're all flying to Biarritz on Sunday to stay a couple of nights, then I thought I'd rent a car and go on to Arcachon on the Tuesday."

Dick entertained a brief fantasy of a weekend in Biarritz with Jennifer. He could just imagine the two of them running down a big sandy beach into the rollers, her glorious body in a bikini . . .

"So you'll want that introduction to Arlette and Jean Paul?"

"If it's not too inconvenient for them, yes please."

"Well, I know they're going away at the end of July, but that leaves almost two weeks still, well, one week starting next Monday. And really it's not a very big place. I'd have thought that Arlette could show or tell you what you needed to know in a day or two. Let me have a word with Jean-Paul, and I'll get back to you after lunch, if that's all right?"

"Wonderful. And I really am grateful for your support, Dick."

How grateful is grateful? Of course he couldn't possibly go to Biarritz for the weekend. But he could certainly see a requirement to go to the factory in Belin quite soon . . . might she still be in Arcachon?

He stretched, and walked next door to Elizabeth's office. "Elizabeth, it's time I called Jean-Paul for an update on Alain. Could you get him for me please?"

Within half a minute Jean-Paul was answering.

"Ah, Dick, but quelle coincidence! I was a ce moment about to call you!"

"So, is there some news?"

"Oui, oui, and ver' bad news, I'm afraid. Alain est mort. 'E died a few minutes ago, still unconscious. The 'opital, they make an emergency surgery, but they could not save 'im. Je suis desole. Sa femme, Viola, she was there by the bed, she telephone me of course. We were all good friends, you know, Arlette also. C'est terrible, terrible."

"Jean-Paul, I am so sorry. Of course I didn't know him well, but he was a very good man, no doubt at all. I would like to be told about the funeral, in case one of us can come from here to represent ACP?"

"Funeral? Ah, oui, l'office des morts. Je regrette that there can be no date for that yet. Viola tells me that there must be une autopsie, and that no-one knows when the police will give back le cadavre. This is now une homicide, vous comprennez?"

"Murder, yes." Dick's brain was racing, trying to calculate how much the situation had now changed. He decided to plunge in with the truth. "Jean-Paul, I think you know that I had a short meeting with Alain at my hotel on Thursday evening?"

"Oui, 'e told me. 'E was distrait, an' tell me that you suspect something bad. I am ver' sorry, Dick, to know that you do not trust my explaining."

"Jean-Paul, if I have upset you I apologise. From my point of view it seemed perfectly possible that you were telling me just what Alain had told you, without perhaps having had the time to investigate thoroughly for yourself. Anyway, I do need to know if the police have been told about my meeting with Alain?"

"Not by me, Dick. When I talk to the inspecteur, I am believing that Alain has been attacked by a voleur or some terrible madman, so I saw no reason to mention our little betise." There was a perceptible pause before he continued. "I do not think it would be wise at this time to raise such a matter with the police, do you?"

Dick wondered if that was just strain he heard in Jean-Paul's voice, or was it even a note of pleading?

"I agree, Jean-Paul, there is no reason for me to involve myself at this time." He remembered Ben's e-mail. "You know that our senior managers are covered by a very generous company insurance policy? Perhaps you may find an occasion to tell his wife, what was she called?"

"Viola."

"Viola, yes, pretty name. Perhaps you could tell Viola that there will be a large sum of money to help her. Any children?"

"No children, non. Mais Alain say to me last week when 'e came to diner chez nous that they were so 'appy in Bordeaux an' confortable wit' 'is work an' ze company, an' that now is a good time to start a family. So per'aps they are already trying, si vous comprennez?"

"Yes, I see. Well, tell Viola she will be well looked after, and I will get Jean Savage to send some detail to you by the end of the week. Jean-Paul, I know this is a very bad time for you, but can I ask you a personal favour please?"

"Naturellement. 'Ow can I 'elp?"

"You remember I mentioned about a family friend, a widow with a young son, Mrs. Jennifer Hawkins?"

"Oui. She was thinking of coming to Arcachon, non?"

"That's it. Well, she'll be flying over to Biarritz on Sunday with her son and his nanny, and coming on to Arcachon by car on Tuesday. I wonder if you could find them rooms in a good hotel for, say, Tuesday through Sunday of next week? Money's not a problem for her, I think, so somewhere special if you can. And I was wondering if Arlette . . .?"

"Of course, Arlette will be very pleased, no problem. It will take her thinking away from this terrible affair, sans doute. I will talk wit' her about the lady ce soir. I will book the 'otel, an' e-mail you with her ideas tomorrow, and send you also our mobile telephone number so that Madame Jennifer can call us from Biarritz Dimanche soir to make arrangements. Ca va?"

"Excellent, Jean-Paul, you are a good friend. Please, remember to give my deepest sympathy to Viola. I will get things moving about the insurance I mentioned. And of course I will be in touch again by Friday with the information about the Interim Finance manager. A bientot, then."

Dick put down the telephone, and immediately Elizabeth came in and picked up his tray. "While you were talking to Jean-Paul a lady telephoned from Stockholm. She said she was just returning your call, and would not leave a name or a message. Is there a number I can get for you?"

Elizabeth's disapproval was almost palpable. Dick knew how proud she was of her status in the company – it could be very awkward indeed if she were tempted to say something about Stockholm to any of her wide circle of friends and relatives in Lynchester. A thing like that could easily get back to Rosemary.

"Not for the moment, thank you Elizabeth. I was just calling the Town Hall there to ask them to send me in any information they might have about factories for sale in Sweden. But I don't think I'm up to doing any more for the time being. That was bad news from Jean-Paul, by the way. Alain has just died without regaining consciousness. So the police are now treating it as murder. I need to think things through a bit, so I would be grateful if you would treat this information as confidential for the time being. I'd like to tell the Chairman myself after lunch, when I'm ready. One thing that would be nice though. I wonder if you could get me a sandwich from the canteen? Anything with ham or any other cold meat in it. And an apple, please. I'd like to take it out and have a quiet picnic by the river."

The stretch of grassy bank with a low stone wall between the river and the factory building was the site of the old mill wheel that used to power the factory, and was still part of Strongwheat's land, and so technically private. But by long tradition it was open to the public as part of the walk along the river bank, and was also popular as a good spot to fish. It was empty though today, apart from a young couple whom Dick thought he recognised from the factory. He sat on the grass ten yards away from them, and noticed that they got up a minute or two later and walked on, leaving him alone with his thoughts. Across the river was Crabbe's Marsh, so called because it had usually been flooded during the winter, when the river rose. Now however the banks had been raised and stabilised by the construction works for the Hawkins Mall, which was just upstream to his left. It was a tall T-shaped building faced with cream stone, with groups of four high narrow windows at regular intervals all around, giving it an almost Gothic look. He chewed a very good ham sandwich on thickly-buttered crusty new bread, and looking at the Mall made Dick think of Jennifer Hawkins. He realised that he was actually looking forward to hearing that soft, warm voice again. Should he feel guilty?

I've got to call Jennifer this afternoon, and she's sure to be very pleased with the promise of help from Arlette when she gets to Arcachon. Pleased and grateful, no doubt. Am I just fantasising to think that I might take things further? Dick smiled at his own euphemism. *By 'take things further' I mean 'get into bed with her, add her to my harem', don't I? Rosemary is a lovely wife, I'm sure no man could ask for better. And she's bringing up two fine sons for me.* He crunched a final bite from the apple, and threw the core far out into the slow-moving stream. *And yet I've allowed myself to be drawn into a relationship already with Brit. What would Rosemary say about that?* Try as best he could, he could not imagine what would happen if she ever found out. *I really don't need any more complications at the moment. When I talk to Jennifer I'll keep it cool and friendly. Perhaps I might even suggest that she should come over and have dinner with us sometime, maybe with Mum and Dad there, and we could gossip about the Hawkins Wing and Princess Anne . . .*

Dick stood up and dusted himself down. *On the other hand, perhaps the farther apart I can keep them, the safer it's going to be. But then why does that matter, as I'm not going to get involved with Jennifer anyway. Am I?*

Chapter Thirteen

Jennifer Hawkins was not accustomed to being kept waiting, and by two o'clock she was prowling restlessly around the house, willing the telephone to ring. She finally sat down on the big swing-seat outside the french windows of her dining room and leafed through a copy of 'Country Life'. Those impossibly immaculate, so desirable houses in acres of pristine English countryside . . . who could afford such outrageous prices? *You could, Jennifer, if you wanted to. Perhaps not immediately, but after the Mall has matured for another couple of years you should be seriously rich. And lonely?*

She was intuitive enough to admit to herself that Billy having started school was probably a big contributor to her feelings of restless uncertainty. Already he was starting to chatter more and more about his classmates in the nursery school, his teacher and the events of his day, and to resist her attempts to cuddle him. She could foresee the inexorable widening of the distance between Billy and herself as he became more self-reliant. *And that was how things should be. A mother's love should enable a boy to stand tall and confident of his place in the world, not strangle him with her apron-strings. But lacking a husband, lacking other children to worry about, what am I to do with my life?* Was Dick Routledge too a cause of this tumble of disjointed feelings that surged through her? *If he'd been offhand, or just been ordinarily polite, I wouldn't have thought twice about him. But there's something else there, I felt it when we were together yesterday. He's reaching out for something. Perhaps he doesn't know it, but he is. And I think it could be me.* She grinned to herself as she turned a page to look at a photograph of a very nice looking girl from Hampshire who, it seemed, was about to marry some sprig of the nobility from Sussex. *Just suppose a Hawkins ran off with a Routledge . . . wouldn't that cause a stir in Lynchester!* She jumped convulsively as the telephone rang at last, and glanced at her watch – almost three o'clock. She walked slowly through to the kitchen, took a deep breath, waited, and then picked up the receiver on the sixth double ring.

"Hullo, Jennifer Hawkins."

"Jennifer, hullo, it's Dick Routledge. Sorry not to have got back to you earlier, but things have been a bit fraught."

Jennifer wondered out of curiosity what 'fraught' implied, but decided not to ask.

"It's very good of you to call anyway, Dick. I know just how hectic things can get in business. So, what's the news?

"Good and bad, I suppose. Jean-Paul will find a nice place in Arcachon for you to stay next week, and he'll e-mail me probably tomorrow the details and a telephone number where you can get hold of him from Biarritz over the weekend. He's sure Arlette, his wife, will be delighted to show you around."

"That's everything I could have hoped for, Dick, and I'm really grateful."

There was an unmistakeable warmth, an invitation even, in Jennifer's tone. Dick tried to ignore it and remain calm.

"There is a problem that you should be aware of, which could be awkward for you next week. Jean-Paul has just lost his financial manager, a man called Alain Roberte. When I say 'lost', I should tell you that he's been murdered. He was bludgeoned about the head by the river bank in Bordeaux on Saturday evening, and he's died now in hospital, this morning. So don't be surprised if Jean-Paul seems a bit distracted, he's under a lot of pressure. Well, to be honest I suppose we all are."

"Oh Dick, that's so awful. A murder? Wouldn't it be better if I just looked after myself? I'm sure I can manage, and there'll be lots of estate agents keen to help."

Dick thought for a moment. He had actually expected Jennifer to make this offer. Probably it would indeed be better for Jean-Paul not to have Jennifer to worry about. On the other hand some instinct urged him to maintain contact – provided of course he was simply being helpful to a fellow member of the Lynchester community . . .

"I did press Jean-Paul about that, but he insisted there would be no difficulty in looking after you. To be frank, I expect that Arlette will be the one to do anything that needs doing, and she's got this little boy too who's about a year older than Billy. It might be fun for you to see how Billy copes with a French boy, and vice-versa. I think you could reasonably expect Arlette to be with you for a day or so to help you look around, and perhaps she'll ask you to dinner at their house."

Jennifer saw no need to press Dick any further about taking up Jean-Paul's time. Instead she thought this might be the opportunity to put to the test her intuition about Dick's interest in herself.

"I'll take your advice, Dick, and call Jean-Paul on Sunday evening, but I'll try hard not to be too much of a nuisance. I expect I'll stay in Arcachon for a week at least, possibly two. Is there any likelihood that you will need to come over? I was thinking, dinner in the best restaurant would be the least I could offer, to say thank you for being really helpful."

'*The least I could offer*'. As Dick listened to her voice he was reminded of Jennifer's profile as she had sat beside him, the huge dark eyes and the full lips, the hint of voluptuousness in her body. He was tempted to give her a 'strong maybe', if nothing else as a way of keeping the conversation going for a few minutes more. But he remembered his decision on the river bank, and kept his answer cool but friendly.

"Wouldn't that be nice, Jenny! But I'm off on holiday myself for a fortnight with the family, leaving at the end of next week. We've rented an apartment in Salcombe and booked the boys onto a week's sailing course. Do you know Salcombe?"

Jennifer tried her best to hide her disappointment. "I don't, no. Where is it?"

"It's the most southerly point of Devon, about halfway between Dartmouth and Plymouth. Nice sheltered estuary, old port and one-time wooden ship-building town. Now a super dinghy-sailing place. And the boys will be having sailing lessons from this old Mersey ferry called 'Egremont' for their first week, so Ros and I will have some time off. We're going to play some golf, and she's promised to come sailing with me too, as long as there's not too much wind."

Jennifer recognised that he was regretting some of the previous day's openness, and, guessing that her timing had been wrong, decided to cut her losses.

"Sounds lovely. I must go, Dick, I can hear Greta arriving back with Billy. I look forward then to a call from you later in the week with the details about Jean-Paul."

The hour between the end of Dick's peaceful lunch by the river and his call to Jennifer had indeed been very fraught. Elizabeth had come into his office as soon as she heard him return.

"Oh, Mr. Dick, I'm so glad your back. There was an important call from France, and I didn't know where to find you."

Dick had never seen Elizabeth so agitated – she prided herself, he knew, on being a model of calm competence. He tried to be soothing.

"Now, Elizabeth, you know I never go far without telling you. I was just sitting on the grass by the river, enjoying that very good ham sandwich from the canteen. Anyway, I'm back now, so how can I help?"

"You had a call from Bordeaux, a policeman, M'sieur St. Just. I've typed everything on this sheet of paper for you. Perhaps you'll let me know when you want me to call him back."

She placed the typed half-sheet in front of him on the desk and left. Dick knew that she was far from mollified, but decided as he read the note that he could understand why.

Monsieur St. Just telephoned at 13.35pm. He said that he was the Commissaire de Police in Bordeaux and in charge of the investigation into the murder of Alain Robarte. He wishes to interview you urgently on a matter of grave importance. If he came over to England, could he meet you in your office at 9 a.m. tomorrow?

Interview? Murder? Grave importance? Tomorrow! No wonder Elizabeth's alarm bells had started ringing! Dick knew that he had no choice but to meet this St. Just. The question was, what was he going to ask? And if it was about Alain's visit to his hotel room, how much should he reveal about the reason for it? First things first – an early call back to Bordeaux would suggest he had nothing to hide. He looked down at the pad on his desk – he had been absent-mindedly doodling while he thought it through – a circle, with arrows entering it from all sides. *That's me, Saint Sebastian of Lynchester!* He walked into Elizabeth's office.

"I see the Chairman's office door is closed. Is he in?"

"He had a salad at his desk, Mr. Dick, but I'm sure he's finished now. You could just knock and go in, I'm sure. Isn't it awful to have the French police . . ."

Dick cut her short. "It's just routine. Perhaps this Commissaire fancies a trip to England, who knows? Anyway, can I leave him to you? Tell him nine o'clock is fine, and I'm keeping the morning clear for him. If he's intending to travel directly here for nine, he's going to be catching the Bordeaux to Paris flight soon after six in the morning I should think, so you could offer to have our driver meet him at Birmingham Airport. Or if he's coming over this evening, you could offer to book him a room at the Belfry, and have him collected in the morning. Let's try to make him welcome."

Elizabeth looked pleased to have the responsibility handed back to her, and was picking up the telephone as Dick left her office. He decided to look in on Jim Helvin first, just on the off chance that there might be some progress. Jim looked up balefully from the mass of paper on his desk.

"I said it would take some time, Mr. Dick, but it won't get done at all if you keep interruptin' . . ."

Dick raised his hands palm out to signify a truce, and put Elizabeth's little note down in front of him. Jim read it carefully and nodded.

"Murder now, is it? When did Alain die?"

"About an hour ago. No, two."

"I see, and now it's really gettin' serious. You're goin' to be asked if we have any evidence of anythin' that could suggest a reason for murder, a motive, right?"

Dick sat down heavily. "I don't want to put words in your mouth, Jim, but if there's anything at all coming out, could you tell me, please?"

Jim was willing to be helpful, but his natural caution would not let him say much. "I've been at it two or three hours only, and you're not the only one who's found it necessary to interrupt me, so there's nothin' yet definite at all. Nothin' definite, y'understand? Not the sort of thing you'd want to go blabbin' off to the police about."

"But there is something?"

"Aye, there's somethin'. When I go through the statements I can see that, over the last four months, the gross payments through the account have gone up about thirty percent. That's quite a bit more than the growth of the sales, so there's somethin' a wee bit odd to look into. But it's no more than that at the moment, somethin' to be looked into."

"How long, Jim, before you know more?"

"I canna' say for sure, an' this is no time to rush to judgement, you'll agree." He looked down at the e-mail again. "This Commissaire chappie is coming at nine tomorrow. I'll be workin' at this till late this evening, and in here early tomorrow, so why don't you look in just before your meetin', and I'll give you the best steer then that I can. Will that do?"

"I'll owe you one, Jim."

Dick knocked and walked into his father's office. The lunch tray had been pushed to the side of his desk, and he was reading a bound document with a red cover, which Dick recognised as John Savage's report about the pitfalls of doing business in Italy. He looked at Dick over the top of his gold-rimmed half-glasses.

"I was thinking that I might have put the fear of God into you about Italy. If you read between the lines you get the impression that John is really just being ultra-cautious. I don't suppose . . ." His voice died away as he saw the grim expression on Dick's face.

"I should have come in to tell you straight away after I'd spoken to Jean-Paul, just before lunch, but, well, I suppose I was a bit upset. It's Alain, Dad, you know, the financial guy in Belin. He's died. So now it's a murder case."

"Damnation! And that changes everything, doesn't it."

"It does. Elizabeth took a call during the lunch hour from a M'sieur St. Just. He's the Commissaire de Police in charge of the case. And he's coming here to interview me at nine tomorrow morning. His telephone call sounded quite serious, I'd say."

He gave his father Elizabeth's note to read. James took off his glasses and rubbed his eyes. "He can't make you talk to him."

"No, but I'm sure I should."

"Yes, I think you should too. We don't want to give the impression that we have something to hide . . . But should you have a solicitor with you? Frankly, Dick, I'm out of my depth here. Any ideas about getting advice?"

Dick stood up and walked to the window. His father had dropped the venetian blind to cut out the glare of the afternoon sun, but through the half-closed slats he could see two swans swimming in stately line astern across the river, breaking up the glitter of the sunlight as they moved and leaving behind a shimmering wake. Everything was so *normal* out there!

"Well, I can't see Henry Lovatt being much use." Henry was the company's solicitor in Lynchester, and had been for twenty years.

"Henry's sound on wills, contracts and property, but he'd be faffing in the deep end like us in a murder case. Especially a foreign murder case. And somehow I dont see this being up John Savage's street, either."

"Which leaves us with Oliver?" Dick sounded very uncertain.

Oliver Sedburgh had been a non-executive director of Strongwheat up to the time of its acquisition by ACP. He was one of James' oldest friends, and a senior partner in London in one of the top six accountancy firms.

"Well, it's certainly not Oliver's area of expertise. But his judgement is pretty sound, and he'll definitely know where to get good advice. Sit tight there for a minute and let's get Elizabeth to call him."

Dick sat back and looked at his scratch pad with its scrawled list of 'things to do'.

Call Jennifer and Brit

Call Pietro in Parma. Go next week?

Confirm recruitment details for Wuppertal, Germany, to ACP Corporate

Talk to Jean about company insurance for Alain's wife, Viola.

Check that there are no hitches re Interim Manager CVs – due tomorrow.

Talk again with Jim.

?Tell Jean-Paul about St. Just coming?

Get back to Jennifer before Friday with info from Jean-Paul.

Check with Ros that everything was fixed for the holiday.

"Hullo, Oliver? It's James. I trust you're in rude health? Yes, indeed. Can you spare us a few minutes to talk, we've got a serious problem? I'm grateful. I've got Dick here, and he knows more of the detail than I do. I'll just put him on."

Dick went over the history of the peculiar monthly figures, Jean-Paul's not entirely convincing explanation, the meeting with Alain Robarte and the subsequent murderous attack on him.

"You can see, Oliver, that it's all a bit circumstantial. I mean we don't know if there's really anything amiss with the figures yet, and we don't know if there's any connection to the murder. But now the Commissaire de Police from Bordeaux wants to come over tomorrow to interview me, and it's getting serious, I think. So we're wondering, is there anyone you know who could advise us, well me particularly, what I should be saying tomorrow to this Commissaire when he comes?"

Oliver was silent for a few seconds. "I agree, Dick, that if a Commissaire de Police thinks it worthwhile coming to Lynchester at the drop of a hat, then it's serious and you need specialist advice. Let me dig around for an hour. I play bridge with a man who works in 'Fair Trials Abroad', or something like that. I know that's not quite the situation, at least not yet, but he'll be bound to know how French police enquiries work. I'll get on to him now, if he's in his office, and ask him to call you himself or suggest someone else. Don't worry too much, Dick, there are worse things than a month in a courtroom in Bordeaux! My regards to your father."

Dick thanked him and told his father the gist of Oliver's remarks.

"Sounds pretty good. I'd guess that they couldn't make you give evidence in person, if it came to it. I mean, you are not a material witness, are you? A sworn affidavit ought to be enough. Can we talk again after Oliver's pal has called you?"

"Should I tell ACP that Alain has died?"

"NO!" Dick looked up from his scratch pad, surprised by the vehemence of his father's reply. "At least, not yet. Let's see if Jim Helvin makes some progress, get the advice from Oliver's friend, perhaps wait until after your interview with the Commissaire. I like to be giving Ben solutions, not problems, if you see my point?"

"Fine then Dad. I'll get on, and look back before the end of the day."

Chapter Fourteen

For the rest of Tuesday afternoon, Dick was almost continuously on the telephone, working steadily through the list of 'things-to-do' from his scratch-pad.

He had felt distinctly virtuous as he finished the call to Jennifer. *I'm sure that was an invitation to something more than a dinner. And I turned it down. I suppose, if she likes Arcachon, she might move in there early in September. I'll bet the sea will still be warm, and you could easily lose yourself in those gigantic sand-dunes. Well, I will certainly have to be going over after the holidays. I will need to be touching base in Belin with our Interim Finance Manager. Jennifer's a really interesting woman though. But dangerous too, I should think. Not the sort of woman you could have a light-hearted affair with. Which reminds me . . .*

This time the telephone number was firmly in his memory.

"Brit? Hullo, it's Dick Routledge. I'm sorry I was not there when you called back. Are you recovered from the trip to France?"

"Just about, thank you Dick. I was going to stay on, but it didn't seem the same after you had gone, so I came back on Saturday afternoon."

Dick took a moment to digest this. *Was there something being left unsaid, a hint that Brit was perhaps not quite so light of heart as he had thought?* He pressed on nonetheless.

"I've missed you too, darling. In fact I thought about you this morning, which is why I called. I might be going to Parma next week, and I remembered you saying that you were due a trip to Milan. So I wondered if we could get together again?"

Since Dick had left her in that nice Bordeaux hotel bed, Brit had been thinking about him a lot, returning over and over to the affectionate way he spoke, the way he caressed her body, the attention he paid to her thoughts and opinions. He behaved like a man in love. But was he in love with her, or just with the idea of having a compliant mistress? How could she tell? She only knew that her heart bumped with excitement at the thought of seeing him again so soon.

"Well, I have finished my report on the trip to Paris, and things are winding down now in the office here as we get ready for our month of holiday in August. I will need to find out if the sales people in Milan would be ready to talk to me, though they always seem very, very, what's the word? Anxious? Wanting?"

"Eager?"

"Yes, thank you Dick, eager. Did you have any particular days in your plan?"

"I thought that I would fly to Milan on Tuesday morning, and come back on Thursday evening. So we could have two days and two nights together, though I would have to spend all day Wednesday in Parma."

"Sounds wonderful, Dick. I'm just looking in the little book I keep, and I see that both Gucci and Versace have written to me this year, asking me to come to Milan. So I'm sure I can fill up the day you are away in Parma. I will ask one of them to propose a hotel for us, so you can leave the booking to me this time."

Dick thought of Elizabeth's reaction to being told that the hotel was already booked. Not ideal perhaps, but he could tell her that Pietro was fixing things.

"That's fine, darling. I'll try to get an early flight on Tuesday so that we can meet by lunchtime and maybe see the sights. I've never been to Milan before."

"I will call you later today or tomorrow with the hotel where we will stay."

"That's good. Oh, I see from my diary that tomorrow morning I have an important meeting. I'm here all the rest of today, but if it's tomorrow that you call could it be in the afternoon, please."

"Of course. Arrivederci, darling."

Dick was still smiling as he put down the receiver. *Arrivederci! That's one word of Italian more than I know!* Next job was to talk to Jean Savage about the corporate insurance for Alain's wife, Viola. He wasn't altogether surprised to find that Jean was already up to speed when he mentioned insurance.

"I should think that Ben must have alerted ACP's Human Resource people, because I've just received an e-mail with a summary of the terms of the compensation for an executive laid off work by illness or injury. Saves me looking it up in the big blue book of staff conditions. Basically he's guaranteed full salary for six months, then two-thirds pay for another six months. Any news of Alain's progress?"

"Jean, I'm so sorry not to have told you yet, but I've been chasing round a bit. Alain is dead. He died just before lunchtime today, without ever recovering consciousness. So it was really death benefit for his wife, Viola, that I wanted to ask you about."

Jean was silent, and Dick saw that her large brown eyes were filling with tears.

"How awful. That's so sad, Dick. He was so full of life. I remember him saying how much he was looking forward to being near the sea, because he liked swimming so much. Are there any children?"

"Jean-Paul says no, but they were probably trying for one, so she could be pregnant and not know it, or not have told Jean-Paul."

"Well, I know the policy entitles the widow to a lump sum of several years' pay, plus any accrued company pension, though that wouldn't be much in Alain's case. I think there would be more for a child of Alain, if one came along, but it might be as well not to raise that possibility for the moment. I mean it could be incredibly painful for the wife to even think about – what's her name again?"

"Viola."

"Viola, right. Dick, can I suggest that you leave this to me now? I'll write, or rather e-mail to Jean-Paul, and he can then communicate as he thinks appropriate with Viola. And I'll keep you posted, of course. You will convey my deepest sympathy, won't you?"

"I will, Jean. I'm feeling pretty bad about it myself."

Dick was on his way back from Jean's office when Elizabeth came out to find him.

"There's a Mr. Sullivan on the telephone for you. Says he's calling in response to a request from Mr. Sedburgh?"

Dick caught the note of enquiry in Elizabeth's tone, and decided to try to continue to rebuild bridges by taking her into his confidence.

"Ah, yes. The chairman asked Oliver if he knew someone who could advise us about dealing with the French police. You know, the Commissaire St. Just who's coming tomorrow morning to see me? This Mr. Sullivan must be Oliver's friend. Put him through, please, Elizabeth."

Dick recognised Sullivan's accent as Southern Irish, but obviously overlaid with a lengthy exposure to upper-class English. He was brisk and business-like.

"Mr. Routledge, my name is Sullivan, Michael Sullivan. I'm a practising barrister, specialising in representing clients in criminal and civil courts on the continent of Europe. I owe Oliver Sedburgh a favour, or to be precise I owe a favour to a friend of Oliver's, so this telephone call is by way of being a free consultation for you. How can I help?"

Dick felt constrained to be as concise as possible.

"Thank you for calling, Michael. We are a breakfast cereal manufacturer, the European subsidiary group of a large US corporation called ACP. We have a newish subsidiary in France, near Bordeaux. Recently we began to suspect that there might be a financial discrepancy, but there is nothing certain about that yet, just a reasonable possibility. I went over there myself last week, and had meetings with both the Finance Manager and the Managing Director, which were . . . ah . . . inconclusive. Our people here are going through the accounts and bank statements now with a fine toothcomb, and we hope to come to a better understanding in a few days. However we have now heard that, over the weekend, the Finance Manager was the subject of a violent attack while he was out for a walk, from which he has died just this morning, making it a case of murder. A couple of hours ago we had a request from the Commissaire de Police in charge of the case, who wants to come here tomorrow first thing to interview me. I have already said 'yes'. So the question is, How should I respond? I mean, should I be totally frank? Should I have a solicitor present? I would be very grateful for your advice, Michael. By the way, I'm Dick Routledge."

"Fine, Dick. Very clear, yes." Dick waited patiently during an apparently endless interval, which was probably in reality less than a minute. "I see your difficulty. You suspect something has been going adrift in your French subsidiary, but you are by no means certain. On the other hand, if there is a problem, you're wondering if this murder is merely a coincidence, or if just by starting to investigate you may actually have triggered the attack on your Finance Manager. Without meaning to, of course?"

Dick took a deep breath before answering. Sullivan had put into words his own deepest fears. "Something like that, yes."

"Yes. Well, your Commissaire thinks it's important enough for him to come over at very short notice, and you certainly don't want to appear obstructive, that's for sure. I should warn you that, in certain types of enquiry, the French police would have quite extraordinary powers to subpoena witnesses and records, with the full support of an English court."

"What sort of cases?"

"Oddly enough, not simple murder. That's if murder ever is simple. But if it turned out to involve drugs, or international trafficking, their powers are quite tremendous. Draconian, you might say."

"I hardly think this is that sort of affair . . ."

Sullivan cut him short. "With respect, Dick, what you think is not evidence, as we say. It's what the Commissaire and his examining magistrate think that matters. Anyway I'm going to have to abbreviate our discussion, unfortunately. I have a client who has arrived slightly early for a four o'clock meeting, and I've already kept him waiting ten minutes. Not good when he's paying, if you take my point. I'll sum up, Dick, and perhaps you might like to call me again after your Commissaire has been, tomorrow. First of all, I would suggest that you do not have a solicitor present, – solicitors can make policemen feel you are trying to hide something, which may not be a good idea in this particular case. Ask him first why he needs to see you – he'll tell you the truth, I'd expect, but not necessarily the whole truth. Assuming he wants to know if there was any special reason for your visit to Bordeaux, show him whatever signs or evidence you have for being suspicious. The simple fact is that you can have absolutely no idea if there is any connection between your investigation and this crime. If he feels confident that you're being frank and open, he'll have less excuse to go on a general fishing expedition. And don't worry too much. Sounds to me as if your involvement is pretty peripheral. Bye for now."

Dick was left holding the silent telephone. He looked down at his pad, where he'd scrawled,

No solicitor. Ask why. Show evidence. Be open. Call tomorrow.

Not a lot, really, but I do feel a bit less worried, so Mr. Sullivan seems to have done the trick. Let's hope Jim Helvin has something clear and simple to show us in the morning.

Dick turned back a page on his pad, to the list of 'things to be done'. He glanced at his watch. Four-fifteen. Damnation! That meant five-fifteen in Parma, and Pietro might already have left the office. *Good job I don't have to deal with businesses in Tokyo or Los Angeles!*

"Elizabeth, could you get me Pietro Cavalli in Parma, please?"

She rang a minute later. "Signor Cavalli is visiting a client in Rome today, but will be back in the morning. His secretary is called Olivia, very helpful, speaks nice English. Is there a message?"

Dick thought quickly. Why not? "Say that I'd like to come over next week to talk about the possible breakfast cereal introduction, and could he be free on Wednesday? If his diary's clear, I'll call or send him an e-mail tomorrow."

Elizabeth came back into his office a minute later. "Wednesday next week is clear in his diary, so Olivia has reserved it for you. Would you like me to book the flights and hotel?"

"Flights, yes please. I'd like to go Birmingham/Milan, first thing on Tuesday morning, coming back Thursday afternoon. Let me talk to Pietro tomorrow about the hotel. He may have a suggestion, somewhere special. Do you know I've only ever been to Italy once in my life? And that was a school trip to Rome. Oh, Elizabeth, there is one other job, if you could help me, please."

He found the letter from Wuppertal in his in-tray.

"Werner has sent over the CV's and starting salaries for the German management team, which is complete now. Would you ask Mrs. Savage to copy it for herself and forward it to ACP Personnel for their records."

Two more items scratched off his 'to do' list. Was there anything else that wouldn't wait until the morning? Jean-Paul . . .? He decided there was every reason to keep Jean-Paul believing that he was still a trusted colleague. Should he telephone? *I don't feel strong enough for an argument with Jean-Paul.* He switched on his PC and raised the e-mail programme.

M. St. Just, the Commissaire de Police in charge of the investigation into Alain's murder, has asked if he may come here to interview me at 9 a.m. our time tomorrow, Wednesday. It seems likely that he will want to know why I came to Belin last week, and I think I must tell him about the betise *with last month's numbers. Please let me know if there is anything else you want said – or not said – at this time. warmest regards, Dick*

He read it through twice. *I bet that gets him worried!* He pressed 'send' and sat back, rubbing his eyes. *Should I talk to Dad again? Leave it till after the policeman's been . . . Just a quick check with Jean, about the Interim Finance Manager.*

He found Jean standing behind her desk, which was clear. She looked embarrassed.

"Dick, Hi. You've caught me sneaking off early. John's promised to take me to Stratford tonight. Quiet dinner by the river – it's a sort of anniversary for us. Was there something urgent?"

"Not really, I suppose. I just wanted to know if the agency was still on track to produce the CV's tomorrow for the interim for France? And does it make any difference to the plan, now that we've got to think about recruiting someone permanent?"

Jean moved firmly towards the door. "CV's are definitely coming in by hand, tomorrow morning. Shall I come in with them to you? We could think through the recruitment problem at the same time, when I've got my brain in gear."

"Well, I've got this French policeman to talk to first thing. Shall we say around eleven, please?"

He found Elizabeth clearing her desk also. "It's such a lovely evening, I called my husband and he's going to meet me in the garden of the 'Feathers' for a drink, and we might have a bite of supper there. The Chairman's already left – is there anything you need done?"

"Nothing that won't wait, Elizabeth. Have a nice evening."

"You too, Mr. Dick"

So, I seem to be forgiven there. Time to see if I'm still in Rosemary's good books.

Chapter Fifteen

Rosemary Routledge had torn up the business card she had found in Dick's pocket, and dropped the pieces with a symbolic flourish into the kitchen waste bin. But it was not so easy to put out of her mind the nagging doubts, the gnawing uncertainty of not knowing if the card had any significance. She wished now that she had simply told Dick she had found it, and asked then if he wanted it kept. That would have elicited some response, and she could then perhaps have seen through to any underlying embarrassment. But he would certainly have guessed that she was suspicious – and where was the benefit from that? They had a good, loving marriage, she thought, no money worries, two fine sons. The Routledges had a place in Lynchester society. Strongwheat was already the town's largest employer, and now Dick's father was the largest contributor to the new Childrens' Wing of the local hospital. Of course it was only a small town, but Rosemary quite enjoyed the little tokens of recognition, even deference, that she received when she was recognised in the local church, or the supermarket, or the Tennis Club. And there were the not inconsiderable perks of Dick's position. She had been to America twice now with him, once to ACP's headquarters, a trip which had included a couple of nights in Chicago, and once to New York, when Dick had attended some sort of global corporate conference and she had been entertained royally with him in the evenings, and had two days to see the shops and the sights as well. Later in the autumn there was to be another meeting of ACP's management, this time in San Francisco, which they were both looking forward to. *So why do I feel so restless, so uncertain?* She would have liked a third child, preferably a girl of course. But there had been those hard years when she was stretched to the limit coping with two small sons and with Dick, when he seemed to be so deeply depressed after it became apparent that his flying days were over as a result of that rugby injury. Then came the call to leave the RAF and come to Lynchester to take over from his father; and the frantic years of making a new home here, and Dick being more or less forced by his father to gamble everything on the success of the new cereal product. And the long, tense excitement of selling the company for what turned out eventually to be a very handsome price, and the pressure of Dick's new job. Somehow the months of putting off starting another baby had become years – and now? Now she was almost forty-four. *Not really too old perhaps* . . . Rosemary was going around the boys' bedrooms, picking up discarded socks and shirts and tidying up. *Do I want to go through all that again, the discomfort of morning sickness and a swollen body, that deep, soul-grinding anxiety about the viability of the new foetus, the pain of giving birth, the sleepless nights? I suppose though if I wanted it we could easily afford a nanny, and some help around the house. Really, if I wanted I could be a lady of leisure. I could get used to that* . . . The sound of a car-door being slammed on the driveway ended her private daydream. She looked at her watch – five-thirty. Dick was early for once. The boys had finished tea, and were watching a video of 'Lord of the Rings'.

"Daddy's just coming in. James, would you stop that just for now, and get out your homework please? Peter, you can come and help me get the supper. Perhaps you could start by laying the table."

Normally, Dick Routledge was the least nervous of men. Confident in his powerful physical presence, the very thought of 'looking over his shoulder' was totally alien to him. But as he had driven out of the factory gates for the short journey home he became aware of a grey Volvo estate parked across the road, which started moving soon after he had turned onto the busy road along the river. He turned right as usual to cross the Town Bridge, and as he reached the far side he glanced in the mirror. There was that car, with the usual Volvo 'lights on in broad daylight', just turning onto the bridge. He drove up the slope, passing the Hawkins Mall and the Tennis Club, and turned left into his own quiet street, shaded with pollarded lime trees in dusty leaf, and with handsome detached houses on both sides. He checked momentarily behind as he turned right off the road onto his gravelled drive, and was relieved to see the Volvo continuing innocently up the hill. He opened the back door of his Jaguar to pick up his jacket and briefcase, and had just slammed it shut when the car came cruising past his house, this time from the other end of the street, and turned right, back towards the bridge. He caught a glimpse of two men inside, both in shirtsleeves. Neither looked towards him as they passed. The one on the passenger side had his head down, apparently writing on a pad. The driver's face was in deep shadow.

His mind leapt immediately to the attack on Alain Robarte last Saturday in Bordeaux. *What if these men were part of the same gang that had killed Alain? Now they knew where he lived. Might he be the next target? Or his family even? Should he call the police? Would it make sense to go through all that rigmarole of explaining why they were worried about the French accounts, and what had happened to Alain? What would the local police be able to do anyway? Damn, he should have taken the number of that car!*

He realised that he was breathing hard, and guessed his pulse-rate was up. *Silly nonsense. It's probably just some visitors to the town, trying to get their bearings. The last thing I need to do is alarm Rosemary and the boys.* He looked up and down the empty street, silent and basking in the calm evening sunlight. A murder in the south of France seemed a million miles away. But as he pulled out his key and shut the front door behind his back he was suddenly aware that his legs were trembling.

He took several slow, deep breaths and walked into the kitchen to hug Rosemary from behind and nuzzle her long neck beneath the mane of auburn hair.

"Watch it, I'm peeling onions! You're home nice and early for once. How was your day?"

Dick thought back over the events of the day. Brit, and Jennifer, and Alain of course, and the French policeman coming tomorrow.

"A bit tough, actually. The worst news is about Alain Robarte, you know our Finance Manager in France? He died this morning from that attack on Saturday, without regaining consciousness."

She turned to face him, pushing her hair out of her eyes with the back of her hand in a little gesture he loved. "Oh Dick, that's so terrible. His poor wife – he was married?"

"Yes. But no children, we think. I'll go see what the boys are up to, and we could talk some more about it after supper?"

* * *

Ellen Routledge was in a daze of excitement, which suited James, as he was feeling anything but talkative at supper.

"Just think, Jim, the Princess Anne coming to Lynchester. I mean, you're the biggest donor, so you're bound to be introduced to her. Me too, I should think? What shall I say to her? How do you address a Princess? Whatever should I wear? I said to Dick that he was to help me insist on getting someone with a bit of class to do the opening, but I never thought for one minute that we could get the Princess. It's the next best thing to getting the Queen herself. Dan thinks there's bound to be TV coverage. You know, you could be in line for a knighthood. Or at least an OBE. 'Sir James and Lady Routledge'. Sounds well, don't you think?"

"Sounds like a modest return on an investment of one and a half million, I'd say. I often think that if father ever knew what I'd done with some of the money we got from selling his business he'd never stop spinning in his grave." He paused while he cleared his plate of shepherds' pie. "Which reminds me . . ."

Ellen caught the change of mood immediately. "Something wrong, Jim?"

He told her about the trouble at the French factory, and the murder of Alain Robarte. "And the French police are coming first thing tomorrow morning to interview Dick."

"They don't think . . .?"

"No, no nothing like that. But they obviously think he's involved in some way, which means we're all involved. I'm just praying that we can keep the Yanks out of it. They're surprisingly strait-laced about the business – senior executives should be whiter than white is the impression they give. Of course the reality is no doubt something else."

After supper they walked out into the soft sunlight to look at the garden that Ellen was so proud of. Judging that James was both in a mellow mood, and at the same time not particularly enamoured of business life at the moment, she broached a subject that was always close to her thoughts these days.

"James, when you were recovering from your stroke, we never thought you'd get back to work. And then after Dick came in, I could understand you wanting to set an example to him. Then you sold the company, and for the life of me I can't understand why you wanted to soldier on. I mean you're coming up to sixty-four now. How much longer do you want to go on? We certainly don't need the money. And now this terrible thing in

France is going to give us all sleepless nights, with Dick being sucked into it. God knows you've had your share of hard work and worry. Couldn't you just walk away and retire? Please? While we've still got some years left for ourselves?"

James was not by nature the most sensitive of men. Probably he would not have been successful if he were. But he was very fond of Ellen, and had never realised before that she wanted their lives to change.

"What would I do if I retired? Play golf all day? You'd pretty soon get fed up with having me under your feet, I'd guess."

Ellen had thought about this, and was defiant.

"We could travel. I mean really travel. Live abroad in France or Canada or . . . or Ceylon for a month or more at a time. Try to really get to know a country. Go on a cruise. Several cruises, to the Caribbean or the Greek Islands. Get properly involved in the Children's Wing, leading more fund-raising. You might stand for the Council, be Mayor even. After all, you're certainly Lynchester's leading citizen. And you could play some golf, if you wanted. Believe it or not, I married you because I wanted to be with you, and I still do. Mostly that is, when you're not being a grouch. And who can say how much longer we've got to be together?"

She sat down on a wooden seat in an arbour that caught the last of the setting sun. Her face as she looked up at him seemed suddenly youthful. "Come on, James, let's do it!"

Deeply touched by Ellen's impassioned plea, James sat down beside her and took her hands in his.

"I never knew you felt so strongly about it, love. Not that I'm saying 'yes' mind. At least, not just yet. This is the first real trouble we've had since ACP came in, and it goes against the grain to up sticks and run away. I just couldn't do it, d' you see?" He thought in silence for a few moments, then continued. "Here's a promise. I'll help Dick through this crisis, and we'll take a bit of holiday ourselves next month, when Dick gets back from his. A couple of weeks in Scotland or Devon would suit me. Then we'll all go to this next ACP management get-together in San Francisco, that's in the middle of October I think, and I'll tell them then that I'm retiring. Give them six months to find a successor, and I'll finish in the Spring. How does that suit you?"

Ellen was secretly triumphant, having got much more than she had expected, but she kept her tone cool. "It'll have to do I suppose. And don't think for one minute that I won't hold you to it, because I will. I'll call your loving daughter Ruth and Andrew this very evening and tell them what you've promised. Now then, whilst I've got you out here, there's this big clump of couch grass that's too much for me to shift. I'll fetch you the garden fork."

Long after Dick had fallen asleep, Rosemary lay stiffly awake. She hadn't raised the idea of another baby with him. What with the awful news about Alain and the French policeman coming tomorrow it seemed definitely not to be the right time. *Would it ever be? My monthly is about due, so I could just stop taking the pill. Without telling Dick?* And that card kept sticking in her thoughts, like a small, sharp fishbone in the throat. *Damn, damn, damn, damn, damn.*

Chapter Sixteen

The Commissaire de Police from Bordeaux arrived promptly at nine o'clock the next morning, having been collected by the company driver. For some reason Elizabeth seemed to be very impressed that a French policeman should have come all the way from Bordeaux to see Dick, and she ushered him into the boardroom, where Dick was already waiting, as though he were visiting royalty.

"Mr. Routledge, this is Commissaire St. Just. Commissaire, Mr. Richard Routledge."

Dick rose from the comfortable armchair at one end of the coffee table. "Bienvenu a l'Angleterre, Commissaire. Vous prenez du cafe?"

Commissaire St. Just looked about forty. He was short and chubby, with a fair complexion and sandy brown hair cut militarily trim. His dark grey pinstripe suit could well have come from London. He smiled warmly as he shook Dick's hand, placed a business card on the coffee table, and sank into the other armchair opposite.

"Yes, thank you, coffee would be fine. Black, no sugar, please."

His English accent was almost perfect. Perhaps a hint of America?

Dick heaved a silent sigh of relief that his French would not be further tested.

"How was your journey? I asked Elizabeth to arrange things for you, if possible."

"She did excellent work. I came over last night, Air France to London, then BA to Birmingham. Your charming company driver met me quite late in the evening off the flight, for a good night's sleep and of course an English breakfast, at the Belfry Hotel. And he collected me as you see this morning. I must thank you, M'sieur Routledge, for your kind consideration, and especially that you have made time in your busy schedule to see me at such short notice."

"Well, M. Robarte was a valued colleague, and we want to be as helpful as we can to your investigation." Dick paused to finish his cup of coffee, and sat forward attentively. "So, M'sieur St. Just, what makes it worthwhile for you to come over to England? Do you think there is some connection between Alain's work and his murder?"

The Commissaire reached into his leather attache case and pulled out a small voice-recorder, which he switched on and placed between them on the coffee-table.

"Entrevue en Angleterre avec M'sieur Richard Routledge, Mercredi, vingt-deux Juillet. I hope this will not make you feel uncomfortable, M'sieur Routledge, but I dislike to write when we are talking?"

Dick shrugged. "Not at all."

"Good. Now, as to what brings me here. I understand that you had a private meeting with M'sieur Robarte last week, on Thursday evening, I think?"

Dick nodded. *How did he know that? This was becoming distinctly 'up close and personal'.*

St. Just continued. "Would you be kind enough to explain to me the purpose of this meeting, and why it took place in your hotel room, rather than in the office?"

Dick thought quickly. It seemed important to demonstrate that the meeting with Alain had a legitimate business purpose, even though it had taken place out of office hours. But first he needed to know more about what the police thought they knew.

"If you agree, M'sieur St. Just, I would like to bring in one of my colleagues, our Financial Director, who can certainly explain more exactly than myself what the meeting was about."

Dick stood up and pressed the bell alongside the fireplace, which brought Elizabeth to the boardroom door a few moments later.

"Elizabeth, would you be kind enough to ask Mr. Helvin to join us? Ask him to bring with him the file he's been working on about the French business. And I'm sure some fresh coffee and an extra cup for Mr. Helvin would be appreciated."

Jim Helvin appeared with a thick file of papers in his hands. "Good morning, Commissaire. Dick here has already asked me to open our books totally to yourself, but I don't need to remind you, I'm sure, that much of this material is commercially confidential."

"Of course, M'sieur 'Elvin. My only concern is to understand if there may be some connection between this business and the murder of Alain Robarte."

"Yes, quite so. Dick, I think it will be easier to look at documents if we all sit round the board table?"

Dick had spent almost an hour with Jim Helvin going through his analysis, before St. Just had arrived. He waved his Finance Director into the big chair at the head of the table, with himself and the Commissaire on each side. The little recording device was moved to the end of the big polished table. Jim produced a set of copies of the principal evidence.

"As you may know, our subsidiary at Belin has been in business just over a year. Sales have been growing a little ahead of plan, and though it will be a while yet before we see a profit, because we are investing quite heavily in the marketing, we felt that prospects were good. This analysis shows the sales, in cases and Euros, gross margins, overheads, head-count and so on, month by month since we started, up to May of this year. You can see that the numbers progress quite steadily."

He paused while St. Just studied the page he had handed out. "But in June something changed?"

"Indeed. The standard practice is that summary results are sent by e-mail to us and to our US parent company by the end of the second week after the end of the month. So this is a copy of what we received Monday of last week. You can see that sales value jumps, but sales in cases increase just a small amount. Overheads and head-count also rise sharply, so the end result is a nasty loss."

"I see, yes. So you were concerned?"

Dick intervened here. "Very concerned. This business was the first major expansion for which I was responsible, and to some extent we have been using it as a model for further developments across Europe. So I arranged to fly over last Wednesday evening to see for myself what was going on."

"With what result?"

Dick sat forward in his chair with his elbows on the table, and rested his chin for a moment on his clasped hands. He was careful to speak slowly, as though he were weighing his words very carefully.

"Our Managing Director, M'sieur de Clavignon, offered a very simple explanation. He said that, together with Alain Robarte, he had over the previous week been looking at the effect of varying the way the company operated – increasing the sales force, changing the pricing, altering discounts and so on. All these alternative ideas were worked through and stored as dummy trading months on Alain's computer. Last week, when the time came to send us the results for June, the MD was away on business, and Alain had been told to send off the figures as soon as they were ready, by e-mail to us and to the American parent company. A couple of days later, when the MD looked at what had been sent, he realised immediately that a mistake had been made and one of the 'dummy' monthly sets of figures had been sent. He arranged at once for the correct figures to be sent. Jim?"

Jim handed over another sheet to St. Just, who studied it closely. "It looks much more like the previous months?"

"Exactly. Much more like the figures we had been expecting."

"But you were not satisfied. Why was that?"

Why was that? Instinct? Gut feeling? The way Jean-Paul had waited for him at the airport? Body-language?

"It's not easy to explain. I guess I just felt that something wasn't right. Bear in mind too that I had already made the journey over to Belin to investigate, before the MD returned, well on the same day actually. So it was not a great matter to stay on for an extra day or two to be absolutely sure there was no problem."

"And M'sieur Robarte's visit to your hotel on Thursday evening?"

Jim intervened. "It was at my suggestion that Dick arranged to see him privately. I thought there was a chance that Alain would say more without his boss breathing down his neck. I should have said too that my role as Finance Director for ACP's European subsidiaries means that I have what we call 'dotted-line responsibility' for the Financial Managers in each business. That means that they each report to their local MD of course, but I am responsible to ACP for ensuring that they maintain U.S. professional standards in their accounting. D'you follow me?"

"Perfectly. And no doubt they can come to you for advice and support if the need arises?"

"They can."

"Did M'sieur Robarte ever consult you on any matter whatsoever?"

St. Just's questioning was suddenly hard and direct. Jim paused, with a glance sideways at Dick. "Just the once. I never mentioned this to you, Dick, but he called me from Paris the day after we'd interviewed him here, and he'd been offered the job. He wanted my honest opinion on the salary he was being offered, and whether he should ask for more. I told him it was a wonderful opportunity, and he should just grab it with both hands."

"So he saw you as a friend, as well as a colleague?"

Jim nodded.

"And you suggested to Mr. Routledge that he should meet M'sieur Robarte privately, out of the office. So now, Mr Routledge, what happened when he came to your hotel room?"

Dick pulled one ear reflectively. "Not much, really. I got the impression that he was almost prepared to make some sort of confession, and then something I said made him very nervous, afraid even, and he just refused to say any more without M'sieur de Clavignon being present."

"You say afraid. Do you mean that literally? Afraid of whom, or what?"

"I have no idea."

St. Just waited, then realised that Dick was not going to say any more.

"So, he left you. What happened after that?"

"I had some dinner in the hotel and then an early night. Next day there was another meeting with M'sieur de Clavignon in the morning, this time looking at factory developments and so on."

"The strange figures were not discussed again?"

"No. And M'sieur Robarte had been most insistent that I should not mention his visit, so I didn't, of course. In the afternoon I visited one of your Bordeaux wine merchants for a tasting, and bought a few bottles. I had dinner in the evening in a good restaurant . . ."

"Can you recall which one?"

Dick hesitated. If they checked at the restaurant, he was sure that Brit would be remembered. On the other hand, it would seem very odd if he said he'd forgotten . . .

"I think it was 'Le Chapon' – something or other?"

"Ah yes, Le Chapon Fin. A very good choice. And afterwards?"

And afterwards Brit and I made love, until we were completely and utterly exhausted with pleasure.

"Afterwards I walked back to the hotel, and then caught the flight back the next morning."

"Bien. So, if we exclude casual contacts with airport staff, taxi-drivers and hotel people, and the wine merchant, your only meetings in France were with M'sieur de Clavignon and M'sieur Robarte?"

"Yes. Well, I did meet M'sieur de Clavignon's wife with him on the beach on Thursday afternoon."

"I'm sure that was a pleasure, but it need not concern us today. Do you have anything more to tell me that might be relevant to my enquiry?"

Dick looked at Jim, who nodded. "We have no idea whether or not what I'm about to tell you has any relevance to your case. But I cannot emphasise too strongly that this must remain absolutely confidential."

St. Just rested his elbows on the table and steepled his fingers against his lips, but said nothing.

Jim continued, "We have obtained from the bank in France that looks after our business there these copies of the last few months' bank statements. It's not possible to be certain, but there are a series of payments into and out of the account recently that do not quite fit the usual pattern. I've tried to establish a connection, some correspondence, with the peculiar figures we received initially for the month of June, but because of the irregular way that payments lag behind trading it's proving very difficult."

"Can you say though what it is that you suspect?"

"No. Someone, or several people, seem perhaps to be using this account to receive funds and pay bills that may not relate to our business. For what reason or purpose, I canna' say."

"Who are the approved signatories for your account?"

"de Clavignon and Robarte. Either can pay in, but it needs two signatures to pay out. We are hoping to have a temporary

Finance Manager start on Monday, and he will be the second signatory instead of Alain."

"M'sieur Routledge, can you help to solve this mystery?"

"I can't, unfortunately. Jim has told me that we would need to go across to France and study the actual paying-in slips and debit instructions to make any more progress. Frankly, as there is no evidence to suggest we are actually losing money overall as a result of these transactions, I am wondering whether it is going to be worth our while to spend any more time on this particular enquiry."

St. Just pursed his lips, and looked at Jim Helvin again. "I wonder if I may be able to help you? For instance, if you could let me take away a copy of the bank statements in question, ideally with the transactions that seem suspicious duly marked, I could have one of our police specialists make a study. I am sure that your bank would be willing to give me access to the necessary additional information to trace the payments in and out."

Jim looked to Dick for a decision.

"I think that this is something I should refer to our Chairman. Will you excuse me for a moment, please?"

Dick returned quickly. "The Chairman is quite agreeable, provided you sign for what you take away, together with a commitment to maintain commercial confidentiality."

"With pleasure."

Jim made up a folder of documents, while Dick went back to his office with St. Just to produce a short note for him to sign.

"Voila, M'sieur, and thank you. I think that concludes our business for today."

Dick looked at his watch. Almost midday.

"Can I offer you some lunch, M'sieur St. Just?"

"You are very kind, but I already have an invitation to lunch at Wadham, my old college in Oxford. So if you could call a taxi for me, please?"

"Oxford? So that explains your very good English."

"That, and my American mother."

"Ah, yes, of course. But you won't need a taxi. I haven't got any work for our driver this afternoon, so he will take you of course. It's only about a forty minute drive. Just before you go, there is one other thing I'd like your advice about. It may be nothing, but I am a bit worried."

He described the Volvo and its occupants.

"It's hard to be certain, but I think they followed me home, for some reason."

St. Just sat in the chair at the corner of Dick's desk. "You seem very calm, M'sieur Routledge, but I suspect you are thinking of what happened to M'sieur Robarte?"

"I have a wife and two young boys to think about."

"Let me be frank with you, M'sieur. If you are worried for your safety, you should talk to the English police. Show them my card, if you think they may not be taking you quite seriously." He paused, as though to consider some options, then paced around the small office as he continued.

"You have been very open and trusting with me, so I feel that I owe you some more of an explanation about the direction our enquiry is now going to take. Do you understand what 'money-laundering' means?"

"I can't say I've ever thought much about it. I suppose it's the business of accumulating illegal funds, and processing them in some way so that they can be banked legally and without arousing suspicion."

"Very good, M'sieur. Now, have you heard of ETA?"

Dick felt his heart beating faster. "The Basque terrorist organisation?"

"Terrorist or fighters for independence, depending on your point of view. The Spanish police and military have been very successful at restricting their ability to operate in Spain, partly by good detective work, but also by giving the Basque people political concessions, so that only the most fanatical hard-line supporters will help them now, and most ordinary citizens think they should make peace altogether. As a result many active members have found it impossible to stay in Spain, and have moved their base into France."

Dick's mind was racing. "So you think that our business in Belin . . .?"

"We are aware of one or two alleged members of ETA living in Biarritz, apparently very quietly. But they may be more active than we thought. It is a possibility that occurred to me when you told me the story of the strange numbers, and the unexplained entries in the bank statements, yes. It fits too with the attack on M'sieur Robarte, if he had become a partner to them in some way, and was suspected of changing sides."

"And it could have been his visit to me that caused them to attack him. To murder him."

"It could, yes. But if he was thinking of trying to get out of the affair, his life was at risk anyway. I would suggest that you can have absolutely no reason to blame yourself in this matter."

Spanish terrorists! Illicit funds moving through our little company's bank account! A murder – to stop Alain talking . . . and where did that leave Jean-Paul? Was he part of the conspiracy – or the next victim, perhaps? And what about me? Am I at risk? I need to talk to Dad, and quickly.

"I am very grateful for your frankness, M'sieur St. Just. Shall I walk you to the car?"

After St. Just had left Dick sank into a leather armchair and savoured the forbidden pleasure of another cup of coffee. *I think he was satisfied . . . I didn't mention Brit of course, but with Jim Helvin there I couldn't, could I?*

Chapter Seventeen

As the company Jaguar crunched across the gravel drive and turned out of the gates of the factory, Commissaire St. Just turned to wave a friendly hand from the rear seat. Dick watched him go, and looked up at the lowering sky. The morning's calm and bright sunshine had given way to a cool breeze that was now driving in layers of dark, ragged clouds, with a promise of rain before long. *An omen of things to come?* He ran up the steps and turned into his father's office, to find him dictating to Elizabeth.

"Just a moment, Dick, I'm almost done. '*and I look forward to seeing you in England soon. Best regards.*' That'll do for today, thank you Liz. I'll be off home for lunch after Dick has finished, and back in on Friday morning. So, Dick, how did you get on with your Chief Inspector Maigret?"

Dick waited until Elizabeth had closed the door behind her. "This one's a bit younger than Maigret, but just as sharp. He's taken the French bank statements away with him, as we agreed, and he actually opened up a bit at the end. From what Jim told him about the movements in the account, he suspects that it might have been used for money-laundering. That's where . . ."

"Yes, yes, Dick, I know what money-laundering is. Did he connect that with the attack on Alain?"

"He thinks it's possible, well probable, that there is a connection. The hypothesis is that Alain was involved, and they thought he might be wanting to get out."

"Who's 'they'?"

"He doesn't know for sure yet, but he says that some of the ETA people from Spain have retreated into that part of France, so that's one possibility. I don't think he'll know more until he traces where the money has come from and where it's been going."

James looked thoughtful, took off his gold-rimmed spectacles and rubbed his fingers into the corners of his eyes.

"All of which must leave us wondering what part Jean-Paul might have played in all this. I mean, he's one of the two signatories to the account. Could this money just float in and out without him being aware?"

"I don't know, Dad. Do you ever look at Strongwheat's bank statements these days? I know I don't."

"Not for a good number of years. Jim looks after all that stuff, and anything important about our cash position is reported at the Board meetings. I hate to say this, but I think we should go forward from now on the assumption that Jean-Paul may not be entirely innocent, to put it kindly."

"Right. I told St. Just that we couldn't expect to do much more from this end, so it may not be necessary to involve J-P too much. He'll be kept pretty busy helping our new Interim Finance chap to find his way round next week. And like me, he's off on holiday at the end of that week."

"Fine, well, I'm still against telling the Yanks anything we don't have to, but now that the French police have come to us officially it may be necessary for us to come clean."

James looked at his watch, and Dick could almost feel his father slowing down. He wanted to spare him as much as possible, but some things wouldn't wait. He pressed on.

"I'll leave you to decide what to tell Ben, and when. But there is just one thing more I need your input on, please Dad. Tomorrow we'll be interviewing the candidate Interim Financial Managers to replace Alain for, say, six months. How much, if anything, do you think we should tell them about all this business?"

"That's an easy one, Dick. Tomorrow, say no more than that our incumbent guy has died, after an accident. On Friday, I'm coming in especially to meet your chosen man – I guess it will be a man? Anyway, whoever it is will need a full brief, and that's what we'll give him. He's going to find himself pig-in-the-middle between Jean-Paul, Jim Helvin here, the French police and you, so he's going to need all the information, advice and support he can get. We'll have no room down there for any wet-behind-the-ears bean-counters, so make sure you get someone who is tough and mean. Can I go home to lunch now?"

Dick returned to his own office to find the first drops of rain pattering against his window. *No nice picnic in the sunshine by the river today!* He rang through to the canteen. "Could you bring me in a hot beef pasty please? And I'd like an apple and a pot of tea as well."

He reached for his scrap-pad, and began to make a list of things-to-do.

1. Call Brit re Milan hotel – *safer than waiting for her to call*
2. Check for e-mail from J-P about Jennifer.
3. Talk J-P about capacity to supply Italy next Spring. Have new Italian cereal boxes printed together with next run of French? Who decides finished product transfer prices? Me? Tell J-P about St. Just coming in?
4. Arrange for new German managers to visit Belin after the holidays.

There was a faint knock at his door, and he called out a cheery 'Come in'.

There was a pause while the door handle rattled, and he jumped up to open it himself. She was in her early twenties, he guessed, tall, even in sensible flat shoes, slim in a tightly-belted white overall, and with wisps of blonde curls that had escaped from beneath her white cap. Her large, pale blue eyes widened just slightly as he took the big tray from her and put it down on his desk.

"Pasty smells nice. Are you new here? I'm Dick Routledge."

She took his proffered handshake and smiled. *A smile to soften a statue.*

"Nice to meet you, Mr. Routledge. I'm Jan, Janice Craig actually." Dick thought she sounded very well-spoken for a canteen assistant, but the mystery was instantly solved for him. "I'm here on six weeks of work experience from Birmingham University. Business Studies. Three years at college, plus I could choose either a one-year sandwich course, or the two summers of work experience, six weeks a year, which is what I'm doing.

Mrs. Savage has made it 'a little challenging', as she put it. This is the third week. I've had two weeks on the Production floor, and this week I'm in the canteen. I made those pasties myself at eight o'clock this morning, so I hope you enjoy it."

This last was said almost defiantly, and Dick found himself not wanting her to go.

"I'm sure I will, especially now I know where it came from. What's in your programme for the next three weeks? Something more exciting than the canteen, I hope?"

"Oh, don't knock the canteen. You get to do a bit of everything, and you meet everybody. I'm enjoying it. But next week should be really interesting, I'm to shadow Mr. Wythe, the Managing Director, for a week. After that I've a week in Marketing and a week in Finance."

"And then do you get a holiday?"

"You bet. My boyfriend is renting a motor home, and we're going to potter around France for a whole month. And thanks to Strongwheat I'll have some money to spend. Should be absolute bliss."

Dick held the door open for her to leave. He watched the swing of her hips as she strode athletically across the reception hall and through the swing doors that led into the factory.

Not another one, for God's sake! I'm actually jealous of her boyfriend, aren't I?

He turned on the light in his office as a gust of wind lashed the rain against his window. He bit into the pasty, and smiled as he imagined Janice folding the pastry around the meat and vegetables. *I suppose those are her fingerprints baked into the crimp. Stunningly pretty, very bright, and makes a mean pasty too. I like her attitude. What a combination! Perhaps she'll come back here when she graduates . . .*

Almost reluctantly he focussed on his 'jobs to do' list again. He looked at his watch – almost half past one. An hour later in Stockholm, so Brit should be back from her lunch-break. He dialled her number. Four long rings, he actually could feel his heart beating.

"Hullo, Steen und Strom?" *It was her!*

"Hi, Brit darling, it's Dick. I hope you are well?"

"Very well, especially now that I talk to you again. Excuse me, we have here some sun today, just one hour, and I am now come back from a long walk into our Altstadt, that's the old part of Stockholm, and I am losing some breath. Let me sit down . . ."

There was that irresistible warmth in her tone again, and the memory came back of that last kiss in Bordeaux.

"I'm looking forward to next Tuesday in Milan very much, Brit. I hope you don't mind me calling you rather than wait for your call, but this afternoon could get very busy for me."

"Of course not, Dick. I was going to call you straight away. I have booked us for two nights, Tuesday and Wednesday next week, at the Gran Hotel Duomo. It faces onto the cathedral, and it's just around the corner from all the shops in Monte Napoleone, and La Rinascente, the big department store is near also. I don't suppose you'll want to do much shopping?"

There was a little chuckle in her voice, that seemed to promise so much.

"None at all, if I can help it. But being so near means you won't have to get up too early, so that will be helpful." He scrabbled in his in-tray. "I know I definitely saw a note of my flight times . . . yes, here it is. BA goes direct from Birmingham to Malpensa airport next Tuesday at eight thirty-five, gets there at eleven fifty five – just right to arrive in town for lunch."

"That's marvellous, Dick. My Scandinavian gets in at eleven forty, so we could meet at the airport and share a taxi?"

Dick ticked off the first item on his agenda, and added another note, to call Pietro Cavalli in Parma to finalise the arrangements for their meeting. *I could ask him to send a car to Milan to collect me first thing Wednesday morning. A day together with Pietro in Parma should be long enough to get them started. Must take that European Breakfast Cereal Research Study with me . . .*

He checked his e-mails. As usual, lots of 'spam'. He wondered how they got his e-mail address. *Yes, here's the message from Jean-Paul. He's booked her into a hotel from Tuesday of next week, two rooms for three nights – I'll ask her if that's long enough. And there are three, no four 'phone numbers, one for the hotel, one for wherever he is over the weekend – looks like a mobile number, one for the office, and one for his house in Arcachon. Couldn't be better.*

"Hullo, Jennifer? It's Dick, Dick Routledge. How are you? Good. Look, I've got the info. from our chap in Arcachon, Jean-Paul. Shall I forward the e-mail to you, or would you like to take the details down over the 'phone?"

There was a perceptible pause before she answered. "You're very kind, Dick. Look, I'm staying in because it's a foul afternoon, but I've still got some of that cake you liked. Why not come by with the e-mail at tea-time?"

It was Dick's turn to pause and think before answering. He was mindful of his resolution not to encourage Jennifer to believe that he might be interested in her. *But it wasn't necessary to be churlish . . .*

"I don't think I can get away early enough for tea, but I could drop by for a minute on the way home – say about five-thirty?"

"That will be lovely, Dick. I'll look forward to seeing you then."

Dick decided he didn't particularly want to talk to Jean-Paul at the moment. He wanted to think a bit more about what his father had said. *Obviously Jean-Paul had to be under suspicion. Might that imply that he had even been involved in Alain's murder?* He clicked his e-mail facility to 'Reply'.

Dear Jean-Paul,

Thank you very much for the help with the hotel for Mrs. Hawkins. I'm sure she will be very grateful too, and I know you will like her.

You will remember that we discussed the possibility of packing product for Italy? We have had the go-ahead in principle, and I am going to Italy next week to discuss planning for a Spring launch there. I would be grateful for some preliminary figures by Monday morning latest:

1. A forecast of your spare capacity by month for next calendar year, assuming (a) current hours, (b) extended day shifting, (c) double shifts.

2. Best estimate of marginal costs of production and delivery in container-loads to Parma under each of these conditions. I will of course add a profit for Belin to your cost, to make up the proposed transfer price.

You will be interested to know that Commissaire St. Just of the Bordeaux police has just left us. He already knew about Alain's visit to me, so I had to tell him the reason. He will probably want you to tell him again about how the wrong figures were sent! Best regards, Dick

He read it through twice, decided it would apply just enough pressure to Jean-Paul, and pressed 'Send'.

He checked his 'to do' list again. *Damnation! I should have stayed in that e-mail programme.*

Dear Jurgen,

I am delighted that the management team is now in place, and look forward to coming over again to Wuppertal towards the end of next month. In the meantime would you give some thought please to picking a suitable time for the whole team, including yourself, to come for two or three days to the French factory in Belin, near Bordeaux? They are closed for a month from the end of next week, so mid-September would be good. Please note that I am away on holiday for two weeks also from the end of next week. Best regards, Dick.

And last but not least, Italy.

Dear Pietro,

I would be grateful if you could arrange to collect me from the Gran Hotel Duomo in Milan at 8a.m. next Wednesday. I will also need transport please back to Milan at the end of the day as I have a dinner engagement there. Best regards, Dick

He wondered briefly if he was being somewhat imperious, and decided that it was time he started flexing his 'European Director' muscles anyway. He sat back, and remembered that Jean Savage was expecting to have received the CVs of the prospective Interim Finance Managers for France. *That should be interesting!*

"Elizabeth, if anyone wants me desperately I'm with Mrs. Savage".

Chapter Eighteen

"Charles Harrison, please. Tell him it's Mrs. Hawkins. Charles? Hullo, it's Jennifer Hawkins. I hope I'm not interrupting something important? Your receptionist said that you were alone, but had asked not to be disturbed unless it was something vital. Then she said she'd put me through anyway, so that's quite flattering, I thought."

"I must congratulate her on recognising my favourite client, Jennifer. I hope you are well? How are things going with the move to France?"

"That's just what I'm calling about. I'm going over with Greta and Billy on Sunday."

"You're not moving house already?" There was alarm in his voice.

"No, no. This is just a few days' exploration. Actually Dick Routledge has been very helpful in suggesting that I should look at a place on the Atlantic he knows, called Arcachon. Do you know it?"

Like most men in his profession, Charles Harrison had a naturally suspicious mind, and he tucked away for future consideration the hint of a connection between Jennifer and Dick Routledge. *Jennifer has a reason for mentioning Dick to me. I wonder what it is?*

"No, I don't. Would you like me to do some research for you?"

"That's a kind offer, Charles, but I don't think I need trouble you. I've already got masses off the internet, and Dick has arranged for a colleague of his who lives there to show me around. And there are lots of local agents too who will be showing properties for me to rent."

"So how can I help?"

"I suppose really I just wanted to keep on top of this business of a settlement for Billy. I've looked through the stuff you did for me, and it all makes sense now. Not necessarily the actual investments you suggest, I think we might look at those again together, but the strategy and the structures look right. So I was thinking, if I came by your office on Friday, could we press the buttons on actually liquidating some of my holdings, if that's the right thing to do? I guess that selling some of my shares in the Hawkins Mall may not be quite straightforward? I think there's something restrictive in the shareholders' agreement, about pre-emption rights. And we could sign the papers and so on to set up the Trust, and you could then have a couple of weeks while I'm away to look again at the investment plan and to be sure we know what's the best thing to do. How does that sound?"

Not for the first time, Charles thanked the lucky stars that had given him a client as charming, intelligent and business-like as Jennifer Hawkins.

"How does Friday at 3p.m. suit?"

"Fine, see you then."

Jennifer sat for a moment by the telephone. She had been busy in the garden since lunch, weeding and tying up the climbers. *Dick will be here in a couple of hours. Just time for a nice soak in the bath. Shall I wash my hair or just pin it up?*

Jean Savage looked up and smiled as Dick came into her office. "You must be psychic, Dick. The CVs came in an hour ago, and I was just about to come and see you with them." She handed him a red file. "You'll see there are three people, who all fit the brief, I'd say. And there's a covering letter with the Agency's quotations for them, and the interview programme they've set up for us for tomorrow morning. First one's at nine, then ten-thirty and the last at midday."

Dick glanced through the letter and the file. "Four-fifty, five hundred and six hundred pounds a day! If we have him for six months that's . . ."

"A lot of money, I know. In fact they told me in advance what the rates would be, and I worked out that the six-hundred guy would cost twelve thousand a month, allowing twenty working days, plus another thou' or two for expenses. So I think we should definitely put in hand straight away the recruitment process for a permanent successor to Alain. With any luck we should be able to get someone within three to four months. And don't forget we don't have to pay the Interim during their shutdown, which saves us four weeks."

"But we are still looking at a budget for this lot of forty, no fifty thousand if we include the fee for the recruiting the permanent chap."

"We are. Equally there's a brand new ten million pound business over there that's technically at risk until you've reinstated adequate financial controls. Jean-Paul is really still just a promoted marketing guy; promising, but without solid management credentials, and the other director, Louis Bromberg, is basically a Production manager. You've got a new venture in Germany which is supposed to use Belin as a model, and I hear you're off to Italy next week to start the ball rolling there. So within a couple of years you could have a fifty million business on the Continent. Think of it as a fifty thousand pound insurance policy. One-tenth of one percent."

"Can I take this away and ponder?"

"Of course. But come back in an hour, say, and let's take a view then on the idea as a whole, and also what we want to find out about each candidate."

Back at his desk Dick bit into the green apple, thought momentarily of pretty blonde Janice again, made a face in exasperation at his own alpha male reactions, and started to read through the CVs, making notes on his pad as he read. After about ten minutes there was a knock at his door, and he looked up to see Paul Williams, who was recently promoted to be Sales and Marketing Director for the UK Strongwheat business. He was in his late thirties, stocky with dark, curly hair and just a hint of his Welsh parentage in his voice.

"Afternoon, Dick. Elizabeth said you might not be too busy for a quick chat? Frankly, I need some good advice."

Paul had joined the company five years earlier from its advertising agency to be Marketing Manager, had then been promoted to Director of Marketing soon after the sale of Strongwheat to ACP, and had risen to his present position, taking on the responsibility for the Sales Force, when Walter Hurd had retired three months ago. Dick had a sneaking admiration for Paul's instinct for survival. If he was asking for advice this early in the game, it was because he wanted to be sure that the responsibility for some decision was equitably shared around.

"Paul, of course, come in and sit down. I liked the look of our last Nielsen report on sales through retail last week – another half-point share gain, up to eight percent now."

"And ten percent here in the Midlands area. May sound daft, but it's the share gains that I'm a bit worried about. Or at least, the competitors' response."

"Competitors?"

"Weetabix, to be exact. If you look back over the last twelve months, they've dropped a full point down to seventeen percent share, mostly lost to our two Strongwheat varieties, especially Strongwheat Light. Talking with our salesmen, it's apparent that Weetabix are responding by switching the pattern of their spending on Marketing. It was eighty/twenty advertising to sales promotion, similar to our own, now it's more like sixty/forty, or even fifty/fifty. So there's literally millions flowing into extra price-discounting, and they're getting a lot of the major chains to give them feature price promotions. It must hurt our sales, at least in the short term."

"Is it? Is it hurting volume?"

"Hard to be certain, but we've certainly not grown as fast over June/July as we did in the Spring. And our salesmen are making gloomy noises about August and September."

"And you're asking, what precisely?"

"Simple question, really. I know it's my responsibility, but I'd like to have your views. We're due back on television at the beginning of September – five weeks away. Advertising funds are becoming non-cancellable every day. Do we hold our nerve and spend as we budgeted, or should we hold some money back and become more aggressive on price discounting?"

Dick thought carefully before answering the question. Strongwheat UK was the jewel in his crown, the cash-cow that financed his investment plans across Europe. He was already committed to reinvesting into Germany this year's planned earnings from the UK, and a shortfall would be seriously embarrassing.

"Walter told me once that salesmen are paid to represent two bodies – the company to its retailer customers of course, but also the customers to the company. And customers *always* want bigger price discounts. We've fought a long battle to afford today's advertising budget, and I'd be very reluctant to see it cut back now. I mean, even if they've cut back to fifty/fifty, I'd guess that Weetabix would still be spending more than us on advertising?"

"Just about, yes. One other consideration, we're now already inside the TV cancellation period, so money is becoming irrevocably committed as we speak at the rate of fifty thousand a week."

"A sobering thought, indeed." It put his own agonising about the cost of an interim for France into perspective. He looked at his diary. "I'm tied up tomorrow morning, well, till say mid-afternoon. Could you put together the latest possible information about sales and commitments, and let's sit down with Phil about four o'clock, if that suits?"

"Fine, thanks Dick. I suppose I should have talked to Phil before I came to see you, but I just took advantage of the moment when you seemed to be free."

"No problem." *Not much! If you're going to short-circuit the chain of command, Mr. Williams, you're going to have to learn to live with the consequences.*

At four o'clock Dick was back in Jean Savage's office. She stood up and pressed her hands against her desk, with her eyes closed.

"Don't worry, it's nothing serious. Just gets a bit uncomfortable if I sit in one position for too long, and Baby starts to kick. So, there, that's better! You sit down, I'll stand for a minute longer. Have you come to some conclusions?"

"Yes. First thing, they are an impressive bunch, so I agree we go ahead and meet them. I'll talk it through with the Chairman on Friday first thing, and he'll probably want to tell the Yanks what the damage will be in total. I'll suggest he quotes them a round hundred thousand dollars, and they can decide whether it's capital or revenue. Shall we have a quick run through the CVs together?"

Jean sat down with a small grimace of discomfort, and opened her copy of the red file. "You start, then."

"First up, Henri Besant. He's forty three. French born and trained chartered accountant with Price Waterhouse, Paris. Then ten years with IBM France, and four years in England working for a French wine business. Been independent for two years now, during which he's had two assignments, both back in France, four months and six months, for two different English engineering companies. Do you think he was fired from the wine company?"

"I asked the agency that. Apparently they just decided they could run it without a UK office, from Nantes. He has an English wife and a couple of children, so he got a reasonable redundancy settlement, stayed on in England and went self-employed."

"Fair enough. I'd be interested to ask why he's gone independent, rather than getting another job."

Jean made a note. "That should be interesting. It wouldn't hurt to ask all of them that. We ought to try to establish how close our Henri has really got to the nitty-gritty of the factory floor. On the face of it, only his last two assignments look really relevant."

"And there's one other thing that's really important, which is quite difficult to establish. I'm wondering what the danger might be that Henri will go native on us. You know, he's French, we're a combination of 'perfide Albion' and the 'defi Americain,' and Jean-Paul can be pretty persuasive if he puts his mind to it."

"I'll think about that. I suppose it's going to come down to judging the weight and quality of the man at interview."

"Right. Number two is a lady, Charlotte Aston, fifty two. English. Chartered Accountant, several blue-chip employers, ending up with five years as Finance Director in France of a

Unilever Foods subsidiary, which was sold off so she took a no doubt handsome redundancy settlement three years ago. Has a French partner – male I suppose – who lives in Bordeaux – that's handy. She claims to be 'virtually bi-lingual', and has had . . . seven Interim assignments in the three years, five in France including two food manufacturers, and two in England. All very impressive, but I must say I'd have severe reservations about sending a woman into Belin, knowing what we do about what happened to Alain. I didn't tell you, by the way, but our French policeman this morning suggested we *might* be dealing with a bunch of ETA terrorists, using the company for a spot of money-laundering."

"That sounds plausible. Terrorists . . . definitely not funny. On the other hand they're not likely to persist with this game if they know we're watching, are they? I like the look of Charlotte – let's not rule her out just yet. Though I have to say, number three looks the likeliest."

"He does indeed. William Jameson is sixty two next week. Lives in France. Cambridge graduate, management trainee in Rowntree, twelve years in marketing with them, then INSEAD Business School in France – looks like he paid for that himself, because he doesn't return to Rowntree but joins Dunlop in Paris as Manager of Administration and later Finance Director, then Managing Director of his own business, five years as a publisher in Rouen – very enterprising. Says he sold out intending to retire with his wife to his house on Cap Ferrat, got bored, and has been 'trouble-shooting' as an interim all over the UK and Europe for almost ten years now. Lots of corporate rescues, small companies and big. I suppose one might ask if he's too grand for our business, too heavyweight for the job?"

"He's also the most expensive. But the agency says that for a short assignment it's actually quite important that the interim should be overqualified for the job. Lets him have a very short learning curve, because he's been there, done it and got the stripes. Sounds sensible to me – I mean he's not going to be there long enough to get bored, is he? And he doesn't have to fit into the management hierarchy either."

"Right. There's one problem we haven't talked about, that's the shut-down for the holidays in Belin. That's four weeks from the end of next week."

"As I understand it, Dick, they don't totally shut down. Just the manufacturing. There's cover in the sales office to take orders and issue invoices, and the warehouse will still despatch. So our Interim could still carry on working, if we thought it worthwhile. Might even be easier to get to grips with the numbers, with no one to interfere."

Back in his office, Dick printed off a copy of Jean-Paul's e-mail for Jennifer, which he put safely into his brief-case, and checked his in-tray. Elizabeth had printed out a reply from J-P to his own e-mail.

Dear Dick,

Looking forward very much to Mrs. Hawkins. Working through the weekend to produce the figures for you on Monday. Do not recognise your Commissaire St. Just. The one who has been here was called St. Josephe.

Jean-Paul.

Elizabeth had written a note on the bottom:

I had a call from a rather irate manager at the Belfry Hotel. Apparently his clerk didn't bother to run a credit check on M. St. Just's card this morning, and it has now been rejected. He feels that as we made the reservation we should guarantee the account, "Rather than have him call in the police". I said you would speak to him tomorrow.

Dick immediately put two and two together, and his heart sank as he came up with a very, very unpleasant answer. *St. Just was a fraud, a very plausible fraud too. And he's gone off with a set of our bank statements. Was there to be no end to this affair?* He checked the time – quarter-past five. *I'll call Dad this evening, it's getting too much for me to handle by myself.* Time he was on his way home – or at least as far as Jennifer's.

He looked both ways as he waited at the gates for a gap in the traffic – and there was that grey Volvo estate again, parked on the verge a hundred yards back. And as he turned out onto the road down to the river he glanced in the mirror, and saw it start to move forward to follow him.

Chapter Nineteen

Dick's eyes hardly left his rear-view mirror as he drove from the office. The grey Volvo stayed in full view, one or two hundred yards behind him, as though wanting to be seen, but just too far back for the registration to be read. Jennifer's double-fronted Edwardian house was three houses in from the corner of the road that led down to the Town Bridge, and Dick could not restrain a sigh of relief when he had pulled onto the half-moon of gravelled drive behind her stone pillars. This time the grey Volvo had not turned behind him. Instead he saw it had stopped in the main road opposite, apparently just waiting and watching. As he knocked at the door he was filled with a sense of helpless outrage – *he was being targetted! In his own town! Threatened, intimidated!* He knocked again, and the door was opened by a slightly flustered Jennifer, pressing the last pin into her lustrous dark hair.

"Dick, I'm so sorry to keep you . . ." He pushed past her and banged the door shut behind him. "What is it? What's happening?"

Instead of answering he stepped into the dining room and peered sideways between the velvet curtains. *It was gone, thank God! He drew a deep breath.*

"Jennifer, I must apologise . . . you must be thinking I've gone absolutely doolally. It's been a . . . a very odd sort of day. Some very strange things have been happening."

He stopped and looked at her. The mass of dark hair, pinned up and swept back, served to emphasise the high cheekbones and the fine modelling of her mouth. She was wearing a plain grey dress of some soft worsted material that clung closely to the contours of her body, with a thin red belt to cinch in her waist, and high-heeled red sandals. Those huge dark eyes seemed to be full of genuine concern, and it was very tempting to tell her everything and enjoy the pleasure of her sympathy. *Damn it to hell, why not? I just need to be careful not to put her off Arcachon and Jean-Paul.*

"Just let me organise myself, and I'll try to tell you what's going on, at least as much as I know myself. First of all though, I've got the e-mail with me from France. Can we sit down somewhere and go through it? In case there are any questions still?"

She gestured to a handsome panelled door. "Why don't you go into the living room. I'll get some tea, I'm sure that will help."

The living room, like the dining room on the other side, went from front to back of the house, with a large bay window at the front, and double french windows at the back, now filling with light from the returning sun. The floor was of polished pale oak strip, with a large yellow and blue Persian rug in front of the white marble fireplace. Two comfortable settees and an armchair looked as though they had been recently re-covered, and the plain yellow slub silk glowed warmly in the evening light. There were several vases of fresh roses on side tables, a large, slightly faded photograph of Jennifer with an older man – the original Hawkins? And three photographs in silver-gilt frames of Jennifer with Billy at various ages. *Billy's birthdays?* Standing by the mantelpiece, Dick had just about regained his composure when she returned carrying a tray of tea with two pieces of cake that he thought he recognised.

"I didn't bring the rest of the cake in, because I'm sure you'd be thinking of your waistline, but I thought one piece wouldn't hurt." She put the tray down on a coffee table and sat on the settee. "Come here and sit by me, have a cup of tea, and tell me what on earth is going on."

He pulled the e-mail from Jean-Paul out of his brief-case. "Perhaps we might just get this out of the way first, please?"

She read it carefully. "That's perfect, Dick. I'm so grateful for your help. I remember seeing the name of the Hotel Arc on the website, best hotel in Arcachon, right sur la plage. But it's much more reassuring to have someone local pick it out for me."

"He's booked the two rooms for three nights from next Tuesday. Do you think that will be enough?"

"I should think so. I mean, it's not as though I'm looking at property to buy. So a quick look round a dozen places should be enough for me to pick one for a six-month rental, or a year even – I haven't really made my mind up about how long to stay. I'll call Jean-Paul over the weekend, probably before I go, and try to arrange to meet him or his wife – what's she called?"

"Arlette. And the little boy is Henri."

"Right, I think you told me before." She wrote the names on the e-mail. "So I'll try to meet them on the Tuesday, and that leaves Wednesday and Thursday to trot round with the agents, make a decision Friday morning, then back home till the beginning of September. I'll get on the internet later for our return flights. So, that's me all nicely sorted. Can we talk about you now? If there's any way at all I can help, you only have to ask."

Her hand was soft and cool as she rested it on his. Since he had decided to talk to Jennifer about his problems, he had been rehearsing in his mind what to say, and, more importantly, what to leave out.

"You probably remember me telling you that our accountant over there, Alain Robarte, had died?"

"Vaguely, yes."

"There was a bit more to it than that. He lived in Bordeaux, about twenty miles from the factory. And he was out walking in Bordeaux on Saturday evening when he was attacked. At the time it seemed like a random mugging, and he died without regaining consciousness."

"How awful. Did he have a family?"

"Wife, but no children. Anyway, I had gone over there earlier last week to investigate a financial problem, and it begins to look as though there may be some sort of causal connection between my visit and Alain being killed."

"Oh Dick, no wonder you're upset."

"It gets worse. This morning I had a visit from the Commissaire de Police from Bordeaux, who's investigating this case. I told him about our own financial investigation, and he indicated we might be looking at a case of attempted money-laundering. But just before I left the office some more information came in to suggest that this Commissaire might himself be a fraud, probably part of the same conspiracy, in which case I've been pretty indiscreet. And to cap it all, the last two evenings I've been followed from the office by two men in a grey Volvo estate."

"To your house? And here?" Dick nodded, half expecting her to blame him for exposing her and her son to danger. But she remained warm and reassuring.

"Now I can see why you acted so strange when you arrived. You must be out of your mind with worry."

"I really am sorry about that, Jennifer. I suppose I shouldn't have come with them behind me . . ."

"Nonsense, of course you should. What are friends for?"

She took his hand again in both of hers, and this time he did not take it away, but responded instead to the pressure of her fingers with an almost imperceptible pull on her wrist that brought her face very close to his. The temptation to kiss that wide soft mouth was irresistible, and he saw her eyes begin to close as he touched his lips against hers. She held his hand tightly, and the kiss became less gentle, until she broke away. Her cheeks were flushed and she was breathing heavily. *Did I want that to happen? What are you, Jennifer Hawkins, a schoolgirl on her first date? Of course you wanted it! Very much indeed!*

She sat back into the settee and smiled. "That was strictly for comfort and reassurance, Dick. My well-known therapy system, works better than psychoanalysis every time. I'm applying for a patent."

Dick was not deceived by the light-hearted tone. He had felt a moment of real passion in that kiss, he was sure of it.

"It's me that's really grateful now. You know, I can't talk to Rosemary about this, at least not the way I talked to you."

He stood up, and she rose beside him, as tall as himself in her high heels, warm and infinitely desirable, and now suddenly accessible too.

She tried to keep the tremor out of her voice. "You should probably go now."

Dick wondered what that 'probably' meant. If he offered another kiss, would she say 'stay'? He thought of his car parked in her drive, and of the sharp eyes and wagging tongues of Lynchester. *Time to get back in control.*

"You're right, Jennifer. I don't want to, but I will. I probably won't see you for a few weeks now, but I do hope everything goes well in France."

He squeezed her hands and pecked her cheek. There was an irresistible schoolboy grin as he said, "Thanks for the tea. And the sympathy."

Chapter Twenty

Dick could still taste and feel that kiss as he pulled shut the door of his Jaguar with its usual reassuring 'clunk', and buckled up his seatbelt. He looked carefully both ways before easing out into the road, and was relieved not to see the Volvo. On the short journey to his house he asked himself why he was so concerned about being followed. *Obviously there may be some threat, perhaps a threat of a threat. But it's nothing like the threat from that flight of Migs when you strayed too close to the Russkis' airspace, is it? Am I just getting old and nervous? Or perhaps it's the possibility that the threat might reach out to my family, to Rosemary and Peter and James? And Jennifer?*

As he opened his front door he almost bumped into Rosemary, who was poised like a model, one foot in front of the other, looking at herself critically in the long hallway mirror.

"Ah, Dick, I'm glad you're back. Your mother called me this morning, asked if I would go with her for a meeting in the Town Hall about arrangements for the Lynchester Winter Ball in December. I think she wants me to come onto the committee. She's collecting me any minute now."

Dick wondered why she was now interested in civic affairs, when she had previously refused steadfastly to get involved, but decided not to ask just now. She was wearing the new linen suit bought for their holiday, pale green, long jacket, short pleated skirt, and there was definitely something different . . .

"You've had your hair cut."

"Yes, it was getting too long. Do you like it?"

She had a centre parting, and her auburn hair swung just above her shoulders in a gleaming page-boy bob.

"Very nice indeed. I wish you were going out with me, so that I could show you off to the town on my arm."

"You say the nicest things sometimes." She kissed him on the cheek, just as the front doorbell rang. "That'll be your mother. I've left you some Bolognese in the pot, you just have to warm it gently and cook yourself some spaghetti, say three ounces?. The boys are watching a video, they've had their tea. There's a good detective series you could watch on the TV tonight, but I won't be late."

She opened the front door, greeted Ellen Routledge with a smile and they walked to the car. *I suppose I should be glad she only kissed my cheek. She might have tasted Jennifer's lipstick too.* He looked into the TV den – Peter and James were curled over the armchairs, intent on a space adventure. He received a casual 'Hi Dad', and retreated to his study to telephone his father.

". . . I suppose I might be putting together two and two and making five, but the fact that Jean-Paul doesn't recognise the name St Just, and the hotel are saying that his credit card is dud, well . . . what d' you think?"

"I'd say its odds on you're right, this St. Just has fooled us all, got us to tell him everything we know, and made off with a set of our bank statements, cool as a damned cucumber." James let out a huge sigh. "Nothing else for it, I'm going to have to tell Ben what's going on. I'll give it some thought, and dictate an e-mail to Elizabeth in the morning. I think you should telephone the police here this evening, and see if you can have an appointment with someone fairly senior in the morning. I suggest you take Jim Helvin with you to add a bit more weight."

"Right. But it'll have to be tomorrow afternoon, or Friday. I'm needed with Jean Savage to interview those interim guys until lunchtime. I really feel worried not having a competent Finance man in Belin, someone we can absolutely trust. Do you think I should ask Staffordshire H.Q. for a Chief Inspector?"

"Why not? You're a senior director in the town's biggest employer, and you're up to your neck in a multinational financial swindle, to say nothing of a murder."

"Thanks, Dad."

Jennifer Hawkins raised a hand in farewell as Dick drove away, and stood for a moment in the shadow of her porch. *Dick Routledge was no pushover, but, when it came down to it, he was a man who liked women. And he likes me! If I settle in Arcachon for a few months, sooner or later he's going to come knocking at my door. And that'll be interesting, won't it?*

She climbed the broad staircase into her study, and sat down in front of her PC. *Now then, we're arriving in Arcachon next Tuesday, and staying three nights. So a flight back from somewhere not too far away on Friday. Biarritz again is the obvious place, then there's no complication about returning the rental car. Of course we could stay on a few more days instead of rushing back on Friday . . .*

Rosemary had several reasons for deciding to accept Ellen's invitation to the Town Hall meeting. Not that she really thought through her decision before accepting, so it seemed more like an impulse at the time. But reflecting about it during the day, she realised that those nagging doubts about Dick and that business card played a part. She felt an urge to strike out on her own for once, instead of being just an appendage to her husband's or her children's activities. Ellen had chattered over the telephone *in absolute confidence, dear, you mustn't even tell Dick yet*, about James' imminent retirement, and her plans to keep him occupied with local politics and so on. So if the old man retired, Dick was likely to become even busier. *Unless he retired too, of course . . .* She tried to imagine Dick as a gentleman at leisure, but somehow that didn't seem very likely. James would be going to the Grammar School in September, and little Peter was becoming more independent by the day. So Rosemary too started to think about being more involved locally. *At the end of the day, you only get something out of the community if you put something in. I'm intelligent, energetic, with good experience of managing men and organising projects. They should be very pleased to have me!*

Chapter Twenty-one

The meeting about the Lynchester Winter Ball was held in a pleasant oak-panelled committee room in the Town Hall, and was chaired by the mayor, Dan Gundry. Before proceedings began the members of the committee were standing around, exchanging the gossip of the day, and Ellen Routledge made a point of congratulating Dan very publicly on getting the Princess Anne for the opening of the new Hawkins-Routledge Wing in October.

"An outstanding achievement, Mr. Gundry, a fine piece of leadership."

Dan was experienced enough as a politician to guess he was being softened up for something, but accepted her praise with good grace.

"To be honest, I gave my PA a list of possibilities, and she did the rest. We're waiting for the letter of confirmation before we tell the Press, and I would ask everyone present not to talk about it outside this room, please. But it will be a wonderful boost for the town, no doubt about that, Mrs. Routledge."

"I wonder if you know the other Mrs. Routledge, Dan, my daughter-in-law Rosemary, Dick's wife?"

"Rosemary, good evening and welcome to the committee. I think we may have said a shy 'hullo' once or twice, but it's a great pleasure to be properly introduced. May I hope that you will be able to help us with the plans for the Winter Ball, Rosemary? Dick stood in very well for his father at our last meeting about the new wing. I must say that the more cooperation I see between the Hawkins and the Routledges, the more optimistic I become for the future of our town."

Rosemary had no prior experience of civic politics, but her years as an RAF Station Adjutant, arranging every kind of function for officers and men, stood her in good stead and by the end of the evening she found herself 'volunteered' to be in charge of hiring two bands and a disco. Afterwards she went back for coffee with Ellen. The house was in darkness as they came in the front door with its handsome stained glass panels.

"Where's James tonight?"

"Oh, he'll be already in bed. He gets tired early these days, probably the after-effect of that stroke, though there's been no other symptoms, thank heavens."

Sipping milky coffee on the sofa beside Ellen, Rosemary felt encouraged to offer a confidence herself.

"I haven't talked to Dick about it yet, but I was thinking about going for another baby. Or do you think I'm too old? Be honest now, please."

"No, no, of course you're not too old, dear. In these days of careers for women lots of wives have babies when they're older than you. Naturally I'm biased, but I think another grandson or granddaughter would be wonderful. And I'm sure Dick will love the idea too. I mean, you're not short of money now, are you, so you can have as much help around the house as you want. I was talking to Jennifer Hawkins the other day, she has a live-in nanny, a nice Dutch girl, I think. Something like that would make life so much easier for you. And I'll tell you something else, Peter and James will be thrilled, especially if it turned out to be a girl."

She thought for a moment, then her smile was definitely girlish. "You're off on holiday next weekend, aren't you? I've always found that holidays are a good time for these things. Salcombe isn't it? Such a romantic place . . ."

Rosemary insisted that there was no need for Ellen to drive her home, as it was less than ten minutes to walk, the street was well-lit, and the exercise would do her good on a warm, fine night. She felt almost exuberant as she walked. *A new baby! If we're lucky straight away, she'd arrive in April or May – just right. Shall I talk to Dick tonight? Perhaps not too directly . . . I should try to find a way to get the idea gently into his mind, so that it doesn't come as a total surprise. Perhaps it could even be his idea? My period is due, which is good, because it will be over by the time we got to Salcombe a week tomorrow. All I have to do is stop taking the pill, and let nature and Dick and Salcombe do the rest . . . Next door have got a new baby . . . I should start mentioning to Dick how lovely it is, how happy they seem to be. And I should ask how Jean Savage is getting on with her baby too. I'm sure he'll get the message.* In her cheerful reverie, she was quite unaware of the grey Volvo estate that eased along about a hundred yards behind her, and sped away as she turned the key in her front door.

By the time the three interviews with the candidates for Interim Finance Manager in France were completed it was almost one-thirty on Thursday afternoon.

"I don't know about you, Jean, but I'm exhausted. What say we collect up our stuff and retreat to a corner of 'The Feathers' for a pie and a pint?"

Jean sat back with a sigh. "I'm a bit tired too. It's not going to be easy to choose, is it? Three very good candidates, I . . ."

Dick stood up to cut her short. "And if we don't get moving now, I can tell you from bitter experience that the kitchen at 'The Feathers' gets closed sharp at two, and we'll be left to starve."

The main bar in the pub was busy as usual, but Dick edged his way through with Jean close behind, both raising a hand frequently to acknowledge slightly startled greetings from acquaintances. Before she married John Savage, Jean had lived for three years in a little cottage nearby, and paused to chat for a moment with a former neighbour who asked after progress with the baby. "All going well so far. If it's a boy, I can guarantee he'll be kicking for England when he grows up."

Dick found a table in the Snug which had just been vacated. "What'll you have? I'll get the girl to clear these plates off for us too."

"Pint of orange juice and lemonade, please. And a cold beef salad if they've got one left."

When he got back with the drinks, she was already re-reading her notes.

"Food should only be a few minutes. She thinks there's beef still."

He took a long pull from his pint of bitter. "That's much better. OK then, you first."

"As I was saying, three good candidates, and in ordinary circumstances any one of them could do the job, so we would take the cheapest, I suppose."

"But these aren't ordinary circumstances."

"Exactly. So I crossed off the Frenchman, Henri Besant. He reminded me of Jean-Paul. Not the looks, I mean J-P is lean and dark, and this chap is positively tubby. But the same air of absolute superiority. I think they'd recognise a kindred soul in one another straight away, and bang would go our hope for a counterweight."

"Though I liked his reply to the question of why he'd gone independent."

"Yes, 'I was looking for a proper job, then someone offered me a six-month assignment for the same money I'd just worked a year to earn. To be paid to me gross, with a year to work out my own tax. Que faire?' And that charming smile accompanied by the Gallic shrug. So, how about Charlotte?

"Absolute cracker. As a candidate, I mean. Personally she comes across as a bit of a battleaxe, if that isn't too politically incorrect?"

"I'll let it pass this time, but don't make a habit of it."

"I was impressed by her story of her first assignment, near Geneva wasn't it, when she discovered that the management had been robbing the owners blind for years. She made light of it, but I'd say it took some guts to go straight to the Swiss police, in a small town where the managers had lived all their lives."

They sat back as the waitress arrived with their food, the beef salad for Jean and a steak and kidney pie with green peas for Dick.

"Notice that I'm not having potatoes," he said smugly.

"Nor am I, and I'm eating for two, don't forget."

Dick attacked his pie in happy silence for a couple of minutes. "I have to say though that I can understand why Bill Jameson is the most expensive of the three. Big corporations, small companies, rescues, takeovers, frauds and public offerings, he's done the lot."

"And he wasn't shy about letting us read his file of 'Thank-you and well done' letters, either."

"Yes, a bit unusual that."

"But perfectly understandable. He was making a sales pitch to us, wasn't he? I suppose it came across as unusual to us because very few candidates have that weight of recommendation to offer."

Dick finished his beer with a sigh. "So either Charlotte or Bill will do us very well. Big difference in cost though. Even more if we assume that Charlotte will stay at her French home in Bordeaux, so minimal travelling and accommodation costs. That would make, say, fifteen thou. difference altogether, give or take a bit."

Jean was more cautious. "But will the Chairman accept a woman, especially as she'll have to be working in the front line, as it were?"

"With a fifteen thousand pound differential at stake, my guess is that the Chairman will swallow his chivalrous principles, but let's just put it to him, and ask him to meet both candidates. Do you think you could put together a summary of our recommendation, including the comparative costs of course, say for 100 days, together with the two CVs, please? And give it to Elizabeth, ask her to get it to the Chairman this evening, or else see that he reads it as soon as he gets in."

Jean checked her watch. "Almost three already. I'll call the agency as soon as we're back and set everything up for tomorrow. What time will the Chairman want to start?"

"Let's say eleven, to be on the safe side. Rosemary told me he's starting to go to bed quite early now, so he might not be rushing in too early either. I think the plan should be to let him meet each in turn, then we'll have a decision, and the one selected can stay on with us for a bite of lunch in the office, and we'll unwrap the whole situation then."

Dick had put off talking to the local police that morning, but knew he would have to do it when he got back to his office.

"Afternoon, Elizabeth. Any messages?"

"Only Mr. Egan, the manager at the 'Belfry'. He'd appreciate a call back, please."

It went against the grain with Dick for the company to have to pay the hotel bill for a crook, but he was reluctant to start what could well become an unpleasant quarrel with the 'Belfry'. Being on one of the best golf-courses in the country, it was very popular with visitors from America, especially Ben Camena. His father would not thank him if they lost their privileged status of virtually being able to guarantee a convenient tee-off time, any weekday . . .

"Mr. Egan? Good afternoon, it's Dick Rutledge, from Strongwheat. You wanted to speak to me, I believe?"

Fortunately St. Just, or whatever his real name was, had not been extravagant during his stay, just room, breakfast, a brandy from the mini-bar, and a late-night film. A total of just over £250.

"I wouldn't like this to be seen as a precedent, Mr. Egan, but on this occasion Strongwheat will accept responsibility. Will you be sure to mark the invoice for my attention, please?"

Not wanting Elizabeth to know more than was absolutely necessary, Dick looked up and dialled the number for the local police himself, and was slightly disconcerted to be put through to a call-centre. He decided to press on.

"My name is Routledge, Mr. Richard Routledge. I'm a director of the European subsidiary of an American company here in Lynchester. We think we may have been the victims of an international fraud, possibly money-laundering. Would it be possible please to meet a senior officer, the Detective Chief Inspector?"

There was a pause, then "May I put you on hold for a minute, sir? I need to check with the senior officer here."

Dick listened with rising impatience to most of a slow movement from one of the Bach concertos.

"Good afternoon, Mr Routledge, is it? I'm Detective Chief Inspector James Renton. I understand you believe your company may be involved in a serious crime?"

"Yes, well, not involved, exactly. We think we may be the innocent victims."

"I see. Would you like to come in to Stafford CID tomorrow morning to tell me all about it?"

"I'm sorry, tomorrow is impossible. Might you be free on Monday at all?"

"Monday . . . yes, how does ten o'clock suit you? Give me a fax number, and I'll send you a map to find us."

"It's 01827 776677. I'll come with our Finance Director, Jim Helvin, and we'll bring some paperwork too. Ten o'clock Monday then."

Chapter Twenty-two

Rosemary awoke early on Friday morning, her eyes at first dazzled by the sunlight streaming in through a gap in the curtains. Dick was sleeping quietly beside her, his face calm and boyish, one hand under his forehead. She raised her head carefully to check the time on the alarm clock – almost seven. *A quarter of an hour before the morning rush would begin.* She eased down into the bed again, and winced a little. *Well, that's one thing settled, Dick is really enthusiastic about the idea of going for another baby!* After supper she had mentioned next door's baby girl. 'She's so adorable it's enough to make any woman feel broody', and surprisingly he had leapt straight for the idea himself.

"These broody women, might that possibly include you, my love? If it does, I'm all for it."

He kissed her cheek as he collected the plates from the table. One thing led to another, and by ten o'clock they were in bed, and Dick was being very enthusiastic indeed, as she had been reminded by that twinge of discomfort when she moved. *And I can forget once and for all the silly worry I had after I found that Swedish woman's business card. Dick really loves me very much, and if he was having an affair he couldn't possibly be so keen for us to have another baby. Seems a pity really that last night wasn't likely to be the start . . . still, Ellen was right about one thing, those two weeks in Salcombe could be just what we need!*

There was no sign of the grey Volvo when Dick left his house at eight o'clock, and he tried to put it from his mind as he settled down at his desk to check his post and e-mails. The most interesting was a copy of his father's message to Ben Camena at ACP.

Dear Ben,

You will remember that I told you about the attack on our French Financial Manager, Alain Robarte? I very much regret that he has since died, without recovering consciousness, and in consequence the police are treating the case as a murder. It now seems possible that the peculiar figures you saw from them last week for the month of June, which Alain subsequently corrected, were evidence of attempted or actual money laundering. We do not know yet if this may have any connection to the murder. Dick and I are keeping right on top of this, working with the local police, and we will keep you fully informed as soon as there is any news. So far we have been able to go through all the company's French bank statements, and we are confident there has been no loss of funds from the company. Best regards, James Routledge.

Dick read it slowly a second time. *That should be enough to satisfy them, for a while anyway.* There was a message too from Jurgen in Wuppertal.

"*Thank you for the suggestion about visiting Belin. I will contact Jean-Paul directly and keep you posted about the dates as agreed.*"

Dick wondered in passing if there was a hint of aggressive independence in the tone of the message, and decided that, if there was, it was probably a good thing, because that would result in less need for him to get involved. *The German management team is pretty strong, I think, probably more impressive than the French.*

Pietro had not been accommodating.

"*I regret that we do not have a spare driver at this moment to bring you from Milan to Parma. Would it be possible for you to rent a car, or to come by train?*"

Dick bristled a little at this, sensing that Pietro was 'trying it on', perhaps testing the balance of power between them. He stood up to look at the map of Western Europe that covered most of one wall of his office. *Milan to Parma was about eighty miles. Add on time for getting into and out of the cities, and assuming I don't get lost en route I should allow . . . no, damn them!*

Dear Pietro, I have a very stressful itinerary in Italy, and I would not like to be arriving in Parma too tired to help with your planning properly. So I will arrange a chauffeured car in Milan. I hope that will not break the budget! Best regards, Dick Routledge.

Elizabeth came in with a tray of tea and the morning's post.

"There's an interesting fax here for you from the police headquarters in Stafford, with a map and directions off the M6. Compliments of a Detective Chief Inspector Renton."

He thought that it would do no harm to satisfy her barely-suppressed curiosity.

"Yes, the Chairman wants me to tell them all about the mess in France, and our bogus visitor from Bordeaux. If that is where he came from? I'll be going up to Stafford first thing Monday morning, should be back by lunch time. I'm going to take Jim Helvin too. Just a reminder, Elizabeth, this morning from eleven Mrs Savage and I will be introducing the Chairman to two of yesterday's candidates, and we'll be inviting one to stay on for lunch with us. Would you ask the canteen please to lay on a simple buffet in the Boardroom for four people?"

There was another e-mail on his screen, from Italy.

Dear Dick, I have just had a call from an important customer in Milan who would like to see me, so I have arranged a meeting there for 8.30 on the Wednesday morning. I should be able to collect you at your hotel 9.30 to 10.00, and I'm sure we'll find a way to get you back. Looking forward very much to then, best regards, Pietro Cavalli.

Dick smiled as he read the message, and wondered if there really had been a call from a customer, or whether this was Pietro's diplomatic climb-down? *A lesson learned – sometimes it pays to be bloody-minded*! And there was a reply from Ben Camena to his father's message:

Dear James, Truly sorry to hear the news about Alain. I hope the French police catch the bastards. I have a company expert on money laundering, Joss Pienkowski, who is expected back here from Manila over the weekend. I will have him contact you next week to see if he can help at all. All the best, Ben.

He was still browsing through his post when Jean Savage came in.

"Morning, Dick. Bill Jameson has arrived. He's a few minutes early, so I've sat him down in my office with a cup of coffee and the *Daily Telegraph*. Elizabeth says the Chairman has been in for half an hour or so. Would it be a good move to have a preliminary chat with him, d'you think?"

"Good thought. I read through my copy of your briefing document for him just now. Just right."

"And I wondered if we should include Jim Helvin in the interview panel? I've talked him through the CVs, and he's up to speed. I think he's secretly very impressed."

Dick thought for a moment. "Perhaps not, Jean. This morning we're just asking the Chairman to say which one he prefers, not assessing their professional competence. But I would like Jim to spend an hour with the winner this afternoon, getting him or her up to speed with the detail of his reporting requirements, and the latest results of his digging into the financials. Would you tell him that, please?"

He gathered up his papers and Jean caught up with him as he walked into Elizabeth's office. "Jim's happy to leave it to us."

"Is the Chairman free, please Elizabeth?"

"Not . . . yes, sorry, he's just off the telephone."

James Routledge stood up stiffly as they entered his office and walked round to the front of his desk. "Ellen had me doing some gardening yesterday, and my back's saying I shouldn't have. Morning Jean, morning Dick, do sit down. Have you fixed up to see the police?"

"Monday morning in Stafford, a Detective Chief Inspector Renton."

"Renton . . . that name rings a bell . . . yes, Jim Renton, from Stafford. I met him, let me see . . . about four years ago, before I had the stroke. You remember that business with the Hawkins brothers being killed, very nasty. Perhaps you hadn't joined us then? Anyway, he was the man in charge of the investigation, didn't come out of it too well, if I recall aright. People said that Jennifer Hawkins had pulled the wool over his eyes. Or vice-versa was it? Nice-looking woman, though. Of course that's all a while back now."

Dick had a sudden, disturbing vision of Jennifer in a tight wool sweater.

"I thought that Jean's brief about the Interim Finance manager for Belin was pretty good. Have you had time to read it yet?"

James sat back down in his chair. "Of course I've read it, Elizabeth brought it round last night. No peace for the wicked, I thought, but still, a fair piece of work, Jean, thank you."

Dad is certainly getting softer in his old age! First we get a chatty welcome with a hint of sex in his little reminiscence of

Jennifer, then he's nice to Jean. Next thing, he'll be congratulating me on something!

"We're fairly sure we should go for the lady, Charlotte Aston, but we thought it wouldn't do any harm to see the two of them again."

"No doubt you've given due thought to the little matter of sending a woman into what could become a very messy business, dangerous perhaps too?"

Jean intervened before Dick could answer. "You should perhaps ask her what her experience has been of 'messy situations'. I think you'll be impressed. And my expectation would be that, now they know we suspect money laundering, and the police are looking for a murderer or two, they – whoever 'they' may be – are likely to keep well away from ACP France."

"You might be right. Then again you might not. 'They' are certainly going to want to cover their tracks, and, as I said to Dick, we still don't know how deeply Jean-Paul may be involved. Anyway, that's enough guesswork for one morning. Do you want to wheel in Mr . . . um . . . Jameson?"

James took charge of the interview, then for three-quarters of an hour Dick and Jean just listened as Bill told yarns about his assignments.

"Funniest one, well, funny looking back on it, was for the French subsidiary of a US pet food business, down near Arles in Provence. Quite a big factory, double shifting with about three hundred employees altogether. One Thursday teatime the MD, who's French himself by the way, asks the day shift to hang on for fifteen minutes in the canteen, and brings in the evening shift as well, as they arrive. Once they're all assembled, he announces that the brand and the business have been sold to the major competitor, and this factory will be closing in three months' time. Everyone will get statutory severance pay, and a bonus if everything goes smoothly with the shutdown and transfer of production. This is the first anyone has heard of it, including the management, so consternation all round. He tells the shop floor people they are on paid holiday starting immediately until Monday, and asks us managers to stay on for an hour to talk through the plan, identify possible snags and so on. All very business-like and textbook American practice. Then he goes back to his office to call the States to say everything is moving along, only to discover the telephones are dead. At the same time we find that the office doors are locked and barricaded. We're on the second floor, by the way. We open the windows, and find a very angry crowd outside, waving their fists and shouting up to us.

" 'You're going to lock us out. So we've locked you in! And now we are going to warm up your negotiating position.' "

Bill sat back and spread his hands. "When you've been locked in the factory, and it's starting to get dark, and then you see them building what looks like a bloody great bonfire against the walls just below you, 'Industrial Negotiations' takes on a whole new meaning!"

Even James found his curiosity aroused. "So what happened?"

"The MD threatened to get the gendarmes. The leader shouted back. 'Who cares about the flics? This is Provence! We didn't give in to the Germans, and we don't give in to the Americans, either!' This stuff goes back and forth for what seems ages, then the Production Director points out that the bonfire is being built alongside the wall with the oil tanks behind it, and suddenly the MD goes very quiet. He calls the police on his mobile, and is told, 'This is an industrial dispute on private land, it would not be politic for us to intervene until some crime has been committed. Perhaps the MD has himself has provoked this confrontation to avoid paying proper severance?'

"The MD doesn't want publicity, so backs down. 'All right, let's negotiate something better than statutory severance.' To cut a long story short, they kept us in the office overnight, with just the chocolate bars and coffee from the vending machine. Next day just the MD is let out again to negotiate, if you can call it that, and he agrees eventually to pay three times statutory. Works out to be an average settlement of almost twenty thousand pounds a head. Unfortunately I was being paid by the day as an independent, so I didn't get any of the loot."

James did not allow himself to seem too impressed. "Fine, Mr. Jameson, very interesting. Now we have one more candidate to see, so if you would like to go for a walk for an hour we'll find you in our Reception and try to have a decision for you at one o'clock."

After he had left, James stood up gingerly to stretch his aching back, and walked to the window.

"Quite a fellow, quite a track-record. Of course it needs to be pretty impressive to justify charging us £750 per day, plus expenses. Still, I'd be very confident that he'd hold his end up in

Belin, and we could trust his figures too when they came over. Shall we meet the lady, please Jean?"

Charlotte was altogether less flamboyant, and took it for granted that her interviewers had read her CV. Instead she wanted to talk about what she would be doing, assuming she got the assignment.

"I understand that this will be your first experience of using an Interim?"

Jean felt that it was for her to reply. "First time, yes. Quite frankly we know we have a problem in France, and I suggested to the Board that an Interim Manager could be the solution. Do you think I was right?"

Charlotte was a small, wiry woman in her early fifties, sedately dressed in a dark blue cotton suit with a white blouse. Her fading blonde hair was swept up and tightly pinned, but her rather severe expression was softened by a little smile as she listened to Jean's invitation, and she sat up a little straighter.

"You've seen my track record. There's absolutely no doubt that I can do this job. I'd like you to understand though that it's not going to be like recruiting me for a permanent position, where you have to ask yourself if I will fit into the company ethos, or into the long-term management structure requirements. I'm going to be there for a specific number of weeks or months, and I'm going to ask you upfront to agree with me a specific list of things you want me to accomplish in that time. Then at regular intervals, probably weekly, I'll be telling you what progress I've made, what the obstacles are, if any, and what I'll be doing next."

James felt a need to regain control.

"So, Miss Aston, you've heard quite a bit about our difficulties in France, what do you suggest should be your priorities?"

"It's Mrs Aston by the way, Mr. Routledge, though my husband was drowned in a boating accident five years ago. Priorities? First step, to whom will I be reporting? Putting it simply, who wants to know what?"

"I think you might answer that one, Dick."

"Nothing exceptional, really. Alain Robarte, the Finance Manager who has just died, was part of the local management team, reporting to the Managing Director, Jean-Paul de Clavignon. Based here we have a European Finance Director, Jim Helvin, and you would have a dotted-line reporting responsibility to him, for professional standards and so on. Monthly figures are sent here, and simultaneously to the States, by e-mail."

"No hidden agenda?"

Dick was taken aback by the directness of her question, and was relieved when Jean answered.

"We do have some issues that may need resolving. If you are selected we will ask you to stay on with us for lunch, and we could go into that together, if that will help?"

"Fair enough. So, pending that discussion, my priorities will be to establish a good working relationship with M'sieur de Clavignon, then with the rest of the local team, pick up the routine for the July month-end, and take things forward from there. Presumably you will be starting to recruit a permanent Finance Manager, and I'd be happy to help with that, and with breaking him in once he joins. By the way, I'd suggest you might warn ACP that the July figures will be a few days later than usual, but we'll be up to speed for August."

Chapter Twenty-three

"Grazie, grazie." Brit put down the telephone with a little nod of satisfaction. That was her third call to Milan, and now she had three visits lined up for Wednesday of next week, to Armani, Gucci and Prada. *Nothing like going for the top!* In each case she had asked for the Sales Director's PA, and in each case she had been put through to the man himself – well, a woman in one case. Offers of lunch and dinner had been politely turned away. *They'll be quite cross if I don't buy anything. Perhaps I might suggest that our store customers are not yet ready for their latest styles – and the latest prices – but we could be in the market to take some fin-de-saison stuff, if the discounts are big enough, and if it's not too weird.*

She glanced at her watch – just after Friday midday, and a lovely sunny day too. *I could slip out for an early sandwich by the water. Really, I'm overdue an afternoon off. Though I suppose I ought to think of my Milan trip as a kind of advance holiday. I wonder what Dick is doing now?* She was on the way out of the small office, still dreaming aimlessly about her English lover, when the ringing telephone abruptly called her back to reality. She went reluctantly back to her desk.

"Good afternoon. Steen and Strom, Stockholm."

"Hullo, is that Brit Carlsohn?"

An English voice! But not Dick Routledge! Brit was momentarily confused.

"Yes, this is Brit. Who's that?"

"Brit, I'm really disappointed that you don't recognise my voice. How many Englishmen do you know? It's George, George Hosker from Baines Department Stores in London. How are you?"

George, the Buying Director who had so politely propositioned her after dinner on that conference in Amalfi. So rejection hadn't put him off then!

"George, yes, of course I know you now. I'm very well, just looking forward to the start of our holidays next weekend. I have a whole month booked with my mother and my son in a villa in the Algarve."

"Sounds blissful, I envy you. Well, as you might guess, I have a special reason to call you. Our Ladies' Fashions buyer has just given in her notice. She's off to the States in September, to Sears Roebuck in Chicago on some absolutely unbelievable package. I hardly need to say that I've admired you and your work for a few years now, and I wondered if you might be interested to come to London to talk about prospects here in Baines?"

Brit was silent for a long minute. "George, you know I like you. And the job could be wonderful for me. But I have to tell you straight away that I have a special friend now, a man who is important to me, so . . ."

"Brit, it may not sound too flattering, but I swear the thought had not crossed my mind, absolutely not. In fact it's a big 'No-No' in our company now, we're very politically-correct, so even a whiff of suspicion could cost me my job. Strictly a working relationship, and no complications, I promise."

"That is good, George, and I'm sure we could work well together. When would you like to see me in London?"

"I'm just opening my diary. This really won't wait until you get back at the end of August. So, next week sometime. I've got lots on, but all the supplier visits are UK-based, so nothing I can't move around. Which day would suit you best?"

Brit looked at her own arrangements. Tuesday through Thursday was set aside for the trip to Milan, which she was looking forward to very, very much. That left Friday or Monday. Going to England on Friday would be very difficult, with her holiday flight tickets booked from Stockholm to Faro for the Saturday, especially if there were any last-minute problems in the office . . .

"I have some commitments next week that I cannot change, George. Really, the only possible day for me before my holiday is Monday."

It was George's turn to pause. His buyer's instinct and training told him that making room in his diary for her on Monday would suggest extreme eagerness, if not desperation. On the other hand he had in fact already been turned down by three English candidates, and, in all honesty, he was getting a little desperate.

"Could you be here for lunch at, say twelve-thirty? It would be a chance for you to meet some other directors and senior managers, then we could talk afterwards together."

"Let's agree that then. I will e-mail you this afternoon with my flight details, and I look forward very much to our meeting again."

She sat on the desk for a moment and looked out longingly at the bright sunshine that glittered across the silvery waters of Stockholm's old harbour. *I'll walk along the quay to the travel agent and book my flights for Monday. SAS I suppose, or British Airways. Either way, it won't be cheap, and I'll have to put it on my own Visa card. Though I'm sure Baines will pay in due course. What if I called Dick this afternoon and suggested we meet Monday in London, and go on to Milan together on Tuesday? Perhaps not, he might feel a little threatened! Fancy though, just a little while ago I was wondering what he would say if I came to work in London. Perhaps I am about to find out . . .*

In Belin, Jean-Paul de Clavignon sat back in his office chair with his hands clasped behind his head, and slowly re-read the e-mail that had just come in from ACP's Group Director of Human Resources.

> *We have been discussing here with Ben Camina the terrible news of the death of Alain Robarte. We understand he leaves a widow, but no children. Although he has been with the company only 18 months, he was nonetheless fully covered by the*

company's Executive Life Insurance package. This means that we just need you to send to this office the death certificate, and the insurance will be paid to his widow, at the rate of 12 times his annual gross salary. Please confirm that this was 55,000 Euros per annum.

Jean-Paul pressed 'print'. *Twelve times is generous! Viola will be pleased, a tax-free cheque for 660.000 Euros. If she's careful with her investments, enough income from that to live nicely for the rest of her life.* And he knew from experience that Viola was always careful with money. Though not necessarily careful about other things, else how had Alain come to believe that there might be something going on between pretty Viola and himself? Well, the police were still very active in their enquiries into the murder, so this was no time to be thinking of renewing their friendship. *I know the police have not yet released Alain's body for burial. I wonder though if Viola has been given a death certificate?* He imagined for a moment her pert figure, dressed in black silk, then picked up his telephone to call her home in Bordeaux, only to put it slowly down again. *If the police suspect there may be a connection, her telephone may be tapped. Who knows what she might blurt out if I call her? Better to tell the police about this e-mail, and leave it to them to tell Viola. I wonder if they might see the insurance as a possible motive for murder? Alain certainly had a copy of the company staff handbook, and the insurance arrangement is bound to be in there. So she could have found out how much he was worth – dead.*

As Jean Savage and Dick had hoped, James Routledge had accepted their recommendation of Charlotte Aston without much argument.

"On your heads be it, then." Dick had never known his father to be so laid back – usually he would rip into every suggestion he made, forcing him to justify every step. Today he seemed to be just going through the motions. *He's there, but he's not there. Switched off, I suppose you could say. Well, let's not complain!* Jean met Bill Jameson to tell him he had not been successful this time. He was not at all disconcerted. "I see you've got Charlotte Aston – she won't let you down. Give her my best regards."

Charlotte, Jean, James and Dick had a pleasant lunch around the board table, and as the coffee was being passed round James came to life again.

"Mrs. Aston, you know that we are happy in principle for you to do this job in Belin for us. Equally, we want you to go over as well-prepared as possible for what you may find."

He paused, perhaps hoping for something encouraging from her. Instead she sat in silence beside him, quite still, with her fingers laced together. James continued.

"Well then. The problem in France is not just that our Finance Manager has died. The fact is, he was murdered, smashed about the head last Saturday night while out walking his dog in Bordeaux."

Charlotte's hands went up to her mouth, and there was a little gasp. "Oh my!"

"There's more. Up close and personal, as one might say. Dick, would you like to fill in some background, please?"

"Yes, well, you see we have some other odd things going on in France, but we don't know for sure if they're connected or if it's just a series of coincidences."

He explained about the unusual numbers in the June management report, his own visit, and the explanation that Jean-Paul had given, the car that had followed him around, and the bogus Chief Inspector.

"So you see, there may be a full-blown conspiracy over there, or it might be a series of things, some of which may be connected and some not. And you will be pitched into the middle of it. To be absolutely frank, we are not even entirely certain that our Managing Director is not himself involved. Of course the whole place is crawling with French police now, and we don't believe that you could be in any danger yourself. Definitely not. Well, I've tried to be as open as I could be. How do you feel about it all now?"

Charlotte sat in silence again, and looked from Dick to his father and then to Jean, who was sitting opposite. "How much did the agency know about all this?"

Jean tried not to look guilty. "None of it. Just that Alain has died. We regard everything else we've told you as highly-sensitive company information, and we wouldn't want any of it known outside this office."

"Probably not. I'm sure if the agency had known, they would have negotiated a substantially higher fee, or at least a hefty bonus on completion?"

James accepted the implied invitation to negotiate. "What would you have in mind? Mind you, the four hundred and fifty pounds a day plus expenses seems quite hefty enough to us."

"Perhaps. Bear in mind that a big chunk of that is extracted by the agency before I see it. But it would be a fair enough rate for a small-company Financial Manager, competent to operate in France, if that's all it was. But this is much more complicated, isn't it? You need someone with acute political and personal antennae, someone who can function in what may become a very hostile environment. You need me to engage all my skills and experience, not just my routine ability to cope."

James could not resist going onto the attack.

"Do you want this job?"

Charlotte paused for a few long seconds. "Yes, I don't easily frighten. But at the right price."

"Which is?"

"I'm assuming that you're right about there being not much chance that I will be in any personal danger, but I will be talking to the local police there about that next week. It's perfectly normal, you know, for Interims operating in Russia to have a personal bodyguard, but I don't suppose it's got that bad in France yet. So, I must ask for an extra hundred pounds a day, with a minimum one hundred days on contract, and a success bonus when I hand over to the full time replacement that I will help you to recruit and then mentor in. Five thousand pounds at that time would be fair."

In the ensuing silence Dick did the arithmetic on his pad. *Say a hundred days at six hundred a day, plus five thousand at the end, total sixty-five thousand. pounds. At $1.80 to the pound that was . . . $120,000. Bit over budget, but bearable!*

"Can we assume that you'll be living at home in Bordeaux, and the only expense will be your flights and a car which the company will provide?"

"Agreed."

Dick looked at his father, who nodded almost imperceptibly. "Right then, we'll agree that. Now if you would, Charlotte, I'd like you to spend some time with our European Group Finance Director, Jim Helvin. He'll show you where we'd got to in the financial investigation I told you about, and also brief you on the technical requirements for reporting to our parent ACP. At the moment this is a fairly straightforward manufacturing company, although it is to be used as the model for a new factory in Germany, and we are hoping to start planning soon for a marketing extension into Italy, and you will undoubtedly be involved in the initial preparations and planning for that.

While you're talking to Jim, could I have Elizabeth get your flight tickets for Bordeaux?"

"That would be helpful, yes. I'll go over Saturday, that's tomorrow of course. So not too early, Birmingham to Bordeaux, and an open return, please."

Dick handed Charlotte on to Jim Helvin, and found Phil Wythe, Strongwheat's UK managing director, chatting with Elizabeth. After briefing her about Charlotte's flight, he invited Phil into his office. He thought that Phil was starting to look older, just a little harassed. *Well, you wanted the top job, chum!*

"Good to see you, Phil. How are things going?"

"Can't complain I suppose. Looks like July will be on Budget, which leaves us still three percent ahead of budget so far, but the sales people are nervous about the big volumes in the targets for the Autumn, especially with this new price pressure coming in from Weetabix."

"Yes, Paul had a chat with me about his problem. Are we getting together now?"

They were moving into Dick's office, and Phil pushed the door shut behind him as they sat down.

"I wanted a quick word with you about that. I mean, if there was an irreconcilable dispute, it might make sense for us to ask you to help us decide, but that's hardly the case here. The sales people have reported what Weetabix are up to, and suggested that the trade support we need to get the autumn targets is getting harder to nail down. We both know that if we want to increase the funds for trade discounts the money will have to come out of the TV advertising. I think I need to talk it through with Paul today, think about it over the weekend, and make a decision on Monday."

"Meaning you don't really need me involved?"

Phil gave a tiny shrug. "Unless you have very strong views?"

"Not really. We've all fought long and hard to get the TV budget up to where it is, and there is that awful precedent five or six years ago of what happened last time the advertising budgets were cut. If it was my decision, I'd probably try to find some compromise, but it's your baby, Phil."

Phil stood up. "Thanks, Dick. That's just what I wanted to hear. I knew you'd understand. If you don't mind, I'll tell Paul you've got a problem in Europe that won't wait, so we'll just carry on without you."

After lunch James returned to his office and sat down with a little sigh, still feeling his back. He was worried, very worried about sending Charlotte into whatever the situation was in France. Of course Jean was probably right when she'd said that the high level of police activity would be a protective shield. But what if the real danger lurked behind the shield?

He woke up his computer to e-mail Ben Camina, and found a copy of the message to Jean-Paul about the insurance pay-out. *Six hundred and sixty thousand Euros, that's getting on for half a million pounds. Cash. Tax-free. A big enough motive for murder? I just hope she's very, very careful!*

> *Dear Ben, Just to keep you posted, we have been able to find a very experienced and able Interim Finance Manager for France. She is flying over tomorrow. Cost estimate – £65,000. Best regards, James*

He re-read what he had written. I wonder if he'll pick up on the 'she'? He pressed 'send' and sat back *What else? One 'phone call, then I'm going home.*

"Elizabeth, would you see if you can get me Dan Grundy please? He might be at the Council Chamber, or you could try his mobile number."

"James, good to hear from you. You've caught me at home, but I'm not really skiving off. Just catching up on some paperwork before the weekend. Did you hear about the Princess coming?"

"Ellen told me, yes. I think the town will owe you a debt of gratitude. I heard you'd discovered ancient Rome too?"

"Some of it, anyway. We've decided it's going to take weeks to check out the site properly, and I've got more political sense than to propose eliminating a find which might even put Lynchester onto the 'Midlands Heritage' map."

"Will it cost you money?"

"Not too much. I'm just the builder, incentivised for a share of the development profit when the houses are built and sold on, but it's not my upfront capital, thank heavens. At this stage I can switch our people and plant to other jobs, and just sit things out. They've already found a hypocaust, that's the under-floor heating, and part of a mosaic floor with a flying horse, so it's actually quite interesting too. We'll probably end up with fewer houses, but more expensive ones. We'll call it 'Villa Close' or 'Pegasus Mews', or something like that. Anyway, what can I do for you, James?"

That's what I've always liked about Dan Grundy, practical, gets on with things, knows which side his bread is buttered. "This is strictly for your ears only, Dan. I'm expecting to retire next Spring, but I don't fancy doing nothing. I was wondering if you thought I could make myself "useful to the town, some kind of civic or political work."

Dan was cautious. "Anything specific you'd be interested in?"

"I suppose it would make sense to build on the new H-R ward connection?"

"Mm, yes, especially after the grand opening, well, you'd be a natural for the chairmanship of the hospital, or the NHS regional trust, if a vacancy comes up. You could probably slide straight into a deputy chairmanship anyway. Let me drop a word in one or two ears, and I'll get back to you. Would you be interested to come onto the District Council?"

"Not sure. I don't quite see myself knocking on doors, or making speeches to two old ladies and a dog in draughty halls."

"No, nor do I really. I suppose you're a Tory?"

"I've always voted Conservative, yes."

"I've always stood as an Independent myself, but it takes all sorts, no doubt. Council Leader is Tory, of course. Let me have a quiet word with her for you, just to sound out the lie of the land. You're well enough known in the town, born and brought up here, popular main employer, public benefactor too, I'd guess you'd walk it without needing to do much in the way of canvassing. They'd find you a safe ward, put out a leaflet at election time all about what a good chap you are".

"I'm grateful to you, Dan. But keep it to yourself as far as possible. I haven't told ACP or anyone at Strongwheat yet."

Jennifer Hawkins always enjoyed her meetings with Charles Harrison, her accountant. He was attentive, flattering, not so obviously interested in her sexually as Dick Routledge for instance, but still an admirer, in a careful sort of way. On Friday afternoon though, she encouraged him to bring in his new protegee, Rachel Goldman.

"It's lovely to meet you at last, Rachel. Charles speaks so highly of you, I suspect that you do all the work and Charles gets the credit."

This last was, in Rachel's opinion, very close to the truth, but she was diplomatic. "I'd say he points me in the right direction, and I follow his lead. I've learnt a lot since I came out from Birmingham."

Not exactly pretty, but not unattractive either. Nice figure, strong features, good mind. "So, what have you got for me this afternoon? Basically I want to start things moving vis-a-vis setting aside funds for Billy's education."

Charles nodded to Rachel, who took the lead.

"You had our outline proposal, Mrs. Hawkins. Were there any questions before we move on?"

Jennifer reached into her black leather document case and opened the bound document. "Not really. You're recommending that I liquidate a million pounds worth of my holdings in Lynchester Mall Development."

"Right. We're saying that you should do that irrespective of the considerations of Billy's education, because, apart from the house and some bonds, all your assets are tied up in the Mall, and that's not good practice."

"I believe though that the Mall is doing well."

Charles intervened. "That's not the issue, Jennifer. It's just good sense to diversify."

"But I'll be losing out on future gains?"

"To some extent, yes. Equally you'd be avoiding the possibility of some future losses. We did consider borrowing against the asset, but the advantages and desirability of diversifying seemed so obvious . . ."

Jennifer sat in thoughtful silence for a minute. "Supposing we do this, won't I have simply hived off twenty-five percent of the holdings, leaving me with still the same problem of no diversification?"

Rachel smiled. *Jennifer Hawkins was following her idea now!*

"Not really. Firstly we've already been negotiating for you with the Mall Development company, who have pre-emption rights of course. They're actually quite keen to buy you out now, presumably because they can see the time coming when the Hawkins Mall can be floated or sold on for a healthy profit. If you agree on raising a million at this time, we think you would only have to give up seventeen percent of your holding, not twenty-five. And if you read on in the document, you'll see we're recommending a form of discretionary trust for Billy's fund. This means that, with yourself and Charles here as the Trustees, you have absolute control over the fund and its income, on Billy's behalf. Mind you, I think we still feel that you should be thinking about more diversification. And you really should be thinking about the possible impact of inheritance tax, and taking some steps to protect as much of your assets as possible."

Jennifer held up a hand. "Not too fast now, and not too much. Let's go through the draft of the Trust Deeds, and get that signed off. And if we can agree how to invest Billy's million, I'll sign off the sale of enough of my holdings to produce the fund. And then I'm going home."

Charles winced inwardly at the sharpness in Jennifer's tone. *Rachel's pressed her too far too soon. I must teach her something about 'not pushing at open doors . . .'*

After supper with Arlette on Friday evening, with Henri safely tucked up for the night, Jean-Paul emptied the last of the Bordeaux Superieur into their glasses and carried the wine out onto their terrace which looked out onto a corner of the Bassin d'Arcachon. It was warm still, and he enjoyed watching the fleet of dinghies with their brightly-coloured spinnakers catching the last of the evening's sunshine. Arlette stood beside him at the balustrade and leant her close-cropped dark head against his shoulder.

"You're very quiet this evening, my love. Things still awkward in the office?"

" 'Awkward' is not quite the word I would chose. Perfectly awful is nearer the mark. I was just thinking it would be nice to get the boat out tomorrow and go for a sail and a picnic. But I've got to settle down to work the whole day, producing production figures and costs for exporting to Italy."

"I suppose it's much harder for you, without Alain to help." She gave a little sigh. "But think how terrible it must be for poor Viola."

He sat down on a plastic chair, nursing in two hands the glass that held the last of his wine. *Was there some hint there that Arlette knew something? She's very bright, might easily work things out without letting me find out how much she knows.*

"Not-so-poor-Viola now, by the way. She's to get an insurance payout from ACP, twelve times salary."

Arlette stood with her back to the railings looking at him, her slim shape silhouetted now against the setting sun. "Twelve times? Did you say twelve times salary? Are you insured like that too? Perhaps Viola knew, and had him bumped off for the insurance? What a temptation! Sorry, Jean-Paul, a joke in very bad taste." She emptied her glass and sat on his lap, with her arms around his neck. “I think little Henri needs his Daddy, and I do too.”

Chapter Twenty-four

Freed of the requirement to hold the ring in what seemed likely to prove a contentious meeting about retail discounts versus TV advertising for Strongwheat, Dick felt momentarily at a loose end. He called for some tea, and sat at his desk looking through the scratch-pad he used to remind himself of what needed to be done. *France . . . Interim . . .* He switched on his computer again.

> *Dear Jean-Paul, I am pleased to be able to tell you that our Interim Finance Manager will be joining you on Monday morning. Jean Savage and I and the Chairman have interviewed CHARLOTTE ASTON thoroughly – she is very capable and I am sure you will get on well together. I am attaching her CV for your attention. Regards, Dick*

As he was typing the e-mail he remembered that Jennifer Hawkins would be leaving for France over the weekend. He picked up the telephone to call her. *Just to wish her luck on her trip. She’s really very brave to relocate to a foreign country just like that. Be honest with yourself, Dick, don’t you just want to hear her voice again?*

“I’m sorry, there is no one to take your call at the moment. Please leave a message after the tone, and I’ll get back to you as soon as possible.”

“Jennifer, it’s Dick Routledge, three-thirty on Friday afternoon. Just calling to wish you good luck on your trip to Arcachon. I’m not sure when you’re coming back, but I’ll be here next week, then away for two weeks from next Friday. All the best then.”

Not certain whether he was disappointed or relieved that he had only got the answer-phone, Dick decided he might as well go home early for once. *Monday . . . take Jim Helvin to the meeting in Stafford with Detective Chief Inspector Jim Renton.*

Would that damn Volvo follow him there? A visit to County Police HQ would certainly tell them, whoever 'they' were, that he was not pulling back from the investigation . . . might that be a dangerous thing to be doing?

"Elizabeth, I'm just going to have a quick word with Jim Helvin, and then I'm off home for an early night for once. I should be back from Stafford on Monday by lunchtime. Just as a security measure, I'd be grateful if you didn't tell anyone else where I'm going to be on Monday."

He found his European Director of Finance leaning back in his desk-chair with his fingers interlaced behind his head, and wearing a slightly smug expression.

"You're looking pleased with yourself, Jim. Made some progress?"

"Some progress . . . aye, you could say that. I'd like to look through this lot one more time over the weekend, but I'm pretty sure I've cracked it."

He stood up and walked round his desk to the table at the side of the room, thickly strewn with the bank statements that had been faxed over from France, covered now with pencil and red ink scrawls.

"I'll not pretend I've got a perfect match, but my figures fit well enough with the monthly reports. I've identified four, maybe five sources of payments into the accounts which don't seem to be ordinary customers, and two destinations for payments out which are possibly not to genuine suppliers. If we remove that lot from the calculation, the bank current accounts fit well enough with the monthly trading accounts and the overdraft, and the discrepancies I've just mentioned are consistent with increasing amounts each month being laundered through the company. Could be as much as two hundred thousand euros over the last three or four months, and accelerating, it seems. The June figure alone was around a hundred thousand. Still, I'm satisfied that Alain was being honest when he said that the company was not actually losing any money as a result of this activity."

Jim Helvin, normally quite dour, seemed jaunty, almost boyish in his moment of triumph. "Would you like me to take you through the detail, Dick?"

Dick thought about his decision to get home early, and shook his head. "I'll take your word for it, Jim, at least for today, and I'm sure some congratulations are due for the detective work. Why don't you do a summary, and bring it with copies of the evidence to Stafford on Monday? Can I collect you from your house around nine?"

Later on Friday evening the man that Dick Routledge knew as M. St. Just, Commissaire de Police, alias Felix Potin, made his way on foot from the railway station into the business quarter of Bordeaux and stood in front of an old three-storey stone house that had obviously seen better days. Its stone facade was crumbling beneath layers of dirty cream stucco that had not been repaired for many years, the blue paint on the door and window frames was cracked and peeling, and grubby lace curtains prevented anyone seeing in from the street, even if the windows had been clean enough to let light through. But after he had announced himself on the battered intercom the door opened quietly on well-oiled hinges, and he saw a burly figure with close-cropped grey hair peer cautiously out from the room upstairs.

"Ah yes, Felix, about time too. Come on up then, I've just opened a bottle of Calvados."

The man's French was harsh and guttural, his Corsican accent almost incomprehensible to the visitor's Parisian ear. Felix climbed the bare wooden steps of the creaking staircase and followed the man into a large room with a high ceiling and two tall windows that let in through filthy lace curtains a strained evening half-light. The were three beds in the room, on one of which the man had obviously been lying. There was a tall dresser by a sink, and a small table near the window with four wooden cafe chairs tucked into it. On the boarded floor were a couple of thin rugs whose pattern and colours had long since been lost. Felix sat down at the table, and smiled as his host pulled the brown linen drapes and switched on the light, a single bright bulb hanging from the ceiling, before he joined him at the table with the Calvados and two glasses.

"I see you're still careful as ever, Jo-jo."

"Salut. Always careful, always. While you've been enjoying yourself in England we've had the police here, asking where we were last Saturday evening when our accountant friend had his unfortunate accident by the riverbank."

Felix was alarmed, and coughed as he took a long pull from his glass. "Why here? Do they suspect . . .?"

"No, no, you're not at risk. So far, we are not under fulltime surveillance. We know they've interviewed the Basques and the

Catalans and some Arabs, as well as our people. They're just shaking the trees to see what may fall down."

"They were satisfied with your stories?"

Jo-jo shrugged and spread his big hands. "Who can say? At least they've not come back. Yet." He was suddenly authoritative. "So, tell me about England. Foggy and cold?"

"Very sunny and warm, for once. As we agreed, I was M. St. Just, Commissaire de Police, in charge of investigating the murder of Alain Robarte . . ."

He outlined his visit to the Strongwheat offices, omitting of course the little activity at the hotel with the false credit card. He had been told to pay cash, and, when claiming his expenses, would of course say that he had done so.

"I could see that they were well along the road to understanding your work, so I suggested ETA as the likely people involved, just to keep them nervous. When I left they were thinking about the implications of money-laundering, and they gave me these copies of their French company's trading accounts and bank statements to 'further my investigations'. I would say that they are certain to work out what has been going on, perhaps as soon as next week. You should close off all the connections, in and out."

Jo-jo riffled through the papers, and ran his hands through the thick greying stubble of his head. "Already done, after you called us from the airport. They'll just find a lot of dead ends. Pity, that. Still, there are plenty of others to work through. Is there anything else you need to tell me?"

There was a sudden fierce intelligence in his gaze that made Felix shiver.

"Not much. You know I had Pico follow this Dick Routledge a little, just to let him know we are around. He has a father and mother in the town, wife and two sons, and perhaps a mistress too, a Mrs. Hawkins. Widow, very good-looking, according to Pico, said locally to be very wealthy, with a young son. We might find a pressure-point there, if we need it."

Jo-jo smiled. "As long as he leaves us alone, I don't think we'll trouble ourselves with him. If he doesn't, I most certainly know how to apply pressure."

He stood up and fetched a sheet of paper from the dresser drawer. "Make a few notes for me, names, addresses, you know what I need. And what you've spent. Then you can get back to Paris. There's a TGV in fifty minutes."

"Thank you, I'll be on it. The money?"

"There's nothing kept here. You'll be contacted next week in Paris. We know where to find you."

Jennifer Hawkins walked out of Charles Harrison's office into the town square, feeling distinctly elated. Her holding in the Mall was worth considerably more than she had expected, and setting aside a million for Billy's future still left her owning almost five million pounds' worth of equity. She wondered if Grace, Alan Hawkins' widow, and Helen, George's widow, knew just how rich they were now. Dividends would start in a couple of months, the share-value would probably rise again too. *That girl, Rachel. Very bright, of course, but it was definitely too soon to be selling more.* She strolled back across the old bridge with the late afternoon sun warm on her face, her stiffened cotton dress swishing nicely around her bare legs. A little girl stood at the parapet with her mother, throwing pieces of bread down to a melee of squabbling ducks below. *A sister for Billy would be nice. But for that I'll need a man.* When she got home the little light was flashing on the answer phone, and she listened twice to the message Dick had left.

"I'll be here next week." Was that some sort of invitation to make contact? Now why does that make me think again about a sister for Billy? I suppose he's the only eligible male in sight at the moment. I really should get out more!

Chapter Twenty-five

At midday on the following Tuesday, Dick Routledge was standing by a luggage carousel at Milan's new Linate airport, grateful for the air-conditioning. Usually he travelled light for his European business meetings, with a spare shirt and his washbag tucked into the back of the handsome leather briefcase he carried onboard. But today he had checked in a suitcase, to allow for an extra suit, a lightweight jacket and trousers, and a couple of extra shirts. He was watching the bags go past, and reflecting that Murphy's Law required that the one time this year he had checked a bag would be the time it came last out of the hold, *that's providing they haven't sent it to Reykjavik of course . . .* when his contemplation was interrupted by the hint of a perfume that clawed at his memory. *That would be a coincidence, a woman wearing the same perfume as Brit . . .* and he whirled around to find Brit standing demurely behind him, with her cream jacket thrown over the handle of her trolley, which held a large blue suitcase. She looked calm and elegant in a white blouse and cream slimline pants, and then that beautiful smile sent his pulse racing. There was a playful mocking formality when she spoke.

"Good morning Mr. Routledge. I hope you've had a good journey? Will you be staying long in Milan? I can recommend a good hotel . . ."

He pushed her trolley aside to take her hands, and only the drilled-in inhibitions of an Englishman and an ex-officer in a public place stopped him kissing her passionately on the spot. Brit was only too aware of the unspoken message of delight in his face, and she blushed as she lowered her eyes.

"Don't miss your bag! I have mine already."

They kissed in the back of the taxi, a gentle, soft, loving kiss that seemed to go on all the way into the centre of Milan. He registered them at the Hotel Duomo as Mr. and Mrs. Routledge, and waited in impatient silence as the porter insisted on carrying their bags into the first-floor room and opening the french windows to demonstrate the fine view of the Duomo. The porter received his tip, bowed, and left and Dick continued standing on the small balcony that looked straight across the busy piazza to the soaring High Gothic facade of Milan's cathedral.

"Shall I draw the curtains, madam?"

She smiled again, and her own pleasure at being with him shone out as she fixed her eyes on his face, and began slowly to unbutton her blouse.

"Please do, sir, and quickly. Those are saints on the front of that cathedral."

"Are you hungry, darling?"

Dick had just opened his eyes to see Brit leaning over him, her body inches from his lips. He cupped her breast in his hands and kissed the nipple, feeling it harden once more beneath the pressure of his tongue. They had made love twice in quick succession, and Brit felt dizzy still from their passion. She tried to concentrate.

"Only it is almost three o'clock, and the restaurant is probably closing."

Dick sat up. "I'm sure we can find a piece of pizza somewhere. What do you want to do now?"

She slid off the bed and knelt naked on the floor to collect up her clothes, which Dick had helped her to remove in a great hurry.

"Perhaps we should take a cool shower and become very respectable tourists, if you like?"

By the time they left the hotel, the afternoon sun was beginning to be less fierce, and they took a taxi from outside the hotel for the short ride to the Convent of Santa Maria della Grazie, home of Leonardo's 'Last Supper'. As always there was a queue outside, but it was moving steadily, so they tagged onto the end.

Dick stood behind her in the warm sunshine, enjoying the smooth shape of her boyish haircut. Brit guessed that this was as good a time as any to tell him about her trip to London the previous day.

"Do you know where I was yesterday? London."

"Good Lord, I wish you'd told me. Perhaps . . . no, I couldn't have come down. I had to visit a policeman. I'll tell you about that later. So what was going on in London?"

"I got my head hunted. Is that right?"

"Near enough. A good job?"

"As good as possible, I think. They want me to come to London to be the manager of all buying for women's fashions for the Baines Department Stores Group, reporting to the Director."

"Oh, Brit, that's absolutely fantastic." He broke off as they reached the ticket kiosk. "Two, please, and that book about Leonardo looks interesting. English edition, please"

They paused in the cool of the shadowy passageway before going into the Refectory, where the 'Last Supper' occupied most of the end wall.

"Baines have had some ups and downs, but they're a fine company now, I believe. No doubt they've made a good offer to get you?"

"Assuming I make bonus, I will double my present income. They will provide a free apartment in London for six months, and free flights home to Stockholm every two weeks. They want me to start as soon as possible. I have to give my answer on Friday, before I go on my holiday."

She looked up at his face to try to be certain of his reaction. He responded by winding his arms tightly around her and kissing her, a strong, firm kiss that pressed the breath out of her and left her in no doubt of how he felt.

"I'm so pleased for you. You are going to take it?"

"I . . . I wanted to find out first what you thought about me living in England, just a hundred, hundred and fifty kilometres away." Her body was still trembling from his kiss, and she stepped back and felt the solid reassurance of the rough wall of the ancient convent behind her. "You won't feel a little uncomfortable to have me so close to your home? Threatened?"

"Threatened? Why should I?" But he sensed that there was an unasked question behind Brit's cautious enquiry, a question about the future of their relationship that he was not ready to answer.

"I think the crowd in front of the painting is starting to thin out. Shall we go in?"

When she arrived with Billy and Greta on the Sunday, early in the evening, Jennifer Hawkins thought that Biarritz itself would suit her very well, in fact she liked it so much that she seriously thought of cancelling the visit to Arcachon, and focussing her search for a house to rent in Biarritz itself. Their handsome, spacious hotel suite overlooked a calm Atlantic, with the heat of the day being tempered by a soft westerly breeze off the ocean, and later there was a truly spectacular sunset for her benefit. The Hotel du Palais had been the summer residence of Napoleon III and his Spanish Queen Eugenie, and she loved its overblown Baroque grandeur. After dinner she went for a stroll. There were elegant, expensive shops, a beautiful promenade by the beach with stunning views of the Pyrenees, flower-filled parks and an interesting former whaling port. But on Monday she discovered the other side to the town in high season, with hordes of noisy holidaymakers from Paris or Madrid, lines of cars queuing for a space to park, and overworked waiters in the restaurant too busy to look after her table. Still the sand was wide and soft, the water was warm, and there was enough wind on Monday for the board surfers to show off their skills and entertain the enthusiastic audience spread across the beaches. On reflection, she decided that it would indeed be possible to live in Biarritz for a few months, as the main holiday season would be over by the time she came to France again. On the other hand, Dick had been more than encouraging about Arcachon, and a glance at the map showed that Arcachon was a lot more convenient for the factory in Belin. *I'll call Jean-Paul, and arrange to meet in Arcachon, then make my mind up.*

Jennifer rented an open-top silver Mercedes for the drive from Biarritz to Arcachon on Tuesday afternoon. There was a Route Nationale from Biarritz to Bordeaux that was probably a quicker way to get to Arcachon, but she preferred to follow the older road that wound north along the coast through the great pine forests of Les Landes. Sometimes the trees were overwhelmingly gloomy, and then the shade struck chill even on a fine summer's day, and the road was so lonely that she wondered if she had made the right choice. But then the journey was punctuated by a sunny detour round a pretty lake, or there was a sudden glimpse of the blue ocean, and she could relax again. Billy sat happily beside her, strapped on a child's seat, and in the back Greta let the wind blow her hair.

Her hotel was easily found, being marked in the red Guide Michelin, and as she pulled up outside a young suntanned boy with long fair hair tied back in a pony-tail ran down the steps to collect their bags. *Just after six . . . Jean Paul said he would come with Arlette about eight. Time for Greta and Billy to get some food, and then it's me for a long cool bath!*

Dick stood in silence alongside Brit as they tried to absorb Leonardo's most famous painting. She rested her blonde head on his shoulder as he felt for her hand. He drew a deep breath.

"It's very moving, I think. It seems to be about the moment of betrayal, or at least the moment when Christ announces he will be betrayed."

"Have you heard the 'Passion according to Saint Matthew' by Bach? I'm not sure what the words are in English, we sang it at school in German. Something like 'Lord, is it me? Is it me? Is it me?' When you look at the picture you can hear them all shouting and denying."

Dick had been reading his book about Leonardo. "There's a lot of argument about the 'Last Supper'. One problem was that he experimented by painting onto dry instead of wet plaster, so it's not a true fresco, in fact it started to decay almost from the day he finished it. It's been heavily restored, many times since 1498, so that really the only thing you can say for certain is Leonardo's is the composition."

They left the convent and walked in silence back towards the Duomo.

The rush hour traffic was roaring and honking around them as they reached the cathedral.

"Let's go inside now. I think the 'Last Supper' has stirred my spirit, no matter who painted it."

It was suddenly quiet as the leather-padded door closed softly behind them, and they were conscious of a priest saying Mass to the half dozen old ladies who knelt before him in a side-chapel, his voice stirring a thousand whispering echoes inside the vast gothic edifice. Brit sat on a chair near the back and bowed her head in prayer. Dick remembered that he had not been inside a church since his younger son's christening, and felt chastened as he sat beside her. He'd prayed hard a couple of times when he'd got into difficulties flying, and he'd certainly prayed alongside his mother that his father would recover from the stroke. Could he pray now, beside his mistress? What should he pray for? He recalled a prayer of St. Augustine, '*Oh Lord, make me virtuous – but not yet.*' He saw that Brit had opened her eyes.

"What did you pray for?"

A little smile crossed her face. "That is private,"

Returning home after their dinner with Jennifer, it was Arlette who voiced the thoughts that Jean-Paul too had been thinking.

"She is very charming. Very beautiful, and, I think, very rich. And perhaps rather innocent. Do you think that she and Dick Routledge can really be just friends, from the same town? What did he say about her?"

"He said that they had met on some local committee, a charity I think, and she had mentioned that she was thinking of coming to France to live. So he suggested she come to see Arcachon, and then asked me to help her look around. You know how busy I must be with les vacances starting on Friday, and this new English lady Finance Manager who started yesterday. So I must depend on you to show Madame Hawkins around tomorrow."

"Oh, I am going to enjoy that, she's very easy to talk to, and her son can meet Henri later. But do you really believe they are just friends? Why did he suggest Arcachon?"

"Time will tell. Perhaps because this is the only part of France he knows. If he starts coming every week or every month to Belin, and disappearing in the evenings, say, we will know, won't we my love?"

Jean-Paul waited a few minutes after Arlette had gone up to bed, then made a telephone call on an untraceable mobile.

"Jo-jo? It's me, Jean-Paul. We've just had dinner with the English woman I mentioned, you remember? We thought she might be the mistress of Dick Routledge?"

"And?"

"She is very good-looking, as well as very rich. It's too soon to be certain, but I will be very surprised if she's not his mistress. And she's definitely looking around for a house to rent in Arcachon from September."

"Good, we'll know how to reach out for her if we need to."

"May I ask if Felix had a satisfactory visit to England?"

"Satisfactory? Yes, in the sense that there were no suspicions of him and none so far coming our way, and he was given a set of your company's bank statements, together with the signs they had found that our funds had been moving through. Not satisfactory, because we have had to close down all the inputs and outputs, which is giving me personally a great deal of extra work."

"But no loose ends?"

"Like Alain, you mean? No loose ends left, you can sleep easy, Jean-Paul. Our little arrangement is at an end. At least for now. Good night."

When they emerged blinking into the bright evening sunshine the traffic was still as noisy and frantic as before, but Brit was aware that something was changing between them. Her delight in his company was as vivid as ever, and she was sure he felt the same. So what was different? Something had been communicated between them in the Duomo. Was he nervous about her coming to England, in spite of his enthusiasm? Were they perhaps becoming closer, and at the same time less carefree? She took his arm as they walked into the hotel, and he responded with a little squeeze of her hand.

"We've tasted Milan's art and religion, how about La Scala, the Opera?"

"Wonderful, I've brought a new dress that will be ideal. What is on tonight?"

He asked the concierge if he could get two tickets for the Opera tonight.

"A t'ousand regrets, signor, impossibile."

"I'll pay any reasonable price, if that will help."

"Ah, non, signor. It is not the money. The Opera does not go zis week. No performing. But there is a wonderful concert instead tonight at eight-thirty. Music from the operas, Verdi, Rossini, wonderful."

"Can you get two good seats, please?"

"Certain, signor. And would you wish to dine before the concert, or after?"

Dick looked at Brit for a decision. "I'm hungry *now*," she whispered, "Can we get something sent up to the room, say omelette and frites, and tea and cakes, and perhaps he knows a good restaurant he can recommend, for afterwards?"

Chapter Twenty-six

On Thursday afternoon Dick Routledge, feeling slightly worn at the edges, was back at his desk by four o'clock, having caught the lunchtime flight from Milan. Elizabeth came in immediately with the post and messages.

"Nothing of any great importance. Pietro has sent a long e-mail from Parma with confirmation of the figures you negotiated with him. I've printed it out for you. He's quite eager to make a good impression, isn't he? And Mrs. Hawkins called to say she was just back from Arcachon. She thanks you very much for your help and would like to tell you all about her trip if you have time."

The meeting with Pietro on Wednesday had gone well. Dick had received Jean-Paul's costings for supply to Italy from the French factory by e-mail on Monday morning. He had added a quarter to the bare ex-factory cost quoted, to allow for the cost of delivery from Belin to Parma, and for a profit for the French manufacturing. He was impressed to find that Pietro spoke English beautifully, and had done his research into the market for breakfast cereals in Italy.

"Basically it is early days yet, there is business in Rome and some of the northern cities, but it is very patchy – one store does well, another a few miles away does almost nothing. Of course the company to beat is Kelloggs."

He produced an analysis of their pricing structure for Corn Flakes.

"I don't think we can follow our friends in France in building volume by offering private label to the supermarkets, the market in Italy is still too small for them to take an interest. So we must find a good brand name, sell around the same retail price as Kelloggs, offer a little more margin for the trade, and advertise, of course."

There was a lengthy discussion about the transfer price from France, which was concluded only when Dick agreed to reduce the price he had originally proposed by nine percent. He consoled himself with the thought that Jean-Paul did not know what price he had started from, so would not know that his margin had been shaved. Pietro still argued that, on any reasonable projection of sales, there was still insufficient gross margin to pay for advertising and leave a profit. Dick had an answer to this.

"The Americans won't want you to show a profit too soon. Just put up a five year-plan that shows continuing strong spending on advertising, but sales growing even more strongly, so that you are seen to be reaching breakeven in Year 5. That's when you'll get your own manufacturing, which should add fifteen to twenty percentage points to your margin. Everyone will applaud an aggressive plan like that, and you can amend it from year to year in the light of actual results."

He looked through the outline plan that had now come from Pietro, and was pleased to see he had followed his advice. The forecast used for the total market in Italy followed exactly the published figures from the European Breakfast Cereal Market Study, and his share, within a rapidly increasing sector, was projected as growing from 2% in the first year to 6% in the fifth. *That'll please the Yanks!*

He addressed an e-mail to Jean-Paul.

Thank you very much for the very helpful costings for supply to Italy. We will talk again after the holiday, but just to assist with your own long term production planning, please assume that 50,000 cases will be required by February 1st. next. How are you getting on with Charlotte?

He sat back and rubbed his eyes. His stay in Milan with Brit had been . . . memorable. Wonderful music that first evening at the La Scala concert, dinner in a beautiful old restaurant, more love-making, different from before, slower, more tender, more gentle. More . . . loving? On Wednesday morning they had called for a continental breakfast in the room, and he'd had almost literally to tear himself from her and hurry downstairs to meet Pietro. After the meeting in Parma, with its obligatory tour of the modernised olive-oil mill, Pietro had found a driver who got Dick back to the Milan hotel at a very illegal speed, so there was time to take a taxi out for an al fresco dinner on a terrace overlooking the lakeside in Como. Delicious cold salmon mayonnaise and white wine, Brit in a sensational new white silk dress she'd got from Armani, off one shoulder and draped so that it seemed to wind around her body. Kisses in the taxi back, more slow, affectionate love-making that night. Taxi to the airport together. Brit had said that she needed to talk with her mother about the job in England, but it seemed pretty likely that she was going to accept it. He found himself very enthusiastic about her being more easily available in England – and aware that they were growing closer together. *This is no longer just an idyllic affair with a woman I could meet only in foreign countries. Was there indeed a threat to my marriage, to my family?*

Dick brought his thoughts back to reality. *Too difficult before the holiday. And Rosemary wants a baby, so what am I thinking about? Getting her pregnant, and then walking out, to be with Brit? Almost five o'clock. I'm going to come in for a couple of hours in the morning, so anything else can wait . . . except Jennifer, perhaps. She's been thoughtful enough to call to thank me, so I should call back.*

He dialled her number, and as it rang he thought of her warm kiss, 'just for reassurance', last time they met at her house.

"Hullo, Jenny, it's Dick. Thanks for your call. I gather everything went smoothly?"

"Oh, Dick, it's lovely to talk to you, I'm sure you're very busy. Is it tomorrow you start your holiday?"

"Yes, I'm going to come in for just a couple of hours, and try to be on the road before lunchtime. I'm guessing about four hours to get there. We can get into our holiday apartment in Salcombe any time after four."

"Well, I won't keep you now. Just to say that Arlette and Jean-Paul were very nice, and very helpful. I've found a lovely Victorian sort of villa in the older part of Arcachon, which they call the 'winter town'. I would have gone for somewhere right by the sea, but Arlette persuaded me that it could be really terrible in the winter when the big Atlantic storms blow, so I've taken her advice. We're going to be about four hundred yards back from a beach, right by a park, not far from shops and so on. The owner is there now but she's actually leaving in about two weeks, so we'll be going over just before then, as she's very keen to show me around. I'm going to drive down to Plymouth, take the ferry across to Roscoff in Brittany, and then meander down to Arcachon. If I send you the address and telephone number, perhaps you can come and see us when you visit Belin next? Or if you've got a few minutes, why not come by today to look at some pictures over a cup of tea on your way home? Though that cake is all gone now, I'm afraid. Have you got rid of your stalker?"

She doesn't usually chatter on like this. She's nervous, or excited, wound up about something. Is she concerned that I might say 'yes'? What would happen if I did? I would like to know her better of course . . . but perhaps not today.

"Jenny, I'm so pleased it's all working out, but I'm up to my eyebrows trying to get everything squared away before I go off. Can I call you in France when I'm back from holiday, and take you up on that invitation to tea next time I come over?"

There was a file in his in-tray labelled 'FRANCE – accounts' He had taken it with him on Monday, when he had collected Jim Helvin from his home and driven up to Stafford to meet Detective Chief Inspector Rendle. He had half-expected the DCI to dismiss their story as unsubstantiated fantasies, but he had actually been very attentive, especially after Jim had taken him through his own financial detective work.

"I think it's pretty clear that something unusual, possibly criminal has been going on in your French business. And it's at least a reasonable hypothesis that there is a connection to the unfortunate death of your accountant. On the other hand, unless you want me to follow up the credit-card fraud at the Belfry, it's hard to see that any crime has been committed within my jurisdiction?"

Dick shook his head. "I've settled the bill with the hotel, and we really don't need to stir that up again."

DCI Renton pushed back his thinning black hair with his hands, and sat back in his chair. "I think the most useful thing I could do for you would be to send these papers to Bordeaux. I'm sure my sergeant will enjoy finding out who's really in charge of the investigation there."

Dick interrupted. "I think it might be a Commissaire St. Josephe. At least that's the man who interviewed our MD over there."

"Right, thank you. We'll double-check that. I'll put in a covering note to say that we've talked. Better not say too much, otherwise it'll be just asking for a 'not invented here' reply. Will that suit? I wouldn't worry too much about those chaps who appear to have been following you. The fact that they've made themselves so conspicuous is the best proof that they're some kind of warning, rather than a real threat. And now you're off on holiday?"

"On Friday, yes, for two weeks in Salcombe."

"Very nice too. Chances are, by the time you get back two, well nearly three weeks from now the French police will have cracked it, and it'll be all over."

Dick put the file away in his desk drawer and locked it. *I must call Charlotte tomorrow and see how she's getting on. But now I'm going home.*

Brit also put in a brief appearance at her office on Thursday afternoon. Nothing urgent to concern her, but she thought she ought to circulate a minute of her meetings in Milan. The usually arrogant fashion houses there had been surprisingly accommodating when she suggested that she could buy some current season's product for her group, as long as the discounts were interesting. It seemed that business in England was actually much better than in most of their markets, which made them eager to go for any opportunity for wider distribution in high-class department stores, provided they could have the fig leaf of being able to claim that it was old stock they were shifting. It had been interesting to discover, with a couple of discreet questions, that Baines was seen as perhaps a little below the level where they wanted their products to be sold; but perhaps that perception might be changed?

She called her mother to say she was safely back in Stockholm, but would be in the office finishing off for another hour. "Then they can manage without me tomorrow, and I'll be able to help you pack. Everything all right with Stefan?"

"Stefan is fine, doing his homework," her mother said, "And there's a thick letter for you, special delivery from England."

She guessed that was the offer from Baines. "I think that's something you'll both be excited about. I'll tell you all about it when I get home."

She finished up her report on Milan, and wondered if it might be bad luck to draft her note of resignation before she'd actually read through the offer from England? *I can do that on my laptop from home.* Instead she left the report with a note for her assistant:

> Working at home tomorrow. Please read through the Milan report and send it out with any corrections you like, – give me a call if anything seems unclear. Have a great holiday!

Rosemary was sitting at the kitchen table, chatting with her sons about the plans for the holiday when she heard the crunch of car tyres on the driveway. *He's early, for once!* She pulled the clips out of her hair as she hurried into the hallway, and pulled a brush through the thick auburn tresses as she saw Dick pausing outside the stained glass of the door. His key rattled in the lock and she drew a deep breath as the door opened and he dropped his bag.

"Rosemary, darling! You look lovely. I'm glad to be home at last. No more nights away for a while."

There was no mistaking the warmth in his voice, the pressure of his arms about her, the friendly nuzzle of his lips on her neck, and the kiss that went on a little longer than usual. *He really has missed me! And tomorrow we're on holiday!*

"Come into the kitchen and say 'hullo' to your sons. They've broken up from school today, and they've both come back with very good reports. They think James could get a scholarship to Rugby, that's if we want him to go. I think he would quite like to, but I'm still not sure I want them to go to boarding school."

He walked with his arm around her waist into the sunny kitchen. Peter and James jumped up excitedly and he folded them all into a comfortable family embrace.

Chapter Twenty-seven

After their two weeks' holiday in Salcombe, Rosemary came back on Friday afternoon with a mountain of washing to put through. There were piles of letters, some of which required urgent attention, nowhere near enough food in the house for the four of them, and a garden which had run riot with unchecked growth. Dick mowed the grass, and later self-consciously pushed her trolley through the supermarket as she loaded it up with food for the family, but otherwise seemed to feel that the weekend was a legitimate part of his holiday. So on Monday morning, after Dick had left for the office, and the boys had been collected by a neighbour with two girls of her own, to go to the pool, she was at last able to sit out in the garden with a glass of squash, a few Victoria plums from her garden and the newspaper. *That was one of the best holidays we've ever had . . .*

Salcombe was an old fishing and ship-building town, which had probably not changed much in the last fifty years. It was built up the steep western slopes of an estuary, tucked well back from the sea. There was a beautiful walk from the busy little town south along the estuary to their beach. As the brochure had promised, the apartment had a balcony that faced south and overlooked the beach, just two hundred yards away. From Saturday Peter and James were staying for the first week on 'Egremont', an old Mersey ferry moored at the top of Salcombe harbour, which served as the floating hotel and headquarters for the sail-training school. They slept on board and were kept busy sailing all day – which left Rosemary and Dick to relax on the balcony or on the beach, sail and play golf together, and make love. Especially to make love. She smiled as she sipped her squash in the sunshine, bit into a ripe plum that squirted juice onto her cheek, and thought about the sex. Really Dick had been wonderfully passionate, and his enthusiasm had definitely re-awakened her own delight in the finer points of pleasing one another. There was that day when she had got up to make breakfast wearing only her pyjama top, and Dick had crept up behind her in the kitchen and carried her triumphantly back to bed. "*It's all your fault*", *he had said,* "*I was just overcome by lust*". And she blushed to remember the second day of their holiday, when Dick came back after dropping the boys off first thing in the morning at the ferry for 'Egremont', and expressed horror to find her still in bed. "*Woman! You will pay for this sloth!* He stood in front of her and slowly peeled off his clothes . . . *He really was quite excited* . . . then they lazed around the apartment until, after lunch with some Rioja on the balcony,

Dick had suggested that it was very hot outside, and perhaps they should take a Spanish-style siesta . . . and a long time afterwards they strolled down to the beach restaurant for a barbecue under the stars, then back to bed for more very slow lovemaking again.

Her favourite pale green shorts felt tight around the waist, and she eased one of the side-belts a notch. *That's those clotted-cream teas! I wonder though . . . it would be a bit of a miracle if I got pregnant again the first time we tried, after all these years of contraception. Still, if there was a fertile egg there, Dick must have hit it!* She giggled, stretched out her long legs on the padded lounger to catch more sun, and bit luxuriously into another plum. *I should know in two or three weeks.*

Dick was at his desk soon after eight, but Elizabeth was there before him, and he found the contents of his in-tray neatly sorted into three piles, presumably in descending order of importance. On top of the prime pile was an e-mail from Ben Camena, the VP International for ACP. Dated ten days earlier, it was quite brief:

> *Just to remind you that I will need to have draft budgets for next year by September 30th at the latest.*

Dick knew now from experience that Ben would expect to receive by e-mail just the basic numbers to enable his staff to build up his 'global overview', especially of monthly cash-flow, but even so he immediately foresaw a problem arising in France. Jean-Paul and his whole team were on holiday until the end of August – another two weeks. Allowing for some days before the end of September for debate with himself and any necessary re-working, they would have not much over two weeks to complete the plan. His first thought was to ask Ben for more time, then he decided against it. *Only wimps ask for more time!* He looked through the rest of the prime pile, and found, somewhat to his surprise, the e-mailed report for the month of July from France. *Charlotte's got well on top of the job!* He glanced through the three pages of numbers, set out in ACP's standard format. Sales had continued quite strongly, stocks had been built during July so that Despatch could continue to operate during the August manufacturing shutdown, and there was another small, but welcome profit. Cash-flow was satisfactory, and all the trends looked right. *Thanks be, no surprises!* He turned to his computer.

> *Dear Charlotte, thank you for the July figures – they look fine. Please forward to ACP if you have not yet done this.*
>
> *I need to talk to you urgently about the budget-plan for next year. Please call me after lunch today. Regards, Dick Routledge.*

He looked up as he pressed 'send' to see Phil Wythe, the Managing Director of Strongwheat UK, leaning into his doorway. "You look disgustingly brown and healthy, Dick. Lots of sun in Salcombe?"

"Not bad, just a couple of rainy days, when we all had a fascinating time at the Eden Centre. The tan is mostly wind-burn, mind. Good sailing weather."

"Glad you enjoyed it. I start mine this Friday. We're going camping in Wales, so the sun has just got to shine."

Dick picked up the print-out of Ben's e-mail. "Can I show you this little reminder about next year's budget? I think Ben is on the prod a month earlier than last year. I wouldn't want to spoil your holiday, but . . ."

"But nothing. Elizabeth was smart enough to copy it out to us when it came in, and it's all in hand. I give you full permission to talk it through with my people if you feel up to it, while I'm off fighting the good fight with a tent pole. Anything else while I'm here?"

Dick's secretary Elizabeth had been with the company for many years, in fact she was now the longest-serving member of staff, after the Chairman. When Dick walked next door to her office she looked up from reading the *Financial Times*. She folded it very precisely and handed it to him.

"Good morning, Mr. Dick. I hope you don't mind, I like to keep an eye on my shares."

This was the first time Dick had heard that Elizabeth played the stock market. *You never can tell!*

"Morning, Elizabeth, and thank you for sorting the mail. I gather that Phil got a copy from you of the note from Ben about next year's budget. Probably saved his holiday for him."

"He seemed quite grateful, yes. So I took the liberty of copying it also to France and Germany. I hope that was the right thing to do?"

"Absolutely. Well done. I'm going to settle down with the rest of the stuff in my pile. Could I have some tea, please?"

Dick had enjoyed his holiday at least as much as Rosemary. As he sipped his tea, hot and strong, he too thought about the sex. Somehow the thought of deliberately trying to make a baby, after all these years, had been curiously erotic for him, and Rosemary seemed to feel the same, or perhaps she had taken fire from his own excitement. Either way, they had come back more closely attached to one another than when they had left. *Like a second honeymoon, really. Ros is just everything a man could want. So I'm going to tell Brit it's all over, right?*

He stretched his memory back to the moment they had parted at Milan airport for their separate flights. Brit was very cool and business-like in her crisply tailored cream trouser-suit, a new white blouse in a froth of lace below her face, a small blond curl dropping over her forehead.

"I'll call you early in September," he had promised, "Next time we meet it will be in London, I hope."

She smiled, blew him a kiss and was gone around the corner to find the SAS check-in.

But I don't want to let her go. I love Rosemary, I love my family, I'm really excited about another baby, especially if it's a girl. But . . . but I still want to meet Brit. What does that make me?

There was an e-mail from the new business in Germany,

Dear Dick, The plant installation team from ACP are very happy with progress, and we hope to run manufacturing trials later in August. Would you like to be present? Jurgen Weisser.

The set-up and the trials were now apparently ahead of schedule by a week or two. He felt that it was definitely desirable that he show his commitment by going over for the start-up, and turned to his computer to reply. Then he realised that he felt a little guilty that he had neglected the business in Wuppertal, thanks to his preoccupations with France. *And other things of course!*

"Elizabeth, would you see if you can raise Jurgen Weisser in Wuppertal, please?"

She came into his office a couple of minutes later. "Jurgen is out for lunch at the moment, but she'll get him to call as soon as he gets back. It's almost midday, by the way. Would you like me to get a sandwich for yourself?"

As he chewed on a thick cold beef sandwich he came across a short letter from Bordeaux, from a M'sieur St. Josephe – the same policeman who had visited Jean-Paul, he recalled. It was written in English:

Dear M. Routledge,
We have received from Detective Chief Inspector Renton in Stafford a copy of the statement you made to him about your company and the murder of M. Robarte here. We are very impressed with your analysis of the exact detail of the flow of the monies. I understand that you will visit your factory here quite regularly, and I am of the opinion that a meeting in Bordeaux with myself will certainly assist in the progress of our investigation. I propose to take some holiday during the month of August, but perhaps you would be kind enough to telephone my secretary to make an appointment in September.
With sincere felicitations,
Claude St. Josephe, Commissaire de Police

He checked his diary. When Jurgen called he could let him chose a day for a visit to Wuppertal and the trials to be run, anytime before the end of August. Belin would reopen on Monday, August 29th; he would give them a few days to get things together, and later in that week, say Friday, he could meet with Jean-Paul. And Charlotte, of course. So Thursday would be good for the meeting in Bordeaux with the Commissaire. *And Jennifer? If I go over Tuesday afternoon, I could stay in Bordeaux and see Jennifer on the Wednesday. She's probably on the road motoring down to Arcachon at the moment . . . I'll call her later in the week.*

He wrote on the letter,

Elizabeth – please call the Commissaire's office and suggest that Thursday morning, September 1st. would be convenient. Book me to go over on the Tuesday – pm, return Friday evening, plus hotel Tuesday to Thursday nights.' – D.

He put the letter in his 'out' tray, and turned to his computer.

Dear Jean-Paul, I hope you are having a great holiday! Looking ahead, I would like to come in for a general review on Friday Sept.2nd. By then Charlotte should have made some progress with the budget too. I am arranging to visit Commissaire St. Josephe the previous day. Best regards, Dick.

Dear Charlotte, I am intending to spend Friday, Sept.2nd. with yourself and Jean-Paul, for a preliminary look at the budget for next year. Would it be possible for us to meet for dinner the previous evening in Bordeaux? Best regards, Dick Routledge.

Jean-Paul had rented a 40-foot motor cruiser for three weeks in August, but made a point of checking his e-mails most days as they cruised from Bordeaux up the coast to La Rochelle and La Baule. Charlotte had warned him last week about the new requirement for budgeting. His reply had been very precise:

Sales forecast for France to be this year's actual plus twenty percent. Factor in the fifty thousand cases for Italy in February @ cost plus fifteen percent, assume another fifty thousand spread over the rest of the year. Increase Marketing spend by twenty-five percent. Overheads – plus five percent. Look forward to seeing a first draft August 29th. Good luck!

When he picked up the e-mail from Dick about his visit he was immediately concerned about the mention of his planned meeting the previous day with St. Josephe. *Very worrying. What if Dick suggested to the police that there might be a connection between those odd numbers that Alain had so stupidly sent, and myself? After all, how likely was it that a Financial Manager was acting alone? Really, it was quite surprising that I have not been more aggressively questioned . . . it would be risky to call Jo-jo in Bordeaux . . . there's a mobile phone on board of course, but that's hardly secure. We'll be arriving at the Ile de Re soon – I could go ashore with Arlette and Henri for fresh food and a swim, and find some excuse to get away to use a public telephone kiosk. Can I trust Jo-jo? What's the alternative? If Dick's seeing the commissaire on Thursday, and me on Friday, I wonder if he plans to spend Wednesday with his mistress?*

Dick called Jennifer from his office a week later. "I wondered if you were settling in all right? Do you think you will like living in France?"

"Dick! It's so lovely to hear from you. We've only been here a week of course, but everything seems as we hoped it would be.

The house is so comfortable, we've found two good restaurants we can walk to. I've met Henri's new teacher, she's very nice, Greta has made friends with a Danish au pair, and I think there's a French boyfriend already, and I'm taking sailing lessons every afternoon. Scary at first, but I'm getting the hang of it. Are you coming soon?"

There was an irresistible, breathless warmth about her voice on the telephone that seemed to suggest that she was seriously excited about the thought of seeing him again. Any uncertainties just melted away.

"Well, I don't know if this would be convenient for you, but I have to be in Bordeaux on Tuesday evening, August 30th. Then I have other commitments on the Thursday and Friday, but I really would like to spend Wednesday with you . . . and Billy, if that suits?"

Jennifer noted the fractional pause before 'and Billy', and guessed that Dick was being cautious about declaring his interest in her. But she was certain that it was more than just friendly. She wondered if he intended to tell his wife that he would be meeting her in Arcachon? *I'd bet big money against it!*

"Wednesday August 31st . . . sounds fine, Dick. We'll expect you about ten, and if it's fine we'll plan a picnic with the sailing boat. Let me give you the directions to find the house."

After she had finished and said her goodbyes she put the telephone down quite slowly, her thoughts racing ahead to their day together. Dick Routledge was an unusual man, a combination of intelligence and raw power, and she looked forward very much to getting to know him better. *This isn't Lynchester. Here, I'll make the rules!*

Chapter Twenty-eight

On Wednesday morning, August 31st, Dick left the 'Amarys', his Bordeaux hotel, at about nine o'clock in a rented Citroen and drove carefully in a stream of heavy traffic across the Pont de Pierre which spanned the River Garonne, to follow the A63 south for most of the thirty five miles to Arcachon. By ten he had found her street in its 'Winter Town', the Avenue des Abatilles, with a shady park of tall pines sheltering the handsome Victorian 'Villa Mimosa' from the winds. As his car crunched onto the drive through the rusting iron gateway he saw her coming out to stand on the steps – white beach sandals, a flimsy white wrap-around skirt cinched in with a white belt, a loose white blouse that revealed a glimpse of an orange bikini top beneath, and a white scarf that served to tie back her dark hair. A wide smile illuminated her face as she came down to the car, followed shyly by her son, Billy, who was wearing a swimsuit and a bright yellow lifejacket already.

"Dick! I'm so pleased you could come. Stretch your legs for a couple of minutes, Greta is just assembling our picnic. Billy, say 'hullo' to Mr. Routledge."

Dick took her hand in his, and yielded to the temptation to pull her close for a continental-style peck on both cheeks. A whisper of some delicate perfume rose from that perfect cleavage. *What a stunningly desirable woman she is!*

He shook hands solemnly with Billy, who stayed silent with a thumb in his mouth. "Nice to see you again, Billy. I hope you will call me 'Dick', just like your mother?"

Greta appeared, solid, dark-haired and Dutch, carrying beach towels and a straw basket with a flap.

"Right, Dick, we are ready. Weather forecast is good. I thought a sail along the shore, then a picnic lunch and a swim. I forgot to ask, do you have your sailing stuff with you?"

"Yes, well, they're my swimming boxer shorts really, but I'm sure they'll do. Can I come in and change? I've brought an old shirt and some trainers as well."

"Of course. Greta, would you get Billy strapped into Dick's back seat please? Dick, you can come up and use my room to change."

He followed her into the shade of the house, and admired slim brown legs as she led the way up a curving marble staircase with an elaborate wrought-iron banister.

"Of course we've only been here a couple of weeks . . ." She stood at the door of her bedroom to let him pass, and he knew she was as acutely conscious of the tension between them as he was. As he closed the door he realised he had actually been holding his breath. The room had dark brown velvet curtains and bedspread, with furniture of a heavy fashion that he recognised as typically French Provincial, and he guessed that, apart from a large crystal vase of fresh flowers, Jennifer had not changed anything since her arrival. The bed felt firm as he sat on the edge and changed, leaving his clothes neatly folded. *Just suppose we did . . . make some progress, where could we meet? Not here, with Greta and Billy either side. At the hotel in Bordeaux, perhaps? Or shall we just be good friends?*

He bounced down the stairs two at a time, to find Jennifer waiting at the front door. "Not very feminine, the bedroom, is it? Still, there's plenty of time to make some improvements. Anything special you'd recommend?"

Dick recognised that he was being teased a little, and just smiled as he slid behind the wheel. "I passed the marina on the way in. Seemed to be masses of places to park, fin-de-saison now, I suppose."

They drove along the waterfront and followed the sign into the Port de Plaisance, where she directed him to a parking spot just a few yards from the quayside.

"I haven't bought a boat yet – I've been trying several different ones on hire. The one we've got for today is just over here. I think it's called a five-metre – that's the length at the water-line."

The pale blue and white fibreglass dinghy was moored alongside the pontoon, head to wind. It was very similar to the 'Wayfarer' that Dick had been sailing in Salcombe, with slatted seats all round and plenty of room inside. It seemed to be almost brand new. He stepped down first, and lifted in Billy, who was obviously goggle-eyed with nerves and excitement.

"I've been having lessons, as I told you, but I've never yet taken Billy with us, so this is his first time afloat."

Dick sat him towards the bow, just behind the tall mast. "Right, Billy, you'll be fine there. And when we get going you can help me by looking after the foresail. Mummy will show you exactly what to do."

There were three big yellow lifejackets folded neatly in the bottom of the boat, which they put on. Greta climbed in sturdily by herself and sat on the side by the low wall of the quay, and Dick offered a hand to Jennifer, which she gracefully accepted as she hitched up her full skirt and stepped down in a flurry of brown legs and white muslin. There was a good breeze blowing from the west. Jennifer took impressive charge as she raised the mainsail.

"Dick, you take the tiller please. Let the mainsheet right out for now. Mind the boom everyone. Greta, untie us at the front there but keep tight hold of that iron ring thing the rope is tied to. When you're ready, Dick, pull in the mainsheet, and if Greta lets go and gives us a little push off we should sail away beautifully. I'll help Billy raise the foresail once we're under way."

The Bassin d'Arcachon is roughly triangular, about five miles round each side at high water. Arcachon itself is built on a low promontory that extends into the south side of the triangle, and west of the town is a narrow neck of water that runs almost due south and connects the Bassin to the open Atlantic.

As the boat tacked out through the entrance to the Marina, Jennifer checked that the centre-board was securely down, raised the foresail, and gave the foresheet to Billy. "Hold that rope tight now, darling, and you'll feel the wind pulling at it to make us go faster." The boat heeled, and he gasped in surprise and looked at his mother. She smiled, and he relaxed. "We are going faster, aren't we?"

Jennifer directed Dick westward along the Plage d'Arcachon, and played the tourist guide. "That's the pier there, you can get a trip around the Bassin and out to Cap Ferret, that's the long spit of land around the far corner, on the west side of the exit to the sea. Just behind the pier is the Casino – good place to eat, and not too expensive. There's a very interesting aquarium and local museum next door. Around the marina we've just left is called the 'Autumn Town'. All this stretch, with a lovely flowery promenade which faces north into the Bassin, is called the 'Summer Town', then as we get round the corner there that's the 'Spring Town', and after that we're going to be heading down the entrance, almost due south, and you will see all the park and trees that shelter the 'Winter Town' where we live."

Within half an hour they had turned the corner to head south towards the exit. Inside the Bassin the water had been quite calm, but now the breeze felt stronger, and there was a pronounced swell coming in from the Atlantic, which they could now see about a mile away. It was apparent that a strong tide was running out, adding significantly to their speed over the ground. Beyond the entrance, on the left shore, loomed the huge shape of the Dune du Pilat.

"That's the biggest sand-dune in the world, I think, must be five hundred feet to the top and a couple of miles long."

The swells were getting higher, and Billy, still hanging grimly on to his rope, was looking distinctly uncomfortable as they rode up and down the long switchbacks.

"If you could take us in to the beach here, Dick, just before the Dune, we can find a good spot for our picnic. The tide will be going out for another couple of hours, then by the time we want to come back it will be on our side again."

They surfed in on a small roller and Dick expertly swung the boat round to head into wind just before they touched the sand. Jennifer jumped out thigh-deep into the warm little waves, careless of her skirt, and held the bow as Greta stepped out over the stern with the towels and the lunch, and Dick lifted Billy onto the hot sand. Jennifer looked at her watch.

"It's just after eleven. Would you like to sail a bit further, Dick? I can see the swell coming in from the ocean, but there are no whitecaps, so we could go just a little way out of the Bassin, to the end of the Dune perhaps?"

She seemed to be going out of her way to be alone with him. And the end of the Dune would be out of sight of Greta and Billy. "Wonderful." He waded out to take hold of the bow. "You take the tiller, then, and I'll be crew."

Her thin skirt was soaked, and she undid her belt to peel it off and handed it to Greta. The bottom half of her orange bikini was tied with small black bows on each swelling hip. Dick's throat felt dry as he pushed the boat off the beach and clambered in. Within a few seconds they were scudding down the shore. Jennifer eased out the main, and he felt the boat come up onto a plane, with the bow almost out of the water. "Nice boat, Jenny, we must be doing ten, maybe twelve knots."

"There's a notice somewhere that says the maximum speed inside the Bassin is fifteen kilometres per hour, but I don't think they've ever arrested a sailing dinghy. Did you know that the Bassin is the biggest producer of oysters in France – I think it's thousands of tons a year?"

A old-fashioned motor boat with two men with fishing rods was about four hundred yards behind them and seemed content to keep within the speed limit. Side by side they stretched their legs to sit out on the gunwale to balance the boat with the wind from Cap Ferret on their backs. Dick sneaked a look sideways at Jennifer, who was concentrating fiercely, the tiller in her left hand and the mainsheet in her right. Dick eased out the foresheet, and moved his left arm around her waist to rest on her hip. He felt a sudden shiver run through her body, then she relaxed into his embrace, the breeze whipped her hair from her face, and she turned to him to be kissed, warm, salty lips that seemed to melt . . .

It was the sudden rise in the engine note from the motorboat that made him break away. He looked back in alarm. The distance between them was reducing rapidly, and it was heading straight for them. At about two hundred yards away the engine was now a deafening roar, the menacing bow was a fearsome weapon, high and clear now of the water.

"Quick, Jenny, pull hard on the tiller, make for the beach."

She tugged the tiller hard into her, and the boat swung viciously to the left, bringing the boom crashing across above their heads. Dick dived to the other side to steady the boat with his weight, and saw Jennifer follow in the stern. *Fifty yards to the beach. Just a few more seconds to safety!* He looked behind – the noise from the speedboat was a terrifying scream. He bent forward to raise the centreboard, and there was a crash of heavy metal as that sharp bow smashed into the stern of their craft and tossed it over like a toy. It rode right over them as they hit the water on top of the sail. Dick felt a tearing blow at point where his head and neck met, and then there was darkness.

Floating. Floating weightless in a huge sea of palest blue that supported him but did not touch him. Then sinking, slowly at first, then faster and faster until his whole body was wincing for fear of an imminent impact . . .

He opened his eyes, and found he was looking up at a pale blue ceiling, listening to a faint, persistent hum. *What could that be? Air-conditioning, of course*. There was a starched sheet under his nose. *A hospital. He was connected by wires and tubes to a machine that bleeped steadily. Private ward*. He turned his head. A woman with auburn hair, asleep in an armchair. *Rosemary!* An excruciating pain shot through his neck and right shoulder as he moved, and he groaned aloud. Rosemary immediately opened her eyes and came to his side.

"Dick. Oh Dick, darling, we've been so worried."

He breathed deeply and winced again. His voice was hardly more then a whisper. "Where . . . how long have I been here?"

She looked at her watch. "It's nearly lunchtime on Saturday. You've been here unconscious since Wednesday afternoon."

He tried to sit up, groaned again and sank back.

"Now you're to lie still while I get the nurse, I'm sure she'll give you something for the pain. And there's a policeman sitting in the corridor just outside the door. I've promised to tell him as soon as you woke up."

Dick tried to get his mind working again. *Police? Outside the door? Some sort of protection? Or just anxious to hear his story*? He remembered the speedboat suddenly accelerating and coming straight at them . . . *Jenny? What's happened to Jenny?* Rosemary came bustling back.

"The policeman is calling his boss, the Commissaire, so I suppose he'll be in to talk to you. The nurse has gone to look for the doctor. I must say, this seems to be a very good hospital. Very clean and efficient."

She sat carefully on the bed by his left side and kissed his forehead. "You poor darling. Can you remember what happened? Why were you out sailing with Mrs. Hawkins?"

Why indeed? Or why not? It was all perfectly innocent, wasn't it? He thought of that last kiss, the taste of salt on her lips, the feel of her hip beneath his hand. *Not so innocent, perhaps. How do I ask about Jenny?*

"Well, Mother introduced me to her at that committee meeting about the new hospital wing. She said she was thinking of living in France for a while, and asked me if I could recommend anywhere. I thought of Arcachon, and gave her an introduction to Jean-Paul and his wife, Arlette, who live there."

He paused, but Rosemary said nothing, just fixed those cool blue eyes on his face.

"She found somewhere nice and was very pleased, and said that when I came she would like to give me a treat in return. So we all went on this picnic in the boat, that's Jennifer, Greta, who's her Dutch au pair, and Billy the little boy. I helmed first, then we set down Billy and Greta when the wind was getting up a bit and Jennifer took the helm whilst the two of us went on for another little go. And then this speedboat . . ."

His voice faded away, and Rosemary stood up as the nurse came in . . . *white uniform, and a lovely smile* . . . She was followed by a young doctor, fat and moustached, all bustle and self-important efficiency. They co-operated in a lengthy examination, and conferred in whispers. Finally he nodded and the connections to the machine were removed.

"Bien, M'sieur Routledge, you 'ave a ver' strong head. I am certain you will have a guerison parfait. I t'ink you mus' be 'ere deux ou trois jours plus. Per'aps you will leave Lundi ou Mardi. Ma collegue will give you something for les douleurs. A bientot."

The injection worked quickly, and as the nurse left Dick sank deeper into the pillows. Rosemary returned to the bedside, but did not sit down.

"Your mother came over with me. We've been taking turns to sit in. I should call her at the hotel, I'm sure she'll be so pleased to hear what the doctor said."

"Fine. Give her my love". Dick seemed to be sinking into a comfortable softness. *There was something . . . Of course, Jenny. Nobody had mentioned Jenny yet.*

"Before you go, Ros. I assume they've got Jennifer in another room. Any idea how she's doing? And I expect she'd like to know I'm on the mend."

Rosemary looked down at him, her face suddenly expressionless. She sat down suddenly on the bed.

"I'm so sorry, Dick. I forgot. Of course, you wouldn't know. Mrs. Hawkins, Jennifer is . . . is dead. There was a severe blow to the back of the head . . . she never regained consciousness . . . I think she was already dead by the time we got here on Wednesday evening. There's a sister, from Birmingham. She came over yesterday and collected the little boy and the au pair. Poor little mite."

Dick closed his eyes. *She's dead, and it hurts, it hurts. How do I stop Rosemary from finding out how much it hurts?* He could feel tears welling up inside, great sobbing tears. He was sorry for Jenny, sorry for himself, and that poor little boy! He could think of nothing better than to keep still and silent with his eyes shut. After a minute or two he felt Rosemary stand up. She paused for a moment, as if deep in thought, then he heard her walk slowly out of the ward. Her steps echoed down the corridor. Dick opened his eyes and exhaled deeply. And now the tears could flow.

Chapter Twenty-nine

Rosemary rather prided herself on her good sense of smell. She was staying in the room Dick had occupied at the Hotel Amarys in Bordeaux, and when she returned from the hospital she closed the door behind her and breathed slowly and deeply. *Has Jennifer been here? Dick came over on Tuesday, and hadn't told me he was going sailing with her the next day. Did she join him here that night? The bed-linen is still the same – they'll probably change it today.* She pressed her face into the pillows. There was a hint of perfume! She breathed in again, and she recognised it with some relief as her own. *I heard from Charles Harrison that Jennifer was moving to France for a while, but she'd be coming back to meet the Princess at the opening. But I never thought she'd be staying so close to Dick's factory. You're getting paranoid, Rosemary Routledge. Just because you thought you sensed something in Dick's face when you told him Jennifer was dead. Poor man had just woken up from a three-day spell in deep coma, you give him terrible news about a friend, what could you expect but confusion? Still, he hadn't told me about seeing her, had he?*

She went to the room next door and knocked. *Ellen is going to be so relieved that Dick is awake at last. I'll tell her that the painkiller has put him out again, and suggest we go in together later this afternoon. What does one do in Bordeaux on a Saturday afternoon? How about some shopping?*

Dick awoke again and knew that he had been living through some terrible nightmare, without being able to recall anything of his dark imaginings. *Except that Jennifer is dead!* He opened his eyes and turned his head to look at the clock on the wall. Four o'clock. That injection had put him out for three hours . . . he moved a little, and groaned. There was a dull pain in his shoulder, and a vice tightening about his head.

"Good afternoon, Mr. Routledge. May I hope you are feeling a little better?"

There was a young man sitting in the armchair beside his bed. *Fair hair cut short, white open-necked shirt, sports coat and grey flannels. He looks English!*

"Who are you?"

"Dexter, sir, Detective Sergeant Peter Dexter, Bristol Constabulary."

"Police, yes, of course. Where's the Commissaire, – St. Josephe isn't it?"

"Yes sir, Commissaire St. Josephe, head of CID here in Bordeaux. It's the weekend, sir, they take it very seriously here. The Commissaire is, I believe, playing golf today with his wife. But I'm up to speed with this case, don't worry. I've been in

Bordeaux for almost a year now, on a sort of secondment, actually an Interpol exchange, and the Commissaire has encouraged me to make this one of the cases I focus on, being international to some extent. Just one or two questions, sir, and we think we've more or less cracked it."

"That's interesting. Perhaps . . ." Dick groaned again. "Do you think you could find the nurse, and ask her for something for my head, please. Not one of her knock-out injections, just something for a terrible headache."

Dick was disappointed that the nurse who came in with two tablets and a little water was not the rather pretty one he vaguely remembered from that morning, but an elderly Arab lady who offered him the painkiller and left without a word.

Dick chewed and swallowed. *Nasty taste, but I'm sure I'll feel better soon.* "You were saying that you'd cracked it?"

"More or less. Let me fill you in. There were two men in a speedboat. They ran over your dinghy, injuring yourself and killing the lady, your friend."

"Jennifer. Mrs. Jennifer Hawkins."

"Exactly. She was killed instantly, by the way, very heavy impact to the back of the head. Crushed the back of the skull." He saw Dick wince, and hurried on. "Anyway, they drove off at top speed, and turned north, up the coast towards the mouth of the Gironde, which leads down to Bordeaux. Unfortunately for them, their engine seized up just off Royan, something to do with the prop shaft, as we heard later. They drifted onto a sandbank off shore, where they were seen by the coastguard and then arrested when they were brought to land."

"How . . . who found us?"

"You were being watched at the time by a party of four walkers who were picnicking up on that big sand dune overlooking the mouth of the Bassin. They rushed down and pulled you both from the sea. Lucky for you that you were wearing a lifejacket, I'd say. They called the police on a mobile, and you were both brought here by helicopter."

Dick's head was clearing, and he sat up carefully. "What did they say, the men you arrested?"

"They had a silly story about having a bit of fun, trying to give you a fright as they roared past, maybe tip you into the water with their wake. Then you turned suddenly as they came up, and they couldn't avoid hitting you. They say they just panicked then, and drove off."

"Load of bloody lies! You didn't believe that?"

"Absolutely not. Luckily we have the testimony of the four walkers, who swear they saw the speedboat change course deliberately to follow your turn. So we have charged them with murder. We don't actually believe they intended to kill you both – bit of a clumsy method, we thought. So next week the Commissaire is planning to indicate that the charge might be reduced to the French equivalent of manslaughter, if they co-operate with the information we want."

"Who are they?"

"Well, we know their names, and the fact that they both come from Corsica, but not much more I'm afraid. There is a small Corsican community in Bordeaux, mostly criminal we think, or perhaps relatives of criminals. The tradition of the blood-feud is still very strong there, and people leave sometimes just to get away. We called on the man we think is the local head of the Corsican community, a man called Jo-jo Zonza, but he's done a bunk I'm afraid. The Commissaire has put out a general enquiry across France and via Interpol, but without a lead as to where to look we're not very optimistic . . ."

He was interrupted by the sound of female voices outside the room. Dick recognised his mother's firmest tone.

"He's my only son, I can see he's awake, and no nurse is going to tell me when I can see him. No policeman either."

Brit had enjoyed her month in the Algarve with her mother and Stefan very much. *This whole gorgeous coastline is a playground now for people on holiday from Germany, Sweden and England. Yet somehow the Portuguese seem to like us all, and still keep some sort of identity for themselves. Perhaps it's their weird language, that looks like Spanish when you see the road signs or a newspaper, but sounds just like Russian. I can't wait to tell Dick all about it!*

On the Friday evening before they had left Stockholm she had sat around the dining table with her mother and 12-year old Stefan to tell them about the offer from England, and ask what they thought. She had expected her mother at sixty-two to be concerned about the upheaval in her quiet life, and Stefan to be excited about the challenge of a new country. Instead her mother said,

"To be perfectly honest, dear, I've been getting very bored with life recently. Your father spoke very good English of course, and I used to be able to get by quite well when he took me to London. Just find me somewhere nice to live there, and I'll be very happy to make the change."

Stefan was reluctant to say anything, probably because he hadn't wanted to upset his mother and his grandmother, but Brit probed for an answer, and eventually he said.

"Can we live somewhere in London, so that I can go to see Arsenal and Tottenham Spurs on Saturdays?"

Brit promised solemnly to do her very best, and sent off her notice of resignation and letter of acceptance that evening. Now it was Friday, September 2nd, and she had been back in the office for a week. Her Managing Director had accepted her resignation, to be effective at the end of September, and Brit already had planned a month of frantic activity to enable her to get everything possible done in preparation for the department stores' Spring season. Her new boss had been really helpful, and had found her a three-bedroom apartment in Highgate, London. The plan was for her to start in mid-October, living in London by herself at first. *I know Dick will want to come and see my new apartment* . . . Stefan's school was arranging for him to spend most of this term just learning English, and her mother too would be taking an evening class. They were to join her before Christmas. *But where shall we meet once they've come over? Should I wait for him to call me?*

Jean-Paul de Clavignon was appalled when his special contact in Bordeaux police called on Wednesday afternoon to tell him that Dick had been the victim of an attack with a high-powered speedboat, and that the lady with him, Mrs. Hawkins, had been killed. *There were enough problems and questions arising from the death of Alain Robarte. Now the fools have killed a rich and beautiful Englishwoman, and maimed a senior international business executive. The newspapers will really enjoy themselves digging around that story!*

He thought long and hard about possible consequences for himself. Assuming Dick recovered, he was certain to be very, very angry about the death of his mistress. Resentful enough to want to strike out at any and everyone who might be connected. *Of course he has not directly accused me of complicity in the accounting or the murder of Alain. But that was just business. Jennifer Hawkins is personal!* Jean-Paul felt overwhelmed by a feeling of being now a helpless victim of events himself. *Could I suggest to Jo-jo that Dick is a personal threat to him too?* He decided to call Jo-jo that evening, from a public telephone in Arcachon.

Dick's mother fussed around him for a few minutes, but eventually fell silent, which allowed D.S. Peters to return from the corridor where he had discreetly withdrawn after having been introduced when she arrived.

"Mr. Routledge, I think we are almost done for the day. There is perhaps just one thing you might be able to help us with. Can you tell me, please, who would have known that you were coming over to France last Tuesday?"

"Apart from my confidential secretary, who has been with the company many years, the only people who knew I was coming were your M'sieur St. Josephe, or his PA, who were expecting me for a meeting on Thursday morning, and M'sieur de Clavignon, the MD at our factory in Belin, who was expecting me on Friday. Oh and I'd arranged to have dinner on the Thursday evening with Mrs. Charlotte Aston. She's an Interim Finance Manager. We brought her in a month ago to fill in for poor Alain Robarte, until we could recruit a replacement."

"And Mrs. Hawkins?"

"Yes, of course, Mrs. Hawkins invited me to come over to Arcachon for a sail and a family picnic on Wednesday."

"I wonder if you can recall the precise sequence in which these arrangements were made? You see, we're trying to understand how these men could have known when and where to ambush you with that speedboat. We've already established, by the way, that it was hired in Arcachon for a fishing trip, on the Monday, and collected about nine on Wednesday morning."

Dick thought hard. "I see where you're coming from with the security aspect. The first date that would have been fixed by my secretary would have been with the Commissaire, because he'd written to say he wanted to see me. That would have been the Monday I got back from holiday, that was August . . ."

He looked questioningly at the detective, who fished out a battered pocket diary. "That would have been August 22nd, sir?"

"No, I went to Germany that week. So it was the previous Monday, August 15th. That same day I sent e-mails to Jean-Paul about seeing him on the Friday, and Charlotte about meeting for dinner the night before. I told Jean-Paul that I had a date to see the Commissaire, the day before I was to meet him at the factory, but he didn't know, I don't think, that I was coming over on the Tuesday. You see Mrs. Hawkins only called me at the beginning of the following week, the 22nd, and we fixed up the sailing picnic then."

"But *somehow* they worked it out, and they were waiting for you."

The flat statement by the English policeman struck Dick like a blow. *Somehow . . . somehow . . . and it had cost Jennifer her life!* His head was starting to ache again, but he forced himself to concentrate.

"I can think of a couple of sources for them. Firstly, our MD at Belin, Jean-Paul de Clavignon, was away on holiday when I sent my e-mail. It may have been picked up in his office?"

Peters made a note. "We'll follow that up sir."

"And the other possibility is that Jennifer . . . that Mrs. Hawkins told me she had rented the sailboat especially for our trip. It had to be quite a bit bigger than the one she had been learning on. There may be some sort of leak there, at the boat rental. She could have told the renting people that she needed a bigger boat, because she wanted to arrange a picnic. I mean, no one would have thought to keep it secret, would they?" *No one except yourself, Dick. You led those men in the grey Volvo to Jennifer's house in Lynchester, didn't you? What if they came from Bordeaux, and were keeping tabs on her as well? Perhaps someone guessed I was likely to spend some time with her during my visit. Jean-Paul, for instance?*

Ellen had been sitting in the armchair, looking very tired, while the detective sergeant was finishing his interview with Dick. Seeing that he was ready to leave, she took brisk charge again.

"Well, sergeant, I think that is enough to be going on with. Mr. Routledge has had a serious injury, and needs his rest if he is to recover. His wife and I are at the Hotel Amarys if you need us, though I understand that Mr. Routledge may well be able to leave hospital on Monday. Dick, I've told Rosemary to go back to the hotel. She's been half mad with worry, you know. Well, we all have. Your father has been ringing twice a day to see if there was any improvement."

She was silent for a moment while she collected her handbag and a couple of expensive-looking carrier bags, then she seemed to gather strength again as she fixed a stern eye upon him.

"You may say it's none of my business, but Rosemary loves you very much, and I wouldn't want to see things . . . things going wrong between you. I've told her that your day out with Jennifer Hawkins was just that, a friendly visit with a neighbour that I introduced you to in Lynchester. I think she believes that, because she wants to. Your father and I can guess what you must be feeling, with her death on your conscience, and Billy an orphan altogether now. Perhaps . . . perhaps you've just had a lucky escape. And not just from drowning, if you see what I mean."

Dick could think of nothing to say as she bent over to touch her lips to his forehead.

"Bye now, Dick. Get some sleep, and we'll be back in the morning."

Jean-Paul's mood became steadily blacker over the weekend. Especially after another call from his police contact told him that the two men in the speedboat had been arrested, and were being held in Bordeaux on a murder charge. *Those clumsy, stupid thugs!* He had three possible contact numbers for Jo-jo. On Friday evening, all three were on answer-phone. He tried again on Saturday, with the same result. And on Sunday all three had become unobtainable. *He's gone. Probably for good. Now what? No one can prove I told him when Dick was due to come, and suggested that it might be worthwhile keeping an eye on that woman. Keep quiet, Jean-Paul, do a good job, keep away from the lovely Viola. And pray!*

Chapter Thirty

On Sunday morning, after giving up his attempts to contact Jo-Jo Zonza, it seemed clear to Jean-Paul that he needed more information before deciding what he should do. He walked back thoughtfully from the local payphone in Arcachon to his house, called the hospital, and was put through to the nurse in charge of Dick's ward. She was polite, but not immediately helpful.

"Mr. Routledge has a private room, but I cannot put you through to him at the moment, M'sieur de Clavignon. His wife has just begun her visit. I think they are very devoted to one another?"

"Yes, very, I'm sure. Well, I am a close friend and business colleague. Would I be allowed to visit?"

"I see no reason why not, M'sieur. He is a strong man, making good progress now. When should we expect you? M'sieur Routledge has his mother as well as his wife to come in, so perhaps we should try to give him some warning. He will have some lunch at one o'clock."

"I'll try to come in at two."

Jean-Paul leant over his balcony, enjoying the warmth of the early September sunshine and the angled view of the blue waters of the Bassin, alive again with a fleet of sailing dinghies, many flying multi-coloured spinnakers. Arlette came out and rested her sleek head against his cheek.

"I heard you calling the hospital. How's Dick?"

"Recovering well, thank heavens. In fact I've just had a good idea. They say he can receive visitors, so how about an early lunch and you come with me? Put on your sexiest summer frock, and that will cheer him up, I'm sure."

She stood back and looked at him quizzically. "I'll do my best. But he may still be mourning his lost mistress, don't you think?"

Dick was distinctly relieved to find that Rosemary's mood was much less challenging than his mother's. She pirouetted as she came in, to show off the swirl of a new skirt in bright flower-printed cotton that was a riot of greens and pinks.

"Yesterday's shopping. Actually Bordeaux is more expensive than Birmingham, I'd say, but the choice is fabulous." Her kiss was soft and tender. "How are you feeling, darling?"

"Better this morning, and a lot better now I've seen you. I'm sorry I'm not quite up to anything energetic like cuddling yet. How are Peter and James by the way? I assume they're not up to looking after themselves?"

"Hardly. I wouldn't trust them to put the cat out. Your father is staying at your house and doing the honours. He insisted they'd be no trouble – he's probably spoiling them rotten, but I think your mother will be going home tomorrow, and she'll sort them out."

She smiled, and sat close to him on the bed. "Are you strong enough for some news? Good news?"

He suppressed a grimace as he sat up straight. "Definitely."

Rosemary fixed her eyes on his face, then slowly undid two buttons of her dark green blouse, to reveal a white lacy bra and the tops of a rounded and sun-tanned cleavage. She tipped her head coquettishly. "Do I look just a teeny bit different?"

Dick's mind leapt into top gear. "You're . . . you've got a smirk on your face that I haven't seen for a long time. Are you . . .?"

"Early days, of course, darling, but I thought you should know that I am over a week late. And that hasn't happened for a good few years, so I'm guessing our holiday has done the trick. A baby in May, with any luck."

Dick held out his left arm, and received another very warm, satisfying kiss, which seemed a fair reward for the twinges of pain from his right shoulder.

"When will you know for sure?"

"I thought I would find a chemist tomorrow morning and get a pregnancy test-kit."

"Bring champagne if it's good news. I'd be so pleased, darling."

After Rosemary had left, with a promise to return at tea-time with his mother, the young nurse came in with a foul-testing little glass of medicine. She made him sit forward as she plumped up his pillows, and checked the strapping that bound his right arm across his chest.

"Vous souffrez, M'sieur?"

Dick shook his head, and was relieved to note that the pain had more or less gone. "Not so much now, thank you. Vous me gardez tres bien, je vous en remercie beaucoup. Voudriez-vous me dire votre nom?"

She smiled. "De rien, M'sieur. Je m'appelle Jeanne-Marie. Dans une heure je vous apporterez le dejeuner. Et a deux heures de l'apres-midi vous pouvez compter sur M'sieur de Clavignon."

Dick felt slightly resentful that no one had asked him if he wanted a visit from Jean-Paul, but consoled himself with the thought that it would help while away the afternoon. *A new baby in May would be wonderful. Might we get a girl? I'm feeling better. I want out!*

Just before two o'clock Dick's pretty French nurse came in to remove his lunch-tray and plump up his pillows again. She was undoubtedly very impressed with his guests. "M'sieur et Madame de Clavignon sont arrives. Il est gentil, et Madame est tres elegante."

Dick had been wondering whether to look brave or in pain, and had settled on what he hoped would be a subtle combination of the two when Jean-Paul ushered Arlette into the room. She smiled and leant gracefully over him to offer both fragrant cheeks for him to kiss. She was indeed more elegant than he remembered, and wore a white dress in filmy chiffon with a thin blue piping. She sat down on the deep armchair beside the bed, carelessly exposing a long, sun-tanned leg, and Jean-Paul sat on the other side.

"We are so pleased to see that you recover, Dick," he said, "And I was so very sorry to hear about poor Madame Hawkins. How are things now with you?"

"Much better today, thanks. In fact I feel a bit of a fraud to be in bed still, but the doctor insisted. I'm hoping though that they will at least let me up tomorrow." He pushed himself a little higher in the bed, and winced visibly.

"Mais tu suffres encore." There was a delightful warmth in Arlette's tone that Dick found very helpful. He wondered briefly if her 'tu' had any significance. *Have I become hypersensitive to women's feelings and intentions?*

"No, really, it's just because the strapping is so tight. I got a bang on the head, which hasn't done too much damage, and they say that my shoulder is bruised and cracked, but not actually broken."

"Can you remember what happened?"

Dick told the story again, "But they have arrested the two men responsible. The police think they will talk eventually, to avoid a charge of murder."

Jean-Paul thought that this was a convenient opportunity to get more information. "Have the police made an examination with you?"

"I've been interviewed briefly, yes. An English Detective Sergeant actually, working in Bordeaux on some sort of secondment. He went quite gently with me, but seemed most interested to try to find out how those murderers could know that Jennifer and I . . . that we were going sailing last Wednesday. Because they must have known in advance, as they booked their motorboat on Monday."

"Do they have the answer to that?"

Dick glanced up at Jean-Paul as he asked this question, and sensed that it was less casual than it seemed. *If J-P has been involved, there's no point in tipping him off that we're on to him.*

"I don't know. Of course a lot of people, including yourself, knew I was coming. But only Jennifer knew about the Wednesday picnic. And anyone she may have told, of course. I feel so very badly about her terrible death. I mean, it really was my fault that she found herself in harm's way. I just wish there was something I could do. Other than just keep prodding the French police, I suppose."

Jean-Paul became more relaxed. "Arlette and I have been working during les vacances to make our English better. We have books and tapes, and try to use half of each day in English. Do you hear un avancement?"

"Very much so, especially the accent. I'm impressed. Talking of English, how did you get on last week with Charlotte Aston, our Interim Finance Manager?"

"Ver' well, in fact much better than I expected. The accounts for July were perfect, and August will be done next week. She has shown me the draft figures for next year's budget, and I was ready to meet with you last Friday. She sends her best wishes. She has perfect French, even with mes Arabes. Would you like her mobile phone number?"

"No, but I will try to call her at the office tomorrow. I think . . . I've done about enough for today . . ."

Arlette nodded in sympathy, pressed his hand and then produced a bunch of fat white grapes from a capacious straw basket. "These are for you, Dick, with our love and wishes for a quick get better. And now, je regrette, we must go. Little Henri has been out for the day with a club for les enfants, a cheval dans Les Landes. We must be sure to arrive chez nous before he return."

When they got home Jean-Paul saw the message-light flashing on his answer-phone. It was a cryptic message, asking that he call a mobile phone number urgently. Guessing that it must be the Corsican, Jo-Jo, he left the house abruptly to find a payphone in the town.

"Jo-Jo? It's me, Jean-Paul."

"Ah, yes, my dear friend M'sieur *de* Clavignon. I believe you have been trying to reach me. How may I be of service this time?"

Jean-Paul ignored the heavy sarcasm, and the nuance of the sneer in the emphasis on the 'de' in his name.

"The police are going to threaten your friends with a murder charge, to get them to talk. Do you think you can trust them?"

"Trust them? Not in the least, no. But rely on them not to talk about me, yes, I'm sure. They want to go on living. Even if they are in prison. And of course they know nothing about you."

"Good. But for my part, I am very concerned about M'sieur Routledge. I went into the hospital to visit him this afternoon. He is making a quick recovery, but he is undoubtedly very angry about the death of his beautiful mistress, Madame Hawkins. He says that the police are concentrating on trying to establish how your friends came to know about the sailing trip. Unless I am very lucky, they will be getting very close to me, and I believe his grief and rage will make him keep on driving them to make more enquiries as long as he is alive."

There was a silence on the line. "Jo-Jo?"

"I am here, thinking about what you have said. You may depend on me to act before he leaves Bordeaux to protect us all."

The call was terminated with that. Jean-Paul strolled home considerably more cheerfully, looking forward to a walk along the beach with Arlette and Henri, followed by a fine cold salmon and a bottle of Chablis for dinner.

After Jean-Paul and Arlette had left, Dick reflected on his relationship with them. *Arlette was very charming today. Almost as if J-P had put her up to produce a sort of smokescreen, a diversion for me, behind which he could pump me for information about the police and what they are doing. I'm going to have to do some serious thinking about Jean-Paul. Talk to Jean Savage when I get back. I mean, if I'm permanently suspicious about everything he does and says, how can it make sense to trust him with the future of our business in France? Assuming I can't prove he's a villain, do I have to have a good reason to let him go? How about 'personal incompatibility'? Like a divorce on the grounds of 'irreparable breakdown'? Could be expensive if we have to pay him off, but it's not really my money is it?*

He asked the nurse if he might get out of bed. She was reluctant to allow him out, as the doctor in charge was off for the day, but eventually conceded, "*Pour une heure seulement, M'sieur*", and he was sitting in the armchair reading the Bordeaux Sunday newspaper when Rosemary returned with his mother. They produced a sticky almond tart to share, and chatted amiably about their expensive Sunday lunch and a stroll along the river in the sunshine.

His mother was especially pleased to see him out of bed. "I'll definitely catch that ten o'clock flight back tomorrow. I think your father has had charge of the boys for quite long enough, if they're not to be spoilt for good. This weekend, by the way, they've been to the amusement park at Alton Towers. Thank heavens he's got to get them back to school tomorrow."

Rosemary was more cautious. "Do you think they will discharge you tomorrow?"

"Hard to say. I don't suppose they will keep me in for the sake of it, but I think the doctors here are quite careful. And we're front page news! Did you see the local paper?"

The lower half of the front page was taken up with the story. There was a picture of the smashed sailing dinghy on the beach, and a luridly descriptive text about the terrible murder of a beautiful Englishwoman and the lucky escape of a prominent international business executive, all under the headline, 'Assassins Saisis'. Even as he showed them the paper Dick realised that Rosemary and his mother would be reminded again of the fact that he had been out for the day with poor Jennifer, in secret really, as far as they were concerned. Fortunately neither of them could follow the slang of a French tabloid newspaper. He put a brave face on it and folded the paper away.

"I just hope that the press interest will keep the French police on their toes. I doubt very much if they've got to the bottom of it yet. I mean we don't know for sure if there's a connection to the death of Alain Robarte. Jean-Paul was here earlier, by the way, with Arlette, his wife. Very sympathetic and charming, but I don't really trust him."

Much to his relief, Rosemary said nothing about Jennifer. "As far as I'm concerned, the sooner we can get you back in England the less I'll be worried. Any idea what time the doctor might be around, to say whether or not you can leave?"

Dick thought hard. "I've been unconscious Thursday and Friday mornings, and Saturday might not be typical." He pressed the bell beside his bed. "Let's ask the nurse."

"Jeanne-Marie, a quelle heure arrivera le medecin demain, s'il vous plais?"

"C'est pas precis, M'sieur. Vers midi, sans doute."

Rosemary heard the word 'midi' and understood. "Right then, I'll be here well before midday, and apply a little pressure if necessary. We really must get you out if we can."

After they had left Dick felt very tired, and allowed his nurse to shepherd him back into bed. "Vous ferez un bon diner en trente minutes. Et puis, dormez." This last was accompanied by a graphic little activity with a pretend knife and fork, followed by her hands together at the side of her head. Her eyes closed, and then reopened with a sparkle and an infectious giggle that made Dick smile too. *She definitely was a very good nurse!*

Chapter Thirty-one

By eleven o'clock that Sunday evening Arlette had already gone to bed, 'to finish my Gabriel Marquez', and Jean-Paul was just about to follow her when his mobile rang.

"Jean-Paul? It's Jo-Jo. We need just a little assistance from you. Could you walk out west along the beach from your house, please. Just keep walking, and a friend of mine will contact you as soon as he thinks it's safe. He'll explain what we need."

The sandy shore was deserted. To his left was a line of street lights along the road that ran along the promenade, set too far back to illuminate the deep shadows beneath the sea wall, and to his right was the water of the Bassin, dark now until the moon rose, but glittering every few seconds in the flashing light from the small lighthouse on the jetty behind him. It was very quiet, and his steps seemed to crunch exceptionally loudly in the damp sand and stones along the water's edge. He judged that he was almost at the corner where the beach turned south and Ville d'Ete became the Ville de Printemps, when he saw the silhouette of a burly figure clamber over the wall and drop down onto the beach. He raised a hand and Jean-Paul walked up the beach to meet him.

"M'sieur de Clavignon?"

The tone was respectful, and Jean-Paul thought he detected a Corsican accent.

He extended his hand. "Yes. You've come from Jo-Jo?"

The man clasped his hand in a horny grip. "Yes sir. He asked me to give you this."

As he spoke Jean-Paul felt himself pulled violently forward, and as he stumbled off balance a pad of something sweet-smelling was thrust over his face. He tried to struggle but the man was infinitely more powerful, and as he breathed hard his senses reeled, his legs seemed to melt beneath him and darkness engulfed him as he hit the ground.

After supper Dick's nurse brought him a sleeping draught, but left it to him to decide when to take it. He struggled for half an hour to finish the French newspaper, and watched a long and very serious discussion on French television about world poverty. When his head started to ache from the effort of following the French language, he turned it off, and the overhead light too. *I should take that sleeping draught and get some rest*. But in the darkened room his mind kept returning to memories of Jennifer. *That first time we met at Charles Harrison's committee, she was so calm and self-possessed. Very beautiful too, of course, but out of reach. Then that time we were sitting in her garden, and I looked at her profile beside me and knew then that I wanted her. The laughter over her nice cake, and the way she kissed me, 'just for reassurance'. The way she looked, the way she smiled at me as she came down the steps from her house – was it only a five days ago? The tension you could cut with a knife as she showed me into her bedroom. Those long brown legs when she peeled off her wet skirt beside the boat . . . the feel of the life in her body under my hand when we kissed just before . . . damn, damn, damn those murdering bastards!*

Dick was not a man habitually given to introspection and self-analysis, but lying that Sunday evening in a quiet hospital bed there wasn't much else to do. He knew that he was angry – was there self-pity as well? Did regret for Jennifer include rage and simple disappointment, because now he would never enjoy making love to her? Overwhelmingly, he realised that he felt guilty. *It was my fault she was killed. It was me that persuaded her to come to Arcachon. I led those killers to her front door, and it was me they were after in the boat. Am I in danger now?*

He realised that he would actually welcome some threat, some physical challenge. *If only there was some way to turn back the clock!*

And what about Brit? Suppose I go down to London to meet her, and she became involved in this terrible business too? How could I let that happen? What am I really doing with her? Am I actually in love with her? Am I? Just a little, yes I am. But I'm also using her to inject some excitement into my life. Perhaps I was only really happy when I was flying? I'm almost forty-five now. Isn't it time I grew up? I'm sure she's still in Stockholm for a few weeks. I'll call her in the morning and tell her I've had an accident. Just that. Say I'm getting better, but it'll be a few weeks before I'm up and about. And then I'll call her in London at her office. Maybe I should let her down gently.

He stirred the glass and swallowed it down. It tasted as foully as he had expected, but as he sank down into the bed he knew it would work soon. Oblivion would be so welcome.

"M'sieur! S'il vous plait, M'sieur!"

He heard the rattle of curtains being drawn back. Dick struggled to open his eyes. It was morning, certainly. He looked at his watch beside the bed, then at the pretty, agitated face of his nurse, who was now plugging in a telephone handset. Nine thirty-five. He'd been asleep for twelve hours solid. His neck and shoulder felt stiff, but there was no pain.

"S'il vous plait M'sieur. C'est la police! Tres important!"

Dick picked up the receiver while she went back to her desk and put the call through. He recognised the voice of the English Detective Sergeant.

"Good morning, Mr. Routledge. Sorry to disturb you so early sir, but we've got another one dead in this case, and I need your help, please."

The nurse came back with a steaming mug of black coffee, and they exchanged smiles.

"Good morning, sergeant. It's Dexter, isn't it? What's happened?"

"It's your Mr. de Clavignon, sir. His wife called us, about six this morning. She says she went to bed and fell asleep waiting for her husband to come back. He'd told her he was going for a walk on the beach. That was about eleven. Anyway, she wakes up at first light, and he's not come back. She says she went out and looked along the beach both ways but couldn't see him, so she called the local gendarmerie in Arcachon. To cut a long story short, sir, they found him slumped against the sea wall about a mile from his house, dead. There was a pistol beside him, and he'd committed suicide, as it seems. His wife refused to believe it, I mean there's no note or anything like that, and she says they came to see you yesterday and everything has been cheerful and so on. Obviously we'll know more after the post-mortem, but I wonder if you can help us at all. How are things with the company and his work for you?"

Dick tried to think, but his mind was full of imaginings about Jean-Paul. Dead? A pistol? Suicide? He thought of Jean-Paul with Arlette the previous afternoon – poised, calculating, self-confident. A man who was in control of his world.

"I have to say that my first thoughts would be the same as his wife's. He's the last man I'd have expected to kill himself. Young son, pretty wife, doing well in his first big job. Certainly there was no sign of any problem yesterday. They came in to cheer me up, and were very charming, both of them. The company was doing well, he was doing well for us, next year's plans look very satisfactory. Of course we haven't resolved this business of the money washing through the company's bank account yet, and the murder of Alain Robarte, but . . . No, I find suicide very hard to believe. Could it have been faked?"

"We're asking ourselves that of course. But that only leads to another question. Why would anyone want to kill him? Any thoughts there, sir?"

"Well . . ."

"Yes, sir?"

"I'm sure those thugs that attacked us weren't acting alone. Someone tipped them off about our picnic, and Jean-Paul has to be a suspect, even if he was off on his boat at the time. And he could be tied in to the whole business of this money-laundering we talked about. Someone may have felt that he knew too much."

"But there's nothing more specific? Just suspicions?"

"Just suspicions. I . . . no, just suspicions."

"Thank you, sir. Please call me if anything else occurs to you, no matter how trivial it may seem."

The nurse came in and took his temperature, pulse and blood-pressure.

"Bien, M'sieur, vous marchez tres bien. Peut-etre un oeuf pour le petit-dejeuner?"

Dick nodded his appreciation and she bustled away. *I could be in danger here myself. That's childish nonsense, what do I know that isn't common knowledge? Certainly there's nothing I can tell the police that will make any difference. First Alain Robarte, then Jennifer, and now Jean-Paul. I'm sure they'll find he was murdered. Which means he was definitely up to his neck in everything. So I suppose he got what he deserved. Perhaps that'll be the end of this business and they'll leave us alone. I'll just call Jean Savage in a minute and tell her. She'll probably be able to get us a temporary managing director for a few months, while we look for a permanent. When I get out I will go to see poor Arlette though. I suppose she'll have a lot of insurance to come, like Alain's wife.*

He had just finished his boiled egg when the door of his room was flung open with a flourish and Rosemary stood there, holding a bottle of Champagne and two glasses.

"Guess what! It's positive. I'm pregnant."

He stretched out his free hand, and she sat happily on the bed beside him for a long, warm kiss. He tightened his arm around her, and his whole being was filled with simple joy.

"I can't begin to tell you how pleased I am, Ros. I love you so very much."

DESIRE is the cement that can bind a family together – or the explosive that can burst it apart.

In *DEATH IN THE FAMILY* **Joe Hawkins** has left the family business divided between his two sons, **Alan** and **George**, and his beautiful second wife, **Jennifer**. Each has conflicting ideas for the future of their inheritance. As Jennifer and Alan begin an affair, an enquiry into the murder of a young girl is under way, and the Hawkins family is drawn inexorably into the net. The threads of the story are woven ever more tightly together, until they explode in a thunderous climax.

In *A FAMILY BUSINESS* **James Routledge** persuades his son **Dick** to give up the RAF, and make his own mark in a brutally competitive market. A shareholder, De Boissy, is a London Merchant Bank, where **Alex Hampshire** has become impatient to see a profit, and offers his holding and his services to American Cereal Products. **Jean Carey**, Personnel Manager in the Routledge business is drawn to **John Savage,** who represents the Bank on the board. He comes to understand very personally the meaning of 'conflict of interest'. The big players in international corporations make their own rules for the game. And the family must learn to play – or go under.

In *FAMILY MATTERS* **Dick Routledge** is now Director of European Business. He meets **Brit Carlsohn**, a Swedish international executive herself, blond and very desirable. The finance manager at the French subsidiary in Arcachon is savagely attacked, and it seems that dangerous criminals need to cover their tracks. **Jennifer Hawkins** decides she would like to live in France, and Dick is attracted into helping her to relocate. When he visits Jennifer in France the conspirators must ensure that he cannot interfere in their plans. Permanently . . .

PRESS COMMENTS on Dennis Russell's first novel, '*Carew – a story of Civil War*'

"A carefully observed study of idealism cracking under pressure, based on real people in real situations. Our pick of this summer's reading."

"A rattling good tale" . . . "A fast-paced story of intrigue, romance and bloody soldiering." . . . "An engrossing historical novel."

Jacket design by Averil Davies

ISBN 0-9549742-0-4

ISBN 0-9549742-0-4

£7.99

9 780954 974206 >